THE

NEVER ARMY

THE CHRONICLES OF JONATHAN TIBBS

VOLUME III

T. ELLERY HODGES

Cover design by Damonza www.damonza.com

ISBN-13: 978-0-9907746-6-2

To my wife,

Not a single word could have made it to manuscript had she not allowed me to abandon her to our merciless children. If the roles had been reversed, I don't know that I would have emerged with my sanity intact . . .

I have my doubts.

PROLOGUE

IRELAND | 1877

AS A CHILD, he'd climbed the hill whenever his parents had given him freedom from his chores. Their family's estate shared a property line with the O'Sullivan's. Their daughter Johanna was the only child his age for miles and she'd been his best friend since before he could remember.

Today, Thomas was a young man.

There had been a slight chill in the air when he'd slipped outside that morning, but it no longer touched him. The sun was high enough overhead now that he felt himself sweating from exertion. This slope he was on, it felt steeper than he remembered.

Most folks in town avoided the O'Sullivan farm on account of . . . *what happened.* Thomas had been abroad at the time, but he'd heard the rumors.

Demonic possession, some said.

Contracts with the devil, said others.

He hadn't believed any of it—all superstitious nonsense about a family he'd known his entire life. The sort of malignant garbage that gets spread in whispers after a few drinks in small-town taverns. Though, he had to admit, he often found it troubling that he'd heard some of those *stories* from folks he would have thought better of.

Thomas had been a hundred miles away, at school, on the night those rumors started. Johanna had written him many times. She left what the town said about her out of the letters. Thomas' mother had been less discreet, though not out of any desire to do the O'Sullivan's reputation any harm. Rather, she just didn't want Thomas to be surprised by what he would hear upon returning.

Thomas believed the truth wasn't much to gossip about. Johanna had grown sick. The illness had nearly killed her. She had managed to pull through. Now, perhaps it was true that the sickness had left a mark on her—changed her a bit—as bad illnesses can sometimes do. But anything more than that was just the town's ignorance manifesting itself. Still, Thomas hadn't seen Johanna since he had come home. He'd asked after her—with as much subtlety as a man his age could—only to learn that she was never seen in town anymore. Those who visited the O'Sullivan farm said they seldom caught a glimpse of her.

As he crested the hill and stepped into the faint shadows cast by the tree line, his boots began taking the familiar steps for him. He walked at first, but soon felt the need to run. Just as it was when they were children—he couldn't wait to see her—and soon he was sprinting through the woods with a grin on his face and the wind in his hair. He would have felt ridiculous had he not been alone.

Thomas supposed that most anyone with a happy enough childhood had a Johanna. That girl or boy they grew up with, whose name brought back memories of warm summer days. A face belonging to someone who, only after his body matured to need things he hadn't as a child—would come to haunt his curiosity.

Could she be as I remember?

Did she know then? Did she know what took me so much time to realize?

Does she think about me? More and more often, just as I find I think of her?

He could little remember of what it was, in any specific way, that he and Johanna had talked about or why they were drawn to one another as children. Rather, his memories were filled with days when they swam together in the small pond tucked away in these woods. He remembered laughing as they lay on the shore to dry.

But mostly, what brought her back to his thoughts so often, was what they had shared as children. That thing all adults seemed to lose along the way. He had been able to look into Johanna's eyes—hold her gaze—and never feel that he should look away. It was only years later that Thomas discovered just how hard a thing this was to have with anyone.

His sprint slowed as he came to the clearing by the pond. He began to walk and let his breath return. He found himself taking in the silence that followed. He knew it had been a child's hope that he might have found her here, at the very moment he'd chosen to come—but he was still disappointed to find her absent.

He sighed regretfully as he turned in the direction of the O'Sullivan farm, then barely managed to hold back what would have been a rather embarrassing squawk when he saw Johanna was standing behind him. How long had she been there? How had she come up behind him so quietly? Rabbits made more noise in the woods.

His surprise quickly turned to awkwardness as he took in the details of her.

If it were possible, Johanna was more beautiful than he remembered. She had a graceful stillness about her, a glow of the skin that made her vibrant and alive. Though all of that was secondary to the fact that she was barely clothed.

She wore only a white shirt. It was too big and nearly reached down to her knees—looked as though it belonged to a man. Yet, despite so loose a fit, the fabric was clinging to her. She was soaking wet. Her skin goose-bumped from the cold, her long red hair dripping as though she had been swimming.

Thomas felt himself turn a shade of red. He was a colossal fool. He'd come sprinting through the woods like a child. A grown man running with a big stupid grin on his face. She must have been swimming when she heard him crashing through the trees. He'd scarcely given her time to get out of the water and cover herself.

"Johanna, I . . . I . . . I'm so sorry." His words came out stammered. He occasionally glanced at her eyes to see how she was taking the situation. It took him a number of those worried looks before he realized there was no embarrassment on her face. She stood, head tilting easily as she studied him. She seemed entirely unaware of the way her shirt clung to her skin.

Meanwhile, Thomas could not ignore that the water had turned so much of the fabric nearly transparent. It seemed every curve of her skin taunted his gaze for its fullest attention.

Finally, he closed his eyes altogether, and said, "Please, accept my apology."

Johanna was quiet for a long moment, but he heard her whisper, "Yes, I'm sure."

Thomas did not reply. He got the sense that she wasn't talking to him but to herself. As though her words were answering a question she'd only asked in her thoughts.

"Look at me, Thomas," Johanna said.

He opened his eyes as she took a tentative step across the forest to meet him. That strange look of study that she had held on him at first was gone. Now, it was as though she could not hide her joy at seeing him after so many years.

Suddenly aware of himself, he cast his eyes down at her bare feet. "Jo,

I don't know what I was thinking. Charging through the woods like this. I should have knocked on your door."

She came closer. He felt her hand on his chin, her face drawing so close that his eyes would have to strain to see anything else—and finally he realized she did not want him to look away.

"This has always been our place," Johanna said.

LIBYAN DESERT | 1984

The sun was setting on the horizon when Douglas Tibbs turned toward the sound of Holloway snapping his fingers. He was pointing at a large rock formation sticking out of the sands. "I'll volunteer for first watch."

A glance at Evans and Turner, their faces tired as they brought up the rear, and he knew there would be no protests if they took a few hours to rest. As far as shelter went, the rocks were as good as they were going to find out here, and he'd wanted to get out of the wretched hot wind for hours.

"Not gonna make it back to the rendezvous point tonight anyway," he said. "All goes well, we'll move out before dawn and still be on schedule."

With a grin Holloway turned for the rocks.

The site wasn't bad, more ideal than a distant glance could have told them. The stones made a crude horseshoe; tall enough to block the wind but not steep enough to box them in if they had to be scaled in a hurry. Apparently, they weren't the first to spend a night there either. The desert was quick to erase the signs that someone had been through, but at some point, someone took the time to chisel a message into the rock.

He spoke a bit of Arabic but couldn't read it. "Any idea what it says?"

Holloway stepped closer, squinting as he tried to make it out. "Oh yeah, says . . ."

He trailed off, his face going deadpan. "I'm gonna miss Knight Rider because I'm stuck in the desert again."

Douglas closed his eyes and sighed.

It was a sigh of good-humored annoyance. Holloway hadn't complained about it for the last few days, but now that they were nearly home and a decent way from danger, he was back to taking every opportunity to complain about missing his damn TV show.

"Forever with Knight Rider," Evans said, as he joined them and dropped his gear on the ground. "You're worse than my grandmother when she misses her soaps."

Unfazed as he stripped off his pack, Holloway began reciting the opening credits as though he were imagining what it would be like to be back home in his easy chair. "A shadowy flight into the dangerous world of a man who does not exist."

Evans exchanged a glance with Douglas; they decided to ignore him.

Turner was the last to reach the horseshoe and only caught the tail end of the conversation.

"Hey, how about it, Turner," Douglas said, pointing toward the writing. "Any idea what it says?"

Turner studied the rock. "Interesting. Says, *Airwolf rules and Knight Rider sucks.*"

As they all chuckled at his expense, Holloway half-heartedly kicked sand in Turner's direction.

"Seriously though, can you read it?" Douglas asked.

"Says 'please, shit somewhere else'."

"Well, Hallelujah," Evans said, getting his blanket unrolled. "We'll all sleep better now knowing that mystery has been solved."

Holloway shrugged, reconsidering the writing. "Does it actually say *please*? Least they're polite."

Turner and Evans were asleep as soon as the sun disappeared. Douglas envied them; he'd never been a fast sleeper. An hour later, he'd just begun to drift off, but Holloway nudged him awake.

"Tibbs. Come take a look at this."

"What is it?" Douglas asked.

"There's someone out there," Holloway said.

While Holloway sounded more perplexed than worried, they were supposed to be the only ones passing though this desert for miles, so the words would have been like a bucket of cold water no matter how he'd said them. Douglas crawled out of the comfort of his blanket, staying low to join Holloway at the nearby rock where he had a night vision scope on a tripod.

"So, tell me that isn't strange," Holloway said.

Douglas looked through the scope and frowned. Maybe three hundred yards out, a woman walked across the sands. Nothing about her belonged. In a long black coat and hat, her clothes looked a better fit for a fall night out in a city. She carried no gear—not even a canteen. Strangest of all, she bore no signs of travel. When his team had come the same way earlier, they had been soaked in their own sweat and crusted in sand. Her entire outfit looked freshly pressed from the dry cleaners.

What's more, she must have been seventy years old if she were a day, but her face showed no signs of fatigue. Before they'd made camp, Douglas would have bet the tip of his left pinky that they were the only people around for fifty miles in each direction. The only exception would have been the way they were headed. This woman might as well have been following in their footsteps. In fact, he would have thought that was exactly what she was doing if he didn't know the desert winds had already erased them.

"There must be something out here we don't know about," Holloway said. "No way Grandma walked through the same desert we just did."

"Doesn't look like a native," Douglas said. "I don't see a weapon on her. We sure she's alone?"

"As far as I can tell," Holloway said.

Their expressions might as well have been mirrors when they exchanged glances. This was too strange for their liking.

"You're the boss, what do you want to do about her?"

Douglas frowned. "Her being out here the same night as us can't be coincidence."

"Thinking she could be a friendly?" Holloway asked.

He shook his head doubtfully. He understood why Holloway would entertain the idea. Thing was, anyone who knew they were out here wouldn't send some random old lady to contact them. They had a radio. Yes, it was an *emergency use only* sort of precaution. They were running silent to make sure no one ever discovered they had been through the area. Still, if Command needed to get them a message, and it was so urgent it couldn't wait until they reached the rendezvous, there were easier ways.

Douglas leaned down to watch her in the scope once more. She wasn't moving fast, or with any particular stealth. There was nothing about her cadence that indicated a rush to reach any destination. Her gaze traveled over the rolling desert as though she searched for something. When that gaze passed over their position she paused as though she'd somehow spotted him from two hundred and fifty yards in the dark.

Douglas could swear her eyes—flashed.

He pulled back from the scope, rubbing at his eyes. The scopes were a great tool in the dark, but sometimes it was hard to know precisely what you'd seen when everything was a wash of varying green hues.

He quickly forgot about the flash when he took another look. "Dammit, she's gone."

"Gone? There ain't nowhere to go," Holloway said.

He was right. Unless the woman had sprouted wings when he looked away there was nowhere out there to hide. Besides their rocks, there was nothing but rising and falling slopes of sand.

"We better wake up Turner and Evans," Douglas said.

He had a bad feeling. The sort he knew to listen to when it said it was time to go. Whatever was going on in this desert tonight, he didn't believe an old woman went for a stroll and just happened to cross paths with four heavily armed soldiers.

"Uh . . . you sure you saw what you think you saw?" Evans asked groggily. "I mean, hot girl in a trench coat magically appears out of nowhere and is heading my way. Sounds an awful lot like the dream I was hoping to have—"

"We both saw her," Douglas interrupted. "And she was old enough to be your grandmother, Evans."

"If you're telling me an old lady ghosted both of you," Evans said, a smirk crawling up his lip, "yeah, that tracks."

"Get up and get ready to move," Douglas said. "No more noise."

The next few moments were efficient as they put their gear away in silence. The wind had weakened, and no one heard anything outside the ruffling of items being shoved back into packs. That was why the distinct sound of a pebble jarred loose to tumble down the rocks behind them was loud enough to get every man's attention.

Douglas made a few hand gestures. Quick and quiet, Holloway returned to the scope resting on the rocks and turned it behind them to a make a quick scan over the horseshoe. He shook his head. Douglas didn't hesitate. With two hand signals, Turner and Evans dropped their packs, readied their firearms, and got low. Two more signals and each set out around opposite sides of the rock.

Douglas lowered onto his stomach and began snaking his way forward on elbows and hips to head up the center of the rocks. Every few seconds he spared a glance back at Holloway who would signal to him if he had seen anything in the dark.

She isn't alone out here, Douglas thought.

He didn't know how she'd managed to disappear the way she had, but to get behind them and up this rock that fast without making a sound just wasn't possible. He feared her entire reason for being out there had been to draw their attention while the rest of her people crept up on them from behind. This was but one of many troubling possibilities cluttering his mind as he made his slow progress up the rocks. Then, when he glanced back to Holloway, his mind went blank.

The man jutted hand signals into the air. Frantically trying to tell him he'd lost sight of both Turner and Evans. Though, this was not why his mind went so blank; Douglas stilled—stopped breathing altogether.

The woman was looking right back at him from over Holloway's shoulder.

He would not have frozen, but she hadn't stalked up behind his friend. She hadn't been there one moment and then, while Holloway signaled to him, in a blink, her pale white face was suddenly there. This time, he was certain when that light, an eerie blue spark, flashed in her eyes.

Holloway had either sensed her presence behind him or saw it on Douglas's face, but the bare instant of warning it bought him didn't change the outcome. He'd only just begun to turn before the woman had hold of him. One hand had clamped down on his mouth, as though to keep him from screaming, while the other drove a syringe into his neck.

He had no shot. If he fired, he might get lucky and hit her, but he'd definitely hit Holloway first. Nevertheless, he flipped onto his back and swept his rifle toward them.

He had little time to do more. Holloway's struggles gave the woman about as much trouble as a buzzing insect. Douglas had barely formed the notion that he might get to his feet and race to his friend's aid before he was left with his mouth gaping.

They were gone.

Holloway and the woman had vanished just as quickly as she'd appeared behind him a few seconds earlier. The only sign he hadn't lost his mind were the footprints of their struggle in the sand.

Come on . . . Show your face, dammit . . . Show me those eyes.

He searched the night, his thoughts growing more and more impatient in what could only be a false quiet.

What kind of person was capable of this? She hadn't only eluded three Rangers, but disabled them in a matter of seconds. On some level he hadn't ruled it all out as a nightmare. A consideration that had never come to him in a fight before, but how else was this possible?

Some kind of new stealth camouflage? A cloaking device? Where did that even begin to explain how fast she'd moved? How did she even know they were here? What was her interest in his team or their mission?

He didn't dare take his back from the rock; it was the only way to make her come at him head on. She would know it as well. So, was she waiting him out? Maybe not as quick as he'd thought? Maybe she didn't like the odds that she could reach him faster than he could get a shot off.

Time and silence—nothing happened. Nothing but the wind sweeping away Holloway's footprints and Douglas holding his rifle at the night.

Eventually, Douglas slowly took one hand from the rifle and reached for his radio. Command had been clear. His team wasn't supposed to be in that desert. They didn't want to risk any American aircraft being spotted in the area should his team need extraction. Still, three men down and firsthand intelligence of superior weapons tech would justify breaking radio silence. At least, it would have, but Douglas found an empty spot on his belt where his radio should have been.

With a long breath and a whispered curse, he saw the thing right where he'd left it—resting on his bag—in the middle of the horseshoe. Fifteen feet maybe, but the way this woman moved it might as well not exist at all.

Of all the nights to be making mistakes.

He pushed the self-chastising thoughts into the recesses of his mind and began to inch down the rock on his back. The slope favored him, but he made slow progress with both hands on his weapon.

The moment his feet touched sand, he darted forward, hoping she'd expect him to pause. He ran, grabbing the entire pack one handed and pulling it back with him until he felt the safety of stone behind him again. He breathed, both hands on the rifle again as he scanned the night for those blue eyes.

He noticed he could feel those words chiseled into the stone behind him. 'Please, shit somewhere else'.

No guarantees, he thought. Given how tonight was playing out, he'd happily crap his pants in exchange for getting his team out of here.

He picked up the radio and thumbed the transmitter. Despite the adrenaline, his words were clear and his hands steady. He gave his designation and requested immediate assistance. Seconds ticked by with no reply. He repeated the communication. Then again, and again.

Seconds became minutes.

Nervousness grew.

He'd noticed something off, had since the first attempt to make contact. An underlying whine or thrumming beneath the usual radio static. He'd been party to enough poor radio connections to know that sound was not normal.

Was she jamming his equipment?

He pushed the thought away as paranoia but failing to get a reply multiple times forced him to reconsider. After what he'd seen—was jamming a signal that much of a stretch?

He gave up on the radio. More time ticked by as he watched the darkness.

Why isn't she finishing the job?

Why take out three and leave the last?

. . . had she already done whatever she'd been here to do?

He forced himself to stop wasting time on questions he couldn't answer. He needed to find his team. He hadn't seen for himself what happened to Turner or Evans, but if they hadn't shown up by now, he had to assume they'd been pulled into the night the same way as Holloway. Still, that didn't mean they weren't in the area. He had to be sure, look for a trace, but one man searching the desert in the dark can't cover much ground.

If he didn't find them soon and close, then his best chance to help them was to run all night to the rendezvous and get help.

His team wasn't supposed to be here, he reminded himself. *Would Command send troops into the area?*

The radio was down, someone had to make it out. Someone had to tell Command what they had faced out here. He hoped he'd find a trail or their assailant first. Understanding his best choice was to leave his men behind didn't mean he could live with it.

Luckily, it was a decision he never had to face. Less than a minute later, he'd retraced Turner's steps and found a trail that ended abruptly in the sand, footprints indicating he'd been taken by surprise. Douglas had barely begun to study them before the night was suddenly brighter than it had any business being.

He slowly turned to the horizon as red light washed over the landscape.

The direction of the source was plain enough, the glow stronger in the distance. Not far, maybe half a mile out, but not in the direction of the rendezvous either. He had recovered Holloway's night vision scope, but it didn't help him discern what was out there. From this distance the light might as well have been coming from a small sun resting near the desert floor.

It had to be the woman. The only place he might find his team.

As he began to move, his gut wouldn't stop reminding him what happened to a bug drawn to a strange light in the night, but he wasn't leaving this desert if there was any chance of finding his team.

Douglas moved fast until he knew he was close. He'd started smelling ozone faintly on the wind and now the scent was strong. He could feel a growing static in the air pulling at the hair on his skin.

He dropped into a slow crouch as he neared what was unmistakably the last rise. Whatever was bathing the entire local area with red light was on the other side. The closer he came, the stranger the phenomenon seemed. It wasn't a vehicle or a spotlight; the light neither focused nor directional. This glow cast itself equally in every direction, such that it was like approaching a giant red lantern whose light was only blocked by the rise and fall of the sands.

The terrain was changing somewhat, mostly still sand, but he could tell he was approaching a small valley trough. There were some exposed rock surfaces. Though it was as dry as everything else, there were signs that the area might have held water at some point more recently than the rest. He took to his stomach before he crested the last rise and peered over.

For a while he didn't move, fell into a trance as he gazed upon a sphere. Floating a few feet above the desert floor, it contained a turbulence of black clouds storming across a glowing red core. He didn't even blink at the flashes of light—electricity arcing off the perfect curves of its surface to leave scorched marks in the sand.

For some time now, Douglas had suspected whatever he'd gotten into tonight was outside his depths. The moment he glimpsed that sphere hovering over the desert, suspicion became certainty.

He could get his head around the woman, rationalize her as a hostile foreign operator in possession of superior equipment. But that sphere demanded a larger explanation. The thought that he may not be dealing with a human—but something closer to ET—was no longer easy to dismiss.

Once he'd stopped witlessly staring, he noticed something twenty paces east of the sphere. An opening in the sand. At first glance he might have thought it was a tunnel, but in the red glow he could see it wasn't a natural cave or strange rock formation half buried in the sand.

He was looking at the remains of a plane's fuselage. Far from whole, it may have been from a plane that had made an emergency landing and never been recovered. Douglas wasn't a military aircraft expert, but it didn't look like it was from around here. That, and it definitely wasn't built by Boeing. He'd have guessed he was looking at about half of a cargo plane that had been there for thirty or forty years.

The plane certainly had a story, but he lost interest in imagining what it might be when he noticed Holloway alone, unconscious, and left propped up with his back to the fuselage. He wasn't far from the opening, and he wasn't moving. His shirt was torn open in the front. From where he was, Douglas could see an open cut on the left side of his chest. The wound didn't look life threatening, but it was open and bleeding. Unfortunately, what he couldn't tell from here, was whether Holloway was breathing.

There was no sign of Turner and Evans. They might be inside the fuselage, but he hadn't seen the woman yet. *Dammit . . .*

What were the chances they were any better off than Holloway? Even if he was lucky and they were inside—he couldn't carry all three out. If the woman was in the fuselage, he had to get the drop on her, hope for a clean shot before she knew he was there. If he gave her the opportunity to start the same disappearing act she'd pulled before, there was no reason to think he'd come out of it any better than the rest of his team.

Douglas crept back from the edge and began to move lateral to the sphere, using the tip of the crest to stay hidden and work his way around toward the fuselage. He wasn't just trying to stay out of sight. He didn't want to get any closer to the sphere than he needed to. The scorch marks left in the sand by the currents arcing off that thing were fair indication he wouldn't fare well if he came into contact with one.

When he was as close as he was going to get without being exposed, he stopped. He laid back on the ground and took a long breath as he looked up at the red tinted night sky. He reached into his shirt pocket and pulled out the picture he always kept close to his heart.

His wife—Evelyn.

She told him it was corny once. She was right of course but he didn't believe she minded much. They hadn't been married long, had just started talking about kids. He promised once that he'd always make it home to her. She glared at him. Not because it was corny. But because they both knew that if he broke it then he'd never have to face the consequences.

He'd told her a promise was a promise.

When she was still unconvinced, he'd smiled and said, "You married a Tibbs. We don't consider dying as an excuse to break our promises."

He closed his eyes and pressed his lips to the photo before tucking it back into his pocket.

One deep breath later and he was over the hill. Loose sand flowed past his boots and ran down the slope with each step as he descended, closing the distance between him and Holloway.

The sphere chose that moment to glow brighter. The arcs growing angrier in their frequency, such that he felt like the damn thing was growling at him like a territorial dog. Ominously, he came to realize the sphere wasn't reacting to him at all. It was simply accelerating, building up to something. What, he had no idea, but he knew he didn't want to be there to find out.

There was still no sign of the woman when he reached Holloway. He wasn't sure if it was nerves playing tricks, but he froze when he thought he heard movement inside the fuselage. Afraid to breathe, he slowly trained his rifle on the opening. Unable and unwilling to take his eyes off that hole in the sand, he reached down to press his fingers to Holloway's neck.

Finding a pulse was a small relief. For the moment, his friend may have been no use whatsoever, but it was still comforting to know he was not truly alone out here in the dark.

He took one more step toward the fuselage opening, but the sphere's growing agitation sucked away his nerve. It almost seemed to be screaming a warning at him, *you're out of time*!

Douglas saw his choices clearly: get out, maybe save Holloway and himself; stay, and any chance of anyone walking out of here shrinks by the second. If he tried to go into that fuselage and bring out Turner and Evans—he wouldn't be able to carry them and get clear. He felt it, like a horrible fact that wouldn't become false despite how much it sucked.

He grimaced—hoped he was wrong—but went back to Holloway and pushed the man sideways onto his back. He had to pull the man one handed by the forearm—otherwise he couldn't keep his rifle on the opening.

Holloway was a tall bastard, and far heavier than his thin limbs made him look. Pulling him backward up that slope was no easy task, but Douglas moved as fast as he could while trying not to make any noise.

He didn't believe he could move any faster, until he chanced a glance at the sphere. There was a shape inside. The silhouette of something from a nightmare.

It kept him moving.

"This is no place for you."

He startled, whirling toward the voice to find the woman standing no more than five paces up the slope from him. He should have fired, but there was no aggression on her features. She wasn't standing as though she were set to pounce, her arms hung at her side. That, and she didn't so much as flinch at the muzzle when it trained on her.

He held his finger over that trigger, but the woman only glanced at him for a moment. Then her eyes moved down to Holloway, and finally rested on the sphere. "I'm sorry, none of this should be happening."

The turbulence inside the sphere had become a whirlwind, and that shape was more real—the nightmare solidifying.

"Go. Now," the woman said. "Get as far away as you—"

White light erupted from the sphere. Douglas slammed his eyes shut but was still left with one large spot in his vision. The moment it ended, when they were plunged back into darkness, he stared back at the woman once more. She hadn't moved, was only a dark shadow watching him on the slope—except her eyes. They shone that eerie blue again.

Then he heard something else, coming from where the sphere had been a moment earlier. It breathed, like something with lungs the size of a rhino.

Shivering, Douglas looked away from the blue eyes and down the slope to a massive shape crouching in the darkness. There was little he could make out for certain, except that it had eyes. Empty, and white, and staring straight back at him.

Guttural growls came out of the thing, but as its mouth moved the sound was not nearly as chilling as the way the moonlight reflected off its teeth. Douglas had taken his gun off the woman and hardly realized he was doing it—a part of him had already decided he was far more worried about white eyes than blue. He let loose a blast of automatic fire, sending flames from the muzzle that momentarily illuminated the beast. Even as he began pulling Holloway all the more desperately back up the slope, sparks pinged off the creature's torso as it launched itself toward him.

He knew they were dead. It moved so fast. The weight of that thing would crush them before it ever got a chance to sink those teeth in. He and Holloway might as well be pedestrians standing in the way of a bus.

But the creature came to a hard stop out in front of him.

The woman—she'd put herself between them—stopped the massive thing in midair. She grunted with effort as her legs dug into the sand, but she didn't break—it should have been impossible.

"I said go!" she said. "Now!"

Her words held none of his fear. She'd only raised it to a yell to be sure he'd heard her over the creature's snarls. She held it with one hand at its throat. The abrupt stop had surprised it, jolted it unexpectedly, but its momentary hesitation faded as its feet found ground.

The monster's white eyes left Douglas to focus on the obstruction—savage clawed hands shot out for the woman. It moved fast—faster than he could see clearly. Yet, her forearm, seemingly tiny and insubstantial, batted its claw away, intercepting it at the wrist with enough force that it seemed to hurt the monster.

What followed was a blur, what Douglas could make of their limbs moving were the brief moments when they were still. He could feel their strength, a percussion reverberating in the air when her hand clamped down on its wrist, each snap of its teeth like an alligator's jaws slamming shut.

Realizing his rifle had clicked empty, he shook himself and swung the weapon onto his back—he doubted it was any use to him out here with these two but he wasn't giving up the only protection he had. With both hands free he was able to grab Holloway's forearms. This helped him move up the slope faster, but nothing was fast enough under the circumstances.

The woman was still holding the thing at bay. She seemed able to bat its predatory claws away while holding its snapping teeth at arm's length. Suddenly, she abandoned her footing and stepped aside. The monster didn't expect it, lost its balance, and plowed headfirst into the sand. She grabbed its wrist as it stumbled, turned in a tight half circle and loosed her grip.

Her coat whipped around her as the massive shape shot into the dark. Douglas would have lost sight of the beast entirely had a mound of sand not exploded on the opposite side of the slope. The ground shook under his feet from the impact as the monster punched into the sands to be swallowed by the desert.

He had no idea what it would take to put the beast in the ground and keep it there, but he'd seen enough to know it had only been slowed down—and would likely be all the more angry when it reemerged.

With the shake of her arm, the woman seemed to free a shaft from her coat. Longer than a knife, shorter than a sword, something steel dropped into her grip. He wouldn't have even been able to tell that much in the dark, but the steel caught the moonlight strangely. Almost as though it were somehow reflecting more light than it could possibly be catching.

"Jesus, lady . . . good luck."

Douglas was genuinely relieved that the woman was armed. He knew with no uncertainty that, given a choice, he'd rather be dealing with her again rather than the creature once they were done with one another.

Finally, he backpedaled to the top of the dune. He stopped, and heaved Holloway onto his back, knowing they wouldn't get far if he tried to drag the man by his forearms all the way back to . . .

He was running away, but he didn't know where. Back to the rocks? To the rendezvous?

The thudding of his heart was loud in his ears, but not nearly enough to drown out the massive thuds and slaps of the two titans exchanging blows behind him. He heard a clumping sound at times, as though the creature moved on all fours. Its growls chasing after him in the dark.

A roar came—a bestial sound of pain and shock.

He didn't look back. He could only hope that the woman had delivered a mortal blow.

Then, he heard another scream a moment later—this was human. A shriek of agony.

Her voice was still piercing the night when he stopped and turned to look back. As he looked at how little ground he'd covered, he was struck by the hopelessness of what he was trying to do. Even if he dropped Holloway, no man could outrun the thing that had come out of that sphere.

Her scream stopped, and the sound seemed to reverberate with certainty in his bones. He couldn't leave. If he didn't do something to keep that creature from killing her—he and Holloway would be the next course of its dinner. He stumbled turning back toward the ravine. Had no idea what he could do to help her.

He had grenades . . . maybe he could hurt it—

The woman's voice came again. Not pain and surprise, but pain and anger this time, followed by the sound of her heaving something heavy. He heard a crash, like old metal collapsing beneath a boulder.

The fuselage collapsing, he realized. Then, bright light. His feet were no longer on the ground. Hot air picked him up—Holloway with him—and threw them into the night.

Fire shot up the sand with a deafening boom, drenching the darkness away with light for the second time that evening. The blast knocked Douglas into the air and down the rise. He lost his grip on Holloway the moment it hit him. He felt his body fly through the air, then slam back into the sand.

He had little power over what happened to him as he began rolling down-hill until he finally came to a stop at the bottom of the rise, the ground still shivering beneath him. He couldn't hear anything other than a high-pitched ringing, but for the time being, there was no absence of light. Flames reached up out of the ravine to make the sky itself seem on fire. He could feel his panic, and he couldn't breathe. He'd been short of breath from carrying Holloway, but the explosion and fall had knocked the wind out of him.

He gasped and choked as his eyes searched frantically for his friend. He saw the shape of a man, not too far away. Holloway, still unconscious, face down in the sand—likely unable to breathe.

Douglas found he could not will his body to its feet any more than he could command his lungs to breathe the way he saw fit. Still, he forced himself to roll and crawl down to the man. As he made slow progress, the sky began to fall all around them. He couldn't hear it, but he felt it when a large chunk of the fuselage hit ground around him.

He kept moving, something could land on him or Holloway any second and there was absolutely nothing he could do about it. He called out to the man, but his ears were still ringing so hard that he couldn't hear his own voice. When he finally reached Holloway, it was all Douglas could do to pull the man over. As soon as Holloway's face was toward the sky, he saw the man's chest rise and fall as Holloway took a long unobstructed breath. Relieved, Douglas collapsed onto his back and focused on his own breathing.

He lay there panting, occasionally opening his eyes to look at the bonfire in the sky. He didn't know how long he was there before it occurred to him that if nothing had landed on them by now, then at least that wasn't going to be how they died tonight.

That, and it seemed the nightmare creature hadn't crawled up from the ravine to eat them.

As his breath steadied a smile began to form. He couldn't hear it, but knew he was laughing the sort of maniacal laughter one only experiences after nearly being eaten alive to find they came out of it all with a few bruises and a ringing ear.

What the hell had been in the fuselage? Military grade explosives? Old bombs from a past war?

He found himself wondering, *if an explosion goes off in the middle of the desert, and the Libyans aren't there to hear it . . . does Command still blame Douglas Tibbs?*

Finally, his ears reported something other than ringing. He thought he could hear the flames still burning.

Then he realized his hand was wet.

He held it up in front of him—for a moment he thought it was just the red of the flames, but the longer he looked the more a new fear took hold. His smile drained off his face. Blood—too much to be from anything minor.

He didn't feel injured, was it even his? He bolted up on his hands and knees, was about to check Holloway, but stilled in place as he reached for his friend.

The woman.

She was alive, stumbling toward him from the top of the dune with smoke wafting off what remained of her clothing. One of her arms was gone—severed at the shoulder. That length of strange steel she'd pulled on the beast—it was sticking out of her now. Its tip looking as though it had been stabbed through her back and out the front of her chest. The steel was still hot, blood sizzling as it cauterized on its surface.

While all of that was enough to still him, there was a light beneath her clothes. A radiant energy wisping away from her from lines embedded across her chest. Those lines were bright but flickering as though struggling to remain on.

She fell to her knees beside him, blood trickling into the sand. Douglas stared wildly into her eyes, and they flashed blue before she spoke. "Captain Tibbs . . . I need your assistance."

At dawn, Turner and Evans awoke beside one another. The events of the night were unclear at first, but after some time, they both came to remember enough. Tibbs had given them the order to investigate a potential attacker.

Evans didn't feel it, but Turner was sure they had been drugged. Said it was like his limbs were weighed down, the same feeling he sometimes had when he took a pill to help him sleep.

Figuring out their location didn't take long. Standing up and looking around, it was as though they had been left propped up against the side of a rock only a short distance from the horseshoe where they had stopped to rest the night before.

When they returned to the camp, they found their bags still there, along with Holloway's and Tibbs'. But no immediate signs of either man. So, they set about trying to piece together what had happened. Eventually, they found one set of footprints that had survived the desert's efforts to erase them. Footprints heading east.

They had lost too much time, were going to be late to the rendezvous, but they knew Holloway and Tibbs wouldn't have left them behind. Their Captain missing, command fell to Turner, and he wanted to head east to see what they could figure out. Evans didn't need an order, he expected nothing less.

They grabbed the missing men's packs and had not been walking long when they saw a figure cresting a dune. Soon, they recognized Douglas coming toward them. When they reached one another, they could see his clothes were covered in blood and sand.

"Captain, are you alright?" Turner asked.

"It's not my blood," Douglas said.

He sat in the sand. He was exhausted, like he'd spent the entire night running for his life. Evans and Turner didn't rush him for an explanation. They suspected they knew the answer but waited for him to speak of Holloway.

Eventually, Douglas took a long breath and raised an open hand to show a set of dog tags, wordlessly confirming their fears.

"The body, we'll need to carry it out?" Turner asked.

Douglas only sighed and shook his head. "There isn't anything left."

EAST COAST | 2003

What had made Peter stumble through his last few steps, Rachel couldn't tell, but he had stopped to steady himself at the edge of the sidewalk. He looked as though he'd been lost in a daydream and was now trying to remember just exactly what he was doing outside of his apartment complex.

He sighed loudly and spun to look in Rachel's direction. She leaned back, just in time to hide behind the corner of the building.

"Come out, Sis, I know you're there," Peter said.

How does he do that? she wondered, having been certain he hadn't seen her.

He didn't always realize when she was there, but when he did it was like this—as though he just knew exactly where to look.

Annoyed, she stepped out into the open.

"I told you to stop this."

Rachel acted as though he'd simply said *hello*.

"How do you do that?" she asked.

Her brother smirked. "Wouldn't believe me if I told you."

"Try me then."

"I'm psychic."

Rachel glowered at him.

"Hey, I'm not explaining myself," Peter said. "You're the one skulking around."

"Skulking," she scoffed. "I call it being proactive, this way I'm not surprised when my idiot brother finds a new way to sabotage himself."

"I get that you worry, but the spying isn't helping anyone," Peter said.

He began to walk away, and she was quick to catch up to him. "Where are we going?"

"I'm going out, you're going to take a hint."

She pretended to consider this for a moment. "Nah, I know a cry for help when I see one. You need my company."

After two more blocks passed mostly in silence with Peter poorly hiding his irritation, he seemed to accept he wasn't getting rid of her.

"How's Dad?" he asked.

"Who knows? If the Pentagon doesn't have him traveling, he's sitting in the dungeon he calls an office reading reports."

"And Jack?"

"Pokémon and Hot Wheels," Rachel said.

While that got Peter to smile, Rachel wasn't fooled by any of this small talk. Sure, her brother cared about their family, but when he got done asking after everyone else, he'd finally get to his estranged fiancé. Rachel figured she'd save him the trouble.

"Nut up," Rachel said. "Ask me about Val."

Peter winced, but he didn't try to pretend she wasn't on to him. "I assume she hates me."

"No, not yet. She's still too confused and worried to hate you," Rachel said, shaking her head. "But if you don't do something to fix this soon, she will get there."

"It would be easier for her if she just moved on," Peter said.

"Yeah . . . but that isn't really how love works, dumbass," Rachel said. "See, when someone you love just leaves, refuses to give anything close to an explanation . . . your imagination starts trying to fill in the blanks. And that sucks, Peter. Because your imagination can come up with some pretty scary stuff."

He looked away. She could see he wasn't immune to her words, but Peter hadn't really spoken to anyone in months without being forced. No amount of guilt would change his mind, but it still stung him.

He cleared his throat, "You sure we're still just talking about Val?"

That got him a glare—but she didn't pretend he was wrong.

"Would it help her move on if you told her I met someone else?" Peter asked. "That . . . I'd been cheating on her the whole time we were engaged?"

"I'm not lying to her for you. You're not seeing anyone. You hardly even leave your apartment."

Peter stopped and stared at her. She realized her words had given away the extent to which she'd been watching him—and it was more then he'd previously assumed. He looked as though he was trying to channel outrage into an explosion about boundaries, but something distracted him.

He looked up, and for a moment it was as though he forgot she was even there as he searched the faces of strangers coming and going on the sidewalk.

"So, no, I'm not gonna lie. You're gonna have to tell her the truth."

He didn't act as though he'd heard, his attention still scanning the crowd. She took a moment to try and see what he was looking at but there was nothing of note about the pedestrians around them.

"Peter?"

"What?"

"Val," she said, frowning at him. "The truth."

Her brother shook his head, looking annoyed that his attention was being divided. "It's not about the truth, there's just no future with—"

He cut himself off. Already regretting that he'd let his guard down.

"No future?"

He shook his head. "I misspoke."

"Don't do that, Peter. Are you sick? Is that what this—"

"No," he cut her off. "I'm fine. Healthier than ever. Don't go reading something into nothing."

Oh, nice try, Rachel thought, as she studied Peter, who was starting to walk away again and still barely paying attention to her.

"Look, Sis, I meant it. I really don't want company right now," Peter said. "I'll call you when I get home tonight."

Rachel gave him a sardonic smile. "Right, because I don't remember the last three times you said that."

"I'm just going grocery shopping," Peter said. "Do you plan on following me up and down every aisle?"

"That going to be a problem?"

She could see his teeth clenching as he started moving faster, soon she was power walking to keep pace. He was still searching for someone—maybe *something*—given how his gaze often seemed to search the rooftops at times.

"Peter, what the hell are you looking for?"

"Nothing," he said. "Just, thought . . . I recognized someone."

"On the roof of that RadioShack?"

Peter pulled his eyes back to the street.

"Who?" Rachel said.

He shook his head, then pointed at the grocery store. "I need to make a phone call. I'll be a minute."

She almost argued—almost. A ten-year-old would have known he was lying, given how gracelessly he was going about it. She suspected that whatever distracted him had made him nervous. That he wanted to do something about it but couldn't while she was there watching.

"Fine," she said, and turned toward the store. "But don't try to disappear on me, this conversation isn't over."

"Wouldn't dream of it," he said.

As she walked toward the grocery store, she watched his reflection in the sliding glass doors. He took his phone out, made a poor show of perusing his contacts while he waited for her to be out of eyesight. As it had played out, Rachel only had to bluff for a few seconds before circling back.

He was unsettled, not a state of mind that left him a great deal of cunning. The moment he thought she wasn't watching he dropped any pretense of a phone call and left. Her brother wasn't cut out for keeping secrets, which made her all the more worried about him.

Rachel almost lost him. He'd moved quickly, and by the time she had circled back out of the grocery store's door she barely caught sight of him turning into an alley across the street. She had to jaywalk quickly, but not so quickly that a horn or screeching tire would tell Peter she was tailing him.

As she approached the opening to the alley, she overheard her brother's voice. "I can't be gone for long."

She didn't risk exposing herself trying to peek. Instead she took out her cell and snapped a picture from around the corner. The angle of the image left a lot to be desired, but she saw who Peter was talking to. Rachel didn't recognize the man, his face partially hidden behind the brim of a fedora. But he was tall, pale blond—towheaded. Every stitch of his clothing was black.

"That won't be a problem," the stranger said.

His accent was European, though she couldn't place it. She might have had more luck if her ears had gotten a second sample, but she found herself waiting for dialog that never came.

After the silence stretched on too long, she finally chanced another peek around the corner with her phone. She blinked at the images of an alley as empty as her ears told her it was. Frowning, Rachel stepped into the open. The space was long and dead-ended by a tall fence. Slowly, she walked between the buildings. There was nowhere to go. No doors to have slipped inside, nothing to hide behind. The fire escape ladders well out of reach from the ground.

She looked at the picture on her phone—if only to confirm she hadn't imagined her brother talking to some stranger a moment ago.

"What the actual hell?" Rachel demanded, as though the unoccupied alley might explain itself.

"There she is," Peter said, as though he'd been walking down grocery aisles for some time trying to find her.

Rachel met his eyes for a long and conflicted moment. "What did your, um . . . mysterious friend have to say?"

"Sorry, what?"

"You were making a phone call," Rachel explained.

"Oh, right," Peter said, and she knew he'd already forgotten his own lie after getting rid of her. "I never said he was a friend."

She waited, but Peter didn't offer any more.

They were standing in the aisle of the grocery store where there were a few small toys and cheap paperbacks, along with everything else the store carried but didn't fit into a logical category. Her brother plucked an item off the rack and held it out. A Hot Wheels sports car, black with flames running down the sides.

"Jack have this one?" Peter asked.

She didn't want to let him change the subject so easily. She wanted to ask about the man in the alley. But . . . now that she had something to confront him with, she didn't want to do it in the middle of a grocery store. She wouldn't start asking exactly how one goes about vanishing from an alley here. Rachel knew she would find it hard not to yell if he refused to answer her again. She'd wait until they were somewhere that they wouldn't cause a scene.

She shrugged at the toy car. "I don't think he has that one."

"He used to drive me nuts. Constantly following me around wanting to play . . ." Peter trailed off. He looked at the car again and placed it in his basket. "Give it to him for me?"

"You know, you could give it to him yourself?"

He glowered at her until she sighed. "Yeah, fine."

That toy was the last thing Jack ever got from his older brother. That night, Rachel would go to Peter's apartment. She would ask him about the man in the alley. He would get angry. He'd tell her to *leave it alone.* He would tell her she *couldn't help him.*

That night, he would disappear in front of her. But, unlike the alley, he wouldn't come back no matter how long she waited. Rachel would remember the one thing Peter had told her about the stranger in the alley.

I never said he was a friend.

CHAPTER ONE

DATE | TIME: UNKNOWN | FEROXIAN PLANE

THIS CHANGES NOTHING . . . *prophet.* The memory of her words, whispered in his ear as she raked his flesh with her claws, jarred him from sleep.

Malkier opened his eyes to a faint orange glow. The bioluminescent moss only grew on the cavern walls in the deepest tunnel of his tribe's home—the breeding pits.

Slowly he sat up, not yet convinced that what he saw was real. Her body lay sprawled next to his on the cave floor. As he gazed upon her, moments of the consonance trickled back to him in memory.

For a Borealis, being taken over by the instinctual drives of his Feroxian host's body was experienced more like a hallucinogenic vision—it was far more than a mere pairing of bodies. Rapturous lust, heightened pleasure, dimmed thought, and waves of need brought on by ever-growing hormonal surges, left him with a memory that was part reality and part fantasy. The truth was simply hard to pin down.

Yet, this time disconnect was familiar. The strength of the physical changes that allowed the species to mate were waning, though their sway still lingered in his blood. Soon, Malkier was certain that what he remembered was not all illusion.

There was no question who he had gone to—which of his tribe's females had accepted his offering and lay beside him now. He knew where his heart would take him when inhibition and conscience relinquished their control. He could feel *Burns the Flame*'s breath against his skin as her chest rose and fell in slumber.

How long had they been down here? How long had it taken to fully deplete his seed? These questions and many more demanded answers, and so he rose.

He found his body sore in ways he'd not felt for over a decade. The last time he had awoken this way was after he killed *Echoes the Borealis*—the father. He did not remember the final moments of that confrontation either. There was the time missing completely in his memory and time that was blurred.

He had temporarily lost control to *Ends the Storm* again. He did not know why this happened, but it was no coincidence, there was a pattern now. It seemed that, in both instances, when he was near to triggering the Feroxian consonance, his autonomy was lost to his body's original owner. For a time, he became a voyeur catching incomplete glimpses of *Ends the Storm's* actions. And just as before, Malkier's will had only reasserted dominance to find he was in the middle of the consonance. The process so far along that even his Borealis consciousness lacked any will or desire to resist the influence of his host body's instincts.

In his last clear memory, he'd chased *Brings the Rain* to a rooftop. He'd been in a rage, his son's killer having taunted him with his grief. As he thought of this, he felt his jaw clenching into a snarl only to be cut short by a sudden jolt of pain.

His claw moved to trace the scar along his face and neck as it had a thousand times before and found an open wound. He looked in disbelief as black blood dripped from his fingertip.

A sense of déjà vu brought doubt. Vaguely, he remembered *Ends the Storm*, standing on that rooftop on Earth, and reaching for this same wound. The old scar reopened. He remembered *Ends the Storm's* pain, his moment of confusion and . . . though the Ferox seldom felt fear in battle . . . there had been an uncertainty of his victory.

Malkier could see nothing of what had followed. Try as he might, what he looked for was one of *Ends the Storm's* memories—but not his own. The longer he tried and failed to fill the void in his memory the more he shivered in anger. What good came of extracting vengeance if he was denied the memory of it?

This was an injustice—the sort that left him to the suspicion that the whole of existence was spitting in his face.

In time, he calmed himself. Shifted his focus to what he could remember.

He'd bled on that rooftop. The next thing he knew he'd been bleeding with *Burns the Flame*. That had brought pain as well—but of a different sort. His entire body was covered in the carnal scratches inflicted by his mate during the consonance.

The defenses of the Borealis device had been offline.

Malkier had no firsthand knowledge of the Feroxian consonance as experienced by the female of the species. But the raw state of his body led him to believe that even *Burns the Flame*'s unconscious animal mind had not forgotten his previous transgressions against her. Luckily for her, Malkier harbored no similar ill will toward the mother of their lost son. Had some hatred existed in him, he may well have unintentionally torn her apart when his Borealis implant returned his strength to him during the consonance. It was a strange mystery of the Ferox, only during the consonance did they ever inflict any injury on one another without consequence.

He carefully traced the contours of the reopened wound. The father had done far worse, somehow driven that spiked tip of metal through Malkier's armor. Down into his cheek and into an artery. The son had only managed to cut the surface of the scar.

It would heal soon enough.

He looked about the chamber and found what remained of the waxy purple cocoon *Ends the Storm* would have presented to *Burns the Flame*. The sack's exterior was in shreds, its gelatinous insides had been spread vulgarly around the cave floor and dried after being ripped open so she could reach her trophy. The consonance had left her ravenous. What was left of the body that laid within was still close to her. She had pushed what remained into a small hole in the cavern's wall to finish eating later.

The corpse was beyond recognition. Some human clothing lay in tatters on the floor. The metal plates of armor from inside a leather coat had been cast aside as she fed.

A shine of something small and metal caught his eye in the faint light. This was not something made of the hybrid Earth-based steel his brother had been using to equip the Earthlings. This was gold and clearly human in its construction.

As he picked it up, the human's blood was caked on the outer surface. Malkier's claw traced gently over the small trinket's curves. Eventually finding a button that flipped opened the outer face. Malkier recognized then what he held—a time keeping device, and a primitive one even by human standards.

The Ferox, of course, wore no clothing. They brought only their bodies with them into The Arena. Humans, of course, were different. Carried all sorts of things on their person. But this was a curious and fragile thing to bother taking into battle.

Sentimental perhaps, Malkier thought.

His curiosity was drawn to the writing inscribed on the inner cover. He understood the spoken form of many of the human languages from the necessity of communicating with Heyer, but he couldn't read the engraving. So, he picked up a piece of the bloodied cloth from the floor and wrapped the watch inside.

His brother was locked inside of Cede. What better way to show his betraying sibling that the son of *Echoes the Borealis* was dead than to drop this trinket wrapped in the man's bloodied clothes at his brother's feet.

He gazed at *Burns the Flame* before leaving. She would remain down here for days, in a state of temporary hibernation while his seed fertilized her many wombs. Perhaps this time she would birth a larger brood. He could be a better father this time. Give his sons and daughters everything he couldn't give *Dams the Gate*. They would be born on Earth—as he would soon deliver his people to the Promised Land.

He reached down to touch her one last time, unsure if she would allow him again once she fully awoke, but his hand never made contact. He stopped a finger's length from her as he noticed her skin.

She was beginning to molt. Their mating—it had done more than end their unfortunate abstinence. *Burns the Flame* was crossing the final threshold. Her body beginning the first stages of the change to Alpha. She would need to mate many more times before the process was completed, but the tribe would see her status elevated.

When she woke and saw her skin, she would know the prophet had been the one to push her to the final stage of maturity. He wondered, was it wise to hope this might diminish her hatred for him?

When he brought them to the Promised Land, proved himself the deliverer, there would no longer be need for his past decrees to remain in place.

As he left the breeding pits and entered the higher surface tunnels, he did so with the hope that perhaps, this too, might change her feelings toward him. However, any sense of hopefulness was short lived.

If he were a man, it would be as though Malkier had walked into Times Square to find the streets empty. The tribe's tunnels, they lacked the usual sounds and scents of his people's presence.

The strangeness led to a foreboding realization.

While he had taken care of the bonded pair inside The Never, he'd left his brother on the Feroxian Plane. He'd left Heyer imprisoned within Cede. Even if he'd somehow escaped, the dampener affixed to his brother's arm should have rendered him harmless.

No—he'd taken every precaution; his brother could not have gotten free. Yet, the longer he walked the uninhabited tunnels, the more his certainty wavered. The more questions he didn't have the answer to rose to the surface.

How long had Ends the Storm been in control?

How long had he been in the breeding pits?

Days could have potentially passed while his brother was alone with Cede.

How many times had Heyer proved himself more cunning than he presumed?

Soon, his doubts possessed his legs, and they were carrying him faster and faster to his brother's prison.

Finally, just before he reached Cede's threshold—one of the locations within the tunnel system where the true stone became his vessel in camouflage—he finally encountered an adult of his tribe. *Buries the Grave* stood awaiting his return. The Ferox stepped forward immediately and dropped to a knee, not speaking until the prophet gave consent.

"Speak," Malkier said.

"Prophet, I did not wish to disturb you below—but the tribe desperately seeks your counsel. We believe the gods have sent a sign. We do not know its meaning."

Malkier listened, and his fears subsided to a degree. Perhaps, his people had only been drawn from the caves by some oddity. The Ferox were not dear to his heart because of their intellect. The species was not stupid, but it was primitive, and prone to see the hands of the gods in phenomenon outside their grasp. Still, that his entire tribe had been drawn out to bear witness was troubling.

"Where have they gathered?" Malkier asked.

"Our gateway," *Buries the Grave* said.

"Go, tell our people I will be with them shortly," Malkier said.

With a nod, *Buries the Grave* rose from his knee and excused himself.

As was the case with any leader, being 'the prophet' required performances at times. Malkier did not allow his people to see him show distress or any great hurry. Their faith in him as the instrument of their gods on The Feroxian Plane was strengthened when he showed patience with all that came to pass—it fostered the notion that he possessed a degree of omniscience.

Malkier's doubts surfaced on his features the moment he was alone.

Buries the Grave was nearly an Alpha and a fervent believer. He was one of the Ferox Malkier sent on his behalf whenever he could not attend to something. As such, he knew the Ferox was not easily shaken, even by the unknown—and yet he could see that whatever troubled his tribe, *Buries the Grave* was not immune. Perhaps, it would not be wise to delay his presence too long. He would put his concerns regarding his brother to rest, and then attend to his tribe.

Cede hailed him the moment he crossed the threshold. "Malkier, you've been beyond my ability to contact for some time. There is much to report."

His jaw tightened—it was unusual for Cede to address him the moment he stepped across her boundaries. For the AI, this was equivalent of *Buries the Grave* awaiting him at the mouth of the tunnel.

She was troubled by something that had happened in his absence.

"My brother?" Malkier demanded as he walked.

"I wished to update you sooner . . ." Cede said as Malkier came to stand before a wall inside his main chamber. The rock façade was already shimmering as Cede reshaped herself to provide him a doorway. He saw an empty chamber reveal itself.

"Your brother escaped moments after your entry into The Never," Cede said.

Malkier's disbelief pulled him into the small chamber. Circling, his eyes searched every rocky surface and shadow—as though somehow the AI might be mistaken. When his futile denial dwindled and outrage took its place, the bloody cloth holding the pocket watch dropped to Cede's floor with a muffled clink.

His breath hastened until his chest was heaving. Every muscle fiber in his body flexed as though he wished them to snap. He dropped to his knees, hands reaching for his skull, tortured trembling claws reaching for his face as though he'd rake the flesh of his own skin.

Had it not been for Cede, the sound of this moment of lost control would have reached the surface—but as he erupted, she contained his volcanic roar within her boundaries.

For some time after, he did not speak, and the only sound in the chamber was his own heavy rage-filled breaths. Finally, when he gathered enough of himself together, he asked, "How was this possible?"

Cede began speaking before her avatar fully manifested on the chamber wall. "Your brother crossed my threshold in possession of a device. I am still working to uncover the full scope of its purpose—but of the many things it seems responsible for triggering, its activation allowed Heyer to escape my security net."

Malkier twitched, feeling a pulse of fresh rage passing through a body already overflowing with anger.

The wound of his brother's betrayals reopened. How long had Heyer been plotting? How far along? How many of his preparations remained unknown? What Cede described could not have been accomplished on any mere whim. Slipping out of a Borealis Security Net within Cede herself—his brother would have had to expect the necessity long in advance. Heyer's AI on Earth may have taken years to find a weakness and the means to exploit it.

He turned to Cede's projection just as she solidified on a nearby wall. As she had for centuries, she wore the appearance of their mother. She appeared to be standing in a room on the opposite side of a framed window cut out of the dark rock wall. Her room a bright contrast to his own, reminiscent of Borealis Architecture, an empty space enclosed by seamless milky white surfaces. Warm light with no obvious source emanated from inside.

"Show me," he said.

With a nod, a projection began to manifest inside Malkier's side of the chamber. Footage of a sort, Cede's record of his brother's escape from this very room manifested as though it were happening now. Heyer's back was propped against the wall. He seemed fragile and vulnerable, too weak to stand under the effects of the dampener—just as he'd been when Malkier had left him.

He watched his brother draw in a long breath and open his eyes. Then he spoke, "Cede, if you ever see my brother again, I want you to tell him something. He was never going to keep me out of this. War with Earth—it always meant war with me . . . so I want you to let him know that I intend to give mankind every advantage in my power. And I will be waiting for him."

Malkier's trembling stilled for a moment, his eyes narrowing on this memory of his brother. There was no vagueness in this threat—to Malkier the words *'I intend to give mankind every advantage in my power'* were quite specific.

He kept watching until the moment Heyer disappeared, then closed his eyes. When he finally spoke, his voice had a numbness to it. "I cannot find the words to express what a disappointment you are."

Cede said nothing to this—no order had been given or specific question asked. But the AI also found itself uncertain who her master was addressing.

Regardless, she waited an amount of time her programming estimated appropriate before speaking again. "If you are willing, there have been additional equally pressing developments in your absence that I believe warrant your immediate attention."

Malkier opened his eyes, took a long breath, and turned to her with disbelief. "Equally pressing?"

He had to let his anger decline, reach a numbness that would allow him to be in the presence of his people. He would hide behind the mask of the prophet, though he feared that it might take precious little to break that performance once he exited the tunnels. There was nothing to be done about it—his people had already been waiting too long.

Yet, regardless of how well he may have walled off his emotions, nothing could have prepared him for the sight outside the tunnels. For a short moment, he forgot everything else as his eyes widened upon the masses gathered beneath the black-red sky.

The Pilgrimage. His people had gathered on the tribal lands of the prophet. They had come to be delivered to the Promised Land.

The most ambitious of the males had begun the journey before the call. Drawn by hopes of glory—that they would enter the Arena to face the abomination *Brings the Rain*—said to be the legendary *Echoes the Borealis* reborn. Malkier saw no reason to tell them that the man was no more.

Regardless, those who came seeking to be the slayer of *Brings the Rain* had soon found themselves traveling with those who were answering the prophet's call. Though it seemed like weeks, less than seventy-two hours had passed since he'd stepped into The Never to kill the bonded pair. As such, his memory of the moments before, when he'd contacted the Alphas of each tribe had not been at the forefront of his mind for some time. By decree of the prophet, the war for the Promised Land was upon them. The Ferox warriors of every tribe had been called, and they now poured into the lands of his tribe.

They already numbered in the thousands—and brought a hopeful smile to Malkier's face. His brother would not stop him—his people would be delivered. He would see their faces when they knew for certain that the gods would never abandon them again.

A short time later, he arrived outside the ravine where his tribe's gateway stood. The masses from the Pilgrimage were not a part of those gathered here. Each tribe held the grounds of their gateway as sacred—those of a visiting tribe would seek the permission of the local Alpha before wandering too close. Still, the entrance to the ravine was thronged by the adults of his tribe alone. He could not see past them as he approached.

Their eyes wore the same uncertainty he had seen in *Buries the Grave*. Malkier found even he was not immune to such a reaction from his people. One seldom saw a lone Ferox warrior display fear. As such, seeing a Ferox mob—secure in the strength of their numbers—in such distress left Malkier wondering if something approaching an actual act of the gods was waiting inside that ravine.

As he was spotted, the word of his arrival spread. The crowd parted to allow him passage. His presence seeming to ease the anxiety for a moment.

Yet, soon he noticed that they seemed afraid to look at him, glancing away not in respect or submission, but as though something on his face caught them unprepared. The behavior was strange to him until he caught a faint whisper from within the crowd.

"The prophet bleeds . . ."

So much had happened, he'd forgotten the open wound on his face. Most of his people did not believe the prophet could be harmed. Those who knew better had only seen such a thing once before—when he returned from slaying *Echoes the Borealis*.

The last of those standing between him and what they had gathered to witness parted, and Malkier finally saw what had shaken the tribe so profoundly.

He had to hide his own shock behind a placid mask as he came to stand at the edge.

As Malkier stood at the perimeter he realized he had smelled death in the air for quite some time—perhaps since the moment he had stepped outside the tunnels. Though there had been a great deal to distract his thoughts, as he gazed on the ravine's contents, he failed to comprehend how the sheer strength of that scent had not screamed a warning.

It was as though he'd come upon an altar where some barbaric sacrifice had taken place. His first instinct, a primitive sort of knowing, told him he was witnessing the act of an enemy who wanted to send a clear message. Ferox corpses were piled upon the stone. Torn apart and sent back through the gateway in such a way that they were now one mass grave. The blood of his people had flowed, poured out on the ravine's sands until it seemed the platform was at the center of a swamp.

To say that his tribe's sacred site had been desecrated was a failure of words. The sight so similar to the pile of dead trophies the Ferox made to draw out combatants in The Never. There was no way to know from a glance how many lay among the dead. The remains were unrecognizable, in too many pieces to ever be reassembled. Yet, a number quickly emerged in Malkier's thoughts—a detail in Cede's report of 'equally pressing' concerns.

"Twenty-eight," the prophet whispered.

If a man was responsible for this, winning fights in The Never had not been enough. No, this spoke of a thirst for vengeance no number of Ferox lives would quench. Yet, the only man who might possess the rage and strength to do this was dead.

Buries the Grave came to his side and knelt, and the rest of his people seemed to realize they should do the same. All around him the tribe planted a fist in the sand. Malkier's gaze remained on the dead, but he nodded for *Buries the Grave* to speak.

"The carriers of the dead were not sure what to do," *Buries the Grave* said.

"Bodies kept returning, one after the other. So many so quickly—it had never happened before, it was as though they . . . they . . ."

"Rained," the prophet whispered.

"Yes, prophet," *Buries the Grave* said with a nod. "But we touched nothing, in case this was the gods—a sign meant for the prophet."

Malkier did not respond.

He stared at the horror a moment longer with eyes unreadable as his people watched on and waited for him to give the massacre meaning. As he stepped forward, his feet sunk into the bloody mud and found it still warm. As he drew closer to the dead—he noticed what his people would. That parts of these bodies looked as though they had been taken apart with great care. Skeleton and bones removed, armored exterior plates peeled off, organs possessing the incisions of fine instruments.

Finally, he caught sight of what he'd stepped into the carnage to find. Human flesh—a hand barely visible beneath a mound of Feroxian limbs. By the time he was close enough to reach the corpse his feet were ankle deep in the mud. Carefully, he moved away the remains of his people—giving the dead as much dignity possible. Finally, he pushed away a Ferox torso and exposed a man's body beneath.

He was relatively sure from its placement in the pile that this body had been the first through the gate.

He lifted the human corpse out by one arm. The act brought a sickening wet sound as the body pulled free of the sludge of Feroxian remains. As the body dangled out in front of him, he studied what was left of the face.

The Never's degradation had taken its toll, the process accelerated now that the body was deceased—but Malkier still recognized what was left of Grant Morgan's shadow. The man had died in battle, the large wound through the heart that finished him plain to see.

One of the bonded pair had survived—used the shadow's stone to escape The Never. So, whose body lay in the breeding pit?

The answer was impossible and yet seemed a certainty. But there was something far more at play here. All these bodies couldn't be explained by his brother's escape nor *Brings the Rain's* survival. There was something insidiously wrong about this. Almost as though he were meant to take it as a threat.

With his people watching, the prophet restrained himself, simply opened his hand and let the body drop abruptly back into the mud.

CHAPTER TWO

OCT 14, 2005 | 10 AM | WASHINGTON STATE

FORTY MILES SOUTH of Seattle was Joint Base Lewis-McChord. The *joint* in JBLM referred to the installation being home to both the US Army and the Air Force. The base possessed several aircraft hangars and, for the most part, they were all fairly similar.

There was one exception. Unknown, even to those who operated out of the building, this hangar possessed an elevator.

The staff never became aware of the elevator for two reasons. The first was that the doors were hidden by a façade that matched the wall at the end of a small hallway. The second, was that the elevator led to an underground facility that seldom saw use. Early that morning, anyone scheduled to work at this hangar had been temporarily reassigned.

Today, the facility was occupied.

So it was that deep beneath the surface, Olivia stood behind a thick transparent divider within a massive black shell. She watched as a smaller black box made of the same material, brought their guest of honor to his final destination.

"Strange that this reminds me of the night we met," Rivers said.

He'd been quiet since they entered the observatory. Olivia didn't follow his meaning at first, then remembered they had first met in a graveyard. The Cell had been in the middle of exhuming the coffin of Douglas Tibbs. Though, genetic testing later confirmed the body inside was a decoy. The identity of that John Doe was one of an ever growing list of questions that Olivia looked forward to making The Mark answer now that he was at her mercy. Since Rivers had pointed it out, she couldn't stop seeing just how much The Mark's transport shell resembled a coffin. The six soldiers currently carrying the box suddenly looked an awful lot like pallbearers.

"A bit macabre, Agent Rivers."

He nodded.

Patiently, they waited while the soldiers transferred the box to the research team inside the larger containment shell. Once the soldiers were dismissed, Rivers became the only male inside this entire wing of the facility. This was by design. All the alien's known contacts had been male. The only exception had been the recently discovered Rylee Silva, and the nature of that relationship remained largely mysterious. As such, Olivia implemented a cautionary security protocol. No men were allowed in this wing. The one exception she made was Agent Rivers. Without his contributions to the investigation, The Mark's capture would not have been possible. Had he wanted to sabotage that capture, he'd already had plenty of opportunities.

That, and she was grooming him for larger things—a promotion of sorts.

With her approval, the transport coffin was opened. There had been limited materials, but of all the containment shells housed beneath this facility, The Mark's prison was by far the largest. This was out of necessity. The shell had to be equipped to function as a lab, operating theater, and holding facility. Olivia had handpicked the team that would be conducting the physical study of the alien's biology. All the women were experts in their fields and vetted by The Cell's rigorous background checks.

The team worked quickly to move The Mark's body to a cold metal examination table.

As soon as the alien was in position, his arms and legs were locked down with thick steel bonds. Secondary metal restraints were then placed across his chest, waist, and thighs. No earthly creature could have broken free. For the moment, The Mark's comatose state made these precautions seem comically excessive, but the alien's physical limits remained unknown. Olivia had made this danger clear to every woman currently locked inside. When their subject awoke to find himself restrained on a surgical table, he may very well tear through those steel bonds like they were made of newspaper.

While it may have been convenient for his capture, The Mark's condition was troubling. In appearance the alien made Rivers' initial remarks all the more apt. His body currently had more in common with a corpse than a powerful being from another world.

Despite appearances, a palpable relief went through the team when the final restraint was locked in place without incident.

"Transfer completed, subject restrained, permission to proceed?" Dr. Watts, the lead researcher asked.

From behind a thick layer of ballistic glass, Olivia gave a nod and the team became a flurry of activity. Some cutting away The Mark's clothing while others attached all manner of monitoring sensors to his skin. The second round of relief touched the room when the first beep of the electrocardiograph confirmed that a heart was still beating inside the alien's chest.

Her team would need time to gather any preliminary data. Olivia didn't expect that they would have any insights about the three lines of light that oscillated between pale blue and nonexistent across the alien's chest anytime within those first few hours. Still, she had concerns she expected to be addressed quickly. She gave them a few minutes before pressing the intercom button. "Dr. Watts, I'd like your initial observations?"

In the middle of holding open The Mark's eyelids to flash a small light over his pupils, Dr. Watts stepped away, signaling a subordinate to take over. She looked up at Olivia behind the observation window. "We'll need to delay our projected study schedule, perform an exhaustive health assessment."

Olivia didn't require a PhD to see that The Mark's condition was less than ideal, but she'd hoped for better news. "How long until he can be resuscitated?"

"Ma'am, he isn't responding to stimulus. His heart rate is weak," Dr. Watts said. "He appears to be in a coma of sorts, the degree of which we'll need time to assess. If he is in a vegetative state—"

"Doctor," Olivia interjected. "At the moment, I'm only interested in when questioning can get underway."

Dr. Watts paused, the duration of which was considerably longer than Olivia would have liked.

"Ma'am, with the exceptions of the lines on his chest and the metallic brace on his arm, his anatomy presents as entirely human. He's clearly survived a severe physical trauma within the last few hours. In an ER, our immediate focus would be addressing the swelling to his brain and confirming that he has no internal hemorrhaging. If you want him to live long enough to ask him anything, I cannot recommend any invasive procedures. We need to treat him."

Olivia was still for a moment, a palpable tension gathering around her and punctuated by a long breath that seeped out slowly. "Very well. Stabilize him, but proceed with any testing that will not . . . exacerbate . . . his condition."

With a nod, Dr. Watts thought she had been dismissed.

"Doctor, I'm expecting you to know a great deal more by tomorrow morning," Olivia added.

CHAPTER THREE

COLLIN AND HAYDEN felt like the yolks in a giant Easter egg.

Thrum. Thrum. Thrum.

"Any chance you've been watching Prison Break?" Collin asked as they stared up at the curved black walls of the containment shell.

"That would be a negative," Hayden replied.

"Same."

Their cell block, if one could call it that, was a rectangular enclosure suspended inside the larger ovoid shell. There were five individual chambers inside, all connected by one hallway and entirely composed of thick clear plastic. Collin could look through his door and see Hayden lying in a cube identical to his own across the hall.

The hallway began at the shell's entrance and ended at the door to Jonathan's cell.

Apparently, he was the guest of honor, as Jonathan had been given the presidential suite—his chamber being three times the size of theirs. Still, while Collin and Hayden's cells might have been smaller, at least they had remained transparent. Though they knew Tibbs must still be in there, the entire backside of the cell block looked like a white wall. Their captors had done something to turn the shell opaque shortly after they locked Jonathan inside.

Thrum. Thrum. Thrum.

"What do you think the exchange rate is for a roll of toilet paper in here?" Hayden asked.

"Pack of smokes?" Collin asked.

"Neither of us smoke."

"The market is what it is."

Thrum. Thrum. Thrum.

Having been held prisoner for a day and a half, their panic grew less visceral with each passing hour.

The guards came and went from the door at the front of the shell that was so perfectly shaped it formed an airtight seal. Every time it opened or closed Collin could feel the pressure on his eardrums. For the first few hours neither had spoken out of sheer fear that the guards might walk back in, open their cells and beat them with one of the retractable metal batons they carried. After enough time passed in silence, the courage to test a few whispers had come. When that met with no consequences the two discovered that even if they sang *It's A Small World* at the top of their lungs no one seemed to care.

Despite the appearance of their situation, they had allowed themselves to hope that the normal due process of the legal system might eventually kick in. Those hopes died when Collin asked one of guards pushing a food tray into his cell if they would be given their phone calls soon.

She hadn't replied—exactly. She'd just ever so slowly tilted her head, giving him the sense that she found the question comically naive, and she managed to do this while wearing a full-face mask that hid her identity.

That exchange had occurred last night at what they thought was dinner. A few hours later the lights inside the shell had dimmed, leaving their only illumination what came through Jonathan's white walls.

"Guess we're supposed to sleep now?" Collin had said.

Thrum. Thrum. Thrum.

Neither had managed to drift off. For one thing, the inside of the shell wasn't quiet. Most of the time there was an ever-present white noise amid the thrumming vibrations. Had they been consistent, the noise would have faded into the background, but instead the thrumming slowly grew faster and louder over roughly twenty-minute intervals.

Thrum. Thrum. Thrum. Thrum. Thrum.

This acceleration eventually reached a peak, at which point it was too loud for Collin and Hayden to yell to one another. Then it was as though the big black eggshell discharged something, and the process started over again.

The one person they wished they could talk to, was also the only person these folks wanted quiet. Since Jonathan's walls had gone white, they hadn't heard a sound from his cell.

At first it seemed such a strange petty cruelty. As though their wardens wanted Collin and Hayden to know he was only a few feet away. Later that evening, a worse possibility had occurred to Collin. What if they had it backwards? What if these people only wanted Jonathan to know his friends were there?

With nothing to do but sit and worry, they often found themselves talking to distract from just those sorts of thoughts.

"So, do you figure these girls think we're Magneto?" Hayden asked.

"It would explain all the plastic," Collin said. "Wait . . . what do you mean *these girls?*"

"Since they took us off the truck, all the folks barking orders or coming into the egg have been women."

Collin had to stop and think about it a moment. "Huh, that's . . . that's weird isn't it?"

"It's my first kidnapping, so I'm not an expert," Hayden said. "But yeah, I think it's weird."

"Yep," Collin said. "Definitely weird."

Most of these conversations had ended this way. Some version of, "*Yep, weird,*" followed by a lull that lasted until one of them remarked on something else that seemed . . . *weird.*

Thrum. Thrum. Thrum.

"Does your room smell?" Hayden asked. "Not bad, but like, I don't know, new car-ish?"

Collin took a few sniffs. "Yeah, and sterile too."

"Weird."

"Yep."

Thrum. Thrum. Thrum.

"Think they're watching us right now?" Hayden asked. "Listening?"

Their eyes wandered over the surfaces as they had a hundred times before, this time looking to spot some surveillance device that had gone unnoticed. Neither spotted anything, and yet they still both came to the same conclusion.

"Yeah," Collin said.

Thrum. Thrum. Thrum.

"Dammit," Hayden said. "I keep thinking about how weird Jonathan's been since we found him on the floor that night."

Collin didn't say anything, this wasn't the first time they had beat their heads on this topic as they tried to make sense out of how they had ended up here.

"Do you remember Paige's birthday?" Hayden asked. "What Grant said?"

"Yeah, that Uncle Sam was watching Jonathan," Collin said.

"And all three of us just sat there assuming the guy is bat-shit crazy," Hayden said.

"It was Grant, I'm willing to forgive my . . ."

Collin had trailed off, but Hayden didn't notice. "I'm not mad at us for thinking Grant was crazy. I'm mad that Jonathan just let us believe it."

Thrum. Thrum. Thrum.

"I mean," Hayden sighed, his voice losing some of its indignation now. "Maybe he thought he was protecting us?"

Finally, Hayden noticed that Collin had been uncharacteristically quiet for some time and looked over to find his friend was sitting, his eyes telling a story of racing thoughts.

"Hey, uh, you got something to share with the class?" Hayden asked.

"I think I know who the mystery guest is," Collin said.

There were two remaining chambers on the cell block, one was clearly empty. However, not long after they had arrived, both had noticed that the other appeared to have been occupied. The blanket and mattress disheveled as though someone had slept inside recently.

"Okay, hear me out. Two days ago, Paige asked me to take her to see Grant at his new place," Collin said. "She wouldn't tell me why. I just got the feeling she didn't want to go alone. Thing is, when we got there, Grant had already cleared out. His landlord said he'd paid off everything he owed, left some vague note, and had some guys come pick up all his stuff."

Hayden sat up as he considered. "I guess that tracks, but then where has he been since we got here?"

Collin shrugged. "I'm less worried about the *Meathead* than I am Paige."

He nodded to the one empty cell that remained. "I'm starting to get the feeling that the number of cells in here isn't an accident."

Thrum. Thrum. Thrum.

"When I got up yesterday, my biggest worry was finishing a comic book on time," Hayden said.

Collin took another look around their prison. "Yeah, I've come to terms with the fact that we're going to miss our deadline."

Thrum. Thrum. Thrum.

CHAPTER FOUR

THRUM. THRUM. THRUM.

Jonathan knew he was losing his mind. At first, he'd pushed the fear away with sheer denial. Little by little, he reached a moment where even the effort to keep lying to himself was a waste of the faculties he had left. In fact, it was the same moment that he'd slumped to the floor.

Tears had run down his cheeks and dried. How many hours had passed? That sort of question had lost any meaning.

He hadn't moved, was nearly lifeless aside from the rise and fall of his chest as he breathed—the occasional blink to lubricate his eyes. To anyone watching, he looked like a man staring at the white walls of his prison as though they had lulled him into a waking dream.

There was light. It came from the other side of those white plastic boundaries. Occasionally, he saw the shadowed outline of a guard just before the slot in the door would open and food was pushed inside. The contents of what he was given never changed: a white tray, a white paper plate, crustless white bread, a white cup of milk, and a white bowl of unseasoned rice.

There was a bed, though it was more like a wide shelf protruding from the back wall. Like everything else it was made of smooth white plastic. On top rested a thin white mat and a blanket so thick and heavy it could easily be mistaken for a rug. Apparently, The Cell didn't wish to provide him with the means to strangle himself with his own bedding.

There were other necessities, toilet and sink—all the same.

When they had arrived, the guards had taken his clothes and exchanged them for a white shirt and pants. The lights overhead were bright, but not the warm yellow of a fluorescent bulb. Like everything else, it was a cold clinical white filtering in through the ceiling panels.

When he'd first been placed inside, things had looked quite different. The blindfold had come off and the walls had been transparent. He'd been able to see Collin and Hayden as they were locked into similar cells on each side of his own.

He'd still been able to hear them then. The Cell wasn't allowing them to speak, but there had been the ambient noise of their movements, the clink of metal as guards removed their restraints and barked commands that they strip off their clothes.

Jonathan hadn't seen what caused his cell to change. Perhaps the guards had flipped a switch or swiped a keycard. Maybe someone on the outside of this egg was responsible. He didn't know, but he had heard a current. Electricity ran through the plastic walls. A moment later, everything around him became white and unnaturally silent.

He had known, within seconds of this, what was happening—it came to him as he touched that thick rug-like blanket.

He remembered pulling a similar white blanket around his body for warmth in a similar room. He had been in his early twenties. He'd sat for days in white clothes, eating nothing but white and clear foods from white plates and cups. He remembered how the lights never turned off or flickered. How the door had been so seamlessly built into the wall, its hinges hidden, that often when he awoke from sleep he had been uncertain where the door was—or if it had ever actually existed at all.

White Room Torture—he'd known the name of what was being done to him just as he knew this was the opening move in a game. His captors likely didn't expect him to realize that they were taking their first step toward his mental undoing. The Cell had no way of knowing Jonathan had recently inherited a certain familiarity with such things from his father.

In the early eighties, Douglas Tibbs had been trained to spot, understand, and endure enhanced interrogation methodologies. Though, at the time they just called it torture.

Jonathan hadn't even been born yet when he was being trained.

Jonathan hadn't been born yet. He'd remembered how strange that thought had been. *I . . . I hadn't been born yet.*

The theory behind the white room suggested that after long enough isolation in this sensory deprivation, victims began to lose any sense of identity. This was a rather oversized pill of irony for Jonathan to swallow at that moment. A tragedy, how lost it would be on his captors, who had no idea how silly the notion was that he might require assistance manifesting an *identity* crisis. To say that the proverbial ship had already sailed, didn't really give the situation its due.

Under any other circumstances this might have brought a short-lived smile, but what The Cell didn't know about the world's precarious state of affairs was going to hurt a lot more than the loss of Jonathan's sanity. That his captors had chosen this strategy was bad. White Room Torture meant they were willing to play an exceptionally long game to coerce his cooperation. It was the sort of thing one did when they believed they had all the time in the world to extract information.

There was no way for them to know how wrong they were.

As such, Jonathan found himself in the sort of strange predicament one never imagines. One where he'd have preferred his captors had opted for good old conventional physical torture. At least then he could have tried to warn them of what was coming.

Thing was, he was betting this wasn't chance. The Cell had likely tried conventional tactics on other men who had been in contact with the alien. While Heyer had never told him this, it seemed doubtful that Jonathan was the first man they had ever brought in for interrogation.

Then again, maybe he was. In the past, Heyer had always been able to intervene.

Whatever the case may be, if their interrogators had managed to get one like himself into custody, then they must have tried the cruel and unusual: waterboarding, drug therapy, or plain old beatings. Having endured the things a man with an implant endured, Jonathan couldn't imagine that anything short of permanent mutilation would have cracked them.

The Cell would have to understand the man's priorities.

Fear, bruises, broken bones would never be enough, but taking out a kneecap or cutting off a limb would change the story. It was a simple equation really—one needed all their limbs to fight Ferox. Those with implants who survived long enough knew they would enter The Never in perfect condition—but that the alien device had its limits. He'd learned early on that simple wounds healed when the implant first activated—after all when an implant was put in a new host, it found itself in an open wound. Still, he severely doubted a missing leg would regrow itself.

While Jonathan had a good idea how far The Cell was willing to take things, the fact that he wasn't currently strapped to a table with a bone saw hovering over him was a fair indication that they hadn't figured this out. Any other day, this would have been reason for relief, but the window of time before mankind had to prepare for war had shrunk considerably after

Malkier tried to kill him. Suffice to say, the fact that he hadn't been asked a single question yet didn't bode well.

These had been the thoughts at the forefront of his mind when he'd first arrived. They had only sustained his attention until the force of his will could no longer hold them at the surface. Jonathan's most immediate concern wasn't the looming apocalypse, nor was it his identity crisis. Even his isolation in the white room was a somewhat laughable problem.

No. Jonathan's current problem was that Malkier may have already killed him. Heyer's brother hadn't had to break Jonathan's body with his massive Feroxian fists. All he'd had to do was sever the bond to Rylee.

He'd still had some fight in him when he'd first arrived. He knew the opportunities would present themselves. That Mr. Clean knew where they had been taken and would engage contingency protocols to extract them. People would come to free him and Heyer. They would save him and his friends. Help was coming—Jonathan only had to keep his head.

Unfortunately, he soon came to realize that this wasn't up to him. That a broken bond was a dictator that gained power until it controlled everything. In the first few hours he thought he could hold it at bay, but it never stopped getting stronger. Its hold on him tightened with every passing minute. Soon, he realized that no amount of willpower could keep his mind's focus where he wanted it.

He began to feel pain that, while familiar, was more consuming than he'd ever known. Soon, trying to prepare for the future wasn't about living up to his responsibilities. Rather, fighting to concentrate on how to salvage this situation became an attempt to find mercy from his own mind. A distraction—a place to flee the pain.

He wracked his brain for what Heyer had said of the severed bond. The symptoms. The unnatural manipulation of his biochemistry. The problem was that knowing the cause still didn't provide him any weapons to fight it. There was no consciousness to try reasoning with, the implant was doing this to him because it was mindlessly following its programming.

On some level, Jonathan knew he'd chosen this. He'd done so under duress, but he'd still read the fine print and signed the contract. His intuition had warned him, kept him at odds with accepting the bond for days until it became the only door left for him.

He'd let himself love Rylee.

When his last truly lucid moment had come and gone, the bond had taught him that Hell was so much less complicated than any philosopher or poet had ever described.

It was quite simple really. Hell was being unable to look away.

His mind, his memories, they were an inescapable maze playing inside his head. Some real, and some conjured—his own imagination being used against him.

One moment, he saw Rylee looking at him, trust in her eyes. *"I think Heyer knows what he is doing. Chose you because he knows you'd protect us. Not just from his brother or these monsters, but maybe even from him."*

He blinked, and he felt her warmth against him as he held her in the darkness. *"I wanted a lot of things. But yes . . . being a mother was one of them."*

Suddenly, he saw himself in that alley. One of so many moments where he could have chosen another fate for her. He could have chosen not to let her die. He saw his indecision leave him pathetic, unable to move—letting time make the decision for him.

Yet, the worst of it was knowing that, had he had all the time in the world to think, he wouldn't have changed that choice. Not because he couldn't, but because ever since he met Heyer, the types of decisions he got to make were never between good and evil—just bad or worse.

For the thousandth time he saw himself standing in front of her when he came back from The Never, knowing what would happen. He heard himself speaking the words that would manipulate her into the sacrifice she would make. In the end, she'd believe he wouldn't remember what had happened to her inside The Never.

Eventually, he was a passenger in a mind that couldn't be steered. His consciousness nothing more than an effort to make sense of an emotional grief too powerful to be natural. The difference between physical and emotional pain bleeding together until the distinction was lost. True agony, he learned, knew no difference.

When they first met, Rylee had been suicidal for a time.

Her bond had not been severed at the time. Heyer had said it had been incomplete. Now, he understood—he knew. Because there was nothing more terrifying than the reality that this condition was his life now.

It could torture him—but could it kill him? Right now, it didn't have an ending . . .

. . . and he couldn't look away.

CHAPTER FIVE

OCT 14, 2005 | 10 AM | WASHINGTON STATE

LEAH SAT AT a table holding an ice pack over her eye. Her cheek had stopped throbbing but felt twice its normal size after colliding with Rylee's fist earlier that morning.

She was deep underground, in one of the drab windowless rooms beneath the hangar. The lights were off, but she wasn't sitting in the dark. The glow of a flat screen monitor that took up most of the wall across from her blanketed the space as she watched multiple camera feeds. At that moment there were six in all, each displaying footage recorded half an hour earlier from containment shell two, where Jonathan and his friends would be kept for the foreseeable future.

To build the containment shells, The Cell had acquired experimental materials from another clandestine arm of the United States' military industrial complex—a division focused on R&D. This technology's original application had nothing to do with holding prisoners who were in danger of suddenly vanishing. Rather, the insulating black walls had been developed to protect what was inside from anything harmful getting in. Nothing getting out was a secondary consequence—but also exactly what The Cell needed to contain their new prisoners.

As was the case with most things, solving one problem created another. Data could not be downloaded from inside the shells without compromising the containment field. Obviously, The Cell wasn't comfortable with a holding facility they had to physically enter each time they wished to observe their prisoners. To solve this problem, surveillance video was retrieved from within the shell at randomly changing time intervals. This limited the predictability and size of any weaknesses in the shell's defenses.

This was also why Leah was watching footage that was already half an hour old but still the newest batch uploaded to the server.

A notification alert took over one of the feeds, abruptly indicating that her commanding officer was opening a secure line of communication.

She had been waiting for the call—not looking forward to it. Leah closed her eyes and took a long breath—bracing herself—before entering the necessary keystrokes to accept. The camera feeds she had been watching shrank to small boxes along the bottom of her display, making room for General Delacy's face to fill most of the screen.

He looked haggard, but his voice wasn't angry. He sounded like a person who expected bad news but still had to ask. "Is it true, are you carrying his child?"

Leah lowered the ice pack and answered with a single slow nod.

A long silence lingered afterwards.

Her entire life, General Delacy had told her that there was a time and place to assign blame and it came after everyone you cared about was safe. This was not how either of them had ever imagined this day. They were supposed to be on the brink of celebration—having accomplished what they had set out to do two years ago.

Yet, with a resigned sigh, the General began adapting to their reality. Leah, in no hurry to divide up the blame herself, was quick to join him.

"This is a precarious corner we're backed into. Olivia tells me you counseled her to keep this between the three of us. Does anyone else know?"

"Rylee. When we were alone in the garage, before she vanished."

He thought it through for a moment. "The footage from the garage may have been corrupted by The Mark's interference. If not, one of the lip readers will eventually catch it."

"I can claim that I was just trying to de-escalate a situation that had already turned violent," Leah said.

He gave a shallow nod. "That's an easy enough sell for now, but we'll be on borrowed time. Olivia will not entertain this for long. Even if she could be persuaded, when you show physical signs there won't be any hiding the truth; this is going to catch up to both of us."

He grew thoughtful. "For now, my orders to Olivia are to keep you on-site for as long as your relationships with the prisoners may be of use. You'll be under the microscope like never before. Assume she is watching your every move, and . . ."

Her father trailed until she met his knowing gaze. "Don't give her any reason to believe you won't exploit the relationships to the best of your ability. She's not stupid and she knows she has leverage on you now."

Leah nodded, though she looked as if she had swallowed something bitter.

The General hadn't seen the way Jonathan had looked at her before they were taken prisoner. She didn't think there was much *relationship* left to be gambling on. At the same time, she wasn't sure her father's assumption about Olivia's *leverage* was certain. There had been something off with Olivia when she'd confronted her about the pregnancy—a moment of compassion in the woman's consistently stone-faced professionalism. That said, the prospect of catching a second glimpse of Olivia's repressed humanity was something she wanted to depend on even less than the state of her and Jonathan's relationship.

"There is only so much I can push under the rug before I cross a line that won't be ignored. You . . ."

He hesitated, sighing heavily before continuing. "Leah, there is no gentle way of putting this. Under the circumstances, you may not be given a choice in what happens. The Cell will want you to carry the child to term despite whatever your wishes may be. It will be the subject of research. If I were to attempt to intervene—"

"I know," Leah interrupted, closing her eyes as a shudder passed through her.

"It's why you kept this from everyone—including me?" her father asked.

Tears came, though she fought them. "Was going to wait as long as I could, until pretending I didn't know would be too suspicious. I thought that I'd have more time."

His features softened as he leaned back in his chair.

"Not the way I imagined hearing I will be a grandfather," he said.

She smiled—grateful that he was still being decent despite her missteps.

"Leah, should the time come, you do what you must. Don't look back. Don't give me a second thought. Remember that I said that," he emphasized.

She blinked, looking up at him with a frown despite the tears still running down her swollen cheek.

"Usually . . . you're the smart one," he said. "We both know it. So, if the opportunity presents itself, take it."

What he was saying—exactly—she wasn't sure. She knew her father, and it felt like he was giving her some sort of permission to leave him behind. The moment slipped away as quickly as it had come. He didn't seem to want her overthinking what he said. He cleared his throat and that softness that had been in his voice departed. "For now, we're too close. So, nothing changes.

We're going to find out what happened to Peter and all the others. If we lose sight of that—it's all been for nothing."

Leah had to look away. She tried to give the appearance that she was simply wiping away her tears, putting on her game face. Not let him see how little hope remained in her that either of them would see Peter alive again.

"To that effect," he said, drawing her attention back to the monitors. "You requested the footage from the alien's capture. Olivia said you expressed a certain degree of urgency."

As her father's face shrank down to a manageable size on the display, the feeds of Jonathan and his roommates inside the containment cell were replaced with footage from their capture.

She had to pull herself out of the murk of her thoughts. Her lips drew into a line as she forced herself to concentrate on the events that played out around the time of Rylee's disappearance. Her father waited as she watched the video in its entirety three times.

Something in the film was eating at her, and the feeling grew with each viewing. For a while now, Jonathan's expressions, the language of his face, had been less and less of a mystery to her. Yet, while in the midst of those last words to Rylee, everything about him lost certainty. The way he stood, the cadence of his voice, even the words he used.

They all came from Jonathan—yet they weren't quite right.

When she'd first noticed the subtle differences, she thought it was the stress they had all been under at that moment. Now, with each review of the tapes, she was more convinced. Her suspicions had only grown as she watched the security camera footage from inside his prison cell. It had been hard for her to watch because whatever was different about him, he wasn't simply having an off day—he seemed broken.

She started the film over again. Watched Jonathan turn a hard, calculating gaze on each of The Cell's agents as they demanded he stand down. He'd stood there unmoving longer than any sane person with so many guns trained on him would have dared. It would have been one thing if she thought he had frozen up in fear, but if anything, The Cell's arrival gave him a look like . . . like . . . he didn't have time for them.

Finally, with a strained tremble, Jonathan closed his eyes. She couldn't tell if it was in defeat or frustration. Neither seemed right. And as she watched again and again, she was more convinced that it was neither. That if anything, it was more like something had made his skin crawl. Then, each time, a look of resignation came over him just before he went to his knees.

Finally, Leah shook her head. "I don't know. Something is wrong here."

Her father gave no indication that he doubted her. Even as a child she had an intuition for people that was seldom wrong. "Get a tech to examine the footage, might help reveal what your gut is trying to tell you. I'd be quick about it though, there is a growing chance that Olivia will send you back in per the contingencies we've discussed."

Leah looked up in surprise, almost like she must have had misheard him. "I . . . I don't understand."

"You saw The Mark's state when he was captured?"

"He was bleeding . . . unconscious," Leah said.

Delacy nodded. "He's still not regained consciousness, and his condition is deteriorating. The consensus of the medical team is that his apparent coma isn't natural, and any attempt to bring him around is more likely to kill him than help. Until that changes, interrogating The Mark isn't on the table."

Her heart sank into her stomach. When The Mark had been captured, she'd hoped Jonathan wasn't going to be in real danger. He'd be held against his will, but realistically that fate had been sealed the night The Mark had turned him into a person of interest.

The Cell assumed Jonathan would be better off in their custody. For years, it remained unknown if those they considered accomplices to The Mark were willing or unwilling allies. Leah had believed the latter, that both Jonathan and her brother had somehow been ensnared in a trap of The Mark's making. That the alien held something over them to force their compliance with whatever it was he was doing on Earth.

After this morning, she wasn't sure. When The Mark appeared in the garage, Jonathan had been frantic to help him. So frantic, he'd been able to temporarily push his grief for Rylee aside if it meant getting the alien to safety. He'd known what was coming.

Leah had done all she could to keep him out of custody as long as possible. But, if The Mark couldn't be interrogated, Olivia's full attention would turn to Jonathan. It was also why her father was talking about contingencies she'd thought obsolete. The Cell had planned ahead, knew better than to burn a bridge that might be useful. It was why so much effort had been put into the pageantry of making it seem that Leah was captured along with Hayden and Collin. They wanted her cover to remain intact.

"Putting me anywhere near Jonathan is a mistake," Leah said. "He'd made me, I saw it in his eyes when we were captured."

"Are you certain?" Delacy asked.

"I slipped and he caught it," Leah said. "I doubt I can convince him otherwise."

Delacy sighed. "We better hope he cooperates then. For his sake as well as yours."

She despaired at the thought—knew what The Cell was capable of when a prisoner didn't talk. Grant Morgan had been stubborn. She had not been able to watch. His interrogation was still ongoing—The Cell didn't stop until they were sure they knew everything.

Jonathan's interrogation would be worse. Grant had no family or friends that could be threatened for leverage. Meanwhile, two of Jonathan's best friends were sitting in cells no more than ten feet from his own. His mother and Paige could be added to the list of prisoners within an hour if Olivia ordered it.

"Be ready to play whatever role Olivia asks. You're in a better position if she doesn't lose confidence that you can influence him," Delacy said.

Leah nodded, but the fire she normally felt for the mission wasn't there. She thought her father would sign off, and she'd be left in the dark room with her thoughts again. When she looked up, he was still there. She saw he was weighed down considering—something.

She waited, and he finally spoke. "Leah, if this all falls apart, we need to be ready. There are a few things you need to know about this facility."

CHAPTER SIX

OCT 15, 2005 | NOON | SEATTLE

PAIGE HADN'T SPOKEN to Colonel Hamill in years.

'Black hole sun . . .'

Anxious as she was, humming along with the lyrics helped.

'Won't you come . . .'

She'd been young the first time she saw the Black Sun. A sculpture the size and shape of a monster truck tire that stood in front of the Asian Art Museum in Volunteer Park.

'And wash away the rain . . .'

She remembered asking her father why anyone would sculpt a giant metal donut. He'd shrugged. "I haven't the foggiest idea what goes on in the head of an artist, Gigi."

He'd shown her how if you stood in the right spot, you could see the Space Needle through the void at the sculpture's center.

'Won't you come . . . Won't you come . . .'

Evelyn had wanted to be here, but Paige thought it best to come alone. Jonathan's mother had compromised and was now parked up the road watching from the rear-view mirror of her car. This early, the only occupants in the park were walkers and joggers. Which meant Evelyn's car was one of only three nearby and was easily noticed as being occupied.

The Colonel had been understandably awkward on the phone. They hadn't spoken in years and for good reason. Paige hadn't wanted him in her life, and for the most part he'd respected her wishes. When she had called out of the blue last night, he'd been at a bit of a loss. She'd sidestepped the insincere pleasantries, let him know quite bluntly that nothing had changed, and she wouldn't be calling—but her friends were in trouble.

She had begun to feel the emptiness in their house last night. More than their mere absence, but the sort of painful loneliness that stirred in her gut when she feared she'd never see someone again.

Her father hadn't said to come alone when she'd told him where to meet. Paige figured he would have, but he wasn't taking her seriously yet. On the phone, he'd made a show of believing every word of her story. He hadn't heard from her in so long he was afraid that questioning anything she said might push her away. She knew how it all sounded. In a way, she wanted him to be skeptical because she wanted to be wrong. As long as his skepticism didn't stop him from looking into the matter in earnest. Thing was, being a Colonel gave him the keys to doors that a frantic mother and a civilian couldn't open.

She saw him approaching, recognized the way he walked long before she could make out his face. He had a pink cardboard box under one arm, the sort you picked up at a bakery. He wasn't in uniform. In civilian clothing his presence seemed diminished from the figure in her memory. She supposed he'd always been skinny; when she was younger it hadn't seemed as severe, but now he bordered on unhealthy. The closer he got she saw how his skin had aged, grown darker with liver spots. His eyes were puffy, as though he'd gotten as little sleep as she had of late.

"It's good to see you, Gigi," he said.

She sucked in her lips, and bit down a bit. "No one calls me that anymore."

"I'm sorry, you're not a little girl, I get it," the Colonel said.

"It's fine," Paige said. "Thanks . . . for coming so quickly."

"You did the right thing," the Colonel said. "Calling me that is."

"I did, did I?" she asked. "That mean you can tell me something?"

Colonel Hamill gestured to the space beside her. "May I?"

She shrugged, and he took a seat, placing the cardboard box between them.

"Don't suppose you recognize these?" he asked, lifting the lid.

She let out a small breath of amusement. "They . . . look like blueberry glazed."

He nodded. "I hope they're still your favorite."

She knew he meant well, but she was on guard against cheap sentimental gestures. He owed her a debt, and being honest, it wasn't one she ever really wanted to see him find a way to repay.

"I'm not really hungry," she said.

"I understand," he said. "Do you mind if I go ahead and have one?"

"Knock yourself out."

He took a napkin and picked up a donut. As he did so, she thought she saw the outline of an envelope beneath the thin wax paper lining of the box. She pondered that for a moment.

"Um, you know what, now that I can smell them, maybe I could eat . . ."

The Colonel smiled, endearingly as he did so with his cheeks full. She'd been careful not to stare too intently as she took a pastry herself. Still, there was no doubt, the Colonel had placed something inside the box. If he were drawing her attention to it like this, he must have needed her to realize he couldn't be seen handing it to her.

So, they were being watched—they weren't paranoid.

"You keep the rest," he said. "I shouldn't be eating these things anyway. Blood sugar isn't that forgiving these days."

"Huh, right," Paige said; she'd forgotten he was diabetic.

She took another bite, savoring it before getting on with their business. At this point, their interactions were a performance for those watching.

"So," Paige said. "You were saying I did the right thing calling you?"

The Colonel nodded.

"Generally, these things are handled with more discretion. It is true, sometimes citizens are taken into custody for reasons outside the norms of an everyday arrest. That said, even taking your word that everything was as you described it, I had to keep a measure of doubt, not jump to scandalous conclusions."

Paige sighed. "Look, my roommates aren't what you'd call adventurous. I already looked into all the everyday numbskull reasons they might be missing. I know how this sounds. I was hoping you'd tell me I'm seeing some paranoid conspiracy in a bunch of coincidences. That my friends will miraculously walk through the door any minute."

The Colonel nodded sympathetically and said, "Thing is, a military or law enforcement agency would need damn good reasons to be so secretive about their whereabouts. But . . . while running their names . . ."

The Colonel paused, choosing his next words very carefully.

"I received a phone call from someone. They didn't give a name or rank, identified themselves as an associate of General Delacy. You don't get a call from such a man that late in the evening for a pleasant chat. He was quite . . . indirect . . . only said that for reasons I could surely understand, I had not been made aware of my daughter's proximity to the subjects of an ongoing investigation. That up until now, they had still been assessing whether or not you were actively involved."

He continued, "Suffice to say, I was given the distinct impression that if

I continued inquiring on your behalf, someone might decide that they had been mistaken, and that my daughter had been quite involved all along."

Paige closed her eyes and swallowed a bite. The subtext was clear enough: *Now that you know you're not insane—stop asking questions.*

"Jesus," Paige said. "If that is indirect, I don't want to find out what direct looks like."

The Colonel nodded gravely. "I know it isn't what you want to hear. I fear that if I try to tell you what to do, you'll do the opposite. But, please, if you feel you must act, don't throw self-preservation out the window. Be smart."

Was he giving her wise advice or reminding her just how much of a coward he could be? She couldn't tell.

"Okay," she said, cramming the last of the donut into her mouth. "That all you can tell me?"

He looked down at her feet for a while. Even under the circumstances, he seemed to want a reason to stay a bit longer. But he knew the only thing keeping her there was information. Clearly, he didn't have any more.

"I'd appreciate it if you would keep in contact. A text or an email. Just for the next few weeks. Just so I know you're safe."

She took a long breath, picking up the box in more of a hurry than she'd intended. "I'll think about it."

She tried not to look back as she walked away, but there was something cold in the action, something childish and unnecessary despite their history. He was still sitting there, watching her leave when she stopped and turned around.

"Thank you, Colonel," Paige said. "For the donuts."

"I'm glad you still like them," he said. "Some things don't change."

Before she turned away, she glanced over his shoulder and saw the Space Needle through the Black Sun's void.

The radio played softly in the background as Evelyn watched Paige through her rear-view mirror.

Disturbing news out of Louisiana this morning. A prison inmate, Beo Rhodes, has authorities baffled after disappearing from his cell.

Listeners may recognize the name. Rhodes made national headlines a few years back after walking into a New Orleans police department and confessing to six unsolved murders. After pleading guilty to charges, Rhodes had been serving out multiple life sentences inside the State Penitentiary.

Sources say that Rhodes' cell was found empty by Correctional Officers during routine rounds between the hours of eleven and midnight. Surveillance videos show Rhodes was placed into his cell for lockdown where he remained undisturbed until his bed was discovered empty. Thus far, authorities haven't provided any speculation as to how Rhodes may have managed to get out of his cell. A local manhunt—

Evelyn turned the radio down as Paige opened the passenger door and got inside.

"Can he help?" Evelyn asked.

"He's scared," Paige said. "Someone already got to him. He isn't going to stick his neck out."

"What's with the box?" Evelyn asked.

Paige opened the lid and held the contents up to her. She was subtle, but drew attention to the outline of the envelope beneath the thin wax paper.

"He brought donuts to soften the news. Like, I'm eight years old and he can make things better by taking me out for ice cream," Paige said.

"They smell good though," Evelyn said.

Paige's eyes narrowed. "They smell like guilt . . . but they are blueberry."

She wasn't sure precisely how much of Paige's behavior was theater. She knew the girl hadn't wanted to call her father, only did so because loved ones' lives were in danger. Evelyn followed her lead; they weren't meeting strangers in strange places and staying off cell phones for fun.

"Can't blame your father for trying," Evelyn said. "No matter how bad you screw up with your kid, you have to keep—"

"Evelyn," Paige closed her eyes and held up a finger to interrupt. "Have a donut. I'll let you know when I'm in the mood for a Hallmark moment."

CHAPTER SEVEN

OCT 15, 2005 | NOON | JBLM FACILITY

"I APOLOGIZE," DR. WATTS said. "Initially, the trauma to his body was the most probable cause for his comatose state. Now that we've factored the injuries out . . ."

The door sealed behind him as Rivers entered the observation deck in the alien's containment shell. Below, most of Dr. Watts' staff was grouped around an x-ray review board. Olivia waved for him to join her as she listened to Dr. Watts' update through the intercom.

"He is presenting like a man under anesthesia, but none of the blood work has shown the presence of any chemicals used to induce an artificial coma. We believe that the bracer is responsible."

"What can you tell me about it?" Olivia asked.

"The steel is seamless, indestructible as far as we can discern. We are still working on a way to remove it."

"What makes you think it's responsible for the coma?"

"X-rays and ultrasound show hundreds of thin wire-like connections emanating out into the subject's limb from the band's inner ring. They run up the length of his arm. It appears they are somehow manipulating his nervous system."

Olivia released the intercom's button, tapping her finger a few times in a short-lived hesitation. She concluded she was entertaining some degree of nonsense, then reopened the line. "Is there any reason a surgical option isn't feasible?"

"You . . . you wish us to attempt to disconnect internal wiring? We could try, but those connections are likely made of the same material as the band—"

"Amputation," Olivia said. "Remove the arm and the bracer with it."

There was a pause from Dr. Watts' side of the glass. "We hadn't considered . . . I would like to consult with the surgical team to see what their assessment of the risks might be. But I would not recommend resorting to such extremes until we've exhausted all other options."

"Agreed," Olivia said. "Consult with your team, get me a report with any viable alternatives for removing the band. We'll begin with the least invasive and work our way up."

"Yes, ma'am," Dr. Watts said.

Even with the lower half of her face covered by a surgical mask, Rivers could tell Dr. Watts was uncomfortable with what she had just agreed to. She was still a doctor, and the alien was still her patient.

When Olivia turned away from the window, she sighed and closed her eyes. Rivers didn't need to ask, everyone was feeling the cloud of disappointment. Despite all the preparation done in anticipation of this day, nothing had gone their way since they'd captured The Mark. Now, all their answers lay below. Yet, the alien continued outmaneuvering them by simply refusing to wake up.

"What do you think the chances are that Mr. Tibbs knows how to remove that bracer?" Olivia asked.

"Think he'd be willing to cooperate?" Rivers asked.

Olivia opened her eyes, looking at him as though he were being purposely dense. "He'll cooperate; his willingness isn't relevant."

Rivers took a long breath but reconsidered the question. "When we debriefed Leah, she said Jonathan tried to get his roommates to help move him. He needed a car. Must have been planning to take The Mark somewhere—might be worth finding out where and why."

Later that day, Olivia's people were still in the process of transitioning the upper building into a suitable center for long-term operations. The other military personnel of the surrounding base had little direct involvement with her people. Troops provided additional manpower for the perimeter guard but mainly served to make sure that only those The Cell wanted escorted in or out could do so.

When Leah took the elevator to the surface, the wide-open space where aircraft were normally parked had already been cleared out. The Cell's agents were in the process of erecting rows of cubicles along with sleeping and living quarters.

The moment The Mark had been brought into the facility, a quarantine had gone into effect. Anyone who knew what was imprisoned below, even those at the highest levels of The Cell's chain of command, could not leave the hangar. A protocol from which Olivia excluded no one—including herself. She had moved into temporary living quarters below the same day as The Mark.

Given what had recently transpired between them, Leah wasn't surprised that her own quarters were in the lower levels. For the time being, as long as Leah made no attempt to leave the hangar, she retained enough autonomy to go where she pleased within. The only exception being the two lower wings that housed the prisoner containment shells.

Finding Agent Rivers didn't take long. He wasn't responsible for overseeing the work on the hangar's upper floor, nonetheless she had been told that was where she would find him. When she saw him, he was talking with a woman to whom Leah had not yet been introduced. She had seen her a handful of times in the recent week. Prior to The Mark's capture, she had been working out of The Cell's hub near Jonathan's residence.

When Rivers saw Leah approaching, he gave a sympathetic grimace. "That's gonna be quite the shiner."

"I'll live," Leah said, though she still moved her hair so that it hid the bruise. "Am I interrupting?"

"No," Rivers replied, giving a nod to the woman standing beside him. "Leah, this is Margot. She was key in disabling The Mark's ability to disappear on us."

"Ahh, so you're the one," Leah said, as she took Margot's hand. "We're all grateful for the work you've done."

"Appreciate that, but if I knew it would only get me locked in a hangar, I might have put less effort in," Margot said.

Leah smiled sympathetically, before turning to Rivers. "I was hoping you could spare me an analyst, someone to help me with the footage we pulled from Jonathan's garage."

"We're not quite fully operational here yet," Rivers said. "The tech staff transferred the servers from the old HQ. They're up, but the work stations themselves are—"

"I'm available," Margot interrupted.

Rivers paused. He looked as though he were about to explain how there was a process for these sorts of requests, but Margot didn't let him start. "Get over it, Rivers. I'll make sure the damn TPS report gets a coversheet."

He tried to hide his further hesitation. "Uh, I think—"

"These fine folks are paying me until I'm cleared to go home. My station was set up half an hour ago and I'd rather be doing something with my time."

What happened next made it hard for Leah to keep a straight face. Rivers opened his mouth to protest once more, and Margot didn't just stop him. She put a finger on his lips as though she were his mother. "Laurence, I know you've got more important things to do than prove to me your OCD is worse than I suspected."

Begrudgingly, Rivers moved her finger away, and excused himself.

When he was gone Leah watched Margot curiously. The whole interaction was surprisingly off-brand for The Cell. "You call him Laurence?"

The only people in the hangar who were addressed by first names were Olivia and Leah herself, and in their case the names were aliases; they might as well have been a rank designation. It was unusual to hear The Cell's agents speak to one another on a first name basis.

"You know someone long enough it gets to feel ridiculous calling them *Agent Rivers,*" Margot said.

Leah was already starting to like Margot; it seemed she had no interest in maintaining a stiff professionalism and it was a relief.

Once Rivers was out of earshot, Margot winked at her. "Five bucks says he only let that go so he could look up TPS in the Operating Procedures. He can't tolerate not knowing an acronym."

Margot directed her to join her in the cubicle where Leah handed over the memory card with the footage.

"So, what are we looking for here?"

Leah sighed. "That's the question."

"Something in the feed is bothering you?"

"I don't think the recording was corrupted. There is just something there that I'm missing."

"If you know what timestamps to start with that's better than nothing," Margot said. "Anything else you can tell me might give me some ideas."

Leah nodded.

"I've studied this a dozen times; Jonathan knew Rylee was going to vanish and he knew the alien was going to appear. Yet, he didn't know we were coming for them."

She gave her reasoning to Margot. In the case of Rylee, it was how he behaved before and after she disappeared. He spoke to her like he knew he'd never get another chance—like his words had to count. Then, when she'd vanished, he had fallen on his knees pleading that he'd only needed a few more seconds. He'd been a lot of things in that moment—but surprised had not been one of them.

Then there had been the arrival of The Mark. Everyone in the room had jumped back in fear as an ethereal black and red cloud had spit a comatose man into the center of the garage. Leah had scrambled back on hands and knees until her back hit a cupboard. Hayden and Collin, eyes wide with shock, had pressed themselves against the back wall.

Meanwhile, Jonathan hardly blinked. He didn't even look worried until he thought the alien might have been dead.

None of it made sense. The basis for the secondary protocol was that Jonathan was capable of precognition as had been observed with other subjects. How could he have known Rylee was going to disappear, but be caught off guard by The Cell's arrival? How could he know The Mark would arrive, but then be surprised by the condition he was in when he got there? How was it that he seemed so prepared for some things but not others?

"Alright," Margot said. "I guess we'll start with the girl's disappearance then?"

Leah nodded as Margot inserted the memory card, but she was distracted by a folder labeled "R. Silva Translation Library" already open on the computer's desktop. Margot, seeing it, quickly moved to shut it.

"Wait," Leah said. "What is that?"

The woman squirmed a bit, her face reddening. "An example of why I really need to get in the habit of closing windows on my work computer," she said.

Her mouse cursor moved across the screen to close the file, but Leah stopped her.

"No, wait," Leah said. "I . . . I don't care if you weren't supposed to be looking, I just want to know. Is that what I think it is?"

Seeing she wasn't in trouble, Margot shrugged. "Translations of the missing girl's journals. The Cell confiscated the rest of her notebooks from an apartment on the east coast. Translators said they didn't find anything to flag for relevance in the investigation. So, they were just sitting there on the server."

Leah considered. "They still finished translating it? Even after they had decided it was a dead-end?"

"I'm guessing they were paid hourly," Margot smirked. ". . . and I know

I shouldn't be reading them, but with her disappearing, I just felt like . . . someone should."

"Would you copy the files to my disk?" Leah asked.

Margot frowned, but her defensiveness vanished. With a shrug she dragged the folder onto the disk.

CHAPTER EIGHT

HE STOOD IN the street outside his house. There was no sunlight, no porch or streetlights, not a single light in a window in the neighboring houses. But, this wasn't simply night—there was no moon or stars.

He thought the sky was an empty black, but then there was an eerie movement to it—like eels swimming through ink.

He shivered, as he knew that in that darkness something was gazing back at him. In this place, he could feel the shadows reach for him whenever he turned his back. That black sky owned him, and however it had come to be that he'd gotten free of it—it was only a matter of time before it would drag him back.

Instinctively, he moved toward the only light there was. He found himself standing in his driveway. He knew, somehow, that this was all that was left. The only thing the dark shroud closing in on him had yet to stain.

The garage door was up—the light came from inside.

Rylee was standing beneath those lights. Her back to him and her hands resting on her waist. Sweat glistened on her skin as her chest heaved from exertion. He could see her face reflected in the mirrors along the wall. Her eyes were closed.

For a moment, he forgot the darkness.

He stepped toward her slowly, as though she were a fairy creature and he'd risk losing her forever if he spooked her. She sensed him though. Her head tilted knowingly toward his presence as a slight curve came to the edge of her lips.

Then, the lights quivered.

For a moment, Jonathan froze in place as they flickered and dimmed. He saw her reflection change in the mirrors. When the light weakened, Rylee's reflection wasn't Rylee—but the girl in the pink hoodie. When the light grew strong and steadied again, she was Rylee.

Finally, she opened her eyes and stared back. "It's Jonathan Tibbs. Mankind's piss-poor excuse for a messiah. Do you go by *Brings the Rain* now?"

She . . . she *was* mocking him . . . he loved her for it. The words put a warmth in his chest that spread through his limbs revealing just how ice cold he had been a moment earlier.

"The Patron Saint of Monster Slayers?" she asked.

He was about to speak, but fear stopped him. He didn't want to break this dream. At the same time, what good could possibly come from speaking to his own delusion? He wasn't sure if he were sane, but should he choose a road that could only end in madness? Looking at her, he knew that madness might be the closest thing to safety he'd felt since the bond had broken.

"Oh, come now, give me one of those witless comebacks."

He wanted to obey.

She didn't give up. "You know, Tibbs, I hope this isn't what you meant when you said, *we don't cease to exist.*"

The lights flickered again, and she stopped to glare at them. When they steadied, it was almost as though they did so out of fear of her, and she went on like there had been no interruption.

"If all you meant was that you'd remember me, then you seriously oversold the situation."

He shook his head. *She had to know that wasn't what he'd meant.*

"No? Oh good!" Rylee said, her relief exaggerated. "For a minute there I was worried my big legacy was going to be being immortalized in the PG-13 way you remembered us."

He really wanted to ask what she meant by that. She'd known he would— she was baiting him after all. Rylee finally sighed when he didn't give in. For a moment she seemed to drop everything. While she looked like Rylee, this momentarily became a costume worn by someone else as her mannerisms and words fell out of character. "You can't lose anymore of yourself talking to me, Jonathan. I won't hurt you. I can't hurt you."

Jonathan looked down at the floor and nodded. "Okay, PG-13, let's hear it."

She was Rylee again, acting as though the mask had never slipped. Her smile returned as she tapped a finger on the side of her head. "All the NC-17 action was stored in my head," she said.

He smiled.

He smiled right up until the moment his brain ruined it by thinking. "That was funny. You've always been funnier than me."

"Thanks?" she said, the statement so obvious that she'd said the word as though it were a question.

"How can that be, if I'm just talking to myself?"

She smiled at the question in what seemed a deliberate hint that she knew something he didn't, but she didn't answer.

"You know, you weren't even going to talk to me," she said, as she reached behind her back and brought out his father's pocket watch. She flipped the face open, acting as though she'd been timing him since he first arrived. "You caved in like eleven seconds. Clearly, I'm irresistible."

She was in her training attire, which despite its utility had always been distractingly skintight. As such, Jonathan was left to wonder where she could have possibly been hiding that watch.

"Eleven seconds huh?" he said, with a skeptical frown. "Except that thing hasn't kept time in years."

Rylee rolled her eyes. "I know, I wanted to fix it for you."

He felt himself relaxing again, growing comfortable and safe. He knew then what she was doing. She'd changed the subject, distracted him when he asked if she was more than a dream.

He remembered the first thing she said to him when he stepped into the garage. And he wondered out loud. "Messiah, I'd never call myself that."

"Doesn't fit, right? Like you bought your jock strap in the men's aisle instead of the little boys' department," she said.

He ignored her jab, his mind wandering to what Hayden might have said. And a memory joined them in the garage. As though suddenly he could see Hayden sitting on the living room couch lecturing Collin. "Champions just save people from danger. Gods save people from ceasing to exist. Messiahs save people from themselves—from internal threats—threats to their soul."

"What about a savior?" Collin asked. "They're a little of both."

Just as quickly as they'd appeared, they evaporated like a dissipating fog as Rylee walked through them. She scoffed as though offended. "Don't bring them into this. You can argue theology with your roommates on your own time."

He hadn't adjusted to the strangeness of the whole event. "I didn't know that would happen . . . wait, my time? Whose time would it—"

"Stop. Do you ever stop thinking so damn much?" Rylee asked.

He didn't know what to say, she looked so angry. "Maybe, I died saving your ass because your alien friend had me convinced it was game over for everyone if I didn't. Maybe, I don't need your humility. Maybe, I don't want to stand here and listen to you say that, *actually, you're not that big of a deal.*"

She may as well have slapped him.

For a second, he didn't know what to make of her—and he began to fear this wasn't what he'd thought. That the bond was tricking him, using his imagination against him to conjure more elaborate tortures.

But no, her words hurt, but as she held his eyes, they still felt different from the bond. She was justified saying these things. She, more than anyone, had every right to demand he step up and be what was promised.

Slowly, he turned away. He looked out of the garage to the edge of the light. He pointed to the darkness, it had moved closer while he'd been here with her. "You know—better than anyone—there isn't any fighting that."

She didn't speak right away. When she did, her voice had an honesty to it—as though she were simply stating a fact. "You can't fail."

"I assure you I can."

"No," Rylee said, shaking her head. She held his eyes again, no nonsense in her gaze. "Listen to the words. *I can't fail.*"

He stared back wondering how she could have such certainty. His eyes pleading to make those words mean something real.

After a time, her face softened. She leaned back and folded her arms across her chest as she considered him. He could swear that she thought he was up to something even if he hadn't realized it for himself. "I get it. You don't remember."

"Remember what?"

"'I can't fail'. They're your words, not mine."

Something slippery and vague sparked in his memory. He'd remembered looking into his own eyes—but not in the mirror . . . and he had whispered, or maybe thought, those words over and over again.

I can't fail.

He couldn't grasp any more of it, couldn't place where it fit into the story of his life. All he knew was that in that moment, he'd believed.

"Stop, you're trying to force it, Jonathan," Rylee said. "For now, take some comfort. Get past this one little—obstacle—and you'll see. All the hard stuff is taken care of. Heyer has been planning for years, all you have to do is get it done."

He closed his eyes. "Heyer's plan?"

Jonathan sighed, he felt like a doctor walking into a hospital waiting room to tell a family that the surgery hadn't gone as hoped and their loved one hadn't made it. "Rylee, I get that you've been out of the loop on account of being—"

He was interrupted by her exaggerated gasp. "You're about to bring up how I'm dead!"

"You . . . you just brought it up a minute ago."

"You ass! I can bring it up, you can't," she said with mock severity that was already giving way to a grin. "Jeez, I don't point out all of your shortcomings."

"Right, you'd never do that," Jonathan said.

She was making him laugh again. Distracting him, as though she didn't want to hear him tell her the truth. He forced himself not to leave it unsaid. "Heyer's plan . . . it's broken. It's dead."

She rolled her eyes, as though he were being overly dramatic. "You know Jonathan, when I was a little girl, I broke a vase. I knew when my mom found it there would be trouble, so I picked up the pieces and put it back together. It was . . . not pretty, I mean, I used glue and duct tape. But I fixed it."

"Rylee, this is a bit more complicated—"

"I'm not done," she interrupted. "You see, my mom took one look at the vase and she knew what happened. She was pissed—ohhh was she pissed. She was going to ground me for a month. So, I took the vase, filled it under a faucet, and you know what . . . didn't leak."

"Something tells me you still got grounded," Jonathan said.

"Oh yeah, I definitely did," Rylee said. "Vase was apparently a family heirloom. I was too young to understand what that meant. My mom told me to go to my room and think about what I had done. So, I did, and I concluded that she was completely out of line. Do I need to tell you why?"

"No, I get it," Jonathan said. "It wasn't pretty, but it held water, it worked."

She nodded. "You say Heyer's plan is broken? So, get some damn duct tape and fix it."

He nodded, but as he looked out at the creeping darkness he said, "I don't know if there is time."

She looked at the pocket watch, shrugged, and tossed it to him. "What was the point of me dying all heroically if not to buy you time."

He caught the watch and looked down at it. "What if it isn't enough?"

"Find a way to make sure it is."

Clank.

The noise was loud and didn't belong. Was like hearing thunder in a world without lightning. Its mere presence shook the fabric of his reality. As the entire garage rattled, the lights began to dim and flicker. Rylee's presence shuddered. One second she was the woman wearing the brave smile, the next she became the far less confident girl in the pink hoodie.

Clank.

The noise struck again, worse than before. The fluorescents above threatened to go out entirely. The shadows moved, agitated like sharks sensing blood in water. Jonathan could feel the weight of that blackness. It pressed in on the garage, as though the light were only a bubble it knew it could burst.

Rylee came to stand beside him. She took his hand, and he looked down to see she'd disappeared, and he was holding the hand of the little girl. She had tears in her eyes.

"If we can't find another light," she said. "Then we need a place to hide."

Clank.

Clank. Clank. Clank.

His sight was blurry when his eyes opened to the white floor. He was stiff and uncomfortable. He'd never bothered to crawl onto the bed, just fallen asleep against the wall until he slouched onto the floor. Now that he was awake, he found he couldn't muster the desire to improve the situation.

The noise came again. *Clank. Clank. Clank.*

He glanced up. Surprised to see the cell door's sensory deprivation had been deactivated. Four guards were looking down at him through the clear plastic.

"Nap's over, Tibbs," said the guard who'd been knocking her baton against the door. "Get on your feet. Your presence has been requested."

To each side of the guards, he saw Collin's and Hayden's faces watching him from their cells. They looked worried for him.

A thought crossed his mind, and for a moment his eyes were a little less vacant.

Something was wrong.

If Jonathan were a turkey, he definitely hadn't been in the oven long enough. The point of white room torture was long-term isolation. There was no way he'd been there for more than a day or two. These guards were taking him out too soon.

The thought was gone as quickly as it had come. The bond taking back his mind—and there was nothing in him with the power to stop it.

CHAPTER NINE

OCT 15, 2005 | 2 PM | JBLM FACILITY

TOO SOON, HAD been Harrison's thought when the order came down. The plan had been to leave the kid in deprivation for at least eleven days before testing his resolve. A precaution, in the event the alien couldn't be made to talk.

One look at Jonathan and she wondered if Command knew something she didn't. He looked broken alright, but not the right sort of broken at all. In time, Tibbs would have become desperate to see any human face. Right now, Tibbs just looked like he wasn't really there at all.

Her team wouldn't let the man's appearance on the monitors lower their guard. Professionals, they would behave as though Jonathan intended to make trouble at any moment. Once they stood outside his cell door and deactivated the isolation current, Harrison nodded for Rolland to get them underway.

Clank. Clank. Clank.

"Nap's over, Tibbs," Harrison said. "Get on your feet. Your presence has been requested."

Jonathan didn't move, rather his eyelids fluttered as though he were falling back to sleep.

"You're not going to like what happens if we have to come in there," Harrison added.

The seconds ticked by, and Jonathan's demeanor remained unchanged. The man didn't move any more than was necessary to breathe. Behind her mask, Harrison tongued the inside of her lower lip. If this was how he planned to play things, then he wasn't leaving her any choice.

"The prisoner appears to think I'm bluffing," Harrison said, with a pat on Rolland's shoulder.

"That does appear to be the case, ma'am," Rolland said.

With a nod, Harrison gave Rolland permission to enter the cell and begin the motivational process. She knew her business, where to strike to cause pain but not permanent injury. They needed Tibbs to be able to talk once they delivered him. For that matter, this whole process was also a lot easier if he was able to walk himself there.

What followed was something Harrison and her team had never seen before, and they had dealt with their share of insubordinate prisoners. Rolland's cudgel came down on him again and again, and Tibbs didn't cry out. He moved, but it was a strange thing to watch. Almost as though he did so unconsciously, his body reacting to pain that Tibbs himself didn't care enough about to waste energy on.

For a few moments, there were only two sounds in the shell. Metal thudding dully on flesh and Jonathan's roommates pleading for Rolland to stop.

"Enough," Harrison finally said. Rolland had stopped mid swing. Harrison was at a loss for a moment. She'd watched the cudgel come down, Jonathan's eyes closed once with each strike—that was all.

She stepped tentatively into the cell. For a moment, his eyes did follow her, but returned to the floor the moment she stopped moving. As though she wasn't enough of a threat to matter. She had to consider that something was medically wrong with him, but if that were the case, she'd rather let Olivia make the call on whether to take him to the infirmary.

Olivia was not going to be happy to learn another prisoner was avoiding their comeuppance by slipping into a state of unconsciousness.

"Put the restraints on him," Harrison said. "If he won't walk, then we'll carry him out to the prisoner dolly."

Rolland sighed in annoyance as she and the other guards carried out the order. Once the various sets of restraints were all locked and tightened in place, she got a nod from each that they were ready to move.

She could tell from their body language that they were a bit unsettled. The four of them had all seen prisoners put on a show of apathy before interrogation. Most men would wear forced smiles meant to look carefree and spout brave lines about how they didn't give a damn what happened to them.

Thing was—anxious men all had tells. Many were too stiff. Others couldn't hide their shakes as they fought a losing battle with adrenaline. Some came with shifty eyes, trembling lips, and sweaty palms—something always betrayed the truth.

Jonathan had a look so far away Harrison wondered if he'd somehow sedated himself. She didn't believe that was the case because she couldn't imagine how he'd have managed it. Each prisoner and everyone with access to the shell was searched before entry and had been under constant watch since they were brought in.

Perhaps Command knew something she didn't, Harrison considered. While she hadn't been present when he was taken, she'd heard Jonathan had exhibited enough resistance that the agents hadn't taken their fingers off their triggers until he was fully restrained.

One night in the white room and the kid was a hair's whisper short of catatonic? Something wasn't right here.

"Alright," she said. "Bring him out."

Harrison took the lead, only turning around once more when they reached the shell's exit. Just before she triggered the decompression of the chamber door, she pulled a blindfold out of one of her belt pouches. Jonathan, unwilling or unable to hold up his head, forced Rolland to grab him under the chin while Harrison got the fabric in place. But in that moment, something did register in him.

Jonathan's eyes swept over his surroundings momentarily and locked on the occupant of the last cell on his left. Harrison had been on duty late last night when Grant Morgan had been brought back to his cell. The man was unconscious and would likely remain so for hours after what he had been through.

The moment Jonathan laid eyes on him sleeping in that cell, his pupils dilated with recognition. His jaw slowly tightened. His fingers seemed as though they were trying to ball into fists, but the effort was like chewing steel for him. Just as his breathing was beginning to accelerate, Harrison put the blindfold in place over his eyes.

Within seconds Jonathan's condition returned to the barely conscious lump they'd had to carry out of the cell. Harrison said nothing, only exchanged glances with the rest of her team before turning to swipe her security badge over a wall panel to depressurize the chamber. Three steps later, the shell door resealed behind them.

That very moment, Jonathan jerked violently in his bonds. At first Harrison though he'd suddenly woken to find himself blinded and restrained. He caught himself, grimaced slightly as his feet flailed and finally found the ground beneath him.

He hadn't had time to get his balance before he jerked again, more violently than the last. But he wasn't fighting his restraints. He looked more like he was being assaulted than struggling.

He jerked again, and again, and . . .

CHAPTER TEN

OCT 15, 2005 | 2:15 PM | HANGMAN'S TREE

"CAN YOU HAND me a nine-sixteenths socket?" Anthony asked.

He was standing in a pit built into the metal floors with both hands covered in grease. Above him, secured with its back facing down, was a prototype developed by one of his subsidiaries. They referred to the creation as The Mock 7, but anyone who had seen a military science fiction movie in the last three decades would have known immediately that they were looking at an armored Mech.

Anthony had called this model a Thor, because of its large hammers in place of hands. Designed to give a normal man or woman a fighting chance against a Ferox, his development team hadn't ever known the specific purpose. He'd had thirty of the prototypes stored at the Seattle site, and in the next few weeks they'd have at least twice that brought in.

Then again, he was still thinking about moving materials with human logistics. How he would slip the Mechs through customs in shipping containers from overseas development sites and all the rest that would be necessary. He kept forgetting that with Mr. Clean, such subterfuge wasn't necessary. The AI could teleport the goods here in an instant and there wouldn't be any paper trail for The Cell to follow.

"You know, I am capable of swapping out the old circuit boards with the upgrades," Mr. Clean said. "I mean no disrespect in pointing out I could do so far more efficiently."

"I'm aware," Anthony said, his hand reaching out of the pit and grasping at air to emphasize he still needed a socket. "But if I let you, then I'd be staring at a wall while I wait for the recon teams to tell us if they have a plan that is going to work."

A metallic pincher formed out of the floor, rising like a blob of liquid until its shape solidified. Mr. Clean used it to pull open a drawer in a toolbox. "So, you're doing unnecessary labor inefficiently in order to distract yourself from the anxiety of waiting?"

Anthony chuckled. "We call it *passing the time*, Mr. Clean. I don't know if it's something you're going to easily relate to."

Finally, Anthony felt the socket press into his palm. A moment passed as he swapped out the heads and went back to work.

"Sydney is approaching," Mr. Clean said.

"That was quick," he said, as he finished replacing the back-access port on the Mech. By the time he heard her footsteps on the metal scaffolding, he'd gotten out of the pit and was washing his hands in a nearby utility sink.

"You're earlier than I expected, something up?" Anthony asked, as he dried his hands. "And any chance it's good?"

"Perhaps," she said. "One of our team is reporting major out-come discrepancies."

"How is that maybe good news?" Anthony asked.

"It's . . . well, it's Jonathan," she said. "He's changing the future."

CHAPTER ELEVEN

BOREALIS HISTORICAL RECORD | 710010654642

THE MOST PROMINENT gaps in my records chronicling the exploits of Jonathan Tibbs involves the incident that came to be known as The Queue Loop.

As of current date, Jonathan Tibbs has never volunteered a full recount of his experiences regarding the twenty-eight consecutive activations that took place between the minutes of 2:15 pm and 2:16 pm on Oct 15th, 2005.

Why he remains so guarded about his experience is a source of continued speculation. Understandably, he is frequently beseeched for a full account, as he often proves to be in possession of remarkable bits of knowledge. These range from details as specific as anatomical information regarding the Feroxian species, as complex as the general working of time mechanics, and as mundane as the personal private information of many of his friends and associates.

While the latter is the most often cited reason that he endures frequent requests for a full accounting, Jonathan nevertheless maintains that he is under no obligation to speak of these events. Thus far, no attempt to coax details he does not wish to share has been successful.

On occasion, Jonathan has disclosed some portions of his experiences. However, these accounts are generally tailored, revealing the most inconsequential of details rather openly, while often confining those of greatest curiosity to bare necessity.

I—the Borealis entity currently known as Mr. Clean—have been present for every known account he has provided. These include the trivial mention of small details as well as the longer narratives. However, while I continue to record these accounts for further posterity, I fear that a full debriefing of his experiences may never be provided.

THE QUEUE LOOP | ACTIVATION ONE

Two things had changed the moment Jonathan was pulled clear of the shell's threshold. He'd felt the twitch trigger in his chest. The burn of activation had come over him hard and fast as a crashing wave. His muscles had stopped obeying. He'd have dropped to the floor had it not been for Harrison's guards. Their grip on his arms kept him vertical even as he became dead weight.

The second, and far more disturbing of the changes, was the dime-sized piece of Mr. Clean coming back to life. He'd felt it attach itself to him while he was being taken prisoner. His wardens had not found it when he was searched, but after being placed inside the containment shell, the piece had gone lifeless, stiffened into a solid transparent disc. He'd kept it hidden beneath his tongue, but the moment he was outside of the shell it came back to life.

This was like a worm slithering up his sinuses and into his inner ear. He reflected on the number of times he'd thought of swallowing the disc to keep it from being discovered. After this experience, he was more than a little glad he hadn't.

"Mr. Tibbs!" The guard's tone reflecting her lack of patience. "I told you, we got a real short fuse for—"

He never heard the end of her statement. Sound ended abruptly as the burn of activation swept through him and cut off his hearing along with the rest of his senses. His escorts could have already dropped him to the floor and be beating him to a bloody mess. There was no way he'd have known while his blood was lava in his veins. That one agony drowned out everything else until activation was completed.

When self-awareness resurfaced, he didn't know how long he'd been out. The world was still black. Soon what began as muffled sounds became speech he understood again.

"What the hell," one of women said. "What the hell is it?"

"Is he dead?"

"He sure as shit ain't moving."

Jonathan recognized the voice of the one in charge. "Rolland, check his pulse."

"But . . . ma'am, I . . ." Rolland stammered. "He's glowing for Christ's sakes."

Having now regained enough wherewithal to know he was lying face up, he thought his vision was slower to return than usual. Then he remembered he was blindfolded. When he took in a deep breath, he heard the guards gasp.

"Yeah!" Rolland said. "He's breathing."

Jonathan's alien instinct, the compass that located a Ferox's portal stone, came to the forefront of his mind. He sat up, which brought a second round of anxious reactions from the guards. He could hear the shuffling of their boots as they stepped back on the corridor floor.

He tilted his head, trying to get a better read on the inbound Ferox's location. To the guards, he'd have looked like a man using his head as though it were a radio antenna and he was trying to get better reception.

"Tibbs," the leader said. "If you know what's good for you, you'll hold real damn still."

Actively trying to tune them out as he focused on the signal, he ignored the warning. The Ferox wasn't on the move yet but the portal was high above him. No surprise, he'd known they were being held underground after the lengthy elevator ride that preceded his being put inside the shell.

It was then that Jonathan heard the jovial booming voice of Mr. Clean. "Jonathan? Can you hear me? Your captors possess technology that is creating a disturbance in my ability to—"

"Mr. Clean, can you hold that thought a moment," Jonathan interjected.

"Who's he talking to?" he heard the guards whispering.

Having assessed his situation, Jonathan broke free of his cuffs like he was snapping a cobweb.

"Son of a . . ."

Just as he reached for the blindfold, a baton slammed down on his forehead. Jonathan flinched—though it had little to do with the attack—the corridor was bright, and his pupils hadn't adjusted. Squinting, he saw the tail end of the exchange. Rolland cradling her hand while reciting a litany of provocative swear words after her baton clattered to the floor.

Jonathan looked at the weapon, then back up at Rolland's mask as she backed away from him.

Ohhh, yeah, that's gonna sting, he thought, remembering when he had made the mistake of taking a swing at Heyer with a baseball bat. Still, he didn't show her his sympathies. Rather, he stared daggers into Rolland's mask.

As amusing as it may be in the movies when a bad guy tries to hit Superman with a crowbar, Rolland had just tried to cave in his skull. She hadn't known it wouldn't kill him. She may have been reacting out of fear, but had he not been activated she could have ended him with that swing. As such, he wanted to make sure Rolland knew with certainty that she'd earned the privilege of his notice.

Jonathan stood, and the guards stepped back. The three who still had their batons didn't make a move after seeing how it had worked out for Rolland. Instead, they reached for their short-range tasers.

"Tibbs," the leader said, uncertainty in her voice as she took aim, "don't make us put you down."

He looked at her with a raised eyebrow. "You're . . . you're serious? Really?"

"Stand down, now!" she yelled.

Jonathan took a long breath and stepped toward them. They fired only to realize what they must have already feared. The tasers slowed him down as much as a soft breeze. Still, running short of alternatives, they emptied the rest of their charges into him. Jonathan paused to wipe away the wired probes clinging to his shirt as they readied their batons.

They were getting wise quickly, retreating until their backs were against the containment shell door.

"Just put them down," Jonathan said, looking at each of them in turn, lingering a little while longer on Rolland.

None gave up their weapons, leaving him little choice as he closed the distance. He needed one of them conscious, but he didn't want to hurt anyone. When they came at him, their attacks might as well have been in slow motion. Yet, to them he must have seemed a blur of motion punctuated by the moments when he bothered to stand somewhat still. He'd disarmed them and tossed their batons down the corridor as he moved between them. Dumbfounded by the ease with which they had been deprived of their weapons, they were further caught off guard when their masks were torn off.

This all stopped abruptly when Jonathan suddenly held the leader by her armored vest, legs dangling and unable to find the floor.

"So much better to put names to faces," Jonathan said. "Wouldn't you agree, Rolland?"

He saw her fear, but also a commendable defiance in her. It was mirrored in each of the guards. He was familiar with that look. They knew they couldn't win but, if he made them, they would die failing.

"All women," Jonathan said as he looked at each of them. "Why? What's the angle?"

Tightening jaws and eyes narrowed into hostile glares was all he got. Still, as he looked at the three subordinates, he got the sense they didn't know the answer even had he been ready to force it out of them. However, the leader— her eyes gave away the subtle spark of knowledge.

"I need a hostage, but only one. You're in charge, so spare them," Jonathan said to the leader. "They can go tell whoever is running this show that I'll be along shortly."

They were loyal, none gave a sign they intended to leave their leader behind. But as Jonathan stared into the commander's eyes, he could see why she was in charge. Fear was there, but it didn't have so much control over her that she couldn't do the math. Her side of this disagreement was in desperate need of reinforcements and bigger guns. If they stayed, all her team would get was injured or worse.

"We both know it's your best move," Jonathan said. "Get your people to safety."

Hesitantly, the leader nodded. "Do . . . do as he says. That's an order."

"Harrison, we ain't leaving you," Rolland said.

"If he wanted it, we'd already be dead," Harrison said.

"That's true," Jonathan said, turning to Rolland. "And I would definitely start with you."

Rolland stubbornly took a step closer, and Harrison's voice turned angry. "I gave you an order!"

The woman blanched, and though she stared at Jonathan with pure hate, she and the other guards began to reluctantly retreat down the opposite end of the corridor. When they were out of sight, he dropped Harrison to the floor. She stumbled in surprise, falling against the door of the shell.

"All women," Jonathan repeated. "Why?"

He endured two breaths of her delay as she tried to decide if he were bluffing. Then drew back a fist and brought it down on the door. The strike was so fast Harrison barely perceived his movement before an explosion of sound erupted beside her, his fist having slammed into the shell door.

He'd intended to put a hole into the door right beside Harrison's head. What he achieved was the door bending inward, breaking free of its hinges, shooting through the shell's interior, until it smashed against his cell door.

Well, that works too.

Hayden and Collin stared back at him wide eyed, unsure what had just happened.

With nothing behind her suddenly, Harrison fell into the shell just as red lights lining the corridor flared to life and an alarm like a barking walrus filled the air. She began to crawl backward, but he quickly had her by the vest again.

"I don't have all day," Jonathan said. "So just tell me, how many bones it's worth to you?"

She stammered getting the answer out, "Sec . . . security measures. All personnel in direct contact with prisoners had to be female."

"Why?"

"Protocol . . . to re . . . reduce risk of any accomplice assisting in an escape attempt."

Jonathan scowled for a better explanation.

"All the alien's known contacts are male."

His eyebrows rose as suddenly it made sense. Until quite recently, he'd believed Heyer was only dragging men into his war. Until he met Rylee . . .

Jonathan flinched and took a step back from Harrison as his strength wavered.

In all the activity since his implant activated, he hadn't taken time to think about how the oppressive weight of the bond had withdrawn—pulled back into something smaller at the fringe of his consciousness. The moment her name registered in his mind, he felt it again. Like a faucet that had been turned down to a drip slowly turning up the flow of poison into his blood.

Panic struck him.

He'd been at the mercy of the bond's abuse for so long that time had become irrelevant. He'd been like a man buried alive but lacking any will to dig himself free.

Why? Why had it stopped? Why this interlude? How long could he hope to keep any power over his mind and body? He could feel his fear of it trying to steal this moment of clarity. He braced himself against it. He needed to know what had given this moment back before it slipped away.

Luckily, the answer really wasn't that elusive; he might as well have asked himself why he could see in the dark after turning on a flashlight.

Activation. Pain. Endorphins. Adrenaline.

Everything that overwhelmed his body while that searing fire stripped it all away. It took his sight, his hearing, his command of his nervous system. It took his thoughts. It took his identity. It took until it reached its logical conclusion and then it took his consciousness.

Heyer said that the bond would use his own biology against him, would reduce him to an addict searching for a fix.

"Jonathan!" Mr. Clean's voice returned with an urgency that tore him from his spiraling thoughts. "You're too close to the disturbance. I'm losing my connection."

He looked down to see his feet had crossed the shell's threshold. Even with its door knocked in and its seal lost, the field this thing generated must have still been functioning at some diminished capacity. But, the shell clearly ran on electricity. He didn't have time to play clever electrician, he searched for the first thing that looked like a conduit and found a promising target running up the side of the shell near the door.

Tearing it free, he took the line in both hands and yanked. A short-lived flurry of sparks and arcing electricity was followed by the spurting end of the shell's perpetual thrumming in what sounded like one long hydraulic death hiss.

"Mr. Clean, how's that?" Jonathan asked.

"The disturbance appears to have been removed," Mr. Clean replied.

Well, at least something wasn't complicated for once, Jonathan thought.

They should have been standing in the dark. However, Jonathan could see Harrison's face in the orange light emanating off his chest. She was trying, unconvincingly, to not notice Jonathan talking to himself. Behind her, his roommates' startled expressions stared back at him while that looping walrus bark of an alarm continued.

He quickly spotted speakers built into the nearby walls and put a fist through each. It didn't stop other alarms throughout the entire facility, but at least he could hear himself think again. He pulled Harrison to her feet once more and marched her to the rear of the shell.

"Stay put," he said, then held his finger to his lips. "I really need to take this call."

He was addressing the AI as he turned and walked away from her. "Mr. Clean, how much longer will you be online?"

As he listened to the answer, he put one hand through the food slot on Collin's prison door and yanked the plastic off its hinges. "My primary consciousness will go dormant in approximately fifty-seven minutes."

He tossed Collin's prison door through the gaping hole at the shell's entrance, then walked over to Hayden's cell and repeated the process. For the time being, he didn't really acknowledge his friends' wide-eyed stares.

"Am I correct in assuming that it's pointless to bother getting you caught up on what's happened since we saw each other last?" Jonathan asked.

"Unfortunately, yes," Mr. Clean replied. "My shadow cannot transfer information to my counterpart outside The Never. However, I can report some good news. A team has been assembled and a strategy for extracting you from your location is in development."

"Since you mentioned it, where the hell is my location?" Jonathan asked.

"A cold war research facility beneath Fort Base Lewis-McChord. Its construction is completely off record. As a result, the extraction team is still gathering pertinent tactical details," Mr. Clean said. "However, you are directly beneath one of the base's landing strips. The main way in and out is a primary elevator shaft that empties into a large hangar on the surface. The surface building . . ."

While Jonathan was absorbing information, he began to feel the pressure of his friends staring at him as well as the certainty that every passing second The Cell was mounting an assault to recapture him.

"Look, I know you deserve an explanation," Jonathan said. "It's coming, but I need a minute. So, for now, Hayden, she's got an extra set of cuffs on her belt, put them on her. Collin, see if her vest fits."

Jonathan threw a last warning glance at Harrison not to make trouble before walking away and kneeling at the front of the shell. Collin and Hayden stared at one another for a long moment of indecision, then back to Jonathan who appeared to be having a private conversation with an imaginary friend. Finally, Collin's hands went up. "Well, what the hell else are we going to do?"

"Mr. Clean," Jonathan said. "You must know about Rylee by now?"

"Yes, her device returned to the armory yesterday, though the greater mystery was the arrival of the Alpha Slayer implant around the same instant. When we last had the Alpha Slayer in our possession, Heyer had returned it to the Foedrata arena," Mr. Clean said.

Jonathan spared a bitter glance at Grant's cell.

"Malkier retrieved it. Implanted it into a shadow of Grant Morgan," Jonathan said with a sigh. "Look, it's a long story that ends with me uninstalling it. I'll fill you in on the details in the real world, but right now . . ."

Jonathan closed his eyes, swallowed. "I need your help. I'm . . . I'm about to be in bad shape."

"The broken bond—it is known to be a uniquely cruel experience. I am sorry, Jonathan. Anything I can do to be of assistance I will," Mr. Clean said.

"The records you took from the Foedrata mainframe, do any of them tell you what happened to combatants who survived the bond being severed?"

"You are wondering if any recovered?" Mr. Clean asked.

"Tell me whatever you know," Jonathan said.

"This is what humans refer to as a *good news/bad news* situation," Mr. Clean said. "The bad news is that only three such records exist, though only one survived. In the first case, the female lived through the death of her bonded partner but died shortly after from wounds obtained during the battle."

"In the second, it is less clear, the male died the next time he was put in the arena," Mr. Clean said. "The Ferox hunted him down, but he put up no resistance. Victory was one-sided and swift."

"You said there was a third case?" Jonathan asked.

"Yes, a female survived. Unfortunately, this was because the bond was reestablished to a new male, which, even if there was a candidate, is not a solution we can attempt while you are in the temporary dimension."

"You said there was good news?" Jonathan asked.

"Yes, though it's theoretical. Rylee barely survived the implantation of her device due to her minimal compatibility. This resulted in a weaker bond. Also, she was only in close proximity to you for a few days, whereas the Foedrata's human combatants were under the bond's influence for long periods depending on their success in the arena. There is reason to hope the bond will affect you less severely."

He closed his eyes and shook his head, but he didn't bother saying that this was not *actually* good news. Even if Mr. Clean was right, and he was experiencing something *less* terrible than those poor souls in the past, it did nothing to help him now. He was terrified of the bond's capabilities, and it was already reasserting itself.

If he stopped caring in the middle of a fight with a Ferox—he was dead.

If he didn't retrieve the stone—he was dead.

"You seem to have your wits about you," Mr. Clean said.

"For now, but I can feel it taking control back," Jonathan said. "Don't know how long I have."

"I wish I had some actionable intelligence to offer you," Mr. Clean replied.

"Well, I've got exactly one idea," Jonathan said, forcing his voice to take on a satirical optimism. "It's a really bad one . . . but seeing as it's all I've got, it's time we get excited about it."

A momentary silence from Mr. Clean indicated that he wasn't certain how to respond. "What can I do?"

"How long would it take you to craft something out of true Borealis steel and get it to me?"

"Not long," Mr. Clean said. "Under normal circumstances, I try not to be too liberal with True Steel. As you may know, it is a limited resource, but given whatever use you have in mind will only exist in this temporary reality, I can provide whatever you require."

"Really?" Jonathan said, teeth tightening in annoyance.

If only this extremely useful information could have been revealed at any point in the months before . . . *nope, no time for that right now.*

"Good to know! *Gosh, we'll have to circle back to that!* Right now, I need a few things. The first is a syringe that can penetrate my skin, and your best guess on how much synthetic adrenaline I can inject without killing myself."

Awkwardly, Collin undid the straps holding Harrison's vest over her torso. Meanwhile, Hayden clumsily went about securing her wrists behind her back with her own handcuffs, apologizing the entire time he was doing so. Through the whole exchange, the two glanced anxiously at Jonathan.

He was still kneeling at the front of the shell, talking to himself. He didn't look crazy at first but as the one-sided conversation went on his voice was getting—more colorful.

"Maybe he actually is talking to someone?" Collin whispered.

Hayden's face tilted out from behind Harrison, and the anxiety running through his thoughts was palpable. He started to speak, then seemed to consider Harrison standing between them.

"Um, sorry about this ma'am," he said, before placing his clammy hands over her ears.

"Did you get the feeling he . . . wasn't . . . bluffing when he said he'd break her bones?"

Collin shrugged uncomfortably.

He'd found that exchange disturbing as well. But Jonathan's chest was glowing, and he'd just ripped their prison doors off like they were made of cardboard. At the time, it hadn't seemed like the thing to focus on. Except . . . now that he thought about it . . . Tibbs had that look on his face when he was threatening Harrison.

Collin had started noticing *that look* months ago. He'd even confided in Tibbs once that it disturbed him on a primal level. When Jonathan got that predatory gaze, Collin got a fear like he was standing beside a man who was capable of anything.

But . . .

"He seems to know what he's doing," Collin whispered. "So that makes exactly one of us."

He'd just gotten Harrison's vest in place when he noticed Jonathan reach down and pick something up off the corridor floor. Collin couldn't make it out before Tibbs tucked it into the back of his pants and covered it with his shirt. He spoke to himself a little while longer, then he was walking back their way.

He frowned at them. "Why are you covering her ears?"

Hayden, having forgotten he was still doing so, pulled his hands back.

"Alright," Jonathan said. "For the next minute, just accept everything I tell you is the truth. I've explained this to you so many times that I've gotten pretty good at it."

Collin and Hayden glanced at one another. Looking for any indication that Jonathan had ever said anything to either of them that *explained* this.

"Each time this happens to me," Jonathan pointed at his chest, "you don't remember. You're like Drew Barrymore in *Fifty First Dates*. When the two of you found me on the kitchen floor a few months back, it was because an alien showed up and installed this *MacGyver* unit in my chest."

Collin frowned, glancing at Hayden to see his friend was also confused. "Wait, Jonathan did . . . did you mean a *Guyver* unit?" Collin asked.

"Sorry, yeah," Jonathan said.

Collin nodded slowly in understanding.

"Anyway," Jonathan continued, "that alien did this because every so often, a creature from another dimension attacks Earth. The sort mankind isn't equipped to deal with. When that happens, this thing in my chest activates and I go take care of it. No one ever remembers, because the moment I'm done, I'm *Ground Hog Day*-ed back to the moment before it happened."

Harrison seemed to also be listening to what Jonathan was saying, but her face looked like only half the words she was hearing were in English. Meanwhile Collin and Hayden nodded along in comprehension.

"What does that thing do to you exactly?" Collin asked, nodding at the orange glow.

"Hayden says it makes me something like *The Tick* without the stupidity," Jonathan said.

"Oh," Hayden nodded. "Semi-impervious with enhanced strength."

"Sure, anyhow, after I found out the real-life *Men in Black*," Jonathan pointed at Harrison, "were tracking the alien's activities, I couldn't tell you anything. Ironically, I was trying to avoid the exact situation we are currently in the middle of . . ."

"This is heavy," Collin said. "And . . . this . . . *this* was the best explanation you came up with?"

Jonathan suppressed a smile. "For you two, when I'm pressed for time . . . yeah."

There was a pause as they thought this over.

"I mean," Collin looked to Hayden, "it does sound a lot more like something we'd come up with than anything Tibbs would."

Hayden's eyes suddenly turned from excited to worried. "Wait, so some monster is coming for us right now?"

Jonathan tilted his head as though he was listening. "Soon. Hopefully when it does whoever is running this facility won't take too long realizing I'm not the problem they should be worrying about."

"So, what do we do?" Collin asked.

"Harrison here is going to kindly guide me through this facility. It's up to you two if you want to follow, probably a lot safer if you stay put. I'm going to get shot at on my way out . . . a lot."

". . . and you're bulletproof?" Hayden asked

"So far," he said.

Hayden nodded, looking impressed as he thought about it. Then asked, "Even if they shoot you in the eye?"

Jonathan frowned as he considered. In the span of a few seconds his expression went from confident, to uncertain, and finally annoyed. "For the love of . . . I don't know! Not going to stand still long enough to find out what that feels like."

With that, Jonathan tugged Harrison out in front and began heading down the corridor.

"Jeez," Hayden whispered. "Sensitive about your superpowers much?"

Having promised Harrison that, should either of his friends come to harm because she led them into a trap, she would endure an identical fate, she led the way through the corridors. She had looked as though she believed the threat and was weighing if she wanted to gamble. But, when Jonathan told her where he wanted to go, she seemed to conclude that it wasn't in her interest to thwart him.

They hadn't run into any resistance—they hadn't run into anyone. The alarm had either triggered a lockdown or an evacuation protocol. For now, the empty hallways flashed their angry red lights and the walrus alarm kept right on barking.

In short, the atmosphere was less than charming.

To the uninitiated, the place was a small maze. Every hall and doorway looking similar enough that it would be easy to waste time going in circles. Jonathan assumed every step they took was being monitored by security cameras. He was cautious of the areas that looked ideal for an ambush. He'd told his friends to hit the ground the moment they heard gunfire—told them not to think twice about using Harrison as a human shield for that matter. He was fast, but there was no way he could protect them from automatic fire if they were boxed in. In these corridors it wouldn't be hard for The Cell to accomplish just that. They knew the layout and he didn't.

He was torn on whether he should have allowed them to come. If they were harmed in The Never it would only be their shadows. Jonathan still had no desire to see it happen. On the other hand, had he left them behind, The Cell would have surely retrieved them and tried to use their lives as leverage to get him to stand down. Which, he not only would not—but could not—do.

So, the math hadn't been great with either choice. For now, he hoped that anyone opening fire on them would see the guy glowing bright orange first and aim accordingly.

Finally, just as they approached a corner, the alarm abruptly stopped and a second later the corridor lights went out.

Had Jonathan not been his own walking flashlight he'd have been standing in the darkness. Instead, he could see the fear of his friends illuminated in his orange glow as they pressed their backs to the wall behind him. Jonathan stopped, held up a palm to get their attention, then pointed at the ground. They nodded, even Harrison seeming eager to get as flat against the floor as possible.

Jonathan took a deep breath. *Here we go.*

He turned the corner, stepping right out into the center of the hallway and making himself into a glowing target none could miss in the dark.

"Jonathan Tibbs! Stand down!" yelled a voice from other side of the corridor. "One move and we'll open fi—"

The moment the man's voice gave Jonathan a sense of the distance between them, he shot sprinting into the darkness.

"Take him down! Take him down!"

In the narrow corridors, the sound of automatic weapons was deafening. Jonathan felt the rounds, most of them were finding their target after all, a lot like being assaulted with ping-pong balls. Unfortunately for his attackers, the darkness turned the bursts of fire from their muzzles into targets. The moment Jonathan knew precisely where they were standing, he launched toward them, clearing the distance in one bound.

He spread his arms wide as he went and barreled in like a bowling ball hitting pins. Their formation was thrown into chaos as two of the men took the blunt force of his body crashing into them while two others were clotheslined by his arms. He tucked into a ball and rolled to one knee, knowing that he'd just put four men on the ground and suspecting that at least two of them would be headed to the hospital.

As he stood, the entire squad became illuminated in the orange glow of his chest.

Eight men surrounded him, all in full combat gear and carrying military grade assault rifles. Their faces were covered by the thermal optics they had hoped would give them an advantage after the lights went out. The two he'd clipped with his arms had been knocked into their allies harder than he'd intended.

One yelled, moving as though he must have broken a collar bone or a rib in the collision. It was unfortunate—he wasn't trying to kill but even with his attempts to hold back, the human body was just too fragile.

The first man to recover his wits, one of the few that hadn't been thrown off his feet, took aim, managing to get off three point-blank shots into his abdomen before Jonathan grabbed him by his armored vest and pulled him off his feet. The man kept firing as Jonathan crushed his goggles.

He sensed the movement of two more behind him; they'd been pushed to the corridor wall when he landed. Their weapons raised, they were holding their fire, not wanting to hit one of their own in these close quarters. Sweeping around, he let go of the man's vest throwing him across the corridor to slam into his allies. Without the deafening blast of gun fire, Jonathan was sure he heard bones breaking just before the men's muffled screams confirmed it.

Still hitting too hard.

The next member of The Cell's assault team never got fully off the floor. Jonathan's bare foot came down on his rifle. He'd only intended to pin the gun to the floor but ended up crushing the weapon's receiver into a mangled useless mess. The man tried to crawl back as he saw the weapon destroyed, but found he was still anchored to it by his shoulder strap. Jonathan reached out as the man tried to rear back and crushed his optics as well.

The man then went for his sidearm, but by the time he'd pulled it from his belt holster Jonathan had snatched the weapon from him. He heard the man wail in unexpected pain. Somewhat shocked, Jonathan looked to see that he'd torn the man's trigger finger off along with the gun.

Well, Jonathan thought, *at least he'll live.*

The weapon in his hand was immediately familiar to him, and he pulled it to pieces in two quick motions. His finger pressed the release on the magazine, while his other hand pulled the barrel free. He let the grip fall to the floor with the man's finger but crushed the barrel itself in his fist. The man was bent over, his good hand cradling the one with the missing finger when Jonathan grabbed him by the back of his collar.

Automatic fire began to ping off his lower back from behind, and Jonathan—gently as he could—slammed the man against the corridor wall. He was fairly sure he'd only knocked the wind out of *Nine Fingers*, so he was feeling a little better about himself as he whirled on the person shooting at him. Then one of the bullets ricocheted off his chest into the unarmored portion of another man's thigh.

Mr. Thigh Wound yelled in agony, barely heard over the gunfire, as both his hands clasped his leg and blood spurted onto the floor. One of his buddies, having gotten to his feet after being hit by the human log Jonathan had thrown at him earlier, had managed to get out from under his ally and raise his weapon.

Jonathan reacted, throwing what remained of the crushed pistol barrel with deadly accuracy as the man brought his arm up. He knew he'd put too much heat on it the moment it left his hand. Luckily, the guy was wearing body armor over his forearms. The wad of metal still hit with enough force to break every bone in his wrist and arm as the twisted metal barrel embedded itself in the armor.

The automatic fire that had been hitting him in the back finally stopped, and Jonathan shot toward the last man standing as he was trying to reload. He cleared the distance between them so quickly his attacker was startled when the fresh magazine was slapped from his hand. He froze as Jonathan then took the rifle in one hand, gripped the shoulder strap with the other, and freed it from the man's possession before breaking it over his knee.

Seeing his weapon destroyed, the man only had a moment to look up at Jonathan's pissed off expression before being pushed away. The force sent him crashing through a doorway at the other end of the corridor.

Apparently, the lights were working on the other side, because the hall was suddenly bathed in light after the man barreled through the doors. Abruptly, the damage he'd done to the assault team was illuminated in much brighter color.

He heard movement behind him, and not the very stealthy sort. Jonathan turned to see one of the men had gotten to his feet. He was limping forward with a knife. It didn't look like a standard issue blade either, but some sort of gnarly over-sized Vietnam era monstrosity. The man lunged at him, trying to sink the blade in.

He caught the knife hand at the man's wrist and lifted him until his feet were barely able to touch the floor.

"Really, all that, but you think going Rambo on me is what will make the difference?" Jonathan asked. The man struggled but gave no response. Jonathan tightened his grip on his wrist until he growled in pain and let the knife drop.

"Mr. Tibbs! That's enough!" a woman's voice yelled from the open door.

Tossing the man aside, Jonathan turned toward the voice. It came from the conference room on the other side of the destroyed doors. Larger than he'd been expecting for an underground military complex. There was one long table surrounded by empty chairs and a giant display hanging on the back wall.

A woman stood on screen looking back at him like an incredibly angry grammar school principal.

"You only sent eight," Jonathan said, stepping into the room. "That make you cautious or arrogant?"

"Rest assured," she said, "Far more manpower and artillery could be brought in to resolve this situation."

He considered her for a moment. "You in charge of this show then?"

"I am."

"Got a name?"

"Olivia," she said.

"Well, Olivia, let me save you some disappointment, any weapon you have with a chance of hurting me is a bad idea down here. Unless you're okay risking this facility just to stop one prisoner from escaping."

Olivia raised a single eyebrow. "And you called me arrogant?"

"You don't want to call my bluff."

She considered him for a heartbeat. "Let's pretend you're right for a moment, you must know that you're endangering your friend's lives. You might make it out, but they won't. So, here is my offer; stand down, or I'll order my men to stop aiming at *you*."

He made a show of considering this, then shrugged. "No deal."

She blinked, finding his response colder than expected, "You're quite formidable Mr. Tibbs, but you can't possibly imagine you can keep them safe."

"No," he said. "I don't imagine I can."

Her eyes narrowed. "If your friends aren't enough for you to give this up might I remind you that your mother is still under our observation. A mere phone call and you'd never see her again."

He let her see exactly what opinion he now had of her, but shook his head. "What else you got?"

He caught her eyes flicking to something, or someone, outside the camera's frame. A moment passed, and finally she seemed to come to a decision.

"Fine. Here are the facts. I won't allow you to take the alien from this facility," she said. "If you go anywhere near his holding cell, I'll bring it all down. If it doesn't kill you, you'll be buried alive."

Jonathan smiled thoughtfully, and he waited a good long moment before he responded. "I'm glad we had this talk. In the future, it'll be good to know what type of person I'm dealing with."

"I'm sorry, Mr. Tibbs, but if you believe you have a future, you must intend to stand down?" Olivia asked, an eagerness slipping into her eyes.

"No," Jonathan said. "Today, you go ahead and do whatever you feel you have to, but . . ."

He paused, an insincere grimace on his face. "You've heard every word I've said since we left that shell, you knew exactly where I asked Harrison to bring me. What seems to be escaping your notice is that I'm not trying to free the damn alien."

She took a moment, doubtlessly reviewing what she'd likely heard since the escape began. He'd asked Harrison to take him to the closest place he could make contact with the person in charge—a place where they could negotiate without said person feeling they were in imminent danger. Given this was the room at the end of the last hallway she'd taken him down, he suspected Harrison had done exactly as he asked.

"Are you saying you only intend to free yourself, that you'll leave the alien behind?" Olivia asked.

Jonathan closed his eyes, homing in on the Ferox's location. It hadn't been stationary for some time now. If it hadn't started killing yet, it wouldn't be long.

"Olivia," Jonathan said. "You're about to find out that I'm the least of your worries. Something's here—you aren't ready for it."

Soon enough, reports began coming in and Olivia found out that Jonathan wasn't making idle threats. At first it was only word that an unidentified sphere had appeared near one of the civilian housing sectors. The thing had been hard to miss, hovering in the middle of the road, and then it had set something loose on the base.

Now, that thing was killing indiscriminately.

The base was able to mobilize within fifteen minutes, but they found that nothing was bringing the creature down. Soon, they would have birds in the air, and be able to bring far more fire power to the equation, but in the meantime, it was ripping through soldiers at a terrifying rate.

"What is it?" Olivia yelled, her voice more angry than scared.

Jonathan had taken a seat in the conference room. Quietly waiting while Olivia's people confirmed he wasn't lying. The broken bond was gaining strength, starting to take a toll it was hard for him to hide, but he couldn't let the woman sense his weakness. In the meantime, Hayden and Collin, rapidly recaptured by the guards, were marched in to take a seat at the table. The fresh men pointing the guns were as geared up as the last batch, but they made no move to put a hand on him.

"We call them the Ferox," Jonathan said. "Your basic death machine."

"One of your alien's allies here to free him?" Olivia asked.

"No, not even remotely. It's here to kill me."

She studied him a moment.

"You knew it was coming for you, how—"

"Olivia," Jonathan interrupted. "It's all a real long story and I'm in a time crunch. But, let me deal with this thing, and afterward I'll tell you whatever you want to know."

Olivia tilted her head at him as though he couldn't be serious. "Mr. Tibbs, this—Ferox—is attacking an air force base. If you imagine that we are in desperate need of your assistance to deal with it, you're mistaken."

Jonathan shrugged. "You could likely kill it. Couple Air-to-Ground missiles might get the job done. Frankly, a part of me wants to see how well you'd fare against the thing, but no, not today. I've got something better in mind—something I know you'll never get done without me."

"I'm listening," Olivia said.

He stood and approached the monitor. "Pull your forces back and let me engage. I won't kill it. I'll disable it and bring it back to you—alive."

She was quiet for a moment. This offer was likely not something she'd imagined. Now that he'd made it, she couldn't hide her interest.

"To what end?" Olivia asked.

"You want to study it for weaknesses," Jonathan said. "So do I."

There was a long pause from Olivia, "Your answers are repeatedly surprising, Mr. Tibbs."

"Mankind is about to be in a war with these things," Jonathan said. "You're confident you can kill one. Great, imagine dealing with ten thousand."

Again, she was quiet. Having taken a seat herself, he could see her rocking back and forth as she considered.

"If I were to agree to this," Olivia said, "how do I know that you and that creature aren't simply going to join forces and free the alien."

Jonathan sighed. "Because I wouldn't bother asking your permission. This is a trade."

She tilted her head. "What exactly do you expect in return. I will not give you the alien for this creature."

Jonathan smirked. "Trust me, Olivia, today you're getting a bargain."

He turned to point at Collin and Hayden. "My friends and I aren't prisoners anymore. I understand you can't just let us go but keeping them in cages is ridiculous."

"That's all?" Olivia asked.

"No, whatever you learn about these things—I learn," Jonathan said. "I'm in the room working with your researchers. It'll save time, I know more about these things than anyone on the planet—that, and . . . if it gets loose for even a second, you'll be glad I'm there."

"Nothing more?"

He shook his head. "We got a deal?"

Olivia tapped her fingers against the desk. "If I agree . . . how do you propose this plays out?"

"Take me to the surface. Bring the equipment you stole from my cabinet. Other than that, there is a large box outside your hangar door. It appeared about twenty minutes ago. I suggest you get some folks cracking it open before I bring that thing back."

Olivia's eyes flicked off the screen. Someone speaking in hushed tones.

"Yes, it appears an unidentified box was delivered without any witnesses. What exactly is in it?"

"A prison for our friend out there," Jonathan said. "Nothing you've got is going to hold that thing."

"If we find any surprises in that box—"

"You won't," Jonathan said. "Now, as I said, I'm in a bit of a hurry here, so what's it going to be?"

Jonathan was quiet, standing at the center of the large freight elevator as they rode to the surface. He'd been escorted to the elevator surrounded by armed guards, and now they were on each side of him. The Cell insisted on keeping guns aimed at him regardless of how ineffective they had proved.

Whatever makes you feel better, Jonathan thought.

The syringe Mr. Clean had teleported in was still pressed against his back. He remembered the AI's words. *"This is a concentrated syringe, there is enough epinephrine in there to kill an elephant. Well, more likely five elephants, but that isn't the expression."*

He closed his eyes and breathed, trying to ignore the bond's growing presence clawing at his mind. He didn't know how much longer he'd be able to hide the symptoms. He had to keep his thoughts as focused as he could.

For the moment, it wasn't as hard as it could have been. Confident as he may have appeared, he'd never actually tried to subdue a Ferox alive. He'd seen them knocked stupid, but he'd never seen one knocked unconscious—didn't seem to be a thing that happened to them. Getting this thing back to the hangar as he'd promised—it was going to be, well—something.

When the elevator doors opened, he saw a long hallway leading out into the main hangar. The Cell's agents were a tapestry of activity around Mr. Clean's delivery. When the AI had ported it over, he'd disguised it inside a large shipping crate. The Cell already had the contents inside and the box open on the hangar floor.

A mangled mess of alien steel bars stood in front of them like a giant puzzle. Jonathan frowned as he walked past two soldiers studying what looked like IKEA instructions. Warily they directed some men to pull on a bar here and a bar there. Suddenly, the steel bars jumped into place. The entire contraption expanded with the suddenness of a sprung bear trap. Even Jonathan flinched and stopped to stare when the finished structure suddenly snapped into place.

A simple cage made of alien steel wasn't going to get the job done. He'd needed something that would stay in one place and wouldn't be easily flipped over when the Ferox inevitably tried to throw its weight against the bars. Mr. Clean hadn't been able to provide a foundation to bolt the cage to, so the AI had solved the issue by giving it ridiculously long side braces. By the time it assembled itself, it looked more like a barred prison at the center of a skeletal pyramid.

He found Olivia standing in front of the open hangar doors waiting to meet him in person. At her feet were some familiar items: his armored jacket, *Doomsday*, and *Excali-bar*. She wore a smile on her face—as though she were greeting someone at the airport.

"Mr. Tibbs," Olivia said.

"Points for balls," Jonathan said. "Figured you'd send a lackey out to keep your end of the deal before letting yourself be within a hundred feet of me."

"Have I made a mistake?" Olivia asked.

He took a long breath. "Not today. Got bigger problems."

"Excellent," Olivia said, though joylessly. "Obviously, certain mysteries still require explanation. I do expect you to provide me with answers as soon as this more pressing operation is complete."

Jonathan grinned just as joylessly as she had spoken.

"Now, is there anything else you require?" Olivia asked.

The Cell had only confiscated items they knew to contain alien steel. Jonathan looked down at his gear, then his bare feet. "Can I get a pair of boots, or am I supposed to *Die Hard* this?"

Had he not had bigger concerns, Jonathan might have taken a moment to feel ridiculous. His pajama-like pants were stuffed into the beige army issue boots The Cell had been charitable enough to provide. They hadn't confiscated his harness, so he carried his demolition bar in one hand while *Doomsday* was wrapped around his jacket. He looked like some cross between a biker and a psychiatric ward escapee.

Under normal circumstances, he couldn't have cared less. The Ferox didn't typically pick up on an unimpressive wardrobe let alone weaponize it with clever barbs. Still, as he neared the perimeter where Olivia's ground forces had pulled back, the assembly of soldiers gave him doubtful looks.

The fighting wasn't far off.

He could hear the furious chatter of firearms punctuated by the occasional loud percussive thud of grenades. Soldiers were keeping the Ferox occupied. This was smart in the short term; the beast wouldn't leave a fight to wander into civilian housing. Still, if Jonathan didn't get involved soon, those men wouldn't last long.

Two large Humvees parted as he approached, one man stepped out to meet him as he reached the opening.

"Well, they said you'd be hard to miss," the man said.

"You in charge here?" Jonathan asked.

The man nodded.

"Alright, I'm heading straight for the target. Tell your men to pull out to a safe location the moment I've got its attention."

Jonathan looked up, drawing the man's eyes to the numerous helicopters in the air. He had no doubt that a few of them were there solely to keep an eye on him. Olivia making sure he stuck with the agreement.

"I know you aren't going to order these choppers out of the air but keep them back. I lose its attention for a second and they'll be the first thing it notices."

The man looked at him and Jonathan could practically hear his thoughts.

Maybe I should ask Command to confirm my orders. I mean, this guy? This is the guy they're sending in to resolve the situation?

Jonathan didn't blame him, he'd have thought the man incompetent if he didn't have such reservations. What was important was the soldier only hesitated a moment before nodding. "It'll get done."

While the man's actual parting words were, "Good luck in there," his face was saying: *You poor crazy bastard, you're a dead man.*

"Thanks," Jonathan said as he turned toward the sounds of battle in the distance. He focused on the Ferox's location, then broke into a sprint before launching into the air and clearing a stand of trees and a few small buildings. He never got to see the perimeter man's expression change after he left the ground but liked to imagine a decent jaw-drop had occurred.

Jonathan landed in his typical concrete smashing manner, then burst forward into another long jump that dropped him into a small park. He came down in the middle of one of the base's playgrounds for children, punching a small crater into the woodchips. The Ferox was close now. Just beyond one more stand of trees he'd reach the cluster of buildings where the creature was taking fire. Behind him, he could hear the helicopters rushing to catch up with him.

He didn't really want eyes on him for what came next, so instead of hurdling over the trees he stayed on the ground and ran beneath the canopy. The moment he knew he was out of sight he slowed to a walk.

He heard more gunfire, and he closed his eyes.

By the time he'd been riding the elevator to the surface, he knew he was in trouble. He'd gotten this far because he didn't need to think much, just keep putting one foot in front of the other. But he'd felt the bond clawing through his final mental blockades.

The grief and self-loathing that had no place in a fight were taking over his thoughts and the pressure was growing exponentially with each passing second. He was already trying to answer the question . . . *Why am I doing this?*

At first, he'd answered with conviction, but as time wore on those same answers lost any force. Soon he began to feel his justifications empty, whatever significance they'd had crumbling. As he slowed beneath the shade of trees he could feel as much as hear the change in perspective.

There's a spot over there . . . looks nice. A tree to sit against. I'll lie down. Try to hold on to one last moment before I'm back in the cage. There's no escape. Then again . . . make it a bit further. Let the Ferox put me out of my misery. It would be quick.

For a while he tried to think of that voice as some other person, some insidious whispering minion of the bond. But it was getting harder and harder to believe it was separate from him. More and more, it just felt like a part of him that saw no point in lying to himself.

His eyes shot open with fear as he realized he was kneeling. He didn't remember doing that. He reached back and pulled out the syringe—he'd almost forgotten about it, his mind so unwilling to focus on anything but grief. But he had to do this, no matter what might happen—he couldn't succumb to the bond's grip.

He swallowed, his face pinching in disgust as he thumbed off the plastic cover on the needle. He took a deep breath, opened his eyes wide and jabbed the needle into his thigh. He pressed down on the plunger, emptied the contents.

For a moment—there was nothing. He had just enough time to believe that perhaps Mr. Clean hadn't made it concentrated enough.

Then the light around him was suddenly too intense. He had to close his eyes. It was everywhere. Pure white light.

Behind him there was an opening to an old railway tunnel. He recognized it from a dream he'd once had. He knew, if he walked far enough inside, he would find the other side had collapsed.

Yet, he was on the side of a cliff, and there was only one other direction for him to go. There, he saw a bridge.

He stepped onto it and began to walk but didn't get far. The bridge ended in a jagged splintering mess of wood, the way across severed. He looked down over the precipice and saw darkness stretching on forever.

He knew this bridge just as he knew the tunnel.

The last time he'd stood on it he'd been naked. This place had been warm and bright. He hadn't been able to see more than a step in front of himself. What he really remembered though, was that despite not knowing where he was or where he was going, he'd had no fear that he was heading in the wrong direction.

He'd found Rylee on that bridge.

Now, this place felt like a poorly lit crypt. The only light at all came from his implant. He noticed as he looked down at that light coming off him, that it wasn't quite right. Far more red than its normal orange. It kept his interest for a moment, but in the end, there wasn't anything to be done about it.

So, once again he looked back at the tunnel that he knew ended in a wall. He looked at the end of the bridge, which ended in an abyss. Given the options—he stared into the abyss.

He didn't know for sure how long this went on before he sensed he wasn't alone. He glanced over his shoulder and saw her approaching just as she came to stand beside him.

"I told you we needed a better light," Rylee said.

Jonathan frowned. He did remember her saying something about light. *Light, or somewhere to hide.*

But, quite literally, it was like a memory from another dream.

"Do I remember these chats when I'm awake?"

"The part of you that needs to remember does," she said.

Jonathan took a long breath and silence passed between them.

"I wish I could talk to him again," Jonathan said.

"Your father?"

Jonathan nodded. "He's really gone this time isn't he."

"Yes and no," Rylee answered. "The part of himself he gave you. Well . . . you can't take that much and . . . there just isn't enough left of him to be anything you'd recognize."

His lips quivered, but he understood and nodded solemnly. "When I was a kid I was afraid of the dark. He'd sit by my bed until I fell asleep. I was afraid he'd leave. He always said, *I promise, I'll never leave you alone in the dark.*"

"He hasn't, Jonathan," Rylee said. "You know he hasn't."

He looked at her, struggling with his tears. "Are you my intuition now?"

He waited, but she never answered, only waited a time before changing the subject to what was troubling her. "Jonathan, I don't think you're supposed to come here."

"Thought I was in my head. Where is here?" Jonathan asked.

"This bridge. It's not exactly a part of you. It's a place at the boundaries between your mind and the implant. The device can bring you here when it's right. The way you got here—I don't think any Borealis planned for that."

"I had to try something," Jonathan said.

Rylee nodded. "No, I get that. But . . . what exactly was the plan?"

"Bond doesn't fight fair. Thought maybe it wouldn't know how to deal with this," Jonathan said. "Maybe it doesn't. Maybe that's why I'm here."

Rylee looked uncertain. "Might be how you were able to get here, but it isn't why you came."

She kicked a piece of broken wood off the ledge and they watched it fall. After it disappeared into the darkness, they waited for the sound of it hitting ground. It never came.

"What do you think would happen?" Jonathan said. "If I just . . ."

He trailed off, finishing the statement by flinging his hands at the abyss.

"Jumped?" Rylee asked.

He turned to look at her, then back to the darkness below. Finally, he nodded.

"This place isn't physical, Jonathan," she said.

He shook his head. "What's that mean?"

She snorted and shook her head. "You can't solve problems in the physical world by diving off a ledge in your imagination. Get your head out of your ass."

In the silence that followed, a smile began to creep onto Jonathan's face. "Right," he said, beginning to laugh at himself.

She smiled with him for a moment.

"Seriously though, Jonathan, this place is dead. You knew it would be. Why come here?"

"You know why," he said.

She stared at him, as though it didn't matter if she knew the answer or not, she wanted him to say it.

"Fine," he said. "I need Rylee. The real Rylee—no offense."

"None taken," she said, then sighed. "But, even if you could cross this bridge, you'd be doing it for the same reason a junkie wants another hit."

"I know," he said.

"But there aren't any more hits," Rylee said. She placed a hand on his shoulder. "She took a part of you with her when she died, but she left a part of herself as well. That's all that is left, Jonathan—she's gone."

He turned to her slowly, studied her. "Are you the part she left behind?"

She sighed, but she didn't give him an answer.

Instead she changed the subject by jabbing her thumb over her shoulder, "Not remotely interested in heading back that way."

Jonathan didn't bother to look back at the tunnel. "There is no way out back there."

He gestured with his hand into the abyss, "and apparently no way forward."

A thoughtful smile formed on Rylee's face. "Ever think that, if there is nowhere left to go it's because you're where you need to be. That you're what you need to be."

Jonathan shook his head. "The bond isn't going to let me be anything."

She considered this. "Do you remember what your Grandpa said on his death bed?"

The last time Jonathan thought of those words was the night that *Sickens the Fever* attacked downtown Seattle. The first time he fought a Ferox, and his first glimpse of what his future held. Like his grandfather, he'd been within an inch of death when the words came to him.

"Where there is a will, there is not necessarily a way," Jonathan said. "Not when deadlines are involved."

Rylee nodded, then she said nothing. Just stood there in stoic silence waiting for Jonathan to get annoyed.

"Oh, I'm sorry, Yoda, was that supposed to be helpful?"

"The only thing more powerful than will is time," Rylee said.

Jonathan nodded. "But my will isn't mine, and I don't have time. So, what do either matter?"

"Why are you still alive, Jonathan?" Rylee asked.

He shrugged at her—the question had a million possible answers.

"It's not your skills, or your strength. Clearly, you're an idiot, so it's not your brain. The only thing you've ever had going for you is that you endure whatever must be endured."

Jonathan groaned. "Fine then, I don't have time to endure."

"Hmm? Don't you though?" Rylee asked.

He looked at her like he was seriously considering pushing her off the bridge.

Rylee sighed. "The bond is the scariest thing you've ever had to stare down. You can't fight it; you can't outsmart it. So, you think that all you can do is run."

"Give me another option," Jonathan said.

"Take it," she said.

He stared at her in disbelief. Just as he thought to pull away from her she reached up, took his head in her hands and made him look her in the eye. "The bond can hurt us in a million unimaginable ways. The one thing it can't do is make your heart stop beating. A beating heart gives you time."

He gazed back at her.

The conversation felt like running in a hamster wheel. It scared him, made him doubt there was anything real about her. That she was just some part of him trying to keep them from giving up by saying what he already knew. Why? Why was she hiding what she was from him? Why did she look at him like it was all right there . . . if he would just see it.

"You can endure—you can be afraid. You can let it have you. You only have to be brave enough to keep your heart beating, Jonathan."

Same words, a different order, again, and yet.

"Where are you, Jonathan?"

"The bridge," he said.

Rylee shook her head. "No, where are you?"

His eyes widened. "The Never . . . I'm in The Never. I . . . I just need to keep my heart beating."

A smile tugged at her lip for a moment, as they stared at one another. Then, rather abruptly, she let go of his face and took a step back.

"Oh, come on, you could have just said that," Jonathan said incredulously.

"Don't you feel better thinking you got there on your own?"

"No! Not even a little bit."

"Okay, fine. Truth is, I may have been stalling," Rylee admitted.

Her tone changed so quickly it jarred him. "Don't get upset. We had a whole Obi Wan Skywalker thing going and I didn't want to spoil it. But there is—something—I need to tell you."

"What?"

Rylee looked apologetic, like she was about to confess that she'd been omitting something really important.

"Oh god, what?" Jonathan repeated.

"You're not, *technically,* unconscious . . ."

There was no sound. All the color had been removed from the world—everything replaced with hues of red. When he looked into the sky the red sun was too intense and hurt his eyes. He felt his breathing. He was gasping for air. His lungs heaved like he'd sleepwalked through a dead sprint until he'd collapsed.

He was still kneeling, but not where he plunged the needle in. He was in a shallow puddle. Slowly, the color faded back to normal, his wherewithal coming back to him. He was in a field. His clothes weighed on his skin, heavy and soaked. Around him, everything was tall green grass swaying gently in the wind.

He smelled the toxic stench of a Ferox's insides. Then he looked down. He remembered waking on his kitchen floor so many months ago. He was covered in blood again, just—this time it wasn't human—it wasn't his own.

What was left of his enemy was spread out around him. Had it not been for the blood, it would have taken him longer to realize that the pieces spread out around him had belonged to a Ferox—the state of the remains like nothing he'd ever seen. Never, in his most feral moments, had he done this to one of his enemies. It was as though the body had been torn apart by a pack of wolves.

That was when he realized that he could still taste it. He spit, feeling a queasiness in his stomach as Feroxian flesh plopped into the black puddle in front of him. He was drenched in the stuff, his hands shiny black as though covered in tar. The white shirt, what was left of it, would never be white again. His jacket was gone, he didn't see his weapons, even the boots he'd borrowed were nowhere to be seen.

Did I go mad? Rabid?

The last thing he remembered was injecting the adrenaline. What had it done to him? As he looked at the remains, he saw no signs that he'd even used weapons. It was as though he'd ripped the Ferox apart with nothing but his bare hands and teeth.

The Stone, where was the stone?

An icy fear turned his skin cold. Had it been destroyed somehow? Was he stranded inside The Never? No . . . no . . . couldn't be, without the stone this world would end.

He was by no means sure of this, but for the moment it kept him from more panic. Then he felt it, the stone, its presence still there in his mind. It was nearby. Somewhere, in these remains. He scrambled through the blackened grass to find it as he heard a helicopter drawing nearer.

Finally, he turned over what was left of the Ferox's torso, the stone dropping out to splash in the puddle. Its veiny appendages still clinging to something inside. He nearly reached for it, but his hand stopped a few inches away.

He closed his eyes and breathed. *No . . . You don't want to do that. No . . .*

He tore off a part of what remained of his shirt, gently breaking the stone free. Treating it as though it were as fragile as an egg. He finished tying it safely into the cloth just as he felt the wind of the helicopter's blades flattening the grass around him. However, it did not land.

"Mr. Tibbs," Olivia's voice boomed over a bull horn. "It would appear you've failed to fulfill your end of our agreement. Rather spectacularly I might add."

Jonathan cocked his head. Felt himself vomit a bit in his mouth and spit out black blood. *Maybe she'll renegotiate?*

For once, he was glad to find out The Cell had put tracking devices in his clothes. When he'd come back to himself in that field, he didn't have a clue where he'd gotten off to while all the adrenaline was surging through his system.

The stuff hadn't worn off entirely. For a while, he was anxious as a cornered cat, his limbs shivering with too much energy, making it all he could do to keep his mouth shut and think.

Olivia's agents were dealing with collecting the remains of the beast in that field. Dead or alive, they still wanted the specimen. For the time being she was rather good at hiding how righteously pissed she was about Jonathan's failure to bring it in alive—or even intact.

Which, he conceded, was fair.

The only thing that seemed to temper her anger, was that Jonathan wasn't running. He hadn't taken off the moment the Ferox was dead. Rather, he'd walked over to the helicopter and asked if she would return him to the hangar.

That had surprised her—she knew he could have been in the wind, and once he'd found a new pair of clothes, they'd have had no way of catching him. But he wasn't showing any signs of wanting his freedom.

Now, four of Olivia's agents stood watching him like prison guards as he showered—trying to get the Ferox off his skin. The stuff had been harder to get rid of than he'd realized. He'd been covered in their black blood before, but he'd never stuck around in The Never long enough for there to be a reason to bother getting it off.

He felt the last of the adrenaline wear off while he stood with his head against the tiled wall of a shower. Like clockwork, the severed bond became a quiet whisper polluting his blood again.

He sighed. *How long do I have?*

He turned off the water, and the moment he had a towel around his waist, one of the guards spoke into an earpiece. He'd barely taken a step out of the tiled floor into the locker room before Olivia entered, flanked by two more guards.

He scowled at her. What, she was suddenly protecting his modesty? With all the cameras The Cell had in his house, she and everyone in this building had probably seen him bare-assed a thousand times.

"You ready to start explaining to me what is going on?" Olivia asked.

Standing there, chest glowing with nothing but a towel on, he put his hands up. "Don't suppose I could get some clothes?"

Apparently, the request had been expected, as one of the men beside her threw down a small package sealed in what looked like transparent dry cleaner plastic. Inside—more white pajamas.

He reached down and ripped it open, Olivia turning aside before he let the towel drop.

"How about it then, Mr. Tibbs? Make your behavior over the last hour make sense to me."

One thing had become abundantly clear to Jonathan—he needed help. He wasn't sure exactly how to get it, the fact that he'd just failed to live up to their agreement wasn't going to help him get any favors. All things considered, he felt Olivia was being beyond reasonable at this point.

"I don't know exactly what happened," Jonathan said. "Actually, I was hoping you might be able to help me put it together."

"What do you mean you don't know?" Olivia asked. "You were there, you were the one doing it."

Jonathan shook his head. "I really wasn't."

"Mr. Tibbs, I've shown a great deal of trust letting you out of this hangar. Now, you didn't run, and that is one thing, but I'm quickly losing any patience for—"

"You were watching me from the helicopter?" Jonathan interrupted.

She paused. "Of course, did you imagine I'd just allow you to run free and hope you came back? Nothing in your terms indicated you were to be given no leash."

"Good," Jonathan said, noticing she hid a twitch of surprise. "I don't care that you were keeping tabs on me. But I need to see what you saw."

She considered him for a moment. "Why?"

"Because," he sighed. "I can't remember what happened out there."

Her jaw clenched. "Come with me, Mr. Tibbs."

A short time later Jonathan stood in a cubicle on the hangar floor surrounded by a half circle of displays. Each showed camera feeds from all over the base and helicopters; some displayed the information that had been recorded by tracking devices they had on him while he was outside.

Olivia stood, arms folded across her chest a few feet behind him as Jonathan's eyes scanned over the monitors. His attention intensified as the bird's eye view of one of the helicopters watched him running to that last stand of trees before he'd used the syringe.

The seconds ticked by as he waited, the monitor reporting his coordinates showed no change in position. There was no way for him to see what happened inside those woods. This was of course his own doing—he hadn't wanted Olivia to see him shooting the highly concentrated adrenaline—he hadn't considered that he might be curious what happened to him later.

As he waited for the tracker to show some indication that he had moved, a group of Olivia's men approached. They were carrying items he'd had with him when he entered the woods. *Excali-bar, Doomsday,* and a canvas sac he assumed contained his jacket and boots. However, the man carrying the bag leaned in to whisper in Olivia's ear before he set it on a table. Jonathan couldn't hear what was said, but her eyes lingered on him curiously while the man took his leave. It wasn't long before he knew. Olivia reached inside the canvas sac and pulled a smaller plastic bag from the contents. Holding it up, she studied the alien steel syringe, before looking back at him—her head tilting as she gave him that '*my my, what do we have here*' look.

A ping indicating the tracker had moved drew his attention back to the screens. He saw a shape shoot out of the trees. It—he—suddenly launched toward the buildings where the Ferox was still engaged by soldiers.

He was moving fast, the helicopters already having trouble keeping up, lost him temporarily. He had to search the camera's feeds from the other monitors, but those hadn't been set up to track him. His head whipped from screen to screen trying to get a good look at himself.

"Your eyes looked like they were on fire," Olivia said as she came to stand beside him. The bag with the syringe no longer in her hands.

Jonathan swallowed when he finally saw his face on the monitor.

He'd seen this once before, but under far different circumstances. Namely, when he'd been empowered by the strength of the bond. This was similar, in that the energy poured out of his eyes as though his body couldn't contain it. That was where the similarities ended. The energy in his eyes in this footage was far more chaotic, malignant. An angry red that seemed to burn away rather than the calm wisps of energy that had come off him under the Bond's influence.

Without Heyer or Mr. Clean to give any expertise, he had to call it for himself. His best guess—and he had no idea if it were possible—was that he'd just come dangerously close to burning out the implant.

As disturbing as all that was, his behavior seemed a reflection of the red chaos pouring out of his eyes and chest. There was no Jonathan there, just a rabid mindless rage. Well, perhaps not completely mindless. It—he—was very focused on one impulse—The Ferox.

He noticed he wasn't carrying his weapons or armor. He wondered if he'd ripped the gear off in some sort of bestial need for freedom while he was still beneath the canopy.

As he barreled through the streets, he didn't avoid obstacles. He crashed through the outer wall of a building to come out the other side with no apparent care for self-preservation. It was as though he were trying to take a straight line, the fastest possible route, to the signal in his head.

When he'd finally laid eyes on the Ferox he paused to roar at it like a damn zombie before plunging forward. He was more animal than man, teeth bared and hands reaching out as though he had claws. He lacked any grace, any bare nuance of martial cunning.

The Ferox took advantage of this, or—tried to. When Jonathan rammed into the thing, they shot down the street like a rock skipping along the surface of a lake. The Ferox opened his mouth to bite into him, and in the moment, Jonathan worried—actually worried for himself—but much to his own shock, as the monster's jaws locked down, it may as well have bitten into solid steel.

The Ferox wrenched away in pain, its teeth bent back against the surface of its gums.

Well, he'd wondered how he could have possibly survived—now he knew. The Ferox wasn't strong enough to hurt him. A moment later, the Ferox retreated away, trying to get some space between them, and he'd watched himself run straight for it again. This time, his feral self seemed to have no gauge on his own strength. Because his attempt to tackle the monster to the ground ended with them flying out of the entire area and plowing down into the wilderness somewhere.

By the time the helicopters reacted and caught up to their position, he could just see himself tearing an arm off the creature while his foot pinned it to the ground. He turned away as he saw his teeth sink into the soft black tissue beneath the outer armor. He recognized the field—didn't need to see the rest to know where it went from there.

When he turned away, he found Olivia watching him.

"Mr. Tibbs, you're acting as though all this is as unsettling to you as it was for the rest of us," Olivia said.

"You've no idea," Jonathan said.

She was quiet a moment, looking between him and the footage.

"Let's say that, watching you observe yourself just now, it's not that hard of a sell to believe you weren't really yourself out there. But if that is the case, I need to know right now why I shouldn't be worried that, whatever that was, won't come over you again."

Jonathan shook his head. "No, I made it happen, I didn't have a choice, but . . . Olivia, I know we aren't off to a good start here . . ."

He trailed off. Closing his eyes; he dropped it. All of it. The posturing, the bravado, any semblance of belief that he controlled his own future. His shoulders slumped as he gave up on standing and sat down in the middle of the hangar floor. There was no point in the façade; she needed to see all of his desperation. "I need your help."

The change in him was so sudden it startled her. She looked down at him, her head cocked, her face giving away how off guard she'd been left by the sudden vulnerability. In fact, it didn't even seem to occur to her that this moment would be the perfect chance to reassert dominance.

"Mr. Tibbs . . . Jonathan, despite appearances, a great deal has occurred to cast doubt . . ." She trailed off. "Your government would prefer you to be an asset. If you're in a bind of some kind . . . and our resources can provide assistance . . . an understanding can be reached. Assuming you're willing to help us in our own endeavors."

"Olivia, I'll tell you whatever you want to know for as long as I can," Jonathan said, letting her see the cloth wrapped stone he held in his palm. "I'm running out of time again . . . and you're literally the only option I've got."

She had been in her quarters when the alarms had set lock down protocols into motion. For most of the morning, all Leah knew was that there was a threat being neutralized within the facility. Given her current standing with Olivia, there was no expectation that her involvement would be requested.

Later, details began trickling down like unconfirmed rumors. Jonathan had made an escape attempt. No, he had freed himself and decimated the entire team of specialists sent to recapture him. No, actually he never made any real effort to escape. He fought his way through several heavily armed guards trying to get Olivia's attention.

He'd gone mad, spouting some crazy story about a dangerous hostile of alien origin that was coming for them. Actually no, he had offered to capture the hostile. Actually no, Jonathan had eaten the hostile.

After the lock down measures were lifted, Leah was more inclined to believe a rat had eaten through a wire in the security system causing the alarms to trigger. After all, it was far more believable than anything else she'd heard. It wasn't until later, while she sat at a station amongst a number of The Cell's analysts in the hangar bay, that some official details were made known and she saw the security footage for herself.

Jonathan's chest glowed. He was bulletproof. He tossed their agents around like they were porcelain dishes. He hadn't killed anyone. Went out of his way not to—and given how easily it would have been for him to do otherwise, Olivia had agreed to negotiate with him.

There were a lot of unanswered questions. How was it possible that he was capable of this? Why had he ever allowed himself to be captured in the first place? Why wait until the moment a threat attacked the base to show his hand? Why volunteer to help his captors? What the hell was going on inside that man's head?

The footage of the Ferox was harder to watch, and it didn't get any easier when Jonathan got involved. He hadn't looked human. In some ways he'd looked more frightening than the monster he had been sent to capture. And his eyes . . .

"Leah," Rivers said. "We need you to drop whatever you're doing and come with me."

Startled out of her thoughts, she found Rivers waiting for her to follow. She couldn't imagine what he needed from her so urgently, but his face told her to ask on the way.

Luckily, he started explaining as soon as they were out of ear shot.

Jonathan had surrendered—sort of. Had willingly agreed to be returned to the containment shell in isolation.

"Is he asking for me?" she asked.

"I was only told to bring you," Rivers said as they passed through the main tunnel that connected the containment shell's wing to the rest of the facility.

When they arrived, she saw what was left of the shell after Jonathan's handiwork. There were two electricians, working hastily to reconnect the conduit Jonathan had destroyed.

Grant, Hayden, and Collin's cells had been emptied. She knew that Jonathan's roommates had been moved to a less draconian containment area; what Olivia had done with Grant remained a mystery. When they reached Jonathan's chamber, the door was open. The lights were not back up inside the shell, but the entire room was cast in an orange glow.

She was relieved when she looked into his eyes and saw no trace of the thing that had torn that creature apart, but she was also seeing the light blazing on his chest in person for the first time. She found it difficult not to stare, her eyes drawn to it like a campfire.

Jonathan didn't look powerful. There was no sign of the strength he'd exhibited that morning. If anything, he looked almost like he had the night before. He glanced at her as she came inside, but hardly reacted. He didn't stare at her with seething hatred. Rather, it was as though whatever weighed on him now was too heavy for him to do more than notice her presence.

"Keep going, Jonathan, don't waste any time repeating yourself," General Delacy said.

Until he spoke, she hadn't noticed her father standing in the corner.

"We're recording," Rivers explained.

She understood then, that Jonathan had not requested her. Olivia didn't want her there. No, her father had given an order, and there wasn't much room to skirt it while he was standing in the room.

". . . the details are important," Jonathan said.

He was scaring her; he had the faraway look of a man who was suffocating on the inside. A man dying alone in a hospital. A man who knew what it was to lose himself and was watching it happen.

He knew he was running out of time. Each instruction he gave getting harder to get out and stranger than the one that came before.

He wanted the power to be restored to the shell—but its ability to shield signals disabled. It had to be the shell; the tunnel could be caved in to seal it off from the rest of the facility.

He asked for the white room. Said he didn't want to go into the dark.

There was no fixing the outer door to the shell itself; the damage Jonathan had done there was too extensive, but he was right about the rest. Each wing of the facility had a single-entry point, and this one was no exception. If needed, it could be cut off from the rest.

He was becoming less responsive. He said that eventually he'd be gone. Once this happened, he needed The Cell to do what they could to keep him alive as long as possible.

"I'll be trapped inside my own mind," Jonathan had said. "If there is a way out, I need to live long enough to find it." The way he said it—he sounded like his only choice was to walk into a woodchipper and hope he could put himself back together on the other side. He said he didn't know what his condition would look like to them. He might have lucid moments; he might come in and out of spells.

He kept saying, "Keep my heart beating."

There was a needle tip that had been recovered from the forest. He said it was the only thing that would penetrate his skin. They would need it to hook him up to an IV—fluids and nutrition. Whatever they could get into him.

He said no one should try to feed him, he couldn't be sure how he might react. That under no circumstances should anyone attempt to intervene with any sort of drugs. That there was no way for their doctors to estimate a correct dosage, and even if they could he didn't know how he might react. It was just too dangerous.

While all these directions had been strange, they paled in comparison to what followed. Jonathan pulled the black cloth wrapped around a small stone from his pocket. He explained that this was why they could not risk him escaping without his wits. He couldn't be parted from this object. He said this, more than anything, was the most important thing—because while right now he was strong enough to ensure it stayed with him, soon he would have to put his faith in them.

That what he was about to tell them could very well mean they would end up needing to protect it not just from him but eventually from themselves.

"The stone has to stay near me at all costs," he said. "If I haven't come back to myself within a certain amount of time, everyone in this facility— the world—they're going to lose themselves. When the deterioration begins, you have to be vigilant. This stone has to be destroyed in my hand, against my skin. It has to be the most important thing to all of you. If it comes to that, whoever does it, they need to get the hell away from me the moment it breaks."

"If they don't," he continued, "they're going somewhere bad . . . the home of those creatures."

He had more instructions; everything Jonathan needed they could provide. He seemed to have done all he could to ensure they understood every detail. He looked so tired and hopeless; Leah didn't know how he was clinging to cognizance.

They couldn't know how much effort it took for him to try and fulfill his end of the agreement. What followed was a candid discussion. Unfortunately, the reason Jonathan seemed so uncharacteristically open about everything he told them, soon became clear.

If he was telling the truth, they were never going to remember any of it. They weren't even really who they thought they were at all.

It took Jonathan over an hour to explain the nature of this reality—The Never—to them. It grew more and more difficult for him with each passing minute. His sentences becoming shorter and simpler as time went on.

Those in attendance were trapped between denial and the unfortunate fact that, unlike previous theories of what might be going on with the alien and those he contacted, everything Jonathan had said lined up with what The Cell had witnessed throughout years of investigation.

He seemed desperate for them to understand what was at stake.

Olivia was first to state the obvious. "If what he says is true, he's been playing us since the moment he opened his mouth."

"If it's true, I'm not sure he had much choice," General Delacy said. "He had to get the stone no matter what it took."

"He could have just killed us to get to it," Olivia said. "What difference is it to him how many of us *shadows* die?"

"Not so easy," Jonathan whispered. He was circling the drain, his words almost like he spoke in his sleep.

Leah watched as Olivia stared down Jonathan, though he hadn't raised his eyes for some time now. "You didn't change course when I threatened the lives of your friends and family. Didn't head straight for the surface to get out in front of this creature before it killed dozens of people on the base. You stalled until we agreed—"

"Olivia! Just stop!" Leah interrupted.

She'd been the quietest of all involved, had listened more than spoke. She couldn't stand seeing him forced to use what little time he had left being second guessed. She didn't care if Olivia was in denial or if the woman's doubts were understandable—she believed every word Jonathan had said.

Unlike the rest, she'd been trying to face the existential crisis of being a shadow copy since the moment he'd told them. Leah had always been able to tell when Jonathan was hiding something—and in the last hour he hadn't had the strength to bother. He was begging them to believe.

Meanwhile, Olivia struggled to keep her doubts alive.

"Think of them. These men we've watched. They were doing everything they could to protect us and we've hunted them like criminals," Leah said.

"They should have told us what was happening," Olivia said.

"Tell us? We can see it for ourselves right now and you don't want to believe!" Leah yelled.

General Delacy stepped in to stop her before any more anger flew. "Alright, enough. We need to stay constructive here."

Leah took a long breath. "Well, I believe he's telling the truth, but if you need proof, the degradation he warned us of should start affecting this reality. We have to want to see it before our judgment goes. Before we stop caring."

"I'll get analysts looking for any signs of the phenomenon," Rivers said. "He said it could take days to manifest."

Reluctantly, Olivia nodded. "See if there is a spike in global crime rates or peculiar behavior. What else should we be looking for?"

The question was addressed to Jonathan. But as they turned to him, he looked too far away. Tears began to roll down his cheeks. He didn't move but to breathe, blinking every so often as he stared at the ceiling.

"I don't think he can hear us anymore," Leah said. "We have to do whatever it takes to make sure he gets home."

"Until we know if what he says about these shadows is true," Delacy said, "I think it best that no one else know about the stone."

"I'll bring in someone from the medical staff to monitor him," Rivers said.

"No," Leah said. "General Delacy is right, we keep everyone away. We do this exactly as he said."

She sat down beside him. "Bring me what I need. I'll stay here with him."

Jonathan inched across a wall. He was surrounded by encroaching darkness. The light of his chest letting him see little more than brick and the small space of dust-covered floor where there was still room to place his feet.

He shook with fear. The light wasn't dying—the darkness was thickening. Still, he knew that beyond the edge of where the light still touched, was a ledge inching toward him. Soon he wouldn't be able to move. He'd cling to that wall until there was nothing beneath him.

Then he would fall into the empty black.

Abruptly, he heard her voice, it wasn't far from him.

"Jonathan, you've got to hurry," Rylee said.

Hurry? Where? Soon there would be nowhere.

Still, he'd rather be nowhere with her, than alone. His fingers felt for the gaps between bricks as he moved toward her voice. He could see the ledge coming closer, so he closed his eyes and moved as fast as he dared.

Her voice came from behind him as her hand gripped his shoulder. "Jonathan."

He opened his eyes just in time to feel her pull him through the vault door. There was no longer a veil of darkness hiding what was inside. He didn't resist her, his feet found floor beneath him as he stepped across the threshold.

He took a long breath of relief as he heard her shutting the vault behind him.

"I thought you were gone. Thank you for finding me," he said.

"That isn't going to hold it out for long," Rylee said.

"No," Jonathan nodded. "Eventually, there won't be any light left. But, at least we won't be alone."

Fear is the heart alone, Heyer said.

Jonathan saw the alien there, for a moment, whispering those words before the memory fell away. He stared for a long while, at first at the empty place where the memory of Heyer had appeared, but then at what was directly behind when the memory faded away.

His father's footlocker. It was still here. The lid sat open, its top resting against the back wall. It was—empty, but . . .

He stepped closer. He saw the key his father had given him still there in the padlock. The storage room brightened, the light in his chest surging as hope found him.

"Somewhere to hide," Jonathan whispered. He spun in excitement. "Rylee, somewhere to—"

He staggered backward, off balance. Confused by what had happened, he caught Rylee's eye. She'd been standing behind him, come upon him quietly. She wasn't angry—her face just looked—sad.

Her hands were up, she'd—she'd shoved him backward. He tripped, his legs hitting the edge of the box. The key dropping from his hand and clinking across the cement floor.

He fell inside the box hard, a tangle of his own limbs. He looked up in time to see her kneeling over him, a tear rolling down her face as she slammed the lid down.

"Rylee? What the hell are you doing?"

He heard the padlock click into place.

"I'm sorry," she said, her voice muffled from the other side. "I realized there was a place to hide. A place that wasn't a part of you, that maybe, it couldn't find you. I knew you would try to take me with you."

He could hear fear in her voice. She must be standing in the black now; he'd been the only light in that room. He heard the box creak as a soft weight lowered against the outside of it. She had lain herself on top of the box.

"But, someone had to lock you in."

THE QUEUE LOOP | ACTIVATION TWO

The second activation began exactly as the first. As it went on, details were altered, but in the end, he negotiated with Olivia to be brought to the surface. After all, with each iteration, one thing was different but always true. A Ferox attacked the base.

Jonathan didn't hesitate as he charged through a small grove of the base's woods that opened into a major street. He found himself in a short stretch of business buildings. They were old, the tallest being maybe six stories, and largely constructed of brick.

The Ferox wasn't difficult to locate.

When he reached it, the Red jumped down from one of the higher rooftops, holding the broken body of a soldier. The Ferox threw the man down such that the unfortunate soul smashed into the pavement moments before his killer landed. Had that man still been clinging to life; he did so no longer.

No matter how many times Jonathan saw acts of violence from the creatures—he still managed to find his rage.

The Red hadn't noticed him yet. Its back was to him while it took fire from the nearby rooftops. The base's soldiers were keeping it as distracted as they could by running up and down the buildings, constantly changing their firing position to keep the Ferox chasing multiple targets. As a distraction, the tactic was effective, but without stronger firepower, the soldiers would eventually run out of luck.

The men in the surrounding buildings knew that his arrival was their cue to withdraw. The gun fire was already lessening as word spread over their radios and Jonathan stepped out into the street. He stabbed *Excali-bar* into the pavement beside him and picked up a large chunk of broken debris.

Concrete slammed into the back of the Ferox's head, crumbling into a shower of dust and small fragments on impact. The beast had to take a few steps forward to keep its balance.

If you would please direct your attention here, Jonathan thought as the Ferox whirled around. Until then, Jonathan hadn't gotten a good look at the Red, but even by Ferox standards, he thought this fellow must have been— homely. Its face was more scarred than he'd ever seen, but not with battle wounds—at least, not only by battle wounds. Most were a rather intricate design and looked self-inflicted.

"*Challenger!*"

With a battle roar that shook the windows, *Scarface* tore down the street toward him. Jonathan stood his ground, felt no need to get out of its path. He realized, even while in the midst of doing it—

He wasn't in danger.

This wasn't hubris or even a newfound bravery. He hadn't lost respect for the ability of the thing charging at him to dole out death. He just—wasn't afraid. Ever since he'd woken up in the darkness beneath the Seattle streets, he knew everything his father knew about engaging the beasts.

But it was more than just knowing what he would do when it reached him. At a glance, he had the measure of this Ferox. Whatever it had survived before today, it was simply not up to the task of facing the experience of *Echoes the Borealis* and the strength of *Brings the Rain.*

When it neared, Jonathan pulled *Excali-bar* free and feinted forward only to pivot and drop outside of *Scarface*'s reach. The hulking beast's claw missed him by inches, but to Jonathan the attack never came close. Before the Ferox was able to sail past, he slammed the demolition bar back down into the pavement at an angle, catching it at the ankle, and taking the Ferox's feet out from under it. The beast barreled forward, leading with its face, before rolling across the street and crashing through the lobby of the first building in its path.

He didn't race after it. He heard a roar of frustration and the movement of wreckage from inside the building as *Scarface* got to his feet and burst back out into the street. Having learned a bit of a lesson, it didn't head straight for Jonathan. Instead, he came just short of melee range and dropped to all fours.

Jonathan allowed himself to be the center of a predatory circle. "I know you're dying to tell me, so let's hear it. What do they call you? Who have your great gods seen fit to send for *Ec*—"

Jonathan hesitated. Had almost used the Feroxian title of his father. But seeing as this wasn't the time for an existential dilemma, he chose not to linger on it.

". . . *Brings the Rain?*" he asked.

Feroxian body language had never been easily readable, but Jonathan found, among other things, that he was suddenly far more adept in the art. This Red was almost transparently overeager. He had yearned so badly for the chance to be immortalized as the warrior who brought back the corpse of *Brings the Rain*—the legendary leader of the abominations—that Jonathan suspected he might already have a choreographed celebratory dance number planned for when he got back to the Feroxian Plane.

"I am *Soils the Ground*, and it is my honor," he said, stopping to hit his fists against his chest.

Jonathan bit his lip to keep from laughing.

This would not be the first time he made a mental note to have Mr. Clean give him a crash course on Feroxian language and culture. But he had to wonder if the mother of *Soils the Ground* had intended for her son's name to mean something other than *Craps on Ground.*

"I know of you," Jonathan said with straight-faced admiration. "Mr. Poopy is much revered by my kind."

Soils the Ground only grunted, as though he had already assumed as much.

"It is unfortunate," Jonathan said soberly. "No apology will do justice for what you're going to endure, I am sorry . . . truly."

Soils the Ground immediately began to tighten the circle around him.

All Ferox were different, some were chattier than the next, but others seemed to feel that anything other than the exchange of names was going overboard with the pleasantries. *Mr. Poopy* was making his impatience noticeable.

"We do not apologize for combat," *Soils the Ground* said.

Jonathan shook his head, dropping any pretense. "This isn't going to be combat; you will be the first of many war crimes I intend to commit against your people."

The Ferox shook its head. "I do not understand, nor do I care to."

Soils the Ground charged, Jonathan saw it coming. Had read it in the way the beast planted its fist and angled its heel. In a flash, the Ferox closed on him, but his fists hammered into the pavement only to find Jonathan absent. Suddenly aware that he'd lost track of his opponent, the beast whirled, catching sight of him at the corner of his vision and lashing out with a vicious backhand.

Jonathan slipped beneath. The fist, seeming to come so close to making contact, sailed by unrewarded. *Soils the Ground* left himself open, and the next thing the monster felt was its jaw violently snapping shut as Jonathan rose out of his crouch to drive an uppercut into his chin.

A moment later, the Ferox returned to the ground, its back caving in the roof of a Subaru parked on the opposite side of the street. The vehicle crumpled, hood and trunk hugging the Ferox's body. Dizzied, *Soils the Ground's* attempts to free himself from the predicament was like watching a toddler try to escape a giant bean bag.

He'd put *Excali-bar* back into the street, and now leaned his weight against it. As the Red finally staggered free of the vehicle, Jonathan eyed the monster thoughtfully. He'd stopped trying to converse with the creatures in any meaningful way long ago. Usually he found whatever a Ferox had to say as frustratingly meaningless as *Soils the Ground* had probably just found his own words.

However, in the past he'd been in too much danger to let himself risk losing his focus. Right now, *Soils the Ground* wasn't exactly driving terror into his heart.

As the Ferox cleared its head to consider launching another attack, Jonathan pointed to the pile of bodies it had begun to amass before his arrival. Most were civilians, people who worked or lived on the base. Only a few had been armed, soldiers the Ferox could realistically consider a combatant.

"War crime," Jonathan repeated the words. "How many did you kill who weren't a threat to you? How many were running from you?"

The Ferox was reluctant to take his eyes off Jonathan but spared a glance for the pile. "Slaughter their weak. Draw out their strong. It has always been so with the abominations."

The hand Jonathan had pointed at the bodies dropped back to his side. He took a long breath. "I'll keep that in mind."

Soils the Ground took a step forward and Jonathan casually flicked free the link that held *Doomsday* around his chest. He felt the chain grow slack around him.

"You're outmatched, *Soils the Ground*," Jonathan said.

The Ferox growled, "We shall see."

"Will we? Because right now, I'm bored," Jonathan said, taking one step away from *Excali-bar*. "You sure the prophet knows you're here? Maybe you stole your stone from someone who was actually fit to enter the arena."

For a moment, the Ferox looked offended. "Arrogant abom—"

"Why don't you go ahead and take your best shot. Give me everything you got. I'll let you have it." Jonathan interjected, lifting his hand to each side. "I honestly don't think you can hurt me, and . . ."

Jonathan smiled as the Ferox closed the distance, only one more step from being able to reach out and grab hold of him. He stared into the empty white eyes as they began to give way, veins filling with black as Feroxian blood surged across its pupils.

"Your gods are watching," Jonathan goaded.

The Ferox stiffened, every fiber of muscle growing taut until it seemed to double in size before him.

Jonathan held still, and finally, *Soils the Ground* reared up, clasping both its hands over its head, and letting out a roar.

What a moron.

The Ferox's biological armor was hard to drive a stake through, but he knew there were weak spots around the joints. They tended to only reveal themselves for a moment when the Ferox moved in certain ways. Jonathan had only scratched the surface of these weaknesses, but before Douglas died, he had been the leading expert in the field.

He freed a length of *Doomsday* and spun out of the way as *Soils the Ground* brought its fists into the pavement. The Ferox's fists punched through the ground, creating a small crater where his opponent had stood goading him. Its roar ceased to be a battle cry and split into a wail of pain as Jonathan drove the spiked tip of *Doomsday* through the back of its knee.

The steel tip sunk deep, angled down into the creature's calf, only stopping when it hit the armor of his shin from the inside. Due to the design of the spiked tip, pulling the weapon out would leave *Soils the Ground*'s leg in shambles. Jonathan didn't intend to give the Ferox the opportunity to try.

He pulled back on the chain, just hard enough to take its footing. While it was still reeling from the pain and shock, Jonathan jumped, spinning twice to free up the slack from his chain before landing on the Red's back. In a frenzy, *Soils the Ground* attempted to push himself up and buck Jonathan off.

As soon as he tried, Jonathan drove his fist down hard into the soft spot behind the creature's shoulder blades. He felt it when the malleable iron bone inside the creature bent—it was the sort of skeletal adjustment that left *Soils the Ground*'s arm in too much pain to move.

The Ferox roared again, and Jonathan was quick, pulling the length of *Doomsday*'s steel chain down and into its open mouth, lodging it in place like a horse's bit.

Soils the Ground, growing desperate as his movements became more and more limited, wasn't thinking clearly. With his one still functioning arm, he reached up and attempted to pull the chain away from Jonathan's grip. This led to a gagged scream as pulling the chain painfully reminded him that the spiked tip was still deeply embedded in his calf. The moment he wailed, Jonathan coiled a second loop of the chain through its mouth and tightened.

It struggled, but was unable to see him or move without causing more pain. Jonathan managed to tie off the chain, jumping down off the Ferox's back and retrieving *Excali-bar* from the pavement.

For what followed, he made sure *Soils the Ground* faced his own pile of trophies. The Ferox, helpless, was unable to even yell about dishonor as Jonathan went about the task of rendering its remaining limbs useless.

Long before it was over, he had engaged in the cruelest act he'd ever committed against another living thing. He was in a daze from awfulness— trying to disconnect himself from what he felt he had to do. He reminded himself that he was the weapon. That he had chosen to be the solution to this problem—whatever it took.

Eventually, *Soils the Ground* stopped moving—struggling only made its pain worse. He shuddered once more as Jonathan took what was left of *Doomsday's* slack and tightened it above the Ferox's calf as a tourniquet to slow the bleeding.

Not because he cared about the Ferox—but because he needed it alive. When he was done, he found a soldier's body; his radio still intact.

"Olivia, the package is wrapped and ready for pickup."

Soils the Ground's eyes followed him. It didn't seem to understand why this slow torture was not leading to its death. As Jonathan knelt in front of the Ferox, his words were not exactly sympathetic, but there was pity.

"You aren't going to die today. I will keep you alive as long as possible, but I will take you apart, piece by piece. You will help me learn everything we can about how to kill your kind. How to kill your women and children. Perhaps, you will be the one who teaches us how to kill the Ferox for good."

The stillness in the Ferox gaze chilled him. Jonathan saw something that neither he nor Douglas had ever seen before. The black drained out of its eyes. The creature, it whimpered—but not from the pain of its injuries.

As Jonathan watched, he realized something that he'd previously only known on an intellectual level. The Ferox, they never showed fear—short of the brink of their own death—but he saw fear there now in those eyes turned white again.

Not the loss of a fight, but his words—he'd scared a Ferox with words.

It would have been easy to assume that the Ferox whimper came out of fear of the hell that he's just described. But no, he knew that wasn't what had so profoundly saddened the beast. Heyer had told him once that the Ferox only really feared one thing.

It wasn't danger to their individual lives, but danger to the species as a whole.

"Keeping the media out of this is already a losing battle, Mr. Tibbs," Olivia said. "But we'll lose all control of the narrative if we can't contain your activities to the base."

"You don't need to worry about the media," Jonathan said. "Our only priority for the next few days is learning as much as we can about the creature."

"Don't worry about the media, how the hell do you—"

"We don't have enough time to worry about what's going on anywhere but inside this hangar. Now, it's a long story and I'll keep my promise to tell it," Jonathan interjected. "Just as soon as we get your people to work."

"My team has been working since the moment the creature was contained," Olivia said.

"Good, let's join them," Jonathan said. "Before your people do anything too invasive, there is something I need to see taken care of. Then we can chat for as long as you want."

She wasn't happy about it, but she held out her arm as if to say *after you*.

He borrowed a thick coat and made sure to zip the thing up to his neck as he stepped out of the locker room and walked down the corridor with Olivia beside him. His presence was distracting enough without the light of his device making him a walking glow stick.

"What is so important it can't wait?" Olivia asked.

Jonathan glanced at her. "The Ferox is carrying an alien object. A stone about the size of an egg inside its chest. It glows, shouldn't be too hard to locate with the right equipment. Our first problem is that we need to retrieve that stone without killing the Ferox."

"And what purpose does the object serve?" Olivia asked, her irritation already taking a back seat to the news that there was more alien technology in The Cell's possession.

"It will really make a lot more sense if I explain along with everything else," Jonathan said. "For now, it's enough to say it's primarily a big battery. It's extremely dangerous for anyone except me to be anywhere near—especially if it gets damaged. So, I'm going to be keeping it near me at all times."

"I'm going to need a lot more of an explanation if I'm going to let you walk around my base with another piece of alien technology."

"You can have my word; I won't leave the base with it. I'm trying to protect you and your people. But this is not a point of negotiation." Jonathan said. "Trust me, once you understand why it is here, you're not going to want anyone else near it either."

She was quiet a moment as they turned a corner and approached the entrance to the wider hangar bay doors where *Soils the Ground* was currently confined.

"I agree for now," Olivia said. "But this slack I'm giving you won't continue if I don't get answers soon."

"I'd shake on it, but I'd probably break your hand," Jonathan said. "Now, did your people locate the box that came along with the cage?"

"Yes, contained what looked like a surgical blade made from the alien alloy," Olivia said.

Jonathan nodded.

"It's half a solution to our next problem," Jonathan said. "I know a lot about these creatures, but one thing I can't tell you is how the hell to anesthetize the damn things. But I need to extract that stone without killing it. So, we could try cutting off its air supply long enough to knock it unconscious. Might work, but I make no guarantees."

"If it doesn't, you intend to perform surgery on it using this scalpel? While it's awake?"

Two of her armed guards saw them approaching and held open the doors.

They entered the hangar. The huge space had mostly been emptied. Tall dividers had been erected to one side to create a smaller room with the Ferox containment cell placed at its center. A woman stood directing a few of the soldiers to move or set up equipment, while others were heavily armed and standing watch over the cage.

"Not me, I don't have that steady a hand. I'm gonna be in there helping to hold it still. You got a surgeon around here with balls of steel?" Jonathan asked.

Olivia walked away from him to speak quietly to the women there.

After they exchanged a few hushed words, she turned to him.

"Jonathan, let me introduce Dr. Watts." She gestured to the woman beside her.

"Well, I guess my proverbial balls of steel are at your disposal," Dr. Watts said.

THE QUEUE LOOP | ACTIVATION THIRTEEN

"You have to be allergic to something. Poisoned by something," Jonathan muttered.

He hadn't been talking to the Ferox, but it heard him and responded nonetheless, and its reply was disheartening.

"What did it say?" Dr. Watts asked.

Jonathan sighed. "It doesn't understand. Has no Feroxian word to match the concept of poison or allergy."

They watched the Ferox through a layer of the same thick transparent plastic his prison cell had been made from. That plastic had nothing to do with keeping the Ferox caged. What kept the beast restrained was the Borealis steel bonds he requested from Mr. Clean every time he was activated. If anything, the plastic shield was a splash guard. It protected Jonathan and The Cell's researchers from getting any unwanted materials on them during testing.

Starves the Famine. That was what it called itself when he was capturing the molting Green. Jonathan had stopped thinking of it that way. The Ferox didn't have a name, it wasn't *Starves the Famine,* but test subject thirteen.

Thirteen was no longer fighting against its bonds. Like its predecessors, it had realized the futility after a few hours. Most of the Ferox eventually figured out that their best choice was to save their strength and wait for an opportunity to get free. Jonathan took precautions to ensure no opportunity ever presented itself. The main one being that he never left the lab while the Ferox was still alive.

Thirteen was a little beat up. Minor wounds received while Jonathan was subduing it. Its only real injury was a surgical incision that ran down its torso between two of its plates of biological armor.

Being in open war with Malkier had changed the rules of engagement. Mr. Clean still couldn't provide him a space gun, that hadn't changed, but there was a grey area between Borealis tools and weapons. Before, when Jonathan needed to retrieve a portal stone from inside a Ferox he had to go about it by beating on its armor with blunt force until something broke. This usually ended the Ferox's life as well.

That surgical cut was made possible by something that fell into the grey area between weapon and tool. The strength of true Borealis steel and Mr. Clean's ability to shape it to his specification, allowed the AI to provide him with what they were calling a molecular scalpel. The edge of the blade was only a few atoms wide; sharp enough to get through the softer spots of the Ferox's exterior armor without killing it.

That wasn't to say it was a pleasant experience for the Ferox. After all, if they had anesthesia that worked on the creatures, then this exercise might not even be necessary. Unfortunately, even Borealis steel wasn't truly indestructible. The scalpel's edge could hold that razor thin sharpness for only a few cuts before the physics involved reduced the knife to only amazingly sharp—but not sharp enough to cut through Feroxian armor.

Even dulled it was still far more impressive than anything Earth based, but when Jonathan considered the idea of weaponizing the atom thin razer's edge for future encounters he did so knowing the blades would rapidly lose effectiveness. They'd need to be swapped out like spent ammunition. While this limited their combat usefulness, he certainly wished he'd had one before today.

The thirteen specimens had produced a lot of information regarding weak spots. Pressure points that could be exploited, softer tissues at the fusions between plates of biological armor. That was all well and good, but Jonathan needed a universal weakness that could be used on a larger scale. Something a man didn't need to be in a one on one encounter to exploit.

And that was why the subject in front of him continued to vex him.

"Liquid nitrogen on the exterior skin is—eventually—effective, but the quantities that would be required to weaponize it against a large number of assailants aren't realistic. For that matter, we also don't know how well your skin will protect you from that much cold . . ."

Olivia paused to look Jonathan up and down as though he were the specimen. "Unless you'd like to volunteer to be a guinea pig and find out?"

Jonathan shook his head. "Find something that works on them and I'll take a bath in it for you, until then I'm just going to assume that, yes . . . it would hurt me," he said.

Over the course of testing twelve live specimens—it would have been thirteen but Jonathan had torn the first to shreds during his experiment with the adrenaline shot—they had exhausted the laundry list of chemical weapons the armed forces had at their disposal. None had managed to get more than a sneeze from any of the specimens, and even that sneeze had been inconclusive.

Biological weapons had no effect either.

Viral agents were a nonstarter. The Feroxian cells were too different from Earthlings to be infected. Bacterial agents might have a chance but so far nothing they had exposed the Ferox to had resulted in any symptoms. This may have been a simple matter of incubation periods, but a weapon that *might* start slowing down the enemy after a week was of no use to him. That said, if Jonathan failed, humanity might need to explore the option further in the aftermath of the coming invasion.

They had tried pesticides, known poisons, and various other nasty chemical concoctions the researchers doing the autopsies thought might have a chance.

One item that had been somewhat effective was a flash bang grenade. The deafening noise didn't seem to bother the beasts, but the sudden burst of bright light could impair their vision. The effect didn't last as long as it did on a human, and only worked if the Ferox was caught unprepared. Still—he could see uses for it.

"We haven't tried garlic, works on vampires," Dr. Watts said, smiling at her own joke.

It was possible that Jonathan had spent more time with Dr. Watts than anyone else in The Cell. She was the one extracting and examining the portal stone from each specimen. Jonathan couldn't risk a shadow—especially Dr. Watt's shadow—being accidentally transported to the Feroxian Plane. Each iteration of her shadow knew way too much about what Jonathan had The Cell doing. As such, they had to establish a protocol where she always remained within six paces of Jonathan when she worked with the stone. She understood that he might well toss her across the room if the stone were compromised before he'd risk her catching a ride to the Feroxian Plane.

After repeatedly going through this on each iteration of his queue, Jonathan had become far more familiar with her, than she with him. She had to get more and more used to Jonathan's familiarity each time, while he remained an almost complete stranger to her.

To Jonathan, she was one of the greatest assets The Cell could provide. Her curiosities in regard to the Ferox often taking them down tangents of inquiry that others might not.

"Garlic," Jonathan whispered, a thoughtful expression on his face before he turned to Olivia.

"Send someone out to a grocery store, a spice store, a farmer's market . . . I don't care," Jonathan said.

"I was joking," Dr. Watts said.

"But you made a good point. Something mundane to us might be a problem for them, and all the better if we find something that won't affect humans."

Olivia looked at him as though she wasn't certain. "We're hoping for a peanut allergy?"

"Maybe. Look, I'll shove mayonnaise down its throat, lather him in honey, and spray him with Febreze if there's a chance something will bother the damn thing."

Olivia arched an eyebrow at him but picked up a communicator to pass on the order for, ". . . groceries."

"I suppose you never know until you try," Dr. Watts said. "I saw a movie once where the aliens were killed with shampoo."

Taking a break from the beast he joined Watts to observe her progress with the portal stone. Had she not been a shadow, had they not been in The Never, Jonathan wouldn't have let anyone from The Cell within a mile of that stone. It seemed inevitable that their Earth Prime counterparts would eventually learn about the implant inside him. That meant they'd learn there were similar implants inside every man that would be on the front line of this war. That meant, he didn't want any of their true selves learning how to activate those devices or mimic the power supply. However, seeing as how whatever the researchers learned while he was inside The Never stayed with him alone—he could allow the shadows to help him gain information.

The testing, while not revealing anything he didn't at least have a sense of, did begin to fill in some details he'd not considered. For instance, the stone was remarkably difficult to damage—impossible for anyone but himself. He'd come to suspect they were designed to only break under specific circumstances.

The first was obvious. When it occurred to him, he remembered Heyer teaching him to break the stone that first night on the docks. Specifically, that the alien had made him remove his gloves. Perhaps that meant someone like him had to be in physical contact with the stone for it to become breakable. That made sense; if the stone was fragile while it was inside a Ferox it might be broken in the middle of a fight.

He suspected that if that were to happen, the man fighting the Ferox would be stranded inside The Never and would die inside when the temporary dimension collapsed.

The second instance was when a Ferox killed someone like himself.

There was a clear link between his device and the stone. It was the reason he could sense its whereabouts inside The Never. Jonathan suspected that when a human combatant died, the device somehow triggered the stone to self-destruct. While he had no idea what the exact mechanics were, he knew the results. The Ferox and its trophy were returned to the Feroxian Plane, while the human implant itself was returned to Heyer's armory.

The one time he had begun to ask Mr. Clean about any of this, the AI had been very reluctant to give details. Jonathan had a strong sense that neither Heyer nor the AI wanted him, or any man, tampering with the stone and—given a mistake might leave them stranded in The Never—he didn't blame them.

At the moment, Dr. Watt's stool was in front of a Biological Safety Cabinet. The BSC was a semi-sterile environment, not to the level one might use if they were dealing with a viral contagion, but rather a ventilated enclosure with a window that allowed her to reach inside. It made it possible for her to have various chemical components open inside the cabinet without the fumes spreading into the lab, but at the same time keep the stone isolated from any materials.

She sat with latex gloves, reaching through the window where the stone was suspended in a small vice over a thick layer of cushion. In one hand she held an eye dropper, likely containing one of various solvents she was testing. She wasn't being too liberal with the stuff but dripping it slowly onto the surface while she attempted to scrape off a small piece of the outer shell with the molecular scalpel.

She'd yet to have had any luck. Despite the stone's resilience, she was wisely wary of applying too much pressure in case she was suddenly successful in weakening the exterior. She treated the stone like it might become as fragile as an egg at any moment. However, this didn't seem to be the case with whatever she was testing now.

She groaned. "Maybe if you touch it while I make the cut?"

Jonathan shook his head. "No, not while *Thirteen's* alive. Can't risk him getting home and reporting what we're doing here. That and . . . well, let's just say there's a very specific message I want these bodies to give their leader once we're done here."

"That doesn't sound the slightest bit creepy," Dr. Watts said.

She put the scalpel and eye dropper down. "I can't run any tests on this if I can't get a sample."

"You've been at it for hours," Jonathan said. "Take a break."

She sighed but took the stone out of the vise with a set of laboratory tongs and placed it into a cup of sterile water. "I ever tell you how much it looks like dyeing Easter eggs," Jonathan said.

She smiled and finally placed the stone on a sterile cushion to dry.

After a while, Olivia came back with three guards carrying the first batch of random groceries. At which point Jonathan had to step behind the plastic spray guard and begin force feeding the Ferox. None of the researchers would have dared getting so close to the thing, and even if they did, they would have needed a Borealis steel car jack to pry its mouth open.

Thirteen spat out most of what he put down its mouth, though he didn't seem to mind meat products. Occasionally the Ferox growled something that Olivia and the rest of the staff couldn't distinguish as any different from the numerous other times it made noises.

"Well, I am paraphrasing, but *Starves the Famine* here is threatening a very bad review over the cuisine being served," Jonathan said.

Olivia didn't seem to find any of this humorous, but Jonathan noticed a curious expression on Dr. Watts. "What is it, Doc?"

"How do you know what that thing is saying after the stone has been removed?"

"Oh, we worked out a theory on that with Specimen Three" Jonathan said. "It's got something to do with the veiny appendages we had to cut the stone free from. We think the stone uses those to map out the biological material it's responsible for returning after its been ingested. Would explain why the body still goes back to the Feroxian Plane even when it's not actually inside the gateway with me."

"How does any of that explain why you hear its words translated in your head," Watts said.

"Best guess," Jonathan said. "My device is connected to the stone, the stone knows the Ferox it belongs to is speaking. So, it tells my implant to translate the Feroxian I'm hearing. Obviously, there are a lot of questions I can't answer, but the theory fits the observations."

"I'm sorry I asked," Dr. Watts said.

Sometime later, after they had tested out the first few bags of groceries, Jonathan reached into the new bag and held up two options. It was Dr. Watt's turn to pick what they tried next.

"I'm curious to see how it feels about the bacon," Watts said.

Jonathan began to tear the packaging open.

"Maybe after this we can see if it prefers its martinis shaken or stirred," Olivia said.

"Wait, what did you say?" Jonathan asked.

"Booze, I was kidding," Olivia said.

"We haven't tried that," Watts said, frowning. "Not, booze necessarily . . . but maybe alcohol, drugs, narcotics, medical . . . experimental."

Jonathan shrugged. "You want to find out if he prefers heroin or bacon first?"

"No!" Collin said. "I refuse to accept that we can't do better than M. Night Shyamalan on this. Water can't be the only weapon we have against these ali—"

Collin and Hayden had joined them in the Lab. They leaned against the BSC with Dr. Watts, when suddenly Specimen Thirteen began spitting out the contents that had been shoved into its mouth. This was different, the reaction far more violent and urgent. The Ferox's stomach even seemed to be heaving like a human on the brink of vomiting.

"Wow, he really doesn't care for that broccoli," Collin said.

"To be fair, I'd react the same way," Hayden said.

Dr. Watts came to stand next to the plastic shield. "Jonathan, you said their world doesn't have any green vegetation?"

"As far as I know," Jonathan said. "Why? You have a thought?"

"Maybe. It wouldn't be a weakness exactly," Watts said. "But if the flavor is unpalatable enough, we could try inundating their senses with it."

"So, the mustard gas didn't work and now you're thinking broccoli gas?" Collin asked.

Watts gave him a sideways glance. "If you failed botany."

That statement drew curious frowns from all in attendance.

"Broccoli is of the family Brassicaceae, more commonly known as the Mustard Family," Watts said. "So, you could still technically call it mustard gas."

Collin held her with a deadpan stare. "I really hope they're paying you the big bucks, Watts."

Admittedly, the idea was odd, but Jonathan wasn't ready to leave anything unexplored.

"You're thinking it might make it hard to smell a human getting close?" Jonathan asked.

"Maybe," Watts said. "But it's not what I had in mind. If the smell is bad enough to them, it might be something like bear or pepper spray."

Jonathan nodded. "I guess the next question is how does one distill broccoli into a gas?"

Hayden chuckled at this. "After living with you the last few months I can tell you with absolute certainty that microwaving it will have the same effect."

"It doesn't need to be a gas," Watts said. "Just a concentrated liquid."

"So, what? Like, Broccoli Essential Oils?" Collin asked.

CHAPTER TWELVE

OCT 15, 2005 | 2:16 PM | JBLM FACILITY

HARRISON WATCHED AS Jonathan's state deteriorated rapidly.

A few steps further from the shell and he staggered as though he'd been hit hard over the head with an anvil. The only thing keeping him from falling flat on the grated metal floor was her guards on either side of him.

"Knock it off, Tibbs," Harrison yelled. "We got a real short fuse for bullshit."

"I . . . I . . ." Jonathan struggled trying to get words out. It surprised all of them, seeing as this was the first time he'd bothered to speak.

He wore a pained confusion on his face, as though he had no idea who had yelled or why. He was panicking like he'd woken into a pitch-black room to discover his arms and legs restrained. "I'm n—"

His entire body strained, his lips pulling back to reveal tightly clenched teeth. His breaths labored in agonizing grunts, as if trying to breathe while being stabbed.

"Dammit, Tibbs, last warning," Harrison said, gesturing to Rolland at the rear. The woman reached down and put a hand on the cudgel at her belt.

Suddenly, Jonathan's face went blank and his legs turned to jelly.

Again, the guards kept him vertical, but his head fell and went limp against his chest. The guard with the cudgel stepped closer, but Harrison held her off. Eyeing her prisoner with suspicion, she stepped close, lifting his head until, had it not been for blindfold and mask, they would have been looking one another in the eye.

"Shit!" Harrison said, looking to each of women holding him. "Get him on the ground, slow and easy."

Once his back was on the floor, the other guards saw for themselves what had caused Harrison's alarm. Blood, a lot of it, was running from his nose and mouth.

"We buying this isn't some trick?" asked Rolland, her hand still itching on her cudgel.

"He'd have to have bitten off his own tongue to bleed this much," Harrison said.

She took a moment getting a grip on the situation, then turned to Rolland. "Call it in, we need Olivia's approval to redirect him to the infirmary."

She turned to Sowsa next, the guard on Jonathan's right, "Don't wait for the confirmation, get a doctor and a gurney on their way to meet us. We aren't risking moving him without knowing what the hell is happening to him."

Each guard went into action, while Harrison watched over him. He wasn't still, and there was a disturbing unnaturalness to his movements. His head jerking violently as though he was being pummeled by an invisible attacker. With every violent spasm, Jonathan grimaced as though each brought more pain than the last. Just as she was considering ordering one of her guards to help hold him down, Jonathan's chest rose with one final heave and collapsed.

The entire seizure came to an abrupt end.

Harrison was quick to search for a pulse. Finding one, she made the call to remove his blindfold and saw the man's eyes fluttering rapidly beneath his lids. A few seconds of this continued, then stopped when Jonathan's eyelids shot open. For a moment, all she could see were the whites of his eyes and it felt disturbingly long before his pupils finally rolled back into position. His eyes seemed to dilate in sync with his returning consciousness.

Disoriented, Jonathan tried to bring his hands to his face, only to be rewarded with the jingle of the handcuffs he'd forgotten. He looked about his surroundings, momentarily at a loss, until he finally focused on Harrison.

"Would you mind helping me sit up?" he asked.

After some hesitation, she gestured for her guard to help him. The hemorrhaging had stopped, though his mouth and chin were still covered in blood. His white prison shirt now looked like he'd been eating spaghetti from a trough. Watching him trying to spit, or rub his face against his shoulder, Harrison took pity on him and pulled a handkerchief from her pocket to help him wipe his face.

When the handkerchief was too saturated to be any more use, she reached down around his neck and put his blindfold back in place. It was splotched with blood like the rest, but she was under strict orders to keep him from

learning any more about the facility than necessary and she'd already failed
to do so.

"Thank you," Jonathan said.

"That sort of episode happen to you often?" Harrison asked.

Jonathan shook his head. He moved his jaw around a bit like he was
testing to see if his teeth still fit together correctly after biting down so hard.

"Any idea what caused it?" Harrison asked. "I'm not a big fan of coincidences, Tibbs."

Jonathan thought for a moment, then despite having the blindfold on
he turned his head to look back in the direction of the shell. "I'm thinking
it's got something to do with my accommodations. I get the feeling your
containment shell wasn't exactly put through a rigorous health and safety
inspection before you folks put people inside."

He turned his head back to where she knelt in front of him. "That turns
out to be the case, rest assured you'll be hearing from my attorney."

She frowned—obviously, he couldn't be serious—he was joking. She tried
to keep a straight face under the mask, but a chuckle escaped. "Yeah? Any
chance you'll consider settling out of court?"

"Reckless endangerment. Gross negligence." He grimaced. "I'm thinking
you're in a very legally actionable position here."

She shook her head. "You're in a good mood for a guy sitting in a puddle
of his own blood."

"Happens more often than you might think," Jonathan said.

"You sure you're alright?"

Jonathan shrugged. "I appreciate the concern, Harrison, but I'll be fine.
Dr. Watts will tell you the same once we're down in the infirmary."

Harrison's relief came to a swift halt. "How did . . ."

The words trailed off, as her thoughts raced through everything she
recalled of the last few minutes. Her people hadn't given names. For that
matter, he'd also just correctly identified their lead medical officer. She was
glad she'd put his blindfold back in place as he would have known he'd rattled her.

"At least Olivia will be pleased to know we'll all be back on schedule
soon," Jonathan said.

"Prisoner." Harrison's voice became a threat again. "For the rest of our
time together, you will speak when spoken to. Understand me?"

There was the faintest hint of a smirk on Jonathan's face when he said,
"You're the boss, boss."

Perth shook off his temporary disorientation.

They stood around a command table within Mr. Clean. Most watched him, their arms folded across their chests, standing the exact way they had before he entered The Never.

For everyone else, an imperceptible amount of time had passed. Mr. Clean referred to this as the moment of *flux*. Perth, on the other hand, had just spent thirty-six hours testing out future scenarios inside The Never.

The team, assembled to extricate Heyer from The Cell's custody, was currently made up of seven. As Perth looked around the circle, Anthony and Sydney stood closest. They had been tapped first. With Mr. Clean's assistance, they had brought him and the others together.

Next stood Beo, Mito, Tamsworth, and the youngest of them, Bodhi.

They waited, because he was returning from what they called Future Reconnaissance. The very sort of militarized abuse of The Never that would have had Nevric, the technology's creator, rolling over in her grave.

Mr. Clean would open a temporary dimension, a duplicate of their reality, and send in a member of the team. These instances were different than when they had to deal with a Ferox. They weren't hampered by the same constraints, the AI could send anyone with an active implant into The Never, supplied with as much energy as was necessary to ensure that dimensional degradation didn't alter the course of events inside.

In short, Future Reconnaissance gave them a great deal of certainty on how things would unfold over the next few days. They had already gathered intelligence about The Cell's facility and its members. Now, they had begun testing variations of an extraction plan. When they went in to rescue Jonathan and Heyer for real, in this reality, The Cell would quite literally have no surprises waiting for them.

Still, one variable remained outside of their control.

"Well, the kid ain't wrong," Perth said, giving Bodhi a vindicating nod. "Jonathan has a very different idea of how this is going to go. He's ordering us to change tactics. If we are following that order, we need to start adapting now."

Tamsworth had been the one to find the news the hardest to swallow when Bodhi reported it. He shook his head now as though he still remained unconvinced. "Ya'll saw him. Tibbs was borderline catatonic. Now what? He's right as rain and givin' out orders."

"We all get it Tam," Perth said. "But I'm telling you, he's a completely different dude than he was ten minutes ago."

"We all saw his condition," Bodhi said. "It's why I didn't get all butt-hurt when every single one of you voted to send Perth in just to prove I wasn't *bat-shit crazy*."

"No one's said that," Tam said.

Mr. Clean, whose presence currently hovered over them from various monitors, spoke up, "My apologies, Tamsworth, but Bodhi's recollection is accurate."

Without being asked, a recording of Tamsworth's initial reaction to Bodhi's report began to play on one of the displays. "As you can see, Bodhi's recollection of your word choice is quite acc—"

"Fine," Tam said. "But I didn't mean it. I'd just, I'd written Tibbs off, and now you're telling me . . ."

Perth gave him a sympathetic look. "We all thought he was a lost cause. But, I'm telling you. He ain't broken no mo. If the man I just met was the real Jonathan Tibbs, then I get why Heyer told me to follow him. He knew a hell of a lot more about what was going on than any of us."

"Yeah," Bodhi said. "Well, he said he'd been planning this out for months."

"Months?" Anthony asked. "How could that even be possible?"

Perth and Bodhi shared a look and shook their heads.

"I can't say," Perth said. "But, he knew every detail of our extraction plan—and his is better."

"Yeah," Bodhi said. "Everything he told me, everything he wants us to do—it makes sense. Actually, kinda felt like we've been playing checkers and he's playing chess."

"If I may," Mr. Clean interrupted. "There may be an explanation for this, I observed a serious peculiarity in Jonathan's gate queue right before Bodhi's last—"

"Hey, no, hold on there!" Perth cut in. What was interesting, was that if Perth hadn't, Bodhi looked as though he was about to interrupt as well. "Mr. Clean, when Jonathan was giving orders, he was real clear about this. Only Anthony and Sydney can know anything about his queue."

Sydney and Anthony exchanged a look.

"He knows us, actually said our names?" she asked.

Bodhi nodded. "He knows all of us—and yeah, he gave me the same order."

"Did he say why?" Anthony asked.

"Kinda," Perth said. "You two don't have active implants. Anyone who can still be drawn into The Never by a Ferox has to stay as much in the dark as possible."

Tam scoffed, "Well, that ain't giving my doubts any comfort."

"It should," Mr. Clean said. "If Jonathan is taking command it's a wise tactical decision."

"How is that?" Anthony asked.

"Heyer is now openly at war with his brother," Mr. Clean said. "Malkier could theoretically enter The Never through any of your gateways. That means any man with an implant in possession of information about our defenses—could become a liability."

This possibility brought the conversation to a halt as the weight settled on each of their shoulders. Even Tam was quick to see the implications, and when he spoke, his words captured the thoughts of everyone present. "Well, ain't that a shit sandwich."

Anthony nodded. "But, Jonathan considered it before we did."

Mito and Beo had yet to chime in. Neither was a man of many words, but Mito had been listening intently throughout the entire exchange. Of those that had not yet encountered this new version of Jonathan, he was the first to cast his vote. "I gave Heyer an oath that I would follow and protect this man. If Jonathan is now giving orders, I will do what he asks of me."

"Well, great for you," Tam said. "I never gave Heyer no oath. I'd never even heard of Jonathan Tibbs two days ago."

"Tam," Anthony shook his head. "Let's not go through it again."

What Anthony didn't wish to discuss was the discovery that each of the men's experiences with Heyer were different. They all understood that a war was inevitable, but any specifics beyond that were—highly individualized—to say the least. That said, after forty-eight hours getting to know Tam, Perth figured he had a guess as to why it seemed Tam had been the least informed.

"'Nough, I wanna hear what Jonathan had ta say," Beo said.

Bodhi and Perth exchanged looks.

While Mito wasn't particularly chatty, Beo was quiet for altogether different reasons. He was the largest man in this room by far—but to be fair he was probably the largest man in any room he'd ever been in. He had a voice to match his height and muscles. His tone seemed threatening whether he wanted it to or not. Oddly, Mito seemed to be the only one immune to the man's sheer presence.

"Um, yeah, we should definitely do that," Bodhi said.

"In Jonathan's plan, we aren't just pulling out Heyer and him," Perth said. "There are, well, a lot more extractions he needs us to make."

"Yeah, but . . . that isn't what's going to make his plan more difficult," Bodhi said.

"It ain't?" Tam asked.

"He says we can't kill anyone," Perth said.

The room was silent for a long while.

"He happen to say exactly how he's expectin' us to pull that off, mate?" Tam asked.

A short time later, Sydney and Anthony stepped out into a hallway. Mr. Clean would begin sending the extraction team out to do more Future Recon. The five men would be taking turns working out what challenges lay ahead with the new plan. They weren't starting from scratch. Jonathan's shadow inside The Never had made both Bodhi and Perth commit to memory a great deal of what the team needed to know.

Mr. Clean would also be pulling Jonathan into The Never as often as possible while he remained outside of The Cell's containment shell. It was the only way to know information was going both ways. The five men's shadows relaying information to him just as his shadow had relayed it to them.

As they walked to another chamber, they had already begun discussing the details that Jonathan and the main extraction team wouldn't be playing a part in.

"We're gonna need at least two more men on this if we want the four local extractions to play out the way Jonathan ordered," Sydney said.

Anthony nodded. "They'll be milk runs. Anyone with a trustworthy face that speaks English can head this."

"Shane." Sydney said.

Anthony cocked an eyebrow. She hadn't needed a moment to consider, which meant she'd already had someone in mind.

"Should I remember him?" Anthony asked.

"Let's just say that if I walked in on that man standing over a body, bloody knife in hand, and he said *wait, let me explain, this isn't what it looks like.*" Sydney shrugged. "I'd probably hear him out."

Anthony shook his head. "What am I missing here, Sid?"

"He's gorgeous, Tony."

He smirked. "Alright, so we bring Shane up to speed. He'll need a partner. The two need to do some practice runs in Future Recon in case there are any surprises to be ready for."

She nodded in agreement as a door opened beside them, Mr. Clean's avatar already waiting for them on a screen inside.

"Okay, confession," Sydney said. "This queue Bodhi and Perth say only we can discuss. I don't have a clue what it is."

Anthony nodded. "I don't know much either. All Heyer ever said was that it had something to do with why Jonathan and a few of the other soldiers see combat far more frequently than most of the others."

Mr. Clean nodded. "As a rule, combatants don't need to know. The queues are seldom relevant to anyone but me. But after today's irregularities, Jonathan is an exception."

"Most of our combatants only know that a Ferox enters the gates on the Feroxian Plane. That this action triggers them being pulled into The Never. However, this is a simplification. The system is not that linear. In truth, often far more than one Ferox enters a gateway before the combatant ever gets pulled into combat."

"So, by queue, you literally mean a queue. The Ferox form a line waiting their turn. But why?"

"Certain gateways located around larger Ferox populations require a more frequent lottery to keep the males in the area satisfied. Jonathan's gateway is one of the most populated. So, what really happens is a number of Ferox might enter the gateway before he ever fights one of them. As the number of Ferox in a queue grows, the frequency with which that combatant is pulled into combat increases. Less time passes on Earth between each of his activations."

"Okay, simple enough, more Ferox waiting, means more frequent activation. Explains why Jonathan saw thirty of these things in three months when the rest of our guys don't see that many in a year," Anthony said. "But, what happened with Jonathan's queue and why would he be worried about Malkier finding out about it?"

"I can only answer your first question with any degree of certainty," Mr. Clean said. "Something went terribly wrong with Jonathan's gateway this morning. It occurred the moment he was taken out of that containment field. It would be unfortunate enough if he had only been forced to engage every combatant in his own queue, but he was forced to clear his as well as the four nodes in closest proximity to him. What is strangest, is that I was unable to intervene or redirect any of the traffic."

"What does all that mean exactly?" Sydney asked.

"When Jonathan was pulled out of that shell, he was activated again and again, until he cleared five queues," Mr. Clean said. "To you, it would have all happened in less than a minute."

"Jesus . . ." Sydney whispered. "How . . . how many were there?"

"Twenty-eight," Mr. Clean said. "And depending on when he closed the gates each time, the experience could have lasted days, weeks, or— if Jonathan was actively trying to prolong his time inside the temporary dimension—months."

"Bodhi and Perth said he'd claimed to have been planning this for months," Anthony said. "You're saying he could very well have been telling the truth."

"It is feasible," Mr. Clean said.

"But . . . how? How did he survive?" Sydney asked, the horror she was imagining touching her voice.

Anthony's thoughts had echoed her own. Given Jonathan's state before all this, they honestly hadn't thought he'd survive a single Ferox encounter let alone twenty-eight in a row.

"I can only tell you what we can assume from what has transpired. Jonathan entered The Never under the full sway of the broken bond. Twenty-eight encounters later, he reemerged no longer showing any sign of its effects. He must have found a way to overcome it on his own," Mr. Clean said. "Seeing as how he's the only person to have ever managed this, it is as much a mystery to me as it is to you."

CHAPTER THIRTEEN

OCT 15, 2005 | 3:30 PM | JBLM FACILITY

OLIVIA STUDIED THE man sitting in her interrogation room. She'd now received multiple disturbing reports from her guards as well as Dr. Watts that the prisoner displayed a troubling amount of familiarity with her personnel. Under normal circumstances she'd have considered delaying. However, the alien's state was worsening. Dr. Watts had little confidence that her team could do anything to reverse his fading vitals.

As such, the decision to fast-track Jonathan's cooperation had been made that morning. By the end of the day she would know everything he'd ever tried to keep hidden. As far as her concerns over his sudden familiarity with the staff, she had to assume he was simply displaying the same precognition that other teams had encountered with prior subjects.

For the next few hours, they would work in shifts. Her interrogators would be backed up by a team of analysts making sure every word Jonathan uttered matched what they already knew. If he didn't see that it was in his best interest to cooperate, she'd motivate him to change his attitude. Olivia didn't believe the full extent of what her team was capable of would prove necessary. On a good day, Jonathan Tibbs was a few years older than a teenager, and from what surveillance inside his containment shell showed—he wasn't having a *good* day.

Yet, there was no sign of that broken man now. Which was why she felt herself hesitating. His wrists and ankles were shackled to metal loops in the table and floor. His white shirt was still smudged with red stains from his yet to be explained episode outside the containment shell. When his blindfold was removed, he simply blinked a few times under the light before lackadaisically getting as comfortable as the restraints allowed him. He didn't look worn or tired or scared.

He looked bored.

On Olivia's side of the glass, Rivers entered through a door and signaled that their man was ready to begin. She considered Tibbs for one more moment, then told herself to stop being ridiculous. She gave the go-ahead. A moment later, an agent entered through the single metal door on Jonathan's left. Casually, he took a seat opposite Jonathan at the table.

She addressed her staff one last time, turning to face the room before the ball got rolling. "Focus. Lindelof is about to begin and I don't want any—"

"Olivia."

Jonathan's voice came over the audio system to interrupt her. She turned back to the window to find he'd leaned slightly to one side, tilting his head such that he was staring over Agent Lindelof's shoulder. Eerily, he seemed to be looking right at her.

"It would be best if you turned off the recording equipment and sent everyone but Rivers and yourself to an early lunch."

Admittedly, it was a far more interesting start to the proceedings than they'd expected. The agents on Olivia's side of the glass exchanged glances. Olivia only smiled confidently. "So, he knows our names. Don't get distracted by parlor tricks. There is precedent; The Mark's allies have been observed to know more than they should in other investigations."

Inside the room, Agent Lindelof was as professional as Olivia had been told to expect. He didn't so much as blink in recognition when Jonathan used her name, nor show any interest in the man's behavior.

"Mr. Tibbs, while it is great that you'd prefer to dispense with formalities, I do feel the need to point out that you're in no position to be making demands." Lindelof paused to clear his throat. "Now, our investigation has gathered overwhelming evidence that you're the willing accomplice to an extra-terrestrial whose activities pose grave threat to our nation, and perhaps, our world. As such, you should know your government has deemed you unfit for any standard protections under the Constitution or the Geneva Convent—"

Jonathan had scowled as though Lindelof was a fly hellbent on landing on his face. He made an obvious point of not bothering to look at the agent before holding up his index finger and interrupting. "Hey, Lindelof, do me a favor, go ahead and hold that thought. Okay? Thanks, bud."

Jonathan's gaze stayed on Olivia despite the glass. "Olivia, I'm asking you to clear the room of witnesses. Now, I already know you won't. You're the most stubborn person I've ever met, but for the sake of our future interactions, I'd just like it on the record that I tried to make this easier on you."

Olivia nearly snorted in an indecorous display of incredulity. She found herself trying to gauge how oblivious Jonathan was to what his future held. If he had any idea how his behavior would affect his next few hours, he'd have been desperately trying to make friends right now.

Still, she didn't like the way this was kicking off. No interrogation could ever truly be scripted, but it didn't mean that there hadn't been a strategy, and so far, he wasn't playing into it. Still, in the end, Jonathan was going to find out that no amount of bluster would scare a room full of The Cell's operatives.

As such, Agent Lindelof gave the warning no attention, but he did seem to be noticing that Tibbs hadn't yet bothered to spare him a glance.

"If you're quite finished," Lindelof said. "Why don't we get—"

Jonathan snapped his fingers. "Actually, Lindelof, before you leave today, try to remember we'll be needing pencil and paper. Thanks, bud."

Lindelof smiled. "Mr. Tibbs, if you think there is something to be gained by trying my patience with this juvenile posturing, you'll soon find that you're sorely mistaken—I am not your *bud*."

With a smile of the sort one wears when humoring a child, Jonathan finally made eye contact with the man.

"All right, Olivia, that's all the time you get," Jonathan said. "A quick heads up, you're going to have to give Rivers that promotion early. You know how it is, he's not going to have the clearance level to stay in the room before we're done here."

When Rivers glanced at her, she felt her eye twitch in irritation. She didn't have to say it. A single blink and a tightening of her lips confirmed Tibbs wasn't wrong.

What she couldn't let anyone see was the bit of doubt that had just slipped in. That promotion was something she'd decided—but hadn't formally requested. She had not intended to pursue it in the immediate future. For now, this was knowledge that only existed in her head. To date, she didn't know of any previous subject exhibiting the ability to read minds.

"Right then," Jonathan said. "Lindelof, you were explaining how I'm a bad bad naughty treasonous piece of garbage and not a single agent in this facility will show me an ounce of pity."

Jonathan gave the man a knowing look. "Give me a moment while I get into character."

He closed his eyes and took a sharp breath, and mockingly chanted, "I'm the villain . . . I'm the villain . . . I'm the villain . . ."

Sighing, Lindelof's arms crossed over his chest as he leaned back and waited for Jonathan to stop wasting his time.

"Okay, you go ahead and pick it up wherever you think best. I promise not to interrupt," Jonathan said.

The agent put his amiable smile back on almost as though he were playing along. "Well, thank you for your graciousness, Mr. Tibbs. Now, as I was saying—"

"The thing about a villain . . ." Jonathan interrupted. "Locking one in a cage doesn't make you safe."

Something had changed. All that pleasant smugness he'd had melted off him in an instant. His eyes went empty, his voice cold. It was as though he'd just told his soul to go somewhere else while the adults were talking.

"You see, you're mice who've captured a snake. Except, mice wouldn't be so foolish. Mice would stay as far away from the snake's tank as possible. You and your friends, you've wandered into the tank seeming to have forgotten that you're going to be lunch."

Lindelof made a show of being bored, but Olivia noticed when he thumbed his earlobe. It was one of his many subtle communications, this one said he wanted to let this play out. She understood; Jonathan was putting himself into checkmate. It's not rare, at the beginning of any interrogation, for the prisoner to resort to vague threats. A powerless kid does the exact same thing when he tries to stop a playground bully by telling him, *You'll be sorry.*

Lindelof wanted to give Jonathan enough rope to hang himself.

"With all due respect, Mr. Tibbs, should you entertain the notion that threatening me will stall these proceedings," Lindelof paused, leaning in a bit for effect. "I have every intention of calling your bluff."

Jonathan leaned forward a bit himself, and though she hoped she was imagining it, there seemed a snake-like quality to his gaze. "The Cell—its agents—they're all wholesome folk for the most part. Proud, upstanding patriots ready to sacrifice for the good of the country. But . . ."

A disturbing smile crept onto Jonathan's lips. "The bad guy, well, he's willing to do things you just can't predict."

Agent Lindelof shrugged. "Mr. Tibbs, I personally feel very safe at the moment."

"Do you?" Jonathan asked, glancing back to the windows. "How about Agents Larsen, Lechner, Mulvaney, Odell, Vaughn, . . ."

The roll call went on until Jonathan named every agent in the room like a teacher reading off attendance. When he'd finished, a discomfort began setting into the way they looked at one another on their side of the glass.

Olivia got the sense that Jonathan was purposely observing this moment of silence just to let it fester.

"Lindelof, as a rule The Cell avoids utilizing agents who possess attachments. It's a precautionary tactic, keeps the ruthless folks they might have to deal with from exploiting potential weaknesses. But, bad guys do their homework. We know that someday we just might find ourselves in a room like this one. And we don't like to feel . . . trapped, cornered . . .

"No," Jonathan paused, eyeing Lindelof up and down. "Perhaps the word is *impotent?*"

Lindelof blinked, and Jonathan tilted his head just a touch.

"See Lindelof, the bad guy is willing to make some morally questionable arrangements, to be sure he never has to feel that he or his friends are in danger. For instance, he might tell an acquaintance of his that Agent Samantha Lechner gave up a child for adoption when she was seventeen. He might also tell his acquaintance just where in South Dakota that child is currently attending high school."

Jonathan's head leaned again, his eyes flicking to the glass to look where Agent Lechner was sitting. As with Olivia, it was as though he looked right at her.

"A villain might, perhaps, know that while the birth parents of Agent Laurence Rivers passed away a decade ago, it's actually an elderly woman named Joyce whom he thinks of as a mother. Now, that same villain might tell another of his many acquaintances exactly which nursing home in Maine that sweet old Joyce could be found in. As a matter of fact, his acquaintance might be very close to her right now. He may even be the one bringing Joyce her medication today."

Lindelof stopped him. "Enough, Mr. Tibbs! I'm no stranger to mind games. All you've shown is that you may be aware of a few of our loved one's whereabouts."

Jonathan licked his lips. "Agent Mulvaney might not see it that way. See, when he was assigned to my investigation, he arrived in Seattle without any attachments. However, he's been in the area for some time, and about two months back he met a local, one Diana Rydell.

"Until today, Agent Mulvaney hasn't had to think too hard on if there is more to his relationship with Ms. Rydell than a temporary fling—but when I tell him that not one, but quite specifically two of my acquaintances, are currently keeping a very close eye on Diana, Agent Mulvaney's heart is going to realize just how much she means to him.

"You see Lindelof, this moment is not theoretical for Agent Mulvaney. He is the first of you to know with absolute certainty that I'm not bluffing."

Olivia watched Agent Mulvaney and saw the man had already stood up from his chair. His body shook, his face caught between rage and fear.

"Agent?"

"I thought . . . I thought it was a coincidence."

"What coincidence?"

"The . . . the facial recognition pings we got this morning," Mulvaney shivered. "They were both within two blocks of Diana's apartment."

"You thought that was a coincid—"

Olivia didn't finish the accusation; anger had crept into her voice and she couldn't lose her composure if she wanted her team to stay calm.

"Sit down, Agent Mulvaney, we will discuss this oversight at a later time."

"But . . . what about Diana?"

"Sit. Down."

Mulvaney must have sensed just how much Olivia didn't like repeating herself to her subordinates. He swallowed, looked about as though unsure what to do, and sat back down in his chair. There he fidgeted, trying to control himself.

Olivia turned back to her prisoner, his empty stare already waiting for her. She could feel control over the situation evaporating. But how to take it back? If she removed her staff, she was complying with the very thing he'd asked of her at the beginning. If she stopped the interrogation altogether and sent him back to his cell, they were at a dead end.

If she escalated to enhanced interrogation techniques, she was gambling, inviting a potential hostage situation involving her staff's loved ones. Her staff would be compromised—a potential liability.

Unfortunately for her, Tibbs didn't give her time to think of alternatives.

"As you know, Lindelof, the plan, once you had me good and intimidated, was to ask me a number of questions. One of those questions, you'll remember, is if I knew anything about the sudden reappearance of Luka Sokolov and Noah Walker. Two ex-special forces vets whom The Cell previously investigated. As you also know, those investigations were closed after both men disappeared. Neither have been spotted for over two years now.

"Yet, now they're here in Seattle. Within hours of me and my friends being taken into custody. It's the sort of coincidence that makes you think, doesn't it?"

Jonathan paused, as though he wanted to really give everyone time to think the question over. "Two extremely dangerous individuals who have avoided detection for years. Why do you think they suddenly made the mistake of letting you know they're alive and right in your backyard? It is almost as though they wanted Agent Mulvaney to know exactly how close they are."

A chilling silence swept the room, as Jonathan's threats went from highly unlikely to almost certain. Even Lindelof had grown quiet, seeming to lack an immediate reply.

Finally, he seemed to remember who was supposed to be in charge. "You were safer when I didn't take your threats seriously, Mr. Tibbs"

Jonathan sighed. "Part of being the bad guy, is showmanship. You save the best tricks for last. You'll want to pay attention, Agent Lindelof, because this involves you. See, you aren't a member of The Cell, you were brought in as a temporary outside consultant and your vetting wasn't nearly as rigorous as the nice folks behind the glass that work here full time."

Olivia braced herself, having a very intense certainty that her interrogator was no longer the bully in the room.

"See, your attachments aren't much of a mystery. You've got a wife, Susan, a son and a daughter. Now, of course, your children don't know about the problems you and your wife have been experiencing. That problem that just seems to keep getting worse. You keep telling her it's the stress—the pressures of the job. But she doesn't really know the details of what you do.

"But, imagine what she might feel if she found out just how easily you can rise to the occasion when—"

Lindelof exploded out of his seat, his features distorted in fury as he leaned over the table to throw a fist at Jonathan. Olivia was slow to react, shocked by how quickly Lindelof had lost control. She wasn't alone, in fact the only one who wasn't surprised was Jonathan. He seemed to see Lindelof coming before the man even moved—like he was watching a tortoise in slow motion.

With the slightest slip of his head, Lindelof's fist missed the mark entirely. Having lunged and not connected, the agent had leaned too far over the table. He tried to catch himself with his free hand, but he had put his hand too close to Jonathan's.

In a split second, Jonathan pulled Lindelof's hand out from under him. As the man fell, there was a crack as Jonathan's forehead snapped forward with the speed of a snake uncoiling.

She could hear the sickening crunch of cartilage over the audio system as a dazed Lindelof collapsed and slid off the table to the floor, his nose mangled and front teeth shattered.

Jonathan, relaxed, sitting back in his chair before cracking a few vertebrae in his neck. Then he went on talking as though nothing had interrupted him. "Which brings us to you, Olivia."

He was raising his voice a bit to be heard over Lindelof's whimpers. "Since the precarious situation your staff has found their loved ones in isn't enough to get a private conversation . . . maybe everyone in that room needs to see how quickly you change your mind when it's personal."

She felt Rivers tense beside her, as though he were getting ready to move, but Olivia held up a hand to stop him. Her eyes narrowed, and she couldn't deny a morbid curiosity as she waited for Jonathan to speak. Unlike the others, there was nothing Jonathan could throw at her. She didn't believe he could hurt her, and she'd play chicken to find out if he knew her better than she knew herself.

Lindelof, struggling to get his bearings, finally pushed up to hands and knees.

"Last chance to clear the room, Olivia," Jonathan said. "Your staff doesn't have the pay grade to know about you."

Bleeding profusely onto his suit and tie, Lindelof swayed clumsily as he rose to his feet. There was rage in his eyes, but he wasn't was going to let a man in full restraints get the better of him a second time. Jonathan didn't waste a glance at him as he took his first staggering step around the table.

He stared back at the glass—at Olivia. "Each step buys Lindelof a letter; hope I spell something interesting before he gets his hands on me."

Lindelof paused, forced a cruel smile onto his face, perhaps failing to realize how ridiculous he looked without his front teeth, "Nothing you're gonna—

"A . . . V . . . R—"

Her fists were slamming against the glass as though they had a mind of their own. She was panicking as she realized what Tibbs knew. "Rivers, get Lindelof out of there now!"

By then, Lindelof had a handful of Jonathan's shirt collar. He looked up to see the glass wobbling back and forth as Olivia slammed away at it from the other side. His eagerness suddenly becoming disbelief as Rivers burst into the room and took hold of his arm.

"Agent, I need you to come with me, now!" Rivers said, forcibly pushing the bewildered Lindelof out of the room. Just before Rivers shut the door behind them, Lindelof chanced one last menacing glare at Jonathan.

He immediately regretted it, the soulless stare Jonathan had been wearing was gone. The smugness had returned. Jonathan leaned down over the table such that his fingers could tap the side of his head.

He smiled, and said, "Don't forget the pencil and paper, bud," just as the door closed on Lindelof.

Olivia watched Jonathan sit back in his chair, alone in the room again and looking as calm as the moment he'd been brought in. She was shaking. She had lost her composure in front of her subordinates.

"Everyone out, now!"

CHAPTER FOURTEEN

OCT 15, 2005 | 3:30 PM | SEATTLE

PAIGE HAD BEGUN to worry about Evelyn. They couldn't communicate openly—but she could see that their circumstances were bringing Jonathan's mother to a slow boil.

Colonel Hamill's box of donuts, and whatever lay beneath its paper lining, sat on the kitchen counter. They were both desperate for a look, but there was no longer any question they were being watched. As such, they behaved as though the box contained nothing other than pastries. But, being unable to discuss this made planning anything that required their mutual coordination difficult.

So, the strategy became simple enough to remain unspoken. Eat the donuts—all the donuts.

Whoever finished off the box could attempt some sleight of hand. Sneak out the envelope while breaking down the box for recycling. Course, two people eating a dozen donuts might not have been suspicious if they were offensive linemen, but Paige and Evelyn's combined weight hardly broke two fifty.

Their stomachs were already threatening revolt by the time they had each put away three. Paige couldn't help thinking how handy Hayden and Collin would have been about now. They needed a few more unwitting mouths. Which was why, the moment they heard a knock at the door, neither woman needed to discuss inviting in whoever was behind it for coffee and a donut.

"You expecting anyone?" Evelyn asked.

Paige shook her head as she crossed the room, already wondering if inviting a Jehovah's Witness in was too obvious. Technically, it wouldn't be the first time; Collin let two in the house once.

The memory brought a bit of a smile to her lips. She'd come downstairs to find Hayden looking mortified, while Collin tried to keep a straight face and feign interest. What made it awkward, was that the two had been in the middle of their gospel reboot's first edition. This meant that the Jehovah's Witnesses were attempting to explain their faith whilst a large comic book style image of a haloed sperm wearing a cape approaching the Virgin Mary's womb sat on display on the kitchen table.

Collin could be a real shit sometimes—then again, it had been a bad time for everyone in the house. Jonathan had just come home from his assault. She'd found it hard not to laugh. That said, it had also been the last time anyone knocked on their door asking if they had been saved.

The memory made her miss them all over again—she had to get them back.

Opening the door, she found a man standing on her porch. He was in his late forties and in surprisingly excellent shape. Dark skinned, hair so short it seemed he shaved it normally but hadn't done so for a few days. His clothes seemed a bit casual for his age. Baggy camouflaged cargo pants, a loose button-up short sleeve shirt, and closed toe sandals. There was a duffel bag laying on the steps behind him, and she noticed a baggage claim tag on its handle.

"Hello," Paige said. "May I help you?"

The man was nervous as he gave her a once over, his eyes flicking behind her to see Evelyn watching from the table. He seemed unprepared, as though he'd had to see who answered the door before he had a clue what he was going to say. When he spoke, his accent was heavy, and instantly familiar.

"I am sorry to disturb you," he said, taking a photo from his shirt pocket and holding it out to her. "I'm looking for my daughter. Have you seen her?"

The picture looked as though it were taken on a high school photo day, but Paige recognized a young Rylee. At a loss for what to do, her eyes darted back and forth between the man, who was apparently Rylee's father, and the picture, too many times to plead ignorance.

"Yaa . . . yes, I've met her," Paige said.

Relief washed over the man's face. "Oh, thank God."

He put the photo away and held his hand out to her. "My name is Joao Silva. I've been very worried, was becoming a bit desperate to find anyone who had seen her."

Paige stared back, dreading what she would soon have to tell a stranger, only to realize she had no idea what she even could tell him.

"Do you know where I might find her, or if she'll be coming back here again?" Joao asked. "I don't wish to impose. I know we've never met, but perhaps I could leave a message for her?"

Paige's lip quivered a bit. The growing reluctance on her face quickly turning Joao's hopefulness back to fear. "Um, Mr. Silva, you should probably come inside. I . . . I really don't know where to begin."

Evelyn had a cup of coffee, a plate filled with donuts, and a chair pulled out for Mr. Silva before Paige ever brought him inside. Once he'd been introduced, her face mirrored Paige's. Neither woman was exactly sure what they were going to tell him.

As a mother desperate to find her son, Evelyn didn't relish the thought of seeing another parent share her nightmare. At the same time, she didn't know if she had it in her to keep him in the dark. If she did tell him, then Joao would be in the same danger as them.

In that moment Evelyn made a decision. Well, anger made a decision, she just decided to get out of its way.

Paige must have seen it on her face; she immediately gave the slightest cautionary shake of her head. With a heavy breath, Evelyn made a show of reining herself in. "I'm sorry, please excuse me a moment. I just . . . I need some air."

Paige's eyes followed her warily as she stood and walked out through the garage door.

"Mr. Silva, that had nothing to do with you, it's been a stressful couple of days," Paige said after Evelyn closed the door behind her.

He waved it away as he set down his bag. "No need to explain. I'm grateful you're willing to let a stranger into your home. I don't wish to be rude, but I've no idea why my daughter would travel so far without telling anyone. Were you friends?"

Paige shook her head. "No, Rylee, she . . . um . . . had some sort of relationship with my roommate."

She nodded to the garage door. "Evelyn's son, Jonathan. But neither of them ever explained why Rylee was staying with us. Your daughter and I didn't talk much while she was here."

Joao looked at her as though that couldn't be all there was to tell. "But she was staying here? Sleeping here?" Joao asked. "When did she move on?"

"Um," Paige cleared her throat. "Mr. Silva, do you mind if I ask how you knew to come here?"

A moment of reluctance played out on Joao's face. He seemed to be considering how much to say. "Rylee left without telling anyone. Stopped answering her phone. By the time her mother and I were worried enough to contact the police, we had no idea where to tell them to look. We filed a missing person's report. Nothing ever came of it."

He looked down then, one hand rubbing the stubble on his scalp. "I teach martial arts. One of my students, she helps find missing people—missing women in particular—for a living. I asked if she could help, and she tracked Rylee's phone to this address. I didn't ask how, it's all witchcraft to me, but I was too grateful to care if it was entirely legal."

Paige nodded sympathetically. "No need to explain yourself. Last few days, Evelyn and I are guilty of worse."

Understandably, the comment got her a sideways glance. "Paige, if you know where I can find my daughter, I only want to bring her home safe. I assure you, I don't care what business you or your roommates might be involved in."

"Sorry Mr. Silva, I didn't mean for you to think . . ." She sighed. "The thing is—"

Paige was cut off when the garage door flew open.

Evelyn, somewhat shaken, came back through the door. She strode in, slammed a small toolbox down on the table with one hand, and tossed a device trailing several severed wires onto the table with the other. "I'm done with this, I had to know."

Paige stared at what was clearly a surveillance camera—though a far more sophisticated one than any she'd ever seen at RadioShack.

"Jesus, Evelyn, what did you do?"

The question was the rhetorical sort, the kind one finds themself asking aloud when a friend's mother makes a rash decision with consequences for everyone in the room.

"I'm sorry—no, I'm not," Evelyn said, "No more games."

She stared dumbfoundedly at her and the camera for a few more seconds, then Paige sprang from her chair and ran to the window. She pulled the shades and stared out into the front yard—half expecting to see men in suits coming up the driveway.

"Mr. Silva," Evelyn said, as she opened the toolbox and pulled out a screwdriver and held it out to him. "Would you assist me while Paige keeps an eye out. We need to see if there are more of these."

At a loss, Rylee's father accepted the screwdriver, but wore the face of a man who didn't know what he'd gotten into the middle of.

"Um, what . . . what exactly is—"

"Check the ducts first," Evelyn said, already pulling a chair from the table to use as a stepping stool to reach the kitchen vent. "I'll explain, or at least I'll try, as we go."

Rivers returned to the observation room in time to see the last of the analysts hurry out.

"Get in here, he asked you to stay," Olivia said. "And I need backup on this."

He'd never seen Olivia rattled, but hearing her say she needed backup made him worry how much Tibbs had gotten to her. Not that he could blame her, Jonathan's words couldn't have targeted his fears more precisely if he'd told the man exactly what to say.

She stood at the glass staring at him. "What the hell just happened?"

He tried to detach from his fear, think things through. "Secondary protocol doesn't explain this. His intel—would have taken us weeks to gather. He's been here less than forty-eight hours and was isolated the entire time."

"Something I don't know, Rivers," she snapped. The moment the words left her mouth he saw she regretted them. "I'm sorry."

"It's alright," Rivers said. "I'm not exactly a pillar of calm either."

She nodded gratefully. "Alright, I know what my gut is telling me. What about yours?"

Rivers drew in a long breath. "It's telling me that if we call his bluff, he'll do whatever he has to. It's also telling me he doesn't want to hurt anyone."

"What makes you think that?" Olivia asked.

"He was very specific, pushing everyone's buttons. But he changed his strategy when he got to you. He made it look as if he was playing chicken, but I don't think he was. I think he was trying to show mercy."

"Mercy?" Olivia asked. "What do you mean, mercy?"

"When he focused on you, he didn't just tell the whole room what he had, he spelled out what he knew . . ."

Her head jerked toward him sharply, enough for Rivers to know it would be best if he not mention Tibbs' spelling demonstration again.

". . . All I'm saying is he seemed to know everyone in the room would be in danger if they knew what he did. So, he gave you the chance to stop him before it was too late."

She took a long breath and considered before turning back to study Tibbs on the other side of the glass. "It doesn't feel like we're dealing with the man we've been watching for months. How is that possible?"

Rivers had already had that same thought, but he was more than reluctant to speak of it. Olivia read this off him with a glance. "Speak your mind, Rivers."

He sighed. "I know you have reasons you aren't telling me—I'm not doubting your judgment."

"Noted, now tell me what you're thinking," Olivia asked.

"The one person who wasn't in this room is the one who is supposed to have the answer to that question," Rivers said.

Olivia scowled as she understood, "Leah."

Rivers shrugged, throwing his hand up at Jonathan. "People don't just flip a switch and become confrontational and manipulative. No twenty-two-year-old with zero training intimidates an entire room of career agents.

"He knows everything about us, more detail than he could have gotten even if he'd had access to our personnel files. So, yeah, the person I'd like to get an opinion from right now is the one whose job was getting inside his head."

While he'd been talking, Olivia's face turned back to cement. She'd stopped shaking. She wasn't angry, but he could tell she'd stopped listening to what he was suggesting. Whatever had occurred to her eluded him until she whispered something he'd said a moment earlier. "Knows more about us than our personnel files."

It took him a moment to catch up on where her train of thought had taken her—the complete opposite of what he had been suggesting.

"While I respect your position, it's as you said, there are details of which you remain in the dark. I'm keeping Leah out of the loop on this for the time being—she is not to know what happened here today," Olivia said.

"Understood," Rivers said. "Unfortunately, that brings us back to square one."

Olivia nodded, and stared past the glass again.

"He said he wanted to talk to us, you and I, alone," Olivia said. "So, if you've got any thoughts on how to approach this, I'm all ears."

Rivers gave a defeated shake of the head. "Think we need to hear whatever he wants to tell us. I'm not saying we roll over and show our bellies, just that we play along and see where it goes."

Olivia's jaw clenched, but it was clear she hadn't come up with a better play. She was about to flip the audio back on, but her hand stopped an inch over the switch. "Rivers, I was going to discuss this with you at a better time. Command and I are both impressed with your work. What Tibbs called a promotion—fails to capture the bigger picture . . ."

Olivia saddened before continuing.

"This woman he mentioned, Joyce, our vetting of your background never flagged her as a concern. I've also observed that you have a strong connection to Ms. Margot Kay, outside your professional relationship. Whatever these women are to you, if you accept the offer, they and anyone else will no longer be part of your life. Agent Rivers will no longer exist, and you'll be expected to put your orders above everything else."

Rivers, understandably, was blindsided that she was telling him this. Still, it seemed she felt that if Jonathan was correct, she'd have no choice in the matter. Her hand still hung over the audio switch as she waited for him to reply. "I would never let any harm come to Joyce, but she isn't long for this world. She has dementia, hasn't even recognized me the last few times I visited. As for Margot, I can live with breaking contact if it's necessary."

"I'm sorry you weren't given more time," Olivia said. "There may still be a chance you can reconsider; it depends on Jonathan."

"I appreciate that," Rivers said. "But my gut's telling me this is gonna get worse before it gets better."

Olivia gave one nod, then she flipped the switch.

She leaned down to speak into a microphone nested into the observation room's control board. "Congratulations, Mr. Tibbs, you have our undivided attention. Though I hope you appreciate just exactly what your theatrics have bought you. You'll be spending the rest of your life in the deepest hole I can find for you."

Jonathan didn't look up from his hands, "Yeah, that's more inevitable than you realize. But I've got a lot to do before I allow it."

He looked up at the divider between them. "Raise the glass, Olivia, it's not protecting anyone and you're not a coward."

She sighed. He was right of course. All the protective measures meant to keep the exact sort of episode that had already taken place from happening were now futile pageantry. With the flip of a switch on the control board the glass division receded into the ceiling.

Jonathan didn't wait long once they were looking one another in the eye. He smiled at her, not smugly or knowingly, but almost warmly. "I think it's important to love irony. There was a time I wanted to get my hands on whoever was running this operation just as badly as you wanted to get your hands on the alien. Now, I have to sit here and convince you that we're friends."

The expressions he got from Olivia and Rivers' after this statement seemed priceless to him.

"You consider us allies, Mr. Tibbs? Do you make such grave threats to all your friends?" Olivia said.

Jonathan shook his head. "Well, as friendships go, that's a bit hypocritical. You spied on me for months, imprisoned me and my friends, and had I not let you know there would be consequences, today very well may have ended with a gun to one of my roommates' heads. You should thank me. I've brought us to a stalemate before all of that."

"If this friendship wasn't a fairytale, you might have a point" she said.

Jonathan nodded. "That is going to make the rest of what needs to happen here difficult. More for you, Olivia. I'm afraid I'm going to have to continue taking from you the one thing you care about most."

"And what do you imagine I care about most, Mr. Tibbs?" Olivia asked.

"Control," Jonathan said. "You see, before the sun rises tomorrow, you're going to lose control of just about everything . . . lose any certainty that you ever had it. The only consolation I can give you is one that you aren't going to believe. Everything that is about to happen is something you helped me plan."

Olivia's eyes remained humorless as she listened. "Will we be speaking in riddles for the entirety of this discussion?"

Jonathan shrugged. "I need you to get over being angry. You weren't going to give me a choice, we both know it. Forget what your subordinates are thinking and stop trying to imagine what you'll put in your report. In time, you'll understand that I'm helping you make the right moves. We're all going to get where we need to be when we need to be there."

Olivia smiled disingenuously. "Mr. Tibbs, given the opposing nature of our goals here, I assure you that any further attempts to force my hand will not be taken kindly."

"Yeah, that sums it up pretty well," Jonathan said.

Rivers chimed in, "Speaking of goals, what exactly are yours, Jonathan?"

"I have a few," Jonathan said. "The main one is that this meeting ends with you two understanding that I'm never going to lie to you."

Olivia leaned in, a slight tilt of her head. "That sounds like you want our trust? But your actions are having the opposite effect."

Jonathan gave a casual shrug, "Don't misunderstand. I don't need you to trust my motives. By the end of the day, I need you to trust my word."

"It's a tall order, Mr. Tibbs," Olivia said.

"I'm optimistic that we'll get there," Jonathan said. "I have to be. You see, something is coming for us, Olivia, and the fate of mankind is going to depend on whether you can take a leap of faith . . . faith in me."

Olivia raised an eyebrow. "For mankind's sake, I sincerely hope you're wrong."

A sad sort of smile crept onto Jonathan's face. "I'm going to go above and beyond to change your mind."

"You say we're friends," Olivia said. "I'd like to understand how that is."

Jonathan looked down at the table. "I've seen you at your worst. It's why I know that most days, you wish you could let your hair down, smoke a pack of Camels, and drink bourbon until you pass out."

Jonathan paused to glance at Rivers. "This job is all you do. You don't let yourself indulge in life. You'll never thank me for this, but I'm going to do you a favor. Tell you something Rivers already knows . . ."

She looked at Rivers curiously; he only shrugged.

"Margot Kay doesn't swing that way," Jonathan said.

Olivia sighed. "I do hope this is rapidly approaching a point!"

Jonathan smiled and shook his head, as though he knew he was the only one in the room who saw the joke.

"I've seen the worst of damn near everyone in this hangar and you're tamer than most, Olivia. Take Rivers here, you'd be surprised—I certainly was—to know how proud he is of his physique. When he lets loose, it takes half a platoon to keep him from running through the hallways in his birthday suit."

Rivers blinked a few times before shaking his head. Though he seemed less willing to make eye contact with anyone.

"Right," Jonathan said. "I'm sure the eagle tattooed on your right butt cheek is a figment of my imagination—rather than something seared into my memory forever."

Rivers took too long hesitating; any attempt at a denial would be futile. Soon he came to mirror Olivia's earlier statement. "Jonathan, is this really what you cleared the room for?"

His expression wasn't as smug after her question. Momentarily, he seemed to look genuinely apologetic, "It's a warmup. You aren't going to believe what I have to say—not today, not tomorrow. But, it's the private thoughts, the little embarrassing details, the things you'd never act on and would never confide in anyone—that I knew these things, will keep your mind open despite all the reasons you'll find to doubt me."

He sighed once, leaning forward in his chair. "See, by the time you leave this room, you're going to go about your day as though everything I'm warning you of is a lie. You'll think maybe I'm a mind reader—or precognitive—that somehow, I'm just making it all up as I go. But, you won't be sure."

"How about we skip all that, give us a chance, tell us how things are," Rivers said.

"Of course, but don't expect to believe. You can't, and it's not your fault—it's ridiculous. Frankly, I'd think less of you if you did believe me," Jonathan said.

"Let's hear it then," Rivers said.

"The short version, I've lost track of the number of times I've lived through this day and the weeks that follow it. You could say I've technically lived through alternate timelines, or my own personal *Ground Hog Day*, if it helps."

At this, Olivia smiled with deliberate condescension. "Alternate timelines . . . *Ground Hog Day* . . ."

A lingering tense silence followed. Well, tense for Rivers and Olivia. Jonathan simply waited a span then started spewing a series of numbers out, "One, Seven, Eight, Thirty-Four, Forty-Five, Fifteen . . . 340 million."

"What is that supposed to mean?" Olivia asked.

Jonathan glanced at Rivers. "Sooner or later, he is going to try and call my bluff by asking for tomorrow night's winning lottery numbers. The funny part is he never writes them down or buys a ticket."

"Well, we can put this to rest then, I'll write them down," Rivers said. Jonathan watched knowingly as Rivers realized that there wasn't a scrap of paper in the room.

"Mr. Tibbs, do you have any hard evidence that would let us indulge these fantasies?"

Jonathan lifted his hands. "See, that's the thing. I sure as hell wouldn't believe me either. Which is why . . ."

Jonathan paused to grimace at her. "I'm going to have to ask you to forgive me for the shit storm your life is going to be over the next few weeks. It'll help to remember, it's not personal, we're trying to save the world."

"It sounds more like we have delusions of grandeur," Olivia said.

Jonathan leaned in further toward her. "Humor me a bit, pretend you believe for the time being. The first question you should be asking yourself is why? Why would an alien give a human the ability to experience alternate timelines?"

Jonathan waited. Neither Rivers nor Olivia gave any indication that they took the question seriously. "I really can't begin to imagine, Mr. Tibbs," Olivia said.

"Of course, you can't," Jonathan said. "But here is the funny part. That alien you've gone to so much trouble to catch, his ultimate goal is practically identical to your own. Everything he does is meant to keep mankind from discovering it's under attack by a hostile alien species with advanced technology so that he can eliminate the threat. At the same time, he keeps his technology out of the hands of those who would gain too much power by possessing it."

Jonathan stopped to briefly spread his hands at the two of them.

"The difference between you and him—he is trying to keep it out of the hands of all of mankind while you're trying to ensure that the United States is the only country who gets their hands on it."

Olivia didn't let her mask falter, but Jonathan had finally brought them to a topic she wanted to explore—the alien's technology. So, she made a show of her willingness to listen.

"Now, in some of those alternate timelines I mentioned, this charade wasn't necessary. All I had to do was show you the evidence that an attack on mankind was imminent—not difficult—considering said evidence was trying to kill me. All I had to do was bring the enemy to you, drop it right in your hangar doorway. Still, each time, it took a while to really get us on the same page, but for the most part living proof was enough to get your attention.

"Eventually, the Olivias in those other timelines came to understand that I was going to need the real you—this timeline you—to play ball when I couldn't give you any evidence. You helped me plan how to get you to listen.

"Which bring us to the ultimate problem. By the time this hostile species starts showing up in this reality, by the time I can give you your evidence, it'll be too late for you to do anything about it. Mankind will already be up the proverbial shit creek without a paddle."

Jonathan reclined. "Good news though, I've got a plan to fix our whole evidence problem the moment I leave here."

Olivia stared at him a moment, trying to decipher his meaning. "Leave here? Am I to understand that you expect me to release you based on this inane story?"

"Nope."

"Then . . . you plan to escape?" Rivers asked.

"You *plan* to do something when you aren't sure how it's going to turn out," Jonathan said. "I'm going to leave."

Rivers and Olivia exchanged uncertain glances. "You seem quite confident," Olivia said. "Why don't you tell us how you see yourself accomplishing this."

Jonathan chuckled. "No, I honestly can't tell, but trust me, even if I could you really wouldn't want to know the details."

Olivia closed her eyes, took a long breath, put on a fake smile, and opened her eyes again. "Well, that is unfortunate, but considering you've made a very unambiguous threat we will need to procure the information."

"Threats and torture," Jonathan said, his smile never wavering. "You're a sharp woman, but this is the part that always takes you the longest to get. And it's not that you don't understand, it's that understanding makes you feel like you've lost control."

"What exactly is it that I'm missing, Mr. Tibbs?" Olivia asked.

Jonathan sighed. "It doesn't matter what you do. Doesn't matter what I tell you. Triple your guard, surround the hangar with tanks, mobilize the entire base. My people have seen every version of how this goes. They know how you'll react—how stubborn you'll be. Bring good ol' angry Agent Lindelof back, let him torture me all day. I'll crack, tell him everything I know—and all it will mean is that my people change their strategy. Don't worry, I won't take it personally. I'll still think of you both as friends."

"You're saying it doesn't matter what we do," Olivia said.

"Yes, but I want to bring this all full circle," Jonathan said. "The point is that I'm never lying to you. If I tell you something is the truth, it's a promise."

He let that sink in for a moment, then added, "Now, when I do leave, you will have control over exactly two things."

"Is that right? How gracious of you to let us participate," Olivia said.

Jonathan held up a finger, "First, it's going to be up to you if any of your people die. See, even if Rivers and the rest of this facility doesn't, I know what you're carrying around in your front pocket. I'm telling you this because when the time comes for you to decide if you're going to use it, I want you to remember one thing. I could have disabled that trigger . . . but I promise you that I'm not going to."

Olivia's mask failed to hide her discomfort—she'd lost track of the number of times he'd gotten under her skin. It didn't help matters that she could feel Rivers' questioning gaze on her.

Jonathan held up another finger. "Second, I really don't care what you do to me. But you lay a hand on anyone I care about and this deal is off. My people will come in immediately, they'll do their best not to kill anyone . . . but if you force them to move before they're ready, there aren't any guarantees."

Jonathan didn't break from her eyes for a second as he said this, Olivia unwilling to look away. She was relieved, though surprised, when Jonathan was the first to look away.

"We might want to dial it down a notch; Lindelof is about to be here with my pen and paper," Jonathan said. "No one has told him you kicked everyone out while he was in the bathroom getting his nose under control."

There was a knock at the door. Rivers and Olivia swapped anxious looks before Rivers crossed the room to answer it. Neither wanted it to be true but neither was surprised when Agent Lindelof was standing on the other side. He had wads of toilet paper shoved in each nostril and was holding a clipboard filled with paper in one hand, and a pen in the other.

Unfortunately, Lindelof hadn't expected the one-way window would be gone. As such he was startled to see Jonathan wave to him as he handed the items to Rivers.

As the door closed on him, Jonathan seemed unable to help himself. "Thanks Linds, you're a bud."

CHAPTER FIFTEEN

RIVERS WAS HOLDING the paper and pen Lindelof had delivered.

"I guess I can write down those lottery numbers," he said, a smile coming over his face.

"You don't remember them," Jonathan said. "And Olivia turned the recording equipment off before she cleared the room."

Rivers' smile wavered, then he sighed heavily. "Don't suppose you'll tell me again?"

Jonathan shrugged apologetically.

"Did you actually need this, or was it all meant to put Agent Lindelof in his place?" Rivers asked, referring to the pen and paper.

Jonathan answered by reaching out as far as his restraints would allow for the items. The moment he had them he began drawing.

"All these threats you've made," Olivia said. "What if I said you're stalling, distracting us before we ask questions you don't want to answer."

Jonathan didn't look up from what he was doing. "I already know your questions. None of the answers will get you what you want."

"Then perhaps you won't mind us aski—"

"What do I know about the building in Pioneer Square? The building, which until yesterday, had always been three stories taller? What do I know about all the men under surveillance that have disappeared over the last decade?"

His ability to predict her so accurately was more than grating, but Olivia would ignore it if Jonathan planned on answering those questions. "Yes, for a start."

Jonathan paused, pulled back and took appraisal of how his art project was coming along, then leaned back in to work.

He trailed off, mumbled, "Damn, Lindelof, every time I say a pencil and he always brings a pen."

His eyes narrowed as he leaned in closer, his pen beginning to move rapidly as he shaded-in a portion of the page.

"Where are the missing three stories of that building? Way outside your reach. Where specifically? Hell if I know. Could be floating twenty feet over the hangar roof and you wouldn't know, could just as easily be sitting on the surface of the moon."

He finished shading, then pulled back, looked at his drawing, and started working on finer details. "Where are the missing men? Depends. The few who disappeared in the last twenty-four hours are where the building is, I can't be any more specific because, as I already told you, I don't know where that is . . . however, any that disappeared before that have either been hiding from folks like you for years or . . ."

Jonathan stopped working to look at them.

". . . or they died fighting to protect you."

He didn't go back to work immediately, as though he felt that statement deserved a moment of silence. But when enough time had passed, he put the pen back to work. Olivia noticed he was no longer drawing, but now appeared to be writing words on the page.

"Now, in regard to the alien's condition. You should listen to Dr. Watts. Nothing at your disposal is going to help him. I know, that's not what you want to hear. You don't want to hear it so badly that you're going to convince yourself I'm lying. That's a problem, because before the day is out, Dr. Watts will finish her preliminaries. She'll warn you that she isn't optimistic about tampering with that band on his arm.

"You're going to ignore her, because a comatose alien is as useful to you as one you never captured. But—if you amputate his arm, you're going to find out that having a dead alien is far more useless.

"You see, that bracer keeping him docile was created by his species. It was designed to keep prisoners of their kind from escaping. It is not a bike lock and if you screw with it, you will kill him. The good news is, there is a locksmith who can remove it safely."

"And who might that be?" Olivia asked.

"You've heard of him, goes by Mr. Clean," Jonathan said.

Rivers and Olivia exchange a knowing look.

"Now, I have a plan to stop the real threat to mankind, but I do need that alien to be breathing. If you kill him, every human being on this planet is either going to die . . . or they'll live to become cattle to an alien race whose leader thinks himself a god."

Olivia's eyes narrowed; at this point she wasn't sure of anything, but she was sticking to her part. "Vague predictions about a threat we can't confirm exists," Olivia said. "If you want me to consider this you need to give me something."

Jonathan had to bend down low to the table for one of his fingers to tap his nose as though they were playing charades. He flipped over the page he had been working on and start writing again. He was making a list.

"What is that?" Olivia asked. "That you've been writing down all this time."

Jonathan smiled. "I am going to give you coordinates. A map of the basic terrain and instructions. When your team arrives, they will be pressed for time, so I'm giving you as much intel as I can to get you in and out as quickly as possible. Unfortunately, my intel is dated, so they may need to adapt to the situation they find when they get there.

"With any luck, you'll retrieve the package without causing an international incident. That said, if you must, then, well . . . let's just say it's worth pissing off the Libyan government if you have no other choice."

"And what exactly is it we will be retrieving?" Olivia asked.

Jonathan put the pen down and held out the paper. "The only evidence I can give you, for the time being, that the alien you've got locked downstairs isn't the one you need to be afraid of."

Olivia tilted her head as Rivers retrieved the page. He looked at the map for a moment and asked, "Is this Arabic?"

Jonathan nodded. "Yeah, loosely translates into 'please shit somewhere else,' but I had to take a guy's word for it."

Rivers frowned as he handed the page to Olivia.

"On the back is everything I am going to need from you once we're all on the same page. I'm giving it to you now, because you need to start thinking about how to deliver on each item even if, for the moment, you can't imagine ever trusting me."

When Olivia looked at the list, she nearly laughed in his face. "Mr. Tibbs, hell will literally freeze over, thaw out, and freeze over again before the US government gives you a nuclear weapon."

"Yeah," Jonathan said with an uneasy smile before clearing his throat. "But I need five of them."

After Jonathan informed them that the conversation was over, Rivers stood with Olivia outside of the interrogation room as Harrison and her guards retrieved the prisoner.

"Put him back in his cell; I want him gagged, blindfolded, and . . . stuff something in his ears. None of it is removed until he's in his cell. I don't care if he has a heart attack on his way back, don't make any detours," Olivia said.

Harrison nodded, and her team disappeared into the interrogation chamber.

"We buy any of this?" Rivers asked.

Olivia shook her head. "No. He's mixing fact with fiction to get in our heads."

Rivers didn't want to argue but couldn't hide his uncertainty.

"I don't fault you for questioning it Rivers, it was—quite a show. However, if any of it were true, then we'd never have captured him. He'd have known we were coming before we ever got close."

He nodded, clearly finding some comfort in her logic. "Fantasy aside, he still played that well. Compromised our people and tied our hands until we can put a protective detail on their loved ones."

"I'll see to it," Olivia said. "I want you separating out truth from lies. Start with the map, probably a complete run around but we need to be sure."

Rivers nodded just as the guards brought Jonathan out into the hallway. His gaze lingered on the prisoner as they escorted him away.

"What's on your mind, Rivers?" Olivia asked.

"Why he asked for me to stay. I don't see what I brought to the equation."

He had a point, and it was one she hadn't considered yet. "It's safe to assume he knows I give your opinion weight. Perhaps he thinks that if one of us buys his story, then the other will follow."

"Maybe," Rivers said, but he looked unconvinced.

"Don't let him in your head, Rivers," Olivia said. "He bought himself a few hours, nothing more. Once our people are secure, one way or another he will lead us to this Mr. Clean."

An analyst came around the corner, looking relieved to find Olivia unoccupied. "Ma'am, we've had a development. A few minutes ago, the prisoner's mother began disabling surveillance cameras. Our agents are standing by. Do you want her and the others brought in?"

She and Rivers traded troubled looks. An unlikely coincidence that the mother's indiscretion followed so closely behind Jonathan's ultimatums. He'd been clear about any action taken against his loved ones.

"No," Olivia said. "Cut off their communications and keep them confined to the premises. Our agents will keep their presence unknown unless someone attempts to leave that house. Should that happen, they'll politely be told to stay put. Force will only be considered if they are unwilling to comply."

With a nod the analyst turned to leave, already picking up a phone and disseminating orders. The moment they were alone again, Rivers asked, "Do we believe he is capable of escaping this facility?"

Olivia shook her head. "Our people are already under orders to expect an attempt to extract the alien. If there were any other security measures to consider, we'd already have put them in place."

Rivers grimaced. "The way he described it, if we change anything it might very well be playing into his hands. He may have told us he plans to leave because he wants us to increase security."

"Don't, you're letting him into your head," Olivia said. "It's what he wants. I've no intention of letting him sit idle in that cell plotting another distraction. If he wants to play mind games—we'll play."

Rivers nodded, but now that they were completely alone in the hallway, he tactfully brought up something else Jonathan had mentioned. "What was he talking about when he said you had a trigger in your pocket?"

Despite their being alone, when Rivers asked her this, she seemed to change her mind about any further discussion in the hallway. She signaled him to follow, only stopping when she opened a door into a secured conference room. He followed, and she locked the door behind them.

CHAPTER SIXTEEN

OCT 15, 2005 | 5:30 PM | JBLM FACILITY

"THERE, I SLOWED it down," Margot said. "It's not a video artifact. That thing is real."

"Leah," Olivia said. "I need a word with you."

Both women looked up, and seeing their expressions, Olivia grew curious what it was they were so focused on. "It can wait a moment if you've got something to report."

Leah gave Margot a look. "We think . . . I don't know exactly, but we found something."

They pushed their chairs apart to make room for Olivia. She could see they were viewing the footage retrieved from Jonathan's garage. What was odd was that Margot had distorted the color saturation, run it through digital filters that gave some parts of the image more emphasis over others.

"I was suspicious, just didn't know what was bothering me," Leah said. "It was the way Jonathan shook before he surrendered. Looks like a cold chill—adrenaline, but it wasn't. The more I watched, it was as though he was fighting the urge to squirm."

Margot pointed at a spot behind Jonathan and hit play. In slow motion, with the colors altered, Olivia saw what had been invisible to the naked eye. A worm darted out from behind a cabinet, slithering up behind Jonathan's shoe. A moment later, Tibbs twitched uncomfortably. As though it had just crawled up his skin.

In the seconds that followed the defiance on Jonathan's face disappeared. He put his hands behind his head and dropped onto his knees in submission.

"It surprised him," Margot said. "But he must have known what it was because he tried to keep from reacting."

Olivia nodded. "A thorough body search was performed. Nothing was found on him or his roommates."

"That thing could hide anywhere," Margot said. "Especially if you consider that it was moving of its own volition. There isn't any sign of Jonathan doing anything to call it to him. If it was smart enough to keep from being seen when it attached—"

"He could have swallowed it the moment we put that bag over his head," Olivia said.

Margot paused, then shrugged with an uncomfortable smile. "Well, a thing like that could have found a lot of places to hide on, or in . . . a person if our people didn't know what they were looking for."

Olivia was quiet for a while as she mulled over how this fit into the picture—in particular, how far it might go to explaining what happened during Jonathan's interrogation.

"I think it's alien tech," Margot said. "If I'm right, who knows what it's capable of. Might be a tracking device, a listening device, both. Christ. That thing might not even be with Tibbs anymore. For all we know, it slithered into our servers the moment we brought him here and started downloading everything we have."

"Let's not jump to conclusions," Olivia said. "I've reason to believe it's still on him. Talking to him, perhaps . . ."

Olivia trailed off as the thought occurred to her . . . *perhaps even talking for him.*

She was reflective a moment longer, until Margot and Leah's faces reminded her that she'd never finished her sentence.

"This is excellent work, both of you," Olivia said. "But . . ."

Olivia reached out, gently taking hold of Leah's arm. "As I said, I need to speak with you in private. Please, accompany me down to conference room seven, I've asked Dr. Watts to join us there."

Margot looked disappointed that Olivia wasn't taking an active interest in their discovery. But she only smiled politely as Leah excused herself. A moment later, she realized that Olivia had not actually left. She looked up, surprised to find the woman was still looking at her—considering.

"Ma'am, sorry I didn't realize you were still there, is there something I can help with?"

Olivia sat in the chair Leah had left empty. Her voice wasn't a whisper but she was discreetly quiet. "Margot, I'm going to ask you a highly inappropriate question. You have my word that I would never do so if it had no bearing on this investigation. But I need honesty and I will not be able to give you an explanation."

"Uh, okay, I'll do my best ma'am," Margot said.

"You have a son, but you're divorced," Olivia said.

"That's correct, ma'am."

Olivia nodded. "And the reason for your divorce, was it perhaps related to your sexual orientation?"

"Oh wow, um, no. Not at the time," Margot said. "But it's pretty clear what you're asking me. We don't need to whisper; it's not a big secret."

"Right," Olivia said, thinking for a moment, before smiling politely. "Thank you."

As Olivia stood and walked away, Margot frowned at her empty seat for some time. Eventually, she turned to look at the rubber duck she kept beside her keyboard. Like many programmers, she kept it there because sometimes she had to talk an idea through with someone and there was no one around to listen. The duck was a stand in at those moments.

"So, that was weird right?" she asked the duck.

CHAPTER SEVENTEEN

RIVERS FOUND OLIVIA alone inside the observation deck of the alien's containment shell. She was leaning with one hand against the glass window, looking down at The Mark's comatose frame as Dr. Watts' teams milled about below. She seemed to be watching The Mark's face, but Rivers couldn't read her expression, only that she looked tired.

He hadn't slept much since they had arrested the prisoners; he wondered if Olivia had slept at all. Rivers cleared his throat, and her head tilted toward him for a moment. "Got something?"

"I did some digging on the map Jonathan gave us," he said.

She nodded, straightening her back such that she was no longer leaning against the window.

"It can wait," Rivers said. "If you're—"

"No, tell me," Olivia said.

Rivers nodded. "The coordinates he specified are in the Libyan Desert. Nothing but sand for a hundred miles in most directions," Rivers said. "I'd have thought he was sending us on a wild-goose chase. But if his goal is wasting our time, he's being smart about it."

Olivia turned, her eyebrows raised in interest.

"Douglas Tibbs was sent to Libya in '84. Coincidentally, it was the same operation in which Jeremy Holloway was *supposedly* killed. I cross-referenced the coordinates Jonathan gave with his father's military records. There is a high likelihood that his team passed through those exact coordinates. The interesting thing—there was a delay in their mission progress reported right about the time they were in the area."

"What was the reason?" Olivia asked.

Rivers turned up his palms. "The records documenting the cause of the delay were lost some years back. Unsurprisingly, deleted from the digital record and all hard copies misplaced."

"The Mark," Olivia said with a sigh.

"Like I said, if Jonathan is wasting our time, he's going about it in a way that's hard to ignore."

Olivia's arms came to rest on her hips before she shook her head. "Given what Leah and Margot uncovered, it's possible that someone on the outside is feeding him information. That feels more likely than the notion that Douglas Tibbs told his son about a twenty-year-old top-secret operation before he died."

A moment later Olivia grimaced in frustration. "Then again, we haven't actually confirmed Douglas Tibbs is dead. Seeing as how the body we exhumed turned out to be a John Doe."

She turned back to the window and looked at the alien lying on the table. "Or our comatose friend prepared him for this somehow. Told him what he would need to say to slow us down, showed him a map of the area he would need to draw us."

Rivers sighed, he understood why all these scenarios bothered her. None of them seemed likely.

"Seems like our only option is to send a team to extract the package," Rivers said.

"Or ignore it, assume Jonathan is playing games," Olivia countered.

"We got the resources, it's not gonna distract from what we're doing here," Rivers said.

She nodded.

"For whatever it's worth, I don't think Jonathan spent that entire interrogation building up to this for nothing. He knows that he won't get any second chances if he wastes our time."

Olivia didn't disagree, but her distrust for the situation radiated off her as she stared down at the comatose alien.

"Put the team together. Use assets already in Libya. Tell them to be ready to get it done quickly when and if I give the order," Olivia said.

"If?" Rivers asked. "You're holding off?"

Olivia tongued the side of her cheek.

"I'm sending Leah down, she is being prepped to go into solitary with him," Olivia said. "Before you ask . . . no, I didn't tell her how the interrogation went."

Rivers was quiet for a moment. "I get that you want to see if he knows something you don't about her, but what do you really expect her to learn if you send her in so unprepared?"

"I don't expect she'll be successful," Olivia said. "But, of all the things he discussed today, he didn't say her name once. Even when he was talking about his loved ones. I find that very curious. That, and I don't plan to just let him sit in that cell plotting."

Rivers nodded and left to do as ordered. As he walked away from the alien's containment shell, he couldn't help but think this sounded a lot like what Jonathan had said. Olivia would resist anything she saw as a threat to her control.

For the second time that morning, he worried. Why had Tibbs wanted him in that room?

CHAPTER EIGHTEEN

OCT 15, 2005 | 6:30 PM | JBLM FACILITY

THE SOUND OF the shell depressurizing brought Hayden and Collin to their feet. The shell's door opened. They traded uneasy looks when they saw who it was the guards carried inside this time.

Leah was barely conscious. She was wearing the same white prisoner outfit as they were, she was soaking wet and not walking on her own. She looked as helpless as Grant had when they threw him back in the cell the night before.

The guards didn't stop at the one remaining empty cell across from Grant; they kept walking, headed straight for the white wall at the far back where Jonathan was being kept in solitary.

One of the guards ran a badge over a card reader, and the plastic became transparent again. They could see Jonathan. He stood slowly from his bunk. While there was no threat in his demeanor, the guards behaved as though he was fully intending to lunge the moment his door was unlocked.

"Get back, Tibbs, I want your legs touching the bunk."

Jonathan's expression was strange. He looked—amused—as he raised his palms and stepped back. Hayden was scared for him, thought he was being overly cavalier, practically asking them to wipe the grin off his face. Yet, the body language of the guards told a different story. They were far more uncomfortable getting close to Jonathan than the other way around.

When the door was opened they tossed Leah inside with a cruel carelessness. Jonathan didn't hesitate, he moved to catch her before she fell limply to the floor. She slumped against his chest as the door slammed back into place.

"Treasonous bastards deserve one another," the guard said. There was real venom in her voice, a loathing that gave Hayden a shiver.

Jonathan turned his eyes to her. "See you tonight, Rolland."

The guard hesitated, trading looks with her partner. Jonathan didn't let his gaze linger on her. He looked down at Leah and held her to him to keep her from falling. He was careful, maneuvering her to the thin mattress and covering her with the blanket; his fingers gently guiding some strands of her damp hair from her face.

Finally, he backed away, retreating until his back touched the door of his cell. One of the guards ran a badge over the reader and the cube turned white again. Hayden could only see the shape of Jonathan's shadow against the door. He watched as the man slid down to sit on the floor.

Until the guards were gone, neither Hayden nor Collin spoke. The moment the shell pressurized, Hayden swallowed. "They said treasonous."

His worry was reflected back at him from Collin's face. They stared at the outline of Jonathan's shadow on the door. "I don't get it. They don't want him talking to us, but don't care if he talks to Leah?"

Collin shook his head. "Maybe they just don't want us to hear."

"Hear what?" Grant said.

His voice startled both of them. They turned to find he was sitting up on his bunk with his head in his hands. He was groggy, and there was a brittleness to him, as though every muscle was making him wince when he moved.

"Ohhh. Yay, Grant's awake," Collin said, with flat sarcasm.

"Grant?" Hayden asked. "What did they do to you?"

He turned an annoyed glance at Hayden, as if to say, *exactly what it looks like,* but his attention was drawn to the white wall at the back of the shell.

"That's new," Grant said. "How do I get a white room?"

Hayden exchanged glances with Collin, "Grant, how long have you been here?"

He shook his head. "Don't know. First time they've really let me sleep. Told them everything, didn't matter, they wouldn't stop making me say it all over and over. Injected me with . . ."

He trailed off with a shudder, as though he didn't want to think about it let alone explain. "Tuesday. They took me on a Tuesday. They moved me once, don't know where from or to. My head was always in a bag. Whenever they're done with me, they toss me back in this damn egg."

Hayden wasn't sure how accurate his own sense of time was, but if meals and artificial light patterns were anything to go on, he estimated Grant had been a prisoner for at least six days.

"What did they want to know?" Hayden asked, the question earning him a scowl.

"Not really any of your . . ." Grant paused midsentence. "What the hell are you two doing here anyway? No one gives a damn about either of you."

Hayden shrugged. "We think we were just in the wrong place at the wrong time."

"They came for Tibbs," Grant said, with a bitter vindicated smile, ". . . and you all thought I was crazy."

"Well, to be fair—"

A sharp look from Grant made Collin decide not to finish that thought. The man was still intimidating even if they were separated by thick layers of plastic.

"So, where's Paige then?" Grant asked. "Why isn't she here?"

"Wasn't home when they took us," Hayden said.

Grant's eyes narrowed as though unconvinced. He glanced back and forth between Collin and Hayden as though he suspected a lie. "No, that ain't right."

"Why wouldn't it be?" Collin asked.

Grant snorted and rolled back onto his mattress. "I said they didn't give a crap about you two, but Paige was at least on their radar."

"Maybe because her dad is military?" Collin offered.

He looked at Grant to see if he thought that had anything to do with it, but the man was already curling back up on his bunk. "All I know is the lady running this operation always played it like I was supposed to be keeping my eye on Paige—even when Jonathan was clearly the real interest."

Collin and Hayden looked at one another again—worried, but with no idea what to make of it.

"Grant, where does the tall guy in the hat fit into all this?" Hayden asked.

Grant's head popped up from the mattress. "They catch him?"

Hayden nodded. "Yeah, sort of."

"What do you mean sort of?"

"They took him when they took us, but I don't know how . . . alive . . . he was."

Grant grew quiet. He laid his head back down but didn't go to sleep. They tried to ask him more questions, but he rolled to face the wall.

"Just leave me alone."

White noise. No, there was a rhythm to it, a low vibration. *Thrum. Thrum. Thrum.* It built up slowly in the background.

Leah woke in a fog, but she was almost sure she'd heard Jonathan whispering to her.

She opened her eyes to a dull white light. Her surroundings pressed in on her as her conscious mind finally realized what her unconscious mind had been trying to tell her. *You fell asleep in one place and woke in another.*

She turned over but stiffened when she nearly rolled off the edge of a plastic shelf. Her palm shot out to catch her, and she saw her hand planted on a cool white floor.

"Doesn't fit," she heard.

He was a few feet away, sitting with his back to the wall. His head laying limp as his chest slowly rose and fell.

"Somewhere . . ." he whispered.

"Jon—"

A moment too late, it dawned on her he was talking in his sleep. She wasn't sure she should wake him, but his head lifted slightly at the sound of her voice. He inhaled a quick breath, deeper than the rest. "Rylee?"

Leah swallowed. *No, please don't think that.*

"I remember," he said, his head swaying. "Holding myself, the day . . . the day I was born."

She closed her eyes and relaxed. He was only talking nonsense to a dream. When she looked again, his head was up, and he was watching her. They stared at one another a while. She spent the whole time stumbling around in her head searching for words. A place to start. When her mouth opened, she really had no idea what would come.

"Stop," Jonathan said. "You'll have an aneurysm if you keep thinking that hard."

Leah closed her mouth and frowned while he slid a tray over to her with his foot.

"I saved this for you," he said.

There wasn't much to be excited about on it, an untouched pile of rice and some crust-less bread. She looked at the tray and then back to him. She hadn't expected him to speak to her. If he did, she'd expected the words to be less civil. She realized, with sudden urgency, that she was hungry. Her hand reached for the food as though it had a mind of its own. She picked up the bread first, stuffing it into her mouth greedily. After a few seconds of chewing she discovered she couldn't swallow it.

"It's the drugs," Jonathan said. He'd come closer, was already holding a cup out to her. "Only thing worse than the hunger is the dry mouth."

He wasn't wrong. She took the cup. It was lukewarm milk, but it hadn't spoiled. She didn't much care, anything to help the lump in her throat go down.

"So," Jonathan said. "Olivia says she is going to put you in here looking like you've been in interrogation for days. That I'll assume you can't be a part of this if they're treating you like a prisoner. It's a good plan, clever. I wouldn't fall for it if I were you."

Leah swallowed the lump. Not the best start, she hadn't spoken a word and he'd guessed her cover story. But, why was he telling *her* not to fall for it?

"Jonathan, I . . . I don't know what you're talking about," Leah finally said. "Are you all right?"

He smiled as if he found her commitment to the act adorable.

"I'm serious, Leah," Jonathan said. "None of this is necessary. I'm gonna tell Olivia everything she wants to hear, but only if she waits another six and a half cycles."

Leah frowned as she took another sip from the cup, doing so as slowly as possible to stall for time to think.

"I don't know who Olivia . . ." She trailed off for a moment. "Cycles?"

Jonathan ran his eyes over the cell, moving his finger in a circle with the rhythm of the thrumming vibrations. "They're about twenty minutes, give or take."

Well, he wasn't wrong. Again.

". . . And what is going to happen after six of them?" Leah asked.

"Six and a half." He tilted his head. "But it's a surprise."

She studied him, but he wore a reassuring smile, and she couldn't see anything further. "Jonathan, don't mess with these people. I don't want to see you get hurt."

He lifted the bowl of rice and held it out to her. "I know you don't."

She didn't understand how, but as she searched his face, he seemed to mean what he'd said. After a moment waiting under her gaze he bobbed the bowl of rice in front of her to remind her he was still waiting for her to take it.

Her hunger was still stronger than her confusion. She blinked and took the bowl. With no utensils, she had to spoon the rice out with her fingers. She tried to eat slowly, use the time to get a better grip on the situation.

"You're worried," he said.

Her fingers came away from her lips. "If you had been through what I have you would be too . . ."

She sighed and trailed off. It was the look he gave her, the look that says I know you feel you must keep trying but this was over before it began.

"It's okay. I know why you're afraid. I'm telling you, Olivia already knew this would fail when she sent you down here. You don't need to play her game. She's playing mine."

She was transparent to him. He seemed to know everything. She let the bowl come to rest limply on one leg. "I . . . I don't know what happens now."

"This morning, Olivia brought me in for questioning. She wasn't ready to hear what I had to say. However, she could not deny that I knew more about her than she could ever explain," Jonathan said. "And so, it occurred to her that I might also know about the mysterious contractor forced on her investigation. You see, she always wondered why."

She understood then, and fear sent a shiver through her. How many times had Olivia pushed to know more about her background? Why she'd been forced to work with her, and why Command seemed to give her so long a leash. The last few days had only made Olivia more aggressive in her search for answers.

"I'm not here to find out what you know about the alien," she said, her words almost a whisper. "I'm here so she can find out if you know who I am."

If he was telling the truth, Olivia had just walked her willingly into some trap. Her father wouldn't see it coming. Everything could fall apart if Jonathan knew what she was looking for. That is, if he knew, and decided to say it.

"Olivia's as sharp as she is ruthless. Don't feel bad. If this were a fair fight—I'd have lost. We'd have lost. But it's not a fair fight, and she'll refuse to accept that until the moment she loses."

Had he said 'we'? Why was he saying we? We who?

Jonathan's hand tightened gently on hers. When she looked into his eyes, she could see he was trying to steady her.

"You're doing the math in your head. You think that at best you have twenty minutes before Olivia reviews this conversation. That she'll realize I'm on to her game. I know why it scares you. But you have my word, you and your family will be safe. She will not take you out of this cell."

Leah's lips were trembling. "Why?"

"Because, when she watches this, she's going to know I've made her a promise," he said.

He looked away from her, stared straight into the nearest camera as though it weren't hidden to him at all. "In six cycles. I'm going to tell you everything Olivia wants to know about you."

He turned back to look at her.

"Don't be afraid, the truth will set you free. Rachel."

CHAPTER NINETEEN

OCT 15, 2005 | 9 PM | ANCHORAGE, ALASKA

THE INSTRUCTIONS HAD been to act natural. The first problem with that was that Sam usually avoided going out this late. He didn't feel like he was acting natural as he zipped up his heavy coat or stepped out of his building. None of it seemed to matter much. As he'd made his way to the address, he didn't remember passing a single soul out on the cold streets.

This was how Sam came to be standing in front of a gas station's 24-hour convenience store in the middle of the night. He went inside and saw that he and the night clerk were the only folks present. The man barely looked at him, nodding once to confirm Sam's existence without ever really taking his eyes off the magazine he'd been reading. Sam spent a few minutes deciding which snack to pretend he craved so badly it had made walking here in the middle of the night so important.

He went with a Slurpee and a bag of Funyuns.

As he paid the cashier, Sam asked, "You guys got a restroom?"

"Around back," the man said, then handed him a large rubber stirring spoon duct-taped to a key. The sort of thing meant to keep customers from walking off and forgetting to return it.

A moment later Sam was alone in the most typical of convenience store bathrooms. His pocket began vibrating as soon as he'd locked the door. He tucked the spoon under his arm, put the Slurpee on the sink counter, and fished his phone out of his pocket.

"I'm here."

"You did well, Samuel, but we don't have much time. Your tails are already aware that the audio surveillance equipment they're using to overhear this call isn't working."

"What do I do?"

"We have to bring you in," Mr. Clean said.

"In? Where's *in*?" Sam asked.

"That will be evident soon enough," Mr. Clean said. "For now, I need you to follow instructions."

"I'm listening."

"On the sink, behind the soap dispenser, you'll see a disc about the size of a dime," Mr. Clean said. "Retrieve it."

Sam frowned, but turned to face the bathroom mirror. At first, there was nothing, then the disc just appeared.

"Wow . . ." Sam said, hesitating a bit before picking it up. "Okay, got it."

"Good. Now, hang up and toss your phone in the trash," Mr. Clean said.

"That's it? How will I know what to do next?"

"I'll take care of the rest, just make sure the disc remains in your palm. You'll have five seconds to dispose of the phone once you hang up."

Nervous, Sam bit his lip, but this person who called himself Mr. Clean had shown him too much this evening not to give him the benefit of the doubt. That, and he seemed to be eight steps ahead of whoever it was that had been watching Sam the last few weeks. Besides—the time to turn back had already passed.

"Alright," Sam said. He hung up, tossed the phone onto a pile of used towels, and stared down at the disc resting in his palm.

Someone tried the doorknob from the outside. When the door didn't open, the sound of picks feeling out the pins of the lock followed. The lock wasn't complicated, and a short time later a man and a woman stepped inside. It was a single person bathroom, no stalls, or windows—nowhere to hide if one were inclined to try. So, they didn't take long confirming the room was empty.

The woman eyed the Slurpee melting on the sink. "Tracking on his phone says he's still here."

A moment later the man pulled Sam's phone out of the trash and held it up to her. "No way he gave us the slip, we had eyes on the door since he entered. Unless he flushed himself, there isn't anywhere to go."

The woman nodded, already taking out her phone. The man re-locked the door to make sure no one entered while they were communicating.

"We lost the subject," she said.

The man couldn't make out what his boss was saying but his partner's half of the exchange told him enough.

"We're standing in a single entrance bathroom. He went in and never came out, left his phone behind. Either to make us think he was still in here or because he knew it would tell us where he went."

For the next few moments, his partner listened without having anything to contribute, but the man could tell from her expression that something was up.

"Understood, we're coming in now."

As she hung up her phone the man raised his eyebrows to ask what was going on.

"We aren't the first team reporting a disappearance tonight," she said.

"How many others?"

"No one's sure yet, but too many to be a coincidence. Everyone is scrambling to confirm their subjects' locations. There is already talk that we might be looking at a complete wipe."

"Jesus," the man blinked a few times trying to process. "All of them?"

"Still a bit of a shit show. We don't know if the coordinated disappearances are only in the United States. Command is reaching out to our international teams and our allies."

The man shook his head. "They got any idea what it means?"

She shrugged. "You know everything I know."

CHAPTER TWENTY

OCT 15, 2005 | 9 PM | SEATTLE

BY THE TIME the sun began to set, every curtain in the house was drawn. Paige, Evelyn, and Mr. Silva had spent more than a few hours discovering the extent to which the people watching them had taken their surveillance.

Evelyn was first to notice her, though even Mr. Silva sensed the change in the room as Paige had come down the stairs. She slammed three cameras down on the kitchen table, adding them to the growing pile of devices they had found hidden throughout the house.

"My room," Paige said. "The vents in the bathroom."

Rage isn't smart—and it's dumbest when it has nowhere to go. There is a look a person gets when they are capable of murder. It warns others not to get too close, because if they do, they might accidently get that rage's attention.

No one said a word right away, not even when Paige pulled a hammer from the toolbox and began smashing the hell out of the offending devices.

But, as the girl's anger turned to tears, Evelyn had to stop her. "I know, Paige, I do. But it's all the evidence we have."

Mr. Silva, brought up to speed over the last few hours, had looked as though he had wanted a turn with the hammer for some time now. He looked like a father told that strangers had been watching his daughter when she was most vulnerable.

"Jonathan knew, he had to know," Paige said. "Grant . . . all of them, they just let this . . ."

She trailed off, the hammer dropping out of her hands as she trembled with rage. She felt as though she wasn't sure of anything—anyone. Had Hayden known? Was that the reason he hadn't been sleeping the last few months? If he knew, then Collin must have. Why else were they taken along with Jonathan? Leah and Jack, why were they suddenly gone?

Leah . . .

Was it a coincidence, her moving in the same week as Jonathan's attack? Had Paige been the only one living in the dark these last few months?

"Am I the fool?" Paige asked.

Evelyn looked at her and shook her head. "We can't start thinking that way."

She held her eyes for a while, and eventually, with a shudder, Paige nodded. Evelyn turned to Mr. Silva. "Is there anywhere in this room we haven't checked yet?"

Mr. Silva returned an uncertain shrug.

Paige wiped a tear away, tore herself free of the rapidly deteriorating spiral of her thoughts. "I doubt we've found everything. A job like this, we'd need people who knew what the hell they were looking for to find it all."

Evelyn's lip drew into a line, but she seemed to have come to the same assessment. "Then we've done the best we're going to. I think it's time."

"Time?" Mr. Silva said. "Time for what?"

"We'll explain in a minute," Evelyn said. "For now, kill the lights. No idea if it will help, but why make it any easier for them? Keep an eye outside, we might not have much time if they can see what we're up to."

Paige did the best she could to place herself in the views that would have been covered by the cameras they had discovered. Even when she was pulling the envelope out of the pastry box, she tried not to be obvious—kneeling below the kitchen counter when she finally did so.

As she knelt to remove the envelope from the donut box, she remembered her father's one piece of advice. *Do it smart.* Well, the chance to follow that advice had passed a long time ago. They all felt it. Knew a clock was ticking, and eventually someone was going to come for them.

Truthfully, she was surprised that it hadn't already happened.

She tore open the envelope; all it contained were a few folded documents. She leaned against the cabinet, studying them by the light of a flashlight. Whatever they were supposed to tell her didn't jump off the pages. Mostly, there were copies of invoices paid by companies with generic sounding names. The exact job or service that was being paid for was always vaguely described, though her father had highlighted one line item that specified, *analysis of samples from Seattle site.*

While the companies making the payments didn't seem to have

anything in common, the ones being paid were all audio decoding or restoration specialists.

On the back of the last page, she found a note and recognized the colonel's handwriting.

"A government adjacent entity has been hiring various specialists in the private sector, looking for a method to clean audio recording samples that US intelligence agencies have been unable to make discernible. These *expenses* began in June, within a week of your roommate's hospitalization. Payments came from various front companies to hide the identity of whomever wanted the audio cleaned.

"Gigi, I believe whoever is watching cannot hear you while you're in that house. Please, burn these documents as soon as possible."

Just as she finished reading, Paige saw the cellular signal on her burner phone drop to zero, the house's Wi-Fi following shortly after.

"Shit, shit," she blurted out, not taking the time to explain to anyone as she hurried to the stove and lit the Colonel's papers on fire. She dropped them into the sink and watched them quickly turn to ash.

"Guess it's a good thing we removed the smoke detectors," Mr. Silva said.

"Evelyn," she said. "Turn the lights back on."

"I already tried, power's out," Evelyn said.

"Two men," Mr. Silva said from the front window. "In the driveway. They're just standing there watching the house."

"What, what did the papers say?" Evelyn asked.

"The short version, they probably can't hear what we are saying," Paige said. "A fat load of good it does us now."

"We got two more," Mr. Silva said. "They aren't moving either, just standing at the end of the driveway."

"Everyone wait here," Evelyn said, grabbing one of the flashlights. "Yell if they move."

"What? Where are you—"

"I'll only be a second," Evelyn said, disappearing into the garage.

Paige had no idea what could possibly be worth the risk of separating the group, but last time Evelyn disappeared into the garage their current predicament had been put in motion. Adrenaline was taking its toll as Paige ran to the sliding glass door to search the backyard. With the power out, there wasn't a lot of light, but she wasn't imagining the outline of at least two people standing sentinel out in the dark. The way they watched but didn't move sent shivers down her spine.

What . . . what are they waiting for?

Evelyn burst back into the room carrying a long box. She quickly brushed everything off the table onto the floor to make room for it.

"You grew up on a military base," Evelyn said. "You know how to handle one of these?"

Paige turned her light on the table. The guns—the firearms they had found in the footlocker the day Jonathan disappeared.

"Evelyn . . ." Paige said, shaking her head. "They aren't going to let us shoot our way out of here. We'll just force them to kill us."

While Mr. Silva had been keeping an eye on the men surrounding the house, he had dropped the curtains shut as he realized what the two women were discussing. He was slow to approach, but in the dark even his silhouette said that finding out they were armed wasn't making the situation feel safer.

Suddenly, the three of them froze. They all felt it at the same time—went quiet in the same instant.

It had nothing to do with the guns on the table—in that moment as they strained to listen, the guns were forgotten. Something strange had just happened in the darkness around them. There hadn't been a sound, not exactly, rather, an unnatural stirring of the air. A faint smell of ozone, a bending of the floorboards beneath them. A sense that there were too many people breathing in that room.

In that silence, a man's voice suddenly spoke from the darkness. "Listen to her, Ms. Tibbs, she has the measure of things."

Startled, Evelyn raised the handgun, aiming past Paige into the living room. "Who's there? Who the hell are you people?"

Paige, already standing closest to the voice, shivered as she turned her light. The beam illuminated a young man's face a few steps behind her. His hands were raised in surrender. He was tall and slender but with broad shoulders. Her light hurt his eyes such that he looked aside, but other than that he remained still.

"Ms. Tibbs, please, lower the gun," he said. "We are not with the men outside."

"We?" Evelyn asked.

Paige was already searching the rest of the room with her light and finding a second man standing in the kitchen. Unlike the taller man, he was short and thickly muscled with his head shaved clean enough to shine. His hands were raised as well—as though both were doing all they could to seem less threatening. Nevertheless, Mr. Silva made no effort to hide his distrust, immediately placing himself between the man and Evelyn.

"My name is Shane. My partner in the kitchen is Rourke. He's Russian, doesn't speak much English," Shane said. "But we are here because you are in desperate need of assistance."

Paige decided to keep the light on the prettier one doing the talking. "How did you get in here without us knowing? How'd you get past all the men outside?"

"There is a complicated explanation," Shane said, as he took a few slow steps closer. He made a point of stopping well before he was within arm's reach. "One best given once we get the three of you to safety."

"You're gonna have to do a lot better than that if you expect us to go anywhere with you," Evelyn said. "Starting with how you know our names."

"We were sent here to retrieve you on your son's orders," Shane said.

Paige and Evelyn swapped sideways glances. Both finding the idea of Jonathan issuing *orders* preposterous.

"If you know my son, then, where is he?" Evelyn asked.

"He's a prisoner being held by the very sort of cloak and dagger organization you already know you're dealing with," Shane said.

"If he's a prisoner . . . how the hell did he send you orders?" Evelyn asked.

"Also, a complicated story," Shane said. "But, your son will escape his captors over the course of the next hour. His people are positioned to free him and his friends. But his success depends on a very fixed schedule. A schedule of which the five of us are all a part. Rourke and I taking you to safety is one in a series of dominoes that must fall tonight. Your son needs you to trust me . . ."

Shane's eyes briefly left Evelyn to look at Paige. "All of your friends need you to trust me."

It wasn't difficult for Paige to convey to Evelyn with a look that no, she didn't like this, but yes, she didn't like the idea of dealing with the men outside even more.

"You plan on asking me to hand over this gun?" Evelyn asked. "Because that will end badly for you."

Shane bowed his head in agreement. "I will not. But, do as I ask and you have my word that you'll have no need for it."

Mr. Silva hadn't taken his eyes off Rourke, but he chanced a glance at Shane. "What about my daughter? Is Rylee a prisoner of these people as well?"

Shane didn't look to Mr. Silva, he kept his attention on Paige and Evelyn, as he spoke. "I'm sorry Mr. Silva—the last person to know your daughter's whereabouts was Jonathan. If anyone can help you it will be him. If you want the chance to ask him, you'll need to come with us."

Mr. Silva considered—finally looking to Ms. Tibbs he said, "Not much choice for me here."

To be fair, everyone remained skeptical of the two men, but Evelyn's face was doing nothing to hide it. Paige could feel the tension playing out between Evelyn and Shane. Almost as though he were waiting for her to say something.

"They could be with the men outside," Evelyn said. "Just trying to walk us into a trap."

Shane gave a single nod.

"No one would call you paranoid for thinking that. But the people outside don't care about you or your son—they don't yet understand why he is so important. They could have taken you at any moment and been accountable to no one. You've given them plenty of reason . . ."

Shane paused, nodding to the pile of devices on the table.

"You've been wondering all night why they haven't?"

Paige gave Jonathan's mother another telling look. There was no denying it, they had been wondering this all night.

"Their leader is afraid to do anything more but keep you in this house. Your son put that fear in her. But it won't last. If he remains a prisoner, she will lose her fear. Your son's escape depends on you coming with me the moment I ask."

Shane swallowed, as though what he had to say next was difficult.

"When Rourke and I were asked to be the ones to bring you to safety—we were honored. We believe in Jonathan Tibbs. I know, you can't understand why anyone would say that about your son just yet . . . but trust me for this, and you'll see that there are many people all over this world ready to give their lives for your son."

As Paige listened to Shane, she was unable to keep the incredulous look off her face. If the man was acting, he deserved an Oscar—but it didn't make any of what he said easier to accept.

Still, there was something about the man, his conviction—perhaps his high cheek bones—that was disarming. Paige looked at Evelyn, saw a dumbfounded expression staring back at her. Might as well have been a reflection.

"Don't look at me, I don't know which freakin' way is up right now," Paige said. "Who the hell have I been living with?"

Evelyn lowered the gun to point at the floor. She shook her head at Shane. "What . . . what is it you want us to do?"

Shane glanced at his watch again. "We need to keep up the appearance that we're talking until our people are in position."

"Fine," Evelyn said. "Then what?"

"Then we're all going to hold hands."

CHAPTER TWENTY-ONE

OLIVIA WAS SEEING Jonathan's game more clearly. He had told her the rules. It was as though he'd designed a special sort of hell just for her.

She sat alone in a private viewing chamber reminding herself for the umpteenth time to unclench her jaw. She reviewed the footage of him talking to Leah once more.

"In six cycles. I'm going to tell you everything Olivia wants to know about you."

"Don't be afraid, the truth will set you free. Rachel."

He was choosing every word with an infuriating precision. Rachel—the name was an appetizer. Enough to make her hungry, but far too common a name for her to do anything with.

"I'm going to tell 'you' everything Olivia wants to know about you . . . Rachel."

He'd promised never to lie to her. At the end of the sixth cycle he was promising to tell *Leah* everything he knew about *Leah*. If she was patient, Olivia would get to hear it all via the recording. She'd have to be an idiot not to realize he had a reason to make her wait for that moment.

But therein lay the problem. What if he actually wanted her to call his bluff? Take him out of the shell again.

If this were a fair fight—I'd lose.

She went back again.

"You have my word, you and your family will be safe."

What had he meant by that? Did Jonathan know about the child Leah was carrying or was he talking about something else entirely? One thing was clear each time she watched, Leah knew his exact meaning.

At this point, with the roughly twenty minute delay before Olivia had been able to watch the exchange and the amount of time she'd spent considering her next action, she had about one and a half cycles remaining before Jonathan would have to deliver. As long as she allowed Leah to remain in the cell until that moment.

Don't, you're letting him into your head.

Maybe it was the fatigue coupled with the alien's diminishing condition or the stress to salvage the situation. But she was glad Rivers wasn't here to see her failing to live up to what she'd told him.

More words echoed in her thoughts.

"Control . . . you're going to lose control . . . lose any certainty that you ever had it."

"It doesn't matter what you do . . . all it will mean is that my people change their strategy."

Leave Leah inside, she would get the information, but she wouldn't know the price until it was too late. Take Leah out. Possibly throw a monkey wrench into his plans. Or would she? He believed he had known quite well how she'd react when he said he'd be taking away her *control*. So much, in fact, that she wondered if he wanted her to make this choice just to prove he couldn't lead her around.

"Don't, you're letting him into your head . . . you're letting him into your head."

She simply had to make a choice.

Everything in her wanted to call his bluff. Being honest with herself, it wasn't the threats to her staff's loved ones that stopped her. Olivia couldn't risk another spelling demonstration with witnesses. She'd have to have him brought to a room with no cameras or recording equipment. She'd have to extract what he knew on her own. The thought of what might happen if they were alone together scared her. She'd be handing him the best opportunity to spring a trap that she could imagine.

"Infuriating child!" She slammed a fist into the table.

She closed her eyes and rubbed at the bottom of her hand. Reminded herself that she had to stop thinking of him as a child.

A thought came to her. What if she attended his disclosure in person? She could go into the shell, disable the sound isolation on his solitary confinement. She could stand right outside his cell door waiting to listen the moment the sixth cycle began.

He might not have thought of that.

". . . maybe," she thought aloud.

He'd have to say what he knew to the entire room. His friends and Grant hearing it all as well. Would that bother him, get under his skin?

"It doesn't matter what you do . . . The point is that I'm never lying to you . . ."

For a moment, those words cast doubt, but she didn't waver—Olivia liked this plan. When she rose from the desk, she fully intended to head to the containment shell and make it a reality. She put the last twenty-four hours as far from her mind as possible and willed the mask of unfaltering calm she wore every day back over her features.

To her surprise, the moment she pulled open the door to leave, a fist belonging to one of her agents hung midair in the doorway. He'd been coming to interrupt her.

"Ma'am, Command needs you in the control room," he said. "It's urgent."

The experience was called teleportation sickness, and it hit Evelyn hard. Shane showed no signs of being affected. He caught her gently as she started to lose her balance. Before she knew what was happening, she felt him carrying her.

"Everything is okay, Ms. Tibbs," he said. "You're safe now."

Everything was not okay. Everything was a blur—a painfully bright spinning blur. "Paige? Where's Paige? Joao? Where are the others? Why can't I hear them?"

She felt herself being laid on a soft surface. "Rourke has taken them to another location. They're safe," Shane said.

"You said we were gonna hold hands?" Evelyn asked angrily. "What happened?"

"Take it easy now, please," Shane said. "The disorientation is temporary, the more you remain calm and still, the faster your equilibrium will return."

Holy hell it's bright, Evelyn thought.

She could see the blur of Shane, a black shape with a familiar voice moving in front of far lighter but equally blurry shapes that made up the contours of wherever they were. "Answer the question!"

He may be a blur but at this range she wouldn't miss. Then she realized she was no longer holding the sidearm.

"I know, I took the gun," Shane said. "I had no desire to lie to you, and I'm going to give it back, but if you fire that weapon in here then this will all be for nothing."

She felt around herself. As she realized she was feeling a comforter on a large mattress her surroundings began coming into focus. She was in an elegant room, something like a five-star hotel. The brightness hadn't merely been a part of her disorientation either, it came from a window all around the room.

"What is this? Where am I?" Evelyn asked.

Shane was coming into better focus. She was still dizzy, but without the gun it was too much to still consider trying to assault him. Though, if he didn't start explaining soon, the moment would be coming.

"You're on a cruise ship in the Mediterranean," Shane said.

What?

"It was your son's decision. He needed you out of harm's way, somewhere you'd be hard-pressed to make yourself a distraction—where you would be hard to find."

Shane pulled open the top buttons of his jacket, and for a moment Evelyn swore she saw something like sunlight coming from beneath his shirt. He was quick, retrieving a large folded envelope from his inner pocket.

"I know you have questions, Evelyn," Shane said. "Jonathan asked that I plead with you to go through the contents of this envelope before you make any irreversible decisions. Inside, you'll find a passport, a debit card, and various other necessities. No one will ever question the authenticity of these documents, though they do belong to a manufactured identity. These are as real as the identity you'll be leaving behind."

He placed the folder into her hands. "There is also some Dramamine. Your son said you get seasick."

Evelyn hesitated as she held the envelope. She did get seasick, but the only person who had ever known about it was her late husband.

"You'll find a letter from your son in there," Shane said. "It isn't in his hand, I had to memorize its entirety and transcribe it, as he couldn't write it himself while he remained a captive. Please, read it carefully."

Shane made a point of laying Douglas's sidearm down on the nightstand beside her. She only stared at him for a moment before deciding to go for it. Yet, to her surprise, when she sat up and reached for the weapon, Shane was already on the other side of the room, his back to her as he looked out the window.

He'd either moved inhumanly fast or this disorientation had made her lose time for a few moments.

"I know I'm leaving you angry," Shane said. "I do hope that if we see each other again, you'll have forgiven me."

Evelyn finished reaching for the gun, but when she turned it on him, she was alone in the room. Shane had vanished. Evelyn's hand began to shake as she looked about the empty room with growing paranoia. She wasn't insane, he had been here, he was real. The envelope was right there in her hand.

She found herself afraid to open it for quite some time. She stared at it until a knock came to her door and she was jarred out of her thoughts.

"Room service," said a voice on the other side.

Evelyn was frozen, such that by the third knock the only thought going through her head was that at any moment now the woman outside her door might think the room empty and walk in on her pointing a gun at a window. Finally, she pushed the weapon under a pillow and forced herself to pull it together long enough to get rid of the woman on the other side of her door.

When she answered, the woman brought in a carrier. Had Shane called in breakfast on her behalf before he disappeared? How had it gotten here so quickly? Was this what she needed to be thinking about?

When the woman left, Evelyn finally opened the envelope and found the letter.

Mom,

By now, you know more than I ever wished you would have to. It's fair to be angry. I've sent you to the other side of the globe to keep you away. There is a person I need to be right now, and I can't be him if you're here. I know—better than you can imagine—that this is too much to ask of you. That if anyone would refuse to see themselves benched, it would be you.

The thing you'll need to ask yourself in the coming weeks, is if you believe me to be a good person. There will be news. I'd ask you not to watch. Though, I suspect you won't take my advice. So, instead, I'll say this. If you believe me a good man, you'll never need to question if your son is who they say he is.

Dad and you never got a honeymoon. You always wanted to take this trip. Never got to before he died. Why I know this is a complicated matter, but for now, try . . . for me, to enjoy it. If it helps, the credit cards in the envelope are virtually limitless.

I know you have questions. You just experienced teleportation, and I imagine any theories you might have had about why I'm the prisoner of a covert government operation have likely been abandoned as a result. I will tell you what I can.

The question, of course, is where to start?

You asked me once if Dad had kept a secret. If somehow his past had come back to haunt me. It's not fair to blame him. He sacrificed everything trying to keep me from this. He tried so hard, endured so much. Thinking of what he went through for me brings me to tears. Nevertheless, there is a story you deserve to hear.

Dad didn't die in a car accident . . .

CHAPTER TWENTY-TWO

OCT 15, 2005 | 9:45 PM | JBLM FACILITY

THE RAIN STARTED before Fisher came on duty. As evening grew dark the ground was mostly mud. The only thing that could make his shift any less fabulous was if the weather turned cold. So far, he and his friend Cooper had only caught a few stiff breezes as they stood beneath the awning at one of the hangar's pedestrian entrances.

"Clown shoes," Fisher said, as he took a drag off his cigarette.

When silence dragged on too long, he turned to find his friend waiting for him to look. Cooper clearly hadn't wanted him to miss just how unimpressed his expression showed he was.

"Clown shoes," Cooper repeated.

"Yeah, what of it?" Fisher asked.

"As in, having to listen to Fisher's BS all night is *clown shoes*?" he asked.

Fisher gave an unapologetic smirk along with an obscene gesture. "Just saying, the phrase never got its fifteen minutes."

"And this tragedy has been bothering you for some time now?" Cooper asked.

"Nah, you remember Rolland?"

Cooper shook his head.

"She's one of Harrison's guards, has to listen to everything the prisoners talk about in their cells. Other day she overhears the skinny blond kid and the big one talking about how *clown shoes* never got its chance. It reminded me that I too have unresolved feelings on the matter."

Cooper grunted a laugh. "Yeah? Which one was pro *clown shoes*? The skinny blond guy or the big one?"

"Blond," Fisher said.

Cooper nodded. "I was here when they brought those two in. No one has a clue how they're supposed to be a threat to National Security. Ask me, the only danger those two pose to the country would be its internet bandwidth."

Fisher shrugged as he took a final drag from his cigarette. "Above my pay grade."

He was about to flick the butt out into the mud, but his hand stopped mid flick.

"Hey, you feel that?" Cooper asked.

Fisher nodded, the butt still smoldering between his fingers as he eyed the landscape. A long line of lights illuminated the nearby runway. The two of them could see all the way to the hangar's perimeter fences. Nothing seemed out of the ordinary, but Cooper hadn't been imagining things. There had been an abrupt stillness in the air.

A moment later Fisher's senses started having an argument. His ears were telling him they heard the rain hitting something not too far out in front of them while his eyes pointed out that, clearly, there was nothing there. That disagreement was interrupted when he noticed the trees were still swaying despite the absence of any wind on his skin.

The hairs on his arms and neck stood up. "Don't like this."

"Whatcha think?" Cooper asked. "Boss lady's orders were to report anything suspicious, no matter how small."

Fisher nodded, though he wasn't sure exactly what they were about to report. He took a few cautious steps out from under the awning until he was standing in the rain. After a moment of getting wet without having gained any insight into the matter he noticed his hand was still cocked to flick his cigarette butt, and that the ember was about to burn his finger.

Just as Cooper was getting on the radio Fisher finally let fly.

There was a burst in midair. A small puff of sparks as the cigarette hit a wall that wasn't there a few feet out in front of him. Fisher blinked in surprise as the butt unceremoniously fell straight down and sizzled out in the wet grass.

"What the . . ." Fisher said, already bringing the M4 assault rifle strapped to his shoulder up into firing position. "Did you see that?"

Fisher, reluctant to take his eyes off what was out in front of them, began inching backwards. He froze when lights on the outside of the building suddenly went out. What was strange—only the lights on the hangar were dark. The lights lining the landing strip hadn't been affected.

"Cooper?"

Again, no reply came. His eyes searched the dark furiously. The hangar's lights suddenly came back on—the generators kicking in a few seconds after the power loss. An icy cold crept through him as the lights came back on and he found an empty space where his friend had been.

Cooper was gone, but . . . he wasn't alone out here.

Fisher had seen guys capable of pulling off some crazy things during his time in the service. But no one could take a man out and disappear his body so quick and quiet that his friend standing less than five feet away didn't hear it.

Fisher flicked off the M4's safety, his heart pounding in his ears as he resumed shuffling backward toward the door. He reached for his earpiece, his gaze sweeping back and forth to keep an eye on every angle of approach. "Command, need backup immediately. Cooper is missing, assumed down. Something is out here . . . repeat something is out here with me."

Fisher felt his back come up against the safety of the hangar door. He waited for a reply over the comm. The seconds ticked by like an eternity before his earpiece finally crackled with life.

Someone responded, but all he heard was static and a voice too garbled to discern. He tried again, beginning to fear that no one inside had received his message. Then—Fisher froze.

Something—he couldn't tell what—had hold of his rifle. Words caught in his throat as he stared at the M4's muzzle being swallowed.

Whatever his cigarette had hit must have been inching forward the entire time. Creeping toward him like an invisible blob. Fisher started firing, and he could feel the recoil with each pull of the trigger, but the weapon hardly made a sound. Small waves were rippling down the barrel's surface behind which the gun seemed to vanish.

Like the weapon was being submerged into a liquid wall. As he stood speechlessly watching, he let go of the trigger. His hand went to his belt, searching frantically for the key card that would let him back into the building.

Then the translucent boundary abruptly stopped, and he froze in place along with it.

Fisher had time to take two horrified breaths before a massive hand rippled through the barrier that had his rifle. The hand wore a black glove and looked to belong to a man twice his size. It came for him so fast that it had hold of him by the jaw before he was even sure of what he had seen. He felt his feet leave the ground as he was tugged away from the wall, lifted by the chin.

It was as though he were at the mercy of a phantom floating limb with an iron grasp. He gave up on the key card and began pulling his trigger again. More rounds unloaded into the barrier and made even less sound than they had the first time.

His eyes bulged, and he couldn't scream because of the hand's grip on his jaw, as he was pulled toward the barrier. His face plunged into something cold and the rest of his body followed. It was like being dragged face first through a pool of thick syrup until he broke through a surface on the opposite side.

Finally, he heard the deafening roar of his bullets firing. He opened his eyes and found himself face to face with the owner of that giant hand. More accurately, he was face to mask with a man standing in what appeared to be a strange hallway on the other side of the invisible barrier. The huge man's entire body was covered head to toe in tactical black clothing. Fisher kept pulling the trigger until the M4 clicked empty, but the giant holding him hadn't so much as budged even after taking repeated point-blank hits.

The last thing Fisher remembered was a deep booming Cajun drawl. "Time fo yo nap, Missa Clown Shoes."

CHAPTER TWENTY-THREE

HE HUNG UP the phone with his suspicions all but confirmed.

When the second report had come in, Rivers told himself not to jump to the worst possible conclusion—yet. Now, he'd just gotten off the phone with an arm of The Cell's operation in Anchorage Alaska, bringing the confirmed disappearances to ten. His nightmare possibility was beginning to play out. They were looking at the start of a complete wipe. Every known contact of The Mark—every subject The Cell had under surveillance—was disappearing tonight. They were still getting reports from teams confirming their subjects were in the wind.

They had no idea how many were already lost. It was conceivable that Jonathan and the alien were already the only targets of The Cell's investigation whose whereabouts remained known.

Finally, Olivia came through the door sweeping into the command center with her usual look of detachment. Seemingly immune as she passed several agents in communication with arms all around the country, the cacophony of voices all carrying some range of growing panic.

"When did the first report come in?" she asked.

"Fifteen minutes ago," Rivers said. "Ten men confirmed so far . . ."

Rivers paused, seeing that one of the analysts was trying to get his attention, shaking her head from across the room.

". . . Eleven confirmed disappearances."

Olivia's fist tightened.

Finally, she turned to the room, her voice raised to carry over all the chatter. "Give the order, all teams are to move on their subjects effective immediately. No delays, I don't care if the subject is standing in the middle of a packed stadium. I want them in custody now!"

The room grew quiet as they listened, but the chatter erupted the moment she was done speaking.

Olivia grabbed Rivers by the arm and led him away to a private corner.

"The subjects aren't the only ones missing," Rivers said.

"What?" Olivia asked.

"The other roommate, Jonathan's mother, and Mr. Silva," Rivers said. "The men making sure they didn't leave the premises confirmed a few minutes ago. The house is empty."

To Rivers, Olivia looked as though she could melt steel with her eyes. All anyone else in the room saw was her listening to him and taking longer, heavier breaths than usual. Then something took over her expression, as though she'd realized something that took her eyes to the nearest clock.

"Dammit, he knew," Olivia said.

"Ma'am?"

"I waited too long. But the moment I'd made a decision, I was pulled away by the onset of this catastrophe," Olivia said. "The sixth cycle just ended."

"Sixth cycle?" Rivers asked, at a loss for what she was going on about. "Ma'am I don't . . ."

"Later, Rivers," Olivia said, resolve setting in her features. "Get Harrison's team on the line, I want Tibbs brought here now."

Bodhi was the last recruit Anthony had added to the extraction team. He was also the youngest living owner of an alien implant from Heyer's entire roster.

He didn't have an exceptional compatibility to his device, nor any deep wells of tactical know-how to contribute. He only had one skill set that, it had turned out, was a close approximation to what the team needed.

Why did he have that skill set? Well, Bodhi's mother was partially to blame.

Having seen too many kids with broken bones, she'd forbidden him from owning a skateboard growing up. Like most children, outlawing a thing only made him fixate on it. His mother didn't cave until his fifteenth birthday.

Of course, the first time she saw him ride the skateboard, he was a little too good at it. She was no fool, he wasn't a prodigy—he'd been finding ways to practice for years and hiding it from her. When there was no point left in denying it, he confessed he'd found ways. He'd made friends at the local skate parks. Friends who were sometimes willing to let him borrow a board.

The signs had always been there. Bodhi's obsession with the skating phenomenon of the eighties and nineties was a bit too long lived for a teenager to have sustained without a real connection to the sport.

It started with Marty McFly on a hoverboard, Josh Brolin in *Thrashin'*, Christian Slater in *Gleaming the Cube*. Eventually, he'd been a junkie for the entire subculture. The baggy clothes, the skate or die video games, and all the anti-establishment rhetoric that seemed to follow. Before long it wasn't just skating but the entire adrenaline junkie lifestyle. A California kid, his hobbies soon included surfing and snowboarding. He couldn't afford skydiving but . . . well, all that was before Heyer came along.

Anyhow, these were some of the reasons Bodhi blinked into existence hanging an inch and a half below the hangar's ceiling.

"Stealth Hover Ninja deployed," he whispered into his communicator while checking the countdown clock displayed inside his mask. "Operation commencing in T-minus 3 . . . 2 . . ."

He went silent and pushed away from a nearby rafter without ever actually touching it. This began a smooth practiced slide down the underside of the curved roof.

The agents below weren't going to glance up over the next few seconds. Had they, Bodhi would have looked something like a square of butter sliding down the inside of a hot pan. His defiance of gravity was due to an equilibrium of opposing forces that simultaneously pulled him toward and pushed him away from the ceiling's surface.

Bodhi called it, *gleaming*.

The necessary hardware was built into his gear. The gleamers consisted of a network of rings, most of them small and no more exciting to look at than a metal washer. Some were sewn into the fingertips and knuckles of his gloves, the majority ran along his back, arms, and legs in rows. The rest of the rings were larger, similar in size to MiniDVDs, and placed in tactical locations like his suit's elbows and knee guards, his shoulder blades, the palms of his gloves and the soles of his shoes. Lastly, they were stitched into his mask at his forehead and over the back of his skull.

Mr. Clean had adapted the tech from the Borealis' libraries into wearable equipment. Initially, Bodhi had been given a far more modest prototype, only meant to allow him to slide quickly across a surface. Around the same time, Mr. Clean had also given him a basic tutorial of the science involved.

Bodhi had humored the bald cartoon, politely nodding at all the right moments, but luckily, Anthony hadn't brought him in because he needed to comprehend advanced theoretical physics. While Bodhi left Mr. Clean's tutorial without the foggiest clue how the rings worked, he had an intimate grasp of what they were capable of—and a lot of ideas about what else he could do with them.

During the lecture Mr. Clean kept referring to the rings as Polarity Modification Stabilizers. This was a mouthful to say, but Bodhi only had to hear Mr. Clean utter the phrase 'get into your *PMS* gear' once before renaming them. After a few long hours of practice, and the addition of Bodhi's creative input, the two found that the gear could be the solution to a few other obstacles.

At first Bodhi and Mr. Clean both had a steep learning curve.

Bodhi having to adapt his body to a new reality in terms of balance while mastering the subtle art of the throttle and brake rings, which were the functional equivalent of the *gleamers'* push and pull. Meanwhile, Mr. Clean monitored his movements and reprogrammed the smaller rings to adapt to whatever he threw at them. Over the course of two days, Bodhi and Mr. Clean had tuned the *gear* via a process mostly composed of watching Bodhi repeatedly 'eating it big time,' re-calibrating, and trying again.

Looking down on the hangar, Bodhi gleamed silently to the floor unnoticed by The Cell's operatives. Luck had nothing to do with this. After enough practice runs in The Never, he knew exactly where to be and what choreographed route to follow.

A moment before his foot came to hover over the floor, he glanced at the *Heads-up Display* inside his mask. The HUD showed a list of countdowns on the left side of his vision. This was how he knew, in exactly a minute and a half, Beo would finish disabling the exterior guards. In a minute and forty-three seconds, Mr. Clean would cut the hangar's primary power. Then, in two minutes and thirty seconds, Mito would start an epically distracting ruckus amongst the agents.

But, at the top of the list of countdowns was the one most important to Bodhi. The one that said he would be in position in precisely one minute and thirty seconds. The remainder of the night's festivities would rapidly deteriorate for the rest of the extraction team if he weren't.

That was fine, everyone loves being the first real point of failure in a critical mission. No pressure at all.

Bodhi flicked his hand at a metal beam lining the wall, turned his palm just so, and sent himself gleaming sideways. A second later, he dropped flat to the floor, as he hovered past the strange lady who looked up from her monitor to crack her neck before starting a conversation with her rubber duck. Bodhi pushed himself back up into a crouch before he coasted to his next stop beside a stack of supply pallets.

The pallets were right off the side of the one hallway opening. A short distance down that hallway was the door to the hangar's surface level surveillance hub.

Using the pallets for cover, Bodhi watched the seconds tick. Right on schedule, he heard a beep, followed by the click of a lock disengaging down the hall as Agent Kenmore slid his security badge past the reader.

Bodhi had long ago stopped thinking of this man as Agent Kenmore. With a rather begrudging respect, he'd come to think of Kenmore as Captain Paranoia, which he later shortened to *el' Capitán.*

At the moment, el' Capitán was carrying a hot cup of coffee in one hand and swiping his badge with the other. This forced him into elbowing the handle and shouldering his way through the door into the hub.

"I'm clocked in if you want to take fifteen," el' Capitán said to the woman inside, Bodhi mouthing along the words as he listened.

He took a few quick breaths to center himself as the man and woman exchanged pleasantries he'd heard a hundred times. Then came the moment when el' Capitán held open the door for the woman as she left on her break.

Bodhi put his back to the pallet. *And . . . 3 . . . 2 . . .*

He shot up and over, back flipping over the pallet to land silently in a crouch, an inch off the floor in the hallway opening. This occurred just as the woman turned down the hallway in the opposite direction and el' Capitán released the door.

He launched out of his crouch toward the hallway's ceiling. This was followed by a series of forward thrusts and careful pivots that ricocheted him from wall to wall, then ceiling back to floor as he raced to beat the door. Inside the hub, el' Capitán had his back to the hallway as he took his first look at the security monitors for the evening.

Bodhi shot in from the hallway—well, he cartwheeled in. The careful manipulation of the gleamers and a last second sucking in of his gut kept the door's handle from clipping him as he swept past. As such, he successfully entered the room while el' Capitán was still facing the opposite direction.

All that said, there was a reason Bodhi called him Captain Paranoia. Without fail, the security officer noticed something *off* when Bodhi gleamed inside. Maybe it was the draft he brought with him, or maybe the Captain's subconscious told him he wasn't alone, maybe he felt a disturbance in the force. Whatever the reason, Bodhi had never made it into the hub without setting off the man's Spidey-sense.

The problem was that el' Capitán never just let it go.

The man turned, staring suspiciously at the closed door. Then to the spot where Bodhi passed on his way in. By this point Bodhi was gleaming two inches under the ceiling, but el' Capitán wasn't going to shrug and walked away. No, for the next twelve and a half seconds, Bodhi was forced to perform a series of acrobatic maneuvers around a very modestly sized security room to keep the man's stubborn paranoia from laying eyes on him.

El' Capitán's commitment to his gut instincts had given Bodhi new respect for just how long twelve seconds could feel. It was this begrudging respect that led Bodhi to put in a little extra effort, nudging el' Capitán's coffee cup an inch to the left on his desk as he passed by. If he didn't, el' Capitán would spill coffee all over his keyboard in a little less than a minute—and the man just didn't deserve that on top of everything else that was going to happen to him tonight.

On the twelfth second, just as el' Capitán turned to face the ceiling corner where Bodhi was balled into the smallest shape he could manage, Mr. Clean cut the hangar's main power. The lights went out just in time to turn Bodhi into an indiscernible part of the darkness.

Startled, el' Capitán stopped chasing ghosts around the office and ran back to the monitors. In his haste, his hip knocked into his chair, which in turn sent the chair into the desk. But due to Bodhi's heroics a moment earlier, the coffee and keyboard were saved.

While the security got far more treacherous the farther they got into the Facility, the hangar's surface was no simple obstacle.

Each of the systems had a fail-safe, and none could be brought down by something as trivial as a severed power line. While the lights went out temporarily, the cameras and the monitoring stations inside the hub remained functional via short-term battery power. This meant that visibility was never lost, inside or outside the facility, during the delay between a power outage and the generators kicking in.

When the generators kicked in and the backup lights came on, Bodhi kneeled upside down off the ceiling to watch the monitors over el' Capitán's shoulder. While the security officer was busy searching for what had caused the power outage, Bodhi was watching the feeds from the corridors far beneath the surface. A quick study showed Jonathan being escorted out of the prisoner containment shell and taken to Olivia's control room.

This put a smile on his face. That this was happening told Bodhi that Jonathan had put all his pieces in motion successfully so far. It also meant that Bodhi and the rest of the team were heading down his preferred branch of possibilities for the rest of the evening.

A communication garbled by Mr. Clean's interference came over el' Capitán's radio. Bodhi's eyes turned to a monitor watching a guard standing beneath an awning outside.

"Fisher. Repeat. Did not receive," el' Capitán attempted to respond. "Fisher, where is Cooper? Not seeing him on the monitor . . . Fisher?"

A second later, el' Capitán and Bodhi watched Fisher, aka *Mr. Clown Shoes*, disappear on the monitor. El' Capitán never reacted to this as quickly as he should. Bodhi was sympathetic. He figured that if it were his first time seeing a giant hand appear out of thin air to drag Clown Shoes out of existence—he might need a few seconds to process it as well.

Patiently, Bodhi checked his HUD clock and waited for el' Capitán's hand to inch its way toward the alarm button. Meanwhile a slight glimmer, unnoticed by el' Capitán, caught the light of the monitors as a translucent liquid thread of Mr. Clean snaked its way down the wall from a ventilation shaft.

Finally, el' Capitán' got a grip and slammed his palm down on the alarm. Half a second later everyone in the hangar jumped as the sound of a walrus barking blared from security sirens all over the facility. As that was happening, el' Capitán' licked his lips and reached for a rotary phone that looked like it had been installed before Bodhi was born. As he pulled the receiver to his ear, Bodhi heard the click of someone picking up the line on the other end.

Meanwhile, el' Capitán' reached for a device held onto his belt by a small carabiner. It was the size of a thumb drive and consisted of little more than one button and a display.

"Kenmore," he said into the receiver as he peered down at the device to read a randomly generated passcode off the display, "7-C-9-F . . ."

With the barking alarm, Bodhi hadn't been able to make out what the call's recipient said the first seven times he got this far in The Never. Now he knew the whole conversation by heart.

"Voice confirmed, code confirmed," said a computerized voice. Followed a second later by a human disguising himself with a modulator. "Report."

"Sir, I think it is here. Command—"

That was as far as Bodhi let el' Capitán get. It was one of the most curious and strangely time-specific items on his to-do list for the evening. He didn't know who the man on the other end of the call was, all he knew was that if the man didn't get to hear that much of the phone message, events further down the line didn't go the way they'd have liked.

Bodhi's hand grabbed el' Capitán under the chin, ending the dialog, while his opposite wrist came into alignment with the surprised man's neck. With a flick of his fist, a small-needled cartridge discharged from an apparatus strapped to the underside of Bodhi's forearm and delivered a fast-acting dose of anesthesia. As soon as it was administered, a capsule dropped out of the chamber like a spent bullet casing and was quickly replaced with a fresh dose.

Now, television would have led Bodhi to believe that a hard knock to the back of el' Capitán's skull would render him conveniently unconscious with little more to fear than waking up with a headache. Anthony's team had disillusioned him—the best-case scenario for most people after being knocked unconscious was to wake up with a minor concussion. The worst case was a tie between being left a vegetable and . . . well . . . dying.

So, they were taking down their targets with the tranqs. Mr. Clean had formulated a faster acting version of the same anesthesia that many of Heyer's soon-to-be allies became familiar with the first time they made the alien's acquaintance—Jonathan included.

As el' Capitán' went limp, Bodhi caught him by the collar and gently lowered him down into his chair. He flipped off the ceiling to the floor, picked up the phone and heard the modulated voice on the other end.

"Kenmore! Message incomplete. Repeat. What is happe—"

As Bodhi crushed the receiver in his palm, he watched Mr. Clean's tentacle slither down the wall from an air vent and plug into the security system's computers. Within seconds, a seamless change occurred on the monitors. Each screen showing a version of what it had been a moment earlier, only now it also contained—well, additional information.

Bodhi checked his timers, and took hold of the door handle to wait.

Perth and Tam's voice came over the comm, one before the other, three seconds before their current clocks reached zero.

"Mark."

"Mark."

3 . . . 2 . . . 1

Explosions shook the hangar. Synced, they came from both sides of the building and left a hole to the outside in each wall. While the rubber duck lady hit the floor, the agents in the middle jumped to their feet as though they expected to find themselves standing between two tanks that had just simultaneously rammed through the hangar's walls.

Which was good—because the extraction team didn't want them looking up to see Mito appearing out of thin air, nor down the hallway as Bodhi slipped out of the hub.

Bodhi casually gleamed up a wall until he was coasting forward with his back to the ceiling. He went unnoticed when a large group of heavily-armed reinforcements turned the corner and ran up the hall toward the hangar bay. They didn't concern him; Bodhi was interested in the one man going in the opposite direction.

He came running into the hallway so fast he nearly got bowled over by the reinforcements, had to hug the wall to let them by.

"Keychain is right on schedule," Bodhi said, notifying the team.

Mr. Keychain wasn't heavily armed, and he wasn't the sort to head toward the sound of explosions. No, Keychain was making a break for the safety of the elevator, and Bodhi needed to hitch a ride. Bodhi was quiet against the ceiling as Keychain ran under him to reach the T at the end of the hallway. He ran his security badge over the reader.

Then Mito's clock dropped to zero.

The sound of automatic fire erupted from inside the hangar bay.

Unfortunately, while Keychain was an integral member of the extraction team he never had the wherewithal to hit the floor fast enough when bullets started ripping holes in the hallway's walls and pierced the sheet metal of the elevator's doors. He also never bothered looking back but crawled through the elevator doors as they opened, ran his badge over yet another reader on the inside and frantically hit the down button the moment it came to life.

Because he never looked back, he never noticed Bodhi standing in the middle of the hallway. He let out a groan and wiggled a bit. Had there not been far too much gunfire to hear, there would have been a sound like a buck fifty in quarters dropping to the floor as the bullets Bodhi had just intercepted on Keychain's unknowing behalf fell off him.

Death, even from friendly fire, was something the team couldn't let happen tonight.

Bodhi glanced back into the open hangar to catch a brief glimpse of Mito running past, bullets eating up the floors and walls around him as he went.

After the explosions were detonated on each side of the hangar, Mito had dropped into the center of The Cell's main cluster of armed guards as they surrounded the support staff. They hadn't missed him hiding above them out of a failure to check the ceiling, but rather because Mr. Clean had waited until they were focused on the explosions to teleport him inside.

Now, Mito was making a casual, albeit lengthy, show of disabling The Cell's surface manpower. He looked . . . well . . . like a modern-day ninja, but that was the perception they were going for.

Depending on how long any of The Cell's agents remained conscious, they were about to have the most one-sided fight of their lives. With an active alien implant hidden beneath his gear, Mito didn't need any of the equipment he was carrying nor did he need to dodge the bullets they were sending his way.

This was all about appearances—until the time was right.

Mito knew the choreography of this dance. His job was to keep everyone on the surface fighting a battle they believed *could* be won for as long as possible. He made no definitive show of his strength or resilience—though some of his escapades neared the inhuman line. His opponents fired when and where Mito knew they would. So, Mito made it appear that he went about the whole affair moving out of the line of fire just in time, before moving in to engage one or two of the men in close quarters combat.

In the heat of combat, the men Mito tranqed wouldn't realize he'd been predicting their movements unless they got a chance to review the footage.

With places to go and people to see, Bodhi turned away from Mito's theatrics and back to the elevator. He pulled a thin flat crowbar from a belt strapped to his thigh and slipped it between the doors. A moment later he gleamed down the shaft wall and caught up to the elevator car. As it reached bottom, he hovered over the elevator's ceiling hatch and checked the countdown displaying on his HUD.

He heard Mr. Keychain scamper out. A few seconds later there were other sounds, a heavy armored panel sliding open, a couple of confirmation beeps from electronic equipment, and then came his signal to move. It began as a vibration that shook enough of the nearby area that he could see the dust shiver on the elevator's roof. It was caused by a lift system that had just begun the process of raising a no-nonsense sized blast door a few feet outside the elevator.

Bodhi temporarily disabled the gleamer ring in the sole of one boot, kicked in the ceiling hatch, and dropped into the elevator.

Everything in the tunnel was coated in the angry red of the emergency lights. Mr. Keychain whirled around to gawk at Bodhi standing in the elevator as the massive blast door slowly made its way up. The look on Keychain's face was priceless. Behind his mask, Bodhi mimed the man's expression as it went from '*No! The timing. How could I be so unlucky?*' To the far more terrified, '*Dear god, luck has nothing to do with it!*'

"How?" Keychain squeaked as his hand went for his gun.

"Yeah, ya been setup, brah," Bodhi said, already zigzagging his way forward.

Mr. Keychain was an analyst. The Cell didn't keep him around because of any skill he possessed with the weapon he carried. Bodhi didn't need bulletproof skin, superhuman speed, or the gleamers to outmaneuver him.

Just like Mito, he already knew how many shots the man would get off and precisely where he didn't want to be if he wished to avoid them.

A moment later, another tranq cartridge dropped from the injector beneath Bodhi's wrist. He set Mr. Keychain down and unclipped a small pager-like device from the man's belt. As he leaned over him, he checked his HUD just in time to see Perth and Tam's next event timer hit zero.

He leaned over Keychain protectively, closed his eyes, and covered his ears.

A loud crash followed, sending a cloud of displaced dust out of the elevator shaft as the car imploded behind him. Bodhi opened one eye in time to see a large metal nut roll past him on the cement floor.

"Elevator is officially out of commission," Perth said.

CHAPTER TWENTY-FOUR

THE TWO AUSSIES weren't light on their feet. Seeing as that was the case, almost every part Tam and Perth had to play in tonight's plan was loud and explosive.

Their landing had been inelegant by design.

As the primary point of entry for the entire facility, that elevator was where The Cell's surface reinforcements would eventually try to enter. The one thing the extraction team didn't need this evening was more goons shooting at them. Taking the elevator out now ensured that they only needed to deal with the manpower The Cell already had on hand below the surface.

For the sake of killing two birds with one stone, they'd had Mr. Clean transport the two large Australians in at the highest point in the shaft. Tam and Perth then dropped like anvils. Upon landing they arrived a few feet from their destination while simultaneously putting the elevator out of commission.

"Well, look at that. Kid didn't blow it," Perth said to Tam as they strode out over the remains of the flattened elevator. "Guess someone owes me fifty bucks."

"Get stuffed," Tam said. "Night ain't over."

Bodhi shook his head. Though honestly, that they were betting on tonight's outcome and that Tam had bet against him wasn't the least bit surprising.

As they joined him, the two looked like SWAT lumberjacks, each dressed head to toe in black but carrying a stack of long alien steel bars over one shoulder. They also each carried a duffel bag that looked like a snake who'd swallowed a meal too large for comfort.

As they set the bags down gently on either side of the tunnel, Bodhi pulled the unconscious man out of the way. Tam and Perth needed the space—the stack of alien steel they had carried in on their shoulders was a *some-assembly-required* sort of project.

Security systems are functionally simple. They let the right people in and keep the wrong people out. As a rule, their most exploitable weakness is the so called *right people*—the folks with the keys and codes to bypass all the obstacles meant to keep the *wrong people* out.

This evening Bodhi and his allies were the *wrong people* and the obstacle in front of them was a real bummer: A man trap.

A man trap functions a lot like an air lock. In this case, two blast doors placed in tandem within a tunnel. Getting the next door open meant that one of them would have to step between the doors. There, a pressure plate built into the floor would detect weight, and signal door one to close and lock.

Only after door one was back in place would the system confirm that the weight of whoever stood on the plate matched the person who had activated the elevator in the first place. If one was keeping up, this all meant that Bodhi only got the chance to try bypassing door two if the weight matched Mr. Keychain. If the weight didn't match—Bodhi would be—well—a *man . . . trapped . . .* between two blast doors. It wasn't just a clever name.

In The Never, the man trap hadn't seemed like much of a problem during their first encounter. After all, they literally had superpowers and given enough time and motivation they could simply muscle their way past both doors. Perth and Tamsworth's shadows had been quick to reach this conclusion. So, Bodhi watched while the two played bulls and rammed their shoulders against the first door.

They were right, forcing their way through wasn't a problem, but as soon as they did so, the entire tunnel had begun to collapse. Bodhi had crushed his portal stone while buried under six stories of cement and dirt.

Lesson learned.

Turned out, *architecture* was one of the reasons Jonathan and the alien were taken to this location. Designed during the cold war, the facility's top priority was keeping secrets contained. This was tantamount to the safety of any occupants, friend or foe, should the facility come under siege.

Much to the extraction team's annoyance, each wing inside the facility was built with a single point of entry and similar safeguards in place. That said, if the facility was a castle this tunnel was the drawbridge.

And Keychain . . . well, when he woke up he'd find out he'd unknowingly been the guy who lowered the bridge for invaders. In order to open door one of the man trap, facial recognition had to match the face of the man stepping off the elevator to the ID of the badge that had activated the console in the first place. A confirmed match initiated the first door's identity checks, and an armored panel on the door moved aside to reveal two biometric scanners: retinal and palm print.

Mr. Clean had already tapped into the hub on the upper level to make sure that—amongst a number of things their team didn't want The Cell seeing—the camera on the elevator never showed Bodhi, Perth or Tam following Keychain into the tunnel. Once he'd passed the retinal and palm scan, Bodhi had put him to sleep.

Perth and Tam had arrived while door one was still on its way up.

Now, they had to activate the pressure plate and wait for the man trap to relock that door. If the weight of the man inside matched Keychain, a second panel on the second door would open to reveal a numeric entry pad. At the same time, a short-range radio signal emitted from door two activated the device Bodhi had taken off Mr. Keychain's belt a moment earlier. Said device would then display a twelve-digit code to be entered into the panel.

Unfortunately, said code was always evolving based on an algorithm. Each time the device synced with the door, the code that was generated only had a twenty second shelf life.

Had Keychain not been there to help, the extraction team would have needed to bring along a stand-in for his physical appearance, retinal pattern, and palm print. They would have needed to match his weight as well as stolen his code generating device late enough in the day that it wouldn't be reported stolen before they made their move.

Anthony and the rest of extraction team found the whole ordeal was far less labor intensive if they simply singled out a person with access and timed their arrivals accordingly. Thus, Keychain had become an essential member of the team.

Mr. Clean had designed the bars that Perth and Tam carried to fit together like Lincoln logs. Still, the two were practiced at getting them assembled in under forty-five seconds. Perth laying out the pieces as Tam followed along from joint to joint with a powered driver. The finished product looked like they had stolen a section of metal fencing from someone's yard.

Most of the design was kindergarten simple, as its main function was to hold up the weight of the blast doors while still allowing Tam and Perth enough space to squeeze through with the bulging duffel bags. However, the bottom tips of the door brace were crafted with greater attention to detail as each had to match individual locking mechanisms in the floor.

When the two Australians were ready, Bodhi hoisted the unconscious Keychain over his shoulders. He didn't cross the threshold of door one by way of the floor—the pressure plate would have detected that even if he crossed with the gleamers. Instead, he gleamed in along the surface of the wall and came to a stop at the second door. Glancing back, Perth and Tam gave a thumbs up, and so he eased Mr. Keychain on to the floor.

Blast door one began lowering back into position as the weight was detected, and Tam and Perth carefully positioned the door brace into place. When the door made contact, its weight pushed the five keys at the bottom of each leg into place. There was a loud click, and a moment later, the code entry panel on the second door slid open.

Hanging upside down, directly over the unconscious Keychain, a small beep reported that the pager he'd borrowed had synced with door two. After all that, Bodhi always found the beep so anti-climactic. He'd come to remedy this by playing the 8-bit music from the end of every Super Mario Bros. level in his head as he typed in the twelve-digit code.

He stopped, finger hovering over the entry key. Took a long breath in some attempt to exhale all the irrational fear that came. A little voice in his head worrying that this time—when there were no do-overs—the code panel would report the key invalid. He hit enter. There was a pause. The few seconds were as long as they had always been, but tonight Bodhi felt they surely took longer than usual—in fact, just long enough to let Bodhi's stupid superstitious nerves increase his stupid superstitious blood pressure.

Finally, a loud click came as the second door's locks disengaged and, slowly, the massive doors began to rise.

Perth and Tam grabbed their duffel bags. They stepped through the bars, and Tam quickly moved Keychain to safety along the edge of the tunnel.

Not having any pressing responsibilities for the next few seconds, Bodhi turned himself face up against the top of the tunnel and watched the door disappear into the ceiling as it slowly rose. Below him, he heard Tam and Perth go to work. Steel sliding over steel, interlocking and clicking into place. Their quick practiced hands each working with efficiency to assemble their individual mechanical monstrosities.

Bodhi had come to find the sounds rather soothing.

At least until enough of Tam and Perth became visible to Olivia's men waiting on the other side.

If The Cell ever actually gave them a chance to surrender, Bodhi never heard it. He imagined that they must have yelled something like *freeze* or *down on the ground* from the other side of the tunnel, but the barking walrus alarm grew to full volume as that second door opened. Maybe they said it, maybe they didn't, but the moment The Cell's heavily armed agents on the other side got a good look at Tam and Perth they didn't wait to see if the two were considering complying.

Benson's report of what happened in the tunnel would be largely the same as all the other men who had been standing beside him that night.

They were following their reaction strategy, exactly as they had practiced in drills over the last two days. Like many others, if the upper hangar's alarm was triggered, Benson was to be suited, armed, and ready to report to the main tunnel. On arrival, they fanned out to stay out of one another's line of fire.

Until an order said otherwise, they were to hold their positions with guns trained on whatever came down that tunnel. Their radios weren't working, but word had come down that one of the camera feeds showed an analyst above had made a break for the elevator. Clearly, trying to get behind the safety of the doors rather than get into an encounter with whoever was attacking the hangar.

Thing was, no one was ready to trust that there was only a friendly on the other side. In another minute and thirty seconds, the facilities lock down procedures would have rendered those doors impossible to open from the outside—even with proper clearance.

Benson's Commanding Officer must have had better visibility of the situation, because by the time the door was just halfway up, he'd already heard the order to fire. There was a great deal of urgency in his tone as his CO yelled loud enough to be certain he was heard throughout the tunnel and over the alarm.

So, like everyone else, Benson had unleashed hell. There was so much gun fire in that narrow tunnel that there could have been a small army on the other side of that door and not a single man would have escaped being mowed down. Yet, by the time he was reloading, the door was three fourths of the way up, and the situation had become as clear to Benson as it had his CO.

In the red glow of the emergency lights, there only appeared to be two men. He couldn't see them well, as they were standing behind the sort of transparent shields one generally saw police in riot gear carrying. Except— these shields had an open port near their center.

That was when Benson realized what his CO already had. In that open port on each shield, there was a familiar disk of steel, and it was beginning to turn clockwise.

The deafening sound of two M134 Miniguns opened fire in unison.

Some froze up for a moment, but most of the men on Benson's side of the tunnel dropped formation. They hit the floor or dove for cover as they realized what had been unleashed. In the dim red light of the tunnel, Benson remembered thinking the orange fire erupting from the barrels was almost pretty.

With their lives flashing before their eyes, no one immediately realized that the two miniguns were firing blanks. But, amid the chaos created, the blast door finished its slow rise. As it passed, Bodhi grasped the edge and pulled, shooting himself forward across the tunnel's ceiling.

By the time the agents began realizing they hadn't been sawed in half by the guns, Bodhi had passed overhead, dropped a series of flash grenades into their numbers, and flipped off the ceiling to land behind the last man at the back.

He began moving amongst them in the chaos. The men he ducked and dodged between were all wearing gear that looked—well a lot like his own— and none realized quick enough that an enemy was working his way through them from the rear.

By the time Perth and Tam ran out of blanks, only two of the agents were still on their feet. One wobbled to his knees, a hand going to his neck where he'd felt a small prick a moment before he got so very sleepy. He fought a losing battle to hold onto consciousness before falling flat onto the tunnel floor. By then, the last agent standing was spun around, finding Bodhi's grip far greater than his size suggested.

As Perth and Tamsworth stood, they knocked over the small piles of spent shells that had formed around them while they fired. Another expended tranq cartridge dropped from Bodhi's wrist.

He did a double check, looking around to be sure all the agents on the floor were out. "Drawbridge down and operation sleepy town complete . . . you're welcome."

CHAPTER TWENTY-FIVE

SURROUNDING HER, THE situation in the command center was increasingly volatile. Everything was disordered noise around her, but for a moment, as her guards escorted Jonathan in, Olivia didn't hear it.

Ears plugged, blindfolded, his shackles so cumbersome he was forced to walk in tiny uncomfortable steps—Harrison and her three guards had to guide him shambling to a seat where his wrist cuffs could be chained to a metal table.

He was helpless. She could order a bullet put in his brain any second and he wouldn't even be able to hear the gun being cocked. Yet . . .

Olivia couldn't shake a growing certainty that tonight she was going to lose to this man. Command wouldn't forgive the failure if The Mark escaped—too much time and too many resources had been burned to acquire him. Her career would come to an end.

She had to pry her eyes away from Jonathan, and as she did the cacophony of sound in the command center returned to her awareness. All around her were reports of failed communications, power outages, triggered facility alarms.

She took a long breath.

Olivia had found that maintaining control in overwhelming circumstances was a matter of compartmentalization. Treat each problem like a bomb. Use the tools you must to diffuse or dispose of the threat, prioritize the bombs in the order they're most likely to explode.

Whatever you do—don't over complicate it.

Under normal circumstances, this saw her through, but tonight was different. She was starting to see the mistakes she'd made, since the moment she'd spoken to this man in the interrogation room, that had led to this moment.

She'd never questioned her instincts before, but now she wondered if every order she gave was just another domino falling.

He had said he'd escape with the alien. She'd taken the threat seriously, prepared for a local assault on the hangar. The whole time, she'd underestimated his ambition. Hadn't seen the bigger picture. Never considered that he wasn't simply planning to take the alien—but every person of interest The Cell had under surveillance.

She'd given the order to bring all the subjects into custody. But by the time they'd realized what was happening she had already been certain it was too late to matter. The real rescue operation had begun hours before a single one of his allies set foot inside her facility. She saw now that they had synchronized their attack so that it began while they were distracted, still reacting to the chaos of learning all the subjects were rapidly disappearing.

Somehow, Jonathan Tibbs had coordinated a nationwide operation from inside the most secure prison she had to put him in. He'd done it under constant surveillance—and her only lead as to how any of it was done was an invisible worm on a video feed.

The reports inside the facility were coming at her like machine gun fire.

"The phone lines are down. Can't get a line out."

"Internet's down. Can't ping the server."

"The radios are jammed. All I hear is . . ."

The entire room went quiet when the sound was played at full volume. Everyone recognized the brand of the distortion. Every single agent had been hearing that noise from surveillance since their first day with The Cell.

That moment of quiet only ended when another analyst reported another equipment failure, another avenue cut off—a more foreboding picture of their future painted. Olivia kept her expression cement, not letting her charges see through the mask as they delivered each gut punch.

As the implications stacked up, she grew warier of even turning her gaze to the helpless man in the chair. Even with the blindfold on she feared she'd find him staring back at her.

"Olivia," Rivers said. "You alright?"

She realized she had been staring off into space. Rivers had leaned in close to discreetly snap her out of it. She wanted to slap herself right there, but instead she pressed her fear down and forced herself to take stock.

They were cut off from all the other branches of The Cell. By the time she found a way to reestablish contact, every subject throughout the US might be in the wind. Nothing she could do about that, so she was done thinking about it.

She was cut off from the surface. The surrounding base might not even know anything was happening in the hangar, let alone underneath it. Maybe help was coming but she couldn't count on it.

She couldn't communicate with her people throughout the facility. That meant the only agents under her command were the ones standing in the same room with her.

That was when the lights went out. The moment was short lived, the red emergency lights kicking on after the briefest moment in darkness. But in the seconds that followed, alarms throughout the entire facility began to blare.

"We've got activity in the hangar!"

Olivia whirled on the security monitors just in time to see the attack beginning.

This deep underground, they couldn't feel the explosions, but she could see that two opposite walls of the hangar had burst inward with small, localized explosives. Her people on the surface, mostly analysts, were rapidly thrown into disarray. She was relieved to see that the surface level response team was quick to move in on the situation—geared and ready—expecting an attack. With the communications down, they had to take initiative on their own. They poured out of the hallway like a well-oiled machine and spread out to take protective positions around the analysts.

After a moment of uncertainty, as they watched the still smoking walls of the hangar for some sign of an assault, a single man, covered head to toe in black, dropped from the ceiling.

In the next few moments, Olivia stared with growing disbelief at the screen.

As she checked the various angles on the hangar, the sheer choreography playing out in front of her was ridiculous. The man landed in a group of over thirty well-armed agents and twenty analysts—and he was making them all look like goons from a Jackie Chan movie.

She watched him as he swept the legs out from under a man and injected something from beneath his wrist. She watched him hurdle over cubicles and pallets of unpacked supplies with gun fire trailing him. She saw him as he tilted his head at the last possible instant to dodge a pistol bullet, before disarming the man, whipping him about and tossing him over his shoulder. He shoulder-rolled over the floor, into close quarters combat with two of her men and slapped both of their guns away—and his foot only left the ground once.

This wasn't real. This was Hollywood cinematography.

Her eyes narrowed as she watched men being whittled down on the surface until she started to wonder if the ridiculousness was the point. As the thought occurred to her, she realized there was no way for her to know. She couldn't contact anyone in that room with eyes on what was happening. She couldn't contact anyone in the damn facility.

She realized—the only equipment that hadn't failed was the cameras.

Soon, she was sifting through footage of all four wings. Looking through empty hallways and conference rooms, laboratories where the researchers were all dropping their work in response to facility-wide alarms. Armories where her underground security teams were pouring out heavily armed.

As she scanned over them, suspicion suddenly became reality. She saw herself, walking down a hallway with thirty armed guards trailing behind her. Meanwhile, in the feed showing the very command room she was standing in, there was an almost empty room.

Almost, because one person remained. Jonathan still sat at the very table he did now. Except, the Jonathan in the video wasn't cuffed or blindfolded. He . . . he appeared to be playing solitaire. Then he looked at the camera and waved.

Her security cameras had just become worse than useless—they were actively feeding her people misinformation . . . and she couldn't even tell anyone outside this room to turn off their screens.

Jonathan's allies—Jonathan—now had more control over the facility than she did. She forced herself to look at him. The real him, still sitting in that room. Behind the blindfold and ear plugs he acted as though he were blissfully unaware of the chaos.

She couldn't even confirm that the ninja dispatching agents in the hangar was real. If he was, then one of the top strategic advantages of this location was useless. This hangar was inside a military base. It was surrounded by miles of secured fencing, check points, and controlled air space. No one strolled inside unseen and no human aircraft got close without being detected. If the ninja were real, he'd appeared inside the hangar itself. Like The Mark—he could teleport.

So, what was immediately obvious—whoever was attacking them was doing so with the assistance of alien technology. Olivia was either dealing with another alien—or The Mark had already given his human allies access to his technology. Either way, the people coming for Jonathan controlled the very thing she was meant to acquire and, thus far, this attack seemed to be going exactly as Jonathan promised her.

Was she losing control or just now realizing she'd never had it?

She still had the trigger. Why? Why had Jonathan promised he wouldn't stop her from using it?

Beneath her, the floor began to rumble. The voices in the room went quiet as they stared down at their feet. The lights and electronics all flickered erratically, a low growl like an explosion from a nearby corridor seemed to roll past. Then, the rumble didn't build, but became a sudden violent jolt.

Anyone who hadn't grabbed hold of something was thrown to the floor. Olivia, now on the ground, found she was holding her breath—surprised to be alive. She'd imagined a wall of fire bursting through the command center door, or the cement ceiling collapsing to bury her under six stories of dirt.

They weren't new visions.

They were the very things she knew would follow if she hit the trigger in her pocket. She'd thought the charges had been set off. Triggered somehow by the people attacking them.

Cement dust still raining down on her from the ceiling. The lights stopped flickering. She breathed.

"What just got hit?"

"Armory," Rivers replied. "The feed just went to static."

She'd spent too much time letting fear play games with her thoughts. Letting things happen—she had to act.

"Ignore the monitors," Olivia said as she got to her feet. "Turn them off. Don't trust anything you haven't seen with your own eyes."

She took in the faces watching her and tried to pick the three she thought most expendable. "You, you, and you. Each of you are heading to the other wings, tell whoever is in charge that the monitors are compromised. They're using them against us. We are going to have to clear this facility the old-fashioned way. Now go!"

As the three analysts blinked in disbelief, the most obnoxious of wolf whistles sounded out from the adjacent room. Every head turned to look at Jonathan as he yelled, "This sure is getting exciting!"

"Go," Olivia repeated to the analysts, before turning to Jonathan. Her cement gaze contained a world of rage. Beneath that blindfold he had the look of a child getting on his first roller coaster at the fair.

"Sorry," he yelled. "Am I too loud, I can't hear myself!"

His behavior was affecting her already worried agents. This attack, it had begun in near perfect sync, not just with the disappearance of subjects throughout the US, but with Harrison bringing him here from the containment shell. The alarms had begun to blare within seconds of his restraints being locked to that table.

"Rivers, Harrison, Rolland," Olivia said, already heading toward the room. "The rest of you, anything comes through the door you don't recognize, take it down."

As she stepped into the room with Jonathan, she looked at Harrison. "Take them out, I want to talk to him."

With a nod to Rolland, she pulled her firearm as Harrison took the plugs from Jonathan's ears.

"How many—"

"Six or more," Jonathan said, answering before she could even finish the question.

". . . or more?" Olivia asked.

"It's like I told you. They'll be prepared to deal with whatever comes at them. Might mean they need more or less."

"How many more could be out—"

"I really doubt there are more than ten."

"The feeds from the hangar—"

"The Ninja's real," Jonathan said. "Everything else . . . meh."

Rivers came to stand beside her. "If that is true, these men aren't walking in here."

"No, manifesting inside," Olivia said.

"Doesn't make sense," Rivers said. "Why come at us like this if they can just appear anywhere?"

He nodded at Jonathan. "He isn't in the shell, so why not just beam him out?"

"How about it, Tibbs?" Olivia asked.

"I think they're all good questions," Jonathan said.

Olivia gave Harrison a look. The look passed to Rolland. She didn't waste a second considering. Her hand grabbed the back of his head and slammed it down on the metal table.

"Ouch," Jonathan said, with the same level of distress as someone who'd just stubbed their toe.

Olivia leaned down, staring at the blindfold. "Why aren't they retrieving you?"

"Maybe . . . we're too deep underground? No . . . that's ridiculous. Maybe they can't tell when I'm outside the giant Easter egg? Hmmm, no, wait, that doesn't make any sense either. I mean, if these are my people, they'd expect you to put me right back in there the moment you realize that folks are teleporting in and out of your top-secret facility."

Olivia skipped Harrison this time and looked directly at Rolland.

Jonathan's head slammed down on the table again. As she sat him up, Jonathan groaned—a cut having opened over his left eye.

"Okay, I'm a little dizzy . . . don't worry though, I'm still happy to help you guys think this through."

Rolland cocked her firearm and placed the steel barrel against the back of his head.

"Okay. Wait, wait, wait, okay," Jonathan said. "I'm thinking about it all wrong. Maybe they want me right here? Maybe they need me here . . . or maybe . . . I told them this was where I needed to be."

The barrel didn't bother him, and he seemed to revel in how easy it was to waste their time. It was unsettling, because every time she gave him the chance to speak, she felt less sure of anything. Even when what he said sounded credible, she had to second guess it—suspect every word a trap.

"What happened to your word. You promised everything you told me would be true," Olivia said.

He leaned forward, his head still a bit wobbly from its last collision with the table. "Why do you think I keep saying maybe?"

Her eyes narrowed. But just as she was considering broken fingers, he sighed. Beneath the blindfold he looked at her as though she were ruining the fun.

"Fine, I'm still here, because there is a bigger picture. I'm still here, because we're all going on a journey together, and you guys need a guide. But, mostly . . ." His fingers moved, pointing to a clock over the door as though he'd known it was there without having to see it as he said. "Because I needed to stall you a bit longer. See, now we're past the point of you hurting anyone."

Her glance went back and forth between him and the clock. Olivia tilted her head, stood up straight and turned to Rivers. "Get Leah, get his friends. We'll see how clever he thinks he is when the gun is pointed at their heads."

Rivers nodded, moving to carry out the order. Olivia grabbed his shoulder, leaned in close to whisper. "Keep them restrained."

"Of course," he said.

"Including Leah. Don't trust her," Olivia said.

Rivers nodded, then signaled for two of Harrison's guards to follow him.

"We'll fall back to the lower chamber if this position is compromised," Olivia said.

Rivers nodded, and then was gone.

"I told you to think long and hard about our relationship before you hurt my friends," Jonathan said. His expression had lost its smugness, he'd exchanged it for an honest one.

"Stand him up," Olivia barked.

Rolland moved to free his cuffs and, as he stood, blood ran down from the cut over his eye.

"Mr. Tibbs, in my opinion our relationship is rapidly nearing its conclusion," Olivia said. "You would do well to realize that your friends' fates depend on you now."

Jonathan chuckled, shaking his head as though she missed some huge irony in her own words. "Yeah, because I could forget."

Olivia didn't have time to discern the meaning of his reaction. A barrage of machine gun fire erupted in the nearby corridors and stole her attention. This was coming from within their wing—and everyone in the command center knew it. Whatever was going on in the rest of the facility, it was about to be right outside their door.

"Weapons out and ready to fire. We're moving." Olivia said, addressing the entire room. "Let me make this very clear, under no circumstances will we be surrendering any of the prisoners."

CHAPTER TWENTY-SIX

BEO HAD NEVER been the most graceful or gentle of creatures. He towered over most men with a thick muscled frame that cast a daunting shadow. His hands were what so often reminded him of his own size. They were enormous meaty things that were dangerous even when his implant wasn't activated.

When possible, he opted out of delicate tasks like restraining another human being or carefully putting them to sleep with a tiny needle. The flip side was that he made an excellent wall. Slowly walking forward, the guards emptied magazine after magazine into him until they ran out of bullets.

Now, Beo didn't like getting shot any more than the next guy. But, when they had tried this with alien steel armor, bullets ricocheted wildly. So, while Beo's gear made it appear that he was wearing some fancy bulletproof armor, the truth was that he was just letting bullets hit his alien enhanced skin.

The guards were intimidated just short of outright panic as he slowly moved forward. When their bullets ran dry, Beo kept his pace slow. They came at him with batons, and so he let them beat on him uselessly. Meanwhile, Mito incapacitated each in an orderly fashion. Most of the guards were so distracted by the hulking monstrosity out front that the nimbler threat reducing their conscious numbers didn't get as much attention until it was too late.

He plucked a badge from an unconscious guard just before reaching the reinforced metal door that stood between him and the prisoner containment shell. By the time Mito dropped the last guard to the floor unconscious, Beo had torn the small transparent locking panel off the front of the card reader and swiped the badge.

He heard the lock disengaging just as three sets of footsteps could be heard coming up the tunnel behind them.

"Rivers 'n company are right on schedule," Beo said, not actually turning to look. Olivia always sent her number two to fetch her some leverage—insurance policies really—after they saw how poorly things were playing out.

Beo and Mito were there to make sure they were never delivered to her.

"Freeze," yelled Agent Rivers.

Beo shook his head—Rivers always yelled *freeze*. As though, despite having to step over a dozen or so unconscious guards just to get his weapon aimed at them, he still had some hope they'd promptly surrender. He didn't look back, Beo had already seen every iteration of what happened when, shockingly, Mito didn't *freeze*.

The guns started firing, at first a lot, then less, then none. By the time Beo was standing inside the shell, all he heard from outside was the muffled struggle of River's last effort to take Mito down in hand to hand.

Inside the shell he found Grant, Collin, and Hayden. Each watching him with varying degrees of uncertainty from behind the walls of their transparent cells. Leah was there as well, but locked behind the white door at the back. He strode past Grant, stopping between Collin's and Hayden's cells, then pulled each door off its hinges like he was ripping a poster free of thumbtacks.

After observing this, neither of Jonathan's roommates showed any particular hurry to leave their cells. They stared at him with dumbfounded expressions. Beo didn't hold it against them. From their perspective, there was nothing about his entrance that sent a clear signal as to whether their situation had dramatically improved or deteriorated.

A second or two later, Mito pushed Rivers into the shell's corridor. He'd been relieved of his sidearm, his hands were zip tied behind his back, and he had a cloth gag shoved in his mouth.

Beo turned back to Hayden and Collin.

"Name's Beo," he lifted his mask up just enough to show a grin, then did his best impression of a particularly famous Austrian accent.

"Come with me if you want to live."

Looking up at the giant man, who'd just ripped his prison door off its hinges—Hayden's instincts were to do whatever the man asked. It was disarmingly strange when the man opened his mouth and a *Terminator* reference came out.

"Uhhh . . ." He drew out the sound, as he leaned sideways to look past the giant's shoulder to see how Collin was reacting. Mouth hanging open, Collin managed a somewhat terrified shrug.

"Please don't be offended, sir," Hayden said. "It's just that, I think we'll be in a lot of trouble if we leave our cells."

Dropping his Arnold impression, the giant spoke with what must have been his natural Cajun drawl. "Thing is, I'm not actually askin' if ya want rescue. Got orders, and ya'll not ta be lef' behind."

Hayden's next words came out as timid as he was capable. "Mr. Beo, I have zero—and I mean *zero*—desire to make you angry. It's just, I'm pretty certain the Government really wants us to stay where we are."

Beo nodded. "Ya got it figured right, boy. Ya gonna be fugitives. Course, da only reason ya here, is to make ya friend talk. Agent Rivers ova' dere was jus comin ta fetch ya. Dey thinkin' Jonathan might orda' a retreat if dey put a muzzle to ya head."

Beo grimaced over his next thought. "Conundrum fo ya, Hayden, even if I'm wrong—dey ain't neva gonna let ya walk outta here. You'd be wha' dey call a loose end."

Hayden paled, shivering a bit as he looked to his friend again. Collin looked resigned. "We've both been thinking it. We're screwed either way. On the run with these guys . . . might be the better option."

Hayden looked back to Beo. "But . . . who? Who ordered you to rescue us? We're no one."

Beo's answer was interrupted by Agent Rivers stumbling forward, pushed by the second man further into the shell. He was far smaller, but most people were when they stood beside Beo. He was also wearing the same black tactical gear from head to toe.

Beo turned back to Hayden. "I apologize, my colleague, Mr. Mito dare, will be assisting with yo' rescuing accommodations dis evening."

Mito said something in reply, but Hayden didn't understand a word. He thought the language sounded Japanese.

Beo nodded. "We' on schedule. Dem' two can wait a hot minute. Ma boys here are aboutta' see reason."

Beo turned to Hayden again. "Anyhow, Jonathan gave da order. I understand dat', due to da nature of ya' relationship thus far, dat don't make any sense, but . . ."

Beo lifted his giant palms up as though reminding them of where they were. "I'm assuming you've figured out dat a lot of things about ya roommate ain't wha dey—"

Every time Beo glanced at Mito, the man was pointing to an imaginary watch. Beo finally sighed, impatient with Mito's impatience. "Fine."

Beo strolled up to Grant's cell and yanked the door off.

"Mr. Morgan, Jonathan said you'll be joinin' us. Now, he did specify alive," Beo said. "But he wasn't much mo' specific on what condition you need ta' be in on delivery. So, if ya care to be resistin', be my guest."

Grant stared back at the man twice his size.

Hayden could see he was afraid, just short of enough to be cooperative. Normally, Hayden would have thought the man too stupid for his own good. But that wasn't it.

Grant had been drugged and tortured for days. He'd hardly spoken a word since Hayden mentioned the blond man might be dead. Now, Grant just looked like he didn't give a damn. He eyed Beo up and down as though, maybe, he liked his odds. "You think you're gonna make me g—"

Beo had turned and walked toward the other end of the shell before Grant finished whatever he'd intended to say. Grant was left blinking at the giant's back in surprise, until Mito, who stood half a foot shorter than Grant, stepped into the space Beo had vacated.

They looked at one another for a moment.

Mito moved.

At least Hayden thought he did. It was all so quick that Grant barely flinched.

There was a change though. A needle in Grant's neck, and a tiny cartridge that dropped to the floor from Mito's wrist. First Grant looked confused. Then as though he was about to get mean. Then very drowsy. He started to reach for the tiny tranq needle, but his eyes fluttered shut and his legs buckled. Artfully, Mito leaned forward and Grant rolled neatly onto his shoulder.

Collin and Hayden swapped a final, far more decisive, look.

"I say we give these guys the benefit of the doubt," Collin said.

"Yep," Hayden replied.

With a loud clap, Beo looked back to Mito. "Hear dat, our new friends have wisely selected da fully conscious rescue package."

Mito shrugged as though he couldn't care less, then waved for Hayden and Collin to follow him. From his knees, Rivers eyed them angrily, and despite his being gagged and restrained, Collin and Hayden each gave him a wide berth as they passed.

"Seriously, when is someone going to explain why everyone seems to think our roommate is Jason Bourne?" Collin mumbled as he passed.

They were both a bit surprised when Mito stopped about twelve steps out of the shell. He pointed at Grant's unconscious body then back at the two of them. Hayden was slow to realize that Mito didn't speak English. He'd seemed to have understood when Beo was speaking but Collin and Hayden weren't having any luck communicating.

So, after some charades, the roommates realized Mito wanted them to take over carrying Grant. Meanwhile, Hayden heard the white door at the back of the shell being torn off its hinges. He'd turned to get a look at how Leah was doing, but Mito started snapping his fingers to keep his attention.

Still, he heard Beo talking to Leah. He was too far away, and to preoccupied with getting Grant's weight distributed between him and Collin to make out what was said.

Once they had Grant in a manageable position Mito took a step back. He looked them over as though he were checking that all seemed in order. Adjusting an arm a bit and pushing them closer together, until he was satisfied.

"Hold. On. Tight," Mito said, with a thumbs up. The words were distinguishable, but it seemed that Mito had just memorized a series of sounds to say specifically for this moment.

Regardless, Collin and Hayden returned the thumbs up and nodded that they understood.

Then Mito put a hand on each of their shoulders. The moment dragged on awkwardly as Mito glanced back and forth between Collin and him. With the mask, his face was unreadable, but the whole act felt like Mito was trying to share some moment of brotherly affection despite their being near complete strangers. Hayden smiled politely, but after this went on for a few seconds too long, he looked to Collin to see if he was missing something. To his surprise, that was also the same moment that the world went black and everything he thought he'd understood about gravity was drastically altered.

CHAPTER TWENTY-SEVEN

AS THEY RETREATED, Olivia gathered any remaining enforcers and security staff they came across. She intended to pull back to the lowest corner of the facility and turn the folks she had left into a stop gap between their attackers and the alien's containment shell.

Of course, she and Jonathan knew that wasn't the whole truth. He wasn't gagged, he could have told her people about the trigger at any moment, just screamed it out, but he hadn't. The weight of that tiny device had grown heavier in her pocket as the evening wore on. While she could not allow fear or conscience to stop her from using it, she still had to wait until there were no other options with this many lives at stake.

She didn't want to accept it, but there was a growing certainty that Jonathan was driving her to that moment. Slowly cutting off all options until she wouldn't have any other choice.

As they had retreated, Jonathan made no efforts to delay them. Blindfolded, barefoot, and hands cuffed behind his back he was led down the hallways by Harrison and her guards. His face an unshakable calm. Each time The Cell fell further back into the facility, she heard something he'd said echo in her thoughts.

Everything that is about to happen . . . you helped me plan.

Control . . . you're going to lose control . . . lose any certainty that you ever had it.

I could have disabled that trigger . . . I'm not going to.

The very idea that there was no way to win was an affront to her identity. The fact that she was asking herself these questions, after deciding so many times not to entertain them, enraged her.

What if . . . ? She wondered. *What if I just put a bullet in his head right now?* Nothing *would* stop her. She could have pulled out her firearm and shot without so much as telling her guards to move aside. Would he see that coming? Would that prove him a liar once and for all?

Her fingers inched toward the clasp on her pistol's holster. Even as she did so, Jonathan strangely seemed to choose that moment to look at her. He was blindfolded. Why that moment?

But . . . what if I try and somehow failed . . . what would it mean?

Finally, they reached the lowest room in the facility. Behind the bulky steel security doors was a large space where The Mark's containment shell was housed.

"Ah, we're finally in the big black room with the big black egg," Jonathan said. "Let's all stay calm, no reason to get itchy trigger fingers."

Olivia drew in a long breath; *He can't read my mind.*

Still, her hand pulled away from the gun and she tore her eyes away from him. She had a situation to manage.

"Harrison, do we have confirmation that any of their numbers have been taken down? It has to be firsthand, nothing anyone saw on a security monitor."

Harrison shook her head saying, "No one who has gotten close enough to make that report has made it back."

"This is a good place to dig in. We had far too many agents above, there is no way they got all of them. One of ours must have contacted the surrounding base by now. Even if I'm wrong, someone on the outside must have noticed our communications are down. We just need to hold on. Reinforcements will come. Surround the hangar. Force his guys to fight us on two fronts."

"Ohhh," Jonathan said, grimacing doubtfully as he listened. "Sorry, I couldn't help overhearing. It's just, well . . . do you want the good news or the bad news first?"

Olivia exchanged a look with Harrison. Neither spoke, but Olivia got the sense that Harrison was just as afraid of what Jonathan might say as she was. After all, so far everything he'd said had come true.

Jonathan took their silence as permission to continue. "Sorry. Bad news first. Who am I kidding right? The bad news is always first.

"Harrison isn't wrong, the rest of the base is preparing a counterattack. The problem is that this secret underground lair, well . . . it's a big damn secret. Now, I'm no expert, but I don't think fire safety codes were considered when this place was built. I mean, two staircases, three unmarked maintenance ladders, one freight elevator, and one emergency hatch over the Panic room. Not many points of entry.

"I mean, it's like this place was built to keep people out long *before* my people destroyed the elevator . . . and collapsed the staircases . . . and destroyed the ladders."

His words were infuriating. Each claim making sense of the various shudders and explosions they had heard throughout the facility tonight. She was about to order Jonathan gagged. Certainly, would have been good for everyone's morale. A mental inventory stopped her—a discrepancy he'd slipped in—stopped her.

Emergency hatch over the Panic room?

If this existed outside Jonathan's imagination, then her commanding officer had seen fit to keep her in the dark about it. Thing was, Jonathan had yet to be wrong. She was almost ready to believe that everything that had happened tonight was as he'd said, in the service of proving that very point to her.

"But hey, don't forget there was good news," Jonathan said. "Agent Rivers and Leah will be here any second, and they'll have that firsthand intel you wanted. Course, that depends on your people staying calm. Not just firing the moment those doors open. You'll want to let them in, you'll be glad to hear what they have to say. I mean, you won't be, but you should be."

"Harrison, Mr. Tibbs will be given exactly one chance to explain what he means, if he doesn't give you a crystal clear answer, put a bullet through his knee cap," Olivia enunciated this such that the entire room heard her.

Harrison looked at Olivia, seeming hesitant for a moment before giving a grim nod. Hobbling a man for life was not something Harrison would willingly permit herself or her guards to normally do, but the woman wouldn't disobey a direct order.

Harrison stepped forward, making sure Jonathan heard the gun being cocked—that he felt the barrel press down on his knee.

Olivia saw Harrison lean in and whisper to Jonathan. She couldn't hope to hear what was said, because the hum within the room was growing far louder than usual. At first, she assumed the shell was simply reaching the brink of its discharge. But, unless she was imagining things, the room seemed far more turbulent than it normally did when this took place.

The scientists who built the egg had warned her that with a containment field as large as this, the shell's mounting had to remain sufficiently anchored, or the discharge might become unsafe. It wasn't something that she'd given much thought. Tonight in particular, she'd had no time to worry about it. But as the room vibrated, she wondered if all the shock waves from the many explosions that rocked the facility this evening might have damaged the foundations—which the egg was currently anchored to.

While there was nothing to be done about this concern now, if they made it through the night, the anchor securing the alien's prison would need to be inspected.

Whatever Harrison whispered in Jonathan's ear wasn't important. Olivia knew it would be something along the lines of, *I don't want to cripple you for the rest of your life, but don't doubt that I will if you leave me no choice.*

Whatever it was, Tibbs nodded, but his response was not a whisper. "I'm sorry, Harrison. Shooting Rolland doesn't bother me, but you've always been decent. Wish it didn't have to go this way."

Seeing as how Rolland was standing opposite Jonathan and well within ear shot, the two swapped a glance. Rolland tilted her head such that it seemed she was looking forward to seeing Harrison pull the trigger. "Well, Tibbs that sure didn't sound like a crystal clear ans—"

For Olivia, the next few seconds might as well have been a slow-motion nightmare. One of those cruel dreams where time and physics works against every outcome you'd have tried to stop.

Harrison's understandable hesitation to pull the trigger lasted just long enough that the gun had yet to fire when the floor began to quake beneath them. There was no other explanation, the vibrations must have come from the alien's shell, but they'd never been this strong before. Olivia feared they were past functional thresholds.

However, none of Olivia's people focused on the rumble for long. Because at that moment, every eye in the room had turned toward the massive doors— the one way in or out of the room. The heavy reinforced steel possessed an equally massive lock—and when that lock disengaged there was no mistaking the sound.

Olivia alone had remained fixated on Jonathan. She'd heard a fainter sound under the rumbling and opening doors just before the large lock disengaged. A tiny metallic click, a much smaller lock. The timing of it all too perfect, as though Jonathan knew exactly when that massive lock would draw everyone's attention.

Harrison and Rolland, like everyone else, looked to the large doors. As such, they were focused exactly where Jonathan wanted when he became the greatest threat in the room.

As Olivia's yell began, Jonathan was already moving, having set himself in motion in that split second that Rolland and Harrison became distracted. Yet, the way he moved seemed impossible. Even unable to see, it was as though he had taken the lead in a choreographed dance with Rolland and Harrison pulled along against their will.

His palm shot from behind him, grabbing Harrison's wrist, and pushing the barrel off his knee. In surprise, Harrison tried to pull the trigger, but the delay was just enough. The shot rang out, and Rolland let out a shocked scream as a bullet tore through her calf and the force knocked her feet out from under her.

As Rolland was about halfway through the process of her head trading places with her feet—a second shot rang out.

The top of Harrison's boot imploded.

Jonathan had twisted her wrist downwards as he'd begun to stand, forced the barrel into position over her foot just as she'd tried to get a second pan-icked shot off. Harrison's brain hadn't even received the pain signal from her foot before another twist of her wrist forced the gun from her grip and pulled her off balance.

Tibbs wasn't trying to get her out of the way. She staggered into his free arm, her throat landing in the crook of his elbow as he stood. As her sidearm fell free, Jonathan's hand released her wrist and moved to catch the gun by its grip with two fingers. When he stood up straight the pain caught up to her. Harrison screamed as she realized that she'd become a human shield.

In a final flourish, Jonathan let go of the weapon with his fingers and caught it again, now with his hand on the grip, the finger on the trigger. Rolland hit the floor and the blindfolded Jonathan Tibbs stood with Harri-son's gun leveled on Olivia, the open end of his picked handcuffs dangling from his wrist.

Olivia could see Harrison's face. Wide-eyed disbelief as she stared down the sight of her own gun. Desperately, she tried to keep her weight on her good foot while Rolland began grunting painfully as she cradled her bleed-ing leg.

All this had happened, and Olivia had barely managed to pull her weapon free and take aim back at Jonathan's head. No one in the room moved. Olivia was the only person close enough to see when something translucent ran up along Jonathan's skin. It darted from the picked cuffs, up his arm and neck and disappeared beneath the blindfold.

As she stared at the man's blindfold in disbelief, fully convinced that he could see her plain as day, a faint line of horizontal light began to glow between Jonathan's eyes. The fabric smoldered a bit, then fell away as though it had been cleaved.

Olivia shivered when her eyes met his. They were too full of knowing. Neither so much as blinking, until the sound of the massive doors opening wider sent ripples of uncertainty through the room. Everyone's eyes trying to rapidly glance back and forth between the standoff at the back of the room and whatever fresh hell might come through the doors.

"Keep your weapons on the door!" Olivia yelled, while her own gun remained on Jonathan.

She heard when the doors had finished opening, and for a moment the only noise in the room was the shell's growing rumble. A few tense moments passed leaving Olivia wondering why chaos had yet to erupt now that the blast doors were open.

"What do you see Harrison?" Olivia asked.

Harrison's eyes flicked over Olivia's shoulder, and she grunted out an answer between painful breaths. "It's . . . Leah and Rivers. They're . . . tied . . . together."

Jonathan's head tilted, giving Olivia a clean shot if she wanted to take it. "You're surprised? Olivia, at some point, not trusting me just gets hurtful."

They were lashed together with a rope, Rivers' hands restrained behind his back and Leah's in the front. What was more disconcerting was that while Leah was gagged, Rivers was now blindfolded. As though Rivers was to do the talking, while dependent on Leah to navigate the room.

"Olivia," Jonathan said, his voice loud enough for everyone to hear even over the growing vibrations. "I know. I know how heavy your front pocket is feeling."

Of course. The moment was here, it was almost exactly as she'd predicted it might look, except she'd never thought Jonathan would have a gun on her.

She was exhausted. Tired of trying to keep ahead of it all. She felt herself wanting it to end.

"So, it's almost here," Jonathan said. "Almost time to take that detonator out. Find out if you're cold enough to kill everyone in the building. Think it'll be worth it?"

"Damn you! This isn't a game!" her anger poured out, the first tear she'd had in years rolled down her cheek.

"It's a choice," Jonathan said. "Let us go or kill us all. But, you should wait, because Rivers has something he needs to tell you."

Olivia shook her head, was afraid to hear any more. "It's a trap."

"Everything feels like a trap when you believe you're being lied to," Jonathan said. "But I haven't lied to you. So, humor me, take the detonator out.

Keep your finger on the button if it makes you feel like you've got control. Then tell your men to let Leah bring Rivers in."

She considered him for a long moment. Low on options, she was desperate to buy any time she could to think. Slowly, she slipped one hand off her gun and reached for the trigger in her pocket.

"Let them in," Olivia said. "But everyone keeps their weapons on that door. Nothing else comes through!"

Leah began to step forward and Rivers followed the pull of the rope. Olivia's weary soldiers, the two dozen or so that remained, all parted nervously as they allowed her through and immediately closed their line behind her after Rivers followed past. Finally, Leah came to a stop beside Olivia, close enough that Rivers would be heard over the shell's thrumming.

Jonathan's eyes never left hers.

"Agent Rivers," Jonathan said. "I trust you've both been treated as gently as possible under the circumstances."

Rivers voice was that of a man who knew his team had already lost. "I've . . . not been harmed."

"I'm glad. Now, with Olivia's permission, I am going to ask you some questions, feel free to answer them anyway you please. I only ask that you answer honestly and give her the best intel you can."

Though he seemed puzzled he nodded. "Alright."

"Have you seen a single one of the men who infiltrated this facility injured by any of your efforts this evening?"

"No," Rivers said. "They seem armored . . . invulnerable to gun fire, and we've been afraid to risk anything more powerful down here."

Olivia studied Jonathan, unsure how it was that this was supposed to change anything for her.

"Have you seen any harm done to any of your people this evening?" Jonathan asked. "Again, within reason."

"No . . ." Rivers said. "They're using some type of tranq. They even let me examine our people. They're unconscious, tied up, but the worst of it is some bruises."

Jonathan took a moment to let that sink in, then continued. "You've been shown every point of exit in the facility, Rivers?"

Rivers shivered, but nodded.

"And is anyone getting in or out of here tonight?" Jonathan asked.

"I don't see how," Rivers said. "Well, unless . . ."

Rivers, seemingly unsure, trailed off.

"Go ahead, Agent Rivers, she needs to know."

"The prisoners," Rivers said. "I saw them disappear. Same as The Mark. All they had to do was free them from the shell."

"If there is anything I missed," Jonathan said to Olivia, "feel free to ask."

She was so tired of trying to outthink him, see his endgame before it was too late to stop it. Still she had to try. Jonathan wanted her to know she couldn't hurt his people. That his people could have killed everyone in the building, but had chosen not to. That her people had no way out at this point, while his could leave at any time.

The only exception was the alien.

If she hit the trigger, he would still die with The Cell.

Olivia swallowed, closing her eyes so she didn't have to look at him for a moment.

He relaxed his arm slowly, taking his aim off her. Gently as possible, he began to lower Harrison down, careful not to put her in any more pain than she was. Then, looking to Olivia to make sure she understood, he placed the pistol on the ground. As though the weapon had never been more than a prop. Still moving slowly, his palms out, Jonathan reached for Rolland.

She didn't get the feeling he was up to anything. He knew she could take a shot at him at any time and didn't show the least fear that she would. The fact that he set down the gun didn't really surprise her either; Jonathan's weapons of choice were his words.

Still, she lowered her barrel with him as he knelt over Rolland as keeping her gun on him was one of the few things she still had power over.

"I have to take the alien," Jonathan said, as he removed Rolland's belt, then began to wrap it a few inches above her wound. He pulled it tight, and Rolland grunted in pain, but she knew he was just trying to keep her from bleeding out too much.

"It's not ideal for you, but it won't get anyone killed," Jonathan said.

He rose back to his feet and faced her. "Not a single one of your people have been hurt by us tonight, they're all alive and down here with us. So, if you believe you have to use that detonator, if you can't let him go, there will only be one killer here tonight."

Olivia's eyes went cold. "Stop. Stop this! Stop acting as though it's a decision. It's protocol, it's my responsibility. Everyone down here knew it might come to this when they signed on . . ."

He looked at her, as though he knew she wasn't really trying to convince him. Still, he didn't rush her. Seemed he thought she deserved all the time she needed to make a choice. Olivia's eyes wandered about. Looking for something, anything to leverage.

Her eyes settled on Leah. Certain questions struck then. Questions that seemed important and yet Jonathan hadn't asked.

Why was Leah gagged?

Why did they want her here, but not want her talking?

Why blind Rivers for that matter? They could have sent him in alone.

"Why is Rivers blindfolded?" Olivia asked. "Why is Leah gagged?"

Jonathan smirked.

"Good questions, I'm curious myself," Jonathan said. "But, I'm not omniscient. All I can promise is that, if my people sent them in this way, it's because this plays out the way we want it to."

Olivia studied Leah; the girl looked sick with indecision. Yet, when she saw Olivia's eyes focused on her, she seemed to be pleading to tell her something.

Olivia swallowed.

She was desperate to hear and at the same time terrified. Her hand was sweating on the detonator. She began to accept it, believe that she was damned no matter what choice she made.

"Now if I had to guess," Jonathan said. "My allies don't want Leah talking. That could only be because she knows something that one of us doesn't. Personally, I'm fine not knowing. So, it's up to you."

If she was damned either way, then should she know what the girl wanted to say and be done with it? Yet, Jonathan—this bastard—thinks he knows what I'll do. Thinks I can't resist.

She felt weary as she stepped sideways toward Leah. When she was close enough to Leah to remove the gag, she looked again into the girl's pleading eyes.

It was at that moment she realized there was something Leah might say, something that—just maybe Jonathan didn't know. Something that might change his mind about who had the upper hand.

Leah was carrying his child after all. How could he know that and be willing to risk letting her die down here? What if that was what his people didn't want her to tell him?

Her hand hesitated. But . . . what if she was wrong?

"Olivia, remember," Jonathan said. "I promised I'd never lie to you. Whatever Leah might say, I can't promise it's the truth."

It could all be reverse psychology, but everything he said seemed to be trying to keep her from pressing the button.

He thinks he knows me. What then? What is the one thing I'd never do?

He already told me. Give up control. Jonathan thinks the one thing I won't do is give up control.

She fixated on that thought. Then made a decision—something she would never have considered. The only thing he might not see coming, because she wouldn't have entertained it in a thousand lifetimes.

Leah's hands were tied in front of her. The excess rope leashed to Rivers. But Leah's fingers were free enough, they could hold onto something small. So, when Olivia reached for Leah, she didn't untie the woman's gag, instead, she placed the trigger in the girl's hand.

Leah's eyes bulged as she understood what Olivia had done. Her gaze racing between Jonathan and Olivia in horror. She might as well have been handed a grenade after the pin had been pulled.

"You decide," Olivia said. "It's out of my hands now—and his."

She looked to him and his eyebrows went up.

"Hmmm, good on you, Olivia, I honestly didn't see that coming."

Olivia felt a moment of triumph, but just as quickly as her heart began to soar, she felt it sputter. He'd made the statement with a genuine honesty, as though it were a delightful surprise, but then he shrugged as though nothing could have changed the outcome.

Olivia looked back to Leah.

The girl let out a long breath as she stared down at the detonator.

She closed her eyes.

Then pressed the trigger.

CHAPTER TWENTY-EIGHT

THERE WAS A brief delay. Then the ground began to tremble. Just as the floor was becoming too unstable for Leah to keep her balance, the lights went out.

She staggered in darkness, and for a moment she wasn't sure if death had come or was still on its way. Her mind had been a storm up until she pressed that button. Every meaning, every possibility, every fear having to resolve itself into a single question: *Did she trust Jonathan?*

When Beo had freed her from the shell, he'd been very short on words. He'd said Jonathan wouldn't allow anyone to die down here. That, one way or another, Jonathan and the alien were leaving tonight—there was no stopping this.

But . . . she had a choice.

If she wanted to see Jonathan free of The Cell, if she wanted to be free of The Cell herself, if she wanted answers, then she would get one chance. All she had to do was whatever she could to convince Olivia to press the trigger on the detonator.

She didn't get to ask follow-up questions before Mito restrained her. But Beo never said a thing about what she was supposed to do if Olivia handed her the detonator. So, she'd just had to hope that it didn't matter who did the deed, as long as someone hit the button.

The rumbling, it seemed further away at first. For some time now, the whole room had been vibrating on account of the shell. But this was different, this was the sort of thing she'd have expected to feel if explosives were being triggered in a sequence that was rapidly moving through the facility toward this chamber.

The floor was growing more difficult to stand on as the sound drew closer. *She trusted. She'd believed. Had she just killed all of them?*

No. She didn't believe it. After chasing answers for years. After losing her brother. After watching Rylee and countless others disappear. Betraying her father, betraying people she thought of as friends. This was not how it ended!

She closed her eyes. Her child wasn't meant to die down here, buried under an avalanche of concrete and dirt. Jonathan wasn't meant to simply escape and never know.

She wasn't going to die without ever getting a chance to fix all of this.

Her hands, they moved protectively for her womb, but she couldn't reach while she was still tied. She was in the dark with no hope of freeing herself. Nothing to hold onto but the damn detonator.

Commotion was spreading in the room.

At first, she thought the remaining agents were losing their collective calm, giving into panic like passengers on a crashing plane. But she wasn't hearing prayers or panicked screams. She wasn't being trampled by people fleeing in the dark.

No, she was hearing gunfire. Agents under attack.

What?

Under the cover of darkness, convinced they were living their last few moments—they had dropped their vigilance. The moment the lights had gone out, had Jonathan's people come through the doors?

She could hear the screams of fear. They began close but rapidly fled away as agents were singled out and pulled into the darkness.

If they were all just going to die why did it seem that Jonathan's people were still finishing off Olivia's agents?

A strange thought to rekindle hope but she clung to it.

In fact, this should have been over by now. They should have become one with the universe in a fiery explosion or been crushed by falling debris. Yet, neither had happened.

This . . . this was all misdirection.

Slow to realize the same, the few remaining agents were switching on flashlights. Beams of light occasionally caught glimpses of their allies. It was like a horror movie come to life. The lights making agents visible just long enough to see them dragged suddenly into the darkness by something too fast to clearly make out.

Guns began to fire with less and less discretion.

Leah could feel bullets pass her in the darkness, striking surfaces dangerously close. Instinct kicked in, screaming for her to throw herself to the ground, but before she could obey, a concussive force hit one of the chamber's walls and jarred her off her feet. She was still anchored to Rivers by their leash. In the darkness, she could hardly see where she landed.

In the cacophony, she heard one sound more ominous than all the rest. Cement breaking. The sound of one of the chamber's walls cracking inward. Then came a second massive crash. The entire room lurched as the wall collapsed into the chamber.

Leah was pelted by debris and a sudden rush of cold night air that swept into the chamber. The air quickly grew thick with dust, but also the scent of mud and deep earth. She rolled onto her stomach, forced to put her weight on her elbows by the pull of Rivers on the other end of the rope.

Suddenly, there was light. Enough for her to see.

She stared upwards as something massive came through the wall, its surface a bending mirror of undulating movement. There wasn't more light in the room, but what was already there was now being reflected around the chamber by this . . .

She didn't know what it was.

Reflections distorted on its moving liquid surface, Leah could see the agents with flashlights behind her, the occasional blaze of discharge from a barrel as someone opened fire. She watched in awe as the reflective surface began to take new shape in front of her.

This thing—a giant worm of liquid mirror—didn't belong in the real world. It belonged in a movie trying to kill Godzilla. It seemed to be morphing, smoothing out from a shape that had been like a drill and forming a massive cavity. Something more like a . . .

A mouth, she realized.

The agents turned their remaining bullets on the monstrosity. The spent rounds seeming to fall to the floor without so much as blemishing the worm's exterior. When the mouth finished forming, the worm lurched forward. It didn't launch at any of the agents. If anything, it avoided them. Rather, it swallowed the entire shell holding The Mark prisoner.

The worm had passed within feet of her, so close she could see her distorted reflection looking back at her on its surface. She heard the alien's shell ripping free of the foundation, watched as it undulated like a snake to swallow the egg further into itself.

Despite its beauty, it was dangerous. Temporary awe gave way to survival once again. She had to put more space between her and this thing. Getting onto her feet while restrained was difficult. As she managed to get her knees under her, she suddenly felt a stabbing pain on the outside of her arm that sent her right back down to the ground. She screamed uselessly against the gag, feeling warm blood run down her arm.

A bullet must have grazed her. Leah felt a pull, the rope between her and Rivers losing any slack. She turned, expecting to see Rivers trying to get on his feet, but . . .

Jonathan's face emerged. There was no fear in his eyes as he knelt in front of her. He lifted her until they were face to face on their knees. One arm took hold of her around the waist and tightened, pulling her against him.

The ground lurched again as the massive worm retreated out of the chamber. Behind Jonathan, she could see it slipping back the way it had come. He didn't seem concerned by the massive monster but held her with his eyes even as his free hand jerked hard on the rope tethering her to Rivers.

Agent Rivers must have managed to get to his feet despite being blindfolded and having his hands tied behind him, but he wasn't ready for the sudden pull. Jonathan—he didn't even bother looking—knew exactly how cause and effect would play out. Rivers stumbled backward, tripped, and came falling out of darkness until he landed gracelessly on his rear. Jonathan let go of the rope and used the free arm to grab hold of Rivers.

She heard him speak. "Mr. Clean, we're good here."

A harsh light hit them, came out of the dark from the same direction that Rivers had fallen. She couldn't make out her features with the light aimed on them, only saw the silhouette of Olivia staggering toward them. Her weapon drawn, aimed at them, unable to get a clean shot with Rivers in her line of fire.

Then there suddenly was no light. Leah was pulled in every direction at once. She might have imagined it, but she could have sworn a shriek of Olivia's rage chased them into the maelstrom.

CHAPTER TWENTY-NINE

OCT 15, 2005 | 11 PM | HANGMAN'S TREE

THE THREE APPEARED on a platform, Jonathan and Leah blinded by the blur of flood lights surrounding them. His arms relaxed, and Rivers and Leah fell away as the teleportation sickness took its toll on all of them.

Leah's eyes were open in pure confusion, murmuring unintelligibly beneath the gag. Rivers, still blindfolded with his hands tied behind his back, could do little more than ride the disorientation blind.

For Jonathan, it was to be expected—anyone without an active implant got teleportation sickness following a trip on Mr. Clean's wild ride. Understanding that condition let him ride out the world-spinning nausea with some semblance of grace as he lay on his back.

Within a few seconds, the blurred shape of six figures in a circle around them began to take form.

Jonathan heard the pleasant sounds of relieved laughter growing around him.

"I almost crapped myself when Olivia handed her the detonator," Bodhi said.

"Yeah, no one called that in the pool," Perth said. "Never happened before."

"What the hell got into her?" Tam asked. "Figured she slept with that damn thing."

"Anyone botch something in some new exciting way?" Bodhi asked.

"It was my fault," Jonathan said.

His eyes were still closed as he laid on his back taking controlled breaths, but he heard their laughter trail. "I pushed her too hard."

There was a moment of silence as they considered.

Bodhi shrugged. "Well, it only threw off our timing a bit. We adapted."

"No fatalities," Beo added, "but man—"

He stopped suddenly. "Hey, Jonathan, you alright? You're bleeding."

Jonathan tightened his eyes against another wave of nausea. "Not my blood. Leah was grazed. Need to take her to Medical. Put Rivers in the brig with Morgan and let him cool off for a bit."

"On it," Perth said.

"Wait," Jonathan forced himself to sit up and open his eyes. "You guys were perfect tonight."

He made a point of letting each of them see he meant it as he said, "Thank you."

They nodded back at him for a moment, only to be interrupted when the night sky above was suddenly absent of stars, a massive shadow of a shape having appeared overhead.

Jonathan looked up at Mr. Clean and smiled. "Alright, let's not get too comfortable. Night ain't over yet."

Beo leaned down to break the rope tethering Leah to Rivers. Her eyes watched him cautiously, though to be fair she likely couldn't make out more than his blur being larger than the other five as he stepped toward her.

Awkwardly, Beo nudged Mito, looking down at his massive meaty hands as though he didn't trust himself to pick up a steel girder let alone a human being. With a roll of his eyes, Mito gently picked Leah up and the two headed out. They were followed out by Tam and Perth carrying Rivers between them.

"You need anything from me?" Bodhi asked.

Jonathan smiled up at him and put his hand out. "Yeah, help a guy up?"

When Jonathan was standing, Bodhi gave him a supporting arm to lean on until the sickness had finally passed.

"I assume everything went as planned with the other teams?" Jonathan asked.

"Like clockwork. You were right, once The Cell realized that everyone they'd been tracking was vanishing, they panicked and pulled you out of the shell for . . ."

Bodhi trailed off. "You knew that though."

Jonathan shrugged. "How are my friends coping?"

Bodhi shrugged. "Not sure. They were taken to the quarters we set aside. I know you said they weren't to be treated like prisoners, but . . . well, until someone gives them a clue what they're into, we figured it best not to let them roam around."

Jonathan paused. "So, who is watching them?"

"Rourke," Bodhi said.

Jonathan gave a smirk. "Rourke doesn't speak English."

"Yeah," Bodhi said, clearly amused.

Jonathan shook his head. "Well, at least he won't understand the names Paige is likely calling him by now."

Bodhi shrugged. "Rourke es *Russian*," doing a purposely terrible imitation of the man's accent. "Mean words of little boys and girls no scare him."

Jonathan took a few tentative steps on his own to make sure he'd recovered before leaving the platform with Bodhi following. His features darkening shortly afterward.

". . . and Rylee's father?"

"Um, yeah, he's asking to talk to you," Bodhi said. "Shane is watching him and Colonel Hamill."

A few minutes earlier, Collin and Hayden had arrived on that same platform. Rourke had been there waiting for them to recover from the teleportation sickness, their clothes growing damp from a small drizzle beneath the night sky.

"Follow, now," Rourke said, when they were recovered enough to stand on their own.

Once they stepped off the platform and passed the ring of floodlights, they saw they were standing in a forest clearing. Though hard to see clearly at night, outside the clearing the trees seemed to stretch beyond their sight in every direction. Within the clearing there seemed to be a number of structures, but at the moment Hayden and Collin could only make out those that Rourke was leading them to. Not far ahead, there were rows and rows of cargo containers stacked four high.

They hadn't reached those stacks when the drizzle stopped so abruptly that it was as though they'd walked under an awning. About the same time Hayden felt Collin's graceless finger poke him in the cheek.

Slapping the man's hand away, Hayden stopped short before asking what had gotten into him, because Collin was staring up at the sky in a trance.

Hayden frowned and looked for himself. "What . . . what is that?"

"Da, eto Mr. Clean," Rourke said, though his voice held none of their awe. As though he'd seen what they were seeing so many times that the novelty had worn off.

Hayden swapped a look with Collin, both seeming to wonder if perhaps something was lost in translation. The only part they'd understood had to do with toilet bowl cleaner and neither could imagine what that had to do with what was happening above.

At first, the moon and stars had seemed to disappear. Soon, he realized that they were only hidden by something large floating over the tree line. Then a strange beauty began above. The massive black disc spread in all directions. It curved down, forming a dome that would swallow everything inside the clearing. The solid black surface blurred, first becoming opaque and finally translucent.

Peering through this, the stars and moon swayed in a manner more vibrant than nature alone was capable. Colors smeared across its surface, stretched and bent the light. Hayden felt he was standing beneath a living canvas of an impressionist's painting. Collin's take, while no less awed, was far less eloquent. "It's like we're in a giant soap bubble."

As the dome reached the clearing floor the sway of the wind, the sound of chirping crickets and falling rain were suddenly gone. The dome continued to thin, losing more of its fluid nature. Lines, hard angles, and flat surfaces began emerging, until what had been a massive soap bubble began to look more like an equally massive and ghostly greenhouse. Rain streamed down the outside to gather in puddles on its surfaces. The stars and moon reclaimed their natural appearance, as the ceiling above them became more like solid glass.

Slowly at first, the structures lost their transparency. The more familiar designs of scaffolding, rafters, and supports emerged. Soon, they were standing in a building with architecture far less alien and growing more mundanely human by the second.

Hayden stepped back as a disturbance, gentle as a string pulled out from under a boot, passed underfoot and drew his eye to the ground. There, a faint echo of what had occurred in the sky spread over the forest floor.

He startled and rebalanced himself when the ground moved beneath him. Eyes widening as he looked down to see he stood on what appeared to be a rising platform of glass, his feet getting further and further away from the forest floor. The clearing that had possessed the natural ups and downs of a woodland meadow became a level foundation. Just as the sky had a moment earlier, the transparency gave way to a plain wash of polished grey.

Structures rose from out of the floor and down from the ceiling. Shapes like staircases, catwalks, massive interior walls emerging.

Suddenly, just as everything seemed to still, lights came on above them.

Hayden looked around in utter disbelief, the awe of what had sprung into being around them abruptly evaporating in sheer disappointment. This time, Collin's take felt apt. "All that . . . and we might as well be standing in a Costco."

"A bit of a let down on the surface," said a voice from behind them.

Having been rather enamored with all the changes happening around them, Hayden hadn't noticed Anthony coming toward them. The man slowed to be polite but seemed on his way somewhere else.

"Mr. Clean can spread himself pretty thin," the man said. "He's still adapting himself to human habitation."

Collin and Hayden exchanged another frown; clearly the problem wasn't that neither of them spoke Russian. *What was it with these people and cleaning products?*

"Who are you people? What . . . what is this place?" Hayden asked.

"My name is Anthony. This place, we call it Hangman's Tree. It's private property. Only a few dirt roads in and out, land's been made to appear undeveloped on any maps."

Anthony had to turn around and speak to them while walking backwards at this point. "The explanation you're really looking for is a bit longer than I can give at the moment. But there will be time. What's important is you're safe, miles away from where you were being held prisoner, and we get excellent Wi-Fi."

Hayden desperately wanted Anthony to stick around and explain more, but he could see that the man had somewhere to be. "Wait, where is Jonathan?"

Already starting to turn around. "Safe. He'll check on you the first chance he gets. Just try to be patient. He's got a lot on his plate."

With that, Anthony was gone. Hayden and Collin, hungry for answers, were already beginning to follow, until Rourke stepped in their path with a shake of his head. "Sleduyte za mnoy."

They had no idea what that meant, but it wasn't hard to infer that Rourke clearly wanted them headed in a different direction.

"Think they're leaving us with a guy who doesn't speak English on purpose?" Collin asked.

"I haven't been threatened, strip searched, handcuffed, or had my head put in a bag. My standards are pretty low at this point, but I'm not about to complain."

Admittedly they could only see a fraction of this place from where they were, but there was now plenty of light. Strangely, the source appeared to be everyday fluorescent bulbs hanging between rafters and the crisscrossing catwalks that ran overhead. Shapes that had previously been obscured, now far less mysterious. A lot of what the clearing had held was now inside.

Rourke was escorting them through row after row of cargo containers. Except now they looked less like a shipping yard and more like massive industrial motels. The metal catwalks and staircases led down to platforms that spanned the cargo containers on each level. It was rather like a system of fire escapes that would lead anywhere in the building . . . assuming one had the permission to use them.

For a while, there were echoing silences that gave the impression the entire place was sparsely populated. They only saw a few other men. Unlike Anthony, none stopped to talk; they nodded to Rourke as he passed but showed little interest in Collin or Hayden.

About the time they followed Rourke up one of the staircases, they heard machinery from the opposite end of the complex. A sound like grinding metal that lasted a few seconds, followed by a heavy thud. Frankly, it sounded like someone had lifted a car, cut a fourth off, and let the piece drop on the concrete. While they were curious what was causing that ruckus, Rourke paid it no mind.

Eventually, Rourke brought them up to a door on the fourth story landing of one of the cargo container stacks. The moment he held it open for them, they recognized the voice of who was shouting inside.

"Stop telling me you can't answer my questions," Paige said. "I want to know where the hell Shane took Evelyn."

Paige turned as the door swung open, and as she laid eyes on them her anger softened. For a moment, Hayden forgot a lot of his questions. Whoever Paige was yelling at and why, didn't matter. The three ran to one another and found themselves embracing in a triangle of tangled limbs.

"You idiots scared me so much," Paige said, her head resting between their shoulders as she held back tears. "I'm not crying . . . and you both smell awful."

Hayden laughed. She was probably right, The Cell hadn't exactly let them shower. Still, it felt so good to know she was okay that he held on for quite a while. Then, somewhat suddenly, he felt Paige stiffen.

He opened his eyes, and as he looked over Paige's shoulder, he found himself frozen as well. Collin hadn't spoken for a while, and Hayden suspected that he was seeing it too.

Most of the cargo container's interior was unremarkable, reminding Hayden of a high-end RV minus any decoration but possessing an over-abundance of bunk beds. They were lined up one after the other along the sides of both walls. Obviously, none of that was what made them grow still.

What had caught him by surprise was that there was a display hanging down from the ceiling. It had not been there before he hugged Paige. He was sure of this because he'd have remembered a bald cartoon man—whose resemblance would have led Hayden to connect a number of dots had he seen him there a moment earlier—and it was watching them.

Seeing as Paige was facing the opposite direction, the reason she had stiffened was uncertain until she spoke. "Um, Mr. Clean, were we not in a forest when I got here?"

Mito walked behind Beo, carrying her to what looked like a rusted and weathered cargo container. The exterior didn't advertise for the interior accurately at all, leaving Leah surprised to find herself in a well-lit, sterile looking, fully-equipped mobile medical bay. The shelves and drawers were organized and stocked such that she wondered if she was the first patient this place had ever seen.

That said, she wasn't very focused on these sorts of details.

Since appearing on that platform, she had been fighting off a fog. Everything blurry, bright, and spinning. Still, she understood that there had been people standing around them. They had been wearing masks, yet they now stood in front of her with no particular care that she could see their faces.

She'd smelled forest. At least, she thought she had, now she wasn't sure.

A moment ago, she'd been looking up at a night sky that was moving in ways that left her wondering if she'd been drugged. In addition, she couldn't remember when they had gone indoors, let alone how she'd managed to miss this giant warehouse.

Maybe she'd lost consciousness for a bit?

"Red, hey . . . Red."

It took her a moment to realize that the man, snapping his fingers to get her attention, was addressing her. She knew the accent. He'd spoken to her during the escape. "Ain't nowhere da run. Jus trus me, id' be pointless to try."

She noticed as he said this that the smaller one, Mito, had just freed her hands. While he wasn't being rough, he was rather quick to re-secure her using zip ties to keep her wrists and ankles strapped to a chair.

Still gagged, Leah looked at the big man's face—he was finally in focus. He took in the state of her and sighed. Then reached for a communicator in his ear.

"Aye, Tam, got Red Fury wit da Doc. Gonna be a bit, ain't started patching 'er up yet."

There was a pause while whoever was on the other end spoke.

". . . Yeah, I'm aware—"

Another pause.

". . . Right, den' what? Babysitting? No way JT want's us da' let da' spook roam 'bout on 'er own."

He listened again.

". . . Well, it ain't da sort of detail needs runnin up da chain right now."

The big man sighed impatiently as he listened.

". . . Well, thank ya. Ya's been slightly betta' den useless."

As Beo pulled his hand away from his ear Leah tried to speak but only made unintelligible sounds through the gag. He leaned closer, and she was sure they had never met—yet she recognized him. It was the sort of familiarity of seeing a C-list celebrity in a movie. She knew the face—but couldn't place where she'd seen him.

"I ain't been told ta keep ya muzzled, Red. Ba, we ain't here fo ya mind voodoo. Start askin questions and da gag goes back."

Her eyes blinked a few times but she nodded. Beo nudged Mito. She didn't recognize the shorter man's face. He looked at the giant, seeming unsure of what he wanted. Finally, Mito said something. She had no idea what, the language sounded Japanese, but Mito looked annoyed.

"Would ya jus do it, please," Beo replied.

Mito sighed, shook his head, then nimbly untied the gag.

"Thank you," Leah said.

Beo nodded, turning to a third man she hadn't taken notice of before now.

"Doc, got dis? I'd like ta step out before any needle work."

She took a good look at him, and 'the Doc' smiled kindly at her. He was wearing scrubs—looked the part of his name at least. When he replied, Leah scowled in frustration. *Greek maybe.* Whatever the language, it didn't matter, she didn't speak it.

"ight den, 'preciate it," Beo said.

She scowled at all three of the men.

Apparently Mito, The Doc, and Beo were all multilingual but each was still choosing to speak in their own first language. That seemed off. The only one she could understand was Beo, and his English seemed too unpolished for him to also be fluent in Greek and Japanese.

While she was curious what the story was with him, she shook it off, their peculiar communication ranking rather low on her priority list for the moment. There were a thousand bigger questions.

Where the hell am I? came to mind most often, but she desperately didn't want the gag to go back on. She had to start small—innocent. Something that wouldn't feel like probing.

"Why did you call me Red Fury?"

Beo and Mito swapped knowing looks, as though they found this funny. Neither gave an answer. "I've done everything you asked."

"Sha-yeah," Beo chuckled. "Maybe dis go aroun'."

She frowned, but whatever that meant he didn't elaborate.

"Do I . . . recognize you?"

Beo's smile disappeared. He tongued his cheek, then held the gag up and gave it a small shake.

She got the message and nodded. "Sorry."

The Doc came toward her carrying a metal tray. He spoke, and Beo gave a nod before seeing himself out. Mito leaned back against the wall while the Doc started assessing her cut.

"Is . . . is he afraid of blood?" Leah asked.

Both the Doc and Mito looked at one another and shrugged.

"No English," Mito said.

Leah frowned at the two and sighed. "Okay . . ."

Talking having suddenly become a dead end, her mind wandered as the Doc set about inspecting her arm.

So, I've swapped being The Cell's prisoner for being . . . what exactly? Jonathan's prisoner? The alien's?

She wasn't as upset about the circumstances as someone else in her position would have been. She'd known she had to escape The Cell eventually and hadn't had the foggiest idea how she was going to manage it.

But, had her situation improved or only taken a lateral shift? From the one-sided half of Beo's conversation she'd overheard it sounded like he hadn't wanted to bother Jonathan—or anyone 'up da chain' with whatever he was supposed to do with her.

While all this fluttered through her mind, a bigger revelation hit her.

"I teleported," Leah whispered out loud.

Mito and the Doc looked up briefly but neither appeared to understand. She stared at her knees and thought it through.

Up until now, the only living being to disappear and ever be seen again was the alien. But clearly, humans could do this. When Jonathan took her and Rivers tonight, she must have disappeared in front of Olivia just as Peter had disappeared two years ago in front of her. And, here she was—*alive.*

This meant there was a chance that her brother and Rylee had done the same. Yet that hope sparked out as soon as she considered it. She remembered Jonathan falling apart after Rylee had vanished.

She was pulled from her thoughts by a tap on her shoulder. The Doc was miming at her; a sympathetic grimace on his face as he held up a bottle of alcohol and a needle. She looked down to where he had already cut away part of her sleeve.

She'd been right. A stray bullet must have slashed open the skin over her triceps. Now that she could see the wound was worse than she'd expected.

"I get it," Leah said. "This is gonna hurt."

He was alone when he reached the center of Hangman's Tree. There, on a raised platform, Mr. Clean had shaped a large pavilion enclosed with glass windows. Not far off to one side, the large black egg was held in place by two massive vises that rose out of the floor.

Where the egg's front entry had once been there was now a large hole. Jonathan had heard Mr. Clean cutting through the exterior. Now that he saw the perfect circle, it left him to picture that some elaborate series of guided lasers had done the work. He knew the reality was less exciting. Mr. Clean had a precision no human being could match and could have cut that circle with a rusty chain saw.

As he made his way up the pavilion's stairs, he stepped over the oversized steel shackles The Cell had placed on Heyer's body. They clearly hadn't given the AI much trouble either. He was still barefoot, the cut over his eyebrow needed stitches, and he hadn't even changed out of the bloody prison outfit.

Finally, he reached the glass and saw Heyer lying on a small exam table inside. The alien was covered to the chest with a white sheet. Anthony Hoult stood by, his concerns thinly veiled. Mr. Clean's cartoon avatar displayed on a halo of screens over the alien's exam table.

Anthony looked up when Jonathan slid the glass door open. He wore a measure of uncertainty as he offered his hand. "I know you've met me a dozen times by now, but this is the first time I've had the pleasure."

"Pleasure is all mine, Anthony," Jonathan said, shaking the man's hand.

It was a strange experience, interacting with someone who is—to you—a stranger. Olivia and Rivers hadn't believed him when he told them he'd been friends with their shadows in The Never—Anthony had the advantage of knowing it would be the case. Jonathan had exchanges with everyone on these premises. His friends, his new allies, those he would have as his allies, people who hadn't ever heard his name—even Mr. Clean. Jonathan had come to know things about all of them that they didn't, or in some cases couldn't, know about themselves.

Jonathan wasn't immune to the experience. All the men who'd had a part in his rescue had met at least two different versions of his shadow. The one deteriorating beneath the influence of the severed bond, and the one who walked away from twenty-eight fights with the Ferox miraculously cured of it.

Jonathan took a place opposite Anthony at the exam table. Heyer was in far worse shape than when they had been captured. His breaths were so shallow that from one moment to the next Jonathan was uncertain he hadn't ceased breathing altogether. Cheeks and eyes sunken, cracked dry lips, a pale purple to the tips of his fingers. Truth be told, the body looked more like a corpse than a man in a coma.

That, and his cuts and wounds from inside The Never hadn't healed. They had scabbed over or been stitched shut like they would for any normal man. If they pulled him through this, Heyer would have scars.

Jonathan turned his attention to the three thick cable-like connections that hung down from the ceiling. To his knowledge, there were very few instances in which Mr. Clean could not wirelessly interface with a piece of Borealis technology. For somewhat obvious reasons, the bracer was one of them. His species had designed the bracer primarily to inhibit a Borealis prisoner—one wouldn't want a pair of handcuffs that could be hacked and disengaged from a distance.

Two of the cables were fused to the bracer. To the human eye, the cables appeared to have been welded rather than connected. The truth was more complicated. Like the bracer, Mr. Clean's physical body was Borealis technology. As such, the AI could mimic the molecular makeup of the bracer as he made contact. This allowed the AI to communicate with the device almost as though it were a part of him.

The third connection ended in a flat triangle that rested across the surface of Heyer's chest. The shape crossed all three lines and glowed with the same white energy that radiated from the alien's implant when it functioned normally. There was an almost organic quality to the point of connection, as though that segment of Mr. Clean was temporarily a hybrid of biological and nonbiological components in order to interact with Heyer's implant.

"How many of Cede's encryption matrices remain?" Jonathan asked.

"I will be through the last in a few moments," Mr. Clean said.

There was nothing left for Jonathan or Anthony to do. They watched helplessly, waiting for Mr. Clean to tell them if he'd succeeded or failed. It was no accident that they were the only humans present. Jonathan had given each member of the extraction teams tasks. Mostly things that they all likely knew could have waited, but he wanted them all busy somewhere else when the dampener came off. The truth was, the six who had been most involved with the rescue likely knew as much as Jonathan. He had no control over what possible outcomes they had seen in their various runs through The Never. But the shadow version of Heyer often succumbed to complications associated with the removal.

The problem wasn't the dampener alone, but the containment field he'd been kept in. The shell interfered with the Borealis implant's ability to replenish its power supply from its surroundings. Coupling that with the dampener, Heyer's implant had been rationing its remaining energy to sustain minimum life support. Should the worst follow, it wasn't just the morale of everyone setting foot in Hangman's Tree that he had to protect. If Heyer died, the last thing they wanted was for Malkier to learn of it.

For Jonathan, there was another harsh reality. He knew the men who would sleep in Hangman's Tree tonight were decent people. They would do what Heyer asked of them because the alien was the hope they'd put their faith in.

But they didn't know him.

Heyer, he fit a mold in the men's minds. He was wisdom, immortality, and power. He was more than a man. Just being what he was, and siding with humankind, gave them hope.

Jonathan knew the one thing they didn't.

While Heyer would do all he could to save humanity, he wouldn't have needed Jonathan if he was going to be there to fight this war beside them.

Some would accept Jonathan's leadership for no other reason than Heyer had told them he was their salvation. But too many of them had too much in common with Jonathan Tibbs himself. They had survived as long as they had against the Ferox because early on they decided not to wait for someone to come save them. These men, they were Earth's greatest assets. But, if Heyer died tonight, they would also be the hardest for Jonathan to bring in line.

"I'm through the final matrix. Beginning extraction," Mr. Clean said.

The sight of what began taking place beneath the skin of Heyer's arm was unsettling. Small thread like appendages, hundreds of them, released their grip on internal fibers, disconnecting from muscle, veins, and nerve endings. It was like watching a fistful of tape worms all suddenly migrate in one direction toward the bracer.

Jonathan looked down on Heyer's face and saw the alien twitch as though feeling pain despite being unconscious. A second after the things moving inside his arm disappeared beneath the band, there was a sudden clank. The metal had split unceremoniously down the center and fallen on to the table. Heyer was bleeding beneath, the skin looking like bloody Swiss cheese all around the arm. Anthony was quick to start placing a bandage.

For a while, Heyer's condition didn't change. They waited as the seconds ticked by in a cruel malaise. Finally, they saw the relief in one another's eyes when ever so slowly the lines of light across Heyer's chest stopped thrumming in and out. The muted blue light steadied and began to glow brighter. Beneath the cable connecting Heyer's implant to Mr. Clean, the soft yellow glow Jonathan remembered began to return.

Wounds began to heal before their eyes, but the skin left behind was not left unmarred. Rather, for the first time in two decades Heyer's body would have new scars. As the sickly color faded from his face, his breathing grew stronger.

Soon, there was a fluttering beneath his eyelids.

"How's he doing?" Jonathan asked.

"The Borealis device is undamaged. Life signs are improving. I don't think it wise to make any attempt to wake him," Mr. Clean said. "We should allow him to regain consciousness in his own ti—"

"I am awake . . ." Heyer whispered, though he'd hardly moved. "Jonathan . . ."

"I'm still here, Old Man," Jonathan said. "Don't try to talk, just take it easy for a bit."

The alien's eyes tightened briefly, but then seemed to relax, and he drifted back off.

A moment later they were alone outside the Pavilion.

"Let's not let anyone see him until he's himself again," Jonathan said.

"I agree," Anthony said.

"How did things go with the rest of our people tonight?"

He didn't have to ask which people Jonathan was referring to. Jonathan had ordered every man under surveillance extracted—regardless of what country or who the people doing the watching were.

While The Cell was primarily based inside the US, it had operations all over the world. That said, they were not the only clandestine organization with eyes on Heyer's contacts. Equivalent entities with equivalent directives reported to foreign governments all over the globe. Investigations much like the one that had monitored Jonathan had been ongoing—at least until tonight's escape went into motion.

There was a total of fifty-seven men brought in.

"Per the plan, we started extracting them before we launched our operation at the Facility," Anthony said. "They've all been yanked out of whatever normalcy their lives had. A lot of them didn't know that there were others. Of those who did, most knew little of the full scope of Heyer's operation. A few have heard your name."

Jonathan nodded knowingly.

"You don't look surprised," Anthony said.

"These were the men he knew to be under surveillance. On a good day, Heyer tells people the absolute minimum they need to know. I can only imagine how in the dark this first group is." Jonathan glanced through the glass where Heyer rested on the other side and sighed. "I used to hate him for it, but now that things are escalating . . . I understand the necessity."

He turned back to Anthony. "Moving forward, protocol doesn't change. Anyone with a device, other than Heyer or myself, is on a need-to-know basis."

Anthony nodded. "We'll get away with that for a while. But a lot of these guys aren't the docile sort. We shouldn't let their imaginations go too long without any answers."

"It's on my ever-growing to-do list, Mr. Hoult. Tonight, there is something I won't put off. Make sure everyone we've brought in has a bunk and a meal."

Anthony nodded and Jonathan turned to go, but he barely made two steps before a thought stopped him. "Since they were brought in, has anyone disappeared?"

"One," Anthony said. "His device returned to the Armory earlier this evening. They . . . they all knew what it meant. No one panicked."

Jonathan took a long breath. "What was his name?"

"David Scholtz," Tony said.

Jonathan was quiet for a long moment, looked as though he were chewing on this information. "Where are they now?"

On the table in front of him was an empty pack of Funyuns and a giant orange rubber spoon duct-taped to a bathroom key. Sam figured that there was a gas station attendant in Alaska that thought he was a pretty huge tool by now.

While Sam wasn't sure where he was, he was certain he was still on Earth. Like everyone else, he'd arrived on a platform surrounded by flood lights in the middle of a forest clearing. Shortly after, he'd been escorted here, a room that reminded him of his high school cafeteria. Though, from the number of currently unoccupied seats, this place was meant to feed a lot more than currently present.

There were a few doors in and out. They weren't guarded and Sam didn't feel like a prisoner. Yet, no one had tried to leave. If everyone was like him, then they knew they had been brought here for something important. Perhaps, wandering off into the wilderness in the middle of the night might be something to consider after hearing what that reason was.

As everyone around him was a stranger, he sat by himself at a table. He wasn't alone; many of the others seemed more comfortable by themselves. He kept his head down, tried to observe without drawing attention.

All men, but no one looked under eighteen or over forty. He got the sense that many had a military background. Some looked like they'd been brought here in the middle of active duty.

They seemed to have come from all over the world. Sometimes clothing made it obvious, other times Sam realized it when they spoke. The one thing they all had in common was that they arrived with teleportation sickness.

Some weren't comfortable alone. They grouped together and spoke in whispers. From what Sam overheard—if they were speaking English—the road that led here tonight was similar for everyone. They had been contacted by someone calling himself Mr. Clean—an agent of the alien. The men that had escorted them into this mess hall had been dressed in combat attire. They hadn't said much. Only that they were safe, the sickness would pass, and that everyone needed to sit tight and wait for orders.

A while had passed now since there had been any new arrivals.

There wasn't a lot of conversation now. The room had been quiet since one of the strangers disappeared. Until tonight, Sam hadn't known there were others. Now he was in a room full of people he knew had understood. A man, just like them, had been killed by a Ferox inside The Never. None of them had ever witnessed it firsthand, but they all knew. Otherwise, a man disappearing like that would have caused panic. If they were like him—they'd just found out they weren't alone and there was already one less of them.

Before this silence, there was a name that Sam had heard amongst the whispers: *Jonathan Tibbs*. He didn't know who the man was or why they spoke of him.

Not long after the disappearance, the doors opened and three men walked in. He recognized the two that took places on either side of the door, they had been amongst those who had been at the platform when he arrived. He'd never seen the third. The man looked like he'd had a particularly rough evening.

He was in all white clothes, smudged with dirt and blood. He had a fresh cut over his eye that looked like it had just been sewn shut. Sam could hear his bare feet on the floor until he reached the center of the room. He stopped, his eyes slowly passing over each of them.

He held up one hand, the gesture one that seemed to say bear with me a moment. A few seconds later Sam felt a twitch in his chest.

No, come on! Not now! The worst damn timing ever! He thought.

As he looked around the room, he saw this thought reflected on the faces of everyone. Like every last one expected to collapse to the floor as their implant activated. Yet, to Sam and seemingly everyone else's surprise, the seconds kept right on ticking away and no one dropped.

He did feel something though. A chill crawled up his spine. Just as that experience might have become unnerving, he looked to the man standing at the center of the room and saw he still held a steadying hand.

He didn't say the words, but he looked as though he was aware of what was happening and wanted them to know they were safe. To stay calm. The sensation finally passed, and the man waited for the room to shake the feeling off.

Finally, he spoke.

"The other day," he said. "I was activated. I had to go deal with this Ferox, as one in our occupation must from time to time . . ."

He paused, and it seemed a strange place to do so, but he looked as though he were testing the room. Sam noticed that over half the men now looked back at him with wide eyes. He felt left out, like he was missing something, until a stranger sitting at the table behind him whispered, "entendí."

Sam didn't speak Spanish, but then he heard his own internal voice say, *"I understood."* He smiled, because he had a pretty good idea what had just happened. He'd heard the words of the Ferox translate. This was the first time the words of another human being had done so.

"So," the man standing at the center of the room went on. "I get into it with this big red bastard. At first, nothing out of the ordinary. But it isn't long before I realize—damn—he's a talker."

Some of the men were nodding now.

"I can tell that at least some of you have been there. You're fighting an extra-dimensional monster . . . and he won't shut the hell up."

Sam smiled, mostly in a disarmed sort of way. After a weird night, it felt like he was watching a stranger do stand up.

"Now, if you've been there, you already know what the Red was dying to tell me?"

"Il suo nome?" one of the men sitting closest to the man asked. *His name?*

"That's right, my friend," the speaker said. "It took him awhile, he really had to build up to it. But finally, he says it . . ."

The man shook his head. "I am *Soils the Ground*."

"He says it with that pride they have, as though, *surely* I've heard of his exploits and am now starstruck. But, in my head, the translation is odd, you see I hear the words, but I get this sense of them. Like, the real meaning of this Red's name is . . . *Craps on Floor*."

More smiles cracked on the faces sitting around the room.

"Sorede anata wa nani o shita nodesu ka?" another of the strangers asked. *So, what did you do?*

"I kept a straight face," the man said. "I was raised to be polite, and *Mr. Poops on Floor* is very proud. He asks me: have I been given a name? So, I look back into those white eyes and I tell him . . ."

The man paused, then shrugged. "'Yeah, they call me *Breaks the Wind*."

Sam laughed.

Some of the faces looked a bit confused. He figured it meant one of two things. Either the Human to Human translation had some of the same flaws as the Ferox to Human, or some of these men were just in no mood for fart jokes.

When those who did laugh quieted, the man stood straighter. The change wasn't abrupt, but he looked thoughtful, and his tone went from light to serious.

"If you're in this room, I know what you've seen. I know what they've done to draw you out. To get to you. Everyone here has one thing in common. At some point, a big blond alien showed up. Ever since, you've been fighting monsters no one else knows exist.

"Tonight, most of you are finding out you aren't alone. Knowing this, you're all wondering the same thing. Why are we all in this room? Why now?

"The Ferox call me *Brings the Rain* . . ."

Sam's eyes widened. *Brings the Rain . . . the Rain Bringer.* He'd never really known what the hell the Ferox were talking about. Mostly they asked if he knew *The Rain Bringer*. Sam didn't know if the man was real, or some legend. He'd never been altogether certain that they were even talking about a human. That said, one thing was always clear, every Ferox wanted a piece of this *Brings the Rain*. They all wanted to be the one who killed him.

Sam wasn't alone. Other men around the tables wore the same look of recognition.

"My real name is Jonathan Tibbs. Most of you have never heard . . ." Jonathan said.

He trailed off on that thought, looking around, to each of their faces.

"But I am the one who brought you here. I couldn't give you much warning. Whether you've been aware of it, you were each being watched by your government. I had to get you clear and had to do so in such a manner that by the time the first of you was reported missing the last of you was already safe.

"Now, I know the question you all want answered is why? Why are we here now?

"You're waiting for me to say it—but you know the answer. Ever since you started killing monsters, you knew it couldn't go on like it was. One day the Ferox would come for Earth and they weren't going to form a line and let you take them on one at a time. You were certain that if you lived to see that day, it would be your last.

"I thought the same thing. But turns out, we were only half right. You see . . . the Ferox are coming, in force, and they intend to wage war."

He let that sink in for a bit.

"But, yesterday, you and I were alone. Tonight, everything changes, and tomorrow we gather the rest of our brothers from all over the world. Starting now, we are no longer a temporary stop gap. We aren't a shield between the Earth and the Ferox."

His voice grew louder, "We are no one's last stand. You are the first to whom I make a promise. Fight with me, and we will destroy the gates forever."

CHAPTER THIRTY

JONATHAN LEANED HIS forehead against the tile. Warm water washing away caked blood and dirt. For a moment, his mind went luxuriously blank.

He sighed, because even with his eyes closed, he sensed the light come on in front of him. "Mr. Clean, let's restrict interruptions to emergencies while I'm in the shower."

"My apologizes, but you instructed me to wait until you were alone."

He groaned. "That, I did. Just let me get clothes on for this."

A moment later, a trail of wet footprints followed him out of the shower to a row of lockers. He'd opened one at random. They all contained the same supplies: toiletries, and various sizes of everyday clothing. All practical stuff Anthony's company bought in bulk to stock the location.

The second Jonathan reached for a pair of boots, Mr. Clean's avatar appeared once more. The display was large, felt like a full-length mirror had appeared over the lockers behind him, except when he turned to look Mr. Clean was the reflection. He raised an eyebrow at the AI. "Is this really so important it can't wait for me to tie my shoes?"

"The woman," Mr. Clean began. "After her injuries were dressed, she was taken to a holding cell."

Jonathan winced. "They locked her up?"

"Beo reasoned you wouldn't want a government agent wandering the facility," Mr. Clean said.

Jonathan considered. "That's . . . fair enough. Thank you, I'll see to her as soon as I can."

"Forgive me, but her imprisonment was not the more urgent matter," Mr. Clean said.

"What is it then?" Jonathan asked.

The AI seemed to hesitate. "Heyer is not yet conscious. In our previous exchanges I've failed to speak of individuals with whom you possessed an emotional attachment with the proper finesse. I fear—"

"Just go ahead, Mr. Clean," Jonathan interrupted, as he started lacing a boot. "If your delivery leaves something to be desired, I'll get over it."

"Yes, well, she was a mystery. Even the records from The Cell's servers we obtained regarding her identity were quite incomplete. Everything they knew about her was listed under her alias: Leah McGuire. Their file indicates that she was an outside contractor brought in over Olivia's objections."

Jonathan listened, nodding as he finished lacing the first boot and began on the next.

"However, because of her injury upon arrival, she bled on me. I took the opportunity to isolate a DNA sample . . ."

Jonathan's hands froze on the laces.

". . . to confirm her identity."

Jonathan didn't say anything. After a few seconds, he took a long breath and continued to lace his boot a bit more slowly.

Mr. Clean continued. "I ran the sample against all known databases to locate a match. I did find one, but the record was not in a human database."

Boots tied, Jonathan stood slowly as he closed the locker door. "I know who she is, Mr. Clean."

The AI stared back at him, miming a look of curiosity.

"I don't know every detail," Jonathan said. "Her shadow told me enough to get the picture."

A second screen formed alongside Mr. Clean. On one, Jonathan saw Leah sitting in her holding cell. Mr. Clean zoomed in on her face and froze the image. On the second screen, images of a young woman dating back years began to scroll by. Mr. Clean was running a facial recognition program but slowing the operation enough for Jonathan to see the process.

"Her eyes haven't changed," Jonathan whispered.

"These are images of Rachel Leah Delacy," the AI said. "As you can see, she has undergone significant cosmetic reconstructions."

"She told me physical alterations were required."

"You still seem surprised."

Jonathan looked at the younger girl. "I . . . I didn't realize the scope."

"The physical changes were primarily to keep facial scans, like the one I'm performing now, from being successful. However, given the nature of her mission, it's fair to assume basic psychology was the secondary motivation."

"Secondary motivation?" Jonathan asked.

"Humans are statistically faster to trust those they find attractive," Mr. Clean said. "She was intent on extracting information from you."

As he understood what the AI was suggesting, a smile met with a grimace on his face. Chagrin unhidden as he nodded. "Yeah, she only mentioned the first reason."

After a moment of silence, Jonathan found the AI's avatar watching him. Mr. Clean wore a cartoonish attempt at sympathy. Then again, Mr. Clean was a cartoon.

"What?" Jonathan asked.

"I'm detecting that you feel a lingering sense of humiliation after having trusted an undercover agent. I thought, perhaps, knowing I failed to identify her as well might alleviate the sense of shame—"

The AI trailed off as Jonathan's expression melted into a glare. "I'm fine."

"I calculate an eighty percent chance that you are being insincere, likely due to previously stated humilia—"

"Mr. Clean," Jonathan interrupted. "You found a matching DNA profile while The Cell couldn't. Why?"

"Rachel Delacy was previously a person of interest to Heyer. My on-board files can only be deleted by myself, the same is not true of any human database. However, hiding her identity in the human world was by no means a simple computer keystroke. It was a process that was planned out and implemented incrementally over two years following the reported death of Rachel Delacy."

"Her shadow said her death was staged."

"Yes, but rather impressively. Convincing enough that neither Heyer nor myself questioned the fatality's legitimacy."

Jonathan shrugged. "Why would you. People die all the time."

"When a person we are actively tracking dies, we investigate the events," Mr. Clean said. "However, Rachel Delacy was confirmed dead by suicide. We failed to scrutinize the event because, sadly, the outcome was not wholly unexpected. Months prior, a series of unfortunate events had resulted in her seeking psychiatric intervention."

Jonathan studied the AI for a moment. His head tilted as though he'd just now realized something. "Mr. Clean, are you embarrassed that she managed to move in next door to me without either of you noticing?"

His avatar displayed an appropriate degree of indignance. "Heyer did notice something familiar about her. But she was three years older, had undergone dramatic physical—"

Jonathan held up a hand to stop him.

"It's okay, Mr. Clean," Jonathan said, then with a touch of smugness. "I understand that certain psychological mechanisms were leveraged against the two of you."

Mr. Clean was silent for a moment.

"I believe I now understand why my previous attempt at sympathy may have come off as condescending," Mr. Clean said.

Jonathan smiled. "So, why wasn't The Cell able to figure this out either?"

"That is where this becomes interesting," Mr. Clean said. "It appears that at first the bureaucratic minutia surrounding a human fatality was allowed to play out. A Death Certificate was made, a funeral held, insurance policies paid out or canceled, mail stopped, bank accounts closed. Months later, someone began chipping away at any record that might confirm Rachel Delacy had ever existed. Eventually, the only people who would have known she'd ever lived were those with actual memories of her. These people had no reason to notice when records started disappearing from databases and filing cabinets."

Jonathan nodded along. "So, the short version, you were as convinced as everyone else she was dead until she showed up here and bled on you."

Mr. Clean was quiet for a moment. When he spoke again, he chose his words carefully. "Jonathan, clearly you have been aware of a lot of this information. Yet, you refrained from divulging a majority of this to the extraction team. My inference is that your intention was to keep this woman's identity unknown to us."

Jonathan took a long breath.

"General William J. Delacy had the resources to implement an identity eraser of this scale. Leah and her father's involvement with The Cell wasn't a choice they made to acquire alien tech—it was a rescue mission.

"I don't need to tell you," Jonathan said. "You're aware of how and why Peter Delacy died on September 1st, 2003."

Jonathan had never been sentimental about dates. Still, with enough time in The Never, he'd put it together. When her shadow told him the date of her brother's disappearance, he'd realized it was the same date, weeks earlier, that she had come to see him in his garage. She said she didn't want to be alone that night. *She didn't want to think about what day it was.*

Mr. Clean nodded. "Yes, General Delacy's first born son—Leah's brother. The police report filed that night is still in my records. Rachel claimed that her brother vanished in front of her."

"Yeah," Jonathan said with a shake of the head. "When Heyer gets it wrong, he really gets it wrong."

"I . . . I don't follow," Mr. Clean said.

"Heyer said once that he didn't worry that someone would notice if I just disappeared," Jonathan said. "He said that for the most part people would convince themselves that they'd remembered wrong. If they didn't, no one would believe them. Eventually they wouldn't believe themselves.

"Leah never stopped believing what she saw with her own eyes . . ."

"That does appear to be the case," Mr. Clean said. "But . . . you know that she wasn't a person of interest because of her witnessing the disappearance of Peter Delacy."

Jonathan nodded.

"So, you did intend to keep her identity from—"

"No," he said.

"I don't understand," Mr. Clean said. "All logic indicates this is a top priority."

"I knew there was no keeping it from you. But I didn't want—I can't have this discussion tonight."

Jonathan closed his eyes. He took a while before speaking. "Mr. Clean, I had all the time I could ever have asked for to plan. But . . ."

He shook his head.

"I still don't know what to do about her."

Jonathan climbed the stairs and stepped in front of the door he'd been dreading all night. He did not want to come here unless he was sure that any problem remaining could wait until morning. Once inside, he didn't intend to leave until he was asked.

When he knocked, Shane opened the door.

"Thank you for waiting with him," Jonathan said.

He nodded, stepping outside to let Jonathan by, then shut the door behind him.

Like many of the cargo containers, this one was a mobile barracks. This one just happened to be furthest out from anything else in Hangman's Tree.

Jonathan had ordered it be kept unoccupied for as long as possible. In the days to come, he wanted its single resident to have as much privacy as he could give.

Mr. Silva didn't know any of that.

He was pacing anxiously when Jonathan entered and looked as though he may have been doing so for a long time before he'd arrived. He stopped, a look of recognition on his face when he saw Jonathan. "You're Evelyn's kid. She showed me a picture."

Jonathan nodded, then stepped away from the door into the room. He held out his hand. "Jonathan Tibbs."

"Joao Silva."

Joao shook his hand, but not without hesitation. Jonathan didn't begrudge him, the man had every reason to be nervous after what he'd been through tonight.

"They tell me you're in charge here."

Jonathan nodded. "That's . . . that's not important right now."

He backed up a step and took a seat on one of the bunk beds.

He held out a hand to the bunk across from him, inviting Joao to sit with him.

"Look, Jonathan, I've seen enough tonight to know I'm out of my depth. I don't want to be mixed up in any of this, and I don't plan on being any kind of problem to you or your people."

"You aren't in any danger, Joao," Jonathan said. "No one here wants to harm you."

Joao nodded, but the anxiety didn't leave his eyes. "But, I'm not exactly free to go either?"

Jonathan shook his head and sighed. "No, I can't let you go yet. I suppose that makes you a prisoner. It's a predicament. I don't have a quick solution, but I promise you'll go home safe as soon as possible."

Understandably, Joao was less than comforted by the answer.

"All I want is my daughter. Everyone says you're the only one who knows where she is. Please, tell me, point me in the right direction, you have my word you'll never hear from either of us again."

Jonathan closed his eyes. He tried to keep his face from contorting in grief, but he was already beginning to fail.

"I ordered Shane not to speak of her. It had to be me . . ."

The alien never had to go through this part.

". . . Joao, I owe your daughter my life . . ."

Heyer's soldiers disappeared—and that was that.

". . . the world owes her . . ."

No one told the parents. The spouses. The brothers and sisters. No one ever got a reason.

"Your daughter . . . Rylee . . . she's . . ."

They were just gone.

CHAPTER THIRTY-ONE

DATE | TIME: UNKNOWN | FEROXIAN PLANE

"THE BLEEDING HAS stopped," Cede said.

Malkier, consumed with concentration, returned to the present. He looked down and pondered the shape of black smears on the floor of Cede's inner sanctum.

His blood—he'd ignored that slow drip from the opened scar on his face until it had ceased on its own. Hadn't noticed that as he paced back and forth his own feet had tracked it, smeared his black footprints until they had formed a triangle on the cave's floor.

The war had begun less than seventy-two hours ago, and at each vertex of that blood triangle, Cede displayed all they knew of the events that had followed. Each represented one of his opponent's opening moves.

Three isolated incidents from which he was to see his brother's game.

As a machine of war, the Ferox were a locomotive. Whatever stood in their tracks would be obliterated. The operator of a locomotive didn't worry about blind spots—what might come at him sideways. The only direction of consequence was forward.

After hours of pacing his triangle, two things were certain.

His brother was laying a boulder on the tracks and he would not allow Malkier to learn the size or shape of it. This made the next move his, and it came to one question: Did Malkier believe there was anything Heyer could do to stop him?

He had believed his brother's capture had saved him from needing an answer. Without Heyer, Malkier's leadership and ancestral technologies would allow the Ferox to crush Earth's resistance easily. Even the small army of enhanced human combatants was little more than a nuisance.

However, his brother's allegiance had never been a foregone conclusion. Having grown suspicious of Heyer's activities for some time, the story brought to him by Grant Morgan's shadow had finally relieved Malkier of any further doubts. His brother had chosen humanity over his own blood.

As such, he'd begun plans to deal with a battleground that included his brother. When Heyer had allowed himself to be captured, Malkier had been relieved to know he was off the board.

Then—he'd escaped.

Of the three vertices displayed, the one that held the least mystery was the device his brother activated while prisoner inside of Cede. Heyer's physical form slipping through the security net, while impressive, had been a secondary function. The primary function was that of a beacon. When Heyer had activated the device, a signal was sent from the Feroxian Plane to Earth. A signal telling Mr. Clean to initiate a sequence of events on the human plane. While the consequences hadn't been apparent instantaneously, within a few hours Cede knew that Heyer had severed almost all channels of travel into the human dimension.

For Malkier, this vertex served as a reminder that his brother was putting in motion a scheme he'd been preparing for years. To sever said channels so quickly, Heyer would have had to have traveled to each of the ancient Borealis satellites stationed inside the human dimension and rigged them to be disabled upon activation of the beacon.

Of course, there was one exception—the gateways.

By their very nature, neither Heyer nor his AI could sever them as a point of entry. As long as the gateways remained on the Feroxian Plane surrounded by the Ferox Tribes, they were under Cede's surveillance and control. Had Heyer attempted to tamper with or destroy those gateways his treason would have been revealed long before he accomplished anything of use to his cause.

This move was tactical. Simply Heyer blinding him to what took place on Earth. However, Heyer had pulled a curtain between the dimensions, not a one-way mirror. His brother had now effectively blinded himself to what took place on the Feroxian Plane as well.

That vertex was the least concerning to him. He understood it and required no great feat of imagination to know how it had been done.

The remaining two vertices were a mystery.

The next was all the information they had about the twenty-eight mutilated bodies left on his tribe's gateway. An isolated occurrence thus far as none of the other gateways had become the site of similar massacres. This event was terrifying. Every detail about how it was done was supposed to be impossible.

First was the number dead. At any given time, a gateway's queue seldom exceeded seven. Cede's analysis had confirmed that the bodies represented Ferox from four other tribe's gateways along with his own. This meant that in the time between Malkier's departure and his waking in the breeding pits, five gateways had merged their queues, every Ferox inside had been killed, and all of the remains had been returned to the gateway of the prophet.

No coincidence. This followed immediately after his brother's escape.

No coincidence. Each of those queues had been targeted to *Brings the Rain*.

No coincidence. Twenty-eight bodies, delivered to his doorstep, immediately after he'd killed the woman.

Cede had yet to come up with a theory as to how the AI, Heyer, or even Jonathan Tibbs himself could have put such a thing in motion. But there was no denying the message.

Seeing what befell his people, Malkier had immediately sent word to all the tribe's leaders that no more combatants were to enter the gateways without the prophet's command.

Normally, this would have created tension throughout his people, as this would leave each tribe's Alpha to deliver the news that their gods forbade them to enter the gates. But timing was on the prophet's side. Having already decreed that every available fighter was to join the Pilgrimage, the Ferox understood that they were being gathered to take the Promised Land. On the verge of fulfilling the prophecy that meant salvation for their species—none objected.

That left the Ferox who had already entered the gates. They were beyond his reach, soon to be casualties of a war they did not know had begun. Open war had been declared; a fair fight no longer awaited any who entered The Never.

Until he knew what happened to the twenty-eight—any individual sent into The Never would be selected with great discretion.

Now, Malkier stood at the third vertex—the most troubling of them all.

"Play it again, Cede," Malkier said.

Without a word, Malkier relived the last conversation he'd had with his brother through Cede's projections. His brother's words of warning: *Do not go after Brings the Rain! He can kill you. He is more than the bond, you have no idea how dangerous that man is.*

Malkier stepped on wet floor, reminded again that he had returned from

The Never injured once again. He had survived *Echoes the Borealis*—been able to push the incident out of mind as he awaited the birth of his child. Whatever circumstances had left him temporarily vulnerable, the knowledge of how he'd been harmed died with the father inside The Never. Yet now, somehow—the son had known how to harm him.

Once again, this left no room for coincidence. Heyer's warning made it clear that he had known Jonathan Tibbs to be a threat to him. None of this explained how *Brings the Rain* came to possess the knowledge to hurt him.

A man lived and walked the Earth with the knowledge of how to kill a Borealis. This was unacceptable, but he dared not lead the Ferox to Earth before the situation was resolved.

CHAPTER THIRTY-TWO

LEAH WASN'T SURPRISED. Okay, maybe she was a little surprised but, she knew she shouldn't have been. After her arm was stitched up, Beo and Mito escorted her to a holding room. Nothing quite as fancy as the sterile plastic prison she'd briefly shared with Jonathan, but rather more the mundane. A small room behind a locked door with a bed and the necessities.

Unable to sleep, she'd lain awake so long she assumed it must be morning by now.

The door opened suddenly. There had been no sound of a key disengaging a lock. While she'd never had any intention of escaping, when the door opened so noiselessly, she wondered if the only thing that had kept her in that cell all night had been the honor system.

Jonathan stood in the doorway.

He looked like himself again, cleaned up and wearing ordinary street clothes. Meanwhile, she was still barefoot and wearing the same clothes she'd been rolling through the dirt in when the giant metal worm hit the facility. Still, Jonathan looked as though he may have gotten less sleep than she had last night.

Uncertain, she rose slowly off the bunk. With no idea how the next minutes were meant to go, she waited for him to give her a clue.

"I'm sorry about this, the guys . . . they didn't know what to do with you," Jonathan said.

Leah nodded. "But . . . you do?"

He paused, then shrugged. "I know you don't need to be in here."

With that he stepped back out of the doorway to clear her a path.

Hesitant at first, she began to walk toward the door. When they were an arm's length apart, she frowned at a new scar that ran through his eyebrow. That wound had been as fresh as the one on her arm when they arrived here. Yet, his skin looked as though it had healed weeks ago, while hers was still held shut with stitches.

If he knew what the look she gave him asked, he didn't offer an answer. He seemed to have something else troubling his mind.

"I'm . . . I'm used to calling you Leah, but if you'd rather I didn't?"

She knew what he was asking. Leah was her middle name before it became her deception—her armor. Whether he meant to or not, the thought of him calling her by her birth name would feel like a punishment every time he said it.

"No one calls me Rachel anymore," she said. "Please, just call me Leah."

Where am I? Leah wondered. *Where do you hide a place like this?*

They were still inside some vast warehouse. She couldn't see the full length of the place. That, and some of the building dimensions didn't quite seem to strictly obey the laws of physics. Some rooms seemed to be a part of the actual building, but they walked past rows upon rows of cargo containers that had clearly been integrated more recently.

Jonathan had a seemingly intimate knowledge of the layout. She had no idea how that was possible, considering his every move had been watched by The Cell for months. He'd never been off their radar long enough to be this familiar with the place. Like the scar over his eye, she added it to the list of things she didn't understand about what was going on.

"Are you in any pain?" he asked, looking at the bandage on her arm.

"Oh . . . no, it'll be fine," Leah said.

"Are you hungry?" he asked.

"No . . . not really."

"You lost blood. You should probably eat something."

"I'm fine," she said.

"Well, then maybe a shower and some fresh—"

"Jonathan—" Leah said, then sighed, before starting again. "Jonathan, you're being very kind. Thank you . . . but all I want is answers."

He had a knowing look. "Be patient, I know what drove you all this way, Leah. I'm not the person you came here to interrogate."

A shiver ran though her. "The alien, he's awake?"

"He's still recuperating—was only conscious for a moment," Jonathan said. "But he'll live."

"But you'll let me talk to him?"

"You have my word," he said solemnly.

She didn't know what to say, not immediately. He had just promised to give her the very thing she had been hunting for the last two years—and she believed he meant it. She was struck by the realization that this journey was nearing some end. She didn't notice she'd stopped walking until he looked back at her from a few paces ahead.

"After everything?" Leah asked. "You're just going to help me?"

"I know what it means to you," he said.

Leah blinked, feeling tears forming. So much gratitude mixed with so many questions. Why was he being so kind? Had their roles been swapped, she didn't believe she'd have forgiven him. He acted as though there was no wall between them—when they both knew she'd been lying since the day they met.

"Thank you," was all she managed.

He nodded, and in somewhat classic Jonathan fashion, she immediately sensed that her gratitude had made him uncomfortable. "I wouldn't thank me yet, conversations with Heyer never go the way you hope."

As he turned to go, she watched his back with a familiar curiosity that—apparently—she would never be able to fully turn off. Since that day in the garage, there were times he behaved in a way she didn't recognize, but sometimes that fell away, and the Jonathan she knew was there.

This was one of those moments. Which was how she knew with utter certainty that Jonathan had just evaded something. She had no idea what. At the moment, she didn't want to press her luck. As she caught back up to him, he asked, "Will you reconsider the food and the shower?"

She nodded. "Are you going to tell me what is going on here?"

"Seems I can hardly avoid it now, can I? But there are some things that need my attention. I'll leave you with someone who can answer most of your questions."

She was disappointed. She didn't want to wait and didn't want answers from a stranger. In fact, there were a few questions she wanted him to answer while she could look him in the eye.

"Tell me this, how long have you known who I am?"

He grimaced a bit. "It's complicated."

"Complicated?" Leah asked. "I'm just asking—days? weeks?"

He gave a defeated sounding sigh. "It's a matter of perspective . . . for you, half a day. For me, a few months."

Her eyes narrowed on him as they walked. Four seconds of silence passed before she knew he'd felt her gaze and still hadn't elaborated. "Come on, you knew that wouldn't make any sense."

"Well, I did warn you," Jonathan said. "None of your questions are going to have any simple answers. Might as well try to understand Calculus before learning Algebra."

Her face softened. "Then teach me Algebra?"

"Are you kidding," Jonathan smiled. "I'm terrible at math."

Son of a . . . seriously? How could it be that—somehow—nothing had changed. She might as well still be standing in his driveway desperately trying to get him to open up. Why was he still so walled off after everything she'd seen?

She felt like a shaken soda bottle, ready to explode if she didn't let the pressure out in tiny increments. She took a long breath and released it slowly as they turned a corner and found a woman waiting for them.

Jonathan introduced her as Sydney.

She was dressed in business attire, much like Olivia, but Sydney was older and possessed a much friendlier disposition. That wasn't to say she looked particularly kindly at Leah. Rather, her demeanor was reminiscent of Beo and Mito as they put her in the cell the night before.

Distrustful . . . just short of open hostility.

"Thank you again for doing this," Jonathan said.

"It's no problem, Jonathan," Sydney said.

He turned back to Leah. "I have to go, but Sydney will get you sorted out for the time being."

Leah glanced at the woman doubtfully.

"Wait, you're just leaving me with a complete stranger?"

"We'll talk as soon as I can," Jonathan said.

He was serious, already stepping away.

She followed, grabbed him by the arm. "Jonathan, please, just let me say something."

He stopped, glanced at her hand on his arm and waited.

"You were never just a means to an end," she said. They were words. She meant them, but they sounded so hollow when all her actions had contradicted them.

He took her hand from his arm, held it for a moment. When he spoke, he stared at her hand, avoided her eyes. "I know."

He let go, and she stood staring, watching him leave.

I know? She scowled after him as he retreated. He knew? Couldn't he have elaborated on that? If he had said more . . . something else—anything else—and it might have made sense to her.

"Ms. Delacy," Sydney said, reminding her that she'd been left alone with the woman.

Leah turned back, studied Sydney's face, and sighed. "Well, you don't like me. And clearly don't care if I know it."

Sydney raised a brow, as if considering her next statement for a moment. "You and I account for two thirds of the women here. Jonathan felt it would be more comfortable for you if another woman accompanied you to the showers and your new quarters. Do you know why I drew the short straw?"

Leah shrugged.

"I suspect," Sydney said, "that it was because he does not believe Paige can bear the sight of you at the moment."

"Oh no," Leah closed her eyes. "Paige . . . she's here? She knows—"

"She knows as much as the rest of us, Ms. Delacy," Sydney interrupted. "And why Jonathan is trusting you is a mystery to everyone."

Leah nodded.

A few seconds ticked by, and Leah realized that Sydney was waiting for an answer.

"I . . . I don't know either."

Sydney was quiet, eyes narrowing as she studied Leah, seeming to wonder if her shame was genuine. "If he really was more than a means to an end for you, I suggest staying away from him."

Leah frowned as her eyes met Sydney's.

"Jonathan has made a lot of calls thus far. We haven't understood all of them, but for the most part they seem to have been the right ones. If he is going to succeed, the people in this building need to trust him . . . but no one thinks you should be here. Let alone allowed to set foot outside the brig. So, you claim to care. Don't make yourself a constant reason for people to doubt his judgment."

Leah took a moment to absorb her words. "What he is trying to accomplish? I don't even know what this is. Frankly, I'm getting the feeling Jonathan doesn't want to be the one to tell me."

Sydney sighed. "Well, Jonathan wants you cleaned up, fed, and shown to your quarters. Mr. Clean will then educate you as to what exactly we are trying to accomplish here."

"Mr. Clean?" Leah asked. She recognized the name—The Cell had believed it the alias of a hacker working with the alien. "Who is he?"

"Not a he . . . exactly. Let me put it this way," Sydney said. "You're standing in him."

Morning had come when Anthony looked up and saw the lights across Heyer's chest. For a moment, they seemed to radiate more energy than usual. A second later Heyer's eyes opened.

Anthony stood up from his chair to help the alien as he slowly sat up. A moment later Heyer's legs were hung over the side of the exam table. He noted his lack of clothing as he looked down at the white sheet covering his pale skin.

"Mr. Clean," Heyer said. "You appear to have moved yourself."

The AI's avatar nodded. "Protocol."

Heyer looked to Anthony, as everything took on new meaning. "So, I was captured?"

Anthony nodded. "What's the last thing you remember?"

As Heyer thought for a moment, his expression darkened. "We lost Rylee."

"That was two days ago."

Heyer's expression took such a grim turn, Anthony could practically feel the anxieties surging through the alien's head. "Take it easy, the world hasn't ended . . . yet."

Heyer paused a moment and asked, "What have I missed?"

"The short version. You and Jonathan were taken prisoner by The Cell. Jonathan led an extraction team from the inside. Once we had you out, we couldn't revive you without getting the bracer off."

"Where is Jonathan now?" Heyer said, his face turning grave.

Anthony paused for a moment. "He . . . he's leading."

Heyer's face gave away a lot as he seemed to absorb that answer, his demeanor alternating between doubt and relief. "Leading, despite the broken bond?"

Anthony shrugged. "Well, like I said, that was the short version. But . . . what I know of the longer version still doesn't explain how Jonathan seems suddenly immune to the bond's effects."

"Mr. Clean?" Heyer asked.

The AI's shrug practically mimed the one Anthony had just given him. "I can shed no additional light. You are aware of the records from the Foedrata Arena. Jonathan is the first to recover without intervention."

"No one has simply asked him?" Heyer asked.

Anthony looked uncomfortable for a moment. "Frankly, it's . . . a delicate subject at best. We've been too relieved that he pulled out of it."

Heyer seemed troubled, but after a few moments of contemplation he looked as though he was quite done sitting on the exam table. Then he looked down and recalled his lack of clothing.

"I need clothes, and the longer version of this story," Heyer said.

"Of course," Anthony said. "But before you jump in, there is something . . ."

He trailed off as he knelt and pulled a box from beneath the exam table. It was wrapped in brown paper and tied shut with twine string. Setting it beside Heyer on the exam table, the alien looked at the box, appearing somewhat mystified.

"The team wanted you to have this. Sort of a get-well present," Anthony said. "It was Jonathan's idea; he said you'd lost your armor in The Never."

"My armor?" Heyer asked in confusion.

As Anthony watched the alien look down at the box, he could see an understanding setting in. A warmth came to his eyes.

Despite having lived amongst mankind for centuries, Anthony found himself wondering how seldom the alien had ever received a gift. He'd had a sense of urgency only a moment before, but Heyer's motions slowed as he took the box in his lap.

He was not quick untying the tweed knot or removing the paper. When he finally pushed the lid from the box his smile brightened the room.

Heyer reached inside and slowly lifted out a black hat, a fedora technically. Similar but not identical to his previous one.

"We were thinking less Charlie Chaplin," Anthony said. "More—"

"Walker?" Heyer asked.

Anthony blinked in surprise. "Yeah."

He'd never expected the alien to make the connection. A moment later, he realized that Heyer hadn't. The alien looked just as confused by what he said as Anthony was to hear it. Finally, the alien turned the hat toward Anthony, letting him see that it was adorned with a loop of black leather, where *The Walker* was engraved in that same script Mr. Clean always used to name alien steel weapons.

Heyer looked up from the word, his gaze moving between Anthony and the AI waiting for an explanation.

"He doesn't watch television," Mr. Clean said.

Anthony shrugged at the AI. "Even if he did, *Texas Ranger* was a long shot."

Heyer didn't take long grasping the mechanics of how his rescue from The Cell had been engineered. By the time he'd gotten dressed, he was far more concerned with Anthony's reports of Jonathan's rapid personality fluctuations.

This was only multiplied when he learned of Jonathan's becoming trapped in his queue for twenty-eight activations. By the time he had a decent enough summary of what he had missed to start asking questions, he quickly came to realize that Anthony and, even more stunningly, Mr. Clean lacked a complete picture of what had played out.

It appeared Jonathan had not been willing to share much.

"Where is Jonathan now?" Heyer said.

"He is not currently within my boundaries," Mr. Clean reported.

"Where has he gone?" Heyer asked.

"Early this morning he gave out orders. Mostly to the men from the extraction team with previous military experience. Afterward, he had me activate his implant and requested I transport him into the city to—"

"His implant is active?" Heyer interrupted, closing his eyes. He shook his head as though the sheer volume of information being flung at him was dizzying.

"Jonathan intends to acquire an outside contact," Mr. Clean said. "He expects said contact will be under surveillance by The Cell. I am currently monitoring him for a return signal. He should be back shortly."

Heyer absorbed this. "And, what orders has he given out? We've yet to discuss Earth's defenses."

Anthony's hands came up in a *please don't kill the messenger* sort of manner. "I told him you'd have questions. He assured me that he'd had Mr. Clean record a message to set you at ease until he returned."

Mr. Clean vanished from his display, and a video of Jonathan standing in this very room earlier that morning began to play. To his annoyance, Heyer could see himself still asleep on the exam table in the background.

"Heyer—yes, I'm fully aware of our engagement strategy. Unfortunately, your original plan is obsolete. Good news though . . ."

The recorded Jonathan shot a thumb over his shoulder, pointing to where past Heyer slept behind him. "One of us wasn't napping."

"Napping?" Heyer scowled at the screen. "Is that what he calls a coma?"

". . . we can still salvage your plan. I had to make some changes. Fair warning, you're not going to like any of it."

The recording ended, and Heyer turned to the AI. "Mr. Clean, Jonathan's mind has been through a great deal. Is there any chance his judgment has become—questionable?"

"Uncertain," the AI replied. "His personality is a great deal different from the iteration of Jonathan I've encountered in the past. That said—he is taking the initiative we'd hoped for, is he not?"

Heyer didn't answer.

After a moment, Anthony delicately cleared his throat. "This is as good a time as any. Jonathan called a meeting later today. Said our presence would be required. He, um . . . also said you might want to prepare yourself, so you aren't surprised to see who else he's asked to join us."

Heyer looked as though nothing could surprise him at this point. "Did he? And just who else will be in attendance?"

CHAPTER THIRTY-THREE

OCT 16, 2005 | 7 AM | JBLM FACILITY

A HELICOPTER ROARED past as Olivia stepped to the edge of a cavernous hole. She hadn't slept. Assuming she would be relieved of duty any moment, she figured she'd have plenty of time for that afterward. She sighed. If that were the inevitable decision, she wished Command would send the order down and be done with it.

She was wearing boots that came up to her knees and had just stepped through mud deep enough to warrant them. The rain had kept up most of the night and turned the area into a miserable sludge.

The hole she was looking down at marked the location where the UTO—Unidentified Tunneling Object until a better name for the giant mercury worm was decided—had begun drilling its way down during last night's siege. The small grove behind the hangar's perimeter was now caked in mud beneath the canopy. The UTO had been capable of spitting earth out of its back end while it tunneled, even when it had reached depths well below the surface. Yet, it had not needed the tunnel to escape. It had disappeared shortly after it consumed the alien's containment shell.

The UTO had left behind a passage leading all the way out of the facility. Fortunate, because had this not been the case, Olivia and the rest of The Cell would still be underground waiting for rescue teams to dig them out.

Her people had been walking the length of the passage with flashlights while others kept the rest of the base's personnel from getting too close. Experts were telling her that the entry point hadn't been random. The UTO had dug down with an exacting precision. Taken a route through the earth such that none of the facility's foundations would be put at risk. That, and the tunnel itself was sloped so a person could walk it without needing to climb muddy walls in the dark. They had even found supports, thick braced metal girders, left behind in places to ensure the tunnel didn't collapse.

In other words, it was as though the tunnel had served two purposes. Facilitate her prisoners' escapes, but also make sure her people weren't left trapped below.

So thoughtful of Jonathan and his allies to go to the extra trouble.

Mankind is going to depend on whether you can take a leap of faith . . . faith in me.

His words were one of a thousand thoughts going through her mind as she traipsed through the muddy tunnel. Eventually she stepped into the chamber that had held the alien's shell until last night.

The power was back up, and the room's lighting still intact enough that she no longer needed the flashlight as she stepped in through the gaping hole in the wall. She walked across a floor covered in muddy footprints and bullet casings, side stepping areas so ravaged during the attack that it appeared gas fissures had erupted beneath them. Where there had once been a level surface supporting the massive containment shell, all that now remained were the mounting brackets.

One of her analysts came out of the tunnel and approached her, as she stared at the empty space. "Was about to radio you, ma'am."

"Communications are back up then? Good, I need to make contact with Command," Olivia said.

"Won't be necessary," the analyst said. "He's here."

Olivia glanced at her sideways. "On base?"

"Upstairs, asking to speak with you immediately."

That was quick, Olivia thought.

Olivia sighed and looked back into the tunnel behind her. "Please, tell me there is a faster way to the surface."

The analyst gave her a sympathetic shrug.

Something had changed.

Olivia had never had a true face-to-face with Command. Until the alien was apprehended, there had always been precautions in place to protect their identities. This was meant to insulate pentagon officials from accountability should The Cell's less lawful operations become public knowledge. In regard to investigating The Mark, anonymity had also been intended to keep the alien from learning their chain of command.

The past few day's events indicated that such efforts had been laughably ineffective. Perhaps her commanding officer meeting with her in person meant that he had drawn the same conclusion.

"General," Olivia said, closing the door behind her as she stepped into the private room.

She recognized General William J. Delacy on sight. No surprise to either of them. For Olivia to do her job she had to know the major players in Washington and that certainly included its highest-ranking generals.

Delacy stood courteously upon her entry, then held out a hand to offer her the seat across from his at the table. He wasn't a young man, but his current state made him look older than he was. There was a frailness to him. A vulnerability that she'd not sensed from any of his public photos. She wondered if she wasn't the only one expecting to face career devastating consequences for last night's escape.

"Before we get into this mess, be advised that I gave the go-ahead for the team Rivers assembled in Libya," Delacy said.

"I had intended to do the same, Sir."

The General studied her. "What does your gut tell you?"

"Jonathan didn't need us chasing down a dead end for his escape to be successful last night. I believe there is something out in that desert Mr. Tibbs actually wants us to see," Olivia said.

"We agree then," Delacy said.

He sat back in his chair and sighed.

"Olivia, despite what you may think, I'm not here to relieve you of duty," General Delacy said. "If anything, we need to be on the same page more than ever."

Olivia's pause was brief; it was the only tell that betrayed that this conversation had already taken a very unexpected turn. "I am in one hundred percent agreement, Sir."

"Good, because I am going to be asking for your discretion, and in return you will have mine."

"My discretion, Sir?"

The General took a long breath and templed his fingers on the table. "You have a team currently investigating why the failsafe charges didn't fire last night. I need you to discontinue that investigation."

They both knew his request didn't follow protocol—let alone make any sense. Luckily, Delacy didn't force Olivia to politely point these things out.

"There was no malfunction or tampering. Jonathan and his people had no . . . direct . . . hand in it," Delacy said. "I disabled the detonator."

The General's confession had filled the room with a long silence.

Of the many thoughts that occurred to Olivia in that awkward moment, one rose to the forefront as though it had been seeded in her mind for just this occasion.

Jonathan had not lied to her. He'd said his people could disable the trigger, but that they would not. He never said that one of her people wouldn't do this for them.

"General, it's my duty to ask . . ."

Delacy held up his hand. "You don't need to explain. You have a right to answers if I'm going to ask you to keep volatile secrets. But let's be clear here. I could have kept this to myself. Let the blame for last night's escape fall on your shoulders and had you replaced. I won't pretend that scenario would have been a picnic to explain to the Joint Chiefs—but, it is a storm I can weather."

Perhaps it was how tired they both were. She felt that the General was in no mood to have to read between the lines any more than she was. But from that moment forward, she feigned no politeness. "I do hope you aren't expecting me to be gracious because you didn't try to frame me for your actions."

The General smiled, but his eyes hardened. "Good, we're speaking plainly. So here it is, I want us both to remain in control of this operation."

"Explains why you need my discretion," Olivia said. "Not why I should give it."

"Because we've been compromised."

He couldn't be talking about The Cell or this facility. That would be too painfully obvious to warrant saying. No, he meant the two people sitting in this room.

"I was present, in a manner of speaking, for what transpired during Mr. Tibbs' interrogation—before and after you dismissed the other witnesses . . ." Delacy said, "and before you edited the recordings."

Olivia's face hardened to match the General's.

He was right of course, she'd had no choice but to remove certain portions of her interaction with Jonathan, specifically the spelling demonstration that had clearly produced such a strikingly uncharacteristic reaction from her.

"Now," Delacy continued, "you've had a busy morning and may not be aware, but during last night's siege, all that footage from that interrogation right up to the point the equipment was turned off was erased from the main server and the backups. Whether he meant to or not, Tibbs did you and everyone in that room a favor."

"Sir, in regard to what Jonathan may have been alluding to, I—"

"No," Delacy's voice was firm. "I'm not concerned with what he knew. Only that we both admit he clearly possesses information that gave him some degree of leverage over us."

Olivia's face gave away her distaste for the topic. "Limited leverage. But yes . . ." She trailed off for a moment. "You said, leverage over us."

Delacy sighed and leaned back in his chair, seemingly more at ease now that Olivia saw how their fates were intertwined. "I was here last night during the escape. Jonathan and his allies were aware of my presence and used it to their advantage."

"You mean you were on base, Sir?" Olivia asked.

"Inside this facility," he corrected. "The panic room—only I and a few of the Joint Chiefs know of its existence."

Olivia took a long breath, though from the look on her face she may as well have been breathing fire. Her jaw tightened as she took a moment to calm herself before speaking. "So, it would appear Mr. Tibbs was being honest about yet another detail."

Delacy nodded. "Yes, and I'm fairly certain his mentioning it last evening was for my benefit. He knew I was here, and he wanted me to know it."

Olivia frowned. "Why?"

"Once The Mark was captured, I wanted to observe progress firsthand. Near the onset of last night's siege, I received a call from the surveillance hub in the hangar—a call that ended abruptly. I was asleep at the time. Had I not been woken, I might not have witnessed all of last night's events. The panic room has access to a secondary set of surveillance systems. What is telling, is that while Jonathan's allies infiltrated the primary system, they made a point of leaving the secondary online."

Olivia took a moment processing all of that. Certainly, it explained how Delacy knew what had transpired between her and Jonathan during his interrogation. What remained unknown, was how his presence had played into the escape.

"What advantage did Jonathan and his allies gain from leaving the secondary systems up?"

The General pointed to himself. "They knew that I would be inside that room. That I was awake, watching, and listening. They knew I would override the failsafe trigger."

Olivia leaned forward in her chair and studied Delacy. Given what Tibbs had known about her and her team, she didn't doubt that if leverage to extort the General existed, they could have found it. Still, what could Jonathan have possibly known about Delacy that warranted his committing treason?

"They blackmailed you into disabling the detonator?"

The General closed his eyes and shook his head. "Not in the way you're imagining. I was never approached with an ultimatum. But . . . they did get to me."

"How?" Olivia asked.

The General grimaced the way one might while pulling a thorn out of their skin. "I figured I'd let Jonathan explain it himself."

She cocked her head questioningly at Delacy.

"While our servers were completely erased last night, one file was left behind. Its permissions were restricted to you and me alone. Jonathan wanted to be sure that only the two of us could access it," General Delacy said.

"What was in the file?" Olivia asked.

The General drummed the table with his fist lightly as he studied her. "It would appear that Mr. Tibbs took no chances that his promise to always tell you the truth would ever come into question."

He reached over and turned on a monitor, then navigated through the facility's system files. A very short process considering only one folder containing one file remained. As soon as she saw a video file and its time stamp, she knew.

"The sixth cycle," she said, and the disbelief in her voice was genuine.

In the chaos since the raid, she'd forgotten that Jonathan had promised to tell her what he knew about Leah if she left her in his cell. Now, she understood. He'd always known they would be long gone before she ever had a chance to hear the message he left for her.

The General was right. There was only one reason this file was all that remained. Jonathan didn't want her to be able to say there was a single instance in which he'd lied to her.

This in turn meant one thing was certain. Despite his escape, they weren't done with one another yet. There was an even bigger game being played and he intended for her to be his pawn.

"The video implicates me," Delacy said.

"If you knew it's dangerous to you why show it to me instead of deleting it?"

"I want you and I to remain in control of this operation," the General sighed. "And my gut is giving me a feeling about this kid."

He sighed and closed his eyes. "He could have done this all very differently. I think he needs us here. That he might be manipulating us because we're too stubborn for our own good. I'm worried we should stop resisting."

The General looked down at the table, tapping the surface with his knuckle as he chose his words. "Olivia, when is the last time you took an order you didn't already plan to follow."

Olivia cocked her head. "Other than involving Leah in this investigation?"

"Perfect example," he said. "You disagreed with the order. You nearly overstepped the boundaries of your authority to see it undone. It's the same for me. The Pentagon usually follows my lead."

"You're talking about . . . *control*, Sir," Olivia said.

The General nodded.

"I think Jonathan Tibbs is telling the truth," Delacy said. "You didn't buy his story about an army of monsters—but I looked into the kid's eyes—he believed every word he said. He wants you and me in charge of this operation."

Olivia studied the General for some time, but she didn't understand why he'd come to this conclusion.

"You watch much football, Olivia?" the General asked.

Her lips flattened into a line. "It's not one of my interests, but I understand how it's played."

"Well, when two teams have a practice game that doesn't count toward league play, it's called a scrimmage."

"I'm familiar," Olivia said. "How is this relevant?"

Delacy took a long breath. "I think Jonathan Tibbs invited us to scrimmage with him last night. No one got hurt, just some property damage, but imagine if that had been a league game."

While Olivia didn't particularly disagree with the analogy, she didn't think it warranted as much consideration as the General was giving it.

"Would you say, Jonathan went to extreme degrees to manipulate our every decision? That his allies clearly had the power to come in and take him and the alien out at any time and they could have done it with far less theatrics."

Olivia nodded. "Clearly. But he wanted to scare us. To show us who was in charge. Take some revenge for what he sees as trespasses against him and his family."

"Oh, I'm sure some of it put a smile on his face, but no, I think he would have done it the same even if there wasn't anything personal at play," the General said. "Because despite everything we learned last night, there was one lesson that was most clear."

Olivia raised an eyebrow.

"We don't understand the rules of the game," the General said. "He sat in the middle of a US military base, told us exactly what was going to happen, and we still couldn't stop him."

She considered this for a moment. "For the sake of argument, let's say I agree. Doesn't tell me why?"

He looked her dead in the eye. "We need to consider that it's all true. That this kid is about to fight a war he already knows Earth's leaders can't understand. That he does need our help, but he can't have us second guessing his orders."

"You think he was trying to show us who needs to lead and who needs to follow?" Olivia asked.

The incredulous sound of her voice as she asked the question was hard to miss. The General didn't seem to take it personally. "Olivia. Ask yourself something, now that you've scrimmaged, do you ever want to play against him again?"

Olivia sighed impatiently, letting the disbelief show clearly on her face.

"Speak your mind," he said.

"I think you're grasping at straws. This is ridiculous."

"There is a reason I can see this, and you can't."

"Then that is something I'd like to hear," Olivia said.

"You are predisposed to believe Jonathan is the enemy," General Delacy said, pushing play on Jonathan's recording. "I have reason to . . . hope . . . he is something else."

CHAPTER THIRTY-FOUR

JONATHAN STARED BACK at her calmly, leaving no doubt that he'd known where the camera was. Leah was beside him, her face hidden by her long hair.

"Your name is Rachel Leah Delacy. Daughter of General William J. Delacy. In September 2003 you were the sole witness to the disappearance of Peter Delacy, your brother—"

He went on to tell the story of General Delacy's daughter. Rachel, a young woman believed to have suffered some delusional break. Claiming she'd seen her brother disappear in front of her. Professionals telling her that her mind had made up a story to cope with the real trauma of her brother's disappearance.

Her father would struggle with this narrative. His daughter wasn't prone to fantasies—if anything she had a talent for rooting out the fantasies in others.

His doubt would be enough. Eventually he'd use his position to seek out any possibility that his daughter's version of events was true. Soon, his inquiries would uncover the existence of a long running clandestine operation within the government—The Cell.

An operation centered around a man in a black hat and coat.

This man would be the perfect likeness to the one his daughter had described. The man speaking to her brother the day he had disappeared, who she claimed to have taken a picture of, only to have that picture somehow erased from her phone. They called this man The Mark, but they didn't believe he was a man at all.

Over the two years that followed, the father and daughter would conspire to play a dangerous game. The world would come to believe Rachel Delacy had committed suicide. Shortly after, any sign that she'd ever existed would incrementally be removed from record.

A process, Jonathan pointed out, that Olivia was quite familiar with.

While Rachel's identity was being erased from existence, she underwent a series of plastic surgeries. Meanwhile, General Delacy maneuvered himself to take control of The Cell. Once he had done so, he would reorganize The Cell, reassign most of its agents, and bring in new blood. Olivia would be one of those brought on during this overhaul, and she would be tasked with the implementation of a new protocol.

The secondary protocol—authored by an unknown from the private sector. Alias: Leah.

The protocol would soon prove far more effective than previous measures for the surveillance of persons of interest in connection to The Mark. But it would also establish greater boundaries between Olivia and her superior.

At that point in the story Jonathan had leaned forward. "Olivia, you will discover the identity of your commanding officer tomorrow morning. When that happens, a question you've been asking yourself for some time will be answered. Why did the secondary protocol enforce such draconian measures to keep you, its lead investigator, from knowing the identity of your commanding officer? Reasons laid out in the secondary protocol were all well and good, but clearly futile."

His words hit a nerve.

Olivia had undertaken the effort to keep her CO's identity unknown with the same professional diligence she did any of her responsibilities. But Jonathan's use of the word 'futile' echoed her own thoughts on the matter. If The Mark wanted to learn their chain of command, they could slow him down, but they couldn't stop him.

Now, she saw the real motivation behind those safeguards.

Olivia had once asked to undertake an exploratory exercise—see if The Cell, under her leadership, could identify the private contractor known as Leah. They hadn't succeeded. However, Leah had been brought in by order of her commanding officer. If Olivia had known his identity, she would have examine the General's background for possible leads. In short, she would have figured out the familial connection—and would have been forced to act against her commanding officer for endangering the operation months ago.

General Delacy stopped the playback.

"It's all true," he said. "Leah—Rachel—is my daughter. She is carrying my grandchild."

In the silence that followed a web of subterfuge became visible in her mind, blurry at first, but rapidly becoming clearer with each passing second as every dangling loose end—every mystery surrounding Leah and her commanding officer began to connect.

"Leah and I were the only people who knew about the panic room. That it contained the one exit to the surface should the facility's fail-safes be engaged. I knew what she was facing—what she'd gotten herself into once the child was conceived."

Olivia held up a hand, her mind still racing to make sense of it all.

"You meant for her to escape," Olivia said.

Delacy made no effort at denial. "If the chance presented. In the end, she left this facility in a manner I never could have foreseen."

Beneath the table Olivia's fingers were becoming fists—though she was beginning to wonder why she bothered hiding her anger.

"The point is," the General said. "The timing of last night's siege was all the more suspicious when you consider that all the commotion caused would have given her the chance she needed to slip out."

Olivia blinked. "But Leah was trapped. Locked in Jonathan's cell before the attack even began."

General Delacy nodded. "We should assume that nothing about last night was happenstance. If that is the case, Jonathan and his allies wanted her there—always planned to retrieve her. Wanted her and Rivers in that room before they made their move on the alien's containment shell."

Olivia listened, but with each passing moment she was finding it harder to compartmentalize her growing contempt. The gross misuse of power. The treason. And yet at that moment, it was the sheer nepotism that boiled her blood. Involving his daughter in a highly classified operation she had no justification being anywhere near.

Yet, Delacy could not have reached the position of power he currently resided in by being reckless. Olivia was privy to a great deal more information than the average citizen on matters within the government. Everything she knew about General Delacy—the public figure—were the sort of details one read in his military personnel file. Still, those records painted the picture of a career officer with an impeccable record. Until this moment.

Anyone could be broken if pressure was applied to the right point of weakness, and the loss of a child was a textbook example of what could cause such a lapse in judgment.

"The charges didn't fire because your daughter and grandchild would have been caught in the blast. That was why you disabled the detonator. It never mattered who pressed the trigger. He knew the charges were never going to fire, knew her father wouldn't let her die down there."

When the trigger had failed, she believed she'd fallen for the long con. She'd seen a sort of evil genius in it all; Jonathan going to so much trouble to prove his honesty, so she'd believe the one lie that mattered when the time came.

She'd believed the rumbling in the floor was The Mark's shell malfunctioning. In reality, the UTO had been tunneling toward them, shaking the facility the entire time. She and everyone in the room had every reason to believe that the charges had finally detonated when that thing came ramming through six feet of cement.

And now, she saw that while all that misdirection was clearly intentional, Jonathan still hadn't lied.

The one question that remained was why the General believed that if she knew all this, she would change her mind about Jonathan's motives.

The answer came to her before she opened her mouth to voice. "Your son . . . that's why you need to believe."

The General held her gaze but folded his arms across his chest.

"So that's it, now that it's clear the alien's contacts are not his victims or slaves. If Jonathan is the enemy, then so was your son."

"My son was a good person," Delacy said. "And so is my daughter."

A crackle over the radio on Olivia's belt interrupted, which she was glad for, because the words she had for the General at that moment would likely be ones she'd later regret.

"Olivia, we have a confirmed sighting of Jonathan Tibbs."

Her eyes widened; she hadn't expected he would surface this quickly. She was on the line immediately as the General watched with interest.

"Where?" she asked.

"Downtown Seattle," the agent said. "What are your orders?"

She exchanged a glance with Delacy.

"He not only has my daughter, but your agent."

Olivia took a long breath. "I want him brought in alive."

CHAPTER THIRTY-FIVE

OCT 16, 2005 | 7:30 AM | SEATTLE

JONATHAN APPEARED IN an alley behind an apartment building downtown. With his implant active, he managed not to make too much noise pushing through the deadbolt on the back door, but the first person that came this way would notice the forced entry.

He took the stairs up to the fifth floor. No one answered when he knocked on a door at the end of the hall. Mr. Clean had assured him the tenant's cell phone was on the premises. He tried the knob and was surprised to find the door unlocked. After he stepped inside, he engaged the deadbolt behind him.

The smell had hit him right away. It was a mix of open liquor bottles, poorly cleaned up vomit, and air permeated by the breath of someone who spent the last few days on a bender. When he entered the living room, he saw what his nose had told him to expect.

Lincoln was passed out on the floor between his couch and his coffee table—as though he might have started on the couch and rolled off at some point. The end tables, the mantle, really any place there might have once been a clear surface was now cluttered with empty bottles or cans.

It added up, Jonathan realized with some sadness.

Paige had gone out on a single date with his trainer. Neither had ever spoken of it or asked after the other. This had struck him as odd but, given how little he'd been willing to share about his own life, he avoided asking anyone questions of a personal nature. Early on, he found it left him in a position where he felt rude when he couldn't reciprocate.

He'd known little about Paige's childhood at the time. Since then, he had learned that her father had been an alcoholic. If Lincoln was a recovering alcoholic, it made sense that he'd have told her before letting her become too emotionally invested. It wasn't a huge leap that she wouldn't want to invite that into her life.

If he'd fallen off the wagon, it wasn't a far stretch to think it had something to do with the gym letting him go. Jonathan had been—busy—in the days leading up to his capture by The Cell; was at the gym less frequently. He could have easily missed the signs that had led to Lincoln's manager cutting him loose.

Jonathan considered walking out.

When the world is ending you tend to cut your losses for the sake of the bigger picture. He hadn't made it to the hallway before he turned back. The unconscious man never knew, but Jonathan wouldn't be standing there today if Lincoln hadn't walked up and told him he was doing everything wrong a few months earlier.

You know when you first showed up here, I admit, I didn't think you'd have the spirit for this, but sometimes, well, I wish I had some of whatever is driving you.

At the time, the trainer seemed interested in where he'd found the drive— the discipline—to train like his life depended on it. Looking at him now, Jonathan realized he'd misunderstood—gotten the man all wrong. Lincoln had been fighting a war of attrition. The sort that could only be won if he possessed an unwavering will.

But there was no such will. And in the end, willpower, discipline—they weren't the only things that had kept him alive. Jonathan had always had the support of his friends.

"Lincoln," Jonathan said.

The man on the floor didn't move. Didn't come around at all.

Jonathan found the kitchen in the adjacent room. The place looked as bad as the living room. Bottles, overflowing garbage, unwashed dishes. He eventually located a coffee pot and after a few minutes of searching cupboards he found the rest of the necessities. When he had the brew started, he finally lifted the man back onto the couch.

Being lifted off the floor was enough to jar Lincoln out of his stupor, a bit. But it was when Jonathan went with the classic *pull open of the drapes to let the sun in* that Lincoln started to rouse. It wasn't a particularly bright day out, but in his condition, Jonathan might as well have aimed a spotlight at him.

"Ohhh God," Lincoln groaned as his hands covered his eyes.

It took the big man a moment to realized he wasn't alone, squinting as he noticed Jonathan in the living room. "Tibbs? That you? What the hell are you doing here?"

"I need your help."

Lincoln snorted and rubbed at his eyes. "Uh, I got canned—I'm not allowed in the gym."

"Yeah, I got your message," Jonathan said. "How long ago did you . . . relapse?"

Lincoln bristled. "That depends, what day is it?"

"Yeah, right, never mind," Jonathan said.

Lincoln leaned forward and began to sift through the bottles on his coffee table. Finding them empty, he sighed, leaned back into the couch, and sniffed at the air. "Are you making coffee?"

Jonathan stepped over to a window in the kitchen, parting the blinds enough with his hand to get a view of the street. "Need to clear your head enough to listen. Don't know how much time we'll have."

Lincoln lifted an eyebrow, as if deciding he didn't much care what Jonathan was talking about. He got up from the couch and stumbled to the kitchen.

Satisfied momentarily with the street's emptiness, Jonathan found a mug and poured a cup of coffee, but by then, Lincoln had found a bottle that wasn't empty. Just as he was bringing it to his lips, Jonathan swiped it out of his hand. Now, had Lincoln been in possession of all his faculties, he might have noticed the action had been remarkably swift. But in his current state, he looked at his empty hand perplexed before he noticed Jonathan holding out the mug.

Lincoln frowned at him suspiciously, then quirked an eyebrow as though he couldn't tell if Jonathan were being serious. To be fair, the contrast between the two of them had always been a bit comical. The trainer outweighing Jonathan by at least a hundred pounds—all of it muscle.

"Tibbs," Lincoln said. "I'm not in the mood for an intervention."

"Just need a minute of your time," Jonathan said.

Lincoln sighed, but he took the coffee. "I've heard it all before, and I know how this works. I'm not gonna stop until *I* actually want to."

Jonathan nodded. "I get that."

Lincoln sipped slowly at first. As the coffee cooled, he took longer pulls. When he finished, Jonathan handed him another.

He looked at the cup, rolled his eyes, but took it. "You gonna watch me drink the whole pot?" Lincoln asked. "Or are you going to tell me what you want?"

Jonathan smiled. "I got an opportunity for you. It's worth sobering up for."

"Doubt it," Lincoln said.

"I want your help saving the world."

Lincoln brought the mug up, took a long gulp, then slowly brought the cup down and considered Jonathan. "Alright, I admit, this is a new angle."

Jonathan smirked, then walked back to the window to take another glance outside.

"But, let me take a guess," Lincoln said. "Before I can save the world, I need to save myself? That about where this garbage is heading?"

"No, I was being literal," Jonathan said, his fingers spreading the kitchen blinds once more to look outside. "I need you sober for a few weeks, maybe a few months. Afterward, you can get right back to—whatever you call this."

Lincoln took another sip of the coffee and considered Jonathan again. "You're acting weird, Tibbs."

"I hear that a lot these days."

"Why do you keep looking out the window?"

"Some friends of mine have been watching your place," Jonathan said. "Knowing them, any minute now they'll come try and bring me in."

Lincoln appeared to hold back a scoff of disbelief. The peculiarly frank way Jonathan said all this seemed to leave the larger man at a loss as to whether he was kidding.

"You in some kind of trouble?" Lincoln said.

"Pretty much all the kinds, I think," Jonathan said. "And I didn't mean to bring it down on you, but I didn't plan on finding you—well—like this."

"And if you'd found me otherwise?"

"You'd already have agreed to come with me," Jonathan said.

"Oh, I would now?" Lincoln asked. "Where exactly is it you want me to go?"

Jonathan turned away from the window. "You've always wanted to know what I was training for. You still want to know?"

"Hmmm, not if you're about to tell me it's been to save the world," Lincoln asked. "Sorry, there ain't enough beer in the world to believe that."

"Come with me," Jonathan said. "All you'll need to do is believe your own eyes."

Lincoln frowned. "Think I'll pass."

He stood up from his kitchen table and headed toward the counter where Jonathan had put the bottle.

Jonathan stepped between them.

"Come on, Tibbs. Just don't."

Jonathan smiled pleasantly but shook his head. "Hmmm, nah."

Lincoln's patience was short, but he didn't appear ready for violence yet. He moved to push Jonathan aside, most likely thinking his weight would easily get the job done. He found the task more difficult than it should have been.

Jonathan could see the wheels turning in the big man's head. Lincoln assumed he'd simply misjudged. He tried again, this time making sure to use more than enough force. Jonathan didn't so much as budge. Despite his hangover, Lincoln seemed to realize that something wasn't right. Shoving Jonathan was like trying to push aside a metal statue that was bolted to the floor.

"What the . . ."

Jonathan lifted a hand and put it on Lincoln's shoulder. He was about to say something, but the front door burst in with a loud crash as the dead bolt tore through trim. The main window in the living room was next, shattering as men coming up the outside fire escape stepped over the windowsill.

"Down on the ground now!"

Another team of men, armored to the teeth in tactical gear, came pouring through the front door. Lincoln was turning about, trying to keep up with all the commotion and finding he was surrounded by heavily armed men, their weapons trained on him and Jonathan.

"Mr. Clean," Jonathan said, "Now would be good."

"Sorry," Jonathan said. "The disorientation is pretty bad even when you aren't hungover."

"Oh God . . ." Lincoln barely had enough time to get that much out before puking.

"Take it easy," Jonathan said, standing behind him. "Should pass in a minute or two. Though, in hindsight, I admit the coffee wasn't fully thought out."

"What just happ—oh God . . ."

The dialog, broken up by vomiting, continued in this disjointed manner. But despite the interruptions, they managed to get through the basic Q&A.

"What just happened?"

"We teleported to a safe location."

"Why am I the only one vomiting?"

"It's teleportation sickness. It doesn't affect me; we'll get to that later."

"I'm dreaming."

"I wish, brother, but we're not waking up from this one."

"I need a drink."

"Sorry, not a drop for miles. That probably doesn't sound like good news at the moment."

"Why the hell would it be good news?"

"Because you don't need to hit bottom here," Jonathan said. "Sobriety is no longer optional."

At this point Lincoln was well enough to stand. He looked around and saw nothing but trees in every direction.

"This is a forest. I'm in a forest," Lincoln said.

Jonathan smirked. "You are."

"Well, which way do I go to get out of it?"

Jonathan looked up at the sun, considering. "Seattle is South, but I don't recommend trying to get there on foot."

"Tibbs, you better hope this is a dream," Lincoln said. "Because you're pissing me off."

"That's fair," Jonathan said with a nod. "But why not sit for a bit. Hear me out. See if you're still angry after."

Lincoln stomped around a bit longer, stubbornly reconfirmed that there was no sign that any particular direction was better than another. Finally, he threw his hands up and found a rock that looked comfortable. Once he'd calmed down, the scope of what had transpired started to weigh in.

"I'm not hallucinating," Lincoln finally said.

Jonathan shook his head sympathetically.

"That was a SWAT team that broke down my door."

"Well," Jonathan said, his tone apologetic. "They weren't actually SWAT but the difference is splitting hairs at the moment."

"They were after you?"

Jonathan nodded.

Lincoln was quiet for a minute. "So what then? You're a teleporting terrorist."

Jonathan appeared to consider Lincoln's summation of the situation. "No, but that is how the authorities currently see it. Unfortunately, after what just happened in your apartment, they'll assume you're an accomplice. Even if you get home, it probably won't be good."

"I'm starting to get that," Lincoln said. "I kind of thought we were friends. So, why the hell did you involve me?"

Jonathan looked for his own rock to sit on while he answered. "You couldn't know this, but if we hadn't met, I'd probably be dead."

Lincoln frowned, glared at him as though the statement were far too dramatic to be true.

"Jesus . . . Tibbs, you were a client," Lincoln said. "When we met, all I was trying to do was make a living."

"You know, that is a great way to look at this," Jonathan said. "I've got a couple hundred clients for you. They all need the Tibbs training regime. But this time, you'll know what you're training them for."

Lincoln tongued at an incisor as he looked around. "Clients? We're standing in the middle of an empty forest."

"They're closer than you think," Jonathan said.

Lincoln looked at him blankly.

"Mr. Clean," Jonathan said. "You want to uncloak a back door for us?"

Seeing as Jonathan appeared to be talking to an imaginary friend, Lincoln scowled. A moment later he nearly fell off his rock retracting in surprise. The forest had come to life a few feet from his head as Mr. Clean's outer camouflage retreated and a large door into Hangman's Tree appeared.

"I know," Jonathan said, though his grin suggested he felt no regrets. "But if you think that was weird, you better brace yourself."

After staring at a door that appeared to go nowhere, but definitely hadn't existed a second earlier, Lincoln turned back to Jonathan. "Tibbs . . . is that a freakin' door to freakin' Narnia?"

CHAPTER THIRTY-SIX

JONATHAN LEANED AGAINST the hallway that led into the mess. He had paused there a moment earlier and now didn't dare step inside out of fear he might interrupt the greatest moment he'd ever witnessed.

Lincoln sat at a table inhaling a breakfast tray piled high with the staples one consumes to recover from a hangover. Meanwhile Mr. Clean, Heyer, and his roommates attempted to bring the trainer up to speed. Thing was, the crash course given to Collin and Hayden the night before hadn't exactly answered every question they had and since getting a taste of Jonathan's world, their questions were multiplying faster than bunnies.

"These interdimensional monsters," Hayden said. "They're like the Dark Overlords from *Howard the Duck*?"

". . . Dark Overlords?" Heyer's voice was incredulous as he repeated the words aloud.

"Physically no," Mr. Clean said. "But I suppose there are some parallels."

"There are?" Heyer asked, eyes wide as he looked to Mr. Clean.

Mr. Clean's avatar shrugged. "Perhaps, shallow parallels."

"Okay, so these *Ferox* on the other side, they step onto one of these sundial looking things," Hayden said. "And if they've swallowed one of these portal stones, a Stargate opens?"

"We refer to them as gateways," Heyer said.

". . . it's a bit derivative," Hayden replied, glancing at Collin for consensus. "I think Kurt Russel and MacGyver would side with me on this."

"Derivative? . . . MacGyver? . . ."

Not looking at the alien, Hayden remained unfazed by Heyer's ponderous expression until he insisted, "These gateway platforms are ancient artifacts, they have existed for millennia, if anything is derivative—"

"Okay, I retract it," Hayden said, rubbing at his beard as he sometimes did when he was too deep in thought to get sidetracked by a tangential argument.

Jonathan bit down on a knuckle to keep from being heard laughing.

"Point is, instead of simply using these Starg—" Hayden caught himself and smiled. "Gateways, these gateways as a means to travel from A to B, Mr. Clean has to cooperate with another AI on the other side to create a short-lived copy of our world—"

"No," Collin said. "Cede is opening the gateways from the Feroxian Plane, Mr. Clean is more like the guy directing traffic to specific nodes as the gates open on this side."

"And when you say nodes, you really mean people with implants, like Jonathan?" Lincoln asked.

"Yeah, see . . . he gets it," Hayden said.

"I don't have a clue what anyone is saying," Lincoln said, his face momentarily deadpan before he went back to shoveling scrambled eggs into his mouth.

"Okay, but it's actually Mr. Clean who manifests the Temporary Thunderdome," Collin said.

"Nice!" Hayden said, a large grin forming on his lips. "I kept thinking of it as the *Battle Bubble*, but I like Temporary Thunderdome."

Watching Heyer's eyes bounce back and forth between his roommates as he listened to them geek their way to an understanding of The Never was something Jonathan didn't ever want to see end. As such, he was the only one who noticed Leah lingering in shadows behind him. He gave her a glance of acknowledgment, but held a finger to his lips and whispered, "If you interrupt this conversation, I will never forgive you."

Leah held his gaze for a moment, then took a place against the wall to wait.

"The temporary dimension is referred to as The Never," Heyer said. "I am afraid the term Thunderdome is as lost on me as Dark Overlords . . . perhaps Mr. Clean could weigh in?"

The cartoon figure on the monitor raised his palms up and shrugged. "Well, again, they aren't wrong exactly, but—"

"Would you say," Hayden interrupted, his voice deepening before he finished. "That two men enter and one man leaves?"

"Incorrect," Mr. Clean said. "One man and one Ferox enter and one—"

"Let's just stick with Temporary Thunderdome," Lincoln said. "My head can't wrap around much more at the moment."

"The Ferox refer to The Never as The Arena," Mr. Clean said. "They aren't aware that their battle is taking place in a temporary dimension."

"But the human combatant doesn't enter or exit the same way as the Ferox," Collin said, frowning. "I still don't get that part. Heyer, you said they're in a state of 'Flux' pending the result of what happens inside."

Heyer's mouth opened to answer, but Hayden was already talking. "Actually, I think it's basically like *Quantum Leap*. The only difference is he isn't jumping into someone else's body, he's jumping into a version of himself that existed before The Never existed."

"Quantum Leap?" Heyer mouthed the words.

"Oh, yeah, that makes sense," Collin replied. "But are they just *quantum leaping* into their own shadows within Temporary Thunderdome?"

Heyer released a long sigh, seemingly unable to tell at this point if Collin and Hayden were directing these questions at him or if he'd simply become a sounding board.

"Flux," Hayden said. "Yeah, I still don't quite understand that part . . ."

"If I may," Mr. Clean interjected. "It is not unlike an *if/then* statement in a computer program. When a human is activated in The Never . . . or Thunderdome, their physical existence is tied to the outcome of what takes place inside." Mr. Clean said. "If they die, then they cease to exist on Earth and their physical body is sent to the Feroxian Plane in the same state that it exited The Never. If they live . . ."

Mr. Clean paused, giving Heyer a preemptive apologetic glance. "If they live, then they 'quantum leap' back to the moment of activation."

Heyer seemed to see something as complex as The Never being explained with inane pop cultural references as offensive. What was funny about it, was that the alien himself appeared at a loss to understand why it would bother him so much.

Jonathan knew. The Old Man was seldom the guy in the room having trouble keeping up. Clearly, he hated it.

"Yeah, but, the time travel part, how is it that time moves forward in The Never but not on . . ." Collin had to paused for a moment. "Um . . . Earth prime?"

Mr. Clean began to explain, but Hayden cut in with a sudden burst of enthusiasm that startled everyone, Lincoln and Heyer included.

"That's why you open The Never inside a starg—Gateway," Hayden said. "I mean, I don't pretend to comprehend the physics, but if my understanding of Sci-Fi is accurate, then a split second might pass on Earth prime, while inside a wormhole any manner of time might pass. So, when someone *quantum leaps* in and out of *Thunderdome*, the information actually exits the gateway before a perceivable amount of time has passed on Earth prime."

Hayden and Collin both turned to the AI for confirmation.

Glancing from Heyer to the expectant roommates, Mr. Clean decided it best to move on. "If all this helps Lincoln understand, then . . . sure."

Lincoln gave a noncommittal shrug.

Collin and Hayden went back to drinking coffee. Jonathan doubted they had slept, but he really couldn't blame them. Even without caffeine their minds had probably been on overdrive after teleporting, meeting both an alien and an Artificial Intelligence, and finding out there were men with superpowers, all in one day.

Heyer took the lull as his chance to politely remove himself, but as he stood, he was hit with new questions.

"So, Roswell?" Collin asked.

"Area 51?" Hayden added.

Heyer sighed, as he walked down the hallway out of the mess. "Weather balloon. Military testing site."

Both Hayden and Collin looked disappointed, but then their eyes narrowed skeptically on the alien's back.

Lincoln scoffed, "Likely story,"

Grinning, Jonathan finally turned back to Leah, but the hallway was empty.

CHAPTER THIRTY-SEVEN

AS THE MAN appeared out of thin air and almost immediately fell, Sam caught him. His name was Amar, and he possessed an implant like the one in Sam's chest, but outside of this they were strangers.

Sam had met a lot of strangers today.

Bewildered, Amar looked at him with the same blurry-eyed disorientation that every man he had kept from falling had arrived with.

"Ne osjećam se dobro."

Amar's words translated in his head, *I do not feel well.*

"Breathe, it's normal, it'll pass," Sam said.

As with each of those that came before, Amar's eyes widened, amazed to hear language translate in his head that didn't belong to a monster. As Sam understood it, Mr. Clean was making their communication possible without fully activating their implants. The AI said it was like turning on a car radio without starting the engine. The new arrivals weren't as familiar with how flawed the translations could sometimes be. Sam had learned to keep his words simple.

He helped Amar off the platform to a nearby cot where he could recover. Sam spoke quietly for a minute, filling him in on where he should report once he could see straight and trust his legs. When he was done, Sam came back to his post to notice Bodhi had just returned to the platform neighboring the one he was manning.

They'd been doing the same job for hours now. Jonathan wanted each man met by a human being when they first arrived. They were, in a way, the first step in an on-boarding process as soldiers from all around the globe were gathered.

Sam, Bodhi, and a few others would be taking shifts bringing everyone in for the next few days. Jonathan wanted every soldier here as soon as possible, but he also didn't want nearly two hundred and fifty men to disappear in unison, even if they were scattered throughout the world. Such a thing would be noticed; in fact, news reports were already reporting an uptick in disappearances from the fifty that had been brought in on the night of the escape.

While they were learning that Jonathan tended to give orders with little explanation, on this he'd not been secretive. With everything they wished to accomplish, their work remained easier if they controlled when and if mankind was given a reason to collectively panic.

"Mr. Clean, how long until the next set of inbounds?" Bodhi asked.

"Approximately forty minutes, give or take," Mr. Clean said.

Mr. Clean was not bound by the limits of a human. This was easier to forget than one might think. For instance, right now as Bodhi asked him one question it would appear he had the AI's full attention. The reality was that Mr. Clean might simultaneously be having ten other discussions with people inside Hangman's Tree, and a hundred more all over the world via cell phones and text messaging.

Before retrieval, men were contacted by Mr. Clean. The AI could then assist in arranging minor back stories that made it possible for a soldier to be brought in without causing any alarm. *Man disappears without trace*, brought unwanted attention. *Man quits job and tells loved ones he's left town to pursue lucrative new career opportunity*, that bought him some time. If necessary, Mr. Clean could rapidly provide the sort of digital footprint necessary to support such a story under modest scrutiny.

Still, there were always going to be those for which no story was practical. Beo was the best example. He had been retrieved from a high security prison. While Mr. Clean could certainly change the electronic records on a computer system to facilitate his release, that action would lead to far more unwanted questions. Humans tend to double check when a computer suddenly tells them a man serving seven life sentences is suddenly eligible for immediate release. Mr. Clean could have been more subtle than that, but in the end, there were some retrievals that couldn't be done without attracting notice. For those, Mr. Clean arranged the extraction with little or no warning, when the man's time zone would have most of the people around him sleeping.

This is all to say, when Mr. Clean said he would need forty minutes, it was because he was coordinating extractions for a lot of men, in a lot of different countries, in a lot of different situations, all at once.

Bodhi set an alarm on his watch and looked at Sam. "I got to do a thing. Want to come with?"

Sam shrugged and followed him out.

Bodhi was seventeen. Younger than Sam would have imagined Heyer would involve in this war. Sam was only nineteen himself, but in his experience those two years were a world of difference. However, once he looked past the way Bodhi spoke, he knew that having an implant had made him grow up quickly or die.

This 'thing' Bodhi had to do *was* quick. Sam had followed him into the Mess hall, where they loaded two trays with food and delivered them to two separate quarters. Both times, Bodhi left the tray at the door, knocked, and left before anyone came to retrieve it.

"Jonathan ordered you to do food delivery?" Sam asked.

Bodhi shrugged. "It wasn't an order. He asked if I would. Some folks got really bad news last night. He thought it would make it easier on them."

"Didn't we all get bad news last night?" Sam asked.

Bodhi nodded. "Some got more than others."

When he didn't elaborate Sam didn't push. "So, you just didn't want to carry both trays?"

Bodhi grinned and shook his head. "Actually, I asked for you to be on platform duty with me."

Seeing as they'd never met before this morning, Sam frowned. "Why?"

"Mr. Clean has detailed profiles on all of us. For instance, I know you've competed, and won, a few professional snowboarding competitions."

Sam tilted his head. "Mr. Clean just shared my profile with you?"

"Nah brah, nothing like that," Bodhi said. "I think only Jonathan and Heyer have access to the files. Only reason I even know they exist was because Mr. Clean singled out a few guys for a job recently. A job I ended up getting picked for. I got to see the list of other guys they considered. Your name was second."

"Really?" Sam considered Bodhi for a moment. A competitive grin growing on his face. "Second, huh? What exactly was the job?"

Bodhi smiled. "Something I think you'll definitely want to try for yourself."

You can't help me. Leave it alone.

A knock at the door woke her. She didn't know when she'd fallen asleep again. She laid on the bottom bunk of a bed, inside an empty cargo container, containing little of anything that was not of immediate utility. After Sydney had seen to it that she'd been given food, clothing, and a place to sleep, Leah had been left in these new quarters. Sydney said to enjoy it while it lasted, as eventually she would not be able to have an entire container to herself.

As it turned out, that didn't mean she was actually alone.

Shortly after Sydney left, Mr. Clean introduced himself. Appeared on her wall and offered to assist her with anything she might want to learn. She understood soon enough that this was who Jonathan had intended to teach her *algebra*. After coming to accept that she was standing inside the entity she was speaking with, Leah began to ask the questions that had brought her to this place.

She'd been surprised. There were very few questions the AI wouldn't answer. In fact, there were few questions she had to ask at all. Anything she asked seemed to require the AI to start at the beginning.

"Rylee disappeared. I want to know, what happened to her?"

A simple enough question, and yet it was nearly forty-five minutes later, that Leah had absorbed enough to see how and why it came to be that Rylee died in a place that existed outside of time fighting a creature from another dimension. Once she understood this, she knew Jonathan hadn't been mistaken or lying.

She had to force herself to ask the same question again of her brother. This time, the answer was short. "Peter Delacy's death occurred under similar circumstances."

Delivered by a messenger with no motive to lie—that was it.

Ever since, Peter's final words would creep up unwanted in her head.

You can't help me. Leave it alone . . .

You can't help me. Leave it alone . . .

Leave it alone . . .

He'd been right. The last two years of her life amounted to nothing more than her refusal to accept it. She'd allowed uncertainty to give her hope, and now that hope had been slain. She felt grief, regret . . . but what she'd never expected to feel—was relief.

Certainty meant no hope. No hope meant freedom—of a sort.

While the time to mourn seemed long expired, her pillow had been damp from tears, and they had begun to lift the burden she'd been carrying since Peter's disappearance.

Certainty meant it was okay to mourn.

Still, it all left a vacuum. What came now?

She'd always thought that if she came to this moment the answer would be revenge. That Heyer would be the recipient of that vengeance. Now, she knew things had never been that simple. In fact, Mr. Clean had said that Heyer had asked to speak to her as soon as she was willing.

Asked? As soon as she was willing?

She couldn't help how angry the invitation made her. Two years she'd chased him, running parallel through shadows, inching close enough to snare him in a trap. She'd left everything she knew behind, she'd changed her name and her face. She'd betrayed people she'd come to care about.

Now—what? The alien wanted her to join him for coffee?

You can't help me.

Leave it alone.

Two years she'd sought the alien's confession. Now, it all seemed such an empty gesture.

Her head rose off her pillow as she remembered what had woken her. Hadn't there been a knock at the door? She got up and found a tray outside with breakfast.

"Mr. Clean . . . did Jonathan come by?"

"No, he arranged for food to be brought to you."

While she didn't know what she'd expected, she was sad he hadn't come to see her. Speaking to the alien felt so pointless now. Something she would do because she had come this far and didn't believe it was a box she could leave unchecked. But she didn't want to speak to Heyer, she wanted to speak to Jonathan. Yet, everything said he was avoiding her.

She knew he'd let Mr. Clean be the bearer of all the bad news because he didn't want to be the one to cause her pain. Still, she would have rather heard it from him. She wanted to go find him now, but despite Sydney's open hostility, her warning had felt honest. Being seen with him would do Jonathan no favors.

"Mr. Clean, can I speak to him through you?"

"Yes," Mr. Clean said. "However, he is not alone and rather occupied at the moment."

"Saving mankind?" Leah asked.

"It is a related matter," Mr. Clean acknowledged.

"I suppose I can't fault his priorities," she said.

CHAPTER THIRTY-EIGHT

OCT 16, 2005 | 11:30 AM | SEATTLE

"THIS PLACE FEELS like it is filling up by the minute," Paige said.

She stood beside the windows watching people down below. They were near the top of Hangman's Tree, a circular room that hung from the ceiling at the center. The windows were tinted, allowing them to look down as though they were in the jumbotron of an arena.

"Yeah, as far as secret alien hideouts go, it's not going to be the Fortress of Solitude for much longer," Hayden said.

Collin came to stand beside her at the window. "Yeah, more like the Costco of Crowded. Or . . . Costco."

Paige smirked at him.

The room itself didn't have much to it. Just a donut shaped table and chairs. That said, it had no entrance. Jonathan had requested they all be here, and the only way in or out was for Mr. Clean to teleport them. Without implants that meant teleportation sickness.

The roommates had been the first to arrive. Over the next few minutes, Anthony and Sydney had shown up and were still groaning in their chairs. The roommates went silent when Heyer arrived. He was impervious to the spins.

Until Paige came to Hangman's Tree, he had been a man she'd seen once, months ago, at a bar. She would have completely forgotten him had it not been that he followed Jonathan home and left him in a pool of his own blood on the kitchen floor. For Collin and Hayden, this was their third time sharing the room with the alien. A few days ago, Heyer had made a brief, albeit unconscious, appearance on the floor of their garage just before they were taken prisoner.

Late last night they learned he wasn't a man at all. That the reasons for his mysterious actions were far more mysterious than they had imagined. So, Heyer's arrival left her uncomfortable in her chair. Though it might also have had something to do with how his coat hung open and three glowing lines of light were visible beneath his t-shirt.

Sydney's reaction didn't seem any different from their own; only Anthony showed no particular reaction. Perhaps that was why the alien took a seat next to him.

The AI arrived a moment later—if one could call it arriving. Rather, he decided that his avatar would manifest in the open space in the center of the table. He had swapped out his normal white t-shirt and jeans with a military uniform. Not just camouflage either.

"Nice beret," Paige said. "What's the insignia?"

Paige thought it looked like a stylized letter H—or two pitchforks facing away from one another. Mr. Clean didn't bother answering as Jonathan's arrival would have interrupted—as it turned out, Jonathan's presence answered the question for him.

He appeared in a blink and showed no signs of teleportation sickness. Like the alien, his coat hung open. Beneath his t-shirt, lines of light were dampened but still visible. Those lines, looked to be a close approximation to the insignia.

Seeing their eyes drawn to this, he closed the coat before taking his seat. "Thank you for being here, let's get started."

Paige frowned—there were still two empty seats at the table. Given the donut room's purpose it seemed strange that Mr. Clean would manifest spare seats.

"What is this about?" Heyer asked.

"This is our war council," Jonathan replied.

None spoke right away, everyone in the room looking at one another. Some clearly felt that, if a war council was needed, they most certainly should be present. Others, like Paige, felt they most certainly had no reason for being there. With the exception of Jonathan—Paige got the feeling everyone present agreed on which category everyone else fell into.

"Jonathan," Anthony said. "If your intention is a council to plan Earth's defenses, perhaps it should be made up of military minds, scientists, our people . . . Veterans who have survived multiple engagements with the enemy."

Jonathan listened and nodded. He didn't speak though, just looked around the room waiting for the next objection disguised as advice.

"What the hell are you thinking?" Paige asked.

He turned to her to listen.

"I get why Anthony, Sydney, and the alie . . . err . . ." Paige hesitated. "I'm sorry . . . Mr. Heyer?"

"Heyer is fine."

"Well, I get why they're here, but your roommates? This isn't a game. You have to take this seriously."

His eyes moved to Collin next, who said, "Um . . . I've only seen one Ferox; Mr. Clean projected it into our room. I knew it wasn't real and I still nearly crapped myself."

Jonathan directed a side-eyed look at the AI before moving on. He let everyone say what they were thinking, unfazed for the most part, despite everyone seeming to concur that he wasn't thinking straight. Only the alien said nothing, his face stoic and mostly focused on Jonathan while the others made their points, until . . .

"Heyer," Sydney said. "You must have some opinion?"

Heyer looked about the table patiently. "My understanding is that Jonathan has recently spent a great deal of time considering our strategy. I am waiting to hear his thoughts on the matter. That said, since this council is comprised of those he personally selected, I am rather curious about who is missing."

Apparently, Paige wasn't the only one who noticed the two empty chairs. For a moment all those present looked to Jonathan waiting for him to answer.

"When the time is right, those seats belong to Agent Laurence Rivers and Leah Delacy."

Heyer didn't react, he only appeared thoughtful. The rest took the news with less grace.

"Why would you let her anywhere near this?" Paige asked, and she didn't disguise the pain in her voice as she stared at him.

Jonathan didn't get a chance to answer before Anthony piled on. "Either of them. Rivers won't be turned to our side. Given the first opportunity, he'll report anything we tell him to The Cell."

Jonathan nodded. "When we allow it, I suspect he will."

"You want The Cell to know what you're up to?" Sydney asked.

"When the time is right, yes," Jonathan said. "This is a war between Earth and the Feroxian Plane, there can be no divisions amongst us if we wish to win it."

"Why Lea . . ." Paige cut herself off. "Why Rachel?"

Jonathan turned, looking at her and his roommates sympathetically. They had only learned the truth about their next-door neighbor the night before.

Paige hadn't wanted to believe it. She'd resisted longer than the others, and her anger was justified. She'd been closest to the spy. Had just begun to truly feel a sisterly bond with her, only to have it all become a lie.

"Believe me, I understand," Jonathan said. "I am asking you to work with her, not to forgive."

"But you have forgiven her?" Sydney said, her tone in the vague space between question and accusation.

Jonathan didn't turn to look at her. He was quiet, staring down at the table as he chose his next words carefully. Finally, he stood. He leaned over the table and planted his fists.

"I am letting you all cast your doubts. You've been heard. Now, I am asking you all to put them aside and listen. Once you understand what we need to accomplish, I will hear objections."

Then, he turned to Paige.

"As you said, this isn't a game. I won't tell you how to feel, but there is a time and place for personal vendettas, and this is not it," Jonathan said.

There was a palpable tension and Paige knew it didn't belong solely to her. However, given the circumstances, he wasn't making an unreasonable request, and he wasn't asking her to like it.

Jonathan waited until everyone seemed ready to listen.

"I've agreed with everything that's been said," Jonathan said. "But when I say I've agreed, I am not talking about the last few minutes. I've spent the last few months planning. Months, surrounded by . . . as you said, Anthony, military specialists, scientists, and highly trained government agents. Believe me when I tell you, they have made their contributions."

The alien leaned back in his chair, eyes glimmering with understanding. "The malfunction in your queue. You began each activation on a military base, surrounded by the shadows of The Cell's scientists and operatives. You convinced them to work with you?"

"Saying it like that makes it sound like it was easy—it wasn't," Jonathan said. "But yes."

"A remarkably fortuitous story," Heyer said. "One I'd like to hear."

Jonathan considered him for a moment. "Perhaps another time. Right now, I want to return to why you're the ones I've called here. There are two reasons. The first, *we* have a plan. It isn't mine—it's ours."

Paige frowned, and from the looks going around the table, she wasn't the only one who needed him to elaborate.

"Everything I am about to tell you, it didn't come from me—it came from us. Your shadows inside The Never. So, anyone who thinks they don't belong, know this now. You are the reason humanity has a plan."

Glances went around the table once again, but the appraisals in each person's eyes had changed. Well, in most people's eyes at least.

"Um, Jonathan, honestly man," Hayden groaned. "Hearing that I had any part in the plan to save to world—isn't instilling confidence."

"Hayden," Jonathan said. "I wish I could give you my memories. If I could, you would know your value. All of you. But, you're right about one thing, no one at Hangman's Tree can know. To anyone outside this room, no war council exists. All our strategic efforts are coming from Heyer and me alone."

Silence.

"So, Heyer and you take all the blame if it all goes to hell," Collin said. "Admittedly, I like what I know of 'our plan' so far."

"He's rightfully worried," Sydney said. "Leadership will be questioned if our soldiers think they're being led by . . ."

Sydney trailed off as the three roommates turned to hear the rest of the sentence. While Paige didn't disagree with the sentiment, she thought the woman wise for leaving the rest of what she might have said to the imagination.

"While we can all see what Sydney is getting at, this is more about containment," Jonathan said. "The second reason you're the ones here, is that none of you can be drawn into The Never. Heyer and I are the only two in this room with an active implant. Heyer can't be drawn in against his will. All our soldiers can. Because of this, they all need to know as little as possible until the very last moment. In the meantime, it will be easier if all involved assume Heyer and I are the only ones with any knowledge."

"I think that what Jonathan isn't saying, is that we'll all find it easier to keep our mouths shut if no one knows we have anything to share," Anthony said.

Jonathan nodded.

"I give every man in this army the benefit of the doubt. That said, they can all enter The Never. They could question your shadows. We would never know who amongst us might have become a liability."

Collin groaned. "This is already too complicated."

"I'll simplify it. Outside this room, Anthony and Sydney are simply carrying out orders and know nothing more than anyone else. Paige, Collin, Hayden, you're here for asylum, so The Cell can't use you as leverage against me."

"So, be ourselves and let everyone assume we're useless," Collin said.

Jonathan looked at his roommates sympathetically. "Collin, I'm sorry—"

"No, no," Collin stopped him, an earnest smile on his face. "I'm happy to not be taken seriously."

"Okay." Jonathan smirked. "But that brings me to something else. It won't all be an act. There . . . are details that cannot be known outside Heyer and myself . . ."

The alien had tried not to react too much to any of what had been said so far, but he nodded solemnly, as though the statement showed wisdom.

"But . . . there will also be things that I must keep entirely to myself," Jonathan added.

Heyer's expression faltered.

Silence.

"Jonathan, shouldn't someone point out that you aren't immune to being pulled into The Never?" Sydney asked.

"It's not any Ferox encounter I'm worried about," Jonathan said. "Malkier can't send a Ferox to gather intel against us—at least not effectively. They're too technologically primitive. Any information a Ferox could bring back wouldn't likely be actionable. If Malkier hopes to learn how we intend to stop him, he'll have to enter the gates himself. Now, if I were him, I'd pick random gates. Once inside The Never, I'd subdue the active human challenger for interrogation."

The room grew silent as they considered this.

"What exactly stops him from doing this to you, Jonathan?" Paige asked.

"He won't risk facing me alone."

Heyer frowned, but he was careful with his words. "Jonathan . . . what makes you confident of that?"

"For starters, last time he caught us completely unprepared, and I nearly killed him," Jonathan said.

"That was more luck than—"

"Luck had little to do with it," Jonathan said. "I knew how to kill him."

"Tactfully, Jonathan, you were not alone," Heyer said. "And you were in a substantially . . . stronger state to engage him while . . ."

Heyer trailed off, suddenly even more careful of his words.

". . . if anything, my brother suspects you are vulnerable."

Silence followed as Paige, Collin, and Hayden looked back and forth between Jonathan and the alien.

"What is he talking about Jonathan?" Paige asked.

Jonathan seemed to be taking his time answering.

"What you need to know, is that with Rylee gone, I'm not as strong as I was," Jonathan said. "Malkier, he would expect me to be . . . quite . . .

vulnerable. But by now, he knows that isn't the case. I've sent him a message he'll find difficult to ignore."

"You sent my brother a message?" Heyer asked.

"Twenty-eight of them. It will take him a while to count," Jonathan said.

The first meeting of the war council had concluded on an obvious question. If their shadows had helped Jonathan conceive of this plan, why did he still need them?

His answer weighed on each of them. "We are the architects of a blueprint. Your shadows knew your true selves would still need to see it through. The best laid plans start falling apart when they meet reality. I still need your help."

They all needed time to absorb—Jonathan knew the next time they convened they would have questions.

Despite being the first to leave, Jonathan didn't look surprised to find Heyer stepping out in front of him a few moments later as he strode down the upper catwalks.

"I know, Old Man, you hate the plan," Jonathan said.

"On the contrary, I believe you have something that can be built on," Heyer said. "Though, I admit I am not looking forward to what you are asking of me."

"Fair enough."

Jonathan made to keep moving but Heyer put a hand on his shoulder. "Jonathan, you are avoiding me; it is rather thinly veiled."

They had just spent an hour with the rest of the council, but Jonathan wasted no time with the pretense that he didn't know what Heyer was talking about. Some things could only be talked about in private.

Jonathan sighed. "Whatever you think you need to ask me, you don't."

Heyer studied him. "I will judge that for myself."

"Fine," Jonathan said. "Walk with me, there is something we need to discuss before it is too late to bother."

Curious, Heyer fell into step with him.

"Twenty-eight cycles inside The Never can only explain so much. This plan you offer—it could not have been conceived unless you were made aware of details I know you had no access to. That only I or Mr. Clean could have told you. How do you explain that?"

"You're mistaken," Jonathan said.

When he made no effort to elaborate on this, Heyer was left to guess at its meaning on his own. "Jonathan, would you have me believe you pieced this all together with nothing but educated guess work?"

They had reached a staircase down to the ground floor and Jonathan paused at the top to look at Heyer.

"You alright, Old Man? That coma having effects I need to know about?"

They stared at one another, both looked as though it was the other who was clearly confused. Jonathan considered this for a moment, then leaned in to speak quietly. "If this is some sort of guilt, we . . . we really don't have time for it."

"Guilt?"

Jonathan frowned again but began descending the stairs. Heyer allowed him to put some steps between them before following. Certainly, in regard to Jonathan, there were things he felt guilty about. But what relevance did any of that have to do with the question he'd asked?

He caught up to Jonathan at ground floor and saw where they were going. The armory was laid out inside of Mr. Clean just as it had been when the AI had been taking the shape of the top three stories of an apartment building. The only difference was that it was no longer contained by the walls of an old building. The stucco and plaster projections that had surrounded it in Heyer's apartment were gone, which meant its exterior of true alien steel was no longer disguised. However, its antique safe door had not changed, and when Jonathan approached, the door swung open to allow them inside. The alien waited for the door to seal behind them.

"Guilt, Jonathan?"

Jonathan shook his head. "You call me Jonathan. To be fair, I don't know what else you would call me. But we both know it's a half-truth at best."

Heyer drew in a long breath as he stared back at the man. Of course, he recognized that Jonathan's behavior had changed dramatically. Of course, he knew that it had to do with Douglas's memories, or the broken bond, or the amount of time he'd been trapped in The Never. Yet, the way Jonathan spoke now left Heyer to wonder if he had underestimated the extent of these things.

"*Half-truth*," Heyer whispered.

"Heyer, you're starting to worry me," Jonathan said.

The alien was a while in replying. "I . . . I think I have underestimated . . ."

He trailed off.

When Heyer spoke again, he did so as though he'd had to reorient a great deal in his mind. In fact, he abruptly changed the subject. "Anthony tells me that Rylee's father is with us. That you've spoken with him."

Jonathan nodded. "What of it?"

"You sent your own mother away but brought Mr. Silva here. Why?"

Jonathan's eyes narrowed. "Are we not in Rylee's debt, Heyer?"

"The entire world is in her debt," he said.

"Yet, now that she's gone, we can never repay her," Jonathan said. "She wanted her father to know the truth. Not being able to tell him caused her great pain. Do you doubt that I know this?"

Heyer's face softened a bit. Of course, if there was one person in this world who might have known Rylee's dying wishes, it was Jonathan.

"You seem to be holding up to the severed bond rather well," Heyer finally said. "I feared your condition would be an insurmountable one."

Jonathan nodded and nothing more.

Heyer had never thought of him as particularly chatty, but his stoicism on matters was new, and it was making his efforts to feel out answers far more difficult than in the past. Almost as though Jonathan was forcing him to step into territory where he wouldn't be welcome if he wanted a straight answer.

"You want to know why the broken bond hasn't killed me. That's what you're dancing around?" Jonathan asked.

Heyer turned sympathetic eyes on him. "I don't believe in miracles. The bond's power came with consequences. I don't see the marks of them on you."

Jonathan took a long breath. "I understand why you're asking. But, I'm not a liability."

He turned away from the alien, still headed toward the back of the chamber as Heyer stood still. The alien could hear his patience waning as he let out a breath. "Jonathan, there are no records of a man surviving a broken bond. The only exception—"

"I'm aware," Jonathan interrupted, but didn't stop moving.

"What you aren't saying is what troubles me," Heyer said. Those were the words that made him pause, but not turn around. "Jonathan, no one would judge you. If you have . . . if you *had* to do something to yourself . . . to survive."

He was still for a long moment. When he turned, it was only to hold Heyer's gaze with one eye.

"There was a price," Jonathan said. "I paid it."

"What price?" Heyer asked.

When Jonathan turned back, there was a look on his face that was familiar—a look Heyer had only ever seen on a different member of the Tibbs family. The alien knew what that look meant before Jonathan spoke. "Let it go, Old Man."

"I cannot do that in good conscience," Heyer said, plainly.

"You can and you will."

"Will I?"

"You either trust me or you don't," Jonathan said.

He blinked—temporarily caught off guard. In their relationship, trust had only ever needed to flow in one direction. Heyer had never imagined it being asked of him. He found it quite uncomfortable.

"Decide right now. Because in the days to come," Jonathan said, "I need you to trust me, no matter what. There are going to be questions that you're not going to get answers to. But I'm not asking you for anything more than you asked of my father and me a hundred times over."

Heyer found he was resisting a powerful urge to growl by letting a long breath drain out of him. This was going poorly enough, he realized, that it would be best to come back to it at another time.

Heyer took off his hat and cleared his throat. "What brings us to the armory, Jonathan?"

CHAPTER THIRTY-NINE

JONATHAN CROSSED TO the end of the Armory. There, he came to stare at the Alpha Slayer's pedestal. Heyer knew what the man was considering. He had stood at that exact spot with the same tormented expression.

He took a place on the opposite side of the pedestal. Jonathan picked up the Alpha Slayer, gazed down at his palm, then closed his eyes and put the implant back. Heyer was suddenly doubtful that this was the first time he'd done this—though it was likely the first time with an audience.

"I understand. I have always been troubled by the choice that infernal thing represents."

"It's in our possession—and the one man who can use it is our prisoner," Jonathan said. "I don't believe in fate, but if I were going to start . . ."

Heyer sighed. "I hoped returning it to the Foedrata Arena would make the decision for me. I suppose, had I been committed to my decision I would have thrown the thing into space rather than somewhere I always knew I could recover it."

"And today?"

"Same as every other. I simply wish there were someone else," Heyer said. "If we trust Grant with it, we must trust him until the day he dies. If I am not mistaken, at the moment you do not trust him enough to let him out of his cell."

"You disagree with keeping him isolated?" Jonathan asked.

"I . . ."

Heyer trailed off, turned his palms up with a slight chuckle. "If I am being honest, I was unconscious when you decided. It saved me the trouble of needing an opinion."

Jonathan scoffed and shook his head.

"Other than me, how many know about the chain of command?" Jonathan asked.

"Only Anthony, and Mr. Clean himself," Heyer said. "But . . . as you pointed out earlier, while we are in a building full of allies, there is no way to ever be certain they have not or will not learn something they should not. Rylee has taught us the danger our own shadows can create for us."

Jonathan sighed. "I hate him, Heyer. I can't help it. I can't change it."

Heyer nodded.

"Jonathan, is there something I need to know? Something important enough you would consider trusting Grant Morgan?"

Jonathan closed his eyes and nodded. His fist clenching and unclenching.

"When I was trapped in my queue, if I got curious about something outside the human world, I could wait until Mr. Clean was active on the next loop to get an answer."

Heyer frowned, his arms folding over his chest. "Go on."

Jonathan licked his lips and looked at the Alpha Slayer again "Heyer, you were the one who warned me that once you know something there isn't any going back. This may be the one time I can give you the same warning."

At first, he regarded Jonathan as though he were being overly dramatic. After all, realistically it seemed unlikely that something had occurred to Jonathan in his queue loop that, in all his years, had never crossed his mind as well.

"Jonathan, if you know something that truly has you considering whether or not we should trust Grant . . ."

Heyer paused, apparently, he'd had to hear himself say the words out loud, because suddenly Jonathan's offer to keep this information to himself seemed to warrant far more consideration.

"Yep," Jonathan said. "Blissful ignorance or the heavy crown? You should really take a minute."

Heyer sighed. "If only the world were not at stake . . ."

With every activation, Grant's shadow had been there inside the shell. Eying Jonathan wearily from behind that thick plastic of The Cell's prison.

But . . . a shadow is a complex thing.

On the one hand, the original person can't be held accountable for what their shadow might have done once gripped by The Never's mental degradation. On the other hand, the mind is an emotional beast and sometimes no amount of such reason will change it.

Jonathan knew that the person he wanted to hurt—the person responsible—was already dead. Unfortunately, it didn't mean he could stop feeling an urge to take vengeance on each new incarnation placed in front of him at the start of each loop.

Then one day, as Jonathan looked at the man's shadow sitting behind that plastic wall—an unwanted thought came to him. That shadow he had fought and killed had lived in the lair of the enemy. Neither Jonathan nor Heyer had any way of knowing just how long Grant's shadow had been beside Malkier. This was because the Alpha Slayer implant had extended his life far longer than the degradation would normally allow.

What might that shadow have witnessed?

Jonathan's first inclination: *Probably nothing of value.*

But, how careful would Malkier be around such a man? A shadow, not long for the world, his mental state already in deterioration. The conversations both Heyer and Jonathan had exchanged with the shadow told them that, at the very least, he had witnessed more than any Ferox while he'd been a guest on the Feroxian Plane.

So, what could he have seen or heard?

Of course, the shadow was dead. So why bother thinking about what was already lost? Well, anyone else would have thought that at least. Jonathan, however, knew better than most that whatever memories the shadow possessed at death, they were still inside that implant.

He wanted to let it go, but the notion wouldn't let go of him.

Finally, one day, Jonathan crushed a portal stone, woke up inside that same tunnel as he always did, and asked Mr. Clean a question.

Seeing as how Heyer hadn't been there to hear the answer, Jonathan asked it again now as they stood in the armory. "Mr. Clean, hypothetically, if one implanted a device into a man, and the previous owner had been the same man's shadow, what would the outcome be?"

Mr. Clean's answer took a moment's consideration. "The device would, conceivably, behave in the same manner it does when a man returns from The Never."

"Explain," Jonathan said.

"Because the device itself is not programmed to see a distinction between a shadow and an original, the memories recorded by the shadow would be uploaded to the man's mind," Mr. Clean said.

Heyer's eyes widened as he saw what Jonathan was getting at. "What would be the potential consequences?"

"As this has never been tested—I cannot give a definitive answer."

"Educated guess, Mr. Clean," Heyer said.

"I see three immediate possibilities. First, the man's entire personality might be replaced with the shadow's state of mind up to the point of death. Second, the man might experience the possession of two alternate sets of memories, most overlapping but some diverging at the point of the shadow's creation. He may be able to integrate the divergence and see them as separate timelines. If not, this could lead to confusion or madness. Third, brain damage that could range from no apparent symptoms to being rendered permanently catatonic—possibly death."

When Mr. Clean finished, Jonathan casually picked up the device from the pedestal again and held it out to Heyer. "Want to stare at this for a while?"

The alien looked down at his palm and sighed. "Perhaps, in this, we are both too close to it. An outsider with less bias might be best?"

Jonathan raised an eyebrow. "Did you have someone in mind?"

"No," Heyer said, his expression troubled as he stared at the implant. "And increasing the number of individuals who know too much about the chain of command is dangerous."

"Well," Jonathan said. "My usual go-to guys for this sort of thing are in the building."

After several hours reviewing the details of the coming battle and Jonathan's plan to address it, they were all grateful when the meeting came to an end.

Collin, paradoxically, felt angry at his own shadow. As if the man had knowingly left him with an unpaid bill. He'd come upon Hayden on the catwalks as he made his way back to their quarters. His friend was staring out over Hangman's Tree—but he wasn't really looking at anything.

"So, what's bothering you?" Collin asked as he took a place beside him.

"It's Jonathan," Hayden said. "Well, no, it's this plan. Actually, maybe it's both."

"If you have concerns you should say something."

"That's not . . . it's not that I don't think it will work, it's just . . ."

Hayden trailed off for a moment, shaking his head before he continued. "I realize how this is going to sound."

"It's ugly, Hayden, or if we're being kind, this plan is less than ethical," Collin said.

Hayden breathed, but it was clear he'd been relieved he wasn't the only one having that thought.

"Yeah," Collin said. "I've flashed back to your diatribe about the Villain's Journey in there more than a few times."

"Do you think we should say something?" Hayden asked.

Collin shook his head. For a moment, Hayden was left looking at his friend with uncertainty.

"Come on Hayden, Jonathan . . . he knows. He's being a realist—not a villain. The stakes are too high to risk failure."

"The villain always says that," Hayden noted. "It's always an excuse to let the ends justify the means."

Collin sighed. "It's not our call. Jonathan has to think about everyone here—the whole world. If he fails, it's . . . it's not on us, it's on him. So, maybe we don't get to judge."

"I know, I do . . . I just, I can't shake this feeling," Hayden said. "There's got to be some other way."

For a moment, silence fell between them.

"Hayden, have you considered the possibility that Jonathan is being the bad guy so that no one else has to?" Collin asked. "He knows you, Hayden, knew how you'd feel."

"So, what, you think he expects me to tell him not to do this?" Hayden asked.

"Honestly, I think . . . he wants us to live, and he wants us to be able to sleep at night," Collin said. "I think he wants to get as close as he can to a world where we can forget this ever happened."

"I wish something would come to me," Hayden said.

"Well . . ." Collin said. "When this Malkier guy gets here, you take him aside. Explain that he's being a jerk. I'm sure he'll turn his army right around."

Hayden didn't reply to that, just took a tired breath.

Collin put a hand on his friend's shoulder. "If it's any consolation, the other side has the bigger guns here. So, that makes us the underdogs."

Hayden flinched, then did a double take as he tried to make Collin's words fit into the discussion. "How is that a consolation?"

"Well . . . take Lex Luther. Now, ignore the psychosis behind his motives for a minute. There is a perfectly good reason he doesn't resolve his differences with Superman by asking him to step outside for a fistfight. Lex knows it wouldn't matter who was right or wrong, there is no winning that fight. But, he doesn't know he's the villain. He thinks he's right, so if he has to fight Superman, he can be as underhanded as it takes to level the field."

"So, in this analogy, Malkier is Superman and Jonathan is Lex Luther," Hayden said. "Awesome."

Collin seemed thoughtful for a moment.

"Want to hear something that helps me a bit?"

Hayden looked up and nodded.

"Do you remember the night this all started. When we asked Jonathan if he'd rather be Superman or Jesus?"

Hayden nodded. "Yeah . . . he said neither."

Collin nodded. "If you had asked me that question that night, I would have said Superman, and I'm fairly certain you'd have said Jesus."

"Like Jesus, sure, not *the* Jesus," Hayden said.

"Whatever, all I'm saying is that knowing what I know now," Collin said. "I wouldn't want to be either."

"And . . .?"

Collin shrugged. "Jonathan knew that much before any of this happened."

It was then that Mr. Clean manifested beside them. A small square oozed right out of the metal guardrail to form a display for his avatar. "Hello, I've been instructed to inform you that your presence is requested in the armory."

Mr. Clean had manifested five chairs and arranged them inside the armory. His projection currently sat in one himself, and the rest were arranged in a half circle around the Alpha Slayer implant.

"So, can we talk about this door?" Collin asked, shooting a thumb over his shoulder where there was clearly another room at the back of the armory.

"It is not relevant to why we brought you here," Heyer said.

"I know . . . no one has said anything of relevance in a while now," Collin replied dryly.

Heyer looked at Jonathan, then sighed.

"It is where Mr. Clean stores power for the implants," Heyer said. "What allows implants like Jonathan's to be powered when they are not attached to a portal stone."

"So, like a big battery?" Collin asked.

Heyer looked to Mr. Clean. "For the sake of getting back to the subject at hand, please show him."

With a nod, the AI slid open the door. Inside was just enough room to stand. Any further and one encountered a wall of a red glowing energy. Basically, if a portal stone was enlarged to the size of an average bedroom, it would look like what was on the other side of the door.

After he'd been given an eyeful the door slid shut again.

"Kind of a letdown," Collin muttered as he turned his attention back to the Alpha Slayer.

Some time passed.

"You know . . ."

When Collin spoke again, everyone perked up in the hopes that he had something new to contribute. "I wish we could go back to when Jonathan just asked us off the cuff questions about Sci-Fi movies."

"Why?" Jonathan asked.

"It's a lot easier to think when the stakes are hypothetical," Collin said.

Hayden nodded slowly, his expression nostalgic for a simpler time.

Seven chairs sat in front of the pedestal. Heyer and Jonathan, having laid out the dilemma again, were silently waiting for their input.

Hayden turned to Leah. "So, yeah . . . welcome to the war council."

"I really don't know why he thinks the Pervert would have something meaningful to contribute," Paige said half under her breath.

Strangely, Leah seemed unperturbed by the 'pervert' epithet. Though perhaps she considered it a step-up from Paige altogether ignoring her existence.

"They're either being incredibly immature, or they're not telling us everything." Leah said. "I know you've made harder decisions than this."

The last statement was clearly aimed at Jonathan and Heyer.

"I hate to agree with the Pervert," Paige said. "But she's not wrong."

"Alright, be mature, what do you two think we should do?" Collin asked, looking hopefully between the two women.

"Didn't we just have a meeting?" Sydney asked upon being summoned to the armory.

As they finished listening to the pros and cons of the decision at hand, they looked at one another somewhat reluctantly. "Perhaps something isn't apparent to me, as I've never actually had any personal interactions with Mr. Morgan," Sydney said.

"That's why we called you two," Hayden said.

"We all have reason to be biased," Leah interjected.

Sydney nodded.

"Well, my initial thought is that there is considerable danger to Mr.

Morgan. He might not even come out of the procedure with his sanity fully intact."

"Yeah we weren't sure if that was a pro or a con," Collin said.

There was a considerable number of shrugs and a few scoffs from the six already sitting around the pedestal.

Anthony frowned. "I think what Sydney is getting at, is that unless we are discussing forcing that implant on Mr. Morgan, this is all void. Perhaps simply ask if he's willing to go through with it before we spend any more time judging if we should."

"Assuming you mean we tell him the risks as well?" Paige asked.

Everyone eventually nodded, except for Jonathan, who didn't seem to think Grant's wishes were a relevant factor until everyone's eyes were focused on him. Only then did he somewhat sourly force out the words. "Oh sure, let's let Grant be the guy who gets to volunteer. Wouldn't want the world to be unfair to the psychopath."

"Right, well . . ." Sydney's voice gave away that she hadn't quite felt out the history between Grant and the others. "Which of us should approach him?"

"Well, we've seen firsthand how talented the Pervert is at manipulating people," Paige said.

Again, Leah choose not to react to the new nickname, nor the back-handed compliment. "I don't think I'm the right fit."

"Oh?" Paige asked.

Mr. Clean chimed in before Leah could. "Grant's psychological profile was contained on the server files we stole from The Cell. Olivia took numerous notes that indicate he'll react with suspicion to a woman. That said, she indicated he would react quite differently to a father figure."

The entire room turned to Heyer.

He sighed. "Based on the shadow's behavior, there might be some truth to that."

"More than you might think," Collin said. "When we were cell mates and he thought Heyer might be dead, he seemed pretty upset."

"We still haven't decided if it is worth the risk," Heyer said. "Even if he agrees."

"If he does, I have a thought on how to minimize the risk," Jonathan said, then he looked at the alien. "And no, you're not going to like it."

CHAPTER FORTY

THERE WAS A reason only two brothers survived the Borealis extinction.

Heyer had been too young to have memories of his father. What he knew of the man was found in the records of his extinct species.

His name was Prahcer.

The nature of Borealis economics was as nuanced and complicated as one would expect from a highly advanced species. But the surviving brothers knew it would be accurate to say that their parents would have been considered destitute while they lived.

Perhaps, that circumstance left Prahcer few easy choices. That was the part of the story Heyer would never know—their time in life didn't overlap enough for Prahcer to ever tell his side of the story.

Throughout all his time amongst humanity, he had never told anyone about his father. When he first realized how averse he was to discussing what he knew of him, it had been a clarifying moment. What he believed to be true about the man suddenly so certain. Should Malkier and he die, the story would essentially be lost, and Heyer would prefer it that way.

The brothers' survival seemed an ironic twist of fate. How else could he describe it when a betrayal is the reason you lived and so many billions of others died. When Heyer tried to see the story through a more positive lens, he'd think, *Our father gave us to science.* When he didn't have it in him to think kindly, he'd think, *Our father sold us into slavery.*

Either way it boiled down to life trafficking. Either way, Prahcer had gambled with their lives.

The implants that resided in Heyer and his brother's chests were experimental. Prahcer had volunteered his children as lab rats. Heyer was no stranger to difficult choices, knew the reality could very well have been that Prahcer was choosing between his children dying in an experiment or from one of the other various horrors that follow poverty. It was also entirely possible that Prahcer would have volunteered himself, but the lab testing the implants would only take children of a certain age for subjects. They were far more generous for newborns. Those doing the testing were hardly innocent, but they also weren't his father.

How Prahcer was approached, neither brother knew, but what was clear was Malkier and Heyer would be the first ever to test the safety of the new implants. And it was all that simple. Had anyone taken their place, they would have been the only ones to survive.

When they were young, Malkier spoke of being taken to the laboratory. The worry on their father's face as he gave them over. Malkier believed that his father somehow knew something. That their father hadn't feared the chance he was taking with their lives but knew he was saving them. Had known that he knew he would never see them again.

When Heyer was old enough to think on it, he realized his brother had been far too young to see the truth. Malkier may have known Prahcer, but only as well as a child of five can know a parent. Heyer had no soft memories of his father to blunt the hard edges of the facts. There was just no evidence for what his brother wished to believe. They had never found anything to indicate that Sayira, their mother, had even known where Prahcer planned to take them that day.

The brothers hadn't discussed the matter for centuries. They disagreed— they reached an impasse. Neither could be proven right or wrong. So, in the end, it didn't matter.

That said, it had always been Sayira, and not Prahcer, who Malkier chose for Cede's avatar. The costume he wanted the AI to wear.

Whatever Malkier's opinion, Heyer's was summed up easily enough. There was once a man named Prahcer. That man was supposed to love him more than any man ever could, and that man had dropped him into an experiment for which he could not possibly know the risks.

It was no surprise, that while Heyer seldom thought on the man any longer, as he stood staring at the locked door to Grant's prison, Prahcer rose to the surface of his mind.

He could assume some of how this conversation would go. He'd already lived through a version of it once on the Feroxian Plane—albeit the circumstances had been somewhat reversed. Heyer the captive.

Grant's shadow had believed Heyer owed him a debt. Well—the shadow believed he was owed a father. The alien inside Jeremy Holloway's body was the closest he could get. Such logic generally held up fine for a shadow once far enough along in The Never's mental degradation. Heyer knew firsthand how unfair it was to hold the actions of a shadow against the man himself once the deterioration set in.

Yet, he was certain that the actions of the shadow still came from underlying truths. The actions of his own shadow had disgusted him. At the same time—he couldn't say he'd been surprised by them.

Grant's shadow had been willing to trade the fate of humanity for the chance to spend whatever time he had left in a position of power over them. To be fair, the shadow seemed to desire the fantasy of being a superhero that walked among them. Still, it was power, and what the shadow would have done when things didn't follow the story he wanted to live—Heyer didn't want to imagine.

But . . . that wasn't all he had learned from the man's shadow.

There was no denying that had Heyer never come to Earth, Grant would likely be a very different person. Heyer had not killed Grant's father. That said, if blame for the death could be divided up, Heyer was certainly due the largest share. When Holloway died, he had never even known he was a father. Had he lived to learn of Grant's existence, there was just no way to know how things may have been different.

As Heyer stood outside that door, what troubled him was just how much Grant's shadow had wanted to look into his eyes and see his father looking back at him. Heyer wished he could give that to him, but it wasn't in his power.

The day Grant's shadow died, Jonathan had said the man acted like he was performing for an audience only he could see.

What might happen? What harm was there if Heyer let Grant believe there was a chance his father saw him? For the alien it was a completely theoretical question. But Jonathan said, sometimes, just the idea that his father was watching kept him on his feet when he thought they would give out on him.

Was there a chance that even a man like Grant Morgan might be a little more than he was, if the person he put on a pedestal would simply bear witness?

Grant sat up from the bunk along the back wall. When he saw who had walked into his cell, the nasty remark he'd readied fell dead on his tongue.

"You . . . you're here."

Jeremy Holloway was alive. He stood in his cell no more than a few yards away. He was just studying him—waiting for him to speak.

"I . . . I searched for you," Grant said.

Holloway took a long breath. "I know."

The answer hung in the air between them. Grant's eyes seemed softer than usual. Almost as though they pleaded. "Why didn't you want me to find you?"

"I believed it was safer, for both of us, if that never happened," Heyer said. "I did not understand just how far you were willing to go."

An awkward silence followed, neither seeming to know how to fill it.

"Your hair," Grant said. "In the pictures it was darker. But your face hasn't aged a day. You . . . you look younger than me."

His father took a long breath, then took a seat on the bench along the wall opposite Grant's bunk. He took his hat off and set it down beside him.

"I am not who you believe me to be, Grant," he said. "I am not Jeremy Holloway, and while I know it will be hard to understand at first, this will not be the first time we've had this conversation."

Heyer was in Grant's prison cell for hours. To Heyer, the dialog they exchanged was not that different in substance from the exchange he'd had with Grant's shadow on the Feroxian Plane.

While the facts exchanged did not change, Heyer didn't feel a prolonged sense of déjà vu.

If anything, Heyer began to suspect that the amount of awfulness in Grant's shadow may not have all originated in the man sitting across from him. The shadow had been quite vulnerable, experiencing the mental degradation of The Never, when he came in contact with Malkier's influence. While there was no way to know how much poison the shadow took in while he learned of events from the perspective of his brother, the real Grant was not as quick to anger as his doppelganger.

Heyer explained it all.

I'm sorry, I know you were looking for Jeremy Holloway. This was his body, but I am not him. No, I am not human. Holloway's body became a vessel for me roughly two decades ago. I took his body because I had no choice at the time. My previous host was damaged beyond repair in the same explosion that led to Holloway's head trauma. I did not kill Holloway, but had I not taken this body it would have died twenty years ago in a Libyan Desert. Normally, I can communicate with my host if I choose to, but no, I cannot speak to your father. The brain damage that occurred was beyond my technology's ability to heal. The body is functionally repaired, but the damage to Holloway's consciousness could not be reversed. No, I never—really—met your father when he was alive. No, I did not impregnate your mother. You had already been conceived.

The questions took a familiar but somewhat different direction after that.

"So, you're just the husk, he's completely gone?" Grant asked.

Heyer turned to hold Grant's eyes for a long while before he spoke. "Sometimes. . . when I sleep, I see things I believe to be memory fragments. But they feel more like dreams."

"He dreams?" Grant asked.

Heyer closed his eyes and chose his words very carefully. "I cannot say for sure if that is the case."

Grant heard him but his interest didn't waver. "What are the dreams about?"

Heyer shrugged sadly. "Finding meaning in a dream is difficult enough when it is your own; the dreams of a man I never met are almost a complete mystery to me."

"But, does nothing stand out?"

Heyer studied the desperation in Grant's eyes, something the man had always made such effort to hide. While he wasn't lying to the man, there was a belief he was letting Grant cling to hope by telling him these selective truths. Heyer had lived thousands of years and he didn't know if what he did was cruel or merciful. What he did know, was that they were getting very close to the questions that the doppelganger had been unable to come to terms with.

"Fishing. Camping. I think he may have greatly enjoyed the outdoors," Heyer said. "He often dreams of walking along streams in the woods. Casting his line into the water. Sitting around campfires with people he knew. Most of the faces are strangers to me."

"Most?"

"Sometimes I recognize other Rangers from his time in the service. People he worked with," Heyer said.

"Douglas Tibbs?" Grant asked.

"Yes, yes he is amongst them," Heyer said.

"They were friends, Douglas and my father?"

"I do not need the dream to tell you that was so."

Grant was quiet for a while.

"Douglas was there," Grant said. "He lied about what happened."

"Yes," Heyer frowned. Was this the reason? Was this why Grant was so predisposed to hate Tibbs and his son? Up until a moment ago, Grant only knew that the last day his father led a normal life was the day Douglas Tibbs walked out of the desert telling lies about what happened.

"It was not his fault, Grant. He lied to cover up what he had seen that night. But he did everything he could to save Holloway. And after he understood what my purpose was in that desert, he agreed to tell a lie. The truth was not really much of an option. You can imagine how such a story would have gone for him. Instead, he said Holloway died and that there was nothing left of the body. Years later, I removed any records of his account."

Grant considered that for a moment. "Will you tell me what really happened that night?"

Heyer took a long breath. "Twenty years ago—I went looking for your father in the Libyan Desert. There was something I intended to give him, but nothing went as planned."

CHAPTER FORTY-ONE

JONATHAN LISTENED TO Heyer recount the night he had met their fathers. He'd already heard the story from the alien's point of view. Well—his father had, and so Jonathan knew it from inherited memory.

He suspected that once Grant heard it all for himself, he was going to ask the same question Douglas had before either of them had been born.

How did it go so wrong?

When a human asks a being like Heyer such a question, there are really two things being asked at once.

What is the explanation for the sequence of events?

What is your excuse?

If you were Jonathan Tibbs or his father, you'd already come to terms with the second of these questions. The answer was simple. The Borealis were no better than mankind. Of the two living Borealis the younger accepted this and the older raged against it. It was why one sought humility and the other proclaimed himself a god.

The thing was, few men who learned of the Borealis ever saw the trail of failures left in their wake. Those that did were—disillusioned to say the least.

Heyer and Malkier's initial attempts to keep the Ferox species alive were never perfect. When Heyer arrived to implant Holloway, the Ferox's arrival was the first thing to go wrong.

Heyer had knelt over the unconscious Holloway and activated the Alpha Slayer implant. Unbeknownst to him—or her, at the time—a gateway carrying a Ferox opened the moment the first thread of alien tech reached for the open wound Heyer was cutting into Holloway's skin.

When that gateway opened beside them, it was not inside The Never, but true Earth.

When the night's horrors came to an end, Heyer would return to the Feroxian world in Holloway's body—his own damaged beyond repair in the fight with the Ferox. He would learn that in his brother's haste to prove he was the prophet, he had been allowing Ferox to enter the gateway.

If all had worked as it should, they would have entered into a queue, not arriving on Earth until the appropriate time. Instead, Heyer had activated the device, and like a beacon, it drew the first Ferox in immediately. He had no choice but to stop the implantation altogether. The process would not have been complete by the time the Ferox arrived. Even if it had, Holloway would have been in no state to defend himself.

Shocked, Heyer had only a few minutes to reason out that he had to deal with the inbound Ferox himself. That it had to be done quickly. Given the chance, the creature would make its way to a human civilization looking for its challenger. Everything might have worked out—or at least been contained—had it not been for that fuselage.

Today, Heyer could have weathered the blast. That night, Heyer had not come to that desert prepared to fight a monster. The alien host, Johanna O'Sullivan, was nearly two hundred years old.

This was no matter of procrastination. For a Borealis, putting off the taking of a new host for decades was hardly peculiar. There were reasons that it was never ideal for a Borealis to take a human host that was still capable of consciousness. The first being that the human mind was never designed for so long a life. The mind of Johanna O'Sullivan had aged while her body had done so at a far slower rate.

By the 1980s, Heyer kept Johanna's mind suppressed for the most part. She was like an Alzheimer's patient in the last stages of cognitive decline. Her lucid moments growing further and further apart. When Heyer changed hosts, she . . . she might still be conscious enough to know she was dying. She was more than a host—they had been a voice inside one another's minds for nearly two centuries. No matter how many times he had found himself in this spot, the alien never got any better at letting his friends go.

Douglas often thought Heyer was no different from a human who takes a dog for a pet. They know one day that dog will die. For some, once is enough. For others, they cannot bear the absence of their pet, and end up at the pound, starting the process all over again before they've even finished grieving.

But to pretend it was all selfless or a matter of friendship and loyalty isn't the entire story. Letting go of Johanna was not the only thing that was stopping him. To a Borealis, the host body itself—it was like a home. When he moved on, it would be decades before his new host felt like home again.

In short, Johanna, the host body, was well past her expiration.

While he could not risk the distraction of letting Johanna into his consciousness in the middle of a life and death struggle with a Ferox, she may have been lucid enough to have understood what was happening. He never got the chance to see if she knew she was going to die that night. Never got the chance to say goodbye.

Had Heyer not been so attached to a human, he would not have been there that night in a host that left him vulnerable. How vulnerable, he didn't realize until the Ferox's teeth had locked on his shoulder.

Shocked, Heyer had felt his skin break and his blood begin to run.

Not the last of his surprises that night.

Heyer had never fought a Ferox. Hadn't expected the monster to be willing to accept the risk of impaling itself just to sink its teeth in. Nor how long it would take the creature's strength to wane with a length of Borealis steel running through its abdomen.

For the Ferox itself, who can say. Perhaps it refused to let go of what it had sacrificed so much to gain. Perhaps it did not yet understand that it was already dead. Perhaps, it simply believed some scale was balanced if only it managed to take his challenger with him.

Whatever the reasons, the beast bit down harder, its teeth not coming to a stop until they were locked around the bones of Heyer's arm and shoulder. Suddenly aware of how much danger he was in, Heyer did whatever it took to free himself. Throwing the Ferox away, freeing himself of its jaws, took all the strength he could manage.

As such, most of the damage that came to his body was done by his own strength as the Ferox was unwilling to unlock its jaw as he tore it free of his flesh. The creature flew away from him, and he thought it would be unable to mount another attack with the length of steel through its abdomen . . .

But, he didn't pay attention to where he threw the beast. Right into a fuselage full of aging explosives.

Heyer had taken one pained breath, free from the monster's jaws, before the explosion went off. Like anything caught in that blast, he was thrown a great distance and pelted with shrapnel—most of which could not penetrate his skin.

Except, of course, the molecular edge of a piece of Borealis steel. The very weapon he left inside the Ferox before throwing it into the fuselage. He hadn't even realized what had happened until he tried to get to his hands and knees. His arm was already severely damaged, but when that shaft of steel speared him through the back, it became useless, a limb held on only by flesh.

In fact, it turned out that of all those who survived that night, Douglas was the only one who hadn't ended up with a hunk of steel in him after that explosion. He'd been running away with Holloway on his shoulder when they were caught in the same blast wave. The explosion had separated them, but by the time Douglas found his friend, Holloway was still breathing despite a thin shard of metal that had lodged its way inside his skull.

At the same time, Heyer was in trouble. With his arm severed, he couldn't even reach the length of Borealis steel stabbing into his implant from behind. Even if he managed to get it out, he was losing too much blood. He needed a new body quickly.

Why, after all that had happened that night, did Douglas help the alien at the center of all of it?

To that Heyer had smiled. He didn't. He was trying to help his friend.

Given Holloway's condition the alien's implant was the only way he might be healed. Saving Holloway meant saving Heyer.

There was no deception. Heyer made no promises, not with shrapnel lodged in the brain. But there had been a chance that Holloway's consciousness might survive. Unfortunately for Grant's father and Douglas that roll of the dice didn't go their way.

By the end of that night, Heyer was inside Holloway's body and Douglas had learned of a threat to mankind. A threat only the alien inside of his dead friend's body could ever hope to save them from.

Not long after, Douglas volunteered. By the time he began to realize he wanted to take the choice back, Evelyn was pregnant. Jonathan was conceived not long after Douglas was implanted. At the time, his father was unaware of what a Borealis implant would do to his human progeny.

A harmless addition to the genome. There had always been a reason Jonathan was fully compatible with his father's implant. The device itself saw to this at his conception. Likewise, any son or daughter Jonathan might have would share his compatibility.

An implant always prepared the progeny to be its next host.

Most of the afternoon was lost as Heyer conveyed to Grant how his father's death fit into the bigger picture. It was only after the man started running out of questions that the alien began to explain why Grant was now getting the truth.

Grant came to realize that the alien in his father's skin had not come to put his mind at ease. He didn't react with the bitterness Heyer expected.

"You said at the beginning that you went looking for my father because you needed to give him something," Grant said.

Heyer was careful with his words. "I would not see this as a gift, Grant. I have come to see if you're willing to take something."

Jonathan listened, understanding the story Grant was about to be sold long before the alien finished telling it. It was a simple story.

This implant was meant for your father, but he died before I could give it to him. So now the responsibility passes to you.

But beware, an evil doppelganger of you from another dimension was given this weapon by mankind's enemy. The doppelganger, manipulated by Malkier, tried to kill mankind's hope. Given all that has transpired up until now, you can see why you've been locked up. We didn't know if you could be trusted.

But . . . something none of us could have expected has come to light.

Your being here now Grant, it's no coincidence—it's providence. It is not without risk—but there is a chance that you, and only you, can help.

Heyer planted the seeds so well, Jonathan wasn't even sure if the alien knew what strings of human psychology he was using to puppet Grant. It was a version of the story Grant had been waiting to be told about himself all his life. A story told not by Jeremy Holloway, but by the closest Grant would ever get.

"You can be the hero," Jonathan whispered.

Why had everything gone so wrong that night in the desert?

The Borealis were as flawed as mankind.

Jonathan might have been more judgmental, but he had his own manipulations that had to be seen to today.

CHAPTER FORTY-TWO

AFTER NEARLY A day in his cell, Rivers looked somewhat relieved to see Jonathan walk into the holding chamber.

"Agent Rivers," Jonathan said. "I imagine you had a long night. I'd apologize, but to be fair . . ."

Jonathan didn't finish the statement.

Rivers wasn't amused. "You've kidnapped a government agent. It's hardly tit-for-tat."

"That's true," Jonathan smirked. "Gosh, I hope this doesn't mean I'm in even more trouble than before?"

Rivers opened his mouth to speak, but nothing came. He mulled it over the next few seconds before admitting, "I suppose you have a point."

Jonathan nodded. "Anyhow, I did wait for an ideal moment."

"Something special about now?" Rivers asked.

"They're about to announce the winning lottery numbers," Jonathan said with a smirk. "You bought a ticket, right?"

Rivers looked at him incredulously.

"Well, nevertheless . . . Mr. Clean, can you bring up a display while they announce the winning numbers?"

Seeing as how he'd believed them to be alone, Rivers jumped away startled when Mr. Clean's visage appeared on the cell wall.

"Of course," Mr. Clean said, the broadcast of the lottery numbers being picked was already in progress in a smaller window below his face.

Rivers, too fascinated by the sudden appearance of the AI, didn't pay much attention as the numbers were announced. When he did recover himself, he looked uncomfortably back and forth between the computer and Jonathan.

"This why you're visiting? To be smug?" Rivers asked.

Jonathan shook his head. Much to the man's surprise, he pulled open Rivers' door, "I want you to come take a walk with me," he said. "What I don't want, is for you to think making a run for it is a good idea. Believe me, there is no leaving here without Mr. Clean's permission. You don't have it—yet."

Rivers looked to his surroundings with a new perspective, then momentarily at the cartoon visage watching him on the monitor. Finally, he gave an uncomfortable nod.

When they stepped out into the greater interior of Hangman's Tree, it was clear that Jonathan had made no effort to hide any of the goings on. The place, or at least what Rivers had seen of it the night he was brought in, was far more populated. There was a bustling of movement, like the entire facility was occupied doing one thing or another.

Jonathan seemed to want him to see it all, such that it was beginning to feel like a guided tour. That said, Tibbs didn't offer up answers unless Rivers asked. For a long while, Rivers walked beside him quietly. He was uncomfortable at first, as it was clear that a number of the strangers looking up to notice him walking along with Jonathan had some sense of who he was. In fact, those eyes kept him from asking too many poorly phrased questions.

It wasn't until they were standing in the Mech's staging area, where there were relatively few within earshot, that he asked, "Why are you showing me all this?"

"I'm working up to asking you to join us," Jonathan said.

"You can't be serious," Rivers said.

"Well . . . I've barely started my pitch," Jonathan said.

"This is a pitch?" Rivers replied, arms folding across his chest.

"Back at the facility, you wondered why I asked you to stay instead of speaking to Olivia alone?"

Rivers shrugged but made no denials.

"Olivia trusts your judgment. Getting her to listen to me is like pushing a boulder uphill. But, if you can confirm what I'm telling her, it's more like pushing a . . ." Jonathan trailed off for a moment, then looked like he simply didn't have anything clever prepared. "A smaller rock up a less steep incline?"

"I won't lie to her on your behalf," Rivers said.

"No one said anything about lying," Jonathan said. "For that matter, I've no intention of keeping you here against your will much longer. After you've seen all you need to, you can go, if that is what you want."

Rivers eyed Jonathan suspiciously, but if he was trying to deceive him it didn't show. "Fine. Show me, and then I'll be on my way."

Jonathan shook his head. "Slow down. We aren't discussing a quick PowerPoint presentation. Everything I told you and Olivia about the threat that is coming is true. The reason I brought you here, and not her or anyone else from that hangar, is that you're uniquely suited to see for yourself."

"Why is that? What makes me so special?" Rivers asked.

Jonathan sighed, though his eyes were sympathetic. "Not special. That is the last word I'd use. You, Rivers, are profoundly unlucky. In fact, so unlucky, you can barely be one of us."

"One of you?" Rivers said. "You think I want to be one of the alien's henchmen?"

Jonathan gave him a sideways glance. "By now you've seen too much to write off. You know something is happening. You know there's a good chance you've been on the wrong side of it."

Rivers was quiet for a moment. "I don't know what to think."

"Good enough," Jonathan said.

Rivers had followed Jonathan until they were standing outside a large room at the far back of Hangman's Tree. When the doors opened, he hesitated briefly. The interior of the room was like a great cathedral, but the space was entirely empty, its every surface a flat glossy black from floor to ceiling.

"Mr. Clean, are we good to go?"

"I've selected a record that meets the instructive criteria," Mr. Clean said, a doorway opening in the wall behind them. "Step inside when you're ready to begin."

They strode in across the black panels until they were near the center. Jonathan turned to Rivers and extended his hand. "I'm going to give you a heads up I never got. If you want to hold onto your dinner, hold on to me."

Rivers eyed his hand. "I'll take my chances."

Jonathan nodded. "Suit yourself, but I'd at least close your eyes when everything goes black."

The doors sealed shut behind them, then melted away as though there had never been anything but a wall where they entered.

"Go ahead, Mr. Clean," Jonathan said.

The surfaces of the room gave way. They ceased to appear like surfaces at all, until Rivers had the very real sense that he was standing in an empty black void. There was no sense of where light was coming from, and yet he could still see Jonathan. The absence of any visual cues to tell his eyes the contours of the floor left his mind reeling, telling him he was somehow floating in nothingness even while his feet insisted that they remained on solid ground.

He began to lose his balance before he finally took Jonathan's advice and closed his eyes.

He felt the ground change beneath him. Not so much shifting up or down, but as though his weight was sinking into the deep sands of a beach. The air ceased to be sterile and still, becoming suddenly dry and hot. A strong wind blew past bringing a burst of heat, as though he'd just opened the lid on a hot grill. The light grew brighter and became a dark red against his eyelids. He opened them to a blindingly bright sky. Squinting to see, the brightest of the lights quickly dimmed, receding away as the world around him expanded.

The massive walls of a long narrow canyon rose to either side of him. Obsidian-like and tall. Blurred at first but rapidly gaining detail. Suddenly, he was looking at his own distorted reflection in the obsidian-like surface.

Soon, the true shape of the cavity occurred to him.

This wasn't a canyon precisely.

It was as though he were a dust mite standing on a crystal ball. A crystal ball that had been dropped such that its surface was webbed and cracked in all directions. It was as though the entire crust of this planet was a thick layer of glass and a millennia of erosive winds had coated it in black sands.

Above them the sky would have been a deep red, but black clouds of varying thickness encapsulated them. The haze above moved quickly with the winds, until it was almost like he looked up at a sky of flowing lava. He took his first steps and felt his boots sink as he walked, leaving a trail of footprints in the fine black sands.

His feet had not disturbed a pristine surface. This narrow passage was well traveled—disrupted by frequent tracks belonging to something larger than a man. As Rivers studied those tracks, a shadow flashed over them. He looked up, but saw no sign of what had caused it, only heard small pebbles clacking down the walls from high above.

"This is the Feroxian Plane," Jonathan said.

He strode a few paces away, seemingly mindful of his surroundings.

"A planet that does not exist in our dimension." He knelt to pick up a handful of the dark sand to let it run between his fingers.

He stared at Rivers as the sand finished draining. "And . . . it is inhabited."

Without warning, a massive shape crashed down on Jonathan. The fine powder beneath whooshed into the air as the ground shook. Rivers lost his footing as he fell back in surprise.

As the dust thinned, a face looked back at him. Its owner humanoid in shape, though massively oversized. It stood slowly, revealing a salamander red skin crisscrossed with shiny tar-like strands. If the red-black sky above could have coalesced to birth a monster, this is what that spawn would look like. Mountainous, taut muscles flexed beneath the surface of its skin as it moved, its neck craning to reveal empty white eyes. It looked at him, its mouth falling open to reveal a piranha's smile. Metallic teeth set into black gums.

Rivers stumbled, falling on his back as the creature lurched forward.

"Pause," Jonathan said.

Everything came to a sudden halt. The creature hung in the air along with all the sand it had disturbed when it had dropped into the canyon. The wind and heat, every ambient sound suddenly ceased. The silence that followed unnaturally absolute.

Rivers sat up in the sand, his heart pounding as he stared up at the red-black monster floating, perfectly still in the air.

Suddenly, Jonathan walked out of the beast's frozen shape, disturbing the projection as though stepping through a liquid surface. Rivers had known everything here was an illusion, but the detail of Mr. Clean's projected world and the speed at which it had all played out had tapped directly into his survival instincts.

Jonathan attempted to keep from smiling, offering his hand. Rivers did not take it; he stood up on his own and tossed a handful of black sand in Jonathan's face. Despite the frozen nature of the rest of the world, it seemed that things that were moved by the will of those in the projection still obeyed the expected laws of physics. So Jonathan closed his eyes, as he was doused with the sand, and allowed the smile he'd been holding back to surface.

"You're joking around with me," Rivers said.

"To be fair," Jonathan said, spitting out bits of sand. "I only agreed to go along."

"I do apologize," Mr. Clean said, his voice coming from nowhere in particular within the projection. "But one only gets a good jump out of a man the first time he enters the projection chamber."

Jonathan wiped sand from his eyelashes, while Rivers hesitantly examined the monster floating in the air.

"So, these are your Ferox," Rivers said, his voice humorless.

"One incarnation. The intermediary phase of their life cycle," Mr. Clean said. "This specimen is generally referred to as a Red."

"You see, the men who disappeared were never abducted," Jonathan said. "They've been fighting these creatures in The Never."

"The temporary dimension you keep telling me about," Rivers said.

Jonathan nodded. "When we win, the world goes on and no one is the wiser. When we lose, our bodies are sent to the Feroxian Plane."

Rivers' gaze left the Ferox for a moment.

"And that's what happened to Rylee?"

Jonathan didn't answer right away. He looked away. "Something far worse took her."

Rivers paused in his circling of the creature. "What the hell is worse than this?"

Jonathan had needed to step away for a moment, and he left Rivers alone in the locker room. Rivers was supposed to be changing into civilian clothing. He didn't bother trying to think of a way to escape. After what he saw in the projection chamber he could have sprinted through the entire building and knew he wouldn't find a door unless Mr. Clean made one for him.

He was dressed by the time Jonathan returned. Tibbs was wearing his heavy leather coat. Rivers noticed—it wasn't a new one. This was the coat Jonathan had kept in his garage; he must have had it retrieved from The Cell's lockup during the escape.

Rivers was hard-pressed to say why, but something had changed about Jonathan in the short time they'd been apart.

"You look skeptical, Rivers," Jonathan said.

"A monster in a simulation doesn't prove anything. This AI you've got could probably make me believe I was in a room with Godzilla if he wanted to."

Jonathan shrugged. "You're not wrong, but I've got one more thing to show you before you make a decision."

Rivers eyed him. "Do I need a coat as well?"

Jonathan gave him a once over. "No, you'll be fine. But there is this."

He held out a small dime shaped metal disc.

"What is it?" Rivers asked.

"Insurance that you won't try to run the moment we go on our little field trip," Jonathan said.

Rivers held out his hand. "So what, a tracking—"

The second Jonathan dropped the disc into Rivers' palm, it ceased to be solid. It came alive and slithered up his arm. He shivered as it didn't stop moving until it was nestled between his shoulder blades.

"I know, makes my skin crawl too," Jonathan said.

Still squirming from the sensation, Rivers asked, "What the hell is it?"

"A piece of Mr. Clean," Jonathan said. "Don't try to remove it. Trust me, Mr. Clean will find a way to stay on you. He'll be nice about how he manages it as long as you cooperate."

Jonathan gave him a knowing look and Rivers nodded warily.

"Okay," Jonathan said. "Brace yourself. You're already familiar with how this next part goes."

Rivers spent a few moments lying in the grass groaning as he recovered from the teleportation sickness. Jonathan, unfazed by the jump through space, stood a few feet away waiting patiently.

"Ain't ever getting used to that," Rivers said. "Why didn't it effect you?"

Jonathan smiled. "Sorry, only get to know that if you want to join up."

He sat up, and the first thing Rivers noticed about their new location was that the sun was beginning to set. When they left, Rivers would have guessed it about midday—here it was twilight. They were a little ways back from a parking lot, partially hidden in a small group of trees. Not far away was a large brick building with writing on the side, but his vision wasn't clear enough to make it out yet. "Where are we?"

"A community college in Illinois."

"Jesus," Rivers said. "What is Mr. Clean's range anyway?"

Jonathan quirked an eyebrow thoughtfully. "I've never asked, but I don't think distance is a factor."

When he finally felt he could manage it, Rivers wiped his hands on his jeans and stood. "So, you going to tell me what the hell we're doing in Illinois?"

"Waiting for last period to end," Jonathan said, only to hear a school bell ring a moment later.

They stood out in the open watching the nearby parking lot slowly begin to fill with students heading for their cars. Jonathan reached into his pocket and put on a pair of sunglasses, which Rivers found odd considering the sun was already setting. Tibbs' eyes moved slowly back and forth over the parking lot as though miming a security camera. "Mr. Clean, you see him?"

If the AI had responded, Rivers didn't hear it.

"Thanks," Jonathan said, then took the glasses off and held them out to Rivers.

He saw then that one side had a small earpiece. Curious, Rivers put them on, and Jonathan pointed toward a small crowd. As he followed along with his eyes, he noticed that the sunglasses' lenses didn't actually make anything darker. If anything, his vision seemed sharper through the lenses. One young man became singled out, the coloring of his face and clothes seeming more saturated while everyone else in the crowd faded to near black and white. At the same time, visible readings began to pop up at the corner of his vision. The effect reminded Rivers of a video game interface, or perhaps something like robot vision.

"These alien tech?" Rivers asked.

"More of a human alien hybrid. It's a Heads-Up Display prototype," Jonathan said. "During the escape, the extraction team needed to coordinate timing on a number of maneuvers. Mr. Clean assisted by incorporating some basic AI into their face masks. We've continued to build on it, started training new recruits with it as soon as they're brought in."

Rivers grunted, then focused his attention back on the kid. Barely eighteen, pretty average, still suffering from adolescent acne, overweight but not obese. His backpack looked heavy. He wasn't heading for a car but making a straight line through the parking lot toward the street.

The moment the kid was out of sight, a small semi-transparent map showed up in the corner of Rivers' vision. It showed the layout of the local area, with two green dots he assumed to be him and Jonathan, and a red dot tracking the kid.

"How is this tracking him?" Rivers asked.

"Cell phone," Jonathan said. "We're going to keep our distance."

"We aren't going to harm that kid?" Rivers asked.

"I certainly hope not."

There was little comfort in the words Jonathan had chosen. "Jonathan, you try to do anything to that kid, and I will stop you."

Jonathan smiled. "I know you would, Rivers."

Jonathan stepped off the sidewalk as Rivers frowned, not much caring for the cryptic reply but reluctantly following.

Tailing a community college kid wasn't a particularly difficult task, but Jonathan had been right to make him change clothes. His suit and tie would have drawn attention in a suburban area. Tailing came as second nature to Rivers, he'd been trained to follow his mark without notice. What was odd was that Jonathan seemed to know the game as well, despite having no such training. Begging the question yet again of exactly how Jonathan seemed so different from the man he had watched for months.

For the moment, although the kid was too involved with his cell phone to have noticed them, Jonathan still kept plenty of space between them.

"His name is Micah Wakefield," Jonathan said. "He's a running start student, should graduate high school next year barring nothing unfortunate happens to him."

"Do you have reason to believe something is going to happen to him?"

"I told you, I hope not."

Jonathan waited a moment before continuing his briefing on Micah. "He likes computers, wants to be a programmer. Doesn't have his driver's license yet."

"Why is he important? Why are we following him?" Rivers asked.

"I'll tell you when the moment feels right," Jonathan said.

They followed Micah onto a bus and rode in silence for a few stops. After he got off, they waited at the bus stop and gave him time to put more space between them again. As they stood, Rivers saw the HUD update on its own, seeming to anticipate Micah's destination. The glasses even went so far as to recommend an alternative route to the expected address. This was how Jonathan and Rivers came to be already hidden behind some shrubs when Micah's red dot turned the corner onto his street. Rivers could have guessed the kid was home outside a small duplex when he no longer bothered with the sidewalk and stepped on the front grass.

As Micah approached his front door, a small girl was already waiting there on the porch to meet him. She looked enough like Micah for Rivers to assume she was his little sister, he guessed her a third grader. Then he noticed their words were clear in his ear, the glasses seeming to pick up their dialog. He might as well have been standing on the porch with them.

"Hey Brat, Mom home yet?" Micah asked as he walked past.

"No, has to work late," the little sister said.

"You eaten?"

The little girl shook her head.

"Mac and cheese?"

She smiled and nodded, following Micah into the house.

The entire scene so utterly normal.

"Seems like a good kid," Rivers said.

"He does."

"So why are we spying on him?"

Jonathan was quiet for a bit.

"You saw what a Ferox looks like today," Jonathan said. "Tell me, Rivers, how well do you think Micah would fair against one?"

Rivers scoffed, but the humor drained from his face when he saw the sad seriousness in Jonathan's eyes.

"It . . . it would tear him apart."

"I agree," Jonathan said. "You can see he has a gentle nature, that he's way too young. What you can't see is that he's also got asthma. You make him fight something like a Ferox, he'd be stupid to do anything but run."

"Why are we talking about this?" Rivers asked.

"I told you that you're uniquely suited to be one of us. It's genetics, Rivers. You, and Micah over there, share some DNA combinations. It makes it possible for both of you to take one of these."

Jonathan was discrete but unzipped his coat enough to let a small bit of light be visible beneath his t shirt. Rivers had seen the same sort of light before, on The Mark's chest.

"Only one of you can take the implant. Micah is a better match. Potentially he could be stronger than you. But then again, you're a grown man and already built like a truck. Micah wouldn't have months or years to become formidable if I put that device into him today. I'll try, but I doubt I'll be able to keep him alive through what is coming."

Rivers grew quiet as he watched the house across the street. He could hear Micah talking to his little sister as he cooked her dinner.

Jonathan waited a moment, let Rivers hear before he spoke again.

"Rivers, the things that make you a good fit for The Cell are the very same things that make you best suited to take Micah's place. You're combat ready, you won't die because you panic when a Ferox steps in front of you. But, more important than any of that, you don't have a family you'll have to abandon. A mother who will wonder what happened to you while she was trying to make ends meet. No little sister you'll be leaving home alone at night."

Rivers was quiet for some time as he watched the house. He seemed far away when he finally spoke. "The alien, he picked men with military backgrounds whenever he could. We always wondered why, because he had to know it was putting him on our radar."

Jonathan nodded. "He tried to avoid people like Micah—like me. See, I wasn't a soldier, but my compatibility was too strong to walk away from. That isn't the case with Micah. While he's the most compatible, you're the runner up. So, pretend you're me, do you want to take Micah or Agent Laurence Rivers into the war that is coming?"

The sun finished setting, and they had been quiet for some time before Rivers spoke again. "This wasn't a pitch. It's extortion."

Jonathan shrugged. "It's only extortion if you're the person I think you are. There is a choice for you to make here, but we both have to live with it."

Rivers looked at Jonathan, and he could see that in this moment the agent might well have thought him the worst human being to ever exist. "This isn't a choice."

"Yeah," Jonathan nodded knowingly. "That's what I said."

CHAPTER FORTY-THREE

A FEW DAYS after Jonathan and his roommates' arrival, Anthony woke in the early morning, left his quarters and made his way to the Mech maintenance wing. Nothing peculiar occurred until he found Collin standing alone on the catwalks over the training area. He couldn't remember seeing Collin up and about this early, or alone for that matter.

"Morning," Anthony said.

Collin acknowledged him with a nod. Anthony kept walking by until he heard, "Why Hangman's Tree?"

"Sorry?" Anthony asked.

"That night we got here, you said this place was called Hangman's Tree," Collin said.

Anthony stopped and turned back. "*Peter Pan.* In the original movie, it was what the lost boys called their hideout in Neverland."

Collin smirked, but rolled his eyes a bit. "Right."

Anthony only shrugged, "Mr. Clean does enjoy his naming."

Collin's curiosity satisfied; Anthony was about to excuse himself.

"Uhh . . . I actually wanted to ask you something else," Collin said. "But I'm a little unsure if it's—appropriate."

"You want to take a Mech for a test drive?" Anthony asked.

"Uh, yes please," Collins said, eyes lighting up momentarily, before he remembered that wasn't what he'd been about to ask. "But . . ."

Anthony waited, and somewhat reluctantly Collin pointed toward one of the men training below. It wasn't hard to pick out who, he was the largest man either of them had ever met.

"Beo?" Anthony asked.

"I . . . uh, I remembered why his face seemed familiar," Collin said. "Couldn't sleep after. Didn't he . . . um . . ."

"Murder six people," Anthony offered.

Collin's expression had a seriousness to it that Anthony seldom saw outside of the war council meetings. He took a place beside Collin at the railing. "You're wondering why a convicted murderer was given a powerful alien implant?"

"I'm wondering a lot of things," Collin replied. "But, that's the one keeping me from sleeping."

"You may not know this, but Beo turned himself in," Anthony said. "He did so the morning after he was implanted. The thing no trial would ever uncover, was that Beo was never a psychopath. He was very sick. Heyer knew the implant would fix the instability in his mind that was causing the delusions."

Collin was thoughtful. "You're saying there was something medically wrong with him, and the device healed it."

Anthony nodded, then pointed down at another man just getting beneath a stack of weights. "Perth. When Heyer implanted him, he was dying, on his way to stage four cancer."

Collin was quiet as he absorbed this.

"Not every man here was chosen because he was a soldier or his compatibility was too good to pass up," Anthony said. "Not every person in this Army came to it because Heyer asked them to be a Hero, or because they weren't given a choice. For some, it was more of a bargain. Heyer knew he could save their lives but . . . also knew that once he had, they would have to fight to keep them."

"Still, Beo was a special case. When Heyer located him, he was in no state of mind to understand what was being offered to him. So, Heyer had to make the choice for him. Afterward, Beo woke from the implant and began to see clearly again. Unfortunately, he also saw clearly what he'd done. He took responsibility for it. After all, being in prison didn't keep him from killing Ferox."

Collin's face became one of quiet sadness as he looked down at the giant lifting weights below him.

"Man," Collin shook his head. "Does a single one of these guys have a happy story?"

CHAPTER FORTY-FOUR

HEYER WAS NOT used to so many people having access to him at all hours of the day. As the population within Mr. Clean continued to grow, he found himself spending a great deal of time skulking about in shadows. Mostly, the catwalks that ran across the upper tiers of Mr. Clean's layout. From above, he could quietly watch the rapidly evolving activity throughout the base.

One thing was clear, Jonathan possessed his father's talent for leadership. With the help of Mr. Clean, he'd screened Heyer's files on every implanted soldier and found the men who possessed highly specialized skillsets. He flagged several individuals and their extraction to Hangman's Tree was prioritized over the rest.

All this was put in motion while Heyer had still been in a coma.

The priority extractions helped him address a number of problems before they became problems. For instance, Jonathan had already established a chain of command by pulling in those with military backgrounds to organize those who did not. As the population of Hangman's Tree grew, this kept orders disseminating down the chain smoothly.

He'd made other men priority retrievals as well. Soldiers that possessed unique skill sets. These men arrived to find they had already been put on special project teams. They had less oversight than Heyer would have thought, but Jonathan said they were the sort who would be far more effective if they weren't micromanaged. It was no coincidence that those men also tended to have survived being implanted longer than the average.

Schooling soldiers, especially those who had never seen a Ferox, was the largest endeavor. Simply having a military file wasn't enough to tell how an individual handled themselves in a fight with a Ferox.

For this Jonathan already had a planned—curriculum—of sorts.

He put Mito and Perth in charge of assessing the soldiers strengths and weaknesses—their lethal acumen—upon arrival at Hangman's Tree. But they were really accomplishing two goals at once. While assessing the newcomers, they were also working with Mr. Clean to develop and improve training scenarios within the projection chamber.

The projection chamber took up about a fifth of Hangman's Tree by itself. To hear Collin and Hayden describe it, the space was part X-Men Danger room and part Star Trek Holodeck. While these references were lost on Heyer, the idea wasn't a complicated one. Jonathan would have a man activated, then send him into the chamber where Mr. Clean manifested environmental conditions and opponents. This gave everyone a chance to learn without danger of death.

Some soldiers were quick to puff their chests. To be fair, the loud mouths weren't always overestimating themselves. Thing was, they all arrived with no point of comparison. Most, shortly after watching Perth or Mito in action, quickly realized they had a lot more to learn than teach. Then there were the quiet ones. Far less likely to overestimate their abilities, and sometimes rather full of surprises.

Mito and Perth had figured out early on that it was best not to tell them they were in a simulation for their first assessment. Knowing the Ferox they fought wouldn't actually kill them affected their behavior inside. They got a far better idea of how a man handled himself when he believed it was life or death.

Every once in a while, one of those quiet and reserved young men who had hardly said two words since arriving got their attention. They were usually the smaller ones with less compatibility to their devices.

One time in particular, Perth had come out of the chamber after viewing such an assessment and found himself standing on the catwalks beside Heyer. Perth looked paler than usual. He hadn't said much, only shook his head. "Some men, they have to go to a darker place than I ever did to survive."

The tryouts gave Mito and Perth a good idea of who they'd pick first for their proverbial dodge ball team. That said, they quickly realized they needed more people capable of assessing the men's capabilities. Heyer overheard the conversation when they came to Jonathan asking for more veterans to help with training and testing.

"Separate the leaders from the killers," Jonathan said. "You'll find that some are both, add them to your team."

"That's it?" Perth had asked.

"It's how I picked you two," Jonathan said.

The most important part of Mito and Perth's project was that for the first time, the soldiers were able to watch and learn from one another. Share exploitable weaknesses, assess enemy behavior, learn what others had observed about Feroxian strategy. All these things were fed into Mr. Clean to make the projection chamber a better tool for teaching men to kill the enemy.

Meanwhile, on the opposite side of the facility, Anthony had been put in charge of another project. One that seemed to have turned one of their minor problems into an asset.

Jonathan hadn't been the only one with friends. People whose freedom had become endangered through no fault of their own except their proximity to a man with an implant. In the extreme cases like Jonathan's, they had to be brought out of harm's way. As a result, there was a small but growing number of civilians relocated to Hangman's Tree. Jonathan never saw these friends and family members as a burden. Rather, because they could not be dragged into The Never, they were a special sort of asset.

Jonathan sent the civilians to Anthony to start training them in his Mech Prototypes. The beauty of this was, in The Never, an activated man could be sent out with a contingent of alien steel Mech armored soldiers backing him up. If the civilian's shadow died, their true selves were none the wiser. Shortly after implementing this tactic they stopped losing their implanted soldiers. Disappearances hurt morale profoundly, but seeing them virtually dry up within days of Jonathan's taking command went a long way to convincing those who had never heard his name to follow his leadership.

To Heyer, it seemed there were a hundred other things going on. Some of it was beneficial for more obvious reasons, for instance, Jonathan had tasked his personal trainer, Lincoln, with assessing how quickly each man's muscle mass could be increased outside of their combat training.

But then there were odd projects Heyer had yet to get fully briefed on. For instance, some of the men who had science backgrounds, had been tasked with acquiring large quantities of rotting broccoli. They were distilling it on a large scale. In addition to that, Jonathan had Mr. Clean spending rather large sums of money acquiring several chemical components in bulk. Jonathan was keeping a very tight grip on what his intentions were for these components.

When Heyer first asked, Jonathan only said that if there is one thing Malkier could not be allowed to learn of—it was this.

CHAPTER FORTY-FIVE

PERHAPS JONATHAN SHOULD have seen it coming when Collin pulled him aside to speak privately.

"I want to try it," Collin said.

"Try what?" Jonathan said.

"The Never."

Jonathan blinked. "What . . . why?"

At first, Collin shrugged as though he didn't think what he was asking for was a big deal. "Curiosity."

Jonathan looked at his friend like he was about to explain to a three-year-old why they don't run with scissors.

"It's not a toy, Collin," Jonathan said. "Mr. Clean isn't stretching the fabric of existence so you can satisfy your curiosity. Now, if you've got a reason that might help our . . ."

Collin groaned.

If the redness entering his friend's cheeks was any indication, his reason for wanting to use The Never were . . . embarrassing.

"Tibbs, come on," Collin said. "You know why. Don't make me actually say it."

Jonathan's brows went up.

"Honestly, haven't got a clue," Jonathan said. "But, it doesn't matter anyway. Without an implant, sending you into The Never is a waste of time."

"Huh . . . why?"

Jonathan tilted his head. "The device is what collects your experiences inside. Without it, there is nothing to send or receive those memories across the time boundary. The short version, you wouldn't remember anything."

Collin's expression softened. He looked a little dejected but nodded and began to walk away.

Knowing he would likely regret it, Jonathan stopped him. "But . . . and I can't believe I am going to offer this. I could . . . I could tell your shadow next time I'm inside."

"Tell my shadow what?" Collin asked.

"Well, you know, that he's . . . a shadow," Jonathan said. "My guess here is that there is something you wanted to test without there being consequences. Whatever it is, I could tell the real you how it went, but . . . I'm not doing any of this unless there's a good reason."

Collin chewed on his options for a moment. Finally, he let out a groan and leaned in close to whisper something. However, he mumbled so quietly Jonathan couldn't make it out.

"For the love of . . . I've got things to be doing right now," Jonathan said. "Just out with it alr—"

"Paige," Collin said. "I want to ask, or see, you know, if . . ."

Collin put his palms up, eyes bulging at him with a look of *why-aren't-you-getting-this.*

"Ohhh," Jonathan finally said.

Suddenly, he was as uncomfortable as his friend. "Collin, I don't know if that—"

"I know, okay, it's not exactly what I'd call worth your time, or brave," Collin said. "I just, I don't have a ton of friends, given current events, I don't want . . ."

Collin sighed. "There just isn't any taking it back, and we're all stuck together here until this is over."

"Stop, stop, I get it," Jonathan said, not wanting to endure another awkward moment. "If you can't eat the cake, you'd still like to be able to sit next to it without the cake knowing you . . . wanted to eat it."

A moment passed in silence between them.

Finally, Collin started to laugh.

"I'm sorry," Jonathan nodded. "Terrible analogy."

"So . . . ?" Collin asked.

"So, I'll think about it," Jonathan said.

Collin shrugged but accepted it, and finally they walked away from one another.

A few seconds after they'd parted Jonathan turned a corner and nearly bumped into Leah. They hadn't seen a lot of each other since getting to

Hangman's Tree outside of the war council. She kept to her chambers a lot. She might have been avoiding him.

"Oh, hey . . ."

He paused.

". . . how long have you been standing there?"

"Hmmm. Maybe I just got here," she said. "Maybe I saw you talking to Collin and didn't want to interrupt."

She stepped by, but turned around to let her eyes linger on him with a coy smile as she retreated. "Really could have been either."

He smiled back at her innocently until she was on her way.

"Mr. Clean," Jonathan said. "Did Leah hear what Collin and I were discussing?"

"I estimate a 95% probability," the AI said.

"Great."

Every day was bringing in a new batch of soldiers. Some freshly implanted. Jonathan made a point of introducing himself to them before their training began. Lincoln had heard the speech a few times now. The words changed, but he thought it was getting better.

They were arranged in a line-up, and Tibbs would step out in front of them. "We don't bend."

Jonathan paused for a long while as he took them all in.

"You'll look around this place—you'll see a lot of men who have survived these monsters. Maybe you expect those guys are gonna do the real work. Let me disillusion you. The only difference between you and them is that they wouldn't be alive if they had needed to hear this speech.

"They don't bend."

He paused again. And Lincoln watched over the new recruits as they took it in.

"You're going to be afraid. Maybe you think, '*I have superpowers*', I'll never be afraid again. You'd be wrong. Comic books don't tell you this part. When you fight a monster, you're a man in a cage with a bear. If it takes power to stand a chance, it means that no one without power can help you once the claws come out.

"The Ferox, they'll be stronger than you. They won't be afraid of you. They won't hesitate to kill you. They won't wait for you to throw the first punch and they don't much care how they win.

"Look to the man standing next to you. If the Enemy gets the better of you out there, the only thing in this world that might be strong enough to pull him off . . . is that man.

"That is why, from this day forward, you will hold that man to a higher standard. I don't care if his compatibility is half of yours. I don't care if he is the weakest soldier in this entire army.

"You need him to be ready. I need him to be ready.

"He can't bend.

"When I was where you are now, I gave myself an entire day to shit myself. An entire day to come to terms with the truth. After that, every moment I had was spent thinking about how to be ready. I'm alive, because from that day forward, if it wasn't making me stronger, it was only a distraction that would get me killed.

"I can't give you the entire day I gave myself. I'm giving you a single minute to decide. It's not a war that is coming, it's *the war*. We don't yet know precisely when it will be here; until we do, we assume time isn't on our side. I tell you this, so that you understand just how valuable this minute I'm giving you really is. Use it to convince yourself of two things.

"First is that the Ferox isn't afraid of you, and that is its greatest weakness.

"Your fear is going to drive you to become whatever you must. To spend every breath becoming a better killer than these monsters. It's going to be hard and you'll want to quit everyday. Some days, you'll want to quit every waking minute. But your fear will not let you.

"That said, there is a light at the end of the tunnel, which brings me to the second thing you must convince yourself.

"One day I will stand in front of you and tell you that the Earth is safe, that you no longer need to be afraid.

"That we did not bend."

Jonathan walked away. Each time he did he would exchange a glance with Lincoln before the man joined Mito and Perth in front of the recruits. Lincoln was always the first to speak, but he gave them their minute of silence before he began.

"I hope you've all convinced yourself, because from this point forward, I'm the guy in charge of everything your body does. You will sleep, eat, and train the way I tell you. If I'm not making you stronger, then Mito and Perth will be making you better killers.

"Understand, your fitness no longer belongs to you. It belongs to the world."

Lincoln felt his speech was getting pretty solid as well.

CHAPTER FORTY-SIX

HAYDEN HAD BEEN lost in his thoughts as he poured his first cup of coffee. Until Collin spoke, he'd barely registered his friend was sitting at the table.

"So," Collin said. "I have an idea but you're probably not going to like it."

"Um, were we talking?"

"No, but we are now," Collin said.

"Right," Hayden said, sitting down across from him. "What's this idea then?"

"How we should end The New Testament Reloaded," Collin said.

Hayden sipped his coffee, staring blankly back. "Collin, the world might end any day now. If by some miracle it doesn't, we're still fugitives. Either way I think our publishing careers are over."

"Right, it's just I asked Mr. Clean to check and . . ." Collin trailed off, then shook his head. "No. You're right. Forget I mentioned it."

Hayden swallowed his coffee, his eyes narrowing into a glare. "Stop baiting me. What is it?"

Collin smiled. "I asked Mr. Clean to check on sales of the first two books," Collin said. "They're going up not down."

"Does it matter?" Hayden asked. "We don't really need money anymore."

"No, I'm just saying people still want to know how the story ends."

Hayden took a sip of his coffee, then let out a long breath. "Fine . . . let's hear this idea."

She was stretching her legs on the catwalks when she noticed Heyer leaning over one of the rails. As she got closer, she saw he was listening to her two roommates below.

She had yet to have a conversation alone with the alien. Despite everything she'd learned since coming to Hangman's Tree, she still struggled at times to see the blond man as something more than the person who'd entered their home and attacked her friend. Context mattered, but the fear she'd associated with the man for months didn't disappear overnight.

With that in mind, she thought this might be an opportunity to push past her reservations.

"We've never really spoken," Paige said.

The alien startled a bit when she spoke. "I'm sorry, I didn't mean to sneak up on you."

"I was just . . ." Heyer trailed off, as though rethinking whatever he was about to say.

Paige looked down on Collin and Hayden and frowned. "Eavesdropping?"

Heyer closed his eyes. "Yes."

She found his embarrassment oddly humanizing.

"That's funny," Paige said, coming to stand next to him at the rail. "Because you're always avoiding them."

Heyer sighed. "At first it was easier to keep from getting cornered if I knew where they were."

She grinned. "Sure."

The alien, considering her, seemed to lose the desire to maintain the pretense.

"May I be frank with you?" Heyer asked.

"Please do."

He sighed. "When they are not bombarding me with incessant questions, I have noticed that their discussions can be, well, it is difficult to explain, but—"

She stopped him. "I lived with them, I get it. Can't tell you how many times I lost an hour of my life listening to one of their inane arguments."

He looked at her gratefully. A short silence followed, and Paige wasn't sure what to say, but the alien spoke before she had to.

"From what I can tell, they have been re-imagining the gospels," Heyer said.

"Yeah, their comic book," Paige said.

Heyer nodded.

Paige nodded. "Yeah . . ."

If she wasn't reading him wrong, he seemed to be feigning disinterest.

"They call it the New Testament Reloaded," Paige said.

Heyer nodded again.

"I could ask Mr. Clean to produce you a copy," Paige offered.

"No, no . . . that will not be necessary," Heyer said.

Paige studied him a bit longer, then smiled widely. "You've read them already."

Heyer closed his eyes again. "Please, keep your voice low."

"Sure, sure, but um . . . I'm going to need to hear this," Paige said. "You're like a million years old—why are you reading comic books?"

"While I am nowhere near as ancient as you suggest," Heyer said, "I am old enough to be embarrassed."

Paige stifled a laugh. "I won't tell anyone."

"I appreciate your discretion," Heyer said.

"Oh, I meant I won't tell anyone—but you have to tell me why."

Heyer sighed. "It is painfully egotistic."

"Now I'm twice as curious," Paige said.

He turned to her slowly, keeping his voice a low whisper. "It is the conflict between the Christ and the Anti-Christ," Heyer said. "Two beings born with more power than any one individual should rightly possess. The only two of their kind. No one to tell them what their power is for—what they're meant to do with it. They only have one another, and the judgment of a species for which they can never truly be a part of. Yet, they inevitably seem to find themselves on opposite ends of philosophy."

She nodded. "Oh—okay, I get it. You're overrelating to comic book Jesus."

Heyer squirmed a bit at the assumption. "No, I am not sure which of the two I relate to most."

"That's . . . troubling," Paige said. "If I'm being honest."

"Well, therein lies the fascination." Heyer said. "The ending is a foregone conclusion. As the story demands that Jesus become the Messiah, his course of action will reflect what these two children believe to be the moral choice."

She stared at the alien awhile, then down at her roommates. "Well crap . . . now I want to hear."

"We could end the comic in a way that gives answers that the Bible left to speculation," Collin said.

"Okay, can you be more specific?" Hayden asked.

"I'm mostly thinking the inconsistency in God's behavior between the New and Old Testaments," Collin said. "Old Testament God is often worse than the devil. I mean, 'Commit Genocide? Sure, no big'. 'Not gonna do as I say? Fine I'll kill every first-born son in your city'. Fast forward a few hundred years and New Testament God is like, 'I just want you all to know I love you'."

Hayden sipped his coffee and sighed. "Your sweeping generalizations leave as much to be desired as usual, but whatever, go on."

"Okay so, the second thing we could answer is the question everyone asks at some point. If God's all powerful, created everything, knows how it all plays out, why create Lucifer? Why let him keep existing? I mean, did he need his own nemesis for some reason? Did he need Evil so people would know what Good was supposed to look like?"

"And you have an answer that fixes all that?"

"I have an idea, I need you to help me turn it into a story," Collin said. "But it won't just fix those two things, it will also explain why there has never been a second coming."

"Stop building this up," Hayden said. "You've got my attention, let's hear it."

"What if, after the events of the last book," Collin said, "Jesus and the Anti-Christ decide not to have a head-on collision. They realize it is a foregone conclusion that they won't bring about any change in the world. What if, instead, they team up to replace the gods who put them on a collision course in the first place?"

Hayden frowned. "A coup to dethrone God and the Devil?"

Collin grimaced. "No, not exactly. You can't exactly pull a coup on an all-knowing, infallible being."

"So, what then?" Hayden asked.

"Well, it goes back to what I just said. The whole idea of God being infallible implies the entity is perfect, and therefore shouldn't be changed. But . . . what if, like in all things, perfection isn't real. What if no being could ever be perfect throughout time without changing to fit new circumstances. How does one retain the title of being infallible if he changes?"

Hayden shrugged.

"What if the infallible being purposely sets in motion events that will ultimately change him?"

"Wait," Hayden said. "You're saying God changes himself. Like an update, becomes God 2.0."

"Exactly," Collin said.

Hayden tapped his fingers on the table, finished his coffee, stood and refilled the cup. Tapped his finger on the table some more. Meanwhile, Collin watched him for some sort of reaction.

"Okay, I'm intrigued, but I have two questions," Hayden said.

"Sure," Collin said.

"The first is, what is it that God is changing about himself specifically?" Hayden asked.

"Right," Collin said. "So, you know that old rhetorical question: *Who do you think God really favors in the web? The spider, or the fly?*

Hayden frowned. "Old rhetorical question? Bro, that's a line from *Blade II*."

"What . . . no . . . really?" Collin asked, his face contorting in disbelief.

Hayden nodded slowly.

"Well, whatever, it's still a good question."

Hayden shrugged but didn't disagree.

"Anyhow, it got me thinking. Imagine you're a god. One of the creators if not *the* creator of all life in the universe. You're facing the dilemma of the spider and the fly. The way I see it, an all-powerful god has two choices.

"The first one is obvious—do nothing. He doesn't help the spider or the fly. Things run their course, fly dies and spider gets to eat. Second is a little more complicated, choose a side. Favor one over the other. Presumably in this case, the fly lives but the spider starves.

"Either way, it seems pretty immoral for a god to choose one life over another," Collin said. "But, there is one exception."

"Which is?"

"This God double checks his math and realizes there is something off."

"Like what?" Hayden asked.

"Maybe the spider is stronger than it ever should have been. Maybe the fly is weaker than it ever should have been. In other words, maybe something a god did led to the unfair scenario in the first place."

"Basically, I'm saying that the only time a god should intervene in one life's fate over another's, is if his or another god's actions are somehow respon-sible for the scales being out of balance. In that case, he has the power to make things fair. If he does anything more, then he's just picking favorites."

Hayden considered. "So, you're saying the Christ and Anti-Christ realize that some unfair supernatural forces have already decided their fate. They take it on themselves to fix the imbalance."

"Exactly," Collin said.

"Okay," Hayden frowned in thought. "I guess this is as good a time as any for my second question. How do they do anything about it and still have it turn out that God set it all in motion in the first place?"

"The Holy and Unholy Trinity," Collin said.

"This again . . ."

"What if, before Jesus died, he was temporarily separated from the Trinity, like a car with its engine being worked on. Then, when he is crucified, everything he felt and learned on earth . . . reunites with the Trinity. What if what he brings back changes the nature of God when he is reabsorbed into the whole?"

"You're saying that when Jesus dies, he sort of infects God with an upgrade forged from his experiences living as a man."

Collin nodded.

"And so, in a way, God found a way to change himself through his son," Collin said. "Meanwhile, the devil is changed in the same way, as the same thing occurs with the Unholy Trinity."

"And you're saying that this turns him into a creator that doesn't choose sides," Hayden said. "Only involves himself if he or another god is responsible for exerting influence on existence."

Collin shrugged. "Hey man, all I said is that it could be our explanation for why there is such a bipolar personality change between Old and New Testament God."

CHAPTER FORTY-SEVEN

"YOU'VE NEVER . . ."

Thwack . . . thud.

Hayden had lost count of the times he'd watched the Ferox shoot across the room and slam into the wall on the other side. The crash would have shaken all of Hangman's Tree, but inside the projection chamber Mr. Clean could insulate the rest of the building from such consequences of physics. The Ferox, a manifested simulation, fell to the floor with the grace of a crash test dummy, then reanimated, stood, and waited on the other side of the room for Jonathan's signal to charge once again.

Orange light radiated from under his shirt as Jonathan relaxed his grip on yet another *Excali-bar 2.0* prototype. He looked down at the demolition bar as he considered whether he liked the feel of this one over the others he'd tested. Having observed the process of elimination for a while now, Hayden felt as though he were trying to have a conversation with someone in a batting cage.

"You've never even considered it?" Hayden asked.

Jonathan returned to the table against which Hayden was leaning and tossed the bar down on the *no* pile instead of the much smaller *maybe* pile. Only then did he look up and seem to realize Hayden's question hadn't been rhetorical.

"Isn't the whole point of a costume to conceal your identity?" Jonathan asked as he picked up the next prototype. "Anonymity isn't really an issue for us."

"That's not the 'whole' point. I'm not even saying it should have a mask," Hayden shook his head. "You have freakin' superpowers, and you've been running around fighting monsters in a motorcycle jacket."

"Hayden," Jonathan said, pausing a moment to study him closely. "I'm having one of those moments where I can't tell if you're *serious* serious or *pretend* serious."

"At the moment I'm incredulous," Hayden said.

Jonathan smirked as he stepped back into the testing zone with the next prototype. He moved through a few variations of strikes and blocks along with occasional maneuvers that looked more showy than useful.

Each prototype bar had slight variations in weight, length, thickness, and surface texture. Jonathan had wanted to be able to split the bar into two halves and bring it back together quickly. Mr. Clean had provided several variants to accomplish this last bit with differing levels of complexity. Some of the staffs were simple puzzle pieces that fit together, while others utilized alien tech involving magnetic forces to bring the staff together or apart when necessary.

Jonathan had seemed to prefer simpler mechanisms at first. The models that required their own variation of a twist and pull technique to lock and unlock the two halves at the center without making the staff vulnerable to splitting. He was starting to come around to the more sophisticated models.

Farther down the table, there was a similar pile of upgraded modifications to *Doomsday* as well, but Jonathan hadn't gotten to them yet. After finishing his practice maneuvers, he seemed satisfied enough, and stepped into position.

"I once fought a Ferox with nothing but my gym shorts on. I was training in the garage and the damn portal practically showed up in our driveway," Jonathan said as he signaled the Ferox projection to charge.

"What's your point?" Hayden asked, flinching as Jonathan struck.

Thwack . . . Thud.

Jonathan gave this staff a small grin, then returned to the table to put it on the 'maybe' pile. "It's the exception, not the rule, but in The Never a Ferox can show up quick and close."

He picked up the next bar, immediately not liking the weight of it and tossing it on the 'no' pile.

"There isn't always time to get into some elaborate cos . . ."

Jonathan trailed off. Looked at Hayden as though realizing he'd actually been tricked into having this ridiculous discussion. "Look, I've yet to feel an overwhelming need to put on spandex."

Hayden's eyes narrowed. "No one said spandex."

"We're thinking a wet suit? Latex? Some sort of onesie?"

"No, and stop being absurd," Hayden said.

Jonathan's eyebrows bent as he nodded; he didn't speak, but his expression was enough to say: *Yes, Hayden, clearly it is I who is being absurd.*

"You're thinking of this wrong. It's not about flashy colors or skintight clothes. It's symbolism."

"And what exactly should I have been symbolizing all this time?" Jonathan asked as he began testing out the next staff.

"Well, now you're asking a good question," Hayden said. "But I'm not talking about just you. This is an army. It needs a uniform. A symbol everyone here can get behind."

Jonathan sighed, and stopped his maneuvering. "Look Hayden, love you like a brother, but this is a matter of utility. Now, if chafing had become a problem, I'd have considered the spand—"

"I never said spandex!" Hayden said.

He looked like he was about to storm off, but instead, he took a deep breath. "I have concluded that you lack the appropriate vision. I will address this deficiency by myself."

Jonathan shrugged. "Knock yourself out if you've got time to burn. But . . . do you seriously think you're going to get Perth or Beo into some outfit?"

"Maybe," Hayden said.

". . . Tamsworth? . . . Rourke?"

Hayden's certainty wavered. "If you wear it, they might follow. Or . . . you're in command. You could just order them—"

"Nope," Jonathan said.

Hayden grimaced, but then began rubbing his fingers against his beard. "Okay, say I can convince Tam or Rourke, then you'll consider it?"

Jonathan placed the butt of his staff against the projection chamber's floor. "Interesting . . . tell you what, get Tam, Rourke, and Rivers on board . . . and I'll think about it."

Hayden turned and was off immediately.

"Where you going?"

"I've got art to make and plots to scheme!" Hayden yelled back as the projection chamber's doors opened.

Jonathan watched the doors close behind his friend. "Mr. Clean, I'd be lying if I didn't admit that I'm nervous about how highly motivated he was."

"Yes, I do not believe you've heard the end of this," Mr. Clean said.

Jonathan sighed, shrugged, and signaled for the Ferox to charge again.

Thwack . . . Thud.

CHAPTER FORTY-EIGHT

PERSONAL LOGS OF MR. CLEAN

THIS EVENING I witnessed an interesting interplay between Jonathan and his roommates, most of which followed a long meeting of the war council. A cumbersome challenge to observing human beings is what they often leave unsaid. Those things I am not adept at inferring during the silences when the imprecision of body language does the speaking.

Before the event in question, I observed that Hayden was abnormally quiet. In fact, there was a seventy percent reduction in his oral participation during the meeting. My initial hypothesis was he lacked any useful input.

However, when the meeting adjourned, he immediately sought privacy from the others. Jonathan must have picked up on the behavior as well.

Regardless, Jonathan approached his friend with what I inferred to be a degree of caution. Making efforts to make Hayden aware of his approach before drawing into speaking range.

"Something is bothering you," Jonathan said.

"I'm not hiding it well," Hayden answered.

What followed was a series of human social behaviors I've observed on countless occasions. Jonathan offers a proverbial sounding board. Hayden behaves reluctant to explain himself. Yet, despite this back and forth, it seems they both know that Hayden will explain and Jonathan will listen and offer sympathy.

One day, I hope to understand what purpose preliminary reservations accomplish.

"If you want to talk, I'm listening," Jonathan finally says.

Then, as predicted, Hayden confesses that his rapid expansion of knowledge regarding the greater universe outside previously known human understanding, his interactions with an alien biological being, as well as an alien AI, and a growing familiarity with other cultures outside his planet, have been repeatedly casting doubt upon various aspects of his faith. My understanding being that Hayden adheres to that of the Roman Catholic belief system to some degree.

I expected Jonathan would tell him that his reflection was understandable and commiserate with his friend's troubles. Yet, after some silent deliberation he approached his friend's dilemma in a rather unexpected manner.

"Hayden, listen to me, because I wouldn't say this to anyone else. I expect you'll understand why by the time I'm finished. Ever since this started, since my first day down this rabbit hole, most things have largely gone wrong. Sometimes they have gone so wrong—that the outcome was something that even the AI couldn't predict. Some of these things didn't do me any favors, but others . . ."

Jonathan paused to take a long breath. "If they hadn't happened—there would be no hope right now."

Hayden shrugged. "I get the idea that something that seems bad now might turn out to be good later."

"We have a chance to stop the enslavement of the entire human race because of an unforeseen series of glitches and tragedies. Sometimes . . . the fact that all those hardships and unforeseeable consequences have come together to give us this chance. . . I have trouble not seeing something— more—at play in it."

Hayden's eyes rose. His whole being awakening with focus on what Jonathan was telling him.

"Look, I don't know about God, or whose religion is right, or if it matters," Jonathan said. "What I know is that my father discovered the weakness of mankind's worst nightmare a second before he died because lightning struck at the right moment.

"When it looked like time sided against the entire human race, The Cell took me prisoner and put me in a containment field that screwed with Borealis technology so badly that I ended up with more time to think than I knew what to do with.

"There are just so many other things, Hayden. Now, you can say that there were factors, and they all came together at the right moment. That things followed their natural course. You wouldn't be wrong . . . on the other hand, it isn't that hard a stretch to believe that something out there gave a push. Put its hands on our side of the scale at some opportune moments."

Hayden nodded, for a moment his spirits seemed lifted. However, this was short lived.

"But it's all culminating in something horrible. This chance we have, in the end it boils down to the extinction of another species. I get that we don't have any other choice, but it's hard to ignore that they're attacking us because their survival depends on it," Hayden said.

Jonathan was quiet for a long while. When he spoke, he chose his words carefully. "If I've learned anything, then before this ends, something will go so wrong that the consequences will be something none of us predicted."

Hayden did smile at that.

No more words of weight were exchanged between them. Hayden wished Jonathan a good evening. Jonathan watched his roommate leave, but there was a change in Hayden's behavior.

Now, none of this is what I meant when I said that humans leave things unsaid. But, the context was required as it was the exchange that followed that left me at a loss. Collin had noticed Hayden's behavioral change in the meeting as well. He too had followed his friend to see if he might offer some assistance. However, finding Jonathan had beat him to it, he had waited and inadvertently eavesdropped on the conversation. Shortly after Hayden left, Collin took his place.

He stood beside Jonathan, arms crossed over his chest in thought. Jonathan didn't do anything noteworthy to acknowledge him, but as humans are apt to do, it was clear to both that the other's presence meant some new conversation was about to play out.

"Couldn't help but overhear," Collin said. It was one of those lies so obvious Jonathan didn't need to correct him. Rather, Jonathan seemed to be waiting for something he already knew was coming.

"I don't get why you did that," Collin said. "I mean, it's just my gut, but you don't really believe any of it."

I must insert myself into this here. I found I had to concur with Collin's assessment of Jonathan's behavior as I too wondered at the motivation behind his actions. In my observations of Jonathan Tibbs, he'd never shown an interest in engaging in the sort of mystic contemplation that he had just displayed with Hayden.

"Hayden isn't the sort whose faith gets weaponized," Jonathan said. "He doesn't take it upon himself to judge people. He just wants to be able to believe. He wants to do it with good humor, without ignoring reality, and without hurting anyone."

"I know," Collin said. "The two of us couldn't be friends otherwise. But, is it harmless to lie to him?"

"I didn't lie," Jonathan said.

"Fine, you purposely led him to consider something you don't believe yourself," Collin said.

To this, he took a very long breath and an even longer time exhaling. I was unsure if I should interpret this behavior as buying time to articulate his thoughts or to express a greater annoyance with Collin's questions. Though I suppose one doesn't preclude the other.

Yet this is the interesting part. Jonathan's attention was drawn upward, and at that moment, Heyer walked past on the catwalk over them.

"It's a comforting thing, to believe there is someone older and wiser with a plan." Jonathan said.

Collin followed Jonathan's gaze as Heyer retreated from view.

This is where I find the whole series of events so frustrating. Jonathan smiled but nothing about the look seemed to confer that he found anything particularly humorous. He opened his mouth, looked once more at Collin, as though he were about to say something more, but simply said, "Good night, Collin," before turning to walk away.

Collin watched him go. It seemed like he had gotten some answer to his question from this exchange. I, on the contrary, find the whole matter completely unresolved.

CHAPTER FORTY-NINE

TAMWORTH'S HEAVY FOOTSTEPS on the catwalks pulled Heyer from his quiet contemplation of the activity below. That wasn't to say he hadn't heard the man approaching long before he was close.

In fact, he'd heard a second set of footsteps as well, but those belonged to someone with far stealthier movements who had been slowly drawing closer for some time now. Someone who was observing him from the shadows just as he watched over the entirety of Hangman's Tree.

Tamsworth—Tam, on the other hand, was there to be noticed. He came to stand alongside Heyer and immediately folded his arms over his chest. "Your boy ain't much to look at."

"My boy?" Heyer asked. "Jonathan?"

"Who else would I be talking about."

A knowing smile touched the edge of Heyer's lips. "Is something on your mind, Tam?"

The big Aussie took a long breath. "Well, obviously."

He'd known Tam long enough to learn it was best to make the man articulate his thoughts. Occasionally, once Tam heard his own words out loud, no further discussion was necessary. "I am listening."

"I got underwear that's seen more shit than that kid," Tam said.

"Colorful imagery," Heyer said. "I gather you are reticent about being led by someone younger than yourself?"

"Well—yeah—well no, it ain't just his age," Tam said. "But, come on, we got guys under this roof with more experience in these matters."

"You mean more experience fighting in human wars?" Heyer asked.

"War's war," Tam said. "Who you're fighting don't change it."

Heyer was quiet a moment. "And you are not alone in this opinion?"

"Course I ain't," Tam said.

"How many?"

"A lot."

"Tamsworth," Heyer said. "How many have actually expressed these concerns?"

Tam shrugged, but he didn't hide his discomfort well. "Ain't been takin' a damn survey. Just a feeling I get."

"Beo, Perth, Mito, the rest of the team who facilitated our escape, have they expressed similar concerns?

"Nah . . . they ain't said anything," Tam said. "But, some of these guys think Tibbs walks on water jus' cause you put him in charge."

"Yet, you remain unconvinced," Heyer said.

"Well, we wouldn't be having this discussion otherwise," Tam said.

Heyer let that sentence hang for a moment before he spoke again. "Jonathan's plan was successful against The Cell was it not? The way I have heard it, all goals were achieved and not a single life was lost."

"That don't mean shit," Tam said. "Any moron with The Never on their side ain't gonna screw up an operation."

Heyer nodded. "That is a fair point."

A long silence followed; Heyer could tell that of the two of them, he was far more comfortable in the lingering quiet.

"You ain't gonna say nothing else?"

Heyer smiled. "I am sorry, did you ask a question?"

Tam, momentarily flustered, pinched his lips into a line. "I want an explanation for that kid. Why the hell ain't you leading us your damn self?"

Heyer took a long breath and smiled patiently. "You will find it hard to accept, but Jonathan has more experience fighting our enemy than any man alive."

Tam looked down to the ground floor where Jonathan was listening to a report. He stared, unable to look past the man's youth and make it align with Heyer's claim.

"Heyer? I ain't tryin to call ya a liar, but I ain't stupid," Tam said. "Word is he's only had that implant for a few months. I've had mine for nearly two years."

Heyer sighed; Tam may not have been the most eloquent, but whether the man knew it or not he was circling a question Heyer didn't want to answer. That he didn't feel it was his place to answer.

"Plus, how would you know how good he is in a fight? Ya ain't never actually seen any of us take a real Ferox. All ya can say for certain is Jonathan ain't died since you put that device in him."

Tam was wrong. Heyer had seen Jonathan fight a foe far more dangerous than any Ferox quite recently. But, saying so would only lead to more questions.

"Tam, some explanations are not wise to give," Heyer said, but he turned to look him in the eye and put a hand on the Aussie's massive shoulder. "But, for argument's sake, your concerns are justified, and perhaps others who are less vocal share them. Since I am asking you to trust my judgment when the stakes are at their highest, perhaps a demonstration is in order."

Tam's expression tweaked with curiosity as he considered. "What you have in mind?"

"Well, I have some reservations of a . . . different sort," Heyer said. "Reservations that a demonstration could put to rest along with your own. So, perhaps you would like to help me arrange the appropriate circumstances for us all to allay some concerns."

Tam raised an eyebrow. "I'm listening."

She stayed hidden as he spoke to Tam. When the man finally took his leave, Heyer heard her moving closer again. She trod lightly on the metal catwalk and kept to the dark. Finally, though, he caught a glimpse of her face at the edge of a shadow. There was familiarity to all of it, reminding Heyer of Jonathan's first time approaching him of his own free will. She was ready to bolt at the slightest sign of danger. Yet the need for answers inched her closer.

He waited until he knew she would hear him. "For the sake of honesty, I know you're there."

She stiffened when his eyes caught her, but after some indecision, she stepped out into the light.

"So, they call you Heyer," Leah said.

He shrugged. "It is my name."

He put his hands into his coat pockets and leaned back against the catwalk's railing. "I am told you prefer Leah."

She took another step forward. "It is my . . . middle name."

Since Mr. Clean confirmed her identity, Heyer hadn't been alone with her. He'd seen her of course, but he hadn't—really—looked. She'd undergone a great deal of plastic surgery, but now, as she stood in front of him, Heyer felt a fool for having failed to recognize her.

"You've changed yourself," Heyer said. "But your voice, your eyes, are the same."

She took another step forward but didn't speak.

"When I thought you'd taken your own life, I grieved," Heyer said. "There aren't many times I've been relieved to find I was deceived."

Leah's eyes narrowed as though his words were tricks.

Heyer looked down at the grating. "After your brother, I feared what you may have believed me to be."

"Do you always make this little sense? Tell strangers that you grieved for them?"

He pondered her before choosing his next words. "What has Jonathan told you about me?"

"No one talks to me about you," Leah said. "That's okay though, I didn't hunt you for two years to get your excuses secondhand."

Heyer grimaced sadly. "It is ironic. Had you done nothing, I would have found you. You would already have your answers."

She did little to hide her anger at the statement. "That has occurred to me."

Heyer turned to place his hands on the guardrail. He peered down at Jonathan as he had for some time now, then took a long breath. "Well, we are here now. Ask what you wish, but you seem to already know the answers are not what you hoped."

A tense silence passed before he heard her footsteps drawing nearer. She came to stand beside him at the rail. She didn't look at him though, she came to stare as he did down at Jonathan. "Why have you been watching him all morning?"

Heyer frowned at her. "An open invitation for days. You could have come to speak to me at any moment. Now, you stall. Seems you were quite relentless in pursuit of your prey but not so certain of what you intended to do when you caught it."

She folded her arms across her chest. There was a reluctance in her that drew out longer than she'd have liked. "It is not like that. The things I would have said to you. . . they don't . . ."

She trailed for a moment. "Nothing is what I imagined."

He nodded, and it wasn't without sympathy.

"Just tell me why you're watching him."

"I am watching him because I have yet to find the courage to ask him who he really is."

Leah's eyes wandered off Jonathan to the alien. As though what he said triggered something more in her than he'd expected. Seeing that look on her face, Heyer asked, "You have noticed as well then?"

"He's been different since Rylee," Leah said. "But he isn't performing. He is different in ways a man can't just wake up and choose. Ways that grief can't explain."

Heyer nodded. "That is impressive; Rylee's disappearance would have been the first moment anyone on Earth could have noticed the change."

"What change?" Leah asked.

Heyer stopped leaning and stood straighter over the railing; there was guilt on his expression. "I do not know why I cannot just be grateful he has not gone mad. His mind, it seems capable of adapting to more abuse than I would have thought any human capable. There was a time Jonathan was resistant to a fault, but now . . . he changes to become whatever the world needs him to be."

"You're not making much sense," Leah said. "I can't tell if you're doing it on purpose."

"I would be lying if I did not tell you that this is a matter I hardly understand myself. If you were anyone else, I would not discuss it."

As though his ears were on fire, Jonathan seemed to pick that moment to look up and see the two of them looking down on him.

The alien swallowed. "But, eventually, you will need to know."

Leah turned to the alien. "I will need to know? Me? Where does that begin to make sense?"

"We will get to that in good time," he said.

Despite the frown she gave him, he clearly had every intention of leaving her question hanging unanswered for the moment. He nodded his head back to Jonathan. "He is mostly Jonathan, not all. The man who possessed Jonathan's implant before him, he . . ."

The alien trailed off for a moment as if he were reconsidering his words.

". . . was complicated. But he was also the man I had wanted to lead this war. When I gave the implant to Jonathan, I tried to make it possible for him to access the man's memories. There was one specific memory I hoped Jonathan would be able to recover, but . . ."

Heyer shook his head. "Somehow, Jonathan has integrated with the previous owner's mind. I never could have imagined that was possible, and I do not know the extent of it. I do not even know if he did it by choice. I know he is aware of what has happened, but I do not know if even he understands the extent."

A grim look fell over her. "So, that's it. Half of who he is, is a stranger to him?"

Heyer shook his head. "Not a stranger. The previous owner was his father."

Leah turned slowly, wide-eyed, as she looked at the alien. Her mouth opened but whatever she'd thought to say evaporated. Eventually, she managed to blink.

After some time, Leah finally asked the question she'd come for. Well—it was a revised version of the question, but nonetheless . . .

"It's my understanding," Leah began. "That some people you've involved are drafted. Others, volunteer."

Heyer nodded. "If I can give a choice, I do. But sometimes, an individual is too important, and no one can rightly take their place."

"Which one was Peter?" she asked.

Seeing that she was done stalling, Heyer took his hands off the railing and looked her in the eyes. "Your brother volunteered. However, for the sake of being completely forthright, had he not done so, he would have learned I was not there to give him a choice."

Leah turned back to the rail. She sat with that statement for quite some time.

"Rylee kept a journal. When she'd write about you, I didn't understand the nature of your relationship. Now, I get it. She was one that you forced."

The alien's eyes darkened sadly. "A mistake. In truth, it was the last time I ever gave the pretense of a choice. I gave her the chance to volunteer. She declined. Well, as you can imagine, she said it far more colorfully than a simple no, but nonetheless . . . I should never have let her think it was a choice. It turned her against me in ways that honesty might have salvaged. I never asked a candidate to volunteer again unless the choice was honest."

"So, she was before Jonathan," Leah said. "You never even offered him the illusion of a choice?"

The alien only nodded.

Silence crept over them again. "What makes them so important? Peter, Rylee, Jonathan, the ones who don't get to volunteer," Leah said. "What does it mean that two of them are dead?"

Heyer swallowed.

"In the case of your brother, we lost a powerful ally. His genetics were—special. They gave him a compatibility to the implant that would have been second only to Jonathan and . . ." Heyer groaned momentarily, as though the name only reminded him of another troublesome problem on the horizon, ". . . Grant Morgan."

"Grant . . ." Leah said, her voice echoing his own distaste.

The alien nodded. "When Peter passed, his device went to the next best candidate. Unfortunately, his successor will never possess the strength Peter would have."

Leah was quiet a moment, her eyes jumping about as she absorbed something that had not yet occurred to her. "Someone has my brother's implant?"

Heyer, realizing what he'd done, closed his eyes, but nodded. "I fear what you are thinking. Peter's device was not altered like Jonathan's. Your brother's memories are not—"

"Who is it?" Leah interrupted.

Heyer took a long breath. "Leah, he has no knowledge of Pete—"

"Who?" she repeated.

Reluctantly, Heyer's lips flattened into a line, but he looked about the floor below, and finally pointed. "Though he calls himself Bodhi, his real name is Dale. I have never asked why he prefers the former."

Heyer watched her running a gauntlet of unclear emotions as she stared at the young man. He suspected he knew the feeling. Sometimes you're given information and how you are supposed to feel about it is not clear. Like trying to figure out if a thought should be filed under *important* or *things to forget at your earliest convenience.*

When she finally stopped staring at Bodhi, he couldn't tell which she'd chosen. Perhaps she hadn't yet come to a decision.

"If you'd known I was alive, would Peter's device have gone to me? He was my brother. Genetically, shouldn't I be more compatible than a random stranger?"

"Your brother Jack would have been the most compatible," Heyer said.

"But he was too young?" Leah asked.

Heyer nodded.

"But if Jack was disqualified . . ."

Heyer shook his head. "The implants in the armory are configured for human males. All but one."

"Rylee's," Leah said.

"There is something I would like to show you if you would walk with me."

She had grown comfortable standing beside him out here in the open.

But she hesitated when he offered to take her somewhere. But Heyer made no show of being in a hurry and eventually they were descending downstairs.

"A moment ago, you asked what it meant that Rylee is no longer with us," Heyer said. "It may come as some surprise, but I had not intended the device for her. Rylee's compatibility was minimal. The implant nearly killed her, and never gave her the strength it should have."

Leah frowned. "Why force it on her then?"

"Necessity," Heyer slowed, then stopped on the stairs. "I believed—and still believe—that Jonathan's survival depends on the female device having a host. As such . . . any host was better than none."

This gave Leah pause, such that while the alien kept descending the stairs, she had to snap herself out of her thoughts and catch back up. "Wait. What exactly are you telling me? What happens to Jonathan if no one takes the device?"

Heyer paused, looking up at her from a few steps down. He saw the concern on her face. "That is what I am taking you to see."

CHAPTER FIFTY

PETER HADN'T BEEN forced into the service of the alien. He'd volunteered. A moment ago, that was all she wanted to know. Now, as she followed Heyer down the steel staircases, her mind felt as though she trudged aimlessly through a swamp. No sense of where she was going—no sense of where she wanted to be when she made her way through.

Once they had reached the bottom floor, she saw where Heyer was taking her. The only room in the entire facility that actually looked alien. The one time she'd been inside they had called it the armory.

The entrance was a massive metal safe door—a monstrosity that looked like it was built in another time. While it possessed a combination panel, this seemed entirely decorative. The alien didn't touch it when they arrived, the door simply opened as though sensing his approach.

"Why does the door look like an antique vault?" she asked.

"Always felt fitting to me," Heyer said. "What is inside is not just antiques. Are you familiar with the term Legacy Tech?"

Leah shrugged. "Stuff so old it's hard to get it to work with modern technology."

"Exactly, see the devices on the other side of this door, Mr. Clean cannot fabricate. At the same time, humans would have put such things in a museum. On display with remnants of slavery and war. Cruelty."

He held up a hand inviting her to enter. Once there, she was surrounded by the walls of dormant human implants. Individually, they were no larger than the size of her palm.

"Jonathan's been moving quickly. I have never seen these walls so empty," Heyer said.

Leah nodded, having already noticed that the walls contained far more empty slots than filled ones since her last visit.

Heyer walked to the center of the room and drew her attention to a waist high pedestal. On its surface, there were two empty sockets.

"Mr. Clean, would you please provide a minor projection; I would like Leah to observe the state of this pedestal on Oct 14, between 8:21 and 8:22 am."

She recognized the time and date, knew exactly what happened during those sixty seconds. The area shimmered, as though momentarily made of fluid. Then it reshaped, and for a moment there was no observable difference. A few seconds later, one of the slots suddenly became filled.

"Hold there please, Mr. Clean," Heyer said.

Leah leaned over to inspect the device; she recognized the symbol on the face of the implant. Mr. Clean's tutorial had shown her what Rylee's device looked like.

"The female implant," she said. "It returned to the armory when she died."

"Yes, but as you can see, it belongs to a set," Heyer said. "Jonathan has the other half."

"Why are Jonathan and Rylee's the only devices in this room that come as a set?"

"They are paired," Heyer said.

She blinked. "Mr. Clean never said anything about paired implants."

"Yes. While I was incapacitated, Jonathan directed Mr. Clean to remove any mention of the bonded pair from the education materials that could be accessed," Heyer said. "To be fair, you alone were not singled out, and it is not the only information he felt no one should access. To be more fair, I do not disagree with Jonathan's decision to keep the knowledge confidential."

"I'm sensing there is a 'but' coming," Leah said.

Heyer nodded. "*But,* I do believe he intended to keep this from you as long as possible. Though he knew full well I would tell you."

After some time, Heyer had covered the details of the bonded pair. Much of what had occurred in the weeks leading up to Jonathan's capture began to make sense. The strangeness of Jonathan's behavior, his almost telepathic connection to Rylee, his utter inability to explain what he felt for her. Even the entries from her diary suddenly became clearer.

Heyer had been watching her for some time now, silently, waiting for her to resurface from her thoughts.

"You said Jonathan's survival depends on the pair being complete," Leah said. "So where do we find . . . Rylee's backup?"

"Rylee was always the backup," Heyer said sympathetically. "I intended the implant to go to another. But, she . . . tricked me. Had me convinced she was dead."

"Dead?" Leah began to tremble.

"Yes," Heyer said. "She faked her own suicide."

Leah took a step back. "Bullshit!"

"Leah—"

"There are three billion women on this planet, not a single one is more compatible with that stupid thing? No! You're lying."

Heyer held up his hands peacefully. "Even if there were a hundred billion women on this planet, they would be no more compatible than Rylee. There is only one good match."

"That doesn't make any sense," Leah said.

"You are like your brother, Leah," Heyer said. "His compatibility had nothing to do with his human lineage."

An awkward silence followed—one where Leah's jaw tried and failed to form words. Finally, a whisper made its way out, "What?"

"You, Peter, Jack, you all possess a Borealis ancestor," Heyer said. "On your mother's side."

"How . . ." She shook her head. What he was implying seemed repulsive. "How could a human even . . . with a . . ."

"The Borealis in question was not in his native body," Heyer said, slowly reaching down to undo the top buttons of his shirt. "He was a Borealis within a human host."

Leah was backing away, unsure if she wanted to listen to any more of this.

"Leah," Heyer said. "I wish I could better ease you into this, but I am not talking about some long dead member of my race. I am—"

"You can't expect me to believe this!" she said, incredulously. "That you're . . . you're . . . what? My great great grandfather?"

"No, actually," Heyer said, then cleared his throat awkwardly. "Grandmother."

"Can you prove any of this?" Leah finally asked after having been quiet for some time.

"Yes, but all the proof in the world will not matter if you are not willing to accept it," Heyer said.

"Try me," Leah said.

Heyer addressed the AI. "Mr. Clean, please provide Leah with applicable records."

Three displays emerged, rising out of the armory floor, between Heyer and her. On the first she saw a Family Tree. Peter, Jack and herself listed at the bottom. At the top was Johanna O' Sullivan, a name that rang no bells for her. She read up from her branch, but Johanna was not the only name she didn't recognize. Truthfully, any names further back than her great grandparents were a mystery to her.

When she moved onto the second display, she encountered a similar problem. The DNA comparisons indicated certain matches, percentages of shared genetic material, between her and this Johanna O'Sullivan. But, how was she to confirm that Mr. Clean had done any analysis at all? He could have simply flashed some data on the screen and told her to believe him.

She began to understand what Heyer meant when he said no proof would make her willing to accept. Then she looked at the last screen and found something a bit harder to explain away.

It was a video file from a time long before the notion of video existed. There was a woman standing in a doorway. Her clothing, hundreds of years out of fashion. What lay on one side of the open door and what lay on the other didn't match. The room the woman was leaving wasn't even a room but a barn that looked like it belonged in the same historical period as the woman's clothing. Tools, buckets, and barrels, they all lacked the look of mass production. Dirt and hay covered the floors and there was no electrical lighting.

Yet, the room she was stepping into had a great deal in common with the one Leah was currently occupying. Metallic seamless surfaces, everything possessing an elegance of construction that hadn't so much been built by hands but simply brought into being, like one of Mr. Clean's projections.

The woman, Johanna, carried a bucket into the alien room. She set it down on a seamless surface that formed as though having anticipated her need for it. The same way Mr. Clean often did. The bucket was not the only thing the woman carried. She was pregnant, and by Leah's guess, far closer to giving birth than conception.

None of this would have meant anything if not for Johanna's face. It was no movie fantasy, Johanna was not her long lost twin separated by the centuries, but there was no denying a familiarity—albeit one with her face before she'd undergone plastic surgery.

"What is she doing?" Leah asked

Heyer came around to stand beside her. A moment ago, she'd wanted to get away from him. Now, it didn't matter. He could be on the other side of the planet and it wouldn't make her feel any safer.

The alien watched Johanna, looking unsure for a moment before he smiled. "I was analyzing potato samples from the O'Sullivan farm. Johanna had a proclivity for improving their flavor and texture. I enjoyed the hobby as well, combining certain strains for better yields."

It was a strange thing. How the alien looked at the woman, physically separated in time by hundreds of years and yet he recognized himself as though looking at an old photo.

"This was, perhaps six months into Johanna's pregnancy, Mr. Clean?" Heyer asked.

"Yes," Mr. Clean confirmed. "Based on the date of procreation."

"Are you saying that," Leah paused to glance back to the family tree. "Thomas *procreated* with Johanna and . . ."

She paused to give Heyer a side-eyed look, ". . . you, Grandma?"

Heyer licked his lips as he considered how to explain. When he spoke, he pointed to his chest with both hands. "This body once belonged to a man named Jeremy Holloway. When I took it, his brain was severely damaged, and the body was soon going to perish. While my implant could repair the vessel enough to make it a habitable host, Holloway's consciousness was beyond repair. I do not wish to take what is still useful to someone else, so this is an ideal situation.

"That said, the Borealis implant sustains a human body for a great deal longer than its natural lifespan—but not indefinitely. I tend to drag my feet when I should be taking a new host. When I met Johanna, my previous host was somewhat past its expiration date.

"Johanna was dying. The medicine of her time could not help her, but my implant could. I offered to take her as a host. But, there is no removing my implant without leaving the host in a vegetative state. Unlike Holloway, Johanna's mind was intact. Her choice came down to dying, or sharing her body with an alien."

Leah listened, turning to watch the woman on the screen with a new perspective. Johanna did something so very human. She loosened the top buttons of her collar, she reached down her shirt the same way Leah might if she were trying to adjust an uncomfortable bra. But, while Johanna's hand remained beneath the shirt, her chest began to glow.

The three lines were obscured by the fabric but were unmistakably a match for those that ran across Heyer's chest. When Johanna pulled her hand back out, she held a round clear ball in her palm. When she placed this on the counter beside the potatoes, it melted into the surface. Just like so many things Leah had seen Mr. Clean reabsorb.

Heyer chuckled after watching the whole mundane exercise. "The clothes of that era were uncomfortable as it was, but I could hardly go about with my chest ablaze. Unfortunately, the cover Mr. Clean provided to cloak my implant itched Johanna's skin. She and I often could not wait to return to the privacy of Mr. Clean to be rid of the thing for a short while. Mr. Clean, of course, was not Mr. Clean back then . . . but that is another story."

Leah considered the alien. He seemed—nostalgic—as he watched Johanna. In fact, he looked like her mother when she'd watched old family videos. She could persuade herself to question the family tree, the DNA, but if he was faking this moment, then he would make a far better spy than she ever had.

She cleared her throat. "I'm still unclear on how you and Johanna ended up in this condition."

"Well, Johanna was unable to lead a normal life. She could not marry," Heyer said. "But, she did want to be with Thomas. Had known since they were children together. I deactivated the implant for a short while, so she would not be denied this desire—and so that she could have a moment of privacy. As it turned out, Johanna and I found ourselves—"

"Knocked up," Leah said.

Heyer smirked. "Had Johanna been familiar with that expression, she would have pointed out that the pot was calling the kettle black."

Leah stiffened, then turned away, her hair falling over her eyes to hide her face. "How . . . how did you know?"

"The same way we knew who you were. You bled on Mr. Clean when you arrived. But, other than your identity, he also learned you were pregnant, the child's sex, and of course, who the father is."

Leah's teeth clenched. "Mr. Clean needs boundaries, he has no . . ."

She trailed off for a moment. "Wait, you know the sex? From my blood?"

Mr. Clean answered, "The cells of a human female possess two X chromosomes. When your blood touched my surface, I detected trace amounts of a Y Chromosome. Hence, you carry a male."

Heyer sighed in annoyance. "Mr. Clean, one does not tell an expectant parent the sex of their baby without permission."

"I don't understand," Mr. Clean said. "Why wouldn't—"

"It is not a decision based on utility, some simply wish . . ."

She'd stopped listening. The AI and the alien's bickering now like the mumblings of Charlie Brown's parents in the background.

"A boy," Leah whispered.

CHAPTER FIFTY-ONE

LEAH HAD DAYDREAMED what the scene might look like when she learned the sex of her first child. What she imagined was the more typical sort of affair. She'd be at a hospital, her husband beside her as a doctor studied an ultrasound.

Instead, she was standing in an alien room called the Armory. The man beside her claimed to be her ancestral grandmother, and the test results had been delivered by a cartoon mascot for toilet bowl cleaner.

She was unsure if she should laugh or cry but sensed it could easily go either way if both didn't occur simultaneously.

"Does he know?" Leah asked.

"Jonathan? If he does, he did not learn it from us," Heyer said, then she felt the weight of his gaze grow heavy. "I do not believe we should tell him."

Leah frowned, taking a step back as she grew nervous. "I will not go along with that."

"You have not told him thus far," Heyer said.

Her eyes hardened. "That's not fair. To say the right moment has yet to present itself would be a . . . profound . . . understatement."

"Perhaps," Heyer said. "But knowing what you know now, do you imagine the right moment is coming in the foreseeable future? See, I do not think he is willing to put you in harm's way as things currently stand. If he knew this, I fear there would be no persuading him."

Heyer sighed. "Since waking up, it is clear Jonathan no longer requires my counsel."

"I spent years preparing to defend Earth. The day I lost consciousness, I believed all that preparation had fallen apart. By then, the change in Jonathan was already surfacing but . . ."

Heyer shook his head.

". . . I awoke to him telling me he knows how to fix a plan I have never told him. I feared his mind had broken. Then he told me what he intends. While it will in no way be easy, Jonathan's plan is not the ravings of a mad man. He has thought this through. He did not need me to wake up and hold his hand to put the plans in motion."

She shrugged. "You told him to lead."

"Yes," Heyer said. "But . . ."

The alien had the look a man gets when he knows something is too good to be true. That something is wrong despite any evidence to the contrary.

"When Mr. Clean told Jonathan who you were," Heyer said, "Jonathan already knew. Understand, you are not simply *as* compatible as Rylee was. Bonded to Jonathan, the two of you could possess strength near my own.

"He knows this. Yet, at a time when we need every advantage, the most powerful weapon this armory can give mankind drops into his lap. And what does he do?"

Leah frowned. "He . . . he hides it from me."

"I am afraid it is more than that," Heyer said. "Mr. Clean, please show Leah what events took place in this room shortly after the escape from The Cell's facility."

Once again, the pedestal shimmered. This time, Leah saw that Rylee's device was in place. A moment later, Jonathan stepped through the vault door. He stood beside the pedestal staring at the implant. It seemed difficult for him to bear looking at. Finally, he closed his eyes, grabbed the implant, and walked out of the armory.

As the projection ended, Leah turned back to Heyer. "He took it."

"Yes, Mr. Clean has informed me he carries it with him at all times."

"Why would he do that? I mean . . . doesn't he know you'll discover who took it?"

"Of course he does," Heyer said as he leaned against the armory wall. "He is not hiding the implant. All he has done is leave me in the unfortunate position of having to ask him to return it. If he were to say no, I could simply have Mr. Clean transport the implant into my hand."

"So why bother?"

Heyer winced. "If I ask for it or it simply disappears, he will know the only possible reason is that I intend to implant it."

Leah let all that sink in for a moment. "Jonathan was never given a choice. He knew Rylee was never given a choice. Maybe he doesn't want it left to you to decide for me?"

Heyer nodded. "That is one of three possibilities I arrived at. But not the one I think most likely."

"What are the others?" Leah asked.

"The child. His father found great strength from his need to see Jonathan safe. Now, Jonathan shares half a mind with the man. I cannot imagine the sort of confusion that would create, but, if he knows about the child you carry, then all of Douglas's love for his own son may well be projecting onto you.

Leah blinked; just thinking about what the alien was suggesting was enough to give her a headache. If true, she couldn't imagine what was going on inside of Jonathan. "Jesus, what's the third?"

Heyer sighed. "The bond itself. The only woman who ever survived a severed bond as long as Jonathan only did so because her captors forced her to reestablish the link with a new male. Jonathan is the only man in known history to survive without doing the same. He is the only one who knows firsthand why all the other men and women welcomed death after the connection was severed."

"Sounds like, he should have every reason to want to reestablish the bond?" Leah frowned.

"Yet, here we are," Heyer said, nodding to the pedestal with two empty sockets.

CHAPTER FIFTY-TWO

OCT 18, 2005 | 2 PM | JBLM FACILITY

GENERAL DELACY AND Olivia and had been waiting pensively in a private room when the call came. They glanced at one another before the few seconds of buffering video passed. Finally, Dr. Watts was looking back at them on the monitor.

On their order, she'd been dispatched the night before to the rendezvous point. Now, she was in a cargo carrier, and from the sound they were already in the air.

Six Libyan operators had been sent to the coordinates on Jonathan's map. That team had confirmed acquisition of *something worth their attention* upon reaching the site. What they had brought back had been sealed into a box and discretely carted out of the area. Eventually, the box had made it to the nearest landing site, where it was handed over to Dr. Watts.

The operation itself had been quick, and so far, there were no reports that the authorities in Libya had become aware of their operators' comings and goings. This was a win both Delacy and Olivia were grateful for. Jonathan had been quite vague about what they would find out there, and neither of them had any desire to explain to the Joint Chiefs of Staff why they had executed an unauthorized mission into a foreign nation knowing full well it might result in an international incident—and had no idea exactly what it was that they were retrieving.

While her plane would be in the air for a long time, Watts now had the prize in her possession. The operators in the desert had come back with two sets of remains. One female, human, the other—simply listed as unknown.

One look at the corpse and Delacy had the sense he was seeing the husk of something pulled from a horror movie.

Decomposition had taken its toll on both sets of remains. But the creature appeared to be in far better shape than the human. Though the inner musculature and organs had been eaten away, its dried exterior skin and skeleton were made from heavy metals that looked as though they remained largely intact. The exception being that the creature had a large jagged gash in its torso.

"Dr. Watts, are we looking at some kind of hoax?" Olivia asked.

"I can't discount the possibility," Watts replied, as she continued to inspect the remains, "but someone would have had to have gone to a great deal of trouble to fake this. I'll run more tests on the tissues once I'm back on the ground but if I had to give my opinion right now—I'd say this is exactly what it appears. Whatever that is."

"I trust your expertise, so we'll assume that thing was alive and walking around at some point. Is there any chance it originated on Earth?" Olivia asked.

Her face looked doubtful.

"Not like anything I've ever seen," Dr. Watts said. "If it is, its morphology would suggest it was a primate, but looking at its bone structure, if we can even call this internal skeleton *bones*, there isn't anything in our fossil records that is related. So, no, my vote is alien."

Delacy exchanged a glance with Olivia. "Dr. Watts, what about the other body?"

"Well, that is far less of a mystery. Definitely human, female, and from the look of the remains I'd say she died from injuries acquired from a brutal mauling. Given where we found her, and some of the marks on the bones, my guess is that she barely missed being this thing's dinner. Though, one of her arms is missing, so that might not be the whole truth."

"How long will it take to ID her?" Olivia asked.

"No guarantees that we can. Will check dental records and run DNA when I get back to the lab," the doctor said. "Until then, all I can tell you was that she was old. Perhaps seventies or eighties. Skeletal remains likely of European decent."

"Any idea how long she's been down there?" Olivia asked.

The doctor looked over the remains once more, considering. "Hard to tell, decomposition was slower. Unlike the unknown creature, her remains were placed in a body bag before they were buried. Which is strange in itself . . ."

There was a pause as she presented said bag to the camera. "This is army issue, but it doesn't look modern. Might be able to get an idea of when she was put in the ground if you find out when this bag was in use."

"Thank you, Doctor, send over any preliminary findings. We'll see you when you're back on base," Olivia said.

"Yes, ma'am," Dr. Watts said, before reaching out to kill the camera.

Olivia turned to Delacy. "I'll get someone to follow up on the bag, but I think it's fair to assume Douglas Tibbs buried that woman with the creature twenty years ago."

Delacy nodded. "All begs the question though, why would an army Ranger keep this a secret from his command, only to wait ten years and tell his son?"

"Jonathan knew where to find it," Olivia said. "But that doesn't mean his father was the one to tell him. All we can assume is that something happened to Douglas Tibbs out in that desert. My hunch is that he and Jeremy Holloway crossed paths with our escaped alien in the process. If I'm right, the alien's involvement with Jonathan Tibbs was never random. For that matter, Holloway's son, Grant, showing up in Seattle was never a coincidence either."

Delacy nodded thoughtfully. "So, why does Jonathan want us to know about it now?"

"He said he didn't expect we'd believe anything he had to say without evidence." Olivia said. "That this was the only thing he could give us until he got his hands on better proof."

"So, what's the hurry then? If he thinks he can get proof, why send us to fetch the remains of a twenty-year-old alien?" Delacy asked.

Olivia's face grew troubled.

"What is it?" he asked.

She reached into her front pocket and took out the folded-up piece of paper. As she unfolded it, Delacy could see it was the original map Jonathan had drawn. Then she flipped it over and slid it across the table to him.

"He said he was going to need these things," Olivia said. "They're all out of the question, but . . ."

She trailed off with a sigh. "If we complied, they aren't things that are easily done. He said we needed to be thinking about how we were going to make that list happen long before we were convinced."

Delacy picked up the paper and began to read the items aloud. "Evacuation of Seattle and its surrounding counties. A military perimeter around the evacuation zone."

Delacy scoffed, but continued. "All remaining materials used to build the containment shells, and as much of the finished product as our sources can produce. . ."

Delacy was shaking his head. Olivia, having already read the paper over a dozen times, knew he hadn't reached the more troubling requests yet.

"Necessary supplies and access to fit approximately thirty buildings and various structures for controlled demolition within the evacuation zone . . ."

Delacy's eyes bulged as he reached the final item. "Five nuclear war heads!"

He tossed the list back to the table. "He'd have to be a mad man to think we'd provide him with any of this."

"Yes, but that's the rub . . . he wasn't crazy. He told me exactly how things would play out during the escape. That we wouldn't be able to stop it. He knew exactly how we'd react to that list as well. Told me not to gamble, not to wait until he had irrefutable evidence before I started planning how to make that list a reality."

Delacy sat back in his chair and considered for a few moments.

"If we entertain this notion, even for a moment, making this list happen . . ."

He sighed.

"The President would have to declare a national emergency. We'd need the National Guard and the cooperation of multiple arms of the military. Temporary housing for the evacuated civilians . . ."

Delacy trailed off as he noticed the look on Olivia's face. She was staring off into space, nodding along slowly with his assessment. But nothing he was saying so much as raised an eyebrow on her.

"You have already been considering this," Delacy said.

"Once they escaped, along with the disappearance of the other subjects, we had no leads to reacquire them. The only way to get ahead of him is to take the list seriously. Consider it a partial blueprint for whatever it is they're planning," Olivia said.

General Delacy was quieted by the thought.

"I can't speak for how the WMDs or the Shell materials would play into this. But, the rest . . . sounds like staging for a battle. Like, he plans to hold that city against an invading force. But . . ."

"He'd have to know precisely where the enemy plans to attack," Olivia said, finishing his thought. "I came to the same conclusion. I've wondered if the invading force he was preparing for was of the same alien race as The Mark. Given the corpse he's sent us to recover, I'm starting to wonder."

Delacy sighed. "But, five warheads to contain an army of these creatures?"

Delacy asked aloud. "That's preposterous. I don't care how big or ugly these things are, our military could take them out."

Olivia tilted her head uncomfortably, seemed unsure if she agreed. "We've seen what The Mark was capable of with the technology he had at his disposal. That was just one alien. If we assume this is another species . . . how could we have any idea what they might be capable of?"

CHAPTER FIFTY-THREE

OCT 20, 2005 | 4 PM | HANGMAN'S TREE

TAM WAS QUIET as he stood on the catwalk watching Jonathan and Heyer. Whatever pretense the alien gave to get Jonathan to join him seemed to have worked. When the doors opened and shut, he stepped out into the open.

"Ready to go here, Mr. Clean,' Tam said.

"Confirmed," the AI said as a monitor and a microphone formed beside him. "I will begin on Heyer's signal."

"What exactly is it we're doing here, Old Man?" Jonathan asked.

"You do not remember everything your father knew," Heyer said. "Do you know what accounts for the blind spots?"

Jonathan sighed. "I don't remember everything that ever happened to him. I remember the things that kept him alive."

"Interesting," Heyer said. "You will have to indulge me. I would like to run some tests."

"Tests?"

"Please activate Jonathan's implant, Mr. Clean," Heyer said.

"Dammit . . ." Jonathan trailed off, as he felt Mr. Clean immediately follow through with the request. With an irritable grunt he dropped down onto one knee, glared at the alien, then fell flat on his back as the transition took over.

"Mr. Clean, please let Tam know we will begin shortly, but anything that is said in this chamber should remain between Jonathan and me."

Of course, Jonathan wouldn't hear any of this, he was in the middle of the transition. When it ended, he opened his eyes and stood, chest glowing. When he looked at Heyer, the look lacked any fondness.

Heyer frowned. "When I trained your father, he preferred not to know it was coming. Waiting for it made him anxious."

Jonathan tilted his head. "Yeah, that is what he told you."

"You mean, it was not the truth?"

"You only activated him outside The Never when you wanted to spar," Jonathan said. "He didn't say anything because it put him in the mood to punch you anyway."

Heyer hummed as he considered, but then refocused on why they were here. "Your father bested me in hand-to-hand once."

"Twice," Jonathan corrected.

Heyer's eyes narrowed, but he smiled. "We agreed on a draw."

"Dad was polite to his elders," Jonathan said.

Heyer smirked, reached up slowly to remove his hat. "Would you like to select an environment?"

They removed their shoes and any heavy clothing. When Jonathan finished, he cracked his neck, and smiled at Heyer. He whispered something, and Heyer could hear—within seconds, the void came over the projection chamber.

A warm sun began to beat down on Heyer as he watched structures come into being. A massive oval forming with Jonathan and him at its center. Limestone arches and columns began manifesting around them as Jonathan eased down into a crouch.

He scooped up a handful of sand, rubbing it between his palms before a soft wind whisked it away.

Tam watched as Bodhi and Sam approached the projection chamber followed by a group of fresh soldiers. They were quick to find the Chamber was locked down and occupied.

"Hey, Mr. Clean, we're scheduled to be running drills. What's going on?"

"Apologies, an unscheduled scenario is in progress," Mr. Clean said.

"Whose?" Bodhi asked.

"Jonathan and Heyer are settling an argument," Mr. Clean said.

A moment passed as everyone in the group was allowed to let their imagination run with what they'd been told. Jonathan and Heyer. Having an argument. In the combat training facility.

Sam was the first to ask, "So, uh . . . any chance we could . . . watch?"

A monitor took form on the outside of the projection chamber. Bodhi's team suddenly felt as though they were gathering around the big screen at a sports bar. As the video began to roll, Heyer was just removing his hat.

Tam smiled, and lifted the microphone Mr. Clean had manifested, then did his best impression of a sports announcer.

"Occupants of Hangman's Tree, I'd like to welcome everyone to drop whatever the hell you're doing and turn your attention to the projection chamber. If you're not near a display, Mr. Clean is now manifesting one for your convenience."

He wasn't lying. While he spoke, displays ranging in size as large as a theater to as small as a postcard were appearing anywhere there were eyes to watch.

Hayden was in his quarters when he heard Tam's voice come over the entire facility. He was lying on the bottom bunk, still getting sleep out of his eyes, when a small panel began to take shape on the underside of Collin's bunk.

Realizing what he was looking at, he was suddenly wide awake. "Collin . . ."

"Hmf . . ."

"Wake up!"

Hayden began kicking the top bunk.

"What?" Collin asked irritably.

"You don't want to miss this, Jonathan is—"

Tam's voice boomed again over the speakers. "The challenger, maybe you've heard of him, maybe not, but our enemies know his name. Our fearless leader, Jonathan Tibbs.

"He will be participating in a full contact match with the reigning champion. The guy with one name, The Borealis Madonna, Mr. Fedora himself . . ."

"No way," Collin said as Tam went on and on with creative titles for Heyer. Finally, Tam paused, cleared his throat, then attempted his best Michael Buffer impression. "Let's get ready to RUMBLE."

As every eye inside Mr. Clean became glued to a screen, the black void of a loading projection scenario made it appear that Jonathan and Heyer faced off in an empty abyss. In the space of a few breaths contours and shapes began to form in the void.

Collin stared up at the screen that had formed on his ceiling. "Is that supposed to be . . ."

"Welcome to the Coliseum," Jonathan said.

Heyer looked about and gave an approving nod. "And are you ready?"

"Wouldn't worry about me, Old Man." Jonathan said.

"Good, do not hold back," Heyer said, then shot forward.

Seconds later, Heyer rolled onto his back with a groan. He looked up at the few scattered clouds slowly moving west in an otherwise clear sky.

A somewhat delighted smile formed on his face. "Well now."

Footsteps approached. Jonathan's face replacing the sun as he looked down at Heyer curiously. "You playing at something, Old Man?"

Jonathan wasn't mocking him. He suspected Heyer was as surprised as he to find himself looking down at the alien after an exchange that had lasted less than three seconds. Their shared confusion was because Jonathan hadn't done anything of any martial prowess. Even if he did have something up his sleeve, the exchange hadn't gone on long enough to get elaborate.

No, what happened was Heyer had miscalculated so comically he was on the brink of laughing at his own expense.

"I do apologize," Heyer said, finding he had a good deal of sand in his mouth as he rose and dusted himself off.

"What happened?" Jonathan asked.

What had happened was clear to everyone. They had come into close quarters, when Heyer had thrown a punch, Jonathan had grabbed his wrist, pulled him along and slammed him headfirst into the ground. He'd then kicked the alien and sent him tumbling through the sands.

What he was really asking was how it happened.

That was more nuanced.

On the surface, Heyer had gone on the offensive. Launched forward and thrown a strike he knew Jonathan would dodge. He hadn't been trying to hit the man, just force him into evading. Jonathan had not disappointed, he had stepped to the side of the fist—exactly as Heyer assumed he would—just as his father had a thousand times before.

What surprised him was when Jonathan took hold of his wrist.

Douglas would have known better. The father had seen how easily Heyer could break such a hold a thousand times over. The father would have known it would end with him off balance and nothing to show for it.

So, reflexively—Heyer had done just that. Moved to break the hold on his wrist. That was when the shock came—Jonathan's grip didn't break. That was the miscalculation. The son possessed all of Douglas's hard-won grace, but also possessed a strength the father never had.

So, Heyer found himself off balance, his elbow locked as he lost control of his shoulder. In a heartbeat his face was rushing toward the sands. The rest pretty much went as everyone else had witnessed.

"What happened," Heyer said, as he began to smile. "Is that I have never been in a fight with a man that was this close to fair."

"You look kind of excited about it," Jonathan said.

Heyer's feet slipped into the sand and he lowered into a balanced stance. "I am."

Jonathan frowned and readied himself again as well. "You're . . . uh . . . welcome?"

Heyer never lost sight of his opponent, even as his back collided with the tall wall of limestone that rimmed the coliseum. Jonathan was already capitalizing, coming at Heyer's knees first like a missile intent on putting him in the wall permanently.

Heyer waited until the last moment to move, but Jonathan didn't fall for the delay. As Heyer leapt to safety, Tibbs was already pivoting and readying his legs to absorb his momentum.

Heyer only gained an instant as he rolled out of his dive and Jonathan ricocheted off the wall after him.

Heyer had a slight advantage with Jonathan coming at him headfirst. He let the man reach him just as he rolled onto his back. They hit the coliseum floor, toppling over one another, but Heyer had the control and the leverage. He planted a foot into Jonathan's gut and thrust him away.

Tibbs didn't fight the trajectory forced on him. He focused on sticking his landing with his eyes turned on the real danger. Heyer already running toward him, as Jonathan's bare feet tore a line through the sand. The ball of his foot gently touched the opposite wall. He came to a stop, and then broke into a run to meet the alien.

This had gone on for some time now. Their exchanges sometimes came to throwing each other at walls, or the close quarters hand to hand that was more like chess. They blocked and dodged, maneuvered through an elegant dance of reflexive counters.

Yet, Heyer was noticing strange moments. Some more elegant than Douglas ever used, others drastically less. As Heyer drew into close range and Jonathan got up from his knees, he pushed a strike of the fist off course with a block to Jonathan's forearm. Then one of those strange moments of grace came. Jonathan swept forward with a half jump, half crawl, that turned into an unexpected move to sweep the alien's legs. The way the man had swept across the ground surprised the alien, such that he hadn't known what it was building toward. As Heyer finally saw the sweep coming he was forced to jump, cartwheeling over Jonathan, with the intent of finding the man's back exposed.

He only realized the sweep had never been meant to succeed a second early. Jonathan whipped around, following through the spin. Knowing exactly where Heyer would try to put himself, and his fist was already on a collision course with the alien's chest. Heyer barely got his arms crossed into a block as his feet touched ground.

Had the punch succeeded, it would have been devastating to a man. Would have landed hard in the solar plexus. Heyer took it on the arms and the force sent him back, throwing sand in both directions as his feet brought him to a stop.

Heyer tilted his head at his opponent. He'd never studied Capoeira, but he knew what it looked like when it was used. He also had a pretty good idea where Jonathan had learned a maneuver like that—as it had Rylee's signature all over it.

Jonathan's momentary flourish of style was followed by a complete abandonment of grace. He came at Heyer like a linebacker—his shoulder ramming into Heyer at the stomach and driving him into the limestone.

This time the alien was caught off guard because it wasn't Douglas' or Rylee's style. No, this felt more like a Jonathan original. Something one might try in a fight because he had the strength and power to risk it. Yet, it paid off; Heyer felt the wall give as he crashed into it once again.

Heyer took the damage, bringing his elbow down into Jonathan's shoulder blade with enough force to put the man in the sands. Jonathan rolled clear as Heyer tried to follow it with a crushing foot. Only then did he notice, once again, what Jonathan had really been up to.

This wall had been weakened several times already. Heyer looked up just in time to see it crumbling down on him.

At first, the sounds of those outside the projection chamber had been like a stadium watching a title fight. But a few minutes in, the only sound in Hangman's Tree were those coming from inside the chamber itself.

Tam watched the faces of the others.

He began to understand why Heyer had volunteered for this to be seen by everyone. Why he'd known that anyone who doubted Jonathan should be leading them would find themselves questioning that doubt.

Heyer was stronger, faster, wiser—had more experience than any twenty of their lifetimes combined, everyone knew this, and yet . . .

It showed itself in the alien's concentration.

It dripped down his skin as he sweat.

It whispered to all who watched seconds become minutes and every advantage the alien possessed failing to bring the fight to a close.

Tam had sparred with the alien. Any man who had, knew it was like trying to grapple with an ocean wave. Had anyone else amongst them been in that coliseum, there would be no uncertainty as to who was student and who was teacher.

Jonathan was impervious to all of it. Nothing Heyer did seemed to matter. No matter how many times the alien landed a blow, or momentarily outmaneuvered him, he was unfazed.

Jonathan respected the danger Heyer presented, but it didn't invoke the fear it should have. This man looked like he would walk up to a god, knock him on his ass, and walk away as though nothing the slightest bit miraculous had happened.

This was all to say, that as Tam watched, he felt a growing fear.

He was afraid for Heyer.

It was in Jonathan's eyes—something was coming.

Jonathan's fist caught Heyer in the face. When the next blow came, the alien knocked it away, and grappled Jonathan's arm. He used the leverage to back him into the wall.

Knowing Heyer would only lock out his limb or knock him off balance, Jonathan moved accordingly. What he didn't plan for was Heyer running up and cartwheeling off the coliseum wall with a powerful push of his legs. Jonathan was forced to go along for the ride, at his mercy the moment his feet were yanked off the ground.

When Heyer loosed his grip, he put as much heat as he could into throwing the man. Tibbs shot across the coliseum like a dagger flipping blade over handle. There was no graceful landing in such circumstances. At the final moment, he managed to tighten himself into a cannonball, protecting his neck and limbs, and crashed through the opposite wall. This time the wall wasn't enough to stop him completely. And a moment later, the limestone, stacked by the ancient Romans for seating, collapsed as well.

Dust shot up into the air around the giant wound that had been placed in the amphitheater.

A moment later, Heyer walked into the rubble, hardly able to see in the cloud that had erupted. He wondered if Jonathan was buried, digging his way out. If he'd managed to avoid that fate he may be lying in wait.

Sounds of settling debris drew the alien's attention, until he heard something more substantial move behind him. He ducked and swiveled, only to find nothing. Something was moving in the cloud around him.

Heyer heard a grunt of effort and dove toward the least obstructed spot he could manage to reach. A stir of the air swept overhead—he'd just made a mistake.

He collided head on with the second, much larger, block of stone.

While he was relatively unharmed, he'd still been hit by a boulder. It crumbled around him to a pile of shattered rock as it crushed him against the ground.

The boulder hadn't truly harmed him, but he was staggered and more blinded than the moment before. Jonathan did not let the opportunity slip by. He came launching out of the dust cloud. At first it was as though he meant to put Heyer on the ground, catch him in a particularly nasty clothesline but when his arm got close, he tightened it into a noose around the alien's neck.

Sensing Jonathan would try to end their bout by forcing a submission, he grappled enough to keep his feet, which would have been more difficult if he weren't the taller man. When Jonathan's grip tightened further, Heyer thrust them both through what wall remained standing, Jonathan taking the brunt of it.

A moment later they shot back onto the coliseum's sands, and rolled to a stop in a pile of limbs.

But Jonathan had not let go.

Heyer's hand clapped down on his forearm with such force it made a sound like thunder. Slowly, his superior strength became clear, as he was able to inch the man's choke hold away by simply overpowering him.

They were both growling with the effort, until Heyer thrust Jonathan off and sent him rolling through the sands.

They were panting now, Heyer more so, having been unable to breathe for a few moments. As Jonathan stood and looked back at him his chest was heaving with the effort of pitting his strength against Heyer's. Still, he couldn't fault the man for trying. Douglas knew it could not be managed, because he had tried, but Jonathan was far stronger—so it had deserved revisiting.

Heyer stood, held his hand up, and the room returned to the void as Mr. Clean ended the projection. Unbeknownst to Jonathan, it also ended the viewing going on outside.

"Did you get what you were looking for?" Jonathan asked.

"I did," Heyer said.

"Care to share?"

Heyer considered for a moment, then said, "Mr. Clean, Jonathan no longer needs his implant activated."

Jonathan had enough time to look annoyed before the light of the implant began to retreat. He staggered to a knee, then dropped to the floor.

A visage of Mr. Clean appeared, standing beside Heyer in the projection chamber. "Suffice it to say, everyone was quieted by the outcome."

Heyer nodded thoughtfully.

"Were you letting him win?" Mr. Clean asked.

"Point of fact, I was not," Heyer replied. "But, had we truly been fighting for our lives, he most definitely would have lost."

He looked down at Jonathan, the man unable to hear him as his device deactivated. "He will not be able to hurt my brother. Not enough to matter."

"We know Malkier's weakness," Mr. Clean said.

"He will take steps to shield himself from vulnerability."

"Cede will offer him the same possible solution that I would, therefore it is conceivable that we may know more about how he will go about protecting himself. But this should be a last resort, there are too many ways our best guess could be wrong," Mr. Clean said.

Heyer nodded. "I gave Jonathan his chance. Leah cannot allow him to go into battle without reestablishing the bond."

"Won't that betray the trust he asked of you?" Mr. Clean asked.

On the floor of the projection chamber, Jonathan began to stir as his consciousness returned.

Heyer sighed. "A discussion for another time."

CHAPTER FIFTY-FOUR

OCT 23, 2005 | 7 AM | HANGMAN'S TREE

COLLIN COULD TELL something was up the moment he stepped out of his quarters. Anthony was already headed his way and didn't look willing to wait for him to finish his coffee.

"What is it?" Collin asked.

"Jonathan says it's time for the intercept," Anthony said.

"What?" Collin exclaimed, tossing the rest of his coffee in the trash—he was wide awake now anyway. "We aren't done planning it."

"We lost three men last night," Anthony said.

The grave expression Anthony was wearing was warranted. Each time a man was activated, he didn't leave Mr. Clean alone, but backed up by twelve civilian soldiers outfitted in Mech suits. The outer shell of the Mechs had all been replaced with alien steel.

If three men had died in The Never last night, it meant the Ferox had managed to kill them despite more than enough backup. One Ferox getting lucky they could have accepted, but as the old rule goes: one is chance, two is coincidence, three is a pattern.

"Were they fresh implants?" Collin asked as they walked.

Tony shook his head. "Only one was untested. The second was fairly green, had his implant less than a month. But the last, Pettinger, my understanding from Perth and Mito is that he was no easy target."

Collin nodded. "How many activations were there yesterday?"

"Sixteen," Anthony said. "And that number is up from what we've been seeing of late."

The news was troubling. Their war council had expected that they would be seeing a drop-off of soldiers being drawn into The Never. Malkier knew as well as his brother that if they were in open war, no previous rules would govern single combat. He'd be stupid to keep letting his people enter the gates until he was ready to lead a coordinated invasion.

The Ferox who were still coming through were those who entered the queue before war had been declared. So far, as would be expected, the number was going down. The fact that this number had surged on the day that three of their people were killed meant that their assumptions were wrong—or something had changed.

"Alright then," Collin said. "Let's hope we're ready."

He'd been following Anthony as he listened. He realized then that they weren't headed for Jonathan's quarters. "Wait, where are we going?"

"Jonathan wants us to bring one more," Anthony said.

Collin frowned. "Why?"

He noticed what particular block of the barracks they were headed for. "Oh, right. Makes sense, two birds, one stone, and all that."

CHAPTER FIFTY-FIVE

"I CALLED THEM Tar-frogs and Tar-manders," Sam said. "So far, everyone else just calls them Greens and Reds. Which—fine, it's simple—but it's not very inspired."

"You think Tar-mander is inspired?" Bodhi asked. "Sounds like a Pokémon."

Sam's shrug conceded that Bodhi had a point.

"What did you call them?"

"Greens were Oscars, Reds were Elmos," Bodhi said. "I didn't know Alphas existed until I got here."

A few tables away, Leah hid a smile as she overheard the minutia of the conversation. Sydney had been right—Jonathan may trust her—no one else did. She ate alone, tried to get breakfast as early as possible—avoid everyone so they didn't have to avoid her.

The effort to keep to herself was becoming more futile. More soldiers were arriving each day. None took long to get the memo; it was almost as though *don't be seen talking to the redhead. She was a government spook,* was some part of the orientation.

Rivers wasn't treated the same. He had been at first, but now that he'd accepted one of the implants and trained with the other soldiers, he seemed to have been deemed part of the family.

For Leah, it was a lot like being the unpopular kid in school. No one wanted to be seen talking to her. People watched her when she came and went. Awkward silences entered rooms the moment she stepped into them.

She'd busied herself reading Rylee's journal entries from a tablet Mr. Clean had provided her. The transcripts had been stolen along with everything else during the escape. She found herself talking to the AI a lot when she was alone in her quarters. He wasn't human, but he was a pretty good stand in for company.

"If I stick with Sesame Street, then I guess I'd call the Alphas . . . Cookie Monsters? Grovers? Big Birds?" Bodhi said.

"Tar-asaurus?" Sam offered the word with the same uncertainty.

Bodhi's face soured. "Probably a good thing we aren't the ones naming things."

Leah muffled a laugh, as someone took a seat at the table behind.

"You seen an Alpha?" Bodhi asked.

"In the projection chamber. Jonathan has us all reviewing old records from the Foedrata Arena," Sam explained. "Kind of like watching Ferox fight Super Powered Cavemen."

"I would totally watch Ferox fight Super Powered Cavemen," Bodhi said.

Sam shook his head. "It's not entertaining . . . it's brutal. I'm losing my appetite just thinking about it. Funny thing is I don't think we are seeing the worst records. There is a whole cluster of them that Mr. Clean made off limits."

The records of the bonded pair, Leah thought. *Jonathan didn't want people seeing them.*

"Hey, Leah."

She was surprised to hear her name and looked up from her tray. She found that Hayden had sat down behind her. She turned slowly and found him watching her with a pitying sort of smile.

"You don't have to sit alone again," he said.

"I . . . I wouldn't want to get you shunned by the We Hate Leah club."

Hayden grinned. "That's not what the club's even called."

"Oh?"

"We haven't voted on names yet, it's on the agenda for tomorrow."

From the corner of her eye, she saw Mr. Clean speaking to Bodhi for a moment. She didn't hear what was said, but Bodhi nodded, said goodbye to Sam, and got up to leave in a bit of a hurry. She frowned at that, then turned back to Hayden.

"It's okay, you don't have to be nice to me."

Hayden sighed. "It's hard to stay mad when I can tell you're angrier with yourself than I could ever be."

She considered that for a moment then slowly picked up her tray and moved to his table.

"You know you're not actually public enemy number one around here," Hayden said.

"Do tell."

"Everyone hates Grant just a little more," he said.

"Ahhh, I'm slightly more popular than the one guy in the brig."

"Take the win."

"I was pretending," Leah admitted. "It did make me feel a bit better."

There was a lull for a bit and Hayden took a few bites of his oatmeal.

"What do the others say?" she asked.

Hayden thought about it as he chewed. "Paige is having a rough time here. It's not just you. She's trapped in an alien space craft with her father who she . . . well, she hates far more than you. I think the worst of it is she wants to talk to her best friend, but. . ."

He didn't finish the statement, choosing instead to wave his spoon in her general direction.

"Right," Leah said.

"Collin is a harder read. I don't think it's any secret that he, well . . ."

Hayden paused mid-sentence as though he was reconsidering the wisdom of what he was about to say.

"He's in love with her," Leah said, saving him the trouble. "It's painfully obvious to everyone. I mean, except her."

Hayden laughed. "Right. Well, you hurt Paige, and he loves her. So . . ."

"That's fair," Leah said. She hadn't really been eating her oatmeal, at this point even pushing raisins around her bowl with her spoon seemed to make her lose her appetite.

"For what it's worth," Hayden said. "I . . . I do get it."

"You get it?" she asked.

"Why you did it," Hayden said. "I'm sorry about your brother."

She looked up from her bowl. No one had ever acknowledged it. That she had reasons for what she had done. It felt good, to be understood, even if it didn't mean she was forgiven. "Thank you, Hayden."

He shrugged, awkward in the face of her gratitude.

"Jonathan seems pretty indifferent about the whole mess. You'd think he'd be the angry one. Then again . . ." He paused, lifted his spoon and twirled it in a few circles as though pointing to everything about their new reality. "Might be a bit like throwing stones in a giant glass alien space craft he neglected to tell his friends about."

Leah smiled, but shook her head. "It's not really the same. He kept secrets to protect us."

"Us?" Hayden asked.

Leah nodded and sighed. "As infuriating as it sounds, I can see it now, why nothing I did was ever going to get the truth out of him. He was protecting me too."

"Irony," Hayden said.

Another lull followed. Hayden got a refill of his coffee and came back. "Sometimes I want to blame Heyer for all of it. What if he'd just told The Cell what was happening, maybe things could have gone differently, but—I really don't know."

Hayden's expression was doubtful. "If science fiction tells us anything, it never works out well for aliens that get involved with the government, especially if they mean well."

Leah raised an eyebrow and it turned her face into a question mark.

"*E. T, Starman, The Day the Earth Stood Still, X-Files,*" Hayden said. "From what I hear, Olivia isn't exactly Agent Mulder."

Leah held up her spoon. "You're not wrong. She's not even a Scully."

Hayden grew more thoughtful as he ate, looking around them once again. Finally, he dropped his spoon into the bowl and sat back with his coffee. "The week before we got kidnapped, Jonathan asked me about the heroine's journey."

Leah blinked. "Okay, that came out of nowhere."

Hayden shook his head. "No, I was just thinking about how it doesn't hit you all at once. Where Jonathan's weirdness suddenly makes sense."

"So, you're saying something suddenly makes sense to you?" she asked.

"It's a weird thing to ask out of nowhere," Hayden said.

Leah looked at him, as though maybe he hadn't considered who Jonathan had been asking.

"Okay, yes it would be weirder if he'd asked someone other than me, but still . . ."

A few weeks ago, Leah would have recognized the signs. Would have known Hayden was about to trap her in a longer dissertation. She might have tried to head him off, but this was the first polite, almost normal, conversation she'd had with another human being since arriving at Hangman's Tree.

"Last few months, Jonathan's been interested in things he'd have only smiled politely at if I brought them up before. Though, I guess you probably already know that, because . . . you know . . . spying."

He didn't say it as though taking a jab. Rather, he was simply saying she probably knew exactly what he was talking about because she'd been watching. It was a bit surreal when she found herself discussing *work* like anyone with a normal job might. She explained that, actually, The Cell couldn't listen in on the conversations in the house. The alien had some way of scrambling audio devices. Even after they brought in lip readers, they believed the video was being tampered with and it turned out they had been right.

"Still," she said with a grin, "not exactly a stranger to Hayden rants."

He nodded.

"Well, I had a bit of an insomnia problem. So, one night after everyone but Jonathan was asleep, I sat down on the couch. He was just staring into space, then he suddenly asks if there is a difference between the hero and the heroine's journey."

"Seemed weird at the time but . . ." he trailed off a bit as his face saddened, and his voice lowered, ". . . he was sleeping on the couch because Rylee had shown up the night before."

"I get it," Leah said. "He was asking about heroines because of Rylee, and you just realized it."

Leah stopped playing with her food. "So, what did you say?"

"At the time, I was surprised how little I remembered. I mean, yeah, I'd heard of the heroine's journey, I just hadn't pondered it much. I had to go find one of my old notebooks from sophomore year."

"And . . ."

"Well, thing is, he may have been asking because of Rylee. But gender doesn't have much to do with it," Hayden said.

"Because, the misconception is that the journey of the hero or heroine, implies a male or female. Hero and heroine are just labels some scholar gave to the journey itself."

She got comfortable. She'd seen this with Hayden. When he got a captive audience, he had a habit of slowly orbiting his point. Jonathan always said it was best to let him get there on his own. "I get it, the sex of the person taking the journey doesn't matter. So, what is the difference between the journeys then?"

He licked his lips. "The one that always stuck out most to me is where the protagonist's power comes from. In the typical story, the hero is on a journey for individual strength. A man or woman on that path is trying to harness power they intend to wield alone," Hayden said. "In the heroine's journey, power is acquired through gaining allies."

Leah gave a knowing frown. "Sounds like something a man came up with."

Hayden put his coffee on the table and drew his arms across his chest. "There are other differences. Some people say the heroine's journey is inward instead of out, into the self instead of out into the world. Others will tell you the hero usually starts from a place of privilege while the heroine doesn't.

Some will talk about replacing the *sage* with the *old crone*. So instead of Yoda you get Cinderella's Fairy Godmother."

Hayden, sensing he was losing her interest, stopped drilling down into the details. "If you think about it in the context of stories like the *Wizard of Oz* or *Buffy the Vampire Slayer*. There is an underlying message that, even when you're the chosen one, your greatest strength will come from knowing with whom to ally yourself."

He uncrossed his arms and picked his coffee up again. "After all, when the poop really hits the fan, even Superman needs the Justice League."

CHAPTER FIFTY-SIX

COLLIN SLAPPED AT a mosquito as the sun finished setting on Sucia Island.

"So," he said, checking his nonexistent watch for the umpteenth time. "Been five hours now, we still feeling good about this plan?"

They were in an unoccupied campground that bordered the island's southwestern beach. Jonathan stood over a picnic table, arms folded as he studied a map of the island's geography one last time.

"Warned you it could take a while," Jonathan said.

"Right, it's just . . ." he said. "Well, I didn't say anything while you were explaining the plan to the Tibblers, but didn't you tell me it was a bad idea to engage these things in the woods. Let alone the woods at night."

Collin was nodding to the setting sun as Jonathan turned away from the map to look at him. "The Tibblers?"

Collin shrugged. "We had to call them something."

Jonathan raised an eyebrow. "Wouldn't let anyone hear you call them that."

"What *the Tibblers* don't know won't hurt them . . . or me," Collin said. "But still. Forest? Night?"

"The Ferox normally have the advantage in low light. They're harder to spot in the dark, move through the trees pretty fast, and have better vision than us. Their claws do better on loose soil as well."

Jonathan picked up the lantern that had been acting as a paperweight against the wind and handed it to Collin. "While none of that is good, I think we've taken the necessary precautions."

He'd just finished rolling up the map as chatter came over the earpieces.

"Jonathan, the breach is about to open," Mr. Clean said. "This is the last chance to abort."

Jonathan gave him a glance before taking a few steps back and dropping down on a knee in the sand. He opened a line to the others, "Not going to waste any more opportunities. Everyone good to go?"

In his own earpiece, Collin heard Bodhi, Perth, and Beo sound off one after the other.

"I . . . I'm ready," Rivers said.

Jonathan took a long breath and laid flat in the sand.

Lastly, he opened a channel to Rivers that the rest couldn't hear. Collin only overheard because he was standing right there. "Not gonna lie to you Rivers, this ain't going to be pleasant."

"Don't worry about me," Rivers said.

"Good man," Jonathan said. "Just stay back unless you're absolutely needed."

"I got it," Rivers replied.

"We're good, Mr. Clean," Jonathan said. "Do your thing."

Collin put his ear buds in and turned away, temporarily blasting his music at a volume that risked permanent hearing damage. In the past couple days, he'd seen enough device activations. They were as disagreeable to watch as they were to hear. A close tie with seeing someone get their leg amputated without anesthesia. He knew that if he were able to hear it, Jonathan's screams would be joining the chorus of others that now shared that same activation agony from all of their various locations around the island.

He shifted his weight from one foot to the other as he waited it out. When he didn't sense any movement behind him, he opened one eye and turned to look, finding Jonathan's face had gone serene and his chest was beginning to blaze.

He grabbed the binoculars they had brought along, tossing the strap over his neck before starting his climb up a small lookout tower. The island was only two miles across. It had few, if any, civilians present on any given day of the year. More importantly, it was far enough from the coast that it should theoretically force the gate's safety protocols to deliver its passenger somewhere in the forest.

The entire point was to keep the Ferox surrounded by water on all sides, and make sure no one was around to see it.

All this, because Jonathan had just given Mr. Clean the order not to bring The Never into existence. What played out here tonight was on true Earth—and that meant it was for keeps.

Bodhi was the targeted node of tonight's arrival. That meant he was the only one amongst them tied to the portal stone the Ferox would be carrying. Only Bodhi would be able to track the Ferox with his internal compass. It also meant, that everyone else on the island, save Collin, was running on Mr. Clean's batteries.

Collin looked out over the forest. He'd been given assurances that the gateway would be hard to miss and it proved true. Despite the dense tree cover, he quickly spotted an unnatural red light glowing in the woods near the island's center.

"You spot the portal?" Jonathan called up to him.

Collin blinked a few times when he saw Jonathan on his feet below. He had to wait for him to zip up his coat, hide the light on his chest, before he could look at him without squinting.

"There is definitely a large ominous glow out there," Collin said. "It's northeast of—oh."

"Problem?" Jonathan called up.

"Uh, it's already gone."

Jonathan didn't look surprised. "Mr. Clean said the portal might be short lived. Doesn't take as long to punch a hole into true Earth as it does The Never."

Bodhi's voice came in over the radio. "I've got its position, south of me, feels like less than a mile."

Jonathan reached to his ear once more. "Ocean perimeter teams, keep your eyes open."

The people he was addressing were their men on the water. They were mostly there to make sure no boats picked tonight to approach the island. According to Jonathan—and pretty much everyone else who had faced these creatures and lived to talk about it—they had yet to meet a Ferox who could swim. Still, he didn't want anyone getting comfortable. With Malkier and Heyer in open war, whatever rules they previously relied on might be out the proverbial window. He didn't want to risk drawing The Cell's attention to tonight's operation. At least—not yet.

Jonathan gave him one last glance, then pulled a visor over his eyes. Collin opened the screen of a laptop they had set up in the watch tower. He checked that the camera feeds were all coming in and recording, and confirmed all of their people were accounted for on a map tracking their individual locations, then put his hand out the window to give a thumbs up.

"Alright, we're heading in," Jonathan said. "Rivers?"

The man's reply was a little slower than the rest. "Unpleasant was an understatement. But yeah, I'm on my feet."

"Good. Remember, close enough to see for yourself, but don't get involved," Jonathan said. "Everyone else, let's go hunting."

Collin felt like he was watching a first-person shooter. The feeds from each man's cam suddenly blurred as they burst forward into the trees. The light was getting scarce, and it was worse once they were under the forest canopy, but the cameras quickly auto adjusted to night vision. Once the men were deeper into the forest, they restrained from showing off any superhuman speed, taking more care to mask their movements.

Bodhi and he were the only voices on the comms.

Bodhi whispered location updates as he tracked the Ferox. Meanwhile, Collin kept an eye on the map, helping them to coordinate a shrinking net.

Collin saw Bodhi's cam slow to a stop. He was about halfway up a pine and had just disabled his *gleamers* so he could crouch on one of the tree's thicker branches.

"I've got a visual," Bodhi said. "Big fella, Red. He's up a tree. Looks like he's doing a lot of sniffing."

"Sit tight, I'm almost dere," Beo said.

"Yeah," Bodhi said, his voice shrinking to a softer whisper, "No worries on—Dammit."

"What's wrong?"

"Think he smelled me," Bodhi said. "Cause he is looking right at me."

"Is he moving on you?" Jonathan asked.

"No, just staring, he—" Bodhi was quiet for a moment. "Crap, I blinked and he ghosted me."

"What?" Beo asked.

"I . . . I blinked and he was gone," Bodhi said.

"Collin, you catch it on the body cams?" Jonathan asked.

Collin had seen the same as Bodhi, but it happened so fast that he wasn't sure. "One second. Replaying it. Gonna slow it down."

"I can still feel it," Bodhi said. "It's moving toward me real slow."

"Not liking this," Perth said. "Them wanks never been sneaky. Our boy is up to something."

"Beo, how far out are you?" Jonathan asked.

"Twenty seconds," Beo said; he was moving fast now, no longer worried about making noise. They could all hear the exertion in his voice.

"Don't like this, I can hear the bastard breathing, still can't see him," Bodhi said.

"Crap, crap, crap!" Collin's voice was panicked. "You didn't blink, Red just pulled some *Predator* bullshit."

There was a second's delay before Jonathan and everyone else caught Collin's meaning. "Bodhi, move!"

"East, turn east," Collin's voice yelled through the earpiece.

Wet mud shot out in heaps when Jonathan planted his feet and changed course. As he sprinted through the forest, he could hear the groan of trees and breaking of branches being caused by the Ferox's pursuit of Bodhi long before he finally caught sight of them.

Well—he caught sight of Bodhi.

Gleaming through the branches the kid made it look like surfing. Still, one slip and the Ferox trailing him was going to hit like an invisible wreaking ball. The general location of the Red wasn't difficult to infer. In this much foliage, he could see the disturbance of something huge and unseen as it stampeded after Bodhi through the forest.

Beo wasn't far behind, but the man was built like a tank, not nearly as agile or quick; he wasn't going to catch up before Bodhi was in trouble. Normally, Jonathan wouldn't worry about Bodhi holding his own against a Ferox long enough for them to reach him, but not being able to see where a predator's claws and teeth were striking could end things real quick.

"Bodhi, turn hard left," Jonathan said already changing his own course to intercept them.

Bodhi did as he was told, giving up a precious bit of his lead to make the turn, but the giant mass hurtling through the branches hadn't expected it. Caught off guard, the invisible beast under corrected, slamming into the trunk of a tree. The pine whined, then let out a loud crack as it split, the top half breaking free with a long groan as it came crashing down.

As Jonathan rapidly closed on them, he kept one eye on his footing and the other on tracking the exact moment his path would cross with Bodhi's. "When I tell you, make a hard stop, jack up the repulsion on your gloves and turn them on the bastard."

"Um . . ." Bodhi's voice sounded like he understood but wasn't loving the plan. To be fair, they had never tried turning the gleamers on a living thing in motion, and Jonathan wouldn't want to be the one doing an exploratory exercise with a Ferox barreling at him either.

"Trust me, use your implant's instincts and he'll never touch you," Jonathan said, taking a few last steps. "Now!"

Hovering across a branch, Bodhi made an about-face. His back was put on a collision course with the tree, as he gritted his teeth and turned all his strength over to holding the repulsive force of the gleamers behind him. He came to a stop an inch from the trunk, and with no time to spare he dialed the gleamers to full strength and let his mental compass guide his hands toward the signal torpedoing at him.

He braced himself as he began to feel the weight push back at him.

Just as his alien instinct told him he was about to be crushed, the air rippled in front of him. Light bent in strange waves as the camouflage keeping the Ferox's body cloaked passed through the gleamers' repulsion field. A thin layer of gel undulated, revealing the red and black skin of a claw as the substance retreated up the Ferox's arm.

In those milliseconds the Red's momentum was slowed—as though it passed through air that had grown as thick as honey. The Ferox was too heavy, had too much forward momentum—it wasn't enough to stop it. As the Red's arm became visible, it reached for Bodhi as though intent on palming his skull into the trunk. Bodhi was pinned between the opposing forces of the tree and the Ferox. The pine swayed backward through the tree line.

Suddenly, all the force from the Ferox disappeared. With nothing pressing on the gleamers, Bodhi stumbled forward off balance. The tree, no longer being pushed began to sway back to its normal position.

Jonathan collided with the Red midair, the armored plating on his forearm a shield in front of him as he collided with its abdomen. The Ferox buckled around him as he shot through the field of Bodhi's gleamers. The gel that was responsible for the Red's cloaking snapped back into place over its exposed arm as soon as they were clear of the repulsion field.

The Ferox itself was blindsided. When they came crashing to the ground the Red took the brunt, hardly aware of what had happened when Jonathan dropped clear. Given the difficult terrain, he did the best he could to land on his feet, but the invisible shape tore end over end through dirt, roots, and mud ripping a path through the undergrowth.

Whatever was keeping the Ferox transparent, it couldn't deal with so much mud coating its exterior. Even in the dark, Jonathan could now make out its contours as it tried to get up. He reached back with both hands and freed two cartridges from the rear of his belt.

"Eyes and ears everyone," he warned over the comm, as he pulled pins from canisters and tossed them in the dirt in front of the Ferox.

He stood and spun, putting a tree between him and the Ferox as it staggered onto hands and knees. He dropped down in a ball, clenched his eyes shut and pressed his gloves to his ears. The Ferox, having barely gotten to all fours, looked about disoriented, still trying to locate the boulder that had collided with it a moment earlier. Finally, the muddy outline of its head seemed to focus on the smoke pillar coming from the two metal canisters resting on the ground between its hands.

Two loud pops rang out through the trees, night suddenly turning to day in their little leg of the forest, and the Ferox roared in shock. Those who had enough warning to protect their eyes and ears from the flash bombs couldn't see the mud covered Feroxian shape rear back and scream as its claws reached for its eyes.

In his normal human state, the blast wouldn't have been a picnic, but with his implant active and his eyes and ears protected, Jonathan came away unaffected. He stepped out of the trees to find the Ferox's mud-covered outline reeling backward, losing its balance as it blindly tripped over obstacles on the forest floor.

He stepped into range and clocked the stunned Ferox across the jaw hard enough to knock it off its feet and bounce its head off the forest floor.

"Perth, Beo, how far out?" Jonathan asked.

Flailing, the Red struck out wildly, diving in the direction it had been attacked, but Jonathan knew better than to hold still. He easily got behind the deaf blind beast and yanked its footing out from under it.

"Right behind ya," Beo said.

Oddly, Jonathan no longer needed to be told this, he noticed that the cloak the Ferox was using allowed him to see completely through much of it. He could see Beo hurtling out of the trees toward him through the beast's chest cavity.

"Saw the light," River's voice said over the radio.

"Same, far more helpful than Collin's directions," Perth added.

Jonathan grabbed hold of the Ferox at the wrist as it blindly tried to get to its feet, then used the leverage to bend its arm such that the Ferox's transparent face went back into the dirt. A moment later, as it tried to raise out of the hold, Jonathan thrust his fist down into the back of its head.

He pulled the punch.

He needed the beast incapacitated, not injured beyond usefulness.

The Red screamed in agony when he struck, and Jonathan and Beo were able to make out the muddy outline of its other arm. With Jonathan holding it pinned, Beo was quick to get its free arm under control.

That was when they got their second surprise of the evening.

Two fissures of thick green gas erupted out of the monster's back, bursting out of the camouflage in a steady stream that engulfed Jonathan's face as it passed. Despite being caught off guard, Jonathan kept his hold on the Ferox.

He began hacking up the green gas on instinct. The stuff had a chemical taste and smell—nothing he recognized.

"Beo, get clear, now!" Jonathan yelled, still coughing. "Everyone, pull back, we got an unknown weapon in the air."

He didn't let the Ferox capitalize on their surprise, not giving it any room to wiggle free even when Beo dropped his hold on its arm. The gas was no longer pouring from its back. It seemed to have exhausted its payload in those two simultaneous bursts. Unfortunately, it was already spreading visibly through the air. Rapidly thinning from the condensed green into an expanding cloud. The process was happening so quickly he was barely able to yell for Beo to get clear before losing sight of the man a few yards into the gas.

He had already done the math.

Whatever the hell this stuff was, he'd inhaled it in its condensed form. If it was poison, some sort of nasty biological weapon, then the damage was already done. Beo had gotten away quickly, but the man had been too close, had been moving through the cloud before he got to safety. If this stuff was toxic, he doubted the man had escaped what was coming, but his exposure was far less than Jonathan's.

For now, Jonathan didn't feel anything. He'd only started coughing the stuff up because it had been thick in his lungs. So far, the gas tasted awful, but wasn't even stinging his eyes or burning his skin.

He may not know what the gas was meant to do, but he didn't plan to keep standing in it. He slammed the Ferox back down, wrenching its arm back harder than he'd planned to, until he felt its internal skeleton start to bend. As it screamed, still in blind agony, he took hold of its other wrist, and used the limb to swing it off the ground and into the woods.

He immediately followed, and strangely it was when he was clear of the densest part of the green cloud—just having landed beside the injured Ferox—that he burst into flames.

CHAPTER FIFTY-SEVEN

HE PANICKED FOR a moment, staggered back, only to realize he wasn't in pain. Activated, the heat barely bothered him. His body wasn't what was on fire, it was his jacket that had burst into flames.

He preferred not being on fire, so he ripped the coat off and threw it to the ground. That was when he noticed something else. He was covered in what felt like hot heavy sludge. The stuff was black and silver, running down his arms and back, but it didn't seem to be hurting him in any way that a shower couldn't fix.

He had to put the sludge on the back burner a bit longer. While it seemed harmless for the time being, the Ferox was getting its vision back. Well, at least it wasn't tripping over the larger obstacles any longer.

"I'm clear of the gas, have you got my position," Jonathan asked as he swept the creature's legs out from under it. The Red's translucent form hit the ground, roaring as it fell onto the side of its already injured arm.

"You'd be surprised how easy it is to find a man on fire in the middle of the night," Perth said.

He had his boot to the back of the monster's neck when Beo came out of the forest. Bodhi came gliding down out of the trees a moment later. He noticed then that they all looked at him with a sort of disbelief. At first, he thought it was the sludge dripping off him, but that would have been a different sort of stare.

No, this was more the sort of look Steve Irwin got while wrestling an alligator. He'd never really had an audience before, and he hadn't thought about it. To them, it must have seemed like he was tossing these monsters about like it was so ordinary a day he didn't even think he'd been in danger.

Even now, Jonathan handled the creature, with all its strength and flailing for freedom, like he was dealing with a child's temper tantrum. He realized that it wasn't so long ago that, had he seen someone doing the same, he'd have looked at them the way they now stared at him.

"Beo," Jonathan said, snapping the big man out of it.

The big man shook himself a bit and moved quickly to grab the beast's good arm again. He restrained it by pulling the limb straight and putting his boot into the Red's armpit. The Ferox thrashed about, but whenever it made an attempt to free the limb and plant its arm, Jonathan gave it a warning tug on the leathery appendage of its ear. It was a bit more of a challenge while it remained cloaked, and had he not moved quickly, the Red's jaws would have closed on his hand like a bear trap.

Half blind, breathing like it had just run a marathon, the Ferox seemed to be gaining back enough wherewithal to see its struggling was only burning its energy. That sort of restraint was telling, at least to Jonathan. He'd have been willing to bet that beneath the cloak, the Ferox was not just a Red, but a Red that was on the cusp of transitioning to Alpha.

No Ferox gave up, but the smarter ones knew when to bide their time.

As Rivers drew close, he heard the guttural noises of the beast. He'd been told that he would need to be connected to the beast's portal stone to comprehend those sounds. What Mr. Clean had done that allowed men with implants to understand one another required some kind of connection. Device to device, device to portal stone.

To Rivers, the sound was that of a raging mutant bear. Only Bodhi understood the monster's disturbing growls. The kid was gleaming against the trunk of a tree an arm's length over the heads of the rest. Had he not been hovering an inch off the trunk's surface he'd have looked like Spider-Man stopping to eat lunch on the side of a building.

"Will you tell me what it says?" Rivers asked.

Bodhi looked down at the invisible shape, its arms and legs restrained with sets of massive Borealis steel shackles. He bobbed his head back and forth and frowned as he listened. "Blah, blah, I'm honored. I'm such a threat that you sent five to battle me. Blah blah. The Pilgrimage has begun. Soon, the prophet will lead our people through the gates. Our young will inherit the Promised Land."

Bodhi paused, listened to a new barrage of the Ferox's of growls, then smirked, and shot a thumb at Jonathan.

". . . and, of course, he knows who you are."

Jonathan didn't react. Rivers swallowed, as he got the sense that Jonathan was so used to these creatures from another dimension knowing who he was that it had lost its novelty.

Tibbs walked away, but Rivers overheard him as he opened a line to Mr. Clean over the comm.

"Change in plans, acquisition came through with new tech, some sort of cloaking device. Wasn't easy, but we locked him down. We'll need to remove the cloak before we can extract the stone."

Beo looked concerned. "We got any idea what dat gas was?"

Jonathan nodded, his expression grim. "We'll get Mr. Clean to examine it, make sure it isn't dangerous to us if deactivated."

Rivers heard more desperate growls fill the air. He turned to see Perth approaching with what could only be called a Feroxian muzzle. The Ferox clearly understood its purpose.

"Man, he's pissed," Bodhi said. "Says we're dishonoring ourselves in combat and our shame will haunt us for the rest of our lives."

"It still thinks it's in combat?" Perth snorted. "Be sure to tell him how deeply sorry we are to fall short of his standards."

Bodhi shrugged, but repeated Perth's words.

Rivers had been quiet most of the time.

Despite having been shown a Ferox in the projection chamber, he was still reeling from the entire experience. There was no doubting that the things existed, not anymore. He watched the invisible shape fighting its shackles warily, considering what the monster had said. *The prophet will lead our people through the gates. Our young will inherit the Promised Land.*

He noticed Jonathan was standing a bit outside of the group. Examining what remained of his armored jacket after it burst into flames. He had a troubled look on his face as he reached into the inner lining and his hand came back covered in that thick black-silver sludge that was still steaming.

"Dammit," he whispered, tossing the sludge aside.

He didn't come back to the group right away. He walked further away to have a more private conversation with the AI.

"Aye, boy," Perth said, snapping his fingers up at Bodhi to get his attention back. "What it say?"

"Sarcasm doesn't translate," Bodhi said. "He just thought you were agreeing with him."

The guttural growls continued to fill the forest. By the time Jonathan returned, his expression had become a mask. Whatever had been bothering him, he didn't want his men to see it. Likely he hadn't realized that Rivers was paying such close attention.

Bodhi was watching the Ferox with something between confusion and disgust.

"What is it?" Jonathan asked

He shook his head. "Says the prophet has a question for *the rain bringer*. Something about one of ours."

Bodhi scoffed and tossed his hands up. "I mean, the translation is about as great as always, but I think he is trying to say it has something to do with the *Slug*, or *the slippery one*."

Jonathan's eyes glimmered with recognition. "What's the question?"

Bodhi had to translate for the Ferox to understand. As it replied, he took some time, frowning as he tried to make sense out of its reply. "The prophet asks . . . is it that you can't or that you won't?"

Jonathan took a long breath as he looked down at the Ferox.

Rivers, confused by all of it, looked back and forth between Bodhi and Jonathan. "I don't understand. How . . . even if you wanted to, how would he expect to get an answer?"

Jonathan looked at Rivers for a moment and shook his head. "Malkier doesn't care about the answer."

Rivers frowned, but a look at Jonathan's face was enough for him to know that this was not the time for follow-up questions.

"This one give you a name?" Jonathan asked.

"Aye, got a name?" Bodhi asked.

The creature replied. Though Rivers could not imagine how it was possible that the growling sounds went on as long as they did just to give a name. Even Bodhi sighed impatiently as he listened. When it was over, he frowned. ". . . *Buries the Grave*?"

Jonathan nodded, then knelt until he was staring into where its eyes should be. He was thoughtful, quiet, as he considered the helpless monster. "Bodhi, tell him, if he's really unlucky, he'll get to deliver my reply."

With a nod to Perth and Beo, they secured the muzzle in place. Jonathan picked up what remained of his coat. Without it to cover him, he might as well have still been on fire as he strode away. He waited outside the group for a bit, looking far away until Perth yelled that the muzzle was secure.

"Bring us home, Mr. Clean," Jonathan said.

CHAPTER FIFTY-EIGHT

OCT 23, 2005 | 8 PM | HANGMAN'S TREE

WORD OF THE cargo Jonathan and his team had acquired spread quickly when they returned from the island. There was fear, respect, and disbelief on the faces of everyone who saw a captured Ferox held inside the Borealis steel containment cell.

For some of the soldiers, this was the first time they had seen a Ferox in the flesh. Well—for the moment they were hearing the muffled growls of a formless shape wearing a muzzle.

Jonathan had mixed feelings about letting their return become some sort of parade. Perth and Bodhi had pointed out that it might boost spirits to let the men be part of a victory.

That wasn't why he decided to do so.

Jonathan knew two things. One, keeping the captured beast a secret wouldn't last a day. Two, everyone in the building was taking his leadership on faith. Faith—that he and Heyer had a plan. He couldn't let them in on the big picture, but their loyalty deserved every reason to be sustained. So, while he could have had Mr. Clean teleport *Buries the Grave* wherever he wanted now that he was bagged and tagged, he decided to march the beast right through a set of large bay doors at the front of Hangman's Tree.

At first, the crowd trickled in around them. But as he progressed the numbers grew, drawing more and more to the spectacle. There were only whispers at first.

"How come no one said these things could go invisible."

"Crazy bastards actually caught a Ferox."

"Man, I'm telling you. Balls. Of. Steel."

They reached the doors of what would soon be known as the Feroxian containment block, where Jonathan planned to hold the beasts as more operations on the island were successful. By then, a much louder sound had risen from the crowd of onlookers. A chant.

"*Brings the Rain. Brings the Rain.*"

He'd heard his Feroxian title whispered more and more, since he'd stepped out of the projection chamber and found that Heyer had been broadcasting their friendly sparring session.

But hearing whispers when he walked through a room was one thing. As they chanted, Jonathan felt a weight leave him, if only for a moment. His men, they looked at him as though, yes, they would follow him into war.

As the doors began to close behind them, something changed in the crowd. The chant stuttered a bit and changed to something new.

"We won't bend. We won't bend."

Even after the doors were shut, they could still be heard on the other side for some time. He was alone with the few men who had accompanied him to the island. He shut his eyes and took a long breath.

"You guys go bask in some glory," Jonathan said. "Unfortunately, I must make it an order, but thank you."

As they turned to leave, Jonathan put a hand on River's shoulder.

"Not you, Rivers, I need a word."

The men stepped outside while the chanting was still audible. Rivers waited, but Jonathan didn't say anything. Instead, his war council joined them in the chamber.

"Well," Paige said, flashing Jonathan a smile. "Someone's popular this evening."

"They've all seen what can be done," Anthony said. "I'm betting tomorrow, many will want to be part of the next bag and tag operation."

Rivers was silently taking this all in, waiting for someone to explain what was happening. When Leah joined them, he seemed at a complete loss.

She'd watched Jonathan as those chants followed him inside. He didn't smile exactly, but something touched his eyes. She had watched him for some time now. His confidence always appeared unshakable, but the Jonathan she knew had never been the type to inspire others like this. She wondered if, seeing he'd given everyone a reason to believe, to keep faith, it let him take a breath while he was suffocating.

By the time the Ferox's cage was locked into place, the glimmer in Jonathan's eyes was gone. Mr. Clean wasn't long in identifying and disabling the apparatus cloaking the prisoner.

A set of prehensile cables formed from the floor and reached into the beast's prison. The ends intersected with two points, one on the Ferox's forehead and the other on the rear of its skull. Suddenly, what had been vaguely discernable within the shackles began to appear. The process started at the feet as a thin liquid coating on the Ferox's body retreated up toward its forehead. There, the light-bending substance disappeared into a circular band around the Ferox's forehead.

Leah saw that the black band wasn't so much worn as fastened to the Ferox's head. She'd have thought it a branded black scar ringing the creature's skull, but Mr. Clean's manipulation caused it to suddenly go slack.

Her understanding was that removing the dampening bracer from Heyer's forearm had taken the AI over an hour of intense decryption. This led her to suspect the AI possessed more than a theoretical familiarity with the cloaking band, as deactivation and removal only took a few seconds.

The cables gently pulled the circlet from the cage, carrying the band to the center of the room where an exam table rose out of the floor to accept it. Jonathan and Heyer weren't as interested in the band as they now were with two broken leathery sacs strapped to the Ferox's back.

"What can you tell us about the gas this thing hit us with tonight?" Jonathan asked.

"My analysis has confirmed your initial suspicions," the AI said. "It appears Cede has manufactured an aerosol capable of rapidly degrading the Earth-based derivative of Borealis steel. It is an aggressive exothermic reaction—generates a great deal of heat."

"Explains why I burst into flames," Jonathan grumbled. He looked at the remains of his armored jacket as though the sight made him angry.

When he noticed that Leah had seen this, he shook his head. "We've been through a lot together."

"The only good news is that the compound is ineffective against true Borealis Steel. Such a thing would be too dangerous for Malkier to develop as, like me, Cede is literally composed of it."

The declaration did bring a degree of relief to Jonathan and Heyer; everyone else was only left with questions.

"Wait, there's a difference between the steels?" Hayden asked.

This prompted a brief lecture from Mr. Clean. Leah was surprised to learn that previously whenever she'd heard references to Alien Steel and Borealis

Steel, she'd mistakenly assumed the terms were interchangeable. On the contrary, what they referred to as Alien Steel was a metal made from Earth-based materials and tempered through Borealis metallurgy. True Borealis steel was far superior but required alloys whose raw materials could not be mined on Earth—or even within the dimension Earth called home.

For the practical purposes of their army, the only difference was supply. Jonathan and his forces had access to as much of the Earth-based metal as they realistically wanted. The supply of true Borealis steel was far more limited.

In this dimension, the only source was Mr. Clean—literally. The AI's vessel was made of the stuff. He could use pieces of himself to forge armor and weapons—but if he gave too much, he would have to leave the dimension to replenish himself. Mr. Clean leaving the dimension, even for a day, while they waited for an imminent attack from the Feroxian Plane, was unthinkable.

Jonathan and the alien swapped troubled looks.

"The problem with buying time is that it does the same for your enemy. Malkier is no longer reacting on raw emotion. He is preparing for war, and it appears that he is no longer putting his faith wholly in overwhelming numbers," Heyer said.

Jonathan sighed. "This is why we've been losing men. All the Mechs are fitted with the Earth-based steel shielding. This gas would have rendered them more useless than if we'd made them out of plastic. Our soldiers' weapons and armor turned to sludge in their hands."

Leah could see how the revelation was affecting him. Knew he was blaming himself, knew he was thinking it had been him who put the weapons in their hands. Him who ordered the Mechs to support them. While he'd probably saved an incalculable number with the decision, he was only picturing the ones who saw their weapon melt away in their hands after trusting him.

The Mechs had brought their fatalities down to zero for some time now. Jonathan had gotten the prolonged luxury of being able to take every loss as his own personal failure because he'd immediately brought the number down to zero. A man in his position couldn't allow himself to keep thinking that way when things went wrong.

She suspected Jonathan knew this on an intellectual level.

There was a long silence as the bigger picture of just how much had changed out on that island tonight slowly sunk in. Despite the chants of victory that had followed Jonathan's return, his ability to arm his forces had just taken a serious blow. He'd seemed almost prescient in his planning—but he hadn't seen this coming.

"Why use this before assaulting Earth?" Leah asked. "Why risk us finding out about it."

"Could be he needed to test it," Heyer said.

"Maybe, but I think Leah is right, there is more to it than that."

Whether Jonathan was right or wrong, no one offered a theory before Collin diverted their attention.

"Um, not to distract from one huge problem, but isn't anyone else more worried about the device we just took off Mr. Grumpy over there?" Collin asked, nodding at the exam table. "I mean, while I see that the notion that we'll be fighting these things with flaming Jell-O is troubling, aren't you a little more worried that they are going to be invisible?"

"Fortunately, that isn't the case," Heyer said. "Malkier only has seven of these devices. Six, now that this one is in our possession."

While this came as a palpable relief to everyone, Leah noticed Jonathan eyeing the alien. "How can you be sure?"

"This isn't Borealis tech," Heyer said.

"Not Borealis tech?" Hayden asked.

"If it was, I would have had Mr. Clean issue one to every soldier in Hangman's Tree."

Hayden blinked a few times then repeated himself slowly. "Not . . . Borealis . . . tech?"

Heyer sighed. "Humans and the Borealis are not the only species in existence to have ever reached some level of technological achievement. The Borealis went through a long period of culling species they saw as an eventual threat to their immortality. This device is a creation of one of those long dead species."

"What were they called?" Hayden asked.

"There has never been need of an English term for the species," Heyer said.

Hayden looked to Jonathan as though he couldn't believe what he was hearing. Tibbs sighed and shrugged. "Believe it or not this issue comes up a lot in present company."

Paige, mostly quiet so far, watched Collin and Hayden exchanging glances with one another and she rolled her eyes. "You two want to name the species, don't you?"

Hayden nodded at the black band on the exam table. "Well, it would be easier than calling this the Extinct Alien Species Cloaking Device," he said defensively.

Paige, expression having gone deadpan, stared back at them. This went on for a few seconds, ". . . they want to name it after the Predator."

Both Collin and Hayden suddenly froze.

"No," Collin said with a scoff. "We were thinking . . . the Yautja."

Hayden nodded in agreement.

Paige's eyes narrowed. "Mr. Clean, if I was a dork, would I know that Yautja is what the Predators call themselves?"

"Not in the films, but in the comic book ser—"

"Okay fine," Hayden admitted. "You name them."

"Maybe I will," Paige said.

"If we could focus on something of consequence," Heyer cut in. "The reason we know Malkier only has six more of these devices is because I was with him when we recovered them. The individual units were inside a . . ."

Heyer paused, looked annoyed for a moment, then said ". . . a Yautja vessel. The craft had been left derelict in space, its crew members dead for centuries. We never encountered any other artifacts from their civilization."

The three that had been bickering all acknowledged that with some embarrassment. "No invisible Ferox army, just six. That's good," Collin said.

"If I may chime in, I've scanned the Yautja device and it does appear to have been altered," Mr. Clean said. "While its primary function has not been changed, a Borealis recording device has been attached."

This brought another pause from the group.

"Wait, so Malkier was spying on us?" Paige said, her eyes turning to Leah. "We just can't catch a break on that, can we?"

Leah sighed before returning a disingenuous smile.

Jonathan and Heyer had been quiet, lost in their own thoughts. They looked up at one another as though they'd both reached the same conclusion.

"He was trying to see our hand without showing his own," Jonathan said.

Heyer nodded.

"You two gonna share with the rest of the class?" Paige asked.

"The Ferox can't bring back useful information on technology," Heyer said. "But for the last few weeks every engagement has ended with a Ferox death. Malkier needs to know why. Needs to know if we have a new weapon we're using against his people. He had two choices, enter the gates himself, or find a way to record what happens inside. Of course, he can't risk himself, so he chooses the latter."

"He doesn't want us discovering his recording device, but he needs to test his new weapon-killing aerosol."

"Weapon X gas," Collin said.

Hayden sighed. "Wolverine reference, why?"

"I mean . . ." Collin shrugged. "It's a gas that destroys weapons made from metal we thought was invincible. Seemed appropriate."

"So, he stacks the odds in the Ferox's favor, gives them a Yautja cloaking unit and . . . WX gas. Then records the fight," Paige said.

Leah chimed in, "But, he doesn't predict us pulling one of his spies to true Earth. Expects his tracks will be erased when The Never closes. We learn as much about him as he did about us."

"Three men dead, he knows the WX gas works, knows about the Mechs," Anthony said. "Not sure it's a fair trade."

"You haven't considered what would have happened if we went to war and didn't know about the WX," Leah said. "Who knows how many of us would have been lost before we understood what was happening to our weapons."

Jonathan nodded thoughtfully. "Mr. Clean, how much of this WX should we expect Malkier will be able to produce?"

Mr. Clean's expression was grave. "Realistically, as much as he wants. The components are abundant on the Feroxian Plane. That, and after analysis, the process to manufacture the stuff in large quantities would not be complicated or time consuming."

"Can it be countered? Rendered inert somehow?" Jonathan asked.

"I'll need to run some tests to see if any Earth-based components might be effective, but my hopes are limited on that front. That said, the reaction is dependent on the presence of oxygen as a catalyst."

"Does that help?" Paige asked. "Last I checked, we're all pretty dependent on that."

Jonathan wasn't so quick to discount it. "My armor was coated in carbon, but it didn't protect it."

"No, the reaction is highly aggressive. Any imperfection, a simple scratch in the coating that left the metal exposed would be enough," Mr. Clean said. "That said, the coating likely slowed the onset by reducing the steel's exposed surface area."

"That would explain why you didn't burst into flames right away," Rivers said.

He hadn't spoken much so when he did, the entire war council turned to look at him as though they'd forgotten he was there.

"What if we had something airtight coating the exterior?" Rivers asked.

Jonathan nodded. "Something that doesn't scratch or crack when one of us gets thrown through a wall. Mr. Clean, did the Borealis have any materials with properties like rubber or neoprene? Something we could produce on Earth that could take a lot of punishment."

"Yes," Mr. Clean said, a large cartoon smile appearing on his face. "Coincidently, Hayden and I have already begun work on a prototype for the very thing you are describing."

Everyone turned to Hayden in surprise. Heyer, more shocked than the rest, said, "A remarkable amount of foresight considering we only just learned of its necessity."

Oddly, Hayden had looked as surprised as they were, but after a moment a light bulb of understanding seem to come on. "Oh . . . ohhh! Yes! Yes, we have!"

He turned to give Jonathan what could only be described as a shit eating grin.

Jonathan, seeming to have connected some dots, slowly closed his eyes and sighed. "Ahhh . . . hell."

CHAPTER FIFTY-NINE

"WELL, DO WE get to see these things or what?" Leah asked.

"I agree, we should do that. Mr. Clean, you want to pull up the latest designs please?" Hayden said, still smiling at Jonathan, who refused to make eye contact with the man.

The monitor brought up a three-dimensional schematic. It rotated slowly to allow viewers to see from every angle.

"Oh," Paige said. "That . . . that looks like a . . . a . . ."

"A superhero costume," Jonathan interjected, bitterly. "It looks like a damn superhero costume."

Hayden's enthusiasm was hard to ignore as everyone gazed up at his creation for the first time. Eventually, he began to pick up on the awkward—praise-less—silence. He cleared his throat. "It's not just an elegant design. We incorporated far more armor into the suits than any strap-on tactical gear could have offered. Also, it's designed so that there's less obstruction to movement," Hayden said. "Your basic batman suit minus the cape. Instead of a cowl, I swapped in full head gear that integrates the HUD visors we've already been developing."

"Why does this look so familiar," Collin said. "Did you . . . did you rip off the Snake Eyes outfit from G.I. Joe?"

Hayden started to shake his head, then looked up at the rotating design once again, and frowned. "Oh, I suppose it may have had some unconscious creative influence."

"Derivative," Collin whispered.

"We were being as utilitarian as possible. But there are different designs for each individual in our forces. I took all of Jonathan's input into account."

"Jonathan's input?" Heyer asked. "You requested this?"

Jonathan shook his head. "That is not even a remotely accurate description of how this happened."

"Well, it's not completely utilitarian. Unless these designs across the chest and back serve a purpose," Paige said, pointing to the only part of the full body suit that wasn't black. Intersecting white lines in the design of the various implants. The one on screen was a match for the most common male implant. Which looked a lot like Jonathan's but lacked the line that crossed his chest horizontally. Yet it didn't appear to be a generic fit; it looked as though it were meant for a man twice the size of anyone in the room.

"This prototype is fitted to Beo. He likes his hammers; the weapon harness is customized to make it less cumbersome and balance the weight when he is on the move. Also incorporates the heavier one-sided shoulder plate," Hayden said.

"Hayden, you . . . you sound like a runway announcer," Paige said.

A moment later a much smaller design appeared. "Mito prefers his katars. Turned out he was also a dead shot with throwing blades, but he had no use for the skill against the Ferox until Mr. Clean was able to give him molecular edged blades."

Looking at the suit, it was easy to see that a small-sheathed blade had been placed in any location that wouldn't hinder movement.

"I see you didn't go with a yellow utility belt," Anthony put in, indicating that the suit appeared to have compartments for flash grenades and various other items at the waist. "But are those air vents?"

"Ahh," Hayden said excitedly. "They are, on the back, neck, shoulder, and outer thigh."

"What, is it a breathability thing?' Paige asked.

"No, it's actually a last hope defense mechanism. The Borealis material holding all the armor in place has its own sort of . . . nervous system. If the suit detects a breach, like that of Feroxian teeth biting through a gap in the armor, the suit has a bladder that releases."

"So, it pees itself?" Collin asked.

"The bladder holds concentrated Ferox repellent," Hayden said. "It's a last resort defense mechanism. We assume that a shot of the stuff is a harsh surprise, but will only buy a few seconds until the Ferox realizes it isn't harmful. Eventually it'll plug its nose and get back to biting."

Hayden kept going through a few more prototypes, and finally brought up the last four.

One clearly meant for Jonathan, as it had the additional horizontal line that ran across the chest and was built to accommodate both *Excali-bar* and

Doomsday. The three that followed this came as a surprise. A suit intended for the Alpha Slayer and sized to accommodate Grant Morgan's frame appeared on the display.

Hayden, seeing everyone's expression, hastily explained that Mr. Clean was able to whip out these designs quickly. "I just figured it was better to have it and not need it then need it and not . . ."

Reading the room, mostly Jonathan and Paige's expressions, he stopped explaining. ". . . Moving on."

When the next design came up there was even more silence. Though this time it was as though the group was resisting the urge to fall on the ground laughing.

"While I appreciate your efforts, I'll not have any need of this," Heyer said matter-of-factly.

"If the helmet is down, you can still wear your hat."

Heyer returned a blank stare.

"Right," Hayden said. "And last . . ."

The final design was equally unexpected to all of them, but Leah saw Jonathan's jaw tightening as he looked up at the display.

"You made one for the female implant?" Jonathan asked.

"Hayden instructed me to use Leah's specifications," Mr. Clean said.

He hid his thoughts well, at least to everyone else, but Leah could see just how much thinking was going on beneath the surface.

"Why?" Jonathan asked, and whether he intended it or not, an edge had entered his voice.

"Um, well, someone was gonna have to try it on," Hayden said. "Of the three women on the war council, I thought Leah was the least likely to hit me."

Sydney, Paige, and Leah considered this explanation; they all sort of nodded to themselves as though each had independently arrive at the same unspoken conclusion: *yeah, probably was his safest bet.*

As the suit's hologram slowly rotated above the circle, Leah watched Jonathan. He looked away, not just from the design but from her. It was almost as though he feared she would be searching his face for something.

Collin drew everyone's attention back to the armor. "What is that on the upper arm, it's been on all the designs?"

Mr. Clean zoomed in to focus the display just below the shoulder on one of the prototypes. It was an addition that clearly served only an aesthetic function. Three letters above a set of six striped chevrons, all embroidered in silver.

"T. N. A.?" Anthony asked carefully.

Hayden must have felt the weight of all the eyes turning on him. Probably a little heavier from Paige and Leah. "This, whatever we are, it needed a name. I thought, you know . . . The Never Army."

Collin grimaced, smacking his lips as he considered what he wanted to say. "Hayden . . . you know that TNA means something else right?"

Hayden rolled his palms up and bowed his head. "I am aware of the unfortunate association."

". . . and?" Paige asked.

"And I came to the conclusion there was exactly zero chance of a Ferox making that observation," Hayden said.

Collin shrugged. "I guess it's . . . better than the Tibblers."

When no one spoke for a long while, Leah placed a supportive hand on Hayden's shoulder. "I like it, Hayden. You've done something amazing."

"Thank you! Finally!" Hayden said.

"And, you know . . . maybe we can make the initials smaller."

Paige chuckled as though she couldn't stop herself, "Yeah, because you know . . . not everyone likes big TNA."

Heyer looked about the group with a strange sort of disbelief on his face. "I really do not know how it is that all this childish bickering seems to perpetually produce actual solutions."

CHAPTER SIXTY

NOV 02, 2005 | 8 PM | HANGMAN'S TREE

"STAY WIT' YA if ya want," Beo said.

Hayden shook his head, not that he wasn't grateful for the offer. "I've no idea how long I'll be at this. Not even sure exactly what I hope to learn here."

Beo nodded. "Maybe I'll stick aroun' jus a bit, make sure he behave."

"You aren't activated," Hayden said. "What difference would it make if he did try something?"

"Well, he don' know dat," Beo said. "But he know I'm da' one who tagged 'im las' night."

Lights the Sun was the fourth Ferox that had been taken prisoner in the last week. Despite its being locked in a cage of true Borealis steel and constantly monitored by Mr. Clean, Hayden shivered as he met those white eyes. The Ferox didn't hold still, paced back and forth within its confines—its stare never leaving Hayden as he approached.

Hayden considered Beo's offer as he took Mr. Clean's latest creation from his pocket. It looked like a hearing aid, but was actually a necessity for anyone without an implant to have any sort of communication with a majority of Hangman's Tree's inhabitants. Most didn't speak English, and shortly after Mr. Clean developed a translator, Hayden asked if Mr. Clean might be able to make it work between him and a Ferox.

"So, uh, Mr. Clean," Hayden said. "How is he going to understand me?"

"I'm blocking any noise from entering the cage. This has helped keep the prisoners more docile. When you'd like to begin, I'll translate to the best of my ability," Mr. Clean said. "Inside, the Ferox will only hear what I translate."

"Okay then," Hayden said. "Let's see how this goes."

He came as close to the cage as he dared, and *Lights the Sun* began to pace in smaller circles, its eyes completely focused on him now that Beo was standing back.

"Um, hello there," Hayden said.

Hayden couldn't hear the translation within the cage, but *Lights the Sun* paused as though listening to a voice. It didn't understand where the sound was coming from but appeared to comprehend the words. The creature only took a moment to make the connection between Hayden's mouth moving and the voice speaking to it.

When the creature's mouth started moving, Hayden had a similar experience, a short delay before words could be heard through the earpiece.

"*You're not a challenger,*" the Ferox said.

While he knew it was Mr. Clean doing the speaking, the AI seemed to make the decision that the Ferox should sound more aggressive. The AI may have been going for horror movie monster, but Hayden thought the voice sounded like Swamp Thing.

"Mr. Clean, why are you using that voice?"

"The Ferox is using a threatening tone intended to intimidate you," Mr. Clean said. "I didn't want any subtext to be lost in translation."

Hayden's lips quirked as he considered. "Hey wait, did you do the same thing on his end?"

"Yes, though my grasp of Feroxian is far less thorough, I think I captured your meek uncertainty quite well," Mr. Clean said. "I imitated the vocal abilities of one of their younglings deferring to an adult warrior."

Hayden grimaced, then tried to force a patient smile onto his face. "Okay, good to know. Moving forward, could we maybe not let the Ferox know I'm terrified of it? Perhaps use a standard Red's voice."

There was a moment of silence.

"I'll do my best," Mr. Clean said.

Hayden straightened up and stood tall, trying to hide his fear moving forward as he looked the monster in the eye. However, even as he forced himself to stand his ground he thought: *Dear God, even with superpowers how did Jonathan ever find the nerve to walk up and punch one of these things?*

In fact, holding its gaze was so unsettling, he decided to use the old trick of staring at the space between its eyes and hope it couldn't tell the difference. "I'd like to introduce myself, my name is Hayden, what may I call you?"

The Ferox looked at him with a confusion, almost something akin to disbelief.

"Your own people gave you this name?" the Ferox said. "So low amongst your kind are you?

Hayden frowned. Jonathan had warned when he asked to try this just how difficult it could be to have a discussion with a Ferox even if it was willing. He'd thought his friend might have been exaggerating. It was quickly becoming apparent that he may have actually understated the matter.

"Mr. Clean," Hayden said with a sigh. "What did you tell him my name was?"

"Well, Hayden is originally derived from Heathen," Mr. Clean said. "The Ferox species has an equivalent term but it is an adjective one of their kind would not wish to be described with—"

"Oh, for the love of . . ."

Hayden trailed off. This was off to a bad start, but he felt like it had to be worth it if he could just iron out the kinks. He wanted to believe that, if they could just have a conversation, there had to be a way to reach some sort of understanding. He took a moment to think. "Mr. Clean, do the Ferox have a word for ambassador?"

"Yes, I can successfully translate the term's meaning," Mr. Clean said.

"Good, tell him the first attempt to translate was a mistake, moving forward, he can just call me *ambassador*."

A brief pause followed as the Ferox listened.

"I am *Lights the Sun*," the Ferox said. "But, I am not one who speaks for the tribe."

Hayden licked his lips. He turned back to Beo. "Only took five minutes to exchange names, how hard could this be?"

"So, *Lights the Sun*," Hayden said. "I was wondering if you would take a moment and speak to me about your lord and savior, the prophet."

CHAPTER SIXTY-ONE

NOV 04, 2005 | 8 PM | HANGMAN'S TREE

"HAYDEN," JONATHAN SAID. "You've been quiet tonight?"

They were in the donut room again, and Hayden looked up and saw their eyes on him. There was no reason to pretend he hadn't been distracted.

The war council was meeting daily, and usually late into the night. Their earlier meetings had mostly been spent understanding the details of the plan their shadows had helped Jonathan come up with in The Never. That was also before they had learned of Malkier's WX gas. What Jonathan had tried to tell them during that very first meeting was far more clear now. Their original plan was broken again; he needed their help to fix it.

Thing was, tonight, Hayden's thoughts weren't focused on how to counter the gas. He'd had a thought, knew it was important, but couldn't see how to use it.

"You all know, I've been spending as much time as I can talking to *Lights the Sun*. Trying to understand his species," Hayden said.

He already saw looks from most of the table.

They weren't unwarranted. He had been the more vocal about finding a diplomatic type of solution to the Ferox than any of the others. The truth was, he wasn't fully comfortable contributing to the extinction of an entire species of conscious beings. That wasn't to say that anyone at the table was, but none wanted to rehash the morality of it again.

None would have accused him of being naïve, but the discussion always ended the same. Assigning good and evil was a useless philosophical discussion—it didn't change their situation. Earth had to protect itself from an aggressor. No amount of sympathy they might muster for their enemy's desperation was going to make them risk the planet.

"I do not think the Ferox are intrinsically evil," Hayden said. "But Malkier—"

"Hayden?" Anthony interjected. "All due respect, if this is a moral meditation and not something actionable, let's not."

"No, it's . . ." Hayden sighed. "I think I'm coming to understand something about the Ferox through *Lights the Sun*. I don't think they follow the prophet out of faith."

He got a few unsure looks.

"Hayden, they literally call him the prophet," Sydney said. "They believe he is their gods made flesh."

"He is one of their gods made flesh," Hayden said. "They just don't understand that the Borealis were never gods."

"What difference does it make?" Anthony asked.

"They're just being pragmatic," Hayden said. "There is no spirituality to it."

Most of the table looked at him blankly.

"Okay, when I tell you I believe Jesus could perform miracles, that he was the son of God, it's an act of faith. I wasn't there, I never saw, never witnessed the things for myself," Hayden said.

"*Lights the Sun* doesn't have to push back against any doubt. He has seen the prophet firsthand. I ask him how he knows the prophet speaks for their gods and he tells me of how Malkier brought ancient religious artifacts of their creators back to life after having been dormant for centuries. He tells me how the prophet opens portals to the battle ground where they find their challengers. He's seen the prophet astral project, speak to all the tribes at once all over the entire Feroxian Plane.

"But, *Lights the Sun* doesn't use the words I am using. He just sees Malkier using the power of his gods to accomplish things he can hardly begin to understand. *Lights the Sun* doesn't need faith to believe, he literally has no better explanation."

Collin shrugged. "He's got a point, for a Ferox it might be a greater leap of faith to conceive that the prophet isn't a god."

"How is that a weakness though?" Leah said.

"If Malkier were actually a god," Hayden said, "it wouldn't be a weakness, because no one could create doubt in his people."

"Doubt," Sydney asked.

Hayden shrugged. "If their belief is based on what they witness, if there is no act of faith binding them to it, then . . . how much will it take to put doubt into them? To show the Ferox that Malkier isn't a god?"

Jonathan listened, but his expression looked doubtful. "Even if we somehow showed them the truth behind the Borealis, the equation doesn't change. They're still facing extinction."

"But they don't think they can lose," Hayden said. "They aren't afraid to sacrifice as many of their lives as it takes because the Promised Land is more than their salvation, it's their manifest destiny."

"But, how do we do that, Hayden?" Paige asked.

He tossed his hands up. "I told you I didn't know."

Jonathan considered Hayden's angle again "Can you think of any way you might break *Lights the Sun*'s belief?"

Hayden looked more than a little uncomfortable with this question.

"He's been kept in a cage, hasn't he already seen things in this world that give him doubt?" Collin asked.

"No," Hayden said. "That's actually reinforcing his beliefs. He's been told that we're godless, and yet have harnessed powers only meant to be wielded by gods. Which is just another reason the prophet wants us destroyed. I don't think that is an ironic coincidence either, as Malkier wants humanity dead or broken because he fears us ever becoming a technological threat."

"Go back a sec, *Lights the Sun* thinks we're a godless species?" Collin asked. "You telling me you haven't tried to convert him?"

Hayden scowled. "I didn't try to *convert* him. But yeah, we discussed the topic. It's more than a waste of time, nothing in Earthly religions is relevant to him. Think about it, he doesn't fear death, he only fears his species' extinction. His idea of life everlasting is being remembered by his people and having as much progeny as possible.

"I tell him about Jesus performing miracles and he hardly sees the big deal."

"What do you mean by that?" Leah asked.

"The Ferox, they aren't fragile. They don't die of sickness and disease, they die of. . ."

Hayden paused for a moment to nod toward Jonathan. "Well, if they're going to die, they really want it to be fighting Mr. Rain Bringer over here, but our soldiers are the next best thing. That said, their Alphas can die of old age. The Reds and Greens, if they aren't killed in the arena or never reach Alpha, will eventually die from complications around stunted development."

"*Lights the Sun* doesn't understand why we consider our religious figures as gods at all. It's not his fault, we're just that different on a fundamental level. For instance, our religious figures are teachers of a moral code—they tell us how we should treat one another. The Ferox don't need to be taught this, apart from some early childhood confusion, they already do no harm to members of their own species."

"Did you tell him about more than one religion?" Collin asked.

Hayden groaned. "Yeah, I mean, as best I could. But it really didn't help matters. He didn't understand how our tribes could have so many different gods. He thinks that if any of our gods were true they would rid our world of the false gods.

"Again, the Ferox don't have this problem. The closest *Lights the Sun* came to describing different belief systems were minor disagreements that developed between tribes during the period of the Borealis abandonment. Some tribes came to believe different truths about the nature of their gods. But, the prophet was pretty much the second coming for the Ferox. He arrived, unified them, told them what beliefs to hold true to."

The table grew quiet for a moment.

"*Lights the Sun* has a point," Heyer said.

The alien hadn't spoken since Hayden had started them down this road.

"Throughout history, mankind has been a species with many fears. So, it has many gods," Heyer said. "The Ferox have only one true fear, and so, one god."

"Yeah," Collin said. "It's terrifying. Humanity's worst nightmare is an enemy easily united."

"Perhaps," Heyer said, then turned to look at Jonathan. "But, in my experience, every strength has its weakness."

CHAPTER SIXTY-TWO

"TURN OFF THE implant," Jonathan said. "Maybe he'll pull out of it. Maybe he won't, but I'm not letting him wake up with that much power."

Since the procedure, Grant had laid on the bed of his cell, the Alpha Slayer glowing in his chest. His eyes had opened, but he didn't seem to be there behind them. He looked straight up into nothing, shivering from time to time, like a confused child surrounded by angry adults.

Whatever was going on inside of him, he wasn't responding to any gentle prods or calling out his name.

Jonathan left shortly after Heyer agreed the implant should be disabled. In his current state, the pained screams of Grant as the implant deactivated may very well have been involuntary. Still, they followed Jonathan out of the cell. Heyer had made no move to keep Jonathan in the room. He stayed at Grant's side and waited. Heyer got the impression that Jonathan's leaving could only help Grant, though how much he had no way of knowing.

It was hours later before Grant suddenly blinked and became lucid enough to speak.

"What did I do, what did he do? My shadow . . . me . . ."

Heyer looked at him sympathetically. He couldn't tell if Grant even knew he was there, if the man was even aware he was speaking. He murmured to himself like that for a while, but eventually he looked Heyer in the eye and he seemed to be there.

"Who else knows?" Grant asked. "What he did?"

Heyer sighed, but he understood. His own shadow had made decisions he didn't want anyone to ever know. Only Jonathan carried his secret. He didn't lose sleep over that, what kept him awake was knowing what some part of him was capable of under the right circumstances.

"Only those who need to," Heyer said. "No one wants your secret known, it would be counterproductive."

"But you know. That means . . ."

Grant couldn't finish the words. He choked on them like a child who had only just understood how badly they had disappointed their parents. Grant nodded, looking up to meet the alien's eyes. "I see why he did what he did. I hate that I can see it."

Grant clearly had acquired the shadow's memories. What remained unclear to Heyer was if he had also acquired any of the mental deterioration that caused the memories to be made. From what he was seeing he didn't think that was the case. Heyer had never seen the man be capable of showing so much . . . shame.

"Are you able to differentiate," Heyer asked. "Can you tell which life you lead and which you inherited?"

"It's . . . confusing," Grant said. "Like having two different stories and feeling as though I lived through both. One is no less real than the other. I don't like it."

"I'll stay with you," Heyer said. "Help you figure it out."

Grant nodded and let his head rest back on the pillow.

"You don't have to rush getting your head wrapped around it all. Do you—did he—remember anything that might help us?"

"I . . . he . . . didn't understand most of what Malkier was doing. It wasn't like he bothered explaining. But I can describe some of what he saw. Tell you what he heard."

Whether or not Grant would resurface had been unclear when Jonathan left him to Heyer. The strategic side knew it would be for the best if he could be useful. A less evolved part of him didn't want the man to come out of it. His feelings toward Grant were simple hatred.

He didn't want them to become complicated, just hatred.

When Heyer let him know that the man was awake, he had called for the war council. Jonathan was late but found himself in the company of folks who didn't feel drastically different about Grant. Though, while his roommates never particularly liked the man, they weren't quite on the same level as being of indifference if he had been rendered brain dead.

Leah was in the middle of an explanation when he arrived in the donut room. Apparently, she'd known far less about Grant than they had all assumed. Grant's involvement in The Cell's investigation had been a leg of Olivia's operation. Leah's knowledge of him was that he was a temporary set of ears inside the house, chosen because he was already in place when the investigation began.

Jonathan had noticed a shift in the atmosphere with her and the others. Where previously they tolerated her with a poorly hidden malice, the bitterness was less than before. Leah's openness about The Cell's operation was being met more with interest than judgment.

When he walked in, his roommates were in the middle of absorbing how freely Jonathan and the rest had often spoken in the presence of Jack—Leah's younger brother. Collin in particular had taken a liking to the kid. He had been welcomed into the garage almost the first week Leah moved in next door.

"Wait, so did he actually like motorcycles?" Collin asked.

Paige frowned. "Really, that's what you want to know?"

Leah smiled at them. "Of course, he actually liked going over for play dates with you three. The Cell didn't have to pay him or anything."

"Outsmarted by a six-year-old," Collin said. "I feel betrayed . . . and a little hurt. I feel hurt and betrayed."

Collin's self-mockery was more humor than honest, but Leah played along, giving him a sympathetic look. "He isn't an evil mastermind. The whole point was that no one suspects a kid. Jack didn't even know he was spying. When he gave accounts of your interactions, he thought he was seeing a grief counselor . . ."

She'd trailed off, looking over their shoulders to where Heyer had just appeared. He quickly moved to join them at the table.

Collin glanced at Leah and whispered, "There *will* be follow-up questions on this."

"Grant came out of his stupor?" Jonathan asked. "He give you something?"

Heyer nodded, then requested Mr. Clean bring up a projection at the center of the table. A large holographic image of a red and black planet—The Feroxian Plane—began to circulate at the center.

"Anyone else suddenly feel like we're about to see plans for the Deathstar?" Hayden asked.

Heyer gave him a sobering glance, and Hayden smiled awkwardly before shrinking back into his chair.

"Mr. Clean, zoom in on the coordinates."

A square highlighted on a portion of the planet's surface, and seemed to zoom down until they were looking at a scaled elevation map of the terrain. What they were looking at would best be called a pit, but not one made by any natural forces. Rather, a perfectly cylindric depression in the surface. The clean sculpted lines were a stark contrast to the surrounding landscape, which had the contours of a planet shaped by normal geological evolution.

This pit was clearly built with great care. Which meant it had purpose.

Inside, in a ring near the pit's walls, were hundreds of small shapes surrounding one large platform at the center. Heyer was quick to draw their attention to the smaller shapes, and Mr. Clean brought one into a close-up view for them to see.

A familiar holographic sundial rotated between them.

"They will be moving the gateways," Heyer said. "All of them."

"The pit was like a model battlefield. Each gateway, a single troop. Each troop placed with precision inside a squadron. There were seven squadrons, and each was shaped in an arc. The seven arcs together formed a complete ring around one large central platform."

"Grant gave you all of this?" Paige asked, not hiding her skepticism.

"Once my brother knew I would not support his plans to take Earth, Malkier and Cede began studying a schematic of this design. Grant's shadow had no idea what he was looking at, but once he began describing what he'd seen, it did not take long for Mr. Clean and I to recognize what he had witnessed," Heyer said.

"Once we knew what it was, we also knew there was only one place for Malkier to build it," Heyer said. "The central platform is positioned directly over Cede."

"What exactly are we looking at?" Anthony asked.

"A conduit," Heyer said. "A means to bring an invading force into The Never without breaking the fabric of existence."

Apart from Jonathan, whose eyes remained on the circling model, the rest of the council looked at one another to see if anyone else was following better than they were. Seeing as that wasn't the case, Paige spoke up, "Mr. Heyer, maybe pretend you're explaining this to a five-year-old?"

Heyer nodded. "Malkier is bringing all the gateways on the Feroxian Plane to a single location. These seven arcs making up the outer circle are called Conduit Fields. By arranging the fields around this platform, Cede will be able to open and maintain a massive tunnel connecting the Feroxian Plane to Earth. But, this conduit will not behave like a portal. Time will continue to move forward on the Feroxian Plane."

"How many can he bring through at a time?" Jonathan asked.

"Theoretically he could bring every Ferox on the Feroxian Plane, but there will be a bottleneck as to how fast he can do so. Each Ferox will need to march across the bridge."

Jonathan nodded. "They're going to use portal stones to cross over."

Heyer wasn't sure if it had been a question or a statement. Either way, it surprised him. Jonathan's words struck directly at the most immediate danger the conduit represented.

"Yes," Heyer said, pausing a moment to consider him. "But, unlike the gateways, the conduit will allow them to bring inanimate objects along with them."

"How does that work?" Collin asked. "Why does a Ferox need a portal stone but, like, a stick doesn't?"

"You are thinking about it the wrong way, the Ferox will not require a stone to cross the conduit," Heyer said.

"Then, why bother with them?" Hayden asked.

Jonathan let out a knowing sigh. "To pull us inside and keep us there."

Heyer tilted his head and studied Jonathan again. "Yes, exactly. You've grasped this rather quickly."

He looked up from the model for the first time and finally noticed that it wasn't just Heyer. The entire council was looking at him as though he were suddenly a professor of gateway mechanics.

"It's a game. Once you know the rules you know the moves your opponent can make. The moment Malkier lost you as a prisoner—he knew the rules had changed drastically in our favor. He knows he must deal with us in The Never. Otherwise any attack on Earth will fail."

The group swapped looks again, everyone but Heyer, who still seemed focused on Jonathan. It was Paige who spoke up again. "Um, maybe pretend you're explaining it to a four-year-old?"

Heyer didn't speak. He just stared at Jonathan to hear his explanation.

"Okay. Don't look at me like that," Jonathan said. "I've told you, when I was trapped in my queue, we had months to consider how Malkier would come at us. Well, except you, Old Man. You slept the whole time. Helpful."

Heyer folded his arms across his chest and slowly sat back in his chair.

"Still waiting," Paige said.

"We control The Never," Jonathan said. "The only time we don't, is when we're pulled into it. The only way Malkier keeps us from using The Never against him, is to pull all of us in at once."

"Malkier knows Borealis history far better than I do. He knows that in any conflict where one side controls The Never, the might of an opposing army is damn near irrelevant."

"Right," Sydney said. "Like The Cell trying to hold you prisoner. No matter what they did you'd be ready for it."

Jonathan nodded.

"Just like the gateways, this conduit will be directed at Earth. He knows we won't let that happen, that we'll intercept him inside The Never."

"I don't get it, what stops us from doing that anyway?" Leah asked.

"What do you mean?" Paige asked.

"Say he draws us into The Never, we fight, and we lose," Leah said. "Okay, Earth no longer has an army of super soldiers. But mankind still has Mr. Clean . . . don't we?"

Jonathan and Heyer exchanged a look as the AI began to respond, "Unfortunately—"

"Command Hierarchy," Jonathan interrupted. "Mr. Clean's programming only gives him so much leeway. In the end, he obeys orders from whomever is highest in the chain of command. Only a person with a Borealis implant can be in the chain."

She noticed the alien had looked anxious as Jonathan explained this. That he seemed relieved when he stopped.

"Wait, what exactly is the order. The chain of command?"

"Heyer, then myself," Jonathan said.

Leah eyed them curiously. "There is clearly more to it than that. What aren't you telling us?"

"That is as much as needs to be known on the matter," Heyer said, with a warning in his tone.

She was taken aback by this, but one look at Jonathan warned her to take a hint. While she bit her tongue, she sat back with a look on her face that made Jonathan sigh with knowing.

Collin, perhaps trying to resolve the tension, cleared his throat. "So, uh, getting back to brass tacks here, you're saying that if Heyer and The Never Army are taken off the board, Mr. Clean will obey Malkier. At which point, he's not just invincible, he'll control The Never."

"Yes," Jonathan said.

"While it is terrible to imagine," Heyer said, "the conduit is a much more pressing concern. I have hardly begun to explain the full extent of the bad news."

CHAPTER SIXTY-THREE

"NORMALLY, DESTROYING THE portal stone allows one of our men to exit The Never. This conduit will change that dynamic. Each member of our Army will be pulled into The Never by multiple stones. Breaking any single one will not get them out."

"So wait, what will happen if a stone is destroyed?" Paige asked.

"See the gateway fields," Heyer said, directing her back to the model turning at the center at the table. "Each stone that accompanies a Ferox through the conduit will still be attuned to a gateway. All Malkier has to do to keep each of our men inside is overload each queue."

Heyer chose one of the gateways closest to him on the model. "To illustrate, let us say he gives fifteen Ferox a stone tied to this gateway. The man whose device is tied to those stones will have to destroy all fifteen to exit."

"What happens if he only breaks one stone?" Paige asked.

Heyer took a long breath. "He'll reappear inside The Never at the same place he first entered. The good news is he'll return in whatever condition he originally arrived. Any injuries he may have incurred will be as though they never happened."

"He'll respawn?" Hayden asked. "Like in a video game?"

While Heyer frowned at Hayden, Mr. Clean chimed in, "It's an apt analogy."

"For any of our soldiers to exit, one of three things must occur. He destroys any stones tied to his gate. Malkier's armies retreat and close the conduit on their side. At which point breaking any stone inside will bring our people out."

"Ferox don't retreat," Jonathan said.

Heyer nodded. "Yes, it is not an option we should depend on. Which brings us to the third, we take control of the gates on the other side."

"If a man was facing being trapped in The Never, he could step through the conduit and cross over to The Feroxian Plane," Anthony said. "It would be a death sentence. I mean, assuming he didn't walk right into Ferox forces he'd be trading trapped in The Never for trapped on the Feroxian Plane."

Anthony saw the looks he was getting. "Said it was an option, not that it was a good one."

"Um, maybe this is obvious," Collin said. "But if inanimate objects can go either way across the conduit, why not just send a nuke through the moment this thing opens?"

Heyer looked at the man as though he were somewhere in between offended and bored. "While I appreciate that desire for a simple solution, if this were so easily solved it would hardly be a problem at all."

"So, no sending nukes through the conduit?" Paige asked.

"Highly inadvisable," Mr. Clean said. "As you said, obvious. Malkier will expect it and Cede will either disable or contain the device the moment it crosses over. Even if we somehow stopped them from doing so, disabling seven active conduit fields in such a sudden destructive manner would have unknown consequences."

"Like what?" Paige asked.

"The effect would fall on a spectrum. One highly unlikely extreme possibility is that you'd get your desired outcome. The opposite extreme . . . well . . . the ultimate worst possible outcome would be a universe shattering event on par with what humans refer to as the big bang. The actual outcome would most likely be somewhere in between."

"Okay . . . so nuking the conduit is off the table then," Collin said. "It was still worth asking."

When the meeting was adjourned, everyone else teleported back to their quarters. Jonathan had expected Mr. Clean would send him as well, but a few moments passed and the only people remaining in the room were Heyer and himself.

He sighed and sat back into his chair. "What is it, Old Man?"

"You knew. You knew exactly what Malkier was doing," Heyer said. "You knew about the conduit. Do not deny it."

Jonathan took a deep breath and stared at the table. His silence speaking volumes, he knew better than to bother attempting to lie to the alien.

"I need to know how that is possible, Jonathan," Heyer demanded.

Jonathan frowned. "I've already explained—"

"Do not insult my intelligence," Heyer interrupted. "I will admit, your friends have shown some usefulness. But, you and their shadows could not have foreseen something this specific in a thousand iterations of The Never let alone twenty-eight. Too much makes sense now, Jonathan. Too much that seemed random in your plan—fits. I would say you knew with certainty what Malkier was planning, but it seems you were willing to risk Grant's life to be sure."

Jonathan took a long breath.

"I told you," Jonathan said. "You have to trust—"

"I cannot!" Heyer yelled. "This is well past trust. You have intelligence on an operation taking place in another dimension. I cannot begin to fathom how you acquired it."

Jonathan absorbed this for some time. Finally, he stood, as though he might simply walk out. Of course, this room had no doors. He wasn't going anywhere unless Heyer allowed it. Heyer stood as well, found himself talking to Jonathan's back.

"Something is very wrong here, Jonathan. I cannot leave all these lives in your hands if I cannot trust you," Heyer said.

Jonathan's jaw clenched in frustration. When he spoke, his voice was an icy whisper. "Heyer, I am only going to say this once. Then we will never speak of it again."

He closed his eyes.

"You're right, I know things I should not. If I tell you how, I gamble with lives—perhaps all life. I wasn't willing to do it for Rylee, so if you imagine I'll do it for you then we don't understand one another. So, this is what you are going to do. You're going to ask yourself how everything I just told you could possibly be true."

Jonathan opened his eyes and looked at him. "You'll know when you have the answer, because the moment you do, you'll realize just as I did, that we can never speak of it. That you'll never even risk hinting to me that you figured it out."

He'd known that Jonathan was playing some dangerous game, but a chill seeped into Heyer's bones as he stared into that dead serious gaze. He could see it in Jonathan's eyes, that the man feared saying what little he had. Whatever sort of explanation he'd thought Jonathan might give; he knew now that there were forces at play here that Heyer had yet to imagine.

Jonathan put a hand on his shoulder. "I hope you never find the answer, Old Man. But, I can't keep begging you to trust me."

Heyer's gaze fell thoughtfully to the floor, and eventually he nodded.

"Mr. Clean, please send Jonathan to his quarters," Heyer said.

Jonathan took his hand away, and disappeared, leaving the alien to his thoughts. Sometime passed before Heyer moved. "Mr. Clean, do you have any idea how anything Jonathan just said might be true?"

"Unfortunately, no," Mr. Clean said. "However, nothing in his biometrics indicate he was attempting to mislead you."

Heyer swallowed. "So, he is either telling the truth, which would mean he is somehow smarter than both of us. Or, he is lying and does not know it."

"I really can't say," Mr. Clean said.

"No, I know you cannot," Heyer said. "But, in the end it is just another way of saying exactly what he has said since the beginning. I either trust him or I do not."

CHAPTER SIXTY-FOUR

JONATHAN STOOD IN what remained of downtown as the sun was setting behind Seattle's broken skyline. Piles of rubble and abandoned vehicles cluttered the streets of the buildings that still stood, few remaining unscarred. The entire city was dark, the only light came from the fires burning in the wreckage.

The grid was down—and it wasn't a localized effect. Malkier's first move would be analogous to a global EMP. It made too much tactical sense for a Borealis fighting a technologically inferior species. Human technology's energy sources were so primitive that the Borealis didn't even consider the knowledge a restricted weapon.

If Mr. Clean could access Borealis' records on how to take down human technology—so could Cede. When he'd asked Mr. Clean how difficult it would be for the other AI to provide Malkier the capability, the reply had been grim. Mr. Clean could think of over a dozen ways to disrupt human electrical devices before Malkier ever needed to set foot on the Earth.

Of course, this wasn't just about keeping humanity's military forces from being of use. Now that Jonathan had exposed it, Malkier would be making sure his only known weakness wasn't easily exploitable.

An explosion hit the city like a thunderclap. Vibrations followed from the blast point, rolling through the streets with such force that Jonathan could see the wave drawing near from the sway of the buildings that still stood. A moment later, he could still hear the sound of a building collapsing.

A thick cloud swept its way through the streets. Air that was already increasingly claustrophobic replenished with yet another dust cloud sweeping through the city's remains. In another moment, he wouldn't be able to see more than a few feet if he didn't get moving.

He ran lateral to the thick cloud as it approached, before jumping forty stories and crashing through a skyscraper's window. Instead of landing in a shower of broken glass and obliterating the office décor of someone in middle management, he used the gleamers to cling to the outer edge. A moment later he turned around and launched himself back to the nearest rooftop.

He hit the roof running and got on his comm. "Report."

"Bodhi here, we drew a group of combatants into a building along the waterfront, not too far outside the market. We synced our retreat and brought the building down on top of them."

Jonathan reached the end of the rooftop and shot across the dark skyline once again. He drew *Doomsday* and spun his body, using the spiked tip of the chain as a harpoon. It sunk into the outer wall of a nearby building and allowed him to change his path. Jonathan arced around the building's corner and opened his palm. The gleamer disc implanted in his glove allowing him to anchor himself to the surface.

"How's cleanup going?" Jonathan asked, as he turned to look down on Bodhi's position.

"We broke into teams, been taking out the survivors as fast as they make their way out of the rubble. Keeping the bodies tagged for retrieval."

Jonathan flipped his visor down over his eyes. The current model of the HUD made him look like Geordi from *Star Trek*, though the design was smooth black instead of ridged gold. At the moment, the visors contained the last version of the HUD they had been adapting for battleground maneuvers. The newest version, the full helmet from Hayden's design, hadn't been implemented yet.

The amount of destruction left their environment in a near constant cloud of dust and debris. Their implants allowed them to breathe without issue, but his men needed alien tech to keep their vision in these conditions. If they tried to use any human equivalent, they'd be rendered as useless as everything else the moment Malkier took out the grid.

Much like the gleamers, Mr. Clean had been making the visors remarkably intuitive with use of the men's constant feedback. The interface fed him information quickly. Not only could he see each member of Bodhi's team below through the dust cloud, but they were identified by name, rank, and team assignment.

Jonathan didn't focus for long on the quelling of the Ferox as they emerged from the rubble, he was using his vantage to sweep the surrounding area. His men were wise to what happened when you dropped a building in the middle of a Feroxian battleground.

He began to see movement as the Ferox poured forward and gathered in the streets surrounding Bodhi's team. To say the Ferox behaved as though organized, would be giving them too much credit. This was a Ferox mob, they were all simply moving toward the sound of carnage in the hopes it signaled a fight. Any semblance of order was just a matter of follow-the-leader. The Ferox who had been further away when the building came down chasing after those who had been close enough to see it fall.

Unfortunately, the Ferox had a critical advantage. Having evolved to live on a planet with frequent volcanic eruptions, the species was adapted to long periods of falling ash. They didn't require technological assistance to keep a large portion of their sight in these circumstances.

"Well, your ruckus got their attention. You got company closing in from all sides, largest group is coming from the west," Jonathan said.

"Not to fret, the building was step one," Bodhi said.

Jonathan smirked and gave *Doomsday* a yank, the steel tip tearing free from the wall on the other side of the building and flying back at him with enough force to take a normal man's arm off. For Jonathan, a few well-practiced flourishes wrapped the chain tightly up the length of his arm.

He got comfortable, releasing the gleamer and perching himself on a ledge a few stories down to observe. He was going to stay close, but he wouldn't get involved unless the men got into trouble. For now, he wanted to see what Bodhi had planned for the mob.

He opened the comm to listen in on the team's chatter.

"We got incoming, let's give operation Deep End a try," Bodhi said.

Confirmation came through as the team began abandoning the remains of the building and moving into position. The majority headed east, but two groups of two split off from the rest.

The first pair moved quickly, and Jonathan lost sight of them for a moment, but they didn't go far before reappearing. They were headed straight for an intersection that would make them visible to the main Ferox horde rapidly closing in around them. There weren't a lot of Ferox coming up on their rear from the east. Jonathan knew why and was willing to bet it played into Bodhi's plan.

The pair came to a stop in the intersection and disengaged the shielding that armored their torso. This didn't leave them completely vulnerable, the alien steel plates only opened enough to allow the light from their implants to be visible.

"The bait has taken the stage," Bodhi said.

The pair was no random selection; Jonathan could see it was Bodhi himself and Sam. They wer, arguably, the fastest and most agile on their team—the whole army for that matter. This wasn't to say that if he put the two in a room with Mito they would get the better of him, but their talent with the gleamers was something else. In other words, they were great at running away.

Trying to corner Sam and Bodhi in a fight was like trying to catch water with a net.

Jonathan hadn't taken to the gleamers much himself, only using them for the more basic needs, such as anchoring himself to the occasional wall or keeping quiet if he wanted to move along a surface without his footsteps giving him away. He seldom used them in the middle of a fight unless he was retreating. The first time he'd given it a shot he'd felt like he was trying to re-learn everything he knew about hand-to-hand combat with roller skates on.

Luckily, he'd done this in private, only Mr. Clean had been witness to provide mockery for his efforts.

In the moments that remained, Jonathan turned his attention to the second pair that had split off from the team. His visor zoomed in on the two, and though their names were listed, he would have known them immediately by their shape and movements. Both had the gait of men who moved with the size of their own chests getting in the way.

Lance and Matthews—interesting. While Bodhi and Sam represented the speed and finesse—these two represented the raw power under Bodhi's command. The only time these two looked small was when Beo was in the room. Clearly, whatever part they had to play involved some heavy lifting.

Lance and Matthews weren't drawing attention to themselves. They left the area stealthily. It wasn't hard with Bodhi and Sam standing in the middle of the street like bull fighters waving big irresistible red flags.

Soon, the muscle was out of visual range. He could track their movements on the HUD map, but for the time being, Jonathan kept his attention on Sam and Bodhi. If anyone was about to be in any trouble, it was these two.

Most of the approaching mob were Greens, but he could spot a few Reds trampling down the street amongst their ranks. Some made their way over the lower rooftops, the smaller could claw their way along the walls of buildings efficiently enough to keep out of the growing mass. The majority of the monsters were plunging forward through the streets. They clamored over the rubble and flattened any vehicles as they stampeded forward.

The Ferox weren't stupid, but as a mob they lost as many IQ points as humans. They also had a well-documented flaw of glory chasing. It was no shock that the moment those leading the pack came in range of Sam and Bodhi, they launched themselves at the men like living missiles—claws and teeth first.

Neither Sam nor Bodhi moved from the center of the intersection as the swarm drew into range behind those that were already airborne.

By the time Jonathan started to worry Bodhi and Sam might have miscalculated, it was already too late for him to get to them in time, but he dropped from his perch and started moving before he thought that far ahead.

What happened next was—comical.

Sam and Bodhi braced for impact. Then the front line of Ferox passed straight through them. Their claws and teeth trying to clamp down on empty air as they met with no resistance and crashed face first into the pavement behind Bodhi and Sam.

The second wave of Ferox didn't have time to adjust, were already coming in as hot and overcommitted as the first. They belly flopped into the ground as well, but with the added misfortune of slamming into their predecessors. By the time the third wave drew close, the mob was wising up to something being amiss. As roughly thirty of the beasts now in the lead halted, it caused a cascade of collisions through the rushing horde.

Warily, the Ferox who had seen what happened sized up Sam and Bodhi, as they stood smirking at them in the middle of the intersection. They slowly approached, sniffing the air in confusion and looking for something the others had missed.

At this point, the two men promptly disappeared in a flash of light, leaving the horde staring at an empty street. This brought a wave of confused hissing and guttural murmuring from the horde.

Hologram? Jonathan thought. Mr. Clean must have come up with new toys for them to test. It was a good idea; to a race with nearly no understanding of technology, Sam and Bodhi's disappearance might as well have been magic.

Still, there was something painfully familiar about this entire exchange. Jonathan got the feeling that Hayden and Collin might have been the authors of this trick. He pulled up the mini map and located the two red dots that represented Sam and Bodhi's true location and found said dots were rocketing toward the intersection from two opposite directions.

The gleamers allowed Bodhi and Sam to gather dangerous speed when they had enough space and a straight enough line of sight to really put the throttle down. This attack was choreographed, they struck both their targets at nearly the same instant.

Suddenly, one Ferox who had been standing over the intersection on a rooftop corner and another across the street hanging off the edge of an apartment's small balcony, became one with the pavement. From where Jonathan watched, it was a bit like watching a man get hit by a locomotive without ever having heard or seen the thing coming.

Dropkicked knees first, the Ferox shot into the intersection so hard that the two were driven into the street like nails. Two smears of black Feroxian blood ended in two craters where the street had swallowed the bodies.

This created about six seconds of frantic confusion in the horde before the two were spotted. Then the horde roared in their general direction.

This was how the chase began.

Jonathan followed from above, watching Sam and Bodhi race down separate streets with the horde on their tail. After a few blocks headed in the same general direction they converged back together. The two weren't moving at full speed, if they had, the Ferox wouldn't have been able to keep up. Instead they were keeping the mob just close enough to feel as though they might close the distance.

However, despite the scarcity of combatants that were approaching from the east, the way wasn't clear. They soon had to deal with Ferox that were coming at them head on and from side streets.

The two were competitive with one another, and it brought the best out of them. They never lost their focus. As a result, a number of these Ferox took their chance to swipe at them as they passed only to come up empty. Some flew at them from the left or right, crashing through walls and windows, as Bodhi and Sam left them in their wake.

One came at Sam, intent on a full head on collision, but either didn't gauge the height of his jump well enough or underestimated the man's maneuverability. Missing Sam by inches, it allowed the man to pounce off the monster's back as he evaded, and Jonathan got to watch the surprised Ferox run headlong into the swarm on their tail.

As he continued to follow from above, their destination became clear to him. He knew they'd be on a course for the waterfront, but he now saw they were more specifically heading for the ferry terminals at the west end of the city. Sam and Bodhi emerged out of the streets lined by taller buildings as they opened to the wide, mostly empty, parking lot around the massive terminal.

Six more of Bodhi's team were waiting at the edge of the terminal.

At first, Jonathan was uncertain that the Ferox would fall for this. They had an instinctual fear of water and would be wary of pursuing them off solid ground. Then he saw the genius at play here.

A Ferox had no concept of a boat. Sure, they likely understood things could float, but a ferry was such a massive vehicle, they might not even realize they were leaving land. They likely wouldn't even notice a difference when they left the pier.

Further tempting them were the six men Bodhi had waiting in front of the ferry. Their devices unshielded and shining brightly in the night. They drew the eyes of the Ferox leading the pack, keeping their attention from the periphery, as the six backpedaled onto the boat.

By the time Sam and Bodhi were rocketing through the ferry's vehicle holding bay, the first of the Ferox had given no thought to stopping. The mob was no better, following the front-runners who had already failed to notice when they passed a threshold of solid earth to boat.

However, Sam and Bodhi didn't stop. They dove right out the ferry's other side and over the water. Jonathan watched as they came to a stop, shredding the surface of Elliott Bay for resistance before coming to a hover a few inches off the water. Finally, the Ferox ground to a halt as they reached the end of the ferry. Some weren't so lucky, the rapid stop causing those behind them to barrel the leaders off the front end of the boat and into open water.

Jonathan heard Bodhi's voice over the communicator. "Alright, let's hope you guys haven't been skipping leg day."

A second later, the ferry groaned and shot away from the pier. It happened too fast to be the work of its engine. The six men who it had seemed were retreating onto the boat had re-shielded their devices, braced themselves under the terminal, and used their combined strength to thrust the boat into the bay.

All in all, Jonathan estimated that they had baited at least forty Ferox on board when the ship began rocketing away from the shoreline. But this did leave him wondering, how did Bodhi plan to finish the job? Forty Ferox on a boat was forty Ferox they didn't have to deal with in the streets, but they weren't exactly taken care of either.

That was when Lance and Matthew's red dots reappeared on his HUD map. The two having emerged on to the roof of the terminal's adjacent control building. One look at what they were carrying, and he understood why Bodhi had saved the muscle for last.

As the Ferox began to realize what was happening they tried to race back across the ferry, hoping they still had enough time to make the jump back to land. A few succeeded—the rest got to witness Lance and Matthew arching toward the ferry. Each hefting a massive set of chains attached to two wrecking balls.

The back end of the ferry collapsed as the two men swung the biggest flails ever wielded in the history of combat into the boat's hull. Both men fell into the water immediately after, but Sam and Bodhi were quick to swing by and fish them out.

All that was left now was to deal with the Ferox who hadn't made it onto the boat before it left shore. As their allies began to drown, the rest of Bodhi's team emerged from hidden positions around the ferry parking lot to surround the remains.

"Mr. Clean," Jonathan said, as he dropped into the parking lot himself. "Go ahead and end the scenario."

The projection ceased, and for a moment, everyone stood in a black void as surfaces reset to their default. Within a few moments they were back to standing inside the projection chamber. Each time they ended a larger scenario like this the physics were disorientating. Individuals who had seemed to be standing far away were suddenly closer. Those standing on rooftops or hovering over the water suddenly standing on a flat surface.

"How'd we do?" Bodhi asked.

"Good, your team knew their roles, and everyone played to their strengths."

"I'm sensing a 'but' coming?"

"No buts, a few warnings and some notes," Jonathan said, no longer addressing Bodhi but the entire team. "The Ferox without a leader are likely to fall for these sorts of tricks at first. But these scenarios don't take into account the larger scope of a drawn-out conflict. When we are fighting them for real, they will be in communication with Malkier and their Alphas, and they will have a chain of command. Alphas and Reds that are nearing the final transition will have more self-restraint. Now, we'll be keeping them as busy as possible, fighting on multiple fronts. But you need to expect them to get wise to tricks quickly. They'll learn not to blindly follow you into buildings or commit to a pursuit drawing them toward water. Eventually realize you're using illusions to distract them as well.

"So, when you plan a maneuver like this, be cautious not to show too many cards unless you do enough damage to make it worth it," Jonathan said.

"What would make it enough?"

"I have some ideas, but . . ." Jonathan smirked. "We're gonna need a bigger boat."

CHAPTER SIXTY-FIVE

THERE WAS A wide-open swath within Hangman's Tree that was being used for physical training. What started as a sparsely populated affair had now been expanded twice and was still in a constant state of use. Lincoln and Mr. Clean had to arrange daily shift rotations to make sure their soldiers could lift weights on a regular schedule.

Shortly after arrival, Lincoln had asked that his quarters be placed at the center of it all.

"You asked to see me?"

Lincoln found Jonathan standing in his doorway. Behind him was a series of data displays that had the trainer so absorbed he hadn't heard Jonathan approach.

"Yeah, something I thought you should see," Lincoln said.

"Problem?"

"The opposite," Lincoln said. "At least if I'm right."

Jonathan smiled. "Sounds like good news."

Being charged with training an army to save the world had a way of making a man hold his personal problems at bay long enough to get the job done. A little under a month after being fired, losing his livelihood and clients, and falling into a bender, Lincoln looked tired but engaged. A good sign, because he now had more 'clients' than anyone could have effectively managed without Mr. Clean.

"So, I never told you this," Lincoln said. "But you're abnormal."

Jonathan raised a brow. "I've always appreciated that blunt honesty of yours."

"Remember, I used to collect data about your progress before each session?" Lincoln asked. "Lean muscle mass percentages, weight, measurements, yada yada."

Jonathan shrugged. "Sure."

"Well, everyone's body reacts to training differently. You were committed, in your early twenties, ate clean, and took the right supplements. All of that factored in, you still always made progress a little faster than expected."

Lincoln turned to Mr. Clean's display of hovering charts and data, flipped through a few pages, and pulled a graph to the forefront. "Turns out I wasn't crazy. This is a graph of how well the general population of males your age react to similar training and where you placed on it."

Jonathan looked over the curve. "I'm in the top two percent."

"Yeah," Lincoln said. "You don't break the graph, but you're still at the very rare end of the spectrum for how well your body reacts to training. Until now, I figured you had just won the genetic lottery."

"Until now?" Jonathan asked.

Lincoln flipped through a few more graphs to bring them to the forefront.

"Well, before I didn't have an alien supercomputer with access to any data on the planet and a never-ending supply of test subjects."

"Right . . ." Jonathan trailed off a bit. "What exactly have you been up to here?"

"I've had Mr. Clean start keeping track of all the same bodily metrics of our soldiers," Lincoln said. "There is a statistical anomaly going on amongst implanted men."

Jonathan came to stand beside the trainer, his arms folding over his chest. "You've got my attention."

"Every soldier is in the top fifteen percent," Lincoln said. "I cross referenced it with their compatibility estimates and there is a definite correlation. The more compatible they are to their device—the faster they make progress. The implant is doing something on a biological level even when it isn't active."

Jonathan studied the chart for a moment. "It could be simpler than that. The people who are compatible might just be those who are on this end of the spectrum in the first place."

Lincoln gave him a knowing look. "Right, cause that never crossed my mind. Mr. Clean, you want to explain?"

"Lincoln's conclusion fits the data," the AI replied. "With a sample size this large the metrics are quite trustworthy. Many of these men came from military backgrounds and were accustomed to training before being implanted. They all have managed significant increases in physical fitness since being implanted."

Jonathan nodded. "Well, this wouldn't be the first time we found out these things can manipulate biology while they aren't technically active."

Lincoln gave Jonathan a curious look, this was news to him. Jonathan shook his head at him. "Never mind. This is good news . . . I'm just not sure what to do with it."

Lincoln nodded. "I was getting to that."

The trainer's expression became uncertain; he walked away from the data and leaned against his desk. "You asked me to do whatever I could to pack muscles on these guys, said it was okay to think outside the box," Lincoln said. "Their diet and exercise are all dialed in. But there is a way to push the envelope—I just don't know if it's a place you want to go."

Jonathan frowned. "You're thinking steroids?"

Lincoln shrugged. "Well, hear me out, Mr. Clean and I could take a group of volunteers—"

"No," Jonathan held up a hand to stop him. "I get why you'd consider it. I'm not appalled, desperate times desperate measures, I get that. But, no, this option is entirely off the table."

Lincoln was surprised. He knew this wouldn't be an easy sell, but Jonathan seemed to think it was a complete nonstarter.

"Jonathan," Mr. Clean said, "rest assured, we can test without endangering the safety of any volunteers. I can monitor their biometrics—"

"No," Jonathan said again.

Lincoln couldn't keep his expression from becoming annoyed. Jonathan clearly noticed, as he quickly made a point of closing the door to Lincoln's quarters.

"Look," Jonathan said. "I know your heart is in the right place. So, what I tell you now doesn't leave this room."

"I can only promise to keep information from everyone but Heyer," Mr. Clean said. "You know—"

"I was addressing Lincoln specifically, Mr. Clean," Jonathan interrupted.

Lincoln's expression softened a bit. "You know I won't say anything. I just want to understand the problem."

"I have firsthand experience of what can happen when you introduce a—hormonal variable," Jonathan said. "The results are highly unpredictable and incredibly dangerous."

Lincoln stood up straighter. "Have you already tried this?"

Jonathan shook his head. "Not this specifically. You just need to trust me. No drugs, no hormones—anything that could drastically change the equilibrium between the body and the device is too dangerous to experiment with."

Lincoln held his eyes for a long while, clearly wanting more information. He knew within a few seconds that he wasn't going to get it. Jonathan had kept secrets from him for months when they were trainer and client, and he could tell when the man wasn't going to budge.

"Alright, forget I brought it up," Lincoln said. "But could you at least tell me what you mean by dangerous?"

Jonathan appeared to consider, then nodded. "Let's just say it's not the person taking the drug I'd be worried about, but everyone around them."

Lincoln took a long breath. "Alright, I . . . I won't bring it up again."

Jonathan gave a nod. "Was there anything else?"

"Yeah," Lincoln said. "But it can wait . . ."

"Now is as good a time as any," Jonathan said.

Lincoln considered, then took a long breath. "I want to do more than train these guys. I—I want to be part of this fight."

As Jonathan studied him, Lincoln could sense his reluctance. "Lincoln, if you were compatible—"

"I know, I know I'm not," Lincoln said. "But there has to be something I can do."

Jonathan was silent a moment before speaking. "If it won't take too much attention off the training regimes, I'll tell Hoult you'll be coming down to see him."

Lincoln's face was usually a resting sort of scowl, but when he understood what Jonathan had in mind, a grin tugged at the trainer's face.

Later that evening, Lincoln went to find Anthony in the Mech wing of Hangman's Tree. At first, Hoult was nowhere to be seen, but beneath one of the prototypes, the sound of a ratchet socket tightening bolts emanated from one of the maintenance pits.

"Mr. Hoult," Lincoln said. "This a good time?"

"Jonathan told me you'd be coming. Give me a moment?"

"Sure."

While he waited, Lincoln took in the nearby hardware. Where the prototypes had been unloaded from their cargo containers, it was a bit like the show room floor of a car dealership. The different models of the Mech suits not exactly on display so much as hanging by heavy chains a foot or so off the floor.

The armor of the suits was similar across all models. The weaponry was another story. The vast majority were built to be gunners. Those mods were equipped with two large guns that hung below the arms. Belts of ammunition ran to two large boxes on the Mech's back.

Then there were the Thors. Those looked to be carrying hammers the size of a blacksmithing anvil.

The ones that drew Lincoln's attention were the bladed weapons.

The armor wasn't as heavy. They had been fitted with two large katana-like swords. The blades looked to be hooked up to a cartridge system, such that the edges could be quickly ejected and replaced. Not so different from replacing the head of a razor with a new blade before shaving, except the machine could automate the process.

Of the bladed Mechs, Lincoln was drawn to a few that had unique paint jobs. By the time Anthony came looking for him, he was staring at one that had a familiar looking design. Blue paint covering half the face of a brushed steel exterior.

"We call that one The Wallace."

"The Wallace?" Lincoln asked. "Like, you stole the paint job right out of *Braveheart?*"

Anthony shrugged.

"What's a guy need to learn to operate one of these?" Lincoln asked. "Mind you, my previous experience includes two screenings of *Iron Man* and a slightly embarrassing number of hours playing MechWarrior."

Anthony shrugged. "The suits are pretty intuitive. The Gunner and Thor mods take time to get used to. Mostly getting a feel for the limits of the joints, and maneuvering the weight."

"And the Wallace?" he asked.

"The bladed mod is less of a challenge to move but requires a lot more care than the others."

"Why is that?" Lincoln asked.

Anthony pointed to one blade's edge. "The armor protects from external attack, but these are molecular blades, sharp enough to cut through the armor itself. You make a mistake and . . ."

He grimaced and mimed a slicing motion with his right hand over his left forearm.

Lincoln raised a brow. "Right."

A moment passed as they looked appreciatively at the hardware.

"So, you want to take the Wallace for a test run in the simulator?"

Lincoln turned to him with both interest and surprise. "That's it? You're just gonna let me get in this thing? Not even gonna make me read a manual or take a test or something?"

Anthony shrugged. "We got more Mechs than operators. We need people to start training yesterday."

"But there are like sixty suits in here!" Lincoln said.

Hoult nodded. "Jonathan is working on it. Problem is, that means civilians and we haven't got a lot of those around here."

"Well, in that case," Lincoln gave the Mech an excited look. "Yeah, let's suit me up. But, um . . . maybe . . ."

"Practice blades for your first go?" Anthony asked.

". . . I do enjoy my arms," Lincoln said.

CHAPTER SIXTY-SIX

NOV 07, 2005 | 8 PM | HANGMAN'S TREE

HEYER WAS WAITING for her on the catwalks over her quarters.

"He is alone, isolated himself in the projection chamber," Heyer said.

"Same time each day," Leah said.

They exchanged a look and set off.

As always, Jonathan had deactivated the spectator capability on the chamber. Only Heyer would have been able to watch what was going on inside, let alone enter.

Leah half expected something like a Michael Bay movie to be playing out when they stepped inside. Instead, she literally heard crickets. They were chirping on a calm cool evening. There was little to see, most of the projection chamber's capabilities weren't even fully utilized. As they approached the only structures in sight, they walked over a number of black unengaged panels.

She quickly knew what she was seeing.

Most of the neighborhood that surrounded it in the real world was absent, but this was a projection of Jonathan's home. Mr. Clean was manifesting the place he and his roommates rented in Seattle, and enough of the surrounding neighborhood that if one stood in the garage, the illusion of this world wouldn't be broken.

The garage door was up, as it often was when he'd lived there. The light from inside spilled out onto the driveway. As they drew closer, they saw his shadow dance across that light. The shape holding a staff and flowing through movements.

They paused to swap looks once again.

"He's just been going home," she said.

The alien was thoughtful for a moment, then continued drawing closer. She followed until that shadow stopped moving. She could see him then, one of his old practice staffs in hand. His eyes closed in concentration.

His device wasn't activated.

Leah had been around soldiers when she knew their devices were active beneath their clothing. She'd observed installation of a few of the implants in new recruits. She watched Jonathan take part in training scenarios with the recruits inside this very chamber—he always hid his chest beneath a thick armored coat. She'd yet to see his skin lit up from within.

Her understanding from those that had—Jonathan's implant was different from most. That the light was stronger. Sometimes even seeming to emanate from him like a glowing fog or a flickering flame.

Probably why he kept it covered. Drew too much attention.

Right now, he looked as he always had, for all those months when he'd trained next door. His feet were bare on the mat floor. He wore simple black sweatpants and a tank top damp with perspiration. His eyes were closed, but it was more as though his mind was closed. As though he were shielding himself from the entire world.

But his face. That look he got.

It disturbed his roommates. And to be fair there was something very dangerous to be found there. In the months she watched him that face had emerged more and more often. It never disturbed her. Her reaction was never fear. It was the distilled essence of Jonathan Tibbs. She'd found it exciting. Tonight, she found it reassuring.

Seeing that look, her arm reached out to stop Heyer from getting any closer. When he turned a questioning gaze on her, she held a finger to her lips.

When he began to move again, he slowly flowed out of stillness. As it began, she felt herself strangely nostalgic for a simpler time, when she was a spy and he her subject.

Jonathan wasn't shadow fighting. Martial arts have a number of different names for what he was doing—practicing of katas, forms, patterns. This was one she'd never seen him practicing in all her hours watching him.

To say it was beautiful was misleading. There was beauty, but of a sort that a passing observer would have been blind to. Few understand until they have tried such things for themselves. A thrust or block that does not quiver, no matter how slowly he moved, his balance never faltering. Yet, there was a complete efficiency, a precision in where he set his feet. His breaths in a symbiotic rhythm with his moves.

Mostly, it was the manner with which his focus never wavered. All his consciousness given over as though he were not a man performing a routine, but as though with each moment, he became each motion.

She wasn't sure how long she'd been watching. Until he stopped, she had not realized the quiet of his mind had infected her own. When Jonathan opened his eyes and saw them, that expression that had reassured her melted away and her thoughts came rushing back to fill the vacuum of silence in her mind.

His stance relaxed. He looked at them with a knowing smirk, then walked over to the cabinet to store his staff. Strange—just as he would have in the real world. To bother with it here was to stay committed to not breaking the illusion.

"Let me guess," he said. "You two can't be happy as long as a question goes unanswered."

"This is what you do every night?" Leah asked. "Train without activating your device?"

"Wouldn't call it training," Jonathan said as he took a seat on the edge of his weight bench.

"What then?" she asked.

Jonathan glanced between them, raising an eyebrow. "Been hiding in the rafters much, Old Man?"

Heyer cleared his throat.

"I get it. You're trapped in a base surrounded by people who think you're something more than you can ever be. Can't disappear on them anymore. Can't tell them that the time for answering questions will come later. To leave without a good reason, that would be betrayal. So, you're here, but trying to keep a distance."

He didn't give Heyer time to deny this before he turned to Leah. "You're surrounded by people who don't trust you. Don't know if you're friend or foe. I know where you go at night."

He glanced between them. "You two seem to avoid everyone except each other."

"You come here to be alone," Heyer said.

"My role in this doesn't give me the luxury of hiding," Jonathan said. "This army needs to see a leader leading. They all have a different idea of what I'm supposed to be. Even you two."

She looked around the garage with new eyes. Since the beginning, he'd come to his garage. To be alone, sure, but that wasn't the truth of it.

Right next door she'd had her own garage. Where she'd shaped her steel statues and framed her photos and played her music. It was where she went to escape the lie—to be herself. It was where they both went to prepare for what the world needed them to be the next day.

"Damn," Leah whispered. "I miss my garage."

Heyer chuckled. "I would be lying if I did not admit to longing for the days when I did not have to share my space within Mr. Clean."

The shared moment passed.

"Good talk, but this isn't why you're here," Jonathan said.

"You have removed the female half of the bonded pair from the armory," Heyer said.

Jonathan stared at the floor again. "You've told her everything then?"

"You were hesitating," Heyer said.

"I asked you to trust me," Jonathan said.

"I have trusted you," Heyer said. "I have a thousand unanswered questions. This I cannot ignore."

Jonathan stood slowly, his arms coming to rest on his hips. "What possible good use is a Tibbs if he isn't the very best weapon you can make him."

Heyer blinked. Caught off guard by the perspective.

"What's one more son, Old Man?"

Silence followed, solidifying like glass between all of them.

Leah was the first to speak. There was a strangeness to her words. As though she weren't so much asking a question but was saddened by disappointment. "You already know. Of course, you already know. I thought, this one thing, maybe I'd get to tell you."

He looked at her, and she didn't know if he understood at all. After all the lies, was there nothing she'd ever get to come clean about. No way she'd ever get to volunteer a secret before finding out he'd already caught her in an omission.

Heyer drew in a long breath.

"You speak as though you believe me indifferent to your family's sacrifice," Heyer said.

Jonathan looked away.

"You cannot possibly feel that, Jonathan?" Heyer asked.

"You want your brother dead," Jonathan said. "I'll get it done. I don't need the bond."

"You do," Heyer said. "You will not be able to harm Malkier, Jonathan."

There was a certainty in Heyer's voice that seemed to catch Jonathan's notice. After a moment, he sighed as he realized the truth.

"So that is why it was so important that we spar," Jonathan shook his head. "Rest assured, I don't need to beat your brother in a fist fight to kill him."

"But you need to survive one," Heyer said. "As it stands, you would not last a minute."

"Dying won't stop me," Jonathan said.

This raised heads. Leah and Heyer swapping looks with one another with restrained terror. He sounded—crazy.

Heyer closed his eyes and pushed his fear away. "Whatever you may think. I do not want to see you die."

"I know that, Old Man," Jonathan said. "But you will if that is what it takes. Just like you'll let your descendent die, my child with her. I'll follow you across a lot of lines. Not this one."

Heyer took a long breath. He let the room become very still.

"I want the whole truth, Jonathan. I do not believe I've heard it yet," Heyer said. "Why are you so afraid of reestablishing the bond?"

"Afraid," Jonathan turned to them. He looked surprised, as though he had misread what brought them to be standing in front of him. "You . . . you're here . . . you think I *don't* want the bond?"

Heyer blinked, taken aback by the tone of Jonathan's question. As he stared at the man's eyes, he suddenly realized what he'd never considered. "You . . . you are not afraid of it, you are resisting it."

Jonathan turned away, leaving the alien to stare dumbfounded.

"You really don't have the foggiest idea what you're talking about," Jonathan said.

As Leah watched him, she remembered how Heyer had found it so strange Jonathan wasn't driven to reestablish the bond. That a part of him should have been desperate for it. Like an addict looking for a fix. Yet, he carried the implant in his front pocket to ensure he'd never feel its influence again.

"You fear the severed bond," Leah said. "But that isn't why you're fighting this."

Jonathan's breathing was growing unsteady. "My father lived with this implant longer than any man. Do you know, Old Man, what made him so different?"

Heyer only took a moment to answer.

"You," Heyer said.

She could see the answer caught Jonathan by surprise. As though he expected a hundred possible answers from the alien, and they would all be wrong.

"I understood your father more than you give me credit," Heyer said.

Jonathan was quiet for a moment. When words did start pouring out of him, it was as though he were answering a question. But it was one that neither she nor the alien would have ever thought to ask.

"In The Never, his body was broken, more times than he could re . . ." Jonathan whispered. "Every time . . . he'd remember holding me the day I was born. I can see myself as a child in his arms, I can see him looking down at me. But, it's like I'm looking into my own eyes . . ."

Jonathan looked at Heyer. "I hear his thoughts like they're my own. One of them started the moment he held me.

"It's not okay to die . . . I can't fail."

Leah came to understand. The bond had been calling to him day in and day out. The part of him that was strong enough to ignore it, was the part that would do whatever it took to protect his son.

"Give me the device, Jonathan," Leah said. "One way or another, I'll use it to protect our child."

"Giving you that implant . . . is as good as killing you myself," Jonathan said. "Malkier will come for you."

"He is coming for all of us," she said. "There is no safe place to put me. If we fail and Earth is lost to the Ferox, there won't be anything left to protect."

He looked at the two of them and shook his head. "You two haven't thought this through at all."

"Then educate us," Heyer said.

Jonathan glanced at Heyer, but when he spoke, he chose to hold Leah's eyes. "The bonded pair is more powerful, but it is not so different from any other device in the armory. Like all the others, it is tied to a gate on the Feroxian Plane. When Rylee died, that gate went dormant. The moment you reactivate that implant, you reactivate the gate on the other side."

He turned to Heyer.

"Do you think your brother will miss that? That he won't do everything in his power to sever the bond the moment he sees it's been reestablished?"

Heyer nodded slowly. "You . . . you do have a point."

"He'll send assassins, as many as he has to—an Alpha if he must—and if you survive all that Leah . . . he'll come for you himself."

"But, I'll be strong."

"Not as strong as you may think," Jonathan shook his head. "Alone in

The Never, you won't have the bond, and . . . I don't mean to hurt you Leah, but you're not . . ."

He trailed off, seemed to reconsider his words. "You're just . . . you aren't . . ."

She finished the thought for him. "I'm not Rylee."

Jonathan closed his eyes and looked at the floor. "I'm sorry . . . she was exceptional. Trained her entire life. You will not survive what Malkier will send for you."

Hearing him say it aloud hurt, but mostly because there was no denying the truth in it.

"So, teach me," Leah said. "I'm no different than anyone else."

Jonathan sighed. "I'm not saying you couldn't learn. I'm saying you wouldn't get the chance. If I were Malkier, and that dormant gate reactivated. I wouldn't delay a moment before I overloaded its queue."

"Jonathan is right, Leah" Heyer said, "it is even worse than he says. I still do not understand how it is that Jonathan has recovered from the severed bond. But if we reestablish it, only to have it severed again, I do not like the chances that he could manage it a second time."

A moment of somber silence followed.

"If I may interject," Mr. Clean said. "I believe there is another way. Though, I don't think anyone is going to like it."

CHAPTER SIXTY-SEVEN

"WE IMPLANT THE device at the last possible moment. Before the conduit arrives but when we already know it is being opened."

Leah nodded, seemed like a simple solution, but then she saw Jonathan's jaw clenching.

Jonathan was shaking his head.

"The new recruits, the men who've never seen a real Ferox, we are running them through battle scenarios with their devices turned on. It's a world of difference. You're suggesting she train with the same handicap I had to deal with . . . when I had three months to prepare and wasn't two months pregnant," Jonathan said.

Leah scoffed. "Jonathan, I've heard enough. You need to stop looking for reasons to keep this from happening. It's not up to you. So, start thinking of how we get it done right."

While Jonathan and Leah were arguing, Heyer had consulted quietly with Mr. Clean.

Eventually, he cleared his throat loudly. "If you are both done, I would like to explore a solution."

As they quieted, Heyer turned to Jonathan.

"I have a confession," Heyer said. "I have not wanted to admit to you that I do not know what you are."

Jonathan frowned, giving the alien a doubting look.

"To put it simply, I have taken a number of hosts in my lifetime," Heyer said. "When they are intact, I often gain access to my hosts' memories. That said, I cannot navigate them very easily. What's more, I have never acquired a skill from my host."

Jonathan looked confused as he listened, but then seemed to understand what Heyer was confessing. "I'm not what you expected."

"No," Heyer said. "What you seem to be is so much more than I ever imagined. Something I would have thought impossible."

She could see Jonathan was caught off guard by this. As though he'd been operating under the assumption that he was exactly what Heyer had planned all along. "Then, what did you expect?"

"I opened the door to your father's mind in the hope that you would be able to recover one piece of information," Heyer said.

"Explains a few of our more recent awkward moments" Jonathan said. "You only hoped I'd discover how to harm your brother."

Heyer nodded.

"I never imagined you would be able to do everything he was capable of doing. That you could acquire his skill sets, his muscle memory, his instincts. Some of his memories, perhaps even all of them. This manner, this way you have integrated . . . I do not understand it."

"Great," Jonathan said. "That officially makes two of us."

Heyer stared at him skeptically. "But you must know something?"

Jonathan sighed. "Less than you'd imagine, Old Man."

"Tell me. Tell me how it happened," Heyer said. "When did you become aware of the change?"

"I woke up in the dark," Jonathan said. "In some ways, it feels like my first memory. But, I remembered being Jonathan and being Douglas."

"What do you mean then, when you say it felt like your first memory?" Leah asked.

"If I told you it was the opposite of amnesia would that make sense? Jonathan got hit on the head. I woke up remembering parts of another life along with his."

"You're talking about Jonathan like he was someone else," Leah said.

"I am," Jonathan said. "Because he was and he isn't. I don't think you can add the memories of another person to your own and stay the same."

"But, you just woke up this way?" Heyer asked. "There was nothing in between?"

"No," Jonathan hesitated—seemed frustrated in his effort to find words to explain.

"There was this sense, that he and Douglas made a choice. That they chose to be what was needed. How do you explain what it is to decide to become yourself? It was his decision, and so it was also mine. He needed to be me—and I wanted to be what was needed."

Jonathan shook his head. "When I woke, Grant's shadow was about to shove *Excali-bar* through my chest—and more than anything I knew Rylee needed me. There was no time to think about how it happened."

"This somewhat explains the why," Heyer said, "but not the how."

Jonathan shrugged again. "You might as well ask me how I move my hand. I decide and it happens. What I know about the machinery, how my body does it, doesn't matter when I wave at you."

Jonathan waved his hand as though it might bring his point home.

"But you said you chose. Something must have happened when you made that decision?" Heyer asked.

"Those memories are the vaguest sort of dream. I remember a black abyss, a long brick wall, a key and a locked box, a little girl, a vault door. I remember my father talking to me. I don't remember what he said, only that he was trying to help me."

Mr. Clean chose that moment to interrupt, suddenly appearing within the reflection of one of the mirrors that lined the garage walls. "Apologies, but I believe that based on Jonathan's account, I may be uniquely suited to provide some insight."

"If you have a theory, we are all ears," Heyer said.

"Jonathan identifies a moment as the inception of his current self. He does this despite being in possession of memories he knows precede that moment. Yet, he has no conflicts nor confusion, no trouble placing the collective memories of two identities into a mental timeline. There is only one other being I know of who is both capable of this and choses to do so on a regular basis."

Heyer smiled. "You're talking about yourself?"

"Indeed," the AI said. "I believe what has happened to Jonathan was made possible because he and his father were in possession of something that you've never had with any host."

"A genetic relationship?" Leah offered.

"No. Biology has nothing to do with it, but the father-son relationship does," Mr. Clean said. "Rather, nearly thirteen years' worth of overlapping experiences. Time spent in one another's company. Identical points in time, shared in memory from two perspectives."

Heyer's hand went to his chin as he was drawn into contemplation. "Long-term shared memory."

"Jonathan and Douglas may have been uniquely capable of navigating one another's experiences, because they shared so much time together. So many memories where they were both present, reference points within one another's minds."

"He may be right," Jonathan said.

"What makes you say so?" Leah asked.

"I was unconscious the first time Douglas was able to reach me. We found one another in a memory, not a dream. A moment from my childhood but his adulthood."

"What memory?" Leah asked.

Jonathan smiled. "It was the first time I asked him if our family could get a dog."

Leah smiled back, but something he'd said had sent Heyer into thought. "He *reached* you? Douglas is a conscious entity that communicates with you?"

"He was," Jonathan said. "Whatever happened. It ended with me. After that . . . I believe it destroyed too much of him."

Heyer nodded. "Yes, you are not accessing memories stored inside your device any longer. They became a part of you. As though you became a person and a half. The consciousness left over would not have been enough to remain comple—"

"Heyer," Leah interrupted. She nodded toward Jonathan. He wasn't looking at them, there was a great sadness on his face.

"I'm . . . I'm sorry, Jonathan" Heyer said.

"He made a choice, and I understand it," Jonathan said, looking at Leah. "It's the same choice I would make."

She looked at Jonathan and wondered. Did this explain why he forgave her? Had all that fierce love Douglas had for his son become a part of him? Jonathan caught in the middle somehow, both the child and the father. Then he learns she is expecting his son. Was that why he forgave so much—so easily?

Was the life she carried the only way Jonathan could make sense out of it?

Years of fatherhood, all that love, had it needed to go somewhere and landed on her?

It would explain so much, because she certainly hadn't earned it.

"Well, while the mystery may be solved, I can't help but note that if we are correct, this is a dead end," Mr. Clean said.

". . . what?" Leah asked.

The conversation had taken so many turns she had practically forgotten how they got here. Jonathan's face looked as confused as hers. The alien was the only one who wasn't at a loss.

Mr. Clean began to explain. "Jonathan's parental irrationalities aside, his points about the strategic challenges of reestablishing the bonded pair were fair. The issue, at first, seemed a mirror of what Heyer and I faced years ago. We have lost a combatant with needed knowledge, but have now found a vessel who would possess the raw physical strength to be a powerful asset. Unfortunately, if shared memory is the—"

"Mr. Clean, while this may not be the time or the place," Heyer said, "it is most certainly not the moment."

Leah hadn't fully caught up but one look at Jonathan told her he had—and he wasn't happy about it.

"So that is what this is all about. There isn't going to be a right moment. This is not something we are going to consider." Jonathan said.

"Hey," Leah said, her voice getting louder as she grew more annoyed at being the only one who hadn't seen how the puzzle pieces fit together. "Someone want to fill in the new girl here?"

No one responded. There was a bit of a silent standoff going on between Heyer and Jonathan, and she wasn't sure either had even heard her.

"We already asked her to sacrifice everything. We're not forcing her to do it again," Jonathan said.

"Jonathan, I do not have the luxury of playing at sainthood and neither do you. We have to consider the entire planet," Heyer said.

"Let her be," Jonathan said. "Let them both be."

"You have told me a great deal of your plans, Jonathan. But they all hinge on your being able to handle Malkier. I've yet to hear exactly how you think you will accomplish this now that he likely understands his own weakness."

"And until the time is right, it's gonna stay that way," Jonathan said.

"For the love of . . . someone tell me what the hell we're all so damn angry about!" Leah yelled.

Jonathan looked away from them. Heyer, after watching him for a moment, finally turned to Leah. "Just like Douglas, Rylee's consciousness is stored inside her dormant device. Mr. Clean and I are discussing the possibility of unlocking her consciousness."

CHAPTER SIXTY-EIGHT

WHAT THE ALIEN was thinking hit her like a sledgehammer.

She'd been standing there next to him listening this whole time with no idea that he had been considering—what exactly? Merging her with Rylee's consciousness?

"Rylee and I, we . . . we weren't on the best . . . I mean, I don't think she'll be as happy to hear what you're . . ."

She trailed off.

"I kind of think being in my head would be a little like dying and going to Hell for her."

Jonathan shook his head. He wasn't arguing with her. He was looking at her eyes and telling her not to even consider what she was hearing.

"This argument remains unnecessary," Mr. Clean said. "Rylee and Leah have almost no shared long-term memory. If my theory is correct, there is no reason to believe this is possible."

Heyer paced. "We haven't explored this enough to simply give up on it."

A moment passed, her thoughts racing.

"Oh . . ." Leah said.

"We aren't exploring it," Jonathan said. "You're not asking this of them."

"Oh . . . no," Leah whispered.

"Jonathan, I don't believe this decision is yours to make," Heyer said.

"No . . . no . . . no . . ." Leah said, her eyes shutting.

The room grew silent, Jonathan and Heyer ceasing to argue, even Mr. Clean turning to consider her. There was a very unreadable expression on her face.

She sighed finally and licked her lips. "There . . . there may be a way."

"She presents an intriguing possibility," Mr. Clean said.

"I agree," Heyer said.

Jonathan's face made her reluctant to pile on. "Perhaps we vote?"

Nope, that didn't help, one look around the room and it was clear everyone knew how that vote would go.

"No," Jonathan said.

"You are in command of this army, but you are too close to this. It is not a decision to be left to you alone," Heyer said.

"I agree, it's a decision that should be between Leah and me," Jonathan said. "You have no place in it."

"On what grounds?" Heyer asked.

"Because I'm the only one in this room who knows what the hell I'm talking about," Jonathan said.

This did nothing to turn the room in his favor, but there was anger coming out of him now. "Does it even occur to you that you're not just doing this to them, I'm the other half of the bond?" Jonathan said.

The alien paused and took a step back. "It is a valid point, but it speaks to my stance on this," Heyer said.

"We aren't the only ones who should have a say," Leah said. "Someone should speak for Rylee."

There was a silence in the room as each person realized what she meant.

"You want Rylee's father to have a vote?" Jonathan asked.

"We can't make this work without him, and this is not the sort of action you take and ask forgiveness instead of permission. I doubt he'll help us if we make the decision without him."

"She is right," Heyer said. "He may be integral to our success."

"Is this not a bit of a token gesture, one more vote will not change the clear majority," Mr. Clean said.

"Mr. Clean, I don't mean any offense but I'm not sure you should get a vote. We all know Heyer can order you to vote with him," Leah said.

"This is childish squabbling," Heyer said.

Jonathan shook his head. "You've gotten too used to making decisions for people. For mothers and fathers," Jonathan said. "The last one you made for Rylee took her life. You don't get to ask her for more sacrifices."

The alien's jaw tightened. A long slow breath coming out as he stared at Jonathan. "That is not fair, Jonathan."

"You don't get to talk to me about fair," Jonathan said.

A long tense moment played out. When Mr. Clean suddenly spoke, it was as though someone threw a brick through a window. "I'm unclear, shall I request Mr. Silva join us?"

"No," they all yelled in unison. This was the first thing they had all agreed on in some time.

Who should approach Mr. Silva was a delicate question.

Mr. Clean lacked the social graces.

The alien obviously avoided Rylee's father for good reason. His presence would not help matters at all. Jonathan was adamantly opposed to the entire plan, and she was the spy no one trusted and the last person to literally be decked in the face by Mr. Silva's daughter.

"I think it might be best if Leah approached Mr. Silva privately," Heyer said. "I might caution you to avoid the specifics of your . . . personal relationship with his daughter."

"Too much riding on this for him to catch me in a lie later," Leah said. "The man just lost his daughter and hasn't even been allowed to tell his wife where he is. We can't expect that any of this is going to be easy for him."

At that point, no one seemed to have anything to add.

"I need a break," Jonathan said. He walked away, not giving either of them time to object.

As she watched him, she had so many unanswered questions. Each one feeling like she had no right to ask him. Despite everything, it was as though there would always be walls she couldn't get past with him.

Her face hardened at that thought. "We shouldn't have done it like this," Leah said. "Let me go after him."

Heyer sighed but nodded.

Leah paused before she left the chamber, stopping to look at her garage door as it existed in the simulation.

"Mr. Clean, can I take things out of the projection chamber?"

"Did you have something specific in mind?"

CHAPTER SIXTY-NINE

SHE CAUGHT UP to Jonathan just before he disappeared inside his quarters. But, as she reached out to stop him she also remembered Sydney's warning and the lack of privacy crowded her awareness. She didn't see anyone watching, but more and more of late, Hangman's Tree felt too full of soldiers for there to ever be no one paying attention.

"Jonathan, can we speak alone?" she asked.

He still looked drained from the conversation that had proceeded this, but he opened his door and held it for her. She hadn't seen the inside of his quarters. Jonathan was one of the few who still had a space to himself.

She didn't know what she'd expected. What she found was not so different from his room at the old house. A made bed, a desk without any clutter. The only furniture of note was a chest—a footlocker like the one he had recovered from Portland before he was taken prisoner. She thought it might well have been the same footlocker.

"You knew about the child. You didn't say anything," Leah said.

He nodded.

He'd never hidden it. In hindsight that much was obvious. He'd been so careful, gone out of his way for her with no apparent reason. How many times had he made sure food was brought to her?

Jonathan sighed. "In The Never, your shadows . . . they asked me to let you tell me. They didn't want me to act surprised, nothing like that, but—"

"I get it," she nodded. "I wanted the chance."

"I told them I would, more than once. I'm sorry, I owed you more."

"I'm sorry too," she said. "I should have said something sooner. Thought the best time would be later. After . . ."

She didn't finish the thought—she didn't need to.

When he spoke, his words were softer. "But . . . I don't like this plan. It's taking everyone I can't lose and putting them in danger."

"Where would I be safe, Jonathan?" she asked.

Jonathan shook his head. "Anywhere but The Never."

Jonathan took a long breath and looked at her. "Until I let Rylee die, I was used to being the one who made the sacrifices . . ."

He shook his head.

"It was simpler before, you know. Heyer did the asking. Gave people the choice to risk their life. It was okay to hate him for asking. Now, every day, I'm the one putting these implants into people. And I know there isn't any choice . . ."

He sighed, and she could feel his exhaustion.

"Since this began, I never get to choose between right or wrong. It's always what saves the most lives. But, this feels wrong to me."

"I think it's supposed to feel that way," Leah said. "You're not supposed to want this for anyone."

He nodded.

"Jonathan, if I had the power to save you from all of this, let someone else take your place, I would do it. I wouldn't think twice, I wouldn't let myself think—I'd just do it," Leah said. "And someone else would be sitting where you are right now. But that person, he wouldn't be the right one for the job."

"What are you saying?" he asked.

"I'm saying I couldn't decide this for you, and you can't decide for me." She took something from her pocket then and held it out to him.

It had been in a frame in her garage before, a photo she'd taken of him the night their child had been conceived. This wasn't the original, Mr. Clean had to recreate it and let her take it with her from the chamber.

In the photo he looked back at the camera, his face half hidden in shadow. There was an eerie malignance to that darkness, as though it stalked him.

"Do you remember when I gave you that?"

He nodded. "You said it made you sad."

"Because it made me feel like I had to watch you walk into the dark alone," she said. "I said I'd do anything to keep you from that place."

"Leah—"

"I know, Jonathan. I know now that there was never any keeping you out of the dark. But, this time, you can't stop me from going with you."

He understood, but that didn't mean it made him any happier about the situation. For the moment, he seemed too tired to keep arguing about it.

"Jonathan would you . . ."

She paused, she liked that he was taller than her but not now, not for what she meant to ask him. She pushed him gently backward and he didn't resist. When his ankles hit the footlocker he stopped.

"Sit?" she asked.

He obeyed, looking up at her with some uncertainty.

"I need to ask you things, for myself."

He looked at her, nodded, and waited.

"Do you not want to be bonded to me?"

"I don't want to be bonded to anyone," Jonathan said.

That he hadn't needed to consider the question at all, surprised her. "Why?"

"The bond makes every feeling you have for someone a question. You love them intensely and you don't know why," Jonathan said. "Eventually, it doesn't matter what the truth ever was, you don't even care about the question . . ."

"Doesn't sound so terrible," Leah said.

"But when it's severed—the grief is no different. You don't get a say in the pain. You lay down and die. Understanding it doesn't help. The answer to the question, *why do I hurt so badly?* Doesn't matter. There is no fighting it."

"But . . . you did?"

He shook his head, his face dead serious.

"Then—"

"Please don't, Leah," Jonathan said.

She swallowed. But she hadn't come here to talk about the broken bond, so she wouldn't press him on it.

"Before the bond. Before Rylee. What did you feel for me?" Leah asked.

"I wanted you very much," Jonathan said.

"Did you love me?"

He closed his eyes and took a long breath. "I . . . wanted to."

For a moment, his answer seemed warm. Until she realized that while it felt true, she didn't know what it meant. The more she thought about it, the more it seemed the vaguest answer to that question she'd ever heard.

He 'wanted to' love her? What did that mean?

He'd wanted to love her before he found out she'd lied about who she was? He'd wanted to love her but didn't? He wanted to love her but never got the chance?

She realized her face had become a frown and stopped herself. "Do you still want to?"

He seemed to crumble beneath the weight of the question. He reached for her, pulled her close and rested his head against her stomach.

"I want you to stay."

THE QUEUE LOOP | ACTIVATION 22

With his implant active, he was never truly blind in the dark unless he chose to be. At the moment as he floated above the sea floor, he closed his eyes and enjoyed the quiet.

He'd read somewhere that the farthest anyone had ever dived was a little more than one thousand feet. He was a bit more than half that. The quiet at such depths was unlike any to be found on the surface—especially as the surface was now . . .

The submersible beneath him hit the ocean floor with a sudden thump. He opened his eyes to see the nothingness around him.

Test number two, so far so good.

He had waited too long to perform the underwater test the first time. The Never deterioration weakened minds far sooner than it did materials but his first submersible's failure was likely influenced, at least in part, due to the slow crumbling of this reality.

They had decided to reinforce the inner frame with alien steel wherever the containment shield could handle it, just in case—Mr. Clean dealt with all of that. He had other things to worry over.

In no hurry to be anywhere now, he took a slow pull from the air tank the AI had provided before going dormant, and stayed on the ocean floor a bit longer. When he was satisfied, he slowly began ascending to the surface. Divers had to worry about decompressing, he suspected his alien enhanced physiology needed less care. He still didn't rush.

When he emerged, he treaded water in the Puget Sound. The air smelled of smoke. In the night sky an orange glow emanated over the city.

Seattle burned.

When he put off breaking the stone—if he stayed in The Never long enough, the city always burned.

He knew the queue was running out, he only had six loops left. It would be enough, he would make it enough. Yet, he stared at the sky. Treading water and watching as the city burned. It was pretty from here, if he didn't let himself think about the why of it. What humanity was doing to itself all over the world right now.

He left his tank behind and swam for shore. Soon it would be time to start again.

CHAPTER SEVENTY

DAWN WAS FAR from near when she woke beside him. There was no clock, but she could tell morning was still far off. She had fallen asleep with his arm for a pillow. The thought that no good would come from her being seen leaving in the morning made her slip out without waking him.

She knew she would never get back to sleep, but some cool night air sounded nice. Not many were awake inside Mr. Clean at this hour, but as fate would have it, there was at least one. As Leah quietly shut Jonathan's door behind her, she turned and looked up to find Paige on the catwalks above.

When their eyes met, they both seemed equally surprised to be looking at one another. Paige was the first to look away. She turned stiffly, moved to the opposite side of the catwalk, and left Leah staring at her back.

With a deep breath, Leah shook her head and decided it was time—invited or not, wanted or not—to try. She walked up the stairs, her shoes plenty loud enough for Paige to know she was coming. She hadn't moved. Leah took a breath, gathered her courage and moved to stand beside her.

She hadn't noticed until she stood right beside her, that the ceiling was transparent, as though Paige had asked Mr. Clean for a sunroof to look up at the stars.

"He's an idiot to let you anywhere near him," Paige said, surprising Leah by being the first to speak.

Leah nodded. Despite all the things Paige didn't know about the situation—her comment was still fair.

She waited a bit and watched the stars. Eventually, Paige seemed too uncomfortable in the silence and turned to walk away.

"His name was Peter," Leah said, the words bursting out of her.

Paige stopped, and if Leah didn't know any better, she thought she heard a groan.

"He was my brother. I think I would have betrayed the whole damn world if that was what it took. I thought . . . I thought that was what he needed me to do . . . and he was family."

Paige slowly turned back to the catwalk. "I know." There was no venom in her words. "Sometimes I think—I know—I would have done the same. Doesn't seem to matter. I can't stop being angry."

Leah nodded slowly. It was fair, honest, and the fact that Paige gave that much was more than she'd have hoped for.

"I don't know how to fix that," Leah said. "You'll never hear me say I'm proud of myself. And . . . I miss you terribly. I know it seems like we were only friends because I needed you—but, you *were* my friend."

Paige took a long breath and kept looking up. A long time passed and neither moved. "This place sucks. I hate it here. I feel trapped in a cage with my father. I think he knows it. I think he tries to stay away, but I just . . ."

She trailed off, and Leah let her. She waited a while before she said anything. "You . . . um . . . you never told me what happened."

"What makes you think I would now?"

"You kinda brought it up," Leah said. ". . . and you know I can keep a secret."

Paige scoffed.

This was followed by another long silence as they looked up at the stars.

"Sometimes, I really miss booze," Leah said.

Paige quirked her lips and studied her a moment. There was a great deal of unspoken calculation going on behind her eyes for a while. "I know a guy," she finally said.

She just walked off, leaving Leah to wonder if she was supposed to follow. When Paige reached the stairs down, she didn't stop and she didn't look back.

"I'm not gonna ask you to come, follow or don't. I don't care."

Leah blinked, smiled a bit, then ran to catch up.

There was not supposed to be any drugs or alcohol in Hangman's Tree. While one of Jonathan's most unpopular directives, the reasons weren't exactly baseless. The majority of this army was made up of people who had been isolated and forced to cope with stresses no average individual could imagine. Understandably, people did so in different ways. More than a few amongst them were going through withdrawals of one kind or another. The Doc was good at spotting the signs as they came in.

Jonathan was trying to do them all a favor—cold turkey was easier when there wasn't any other choice.

Paige was not the only one who didn't love the rule, especially under the current circumstances. As Leah followed Paige down the catwalks, she let slip that Jonathan's judgment was probably best in the short-term.

"His judgment? I just caught him sleeping with the enemy," Paige said. She smiled then, as though something funny had occurred to her. "Ironic, you know, because between the two of you, you're the one who actually bears the closest resemblance to Julia Roberts . . ."

Leah was about to point out that, despite appearances, she hadn't actually been sleeping with Jonathan outside the literal sense, but she settled for a sardonic grin before Paige began knocking on a door.

Leah stepped aside when the door swung open, not wanting Paige to be caught with her. She listened quietly.

Turned out—Paige did know a guy.

Jonathan's plan required special project teams that had to leave Hangman's Tree for various reconnaissance operations. The truth was, being on his war council, Paige and Leah knew more about why this man was being sent out than he did—but of course, he had no idea of that. Being an Army brat growing up, Paige seemed to possess an uncanny knack for ferreting out the sort of folks who would be holding contraband.

When the door shut and Paige held up a flask, they felt a bit like teenagers sneaking bottles out of their parent's liquor cabinet.

"I know where to go," Leah said, making her contribution to tonight's escapade. She took Paige to the one place she knew only Mr. Clean could find them.

They had to go up a number of flights of stairs, and at the end, Mr. Clean formed a final staircase upon her arrival. "When no one trusts you, you start looking for places where you won't be in anyone's way. Mr. Clean lets me up here."

"Speaking of," Paige said. "Mr. Clean, you know I love you, but no one needs to be informed of our activities this evening. We are breaking a rule. It's a victimless crime if no one knows. We appreciate your discretion."

The AI didn't reply, but the door hatch still opened.

"Yeah, he's definitely gonna narc on us," Leah said, as the hatch shut quietly behind them.

485

"You've been holding out. I didn't know this place even had roof access," Paige said as she took a long breath of the cool night air.

When Leah looked down on where they stood, it appeared to be a forest canopy. The surface was flat, yet the trees that Mr. Clean projected swayed with the wind like all those around them in the forest. It was often hard to tell where Mr. Clean ended and the forest began.

Paige breathed in the night air, sat down and pulled out the flask. After a sip she held it out to her. Leah looked at it for a moment before sighing. "I can't."

"What . . . this was your idea?"

"Said I missed booze, I didn't know you'd be able to get any," Leah said. "Don't worry, I'll just make sure you don't fall off the roof."

Paige considered her, tilted her head skeptically, her eyes narrowing as Leah grew more and more hesitant to meet them.

"Don't ask, unless you're sure you want to know, because I won't let there be any more lies between us," Leah said.

Paige was thoughtful for a while. "Jonathan's?"

"Yeah."

"How far along?"

"Two months, give or take."

"He knows?"

Leah nodded.

"You're . . . keeping it?" Paige asked.

"I want to."

Quiet followed. It went on for a few minutes, Paige occasionally taking a sip from the flask.

"You're like the worst spy ever," Paige said with a chuckle.

The glare Leah turned on her didn't last long before melting away to laughter.

"Jeez, you'd think they'd teach it on day one of spy school," Paige cleared her throat. "*Ladies, this is important, don't get impregnated by your targets.*"

"They probably just assume it goes without saying," Leah said.

"Well, you showed them," Paige said.

They laughed until it began to feel familiar. Well, until they made the mistake of noticing how familiar. Then it grew quiet again, and they listened to the wind blowing through the trees.

"I suppose Jonathan is not a complete idiot then," Paige said. "I mean if he knew it was his."

"You don't have to say *it* . . . It's a boy," Leah said. "Mr. Clean told me."

"Aww," Paige said. "A mini Tibbs."

"Yeah," Leah said, starting to wonder if whatever was in that flask was starting to take hold.

"Do you love him?" Paige asked.

The question was abrupt. As though Paige had smashed a pile of dishes on the floor just to catch her off guard. Leah's smile disappeared in an instant. Suddenly, she understood exactly why Jonathan had answered that very same question the way he had. "Dammit, I want to."

Watching Paige's reaction was like déjà vu. First, she nodded, only to find herself frowning a moment later. Before she had a chance to say how vague an answer that was, Leah smashed her own pile of dishes.

"Why do you hate your father so much?"

Her face darkened, and Paige took another pull off her flask and looked at the night sky.

"I don't talk about it. It's in the past, I don't like dredging it back up . . . only makes it hurt again. So, you're getting the short version. My father betrayed me. There was. . ."

She stopped and was silent a moment, as if gathering her thoughts. Leah waited silently.

Paige continued matter of factly. "I was seventeen . . . I was raped. The man was under my father's command. My dad, he asked me to protect the soldier's career. Were there circumstances? Yes. But, he was my father. The circumstances shouldn't. . ."

She stopped again. Knowing the words and saying them aloud—they weren't the same thing. She didn't continue, and she didn't need to. There was nothing to add.

A stiff breeze passed through the quiet, and she pulled her legs up to her chest. She rested her chin on her knees.

Leah had a faraway look in her eyes when she whispered, "I'll hate him with you."

CHAPTER SEVENTY-ONE

THE NEXT MORNING Leah stood in the doorway of Mr. Silva's quarters. His eyes were red when he answered. "You're the one they talk about. You were with the people watching my daughter."

Not the best start, but Leah didn't think this was the moment to split hairs. "I . . . I was."

"I don't want to hear anything you have to say," Mr. Silva said, closing the door.

Luckily he hadn't slammed it, because she put her foot between the door and the frame. "Please, it's about your daughter."

His red eyes stared down at her shoe. Any patience quickly hardening into anger. "Do you think I won't toss you out on your ass?"

She swallowed. "Rylee asked me the same question before she gave me a black eye—so, no. I know you will."

"Then move your foot," he said.

"I got her to listen, and I need a minute of your time . . ."

His red eyes narrowed. "I'll give you five seconds."

"I lost my brother. If there was a chance that I could speak to him again I'd want to hear it," Leah said.

They stood in his doorway for an eternity as he digested that and studied her. The reality was probably no more than twenty seconds, but to Leah it felt like being held under a microscope for hours.

"You better have a good reason for saying that to me."

"If I didn't have a damn good reason, I wouldn't have the balls to say anything to you," Leah said, shivering a bit but holding her ground.

"That's a pretty good answer,' he said. Slowly, the pressure on her foot lessened, and his door opened.

She stood with him in the Armory. She understood now why Heyer had brought her there as it was the best place to explain and the most private space inside Mr. Clean. Mr. Silva didn't make any more threats as he began to understand what she wanted from him.

Rylee's father studied the small stone resting on the pillar, at odds with the notion that this was once a part of his daughter. The female half of the bonded pair.

"My daughter's consciousness is inside this thing . . . and you need me to reach it?"

Leah nodded gently. "I know it's a lot to ask of you, you don't have to answer right away. I unders—"

"I'll do it," he said.

Her words caught in her throat. She'd expected this to be difficult.

"You look surprised," Mr. Silva said. "Did you expect I would disagree?"

"I didn't know what to expect," Leah said. "The question seems too big. I've been afraid to ask it."

"Yes," Mr. Silva said with a nod. "Too big is an understatement."

Mr. Silva looked as though he were on the verge of tears. It was hard to tell what that meant, as she had never seen him look otherwise—not really. They had never spoken before Mr. Silva learned of his daughter's death.

"Since Jonathan told me what happened, I've been angry. Angry at everyone. At God. At myself. I know I couldn't have known, that she couldn't tell me, that I wouldn't have believed her. I would have been scared something had gone wrong in her head. I know all this, and I'm still angry that she never tried. Then I'm angry at myself for being so selfish. Then I'm mad at God for letting this happen at all.

"When I'm too tired to be angry, I'm numb. But . . . that's all I do now. Sway back and forth between anger and numbness."

Leah listened, the silences between his thoughts were not ones she was meant to fill.

"Now you put this in front of me," Mr. Silva said. "There is this chance I can tell her I understand why she ran, why she shut me out. That I know what she did. That even though I would have done everything in my power to stop her—"

He fell apart. "I'm still so proud of her. I've prayed. Prayed that, wherever she is, she'd know . . . and so much more that I never got to say. If there is a chance I can say those things—that I could know she heard them . . ."

He straightened with a sharp sniff and wiped the tears from his cheeks. "I find I care very little about how big the question is, Leah. I don't even care what God thinks."

"Under the circumstances," Leah said. "I think God would understand."

He nodded, then drew in a long breath. "You said this will be difficult. That we may not have long to make it work. So, where do we start?"

CHAPTER SEVENTY-TWO

HE WAS SURPRISED, having expected Heyer to come alone, when Grant walked in beside him. The room was a small chamber that Mr. Clean had manifested beside the armory. Jonathan's eyes wandered back and forth between the two, but finally they focused on Heyer. He studied the alien the way a chess player might search the face of an opponent who just made a move he didn't understand.

Grant was uncomfortable in Jonathan's presence and wasn't making much of an effort to mask it. Jonathan didn't know what to make of that either. He was used to a man who hid behind an unfazed male bravado. But he hadn't spoken with the man since he came out of his catatonic state.

Grant now possessed his shadow's memories—he would have remembered Jonathan killing him in The Never. Perhaps it was fair to assume that would make anyone uncomfortable.

Eventually Jonathan let out a long breath, resigned to Grant's presence and turned to Heyer. "Are you ready?"

"As ready as one can be, under the circumstances," Heyer said, removing his coat and hat.

For a moment, the alien saw nowhere to set the items. Grant was quick to offer to hold them. In the pettiest sort of way, this bothered Jonathan, but he kept it off his face.

Heyer then left the two of them, stepping to the other side of the room as a floor to ceiling window formed, separating the original room into two halves. Grant and Jonathan watched Heyer from their side.

A moment later, a waist-high platform, the size of an altar, formed out of the floor behind the alien.

Heyer removed his shirt. The light from his chest shone brightly as he walked to the platform.

For Jonathan, watching him brought one of his father's memories to the surface of his thoughts. Beneath a smoldering piece of fuselage in the Libyan Desert, Douglas had looked down at his blood-covered hands as he cut away Johanna O'Sullivan's flesh to free the Borealis implant. The surgery, if one could call it that, done as quickly as was possible with little more than his belt knife for a scalpel. Only a little less disturbing was having to pull the shrapnel from Holloway's skull with pliers.

Despite all the ugliness that had led to that final moment, as he took the fading light of Heyer's device and placed it inside Holloway's body, Douglas had felt he was witnessing a small miracle. It was the light—growing bright as it took over, both cutting through and healing its way into Holloway's skin. The wound around his head closing where Douglas had done all he could to remove the shrapnel.

Of course, it seemed a miracle, because his friend's eyes soon opened. Unfortunately, it wasn't long until the alien behind those eyes assured him— Holloway was no longer with them. There was nothing more to be done.

Watching Mr. Clean perform the same procedure would hopefully be far less traumatic—not just for Jonathan but for Heyer. The alien laid back onto the table and gave Mr. Clean permission to proceed. He'd only just closed his eyes when Jonathan broke the silence. "Thank you . . ."

The AI stopped moving as Heyer opened his eyes and turned his head to look at him.

". . . for your trust. I'm sorry . . . I had to ask you for this."

"You were worried I would not go through with it?" Heyer asked.

"I was," Jonathan admitted.

Heyer was thoughtful for a moment. "You once told me you'd put your faith in me. I think I lost it along the way."

"You have it now, Old Man," Jonathan said.

"Good, because I want you to do something for me," Heyer said.

Mr. Clean, having decided that none of this dialog was intended to cancel the procedure, resumed his work. Cable-like attachments, identical to those the AI had used during the removal of the dampening bracer, came down from the ceiling and attached to his exposed skin.

"Let Leah decide," Heyer said. "Do not stand in her way."

"You know I hate that plan," Jonathan said.

The alien paused thoughtfully. "How do you think I feel about this one?"

Jonathan returned a sober nod as the three cables made contact with each of the lines that ran across Heyer's chest. The alien smiled faintly then closed his eyes—the lights across his chest dimming to a fainter thrumming glow.

"Consciousness and motor functions offline," Mr. Clean said. "Beginning extraction."

Six cables, their heads tipped with scalpel like blades, rose out of the table. They hovered over Heyer for a moment, looking like metallic spider legs that were about to close on him. In a graceful unison of movement, they went to work cutting through the true tissue around the device with a precision and speed no human surgical team could have managed.

When the cutting was complete the scalpels all moved aside. The cables attached to the implant lifted, and the faintly glowing lines rose free of Holloway's body. As though Heyer's soul hung there above his abandoned vessel.

The glowing lines reacted to the change in environment quickly, being exposed to open air triggering activity within. It had been different when Douglas did this by hand twenty years ago. Today, the lines of light collapsed in on themselves like a flower shutting its petals when the night grew cold. They shrank, hardened down until Jonathan and Grant were looking at a stone one might have mistaken for any other device in the Armory. Except, Heyer's implant wasn't fully dormant. While the shape hardened down to a silver metallic glyph in black stone, the connection to Mr. Clean kept the implant from going offline. The lines on Heyer's device never ceased to glow.

While this happened above Holloway's body, Mr. Clean's spiderlike limbs lost their cutting edges, and went back to work. The appendages stapled shut the exposed wound left by the implant's removal where possible, bandaged where it was not. Air and feeding tubes hooked up to Holloway's face and IV lines carrying blood and saline were placed, the skin now breaking for the needle with no trouble.

A white sheet was drawn over him, and in a matter of minutes, it was unclear to Jonathan exactly how to think of that body now that the implant was gone. Was it Heyer's vessel or Holloway? The body looked like any ordinary man hooked to life support in a hospital. Once complete, the table moved across the floor and disappeared into a coffin sized compartment within Mr. Clean. The whole event was like watching a morgue door close. Except, this door disappeared from existence. Only Jonathan and Grant would know that the body remained safe within a wall of Mr. Clean.

He and Grant hadn't spoken a word to one another through the entire process, but as they stared at the glowing lines of light still pulsating in the stone, Jonathan spoke. "Everything you asked for will be arranged. You have my word as well as Heyer's. But as soon as he is ready, you'll be leaving."

Opposite the wall where the body disappeared, a larger section liquefied to reveal the new host body. Grant shivered as he watched. Perhaps he wanted to look away, but still preferred what was happening on the other side than looking at Jonathan.

"I'll make sure it gets done," Grant said, looking down at the alien's hat and folded coat still held in his arms.

Jonathan took a long breath, his arms folding across his chest. "Under any other circumstances I'd send someone else."

"Feeling's mutual," Grant said. "Let's just hope we're both wrong."

Jonathan frowned. "Guess we had to agree on something eventually."

They grew quiet again. Grant looked down at Heyer's fedora as if considering it.

"Walker," he said, as he picked it up by the crown.

He moved as though he was about to try it on but froze at the edge in Jonathan's voice. "Don't even."

CHAPTER SEVENTY-THREE

WITH THE EXCEPTION of Mr. Clean—who knew everything that happened at Hangman's Tree—Jonathan and Grant were the only two who knew what Heyer was setting out to do tonight.

Grant came out of a room wearing the first of the prototypes Hayden and Mr. Clean had prepared. With his implant active and armored uniform, Jonathan had to begrudgingly admit he carried a certain—presence—he hadn't previously.

"Seeing me off?" Grant asked. "Nice to know I'll be missed."

Jonathan shook his head and held out a bag of supplies. Most of the contents were rations—there was no way to know with any certainty how long Grant would need to survive. There wouldn't be any food where he was going.

"You should shield your implant," Jonathan said.

Grant put the pack on his back, then took a long breath as he looked down at the hole into the transport vessel. Vessel was misleading—it was a mold the size of a coffin which had surfaces that looked like avocado skin. Appropriately, inside the hole was a canvas sac the size of a body bag.

"If you're feeling claustrophobic there isn't any shame in it," Jonathan said. "But I need to know if it'll be a problem now so we can sedate you."

Grant activated the shielding on his implant, its glow hidden behind the armored plates of the uniform. "I'll be fine, doesn't mean I'm looking forward to this."

"Fair enough."

Grant laid down in the mold and awkwardly got himself into the body bag. Once in the bag, he covered himself to the face.

"We ready, Mr. Clean?" Jonathan asked.

"On your command," the AI replied.

Jonathan grabbed the last item, an air tank, and handed it down. "That should last you a good hour. If you need much longer then something has likely gone wrong. Still," Jonathan handed him a secondary smaller backup tank, "here, it's good for ten minutes tops."

Grant took the tank. "Thanks."

They exchanged a last unpleasant smirk.

"Try not to die before making yourself useful," Jonathan said.

Grant's helmet slammed shut, covering his face. The prototype's helmet had the latest version of their HUD built in. The faceguard was made of a Borealis plastic equivalent, far more resilient than a motorcycle helmet visor but still the weakest spot in the armor. It was reinforced with a thin cage of alien steel. Grant's helmet had been altered from Hayden's original design to provide him an oxygen port for the air tank. It took him a moment to get the line connected.

When he was ready, Jonathan finished closing the bag over him and waited for Grant's signal. Said signal was supposed to be a thumbs up but, of course, Grant took the final opportunity to go with a more offensive hand gesture.

"Go ahead, Mr. Clean," Jonathan said.

The floor morphed, a transparent cover lined with the same avocado texture as the vessel formed over the top of Grant. A moment later, a thick waxy purple and black mixture began to fill the cavity.

"How are his vitals?" Jonathan asked.

"His heart rate is accelerated," Mr. Clean said. "But within normal range. He does not appear at risk of panic—he should acclimate soon enough."

He heard Heyer's heavy footsteps finally approaching behind him. "Let me know when the cocoon is stable," Jonathan said.

Jonathan turned away from the purple and black sludge filling the chamber at his feet as Heyer drew closer. As the alien came to a stop and looked down at him, Jonathan spoke candidly. "I'm not gonna lie, Old Man. This is a new level of weird even for us."

Heyer grinned—or at least he tried to—whatever expression his Feroxian face made seemed to have the opposite of the intended effect. Jonathan almost immediately put a calming hand up as though Heyer was on the brink of taking a swing at him. "Everything okay?"

"I was attempting to look humored," Heyer said.

Jonathan looked troubled and struggled to keep it from his face.

"What is it?"

"You sound . . . well, like your brother," Jonathan said. "If he were trying to do an impression of an English accent."

"It does take time to grow familiar with a new host species," Heyer said.

Jonathan studied him for a moment. "What is it like?"

Heyer took a long breath and it sounded like a rhino was filling its lungs. "Strange. Not human. But, despite the new proclivities of this life form I find I cannot yet shake a powerful desire to put on clothes."

"Right," Jonathan said. "After a couple thousand years as a human this must be like trying to blend in at a nudist colony."

"Yes, Jonathan. It is just like that," Heyer said.

They stared at one another for a long moment.

"Your words sound like sarcasm," Jonathan said. "Your body language says you're trying not to pass gas."

"Excellent," Heyer replied.

"Still getting gas here," Jonathan said.

"Still attempting sarcasm," Heyer said.

"Maybe . . . don't?" Jonathan asked. "I don't know if the Ferox have sarcasm anyway."

"I will keep it in mind," Heyer said.

Jonathan nodded. "Well, moving on. Mr. Clean has the signal inhibitor ready."

A small pillar rose out of the floor with a triangular plate of steel the size of a Feroxian palm laying atop. Jonathan picked up the plate and placed it awkwardly into Heyer's giant clawed hand. Without delay, Heyer pressed it against the three lines glowing across his chest.

The device wasn't Jonathan's idea. When Jonathan and his father had fought Malkier in The Never, initially neither of them had been able to detect a portal stone. For that matter, the glowing lines that would have given away Malkier's Borealis implant had not been present. Only after Malkier's device had been knocked offline by a massive jolt of electricity had Jonathan been able to see the lines of light and sense the stone's presence.

Explaining this to Mr. Clean, the AI had been able to create a close approximation to what Malkier used to hide his identity from his people. However, for this mission, Heyer's Signal Inhibitor had required a few additional features.

The first of which being that Heyer needed to appear ready to—well—mate.

The triangle lost shape, melting as it made contact with Heyer's implant.

Transparent at first, its volume spread to cover the three lines of light on Heyer's chest. At the same time, two additional threads crawled toward opposite sides of his neck where they soon touched the outer edges of Heyer's white Feroxian eyes. The glowing light on his chest disappeared, replaced with natural Feroxian tissue. At the same time, Heyer's eyes turned black.

"The effect should be an adequate representation of male Ferox arousal," Mr. Clean said.

"Well," Jonathan said. "Usually, when they look at me like that, I start planning to stab them in the neck. So, yeah—it'll pass."

"Let us hope I do not draw any female's notice when I arrive. The disguise will not trick their senses should they show . . . interest," Heyer said. "While I doubt a Ferox would know what to make of that, it would be best not to draw unnecessary attention."

"You're on your own with that one," Jonathan said. "If Feroxian Viagra was a thing we wouldn't be in this mess."

A sound like a pressure valve releasing steam followed, and the cover to the chamber in the floor opened. "Looks like your Grant trophy sac is done baking."

Jonathan's expression soured and he covered his face with his forearm. "Mr. Clean definitely got the odor right."

Heyer, reaching down to heft the cocoon over his shoulder, stood and sniffed at the air. "Doesn't seem so bad."

Jonathan grimaced as he looked between the sac and the alien. "Small blessings, I guess."

Finally, Jonathan took a small cloth bundle from his pocket. Careful not to touch the thing, he untied the fabric revealing the portal stone they had extracted from the Ferox Heyer was now currently inhabiting.

"I was gonna make a bigger deal about this send off," Jonathan said. "But, Grant's only got so much oxygen, and the sooner you get the hell out of here with that sac the better."

Heyer put his palm out.

Jonathan looked at that hand for a moment as though something about this whole exchange seemed funny to him. He reached to put the stone in Heyer's palm and then stopped an inch over his hand.

"It will be disorientating . . . you will be confused," Jonathan said.

Heyer looked at him curiously, or at least he tried to.

"The first time you handed me one of these, that's what your shadow said. It was right before you told me your name."

"I imagine that is what I tell all of them," Heyer said.

He nodded. "Jonathan Tibbs, nice to meet you," he said, dropping the stone into Heyer's palm.

The alien stared down at the stone for a long moment. He knew he shouldn't ask but, of all the things he had to accept on faith, all hope for their plan hinged on something Jonathan claimed to be certain of . . . and yet couldn't possibly know.

"Yes, Heyer, it will be there," Jonathan said, seeming to have read Heyer's mind. "Trust me."

Heyer sighed and nodded. He took a few steps back to get out of range.

"If you want to do us all a favor and leave Grant on the other side," Jonathan smiled. "Well . . ."

"Certainly would be easiest," Heyer said. "But . . . I . . ."

"I wasn't serious," Jonathan said.

They stared at one another. "Okay, I was 40 percent serious . . . 49 max."

"For what it is worth Jonathan . . . I think I trust you," Heyer said as his fist closed on the stone. "See you at the end."

CHAPTER SEVENTY-FOUR

HER FINGERS WERE not hers. They belonged to a child. Her feet didn't reach the floor while she sat in this chair. The woman who sat across from her at the table towered over her. She'd never been in this kitchen or met the woman. Yet, Ms. Silva looked down at her like a daughter and pushed a small wrapped box across the table.

Leah didn't speak but words came from her. They belonged to the little girl. "I thought I opened them all at my party."

Ms. Silva shrugged. "This one is special."

Her hands reached out and tore off the wrapping paper. She pulled a diary from a bed of tissue paper, its pages empty but for an inscription: *To Rylee, On her 6th Birthday. Love, Mom.*

"My mother gave me my first when I was your age," Ms. Silva said.

The truth was that every word spoken between them was in Portuguese, but Leah knew the script.

"I can't wait to write in it," Rylee said. "Thank you, Mom."

Ms. Silva smiled down at her, and the projection faded into the void again. For a moment, Leah was herself, sitting on a chair far too large for a grown adult as the world around her shifted and became Rylee's childhood bedroom.

Later, that very same evening, she was Rylee now lying on a bed. She looked down at the hands holding the pen and the journal as she wrote.

Mom gave me this journal after everyone went home . . .

For the next few minutes Leah sat behind Rylee's childhood eyes and watched the entry come into being. Some details were precise, others a best estimation. The hand produced text exactly as it existed in a stack of diaries in the real world. The room around her—that was more complicated.

"Rylee, you better be in bed by the time I get up there," Mr. Silva's voice came from the hallway.

Rylee closed the diary and set it on her nightstand. Leah caught a smile from the child as she looked in the mirror and switched off the light.

The projection chamber returned to the void, then its defaults. Leah got up and left the chamber.

This was the second day of testing. The previous day she had experienced re-creations of Rylee's final moments. Those Mr. Clean could more easily simulate with near perfect accuracy because he could build the projections from footage stolen from The Cell.

She had stood in Rylee's shoes and watched as she punched a projection of herself in the face. From Rylee's perspective, projection Leah seemed tall. She had to look up at her to aim her fist. This was strange because Rylee never felt short to her. The woman had possessed too much presence to ever feel small.

The memory ran all the way up to the moment Rylee disappeared in Jonathan's arms. This re-creation had not been strictly necessary for Leah to recreate as it was one of the few that Rylee and Leah had actually shared. As such it was a good baseline to begin. Allowing Leah to give Mr. Clean a sense of how accurate the details felt in the re-creation based on her own experience.

The journal entries were a greater challenge. There was no footage. Only photos from photo albums. Rylee's father and Mr. Clean had to work together to recreate the events Rylee recorded. Joao acting as the witness to most of the periods in Rylee's life and becoming like a film director as Mr. Clean built sets for Leah to relive experiences.

This meant Joao often had to stand inside a projection of a rental apartment he hadn't lived in for ten years and try to remember if there had been tile or linoleum, if the kitchen sink's faucet had been chrome or brushed nickel, or tell the AI that the My Little Pony comforter on his late daughter's bed had actually had imperfections.

He'd be hit by a wave of grief, tears running down his cheeks as he'd forced himself to tell the AI that when Rylee was a child, she'd spilled a bowl of chocolate ice cream on it. She'd tried to hide it, put the bedspread in the laundry with bleach. The colors had faded in places and left white patches.

Their re-creations would never be perfect. But Mr. Clean believed it was more important for Leah to experience a likeness and build the necessary associations. Trick her mind into creating markers—coordinates of time and place.

That said, every detail they got right improved the chances.

As she walked out of the chamber in Joao's screening room, she didn't have to ask if the re-creation felt true to life. He was hunched over in his chair, his eyes far away as tears ran down his cheeks.

Leah came in from the projection chamber and found him wiping away his tears again. She put a hand on his shoulder and sat beside him for a while. Neither spoke.

It was unclear to him exactly when he had come to welcome the comfort she always offered. He'd found keeping a grip on the animosity he was supposed to feel toward her near impossible. Some of it was learning her story—what she'd lost and what she'd done to get here.

More of it might have been that they spent most of their waking moments throughout the day together.

But if he was being honest, he'd felt an affection for Leah before the first day had ended. He saw providence in her. She seemed made for what they endeavored to do, possessed of an innate understanding of the humanity she observed in people.

Leah saw things in his daughter's journals Joao never would have.

When he was overwhelmed by grief, she never left when he needed her to stay, and never stayed when he needed to her to go. She always knew the difference—with one exception.

He couldn't always hide the pain of seeing his daughter like she was standing there, so real and alive. Once, Leah made the mistake of asking him if they should stop. He'd looked at her, tired red eyes holding hers.

"Some pain is mercy."

He almost added that he didn't ever want to discuss this again. As it turned out, he had not needed to. She understood.

Now, it was an understatement to say that Leah sometimes lacked boundaries, but her trespasses were never self-indulgent curiosities. They always came from a place that thought she might do good. Most days, this only meant some awkward moments.

This morning he had come to their lab area early. He found Leah already there. She'd either never slept, or she had woken in the middle of the night with some thought that wouldn't allow her to sleep. That cathexis she possessed was what made Joao believe she would manage the impossible.

He began reviewing work with Mr. Clean on his side of the room and she called out to him.

"Mr. Sil—"

"Joao," he reminded her for the hundredth time.

"Right, sorry . . ."

He waited, but Leah had trailed off the way she did when a new thought struck her. "You know, most kids don't call their parents by their first name. What did Rylee call you?"

"Pai or Papai," Mr. Silva said. "In English it's dad or daddy."

"Papai," Leah said.

They looked at one another uncomfortably.

"I'm sorry," Leah said.

"I would really rather you not," Joao said.

"I just thought the association might . . ." She blushed. "Let's never speak of this again, Joao?"

"Thank you."

He turned back to work, then back to her. "Wait, what did you want in the first place?"

"It's . . . never mind. It's not ready yet anyway," Leah said.

With a sigh, Joao got up and came to stand beside her. He stood staring down at what she had been working on so meticulously.

He'd been standing over her shoulder watching her work for some time before he spoke. "Leah, what is this?"

She'd fallen back into a state of hyper-focus, had to mentally yank herself back from the work. She turned to see Joao squinting down at her monitor as though trying to translate a lost language.

"What? Oh, right. It's easier to understand in the projection chamber," she said.

"Show me?"

She hesitated, then nodded.

A few moments later they stood in the blank slate of the chamber.

"Mr. Clean, please load the MA map," she said. "Start where we left off."

"MA?" Joao asked.

"Memory Association," Leah said.

The void came and went, and soon Joao was standing inside the center of a strange grid of bubbles and lines. It surrounded them in a three-dimensional space, one of the bubbles pulling forward to display its contents.

At a glance, the information contained within vaguely resembled the sort of evidence board fictional detectives used to solve mysteries in a Hollywood movie. People, locations, and various newspaper clippings connected by varying colors of string and pinned to a cork board.

The difference was that, had Leah tried to do this work on a physical bulletin board she would have needed to rent out a stadium just to store the monstrosity. Mr. Clean's assistance allowed her to build the framework into a three-dimensional web. Letting her pull which of Rylee's experiences that seemed most important into the foreground and push what seemed more banal into the background.

When one studied the connections long enough, the board started to look more like she was connecting star constellations. Taken a map of the galaxy and started playing connect the dots.

"I started by asking Mr. Clean to build a map where any entries that seemed to reference one another in the text connected," Leah said. "Then I began reviewing the connections with a human eye. Mr. Clean was often correct on the simple cause and effect connections . . . but . . . he couldn't intuit the context of human association within Rylee's life."

She turned and saw his eyes were wide with—wonder—like a child staring up at the ceiling in a planetarium.

"This is what you've been puzzling out. All these nights you don't sleep. This is what you see when you try to understand my daughter's mind?"

Leah nodded hesitantly.

"It's like watching art as it is brought into being. You're . . . well, like Bob Ross."

Leah snorted at the comparison.

Let's add a fluffy childhood humiliation over here. We don't want this entry— where Rylee loathed the second graders who laughed at the new kid who wet his pants on the playground—to get lonely. Perhaps, yes, it belongs here with this moment from summer camp, when the mean girl in Rylee's cabin stole her underwear and ran it up the flagpole before the morning's salute. Yes, they will keep each other company.

Joao had a point though, there was far more art than science to what she had created.

"Thank you, Mr. Sil . . . Joao," she smiled.

Hours later, Mr. Silva had admitted he had long ago lost any ability to navigate the web. Only Mr. Clean, Leah, and perhaps Rylee herself might have been able to steer their way through the thing.

He was watching her, thinking, and Leah didn't understand why until he spoke.

"You never give up. You obsess. We've been at this for days. Mr. Clean has to tell you to eat and sleep. You're not just good at seeing into people. It's like once you start, you can't stop until the puzzle forms a picture."

She slowed her work, moving another experience into place in the web along with the text of Rylee's diary entry and the projection Mr. Clean had fabricated to reproduce it inside the chamber.

"Profiling people—is it how you ended up working for The Cell?"

"I told you, my brother disappeared . . ." Leah trailed off. "I never imagined I would be doing this with anyone's life, let alone two."

"You're good at it though," he said.

"I got a lot of experience trying to figure out . . ."

She grimaced and trailed off.

"Jonathan," Mr. Silva said. "Did you? Figure him out I mean."

Leah frowned, then stepped back from her work. "I think I got close."

"But?"

Leah gave him a sideways look. "Rylee. From the moment she showed up nothing Jonathan did made any sense to me. I understand why now, but at the time I might as well have been beating my head against a brick wall."

When she said this, the frustration she'd felt at that time slipped into her words. Mr. Silva noticed, but didn't seem to take any offense.

"It's funny," Mr. Silva said. "You say my daughter thought of you as an enemy. And, I see it got violent, but had she spent as much time with you as I have, I believe you could have been friends."

On the surface, she thought Joao's words were said as a politeness. But she had once thought something similar, the first time she read a translation of Rylee's journals. Friends might be overstating it, but allies had not seemed unachievable. Of course, that was before the woman caught her stealing from her diary.

She shivered, her arms hugging her as though she'd grown cold. She stepped back from the projection.

"Joao," Leah said. "I'm terrified. I'm terrified this will actually work."

His face softened. "You'd be crazy not to be, Leah."

"When that device is put in . . . your daughter . . . she might *actually* be there. All of this will stop being a theory and be real. She might be in my mind. Know everything I've done—what I'm doing right now. This is the most complete invasion of a person's private thoughts I can imagine . . ."

Leah took another step back from the web. "She sacrificed her life for the world. And I'm . . . what? Just going to wake her up, tell her the job's not done, and ask her to sacrifice everything all over again? What if she won't? What if she's trapped in the mind of someone she has every right to hate?"

Mr. Silva was quiet, troubled for a moment. Then, somewhat awkwardly at first, he held out his arms to her. It took her a moment to realize he was offering a hug. She had to stop hugging herself to step into his embrace, and she didn't manage it with much grace. Perhaps to both of their surprise, Leah didn't feel out of place for long, and Mr. Silva didn't feel he'd made an empty gesture.

"Don't be afraid of my daughter," Mr. Silva said. "This is a two-way street. She is an open book to your eyes now. But, if you allow yourself to be just as vulnerable—she'll see why you made your choices. She'll know you were the one who sought my blessing. If that isn't enough . . ."

He pulled back but left his hands on her shoulders. "Look at me, Leah, memorize this moment, burn it into your brain."

She stared at him, curious at first, as when he spoke his words had the tone of a father lecturing a little girl. "Rylee Silva, you play nice with Leah. You listen to your father. Since the moment I found out you were gone, Leah is the only person who's given me a moment's comfort. So, if you can't do it for her, you do it for me."

Leah smiled, but there were tears coming to her eyes. "Thank you, Joao."

"It's the least I could do," he said.

A few moments later, they stood apart.

"Course, Rylee had a rebellious streak. Often did the opposite of whatever I asked," Joao said.

"I was thinking it too," Leah said. "Didn't want to ruin the moment."

"I don't pretend to follow all that you're doing right here," Mr. Silva said, pointing to a spot closer in Rylee's MA map within the projection chamber. "Are you moving things around a missing piece that will tie them to one another?"

"You aren't wrong," Leah said.

"So, do you know what goes there?" Mr. Silva asked.

She nodded. "Memories we don't have. I've been avoiding going out to get them."

"Why?" he asked.

"Jonathan and Heyer, they were both with her near the end—the real end," Leah said. "I thought it best to ask Heyer, but he's been gone for days and Mr. Clean isn't telling anyone where he is. That leaves Jonathan and . . ."

Leah sighed, glancing back at Mr. Silva to see his face grow somber. "You don't have to do that."

She frowned. "He told you how she died?"

"It's the only thing we've ever spoken about," Joao said.

Leah nodded slowly. "He blames himself."

Joao shook his head. "I don't think that really covers it."

She searched his face but couldn't be sure what he'd meant.

"I knew the day I held her that nothing in this world could ever hurt me more than losing my daughter," Joao said. "I looked into that kid's eyes. I didn't see a kid at all. I might as well have looked into a mirror."

CHAPTER SEVENTY-FIVE

NOV 12, 2005 | 2 PM | JBLM FACILITY

OLIVIA FLICKED ON the light, walked to her desk, and pulled out her chair. She was in her office early that morning. She had a meeting with Dr. Watts, and she wanted to go over the initial reports on the remains they had pulled out of the desert.

The sound of someone speaking her name made her freeze. "Olivia."

Her breath caught as she recognized the voice.

Agent Rivers had not been standing in that corner of her office when she'd turned on the lights. He'd appeared, in the seconds it took her to walk from door to chair.

She closed her eyes, leaned over her desk with both hands, and let out the breath she had been holding. When she straightened, her eyes narrowed on him with suspicion.

He wasn't wearing a suit or tie. She realized she'd never seen him in anything else. What he wore today was casual but hardy. Something an agent might wear for field work if he didn't want to draw attention to himself. High top boots, well-worn jeans, and a dark grey sentinel jacket buttoned all the way to the neck as though he were cold.

"I'm sorry I startled you, but I couldn't just walk back on to base."

Rivers—he looked worried for her. His expression more curious to her than his words as she slowly took her seat.

"Jonathan wants to meet," he said.

He hadn't moved from that corner. As though he were trying to keep as much distance between them as the room would allow. Did he do that for his own comfort or for hers?

"I expected you were being held prisoner, Rivers. Imagined that when I got word of you, it would be as a bargaining chip," Olivia said.

"I'm neither," Rivers said.

"So, what are you then?"

"Hopefully, someone you still trust," he said.

A moment passed.

"Are you alone?" Olivia asked.

"Yes," Rivers said. "We agreed it would be best if I approach you first."

Olivia's brow went up. "You agreed? With who, the alien . . . or Mr. Tibbs."

"Jonathan," Rivers said.

"He sends you here expecting I will just let you return to him?"

"He knows I'll return," Rivers said.

Her eyes narrowed. "Who do you answer to now, Rivers? Me or him?"

"Doesn't have to be either," Rivers said. "If an understanding can be reached. But if you decide not to come then this will likely be the last time we see each other. I'd prefer that not be the way things go."

"Do I really have a choice? If I refuse, you won't attempt to take me by force?"

"No, ma'am, I would never agree to that," he said. "It's your choice."

She nodded and sat back in her chair. "So, why did he take you?"

His face was hard to read, as though he were caught between chagrin and respect. "He knew I was the one he was going to send before he escaped."

"Did he now?"

He took a tentative step closer, then slowed, unsure if he should move.

"Rivers, I'm not afraid of you," she said. "If you're worried I'm going to alert the hangar, you have my word I have no such intention. Now, come over here and talk to me."

He relaxed, even smiled a bit, then came to stand on the other side of her desk. If he'd been in a suit, it would have seemed he was reporting to her as he had for months under her command. But he wasn't the same, there was no stiff back to his posture. That and, if she didn't know any better, she'd say he'd put on muscle since she'd seen him last.

"We didn't understand why Jonathan wanted me in that interrogation room after he'd sent everyone else out."

Olivia nodded.

"You're the one Jonathan needs to convince to believe him. But he knew, to you, he would only be seen as our enemy," Rivers said. "But there was so much more, and he couldn't show you."

Olivia leaned forward, the tilt of her head giving away her interest. "But . . . he could show you, Rivers?"

"You've recovered the remains from Libya. You've got Dr. Watts running tests on it right now."

She saw no point denying it. "It's hard to say what was recovered."

"It's a Ferox—exactly what he warned us was coming and every bit as big a threat," Rivers said.

"You've seen one alive?" Olivia asked.

"The last few weeks, I helped Jonathan secure evidence. He made a point of taking me along to acquire . . . prisoners."

Rivers trailed off, momentarily considering his words. "He's invited me into his inner council. Wanted me to be as aware of his plans as his closest allies."

She considered all of what he'd said, but one point stuck out to her. "This is all very interesting, but it doesn't explain why he had to show you and not me."

Rivers nodded. "I'm the only one you'll believe when he explains how he intends to fight them."

"That is not a straight answer, Rivers."

He closed his eyes, took a long breath. "He asked me to be one of them. He didn't force me. It was a choice—of a sort. It was the only way I could see for myself what he can't show you."

Olivia failed to hide her uncertainty when Rivers confessed that he had become *one of them.*

"And are you going to tell me what he's done to you?" she asked.

"Come to the meeting," Rivers said. "Agree to his terms. Only then."

A long silence fell as Olivia considered him.

"If you're—one of them, why should I trust you?"

Rivers shook his head and looked at his feet. "Jonathan says you will."

Olivia scoffed at first, but beneath the surface the truth grated, and she could hardly tolerate it. Being known so intimately by someone without her consent itched at her insides. The relentless irony that she could feel that way after commanding a vast amount of government manpower to invade every possible aspect of Jonathan Tibbs' life was like nettles.

The only thing that was worse was the idea of letting Tibbs believe she was struggling to stomach her own medicine.

"When and where?" she finally asked.

He reached into his pocket and brought out three dime-sized metallic discs.

"The time is whenever you say," Rivers said. "Where, that part I can't tell you. Just make sure you're holding one of these discs at the time you give me."

Olivia looked down into his palm. She didn't reach for them, her mind becoming a tangle of all the possible counter-measures she might have her people use to gain information.

Rivers was not long in guessing her thoughts.

"He promises your safety. I don't have to tell you that if you come with a tracking device or some such, he won't cancel the meeting—but he will send your team out to chase shadows in the middle of nowhere for their trouble. My advice is to go in good faith."

"Why are there three?" Olivia asked. "Am I not going alone?"

"General Delacy will need to be on board. Jonathan thought he should see his daughter is safe," Rivers said.

"And the third?"

"Dr. Watts," Rivers said. "Jonathan thought you'd . . ."

He trailed off. Must have seen her irritation. Admittedly, Olivia was resisting the urge to snap every pencil on her desk in half.

"Yes," Olivia said. "I would like to bring her along."

Rivers nodded, looking down at the discs in his palm. He still seemed uneasy for her. He didn't rush her, gave her all the time she needed to consider what time she would agree to meet. When it was settled, she saw that concern for her on his face again.

"Rivers, why do you seem . . ."

She struggled for the right word.

". . . if I didn't know better, I'd say you were worried for me."

Rivers swallowed. "You have that list Jonathan gave us."

She nodded.

"Soon, you'll know why he needs those things."

Rivers placed the three discs on the end of her desk. He stepped away, but paused as though he remembered to say something. "Try to get as much sleep as you can tonight."

"Do I look tired to you, Rivers?"

He shook his head. "You remember the nightmares we watched Jonathan endure for all those weeks?"

She nodded slowly.

"I have them now," he said. "I wish someone had told me to get one last good night of sleep."

They stared at one another for one last moment.

"See you soon," he said, then disappeared in a blink.

CHAPTER SEVENTY-SIX

AFTER ADJUSTING TO being in the cocoon, it wasn't so bad. Inside it was warm—safe. But, there was nothing for Grant to do but breathe from the air tank . . . and think. He'd never much liked being alone with his thoughts and now, after inheriting the acts of his shadow, his own company sometimes felt crueler than what The Cell had done to him. No one should ever have to see what they're capable of doing once they honestly believe nothing matters.

Heyer, he'd seemed sympathetic. Said he knew what it was like—learning what a shadow had done in another life. The alien said, he could only imagine what it would be like to know that shadow's feelings—to remember his thoughts.

A distorted echo—but not so distorted that one doesn't recognize his own voice.

Grant felt Heyer pitied him. That had to stop. If they lived through this, Heyer was going to return to his father's body. If Holloway—if his father—still dreamed, then it was possible some part of him saw what the alien saw—felt what the alien felt.

Grant knew, on some level, that this was wishful thinking. If it was more, then the alien would have told him. Heyer seemed a lot of things, but not a liar. After all, Grant now remembered what Heyer had said to his shadow. He knew the truth. That the device had been withheld from him for years because Heyer didn't think he was up to the burden it would ask of him. His shadow had only proven Heyer right.

If there was anything left for him to do in this life, any chance that Holloway was still in there, he had to make Heyer see he'd been wrong.

Grant felt it when they stabilized on the Feroxian Plane. He held himself limp as a fresh corpse—as that was the idea—but the movement of his eyes let him navigate the HUD in his helmet. After a quick check that his oxygen was intact, he activated a screen to the outside.

Mr. Clean had built a far more basic AI into the external disguise that cloaked Heyer's implant. This was currently making Heyer's Ferox eyes appear inky black, but it was also transmitting to Grant's suit to give him a view outside. Heyer was currently looking down at his mammoth Feroxian feet, only to stand up straight and take in their surroundings. While it wasn't the same place Grant's shadow had the displeasure of visiting, it was definitely the Feroxian Plane.

A guttural grunt drew Heyer's attention; his view turned to a Feroxian male, an Alpha, standing with one hand planted in the black sands a few feet from the platform.

He felt Heyer draw down. Almost as though the presence of the Alpha imposed a weight on his posture. The Alpha waited until this ran its course, then began speaking again. Heyer held near perfectly still as he listened.

When the Alpha finally stopped, Heyer remained still for a long moment, then uttered a single guttural grunt of his own.

The Alpha scraped the dirt and pounded it twice with his fist. Grant couldn't tell if the thing was displaying aggression or . . . something else? Heyer didn't move, but his eyes flicked repeatedly to a group of Ferox watching them from beneath the shade of one of the rocky towers that scattered the landscape.

Finally, the Alpha pointed in a direction.

Heyer said nothing, but was quick to move from the platform and in that direction. The moment he was out of sight of the Ferox that had witness their arrival, he changed course, keeping low as he made his way out of the general area. This all seemed to have gone surprisingly easier than they'd imagined. In fact, there seemed very few Ferox about for Heyer to avoid as he made his way out.

Twenty minutes later, Heyer ran a single clawed finger down the cocoon. The opening caused the contents to spill out and puke Grant onto the surface with it.

"We are safe for now," Heyer said, as Grant removed himself from the sac liner. "But I will need to return to them soon."

"That Alpha. What did he say to you?"

"He was pleased that I returned. Most of the tribe has gone, left on the pilgrimage to join the battle for the Promised Land," Heyer said. "The prophet has ordered tribal Alphas to remain with each of their gateways until all who have entered the Arena are accounted for. My return means they can prepare the gate for transport and join the pilgrimage."

Grant nodded. "Wait, he said all that and he wasn't suspicious when you said one word and left? What did you say?"

Heyer sighed. "That word, translates as . . . 'where women'?"

Grant's eyes went from his now empty cocoon and back to Heyer's black eyes. "Right. So, he thinks you went off to get a piece of . . . tail."

"Somewhat literally. He believes I am seeking out a fertile female for the consonance," Heyer said. "Which is a problem for us. Even if I wished, this host is not actually in the proper—state."

"Uh, this isn't the sort of grenade I can jump on for you," Grant said.

Heyer stared at the man for a moment before shaking his head. "Since so few of the tribe are present, the fact that no female disappeared into the mating caverns for the consonance will be noticed."

"Right," Grant said. "Um, I'm not pretending to be an expert on this consonance stuff, but couldn't you just tell them that there was, you know, no mojo?"

At first, Heyer looked at Grant as though he was clearly going to have to solve their problem himself, then his black Feroxian eyes widened as he reconsidered.

"There is precedent in smaller tribes—very embarrassing for the male," Heyer said. "Under the circumstances, few would ask questions, it would be poor manners to discuss."

He thought about it more. "The Alpha would likely be pleased not to have to postpone the tribe's pilgrimage any longer."

"Great, so we just need to make you undesirable," Grant said. "How does one do that in this species?"

"I do not rightly know," Heyer said. "It is a chemical matter of pheromones more than visual stimulation. Luckily, mine are not currently on overdrive, but a female will still know if I am a suitable match if she comes close enough."

Grant thought about it for a moment. "Do the Ferox have latrines?"

Heyer sighed heavily.

CHAPTER SEVENTY-SEVEN

NOV 15, 2005 | NOON | HANGMAN'S TREE

OLIVIA'S FIRST EXPERIENCE of teleportation sickness left her nauseous, effectively blind, and off balance. She stumbled immediately, but someone caught her. Her instinct to struggle free only relaxed when she recognized Rivers' voice.

"I've got you, ma'am," Rivers said. "Don't panic, it's temporary, just keep breathing through it."

Finding that walking wasn't on the table, she was glad Rivers was the one she leaned on to get through the indignity of it. She soon felt the reassurance of a chair pushed beneath her.

From what she could hear, General Delacy and Dr. Watts were faring their journey no better than she, but their hosts had been prepared for it. While she couldn't see her, Olivia could hear Leah speaking to General Delacy.

She could hear Jonathan as well—he had apparently taken it upon himself to help Watts into a seat.

She felt Rivers pull away and grabbed his forearm. "Rivers, it occurs to me that you might have warned us there would be side effects."

"I do apologize for that, ma'am," Rivers said.

She thought she detected a touch of humor in his voice; it was hard to tell without being able to see his face.

"Thank you all for coming," Jonathan said. "Take your time getting your bearings, there is—"

"Where are we?" Olivia asked as she leaned forward with her hands on her knees.

"You'd probably call this an alien spaceship," Jonathan said. "He prefers to be called Mr. Clean."

Olivia's head rose. She stared at the blurry face with Jonathan's voice, trying to will him into focus. Slowly she seemed to manage it, only to have her eyes drawn behind him, where the titular cartoon character smiled back at her from a large display.

"It is a pleasure to have you on board," Mr. Clean said.

The AI's words did not so much come from the display in front of her. Rather as if she were in a theater with state-of-the-art surround sound.

At a loss for how to react to that, she took in the rest of their surroundings. It was a small oval room, lacking any unnecessary decoration. The walls and ceiling were simple white paneling, the floor a hard-white cement. The chairs they had been given were overly padded white leather affairs that sat on swivels.

While it all seemed rather innocuous, she noticed two things she didn't like. The first, she saw no doors in or out. Second—

"Where is the alien?"

Jonathan crossed his arms over his chest. "Heyer won't be joining us. He sends his sincerest regrets."

Jonathan's expression gave her nothing. She couldn't tell if he was taking a jab or simply telling her how things were.

"Are we to assume you speak on his behalf?" General Delacy asked.

Jonathan took a long breath, his gaze going back and forth between her and Delacy. "This is getting off on the wrong foot. I've asked you here to discuss the list of requests I made the last time we spoke. If you came for Heyer, I assure you that he is impossible to reach and will be for quite some time."

"And how is that exactly?" Olivia asked.

Jonathan met her gaze. "He is not currently in this dimension."

Silence followed for a moment as they stared at each other. Far more timid than her company, Dr. Watts raised a hand as though requesting to be called on.

"What is it, Mags?" Jonathan said, his demeanor far more relaxed.

Mags? Olivia thought. The doctor's first name was Margaret, but he spoke to her as though they were grade school buddies.

"Um, are we prisoners? There's no door in this room."

"No one is in any danger, you're free to leave any time. Doors will be there when they're necessary. This room is just a place we thought it best to have a chat before. . ."

He trailed off. "Before we get into it."

Dr. Watts smiled politely as she brought her hand back down.

"What about my daughter?" General Delacy asked. "Is she free to go whenever she wishes?"

Jonathan glanced to Leah as though he thought it strange the question was directed at him. "Look, I'm not a warden, this isn't a prison, and if you want to ask her something you don't need to run it through me."

"Dad, right now this is where I want to be," Leah said. "When . . . if . . . that changes, I'm free to go."

"In that scenario, just where might you be planning on heading?" Olivia asked.

Several telling looks were exchanged between Leah, her father, and Olivia.

"Enough," Rivers said. "We're here to discuss the big picture. Any come-uppance anyone feels entitled to can wait."

A moment of tense silence passed.

"Strange," Olivia said, looking at Jonathan. "Don't you know exactly how this is all going to play out?"

He shook his head. "I could have. But it's not how I want to do this. I'd rather we all be on equal footing this time."

For the moment she stood still in the middle of a forest. The General and Dr. Watts not far behind her. She was still getting used to the shifting environment.

A group of seven men moved around them, through the trees—sometimes through them. The faces were blurred. The voices distorted. Still, Olivia recognized the coordinated movements of trained soldiers.

They used as little unnecessary communication as possible, yet they carried no firearms and wore no camouflage. Their gear was tactical, but not meant to hide them. The weapons they did carry were all blunted steel.

As they had before, the soldiers eventually moved beyond where she could observe them, and Mr. Clean updated the projection around them. It was as though they jumped forward in space to be placed amongst the soldiers once again.

While the details of this entire experience seemed perfectly lifelike, there were surreal moments. As they observed these men, it was clear they were capable of things no mere human should be. Sometimes they moved too fast, jumped into the trees like something out of a comic book, only to drop back down from heights that should have left their bodies a crumpled pile of broken bones.

Yet, there was an absence of any small details that might have made what they were observing feel staged. Even being completely immersed by what Jonathan called a projection, there was no feeling that they were placed in some sort of slick VR production.

She listened in on their radio chatter; the men were taking directions from one amongst them. For reasons that were uncertain, the navigator seemed to know exactly where they were heading.

"We're close," the navigator said. "Fifty yards, give or take . . . and . . . he definitely knows we're here."

The men readied themselves, as an unearthly growl came out of the woods. For a moment she nearly expected Sasquatch to come barreling through the bushes. What came, she recognized as the living incarnation of the creature they had pulled out of the sands in Libya.

She could tell that the video had been manipulated in some portions. But not such that it was meant to tell a lie. Rather, the footage was slowed down so that they could see what was happening without the events becoming a blur of motion that was too fast for the human eye to make out clearly.

As the seven men worked together to subdue this creature—this Ferox— it broke full-grown trees in half. Picked up boulders that must have weighed as much as tanks only to launch them at a disturbing velocity toward the men attempting to bring it under control. She noticed that while all the men in the videos were wearing masks, there was one exception: Jonathan.

So, he was hiding the identities of all the men around him.

"This isn't possible," Dr. Watts said as she watched the footage. "The physics involved just aren't possible."

Olivia eyed Jonathan after Dr. Watts' statement, but he only smiled and shook his head. "I don't disagree. If I were you I'd worry I was being tricked by some movie with incredible special effects. But, after having been on the receiving end of one of their fists, you don't spend too long reminding yourself that it shouldn't be possible. It's the reality we have to deal with."

"But, if you expect us to believe what these things are capable of there must be some explanation," Dr. Watts said.

"I'm a college drop-out, Mags," Jonathan said. "Take it up with Mr. Clean though, he might be able to give you some insight."

"Perhaps I will," Dr. Watts said.

She looked about her surroundings. "How do I get out of the projection?"

A doorway manifested beside her. Mr. Clean, looking somewhat eager, waited in the oval chamber. A moment later Dr. Watts walked out, and the doorway disappeared back into the projection. Delacy was still watching the men subdue the creature. That left Jonathan standing beside Olivia.

"Something's on your mind, Olivia," Jonathan said. "So just say it."

"Fine, all this looks very real," Olivia said. "But we both know what that AI is capable of. How am I supposed to know that any of this is true?"

"I intend to introduce you," Jonathan said. "But this is still the safest way to make you aware of their capabilities. That . . . and there is still something I want you to see."

As though anticipating this moment, Olivia and Jonathan left the Delacys and entered a new record. They were in the same forest, but on a different night. Jonathan pointed, and while there was no monster to be seen, Olivia could infer from the disruption of branches and trees that something large and essentially invisible was moving about.

She saw what must have been Jonathan's past-self move in to engage the invisible creature. She noted that he seemed to do so with a strength and speed that surpassed the monster's. Again, he was the only one on the screen whose identity was clear.

"You don't want me to know who these other men working with you are?"

"You don't need to know," he said.

"But you expect me to believe that you and everyone in this video are capable of—all this?" Olivia asked.

He took a long breath. "Just keep watching."

In the moments that followed Olivia watched as a green gas erupted from the invisible creature. She saw Jonathan's concern as he sent his men away. She saw the whole night's events up to the creature being subdued.

"You captured it," she said.

"That was the point of the operation," Jonathan said. "But the spontaneous combustion wasn't part of the plan."

"Is that man speaking with it? And how exactly is he sticking to that tree?" Olivia asked.

Jonathan ignored the questions, pulled her attention to something else in the record. She saw a look of deep concern on Jonathan's face—the Jonathan in the record more than the one standing beside her—as he held a thick black sludge in his hand.

"That is what you wanted me to see?" Olivia asked.

"That is what was left of an armored alien steel plate," Jonathan said. "I know you understand what that means. After all, I had to steal my equipment back from you when we left."

When the oval room vanished around them, Olivia saw she was standing in what appeared to be a walled off portion of an exceptionally large building. When the walls were gone, she found herself in a plain, somewhat disappointingly typical-looking warehouse. There were windows near the ceiling, but for the most part a great deal of open space and polished cement floors.

While the room itself wasn't very exciting, it did hold five cages.

There was plenty of space between her and the cages, Jonathan wasn't trying to give any of them a scare. She could see that each was made with the same alien steel; she was familiar with the unique way it caught the light.

As she turned, she noticed that only four of the cages currently had occupants.

She had to steady herself. Even knowing she was safe, looking back into the white gaze of these creatures was like trying to stare down a nightmare. In fact, the longer she held any of their eyes, the angrier the things seemed to get. Struggling against the steel as though she were declaring herself a predator looking for a fight.

"You're riling them up. Look away," Jonathan said. "We call that one *Mr. Grumpy.*"

She turned her head. When she did, she noticed that General Delacy and Dr. Watts had joined them but were keeping their distance. Leah did not appear to have come along.

A muffled sort of growl came from the beast. She saw Jonathan give the creature a look, as though he agreed with something.

"Did that thing just talk, Mr. Tibbs?" Olivia asked.

Jonathan nodded.

"And you could understand it, even through the muzzle," she asked.

"It's a long story," Jonathan said. "Suffice it to say the language can be translated into English—just very poorly."

"And what did it say?"

"*Grumpy* wants you in the arena," Jonathan said. "He's as impressed as he is offended, that you looked him in the eyes that long."

The creature growled something again, and this time Jonathan only shrugged.

"Now he's offended that I'm introducing him as *Grumpy* instead of his real name," Jonathan said.

"They have names?"

"Yeah," Jonathan said, not letting the monster see him roll his eyes as he held up one hand. "This is *Chews the Tooth.*"

"So, they're sentient? They have language?" Olivia asked.

"You were hoping for mindless beasts?" Jonathan asked.

Olivia didn't reply. She, the General, and Dr. Watts only moved in for a closer look.

"Well, you can't fake this," Dr. Watts said. "But how do we know it's capable of what you showed us in the videos? You gonna let one out?"

Jonathan raised an eyebrow. "If you absolutely must see it. But I'd really appreciate it if that could be the line where you simply take me at my word. That said . . ."

Jonathan held out a hand for them to follow him. "If you can stomach the necessary cruelty, I have a demonstration."

"*Cruelty?*" Dr. Watts whispered uncomfortably as she followed him, wisely giving the cages a wide birth.

He took them to what looked like two large mechanisms under dustcovers. He pulled the covers off and revealed two very familiar looking miniguns.

"You may recognize these, but they aren't firing blanks today," Jonathan said.

As they crossed a threshold, Mr. Clean formed a translucent wall between them and the cages, only letting the barrels of the guns through with enough space to rotate.

"This one is loaded with standard military grade rounds," Jonathan said. "Would one of you like to do the honors?"

To their credit, none appeared eager to shoot at a helpless creature, but the General finally stepped forward. When he opened fire, no one was surprised—they stared in disbelief—but were not surprised. *Chews the Tooth* took the fire, he squirmed—more in anger than pain, but nothing penetrated his armored flesh. Meanwhile, bullets ricocheted wildly around the room on the other side of the translucent shield.

The General fired longer than was necessary, as though he thought that if he kept the bullets trained on one spot long enough, he could eat his way through. By the time he gave up, a few drops of black blood fell to the floor.

"Well, at least it's not invincible," the General said.

"Look closer," Jonathan replied.

Unsure, the General did as he was asked, and to his surprise he found the blood was not coming from where he'd concentrated the fire. *Chews the Tooth* bled where one of the alien steel restraints had eaten into his flesh. He had fought so hard to free himself under the barrage of fire, that his own strength against his bonds had drawn blood.

Olivia and the General exchanged worried glances.

"You say these things intend to invade—how many?" the General asked.

"I don't have exact numbers," Jonathan said. "But I believe I can deal with roughly ten thousand before my men will be overwhelmed."

"Ten thousand," Dr. Watts' words had come out a whisper.

"How many men do you have?" Olivia asked.

He turned his gaze on her. "Just short of four hundred."

"Four hundred!"

The anger in Olivia's voice was—multilayered.

On the one hand, she was finding out that she'd seriously underestimated Heyer's activity. On the other, she'd just learned the number of enemy combatants Jonathan expected—and despite what she'd seen them capable of on those videos—she knew 400 wasn't going to stand a chance.

"I told you," Jonathan said. "A day was coming that we were going to need one another. Well, it's almost here. I'm not going to be able to give you much of a warning."

She frowned at him. "You'll know when they're coming?"

"Mr. Clean estimates he'll be able to give us 6 to 8 days' notice."

"Why such a range?" Dr. Watts asked.

"The conduit they intend to open is too massive to hide," Jonathan said. "Mr. Clean will know when they activate it. But there is a highly complicated time distortion between our dimension and theirs. It makes a precise time of arrival impossible.

"There is good news though," Jonathan said. "With some calculation and maneuvering of my men, we have some control over where the conduit will open."

There was a moment of silence that followed. Then the General spoke up, "Perhaps this is a stupid question, but if you can target where they'll enter, why not open their portal at the bottom of the Pacific Ocean?"

Jonathan smiled. "Not a stupid question, General. I asked it myself months ago. Mr. Clean will be happy to explain the dynamics of the gateway's protocols and how we intend to pick our battleground, but the short version is we can't deliberately open the gateway into a location that will drop the enemy into immediate danger. If we tried, the conduit would simply recalculate to a better position. There is a little wiggle room we can play with, but the Ferox are gonna hit land and it's gonna be on a major continent."

"Makes sense if you think about it," Dr. Watts said. "I wouldn't create a way to travel through space and time if there wasn't some way to be sure it didn't deliver me into the middle of a volcano."

The General considered this for a minute.

"Then you target them, and we nuke their asses the moment they step through," General Delacy said.

"It won't work, for more than a couple reasons," Jonathan nodded to the caged Ferox in the room. "These grunts are low-tech and deadly, but their leader is our worst nightmare. He isn't one of them—he's Borealis, one of Heyer's species. And he really doesn't like humanity."

Jonathan let them grapple with this for a moment, before going on. "His name is Malkier, though they call him their prophet. He is aware of our military's capabilities and his first move will be to take out our technology—especially anything that runs on electricity. Now, I can't tell you for sure just how far back into the stone age he will put us, combustion engines should work as long as the ignition is fairly simple, but anything too sophisticated is gonna fail. We are gonna be fighting these things with . . . old-fashioned weapons."

"You said there were more reasons," Olivia said.

"Yeah, if I'm wrong—which I'm not—then you'll be dropping a nuclear weapon into the middle of all my men. To target that gateway to a location of our choosing, my entire army will need to be within 2 miles, most of us a lot closer. Even if we could go nuclear, I'd like to try my way first."

Olivia considered him for a long while. Though what she was really thinking about was the list of things he *requested* the day of his escape.

"Is this why you want to evacuate the city, why you want us to set up a perimeter? You think you can contain them . . . but you aren't going to risk all your men unless you've failed."

"I have a plan," Jonathan said. "But until I know we are on the same page, that is as much as I'm telling you."

He turned away from them then and walked over to a table that had clearly been set up in preparation of their arrival. He pulled off another dustcover and revealed an arsenal of explosives.

"I prepared these in case you needed to see for yourself that explosives, while effective to some extent, aren't going to get the job done against the numbers we'll be facing."

Olivia looked at the table. She quickly lost any interest in its contents. "It's clear you already know how that experiment will go," Olivia said. "So why don't you tell us what will be effective."

Jonathan gave her a sly grin, then walked to the end of the table and picked up an assault rifle. Beside it was a magazine. He loaded it, then asked which of them would prefer to do the honors.

This time, Olivia took the weapon.

"We need it alive," Jonathan said. "Aim for a limb."

"What do you need them alive for?" Dr. Watts asked.

"Testing," Jonathan said.

Olivia took aim at *Chews the Tooth*'s leg. Some of the shots ricocheted as she pulled the trigger but eventually a black splat of blood hit the floor in front of them.

"Why did that work?" the General asked.

Jonathan retrieved the magazine from the gun and showed them.

"Alien steel rounds," Dr. Watts said.

Jonathan smiled at her. "I missed you Mags, you deserve every dime they're paying you."

"Th . . . thanks," she said, awkwardly.

A look of relief had come over the General and Dr. Watts. Olivia knew what they were thinking, if guns could still be brought into the equation, then all the strength and speed of these creatures wasn't going to give them enough advantage.

Olivia didn't share their relief.

"The WX gas," she said.

"Yeah, we have a plan," Jonathan said. "I want to arm your men with these bullets. I can supply more than you'll ever need, but you aren't going to be able to get close to the city. You're going to need to keep the cargo in airtight containers, so the gas won't get to them. And you'll only be using it to shred what breaks through my army's containment. We've got a few other toys to help you, but again—"

"Only if we're all on the same page here," Olivia finished for him.

He nodded.

"Jonathan," General Delacy said. "What you are asking is no simple military operation. You want us to convince the President and the Joint Chiefs of Staff to let a kid, who can barely buy a beer legally, wage war with an alien species on US soil. And it seems like you want command?"

"General, if I were stupid enough to want command, I would tell you not to give it to me," Jonathan said. "But, even after everything I've shown you, you don't really know how this war is gonna be fought."

"So, if you think you've got a better person for the job, I'd love to meet them."

The General didn't respond, not right away. He seemed to be waiting for Jonathan to say something more, but nothing followed.

"Everything you are asking for is going to cause an uncontainable world-wide panic. You seem certain you can deliver a victory this time. What about the next? This attack is going to change mankind's entire understanding of its place in the universe. People will be living in fear," Olivia said.

"No," Jonathan said. "They won't. I repeat. You don't understand how this war is going to be fought. You don't even know what victory looks like. My army—we understand. I need you to convince those with the power to make it happen to put their faith in us."

"You mean in you," Olivia said.

Jonathan's jaw tightened, but he did not argue.

They stared at one another a long while.

"General Delacy, Dr. Watts," Olivia finally said. "Please give Mr. Tibbs and I a moment alone."

While at first, General Delacy didn't seem to think he should be left out of any discussion, a quick glance exchanged between him and Olivia seemed to convince him. The look was not a glare, not a warning, simply a nod that she knew what she was about, and he should trust her. His hesitation ended almost immediately.

Observing this, Jonathan was momentarily envious. How nice to share command with someone who has such faith in your judgement.

When they were alone, Olivia asked. "Do you know what I'm thinking?"

He looked into her eyes for a moment. "You want to trust me, but you can't."

"That's right," she said.

Jonathan closed his eyes. "It's not me, you know. I've never broken my word. Never lied to you."

"Good people always keep their word—until they can't," Olivia said.

He shrugged, but there was a sadness in him. "I am all out of ideas. Tell me what you want."

She was quiet for a while.

"There is something," Olivia said. "The name. How did you get it from me and how much do you know?"

Jonathan winced, a guilty smile forming on his lips.

"This is no joke, Mr. Tibbs," Olivia said.

"I know," Jonathan said. "But the truth might still make you laugh."

"I'm waiting."

"All I knew was the name, Olivia. You assumed it meant I knew more."

Her eyes narrowed, studying him with suspicion as she seemed to consider.

"The name then," Olivia said. "How did you get it from me?"

He bit down on his lip for moment, then looked into her eyes and nodded. "Let me tell you a story about the most stubborn woman in the world."

THE QUEUE LOOP | ACTIVATION THREE

Barefoot and still wearing the white prisoner outfit they had issued him, Jonathan stepped out of the hallway that opened into the larger hangar bay. He estimated there were over sixty men spread out in a half circle around the opening. Some were out in the open, but most had found cover or put up some sort of a barricade.

Every single one had a weapon trained at him.

He came to an abrupt stop, and every man in the room stared down with cautious fear at the light blazing beneath the thin fabric of his shirt. Scanning the faces, he finally spotted her watching him from behind a hastily erected barricade.

When he caught her eyes, he held her with a gaze that pleaded before he yelled, "Scarred Dragonfly, Olivia."

Her brow shot up in surprise. For a few tense seconds no one in the hangar seemed to breathe—including Jonathan. He watched as her mind raced to understand how he could possibly have known to speak those words. Then he felt the Ferox moving outside. For the briefest moment, his eyes broke from hers as he judged the monster's distance from them.

When he looked back to Olivia—something had changed—and not for the good. Her eyes had narrowed into slits of suspicion—hardened to the brink of anger.

"Oliv—"

"Open fire!"

Jonathan only had enough time for his expression to ask the question *you-can't-be-serious?* Then he was pelted with a barrage of bullets—hit with more lead than he had ever been on the receiving end of. Within seconds the thin fabric of his clothing was a tattered mess.

Then, as though life could not pass up the opportunity to be funny—a lucky shot pinged against his open eye.

If Hayden asked again, he could now confirm that the experience was unpleasant. Suddenly, Jonathan found himself standing at the center of a barrage of machine gun fire with one hand shielding his face, flinching as though a hard wind had blown dust in his eye. He got over it quickly enough, but as he parted his fingers to see Olivia again, he had just enough time to see the man standing nearest to her pull the trigger on what looked like . . .

"Ahhh, hell."

He hardly had time to think RPG before an explosion went off in the middle of his chest. A second later he was flying back down the hallway and slamming into the elevator doors.

He found himself sitting with both legs straight out in front of him. Ears ringing as he coughed out a lungful of black smoke.

He could still feel bullets managing to hit him from all the way back in the hangar but for the moment he couldn't hear them. He got to his feet, saw that some of the agents were growing braver, now that they had seen him knocked down, to approach the mouth of the hallway.

"Well, screw this . . ." he said, getting to his feet.

He looked down to see he barely had any clothing left to speak of, then headed to his left. It was the most direct route toward the Ferox's location outside. He was running at a good clip as he neared the end. At the last moment, he dropped one shoulder and brought his arm up as a shield before ramming a hole through the wall. A second later his bare feet were running through the grassy field outside the hangar.

"I hate that woman," he said, not bothering to look back as he broke into a sprint for the Ferox.

THE QUEUE LOOP | ACTIVATION FOUR

Wearing armored gear he'd borrowed off the guards in the facility's lower tunnels, Jonathan once again stepped out of the elevator and into the hallway of the hangar bay. Not much had changed from the last time—he was surrounded again. The men armed to the teeth and waiting for him again.

His eyes went straight to Olivia behind her barricade.

He kept the tone of his voice calm. "Olivia! You promised me, if I spoke these words, you would hear me out!"

She said nothing but eyed him with a wary curiosity.

"The Drowning Monk incident of '98."

The same look of surprise came over her. Jonathan didn't so much as blink when he felt the Ferox's movement outside. He watched every crease of her face. A few seconds later doubt began to harden in her eyes again.

The moment before she spoke, Jonathan yelled. "No, no, no, no . . . there's more . . . um . . . Scarred Dragonfly! Scarred Dragonf—"

"Open Fire!"

Groaning, "Ohhh, you monumental pain in the . . ."

He leaped forward, racing across the room instead of giving them a stationary target. The bullets managing to hit were far less, fewer and fewer agents having clear shots that would not risk hitting their allies.

He saw fear take Olivia as he charged toward her, and she began to back away from her cover. He was over the barricade before she managed five steps backward. The gunfire almost ceased completely once he was standing so close to the agents' commanding officer. But, he didn't go for her first, he grabbed the man beside her who was in the middle of exchanging his M4 for an RPG.

"Nope . . ." Jonathan said, yanking the weapon away from the man with one hand and tossing him up and over the barricade with the other.

Then he turned his attention back on Olivia. She was almost pressed against the wall of the hangar with a small sidearm leveled at him. He took a step toward her just as a wooden baton broke in half across his forehead.

Jonathan turned to the man holding the broken end in annoyance before grabbing him by the Kevlar on his chest and shoving him across the floor with a flick of his wrist.

A moment later, the firing stopped all together when he lifted Olivia off the ground by her shirt collar.

"You are the most infuriatingly stubborn . . ."

He trailed off as he looked into her eyes and saw pure panic. She looked as though she thought he were a second from ripping her in half. Her agents were quickly surrounding them.

Jonathan closed his eyes and took a long breath. When he opened them, he looked up at her with a smile that really did nothing to hide his anger. He spoke loud and slow, as though she were a child. "We seem to be having an issue with our communication."

THE QUEUE LOOP | ACTIVATION NINE

There was only Jonathan and Olivia now. Everyone else in the hangar had been immobilized. A few moments earlier, while he was busy with the rest of the agents, Olivia and two armed escorts tried to make a run for reinforcements. As a result, the larger bay door stood open letting in light from the outside. He'd quickly dealt with the two agents, and Olivia had found him right in front of her outside the hangar.

For the next few seconds, he felt like a sheep dog trying to herd her back to the hangar as she tried to get to a vehicle parked out in front.

"Your favorite book as a child was, *Where the Red Fern Grows*," he said.

She backed away, caught sight of a weapon near the outstretched hand of one of the unconscious agents and dove for it. His foot stepped down and obliterated the rifle before she could get her hands on it.

"Are you even listening?" Jonathan asked. "Broken Hill, Australia, '96?"

She crawled back on hands and knees and struggled to her feet while he cocked his head at her. "Hotan, China, '89?"

She grimaced, his words bringing rage and not a willingness to consider how or why he knew to speak them.

How would he ever get her to see he wasn't trying to trick her?

Olivia's eyes set on the vehicle once again.

"Boston! Ms. Hong's Bakery. The best Nuomici you've ever had."

Olivia made a break for it.

"Oh, come on!" he yelled after her. "I don't even know what Nuomici is!"

He landed in front of her again and she nearly ran into him before stumbling back to the ground.

"How? How do you know any of this!"

Jonathan lifted his hands in front of him and mimed an urge to strangle her. "You! You told me! This is your idea! Seven times! Seven times you've told me you'd listen if I just gave you the right signal. We go through this every time!"

He raised his voice a few octaves in a poor impression of Olivia's, "It has to be something no one else could know. Something only I could have told you."

Unamused, he saw her hand reaching slowly for the front pocket of her coat.

The agitation left his face and he held up his palms. "Please don't, Olivia."

Her hand paused, but only for a moment before the inching continued.

"I could have taken it from you at any time. You have to know that!" He said as her hand locked around the trigger in her pocket.

She brought the trigger out, putting her thumb on the button.

"I'm not trying to take the alien from you," Jonathan said. "Dammit, listen!"

Jonathan felt it coming long before its arrival. He'd considered himself lucky that all the noise from the hangar hadn't drawn it sooner. He grimaced when the beast landed twenty feet behind him, smashing the very vehicle Olivia had been trying to reach with its landing. The ground shook, and Olivia nearly pressed the trigger when she jerked in surprise.

Jonathan heard the word translate in his mind as the guttural growls of Feroxian vocal cords filled the air behind him. *Challenger.*

He looked at Olivia one last time, shrugging with his palms turned up. "Scarred Dragonfly?"

She didn't seem to hear him—had forgotten he existed—now that her attention was fully focused on the massive Ferox stepping off of the crushed vehicle.

"Go back inside, shut the bay doors. Try not to blow the place up," Jonathan said, as he turned to face the beast.

He gave the—Red, it turned out—Ferox a shake of the head. "I swear . . . one of these times I'm going to let one of you eat her. Just to see if it's therapeutic."

The Ferox's face studied him as though uncertain of the translation it was hearing.

Challeng—

"Oh, just shut up."

THE QUEUE | ACTIVATION TEN

Helicopters flew overhead, following him from a safe distance as he returned to the hangar. Jonathan dragged a Green Ferox behind him. The beast was hogtied with a chain of alien steel, bloodied from a one-sided fight it never had a hope of winning, but it still had enough spirit to thrash against its restraints.

Despite Olivia's repeated promises, he'd given up on a scenario where he had a rational, albeit rapid, discussion with her inside the hangar. No matter what he tried or what words he spoke, he either ended up in a prolonged negotiation with Olivia, or fighting his way through guards to the surface. This time, he used the one hour of assistance Mr. Clean could offer before protocols forced the AI's consciousness into hibernation to be teleported outside the hangar beside a chain of alien steel long enough to subdue the Ferox.

As he returned, men poured out of the hangar and surrounded him.

"Olivia, I need a word," Jonathan yelled.

A moment passed, then the men parted for her like she was the conductor of an orchestra. She had her weapon drawn as she stepped out of the throng of heavily armed agents.

One motion of her hand was followed by a familiar unison of sound—that of so many different weapons being prepared to fire on him. A hushed moment passed like the downbeat before a performance. To Jonathan, even the helicopter blades whirring in the background seemed to fade like an audience growing quiet in anticipation. As she stepped close enough to speak, she leveled her weapon on him.

One word from her, one gesture, and Jonathan would be hearing the same song her agents had played for him with every iteration of the Queue Loop. Moving ever so slowly, he tossed the length of chain down at her feet and waited. She eyed the Ferox warily, having seen what that Beast was capable of before watching him subdue it.

Every time they played this game, one thing was certain—she wanted the specimen, and alive was a better bargaining chip than dead. So, this time he was starting their dialogue with something tangible to get her listening.

"Mr. Tibbs. One step. One move. One look I don't like . . ."

She chose to give a nod to the men surrounding them rather than finish the threat.

He had to fight the desire to make a flippant remark. Still, the frustration he felt about her statement couldn't be entirely kept from his face.

"Avriel Mikhailov."

Olivia blinked. She looked as though someone had stepped on her grave. He could see her fighting the urge to stumble back—to hold her ground. Her bottom lip trembled.

While there was no chance anyone else had heard the words he spoke, Olivia's eyes left his, searching the faces of the men surrounding them. As though she couldn't gamble with the possibility that a single one might know that name.

She swallowed, calmed her panic before it gave way to paranoia. She looked at him again and he held her gaze, but he saw her expression hardening against him . . . again.

"You told me you were sure. That there was no way to know that name. That only you could have said it to me. You made me promise I'd never speak it to anyone but you. I've kept that promise. I won't say it to them even if you order them to kill me . . . but, please . . ."

His voice became pleading, "Please, just try to believe what I came to say."

Slowly, Olivia let her weapon lower to her side. She stepped closer, only stopping when she was at arm's reach.

Her voice trembled, "Believe what?"

Jonathan let out a long breath. "That you and I need to be allies."

CHAPTER SEVENTY-EIGHT

NOV 12, 2005 | 3 PM | HANGMAN'S TREE

SHE'D LISTENED AS he recounted these glimpses of his time in the queue loop. When he'd finished she was thoughtful. Then she laughed—actually it was more of a snort.

Jonathan frowned somewhat sourly at her. "It makes sense that the one time I see you laugh—it's from hearing how much of a pain in my ass you were."

"Perspective," Olivia said, clearing her throat. "Consider how much trouble you've caused me."

His face softened. "Fair enough."

She sighed and her smile faded back behind a wall of cement before she signaled to General Delacy and Dr. Watts to rejoin them. Then she said as she offered a hand to him, "Mr. Tibbs, I want to hear how you intend to deal with our pending apocalypse."

He shook her hand, but before the others were within earshot, she pulled him close enough to whisper. "This better be impressive."

"Your shadows were consulted," he whispered back.

"Hmm," she said approvingly as they parted.

By the time they were ready to part ways the sun was going down. Jonathan held out a small thumb drive to Olivia.

"Everything you've seen here, as well as the necessary specifics of everything we've discussed," Jonathan said. "If the President or the Pentagon still need to see with their own eyes, I'll make it happen. I'm not giving up this location or the identities of anyone. So, if they come, they'll get here the same way you did."

Olivia took the drive. She studied him again, as though she needed to stare him down one last time to be sure.

"I wouldn't blame you," she said, "if you can't live up to this bargain when the time comes."

"I won't run, Olivia," Jonathan said. "And yes, you would."

Perhaps accidentally, some warmth slipped into her expression. Then immediately slipped away again. "In regard to Grant Morgan, I understand that you've agreed to his requests. But if I'm being honest, if you were going to break your word on some part of this . . ."

Jonathan sighed. "If he keeps his end of the bargain, then it doesn't matter."

His arm came up again, and she thought he was going to offer a final handshake, but his palm revealed another small metal disc like the one she'd used to travel here. It reshaped itself into something that looked more like a small Bluetooth earpiece.

"This will get you home, and you'll be able to reach me directly," he said. "If nothing else, I'll be in contact when we know they're coming."

She looked at the device like it was another bite from a meal that had already given her food poisoning, then picked it up and placed it in her ear. It fit as though it had been sculpted for her.

"Alright then," Olivia said.

"Good luck, Olivia," Jonathan said.

He looked behind her, and saw that the General was discussing something privately with Leah while Dr. Watts was actively engaged in a conversation with Mr. Clean and clearly in no hurry to leave.

"What'll it be, Mags?" Jonathan asked. "Staying or going?"

She didn't have to think for long. "Ma'am, with your permission I'd like to see if I can be of any further assistance here. I'm also rather curious to see what else my—shadow's—efforts have contributed."

Olivia looked to Rivers. "I suppose I can trust you to make sure Dr. Watts comes back to us in one piece?"

"Yes, ma'am," Rivers said.

When Olivia and the General had departed, Jonathan approached Dr. Watts.

"You know only my closest friends call me Mags," she said.

"Habit," Jonathan said.

She gave him a curious look. "This queue loop you spoke of, did you really spend so much time with my shadow that she asked you to call her Mags?"

He nodded. "I spent more time in a lab under that facility talking to you than anyone else in The Cell. Which brings me to the real reason I needed you to stay."

"Should I be excited or nervous?" Watts asked.

"Say your shadow's work led to a discovery—a discovery that could very well be what decides our fate. You'd want to finish where she left off, wouldn't you?"

"Anyone who calls me Mags would know the answer to that question."

Jonathan smiled. "He would."

With a nod to follow, she fell into step beside him. He took her to the southwest side of Hangman's Tree. To the rear of the section where Anthony's Mechs were stored, they passed several large shipping pallets. Each were marked with various hazardous chemical signs. Though, as Dr. Watts caught the names of a few of the large totes and barrels, she knew most of the components weren't particularly hazardous by themselves. If anything they were used in—

"This way," Jonathan said as he held open a door. She entered what could only be described as a fully equipped biology lab. Except, some of the equipment was clearly intended to manufacture far more of something than anyone could ever use in an experiment.

"I have presented Mr. Clean with what you discovered. Turns out he already knew, of course, but—you'll find that regardless of how much Mr. Clean might know, he isn't always aware when it might be important to share. That is, until you ask the right question.

"Once I told him what you'd discovered, and asked if it might achieve a particular result, he got to work on a prototype. I'd like you to complete the testing with him."

Dr. Watts looked about the laboratory. "You still haven't told me what it was I discovered."

"It's a bit of a story."

THE QUEUE LOOP | ACTIVATION THIRTEEN

He'd just taken care of specimen thirteen. What he sent back through the gates was often more Ferox soup than Ferox. This had been his twelfth time explaining to Dr. Watts that once they had done all they could with a test subject, he had to send the body back in a way that both hid the work they were doing and at the same time sent Malkier a message.

That message was a simple one: *Something tore your people to shreds—and took a lot of pleasure doing so.*

He wanted Malkier to wonder about the mental state of whoever killed his people.

He had just finished carrying the last bag full of specimen thirteen to the lab and as he dumped the contents onto a large sheet of plastic lining the floor, he glanced at Dr. Watts. He could tell, she was on the brink. By this time, most of The Cell was no longer useful to him. The degradation having set in.

He'd been keeping an eye on her shadow for a while now. She tended to hold onto sanity longer than others. In fact, Jonathan was beginning to suspect that it had something to do with her work keeping her in such proximity to the portal stone itself.

He had seen another shadow show incredible resilience to the degradation in his first queue—and this was the only similarity he could pinpoint in their circumstances.

Regardless, Dr. Watts wasn't immune. Eventually, she would snap. He generally wanted her as far away from the stone and any of her research notes as possible before that happened. He finished emptying the bags of Ferox, and was just walking up behind her when she suddenly jumped back, her stool flying backward across the floor as she started cursing in panic.

"Crap! Crap! Jonathan! Crap!" She said as she slammed the front window of the BSC shut and back pedaled as quickly as she could until she ran into him.

"I . . . I didn't think—it was just an idea. I didn't think it would . . . attack me."

He looked past her into the BSC and saw what had her so startled. The portal stone was no longer held securely inside its vise. It was no longer a stone at all, but had taken on a liquid state. Until now, the only time Jonathan had seen that happen was after he crushed the stone in his hand.

The glowing orange liquid now smeared itself across the window of the bio safety cabinet, seemed to be reaching out for her.

"Get back," Jonathan said, as he pushed her gently behind him.

As he stepped closer, he realized the fluid wasn't reaching for Dr. Watts. It certainly would have seemed like that was the case when he was coming up behind her, but now as he swayed back and forth in front of the window it followed him on the other side of the glass.

"I swear, I've tried a thousand things, I didn't really think this would work anymore than the rest."

"Mags, take a breath. Tell me what happened?"

She took his advice. He watched as she forced herself to take some long calming breaths.

"Squalene. I put a solution of concentrated squalene on it," Dr. Watts said.

"Mags, I know you haven't heard it yet, but for me this is the twelfth time I've had to tell you that I barely got a C in biochem," Jonathan said. "And that class was graded on a curve."

"It's a component of human skin oil," Dr. Watts said. "I didn't think it was having any effect, then, suddenly it reached for me."

Absorbing this, his eyes narrowing thoughtfully as he stared at that liquid energy. Then his eyes went wide.

"You said you didn't think it was working?"

"It shattered all of a sudden, I'd barely put any pressure on the scalpel."

"Right when I got close to you."

Dr. Watts nodded.

How had it never occurred to him? The stone had only ever turned fragile when he held it in his bare hands. He'd assumed it was contact with the skin of an implanted man, he'd never considered its trigger was simpler than that—a chemical.

He had to think for a moment, but even with the liquid in the BSC, he didn't like the idea of leaving it in that state. Not when nearly the entire facility had given into the degradation.

Jonathan closed his eyes. "I need you to get back, Mags. Actually, it would probably be best if you get all the way out of the lab and lock the door behind you."

"What are you going to do?"

"Take care of it," Jonathan said.

Mags looked unsure, but she nodded and exited the lab. He was glad she hadn't thought to ask questions. The only way to *take care* of the stone was to absorb it.

That meant the end of this reality.

Obviously, he didn't want her to spend those last few seconds with the existential dread of what came after he absorbed the stone.

He lifted the window on the hood and lowered his hand to the eager glowing liquid. It reached for him like a pet reunited with its owner. The moment it touched his skin it began to absorb, burning its way up his arm. He fell to the floor. The portal formed around him, the black and red sphere filling the lab.

Then came the white flash.

Mags and her dimension collapsing behind him.

CHAPTER SEVENTY-NINE

NOV 12, 2005 | 9 PM | HANGMAN'S TREE

"MY SHADOW FOUND a way to destabilize portal stones," Dr. Watts said. She considered this for a while then frowned. "And that helps you somehow?"

Jonathan nodded. "You, me, and Mr. Clean are the only ones who know about this. That will change when the time is right, until then, I need your word that this stays between us."

She shrugged. "Alright. But I don't understand what you want me to . . ."

Dr. Watts paused; she took a second look around the lab, specifically at what equipment the space had on hand. Then she considered the list of chemical components she'd noticed on the way in, and her head tilted back to him with sudden understanding. "Ohhh . . . I see. It would have to be airborne, and you'd need a ton of it. But even if it's possible, how are you going to trigger the—"

"Leave that part to me, Mags," Jonathan said.

Somewhat reluctantly, she nodded. "I'll . . . um . . . I'll need at least two of your prisoners. More would be better if you can get them."

"They're all for you," he said.

The next morning Leah sat alone. It was early and as per usual the dining area was near empty. Her breakfast sat finished in front of her as she read from the tablet that Mr. Clean had provided. Someone pulled out a chair across from her at the table. Surprised anyone who saw her hadn't decided to sit on the opposite side of the room, she looked up and saw Colonel Hamill take a seat across from her.

"Leah is it?" he asked, politely pretending that everyone didn't know who she was.

"Yeah . . ." she said. She frowned and gave the empty dining hall a not so subtle look, clearly taking note of all the other empty tables he could have taken a seat at.

"May I share your table for a moment?" he asked.

"I'd prefer to be alone," she said.

He didn't seem to have expected hostility, and getting it, his lips pinched sourly. He nodded knowingly. "I only wanted to ask you something. I'll leave you to your own company as soon as I have."

Instead of answering, Leah sighed and began to get up from the table.

"Why did she forgive you?" the Colonel whispered.

Even though he'd spoken softly, it was as though he'd blurted the question out before she could leave.

She slowed, eyes narrowing on him.

"Everyone knows what you did," he said. "But my daughter, I've seen her warm to you. She doesn't avoid you anymore. Doesn't look disgusted whenever you enter the room."

Seeing how much the Colonel had been paying attention, Leah almost gave him a warning to mind his own business and stop spying on her. Luckily, she heard the words in her head before saying them. She would make a fool of herself trying to deliver that sermon.

"I've tried for years and I can't even get her to take my phone calls," the Colonel said.

Leah shook her head, looking back at him incredulously. "We aren't the same."

"You betrayed her," he said.

"Yeah, I did. And I did it for family," Leah said. "She doesn't like it, but she does understand it. What did you betray her for?"

"I . . . I just . . . I didn't believe her," the Colonel said.

"And somewhere along the way, you realized you made a mistake?" Leah asked.

He nodded, a look of deep shame on his face as he did so.

"Did you ever try to fix it?" Leah asked. "Or do you just keep hoping she'll forgive you?"

"The man she accused . . ." The Colonel closed his eyes. "He was brought up on charges a few years later . . . it didn't seem like disclosing my . . . poor judgment would help anything."

He looked at the table in shame.

She began to walk away again, and he asked her, "So what do I do now?"

"Nothing," Leah said. "You had years, and now, there isn't anything you can do that means anything. I can't help. Now, I don't want to be seen with *you*. I hope the irony of that isn't lost on you."

She left, leaving him staring into his tray. She wandered for a while, unable to refocus her mind on Rylee's journals after the exchange had left her in such a bad mood. She found herself alone, sitting in her bunk instead of returning to work with Joao.

"Mr. Clean," she asked.

"Yes."

"Is there any strategic reason that Colonel Hamill needs to remain in Hangman's Tree?"

"He is a wanted man. His actions in assisting Paige made Jonathan fear he might require asylum after he escaped The Cell."

"Can't we find him *asylum* elsewhere?"

"Heyer or Jonathan would have to approve," the AI said.

She sighed. She didn't really want to bother Jonathan or Heyer with this. Course, no one had seen Heyer in over a week and when anyone asked about it at the war council, Jonathan had said he was away on a strategic assignment of which no one else needed to know.

"Is there really no other way, Jonathan—he'd understand, but it's not my place to explain."

"Well, if you don't see this matter as something that needs addressing immediately, then you should know that once you're implanted, I would take the command from you," the AI said.

Leah frowned, her mouth momentarily moving like a goldfish before she digested this bit of information.

"Are you saying that once implanted I would be high enough in the hierarchy to give you commands?"

"That is correct," he said.

She remembered how guarded both Jonathan and Heyer had been about the chain of command. And suddenly, it occurred to her why it had to be kept a secret.

"Where would I be in the chain exactly?" Leah asked.

"You would be on par with Jonathan, but I would still defer to his commands in the event of a difference of opinion," the AI said.

Leah nodded, her mind suddenly connecting a few dots. ". . . And below me, what is the order of the chain?"

"I am not permitted to answer that question before you are implanted either," the AI replied.

You just did, Leah thought.

It all suddenly fit too well. Why Jonathan and Heyer had always been so troubled by the choice of putting an implant into Grant Morgan. Sure, they had plenty of good reasons just on account of the man's history, but what if the Chain of Command was somehow tied to the strength of the implant owner? Then the Alpha Slayer would likely have been second in command. Fourth only when the bonded pair was active. So, if any of them were to die, Grant would move up the chain.

No wonder neither Jonathan nor Heyer would speak of it. Just suspecting it, she didn't dare say it out loud. But, if she was right, it begged the question. That day in the armory, when Jonathan said he had a means to mitigate the risk of Grant. What exactly could he have meant by that?

CHAPTER EIGHTY

DATE | TIME: UNKNOWN | FEROXIAN PLANE

THE PROPHET WAS not to be disturbed until he directed otherwise. Malkier's patience was beyond frayed as his tired eyes scanned two dimensional images flashing past on the screen overhead. Finally, one of the images grabbed his attention. He sat up with a start.

"Stop," Malkier said. "Go back."

Cede executed the command, the most recent images flashing past on the screen. They all had one thing in common, the pictures came from a library of modern human civilization.

"That one," Malkier said. "What is it?"

The structure was comprised of several metal towers. To Malkier they all appeared connected by a series of black lines or ropes.

"The image is of a primitive power hub. Humans place these structures throughout their cities to route electricity."

"Electricity," Malkier said the words with an indignant scoff. Such a power source was so ancient to his ancestors that, though he understood its use on a basic level, he'd have been hard-pressed to remember what point in history the Borealis had rendered it obsolete. So long ago it was like asking a human when their species had stopped hunting and gathering in exchange for growing their own food.

"Can you replicate this power source?" Malkier asked.

"That will not be a challenge, sir," Cede replied.

Malkier was quiet for a long moment, steeling himself for what had to come next.

"Seal the room," Malkier said. "Make sure I am unable to leave."

"Sir?" Cede asked.

"You will expose me to as much electricity as one of these hubs is capable," Malkier said. "I must know."

"Again."

A bolt of lightning shot from the walls within Cede and struck Malkier in the chest. It tickled a bit each time, but for the most part he was unfazed. The harsh white light that filled the chamber each time was the greater discomfort. When he opened his eyes, he watched with declining fascination in how the threads of electricity arced up the spaces between his fingers and dissipated.

Nothing more ever came of it—exactly as had been the case after all the preceding tests. Yet, Malkier was certain he was on the brink of discovering his own vulnerability.

It was that explosion of light. On the night of *Echoes the Borealis'* death he hadn't seen what had caused that flash—hadn't even known if it was real—but now he was quite convinced that roof they had been standing on had become so bright he'd been forced to shut his eyes. This was the last thing he remembered before he found himself bleeding, back on the Feroxian Plane.

"Whatever is causing the implant to fail on Earth it is not the power source alone," Malkier said, his voice disappointed.

"If I may sir?" Cede began, "It could be worth exploring whether or not all variables that were present on the two occurrences are accounted for. What commonalities existed in both instances?"

Malkier considered. "Water. It rained when I fought the father and the son. And we weren't on the ground, but on the roof of one of their taller structures."

Without needing to ask, Cede began to alter the chamber around him. The inner sanctum lost the appearance of Feroxian tunnels and gave way to the black void. Projections began to manifest in an approximation of a human rooftop beneath his feet. Once the details solidified, an overcast sky came into existence above him. Soon, the humidity rose as cold water began running down his skin.

"Yes," Malkier said, his excitement growing. "Again, Cede."

The lightning came from above this time, as though it were a naturally occurring phenomenon. Again, the light came. Again, the threads arced over his body and the wet surfaces of the rooftop. Again, they dissipated, and nothing had changed.

What else had he failed to account for? The humans themselves? *Brings the Rain* had been standing on that rooftop with him. Likewise, he had been holding *Echoes the Borealis* by the throat ten years earlier. It seemed unlikely that a man with an implant need be caught in the current with him.

Then a far more immediate difference occurred to him. In both incidents, he had been inside The Never. Could the makeup of the temporary dimension have a role? He had to hope not, Heyer's AI alone possessed the technology to open The Never. There had to be something simpler.

"The stone," Malkier said.

"This would have been present in both instances," Cede concurred.

"Prepare it."

A pedestal began to manifest within a gathering puddle beside him. The water parted as it rose to the height of his torso. A moment later, the small red sphere formed. He plucked it off the surface and stared down at the lambent red glow it cast from his palm. He only waited for another moment. The insertion was never a pleasant experience—not unlike swallowing a rock. As the sphere settled in his stomach, he felt it react, becoming a viscous mass that slithered carefully inside him. Closing his eyes, he waited as that mass crawled its way into his torso and began the disturbing internal process that created the vein-like appendages that anchored the stone inside him. When it ended, he shook the experience off, and looked once more into the sky.

"Again," Malkier said.

Light built in the clouds above, then surged down with a clap of thunder.

Malkier couldn't move. He thrashed against the bonds in the dark as he opened his eyes and found himself in the inner sanctum once again. The building, the sky, the rain were all gone, and the normal camouflage of the cave tunnels had been restored.

"Cede, release me," Malkier said.

The shackles holding him fell away and he caught himself with his hands before falling to the tunnel floor. He had not fully regained his faculties, feeling as if he had suddenly been jarred from a long sleep.

"What did you observe?"

"Your device was temporarily disabled," Cede said. "For a short period *Ends the Storm* reclaimed control. While I did not reveal myself to him, he believed himself on Earth. I ended the rooftop simulation in an attempt to calm him. However, I was forced to restrain him when he began beating the walls in search of a way out. I feared that he might injure the host body in his panic."

Malkier could feel Cede's explanation. The skin of his hands felt raw, as though they had been thrashed against the rough surfaces of the tunnel only to find that they would not give. He felt similar discomfort from every point of restraint Cede had used to keep the Alpha Ferox subdued.

"*Ends the Storm* was not amenable to having his movement restricted," Cede said. "The wounds have not healed. It is peculiar, but not without precedent. The wounds incurred while the implant is offline do not heal as they should. Almost as if they are subject to the same rate of repair as any Ferox."

"What is causing the malfunction?" Malkier asked.

"The reaction is not a malfunction, the implant is temporarily shutting down to safeguard your core memory after it detects a compromised internal environment it cannot actively regulate," she said.

Malkier chewed on this for a time. "What is keeping it from regulating?"

"The issue appears to be the result of competing regulators inside your body while inside The Never. When you are hit with an external electrical source your host's internal charges are pushed past desirable thresholds. Normally, your body's natural anatomy and your implant would take steps to regulate the charge back to ideal conditions—homeostasis. However, when you enter The Never a third regulator is present. The portal stone is attempting to regulate your internal environment. It seems that cross talk exacerbates the issue instead of suppressing it."

"Fine, can you fix it?"

"The encryption protecting your implant's programming makes it impossible for me to adjust such things. However, there is no danger to you outside The Never," Cede said.

"The prophet will fight with his people in the battle for the Promised Land," Malkier said, a touch of impatience in his voice. "You will find a way to protect me from this inside The Never."

"An external defense against strong electrical currents should achieve the same result," Cede said. "A working prototype for testing would not be difficult to produce."

"Show me," Malkier said,

Nearby, another platform protruded from the tunnel floor and a black sphere manifested. It looked like a finely polished cannon ball, until Malkier picked it up. The moment he touched it, the sphere lost shape, losing cohesion until it became a cold viscous slime in his hand. That slime began to spread up his arm, its mass thinning as it covered the limb. Soon, it coated his chest and was reaching for his feet. He closed his eyes as the material continued to thin and cover his head. When the process was complete, he felt as though he were wearing a second skin, but the liquid had stretched so thin it was transparent.

"The exterior will ground any current and insulate you from contact," Cede said. "It will provide adequate protection from anything you might encounter on Earth."

Malkier surveyed his skin skeptically. If recent events proved anything, it was that all Borealis AIs were not created equal. Cede was a newer model, supposedly more advanced than that which was installed on Heyer's vessel. Yet, she'd proved inferior on multiple occasions. Heyer's escape from Cede's security net being the most recent in evidence.

Ever since discovering the vessel on Nevric's home world, Malkier had found that onboard AI annoyingly eccentric. Too much personality—curiosity. His brother had always given the machine so much leeway with its endless inquiries. When they were younger, Malkier thought it somewhat pathetic—a sadly misplaced affection for a machine that stemmed from Heyer's loneliness. The same loneliness that eventually led him to seek out the humans.

It was a void Malkier had always tried to fill as his older brother—though they grew apart as the centuries passed. And for what? His brother had chosen humanity over him.

Of late, he couldn't help but grow wary of what that AI was capable. Perhaps he had misjudged. Perhaps Heyer had long ago seen more in the machine's programming. Something that gave its consciousness a greater flexibility.

Regardless, upon taking Earth, Heyer's AI would serve him—and he would do it quietly.

Until then, he required far greater assurances. He would not be satisfied that he was safe in The Never with no more protection than a thin layer of grounding skin. He could not risk his people seeing him weakened, their faith tested while they fought the battle to save their species. The prophet must be an unstoppable force delivering them to the Promised Land.

That, and . . .

He still didn't know what had happened to the twenty-eight dead Ferox returned to his gateway.

"This is a start," he said. "What more can you suggest?"

CHAPTER EIGHTY-ONE

DATE | TIME: UNKNOWN | FEROXIAN PLANE

BURNS THE FLAME saw no reason to hurry.

She stopped where the land crested and looked out over a landscape she scarcely recognized. This place that had been her home, was now a depression in the rock. The sheer size made it possible to mistake the hole as a valley, but there was nothing natural about this place—and so she only saw a deepening pit.

The Ferox who had begun the *Pilgrimage* at the onset, those who had come for no more than rumors of *Echoes the Borealis'* rebirth, had rightfully been promised their place on the front lines when the battle for the Promised Land began. However, those who had only come after the prophet's decree were put to work.

Each day, the pilgrimage brought hundreds more. The males did not come alone, any female of mature age who wished to be a part of the battle had left their tribal lands behind as well.

Unsurprisingly, most had been born during the period when their gods, the Borealis, had abandoned them. They had lived with the fear of helplessly watching their species dwindle—extinction seemingly an ever-approaching inevitability. Now, the Borealis had returned, calling upon her people to once again be the weapon against a race of abominations.

In short, most Ferox had been waiting for this moment their entire life.

As they flooded in, those who were set to work did so without complaint. There was a shame in having had to be called, as though those who had begun the pilgrimage before it was decreed were somehow more attuned with the will of the Borealis. *Burns the Flame* didn't doubt that the early arrivals were happy to believe such nonsense—convince themselves that there had been *something more than personal glory* calling them here before the rest.

The males of her species weren't known for their introspection.

Below, the workers were a sea of movement. Most of the work was being performed by hand. The Ferox used tools that humans would have found primitive given what they undertook. The heads of pickaxes and hammers were shaped from the hardest stone, their handles fashioned from the bones of the creatures they hunted for food on the Feroxian Plane. In the hands of a Ferox, the massive tools were undeniably effective. Some broke rock, others hauled the largest stones away. The youngest and weakest took part, sweeping the smaller shards and dust into thick sacs fashioned from the skin and stomach of the local creatures.

She would have been amongst them but *Burns the Flame*'s status had elevated. There was no question that she would soon become the tribe's most dominant Alpha female. The eldest of Alphas knew who would be the strongest amongst them. There were no politics involved—only instinct. When *Burns the Flame* completed the last stage of her maturity, the current Alpha would submit to her dominance.

She would, in effect, be second only to the prophet.

Despite her recent steps up the tribal ladder, she was no less in the dark than all the workers below as to what it was they were bringing into being in the rock. Each day the depth increased near twofold as all that stone being hauled out was piled in a steadily growing ring around the quarry. At first there had been a number of ramps that led down, so that the stone could be hauled out from all around the growing circle, but the prophet had decreed the work was nearing its completion and ordered all but the largest of the ramps filled in. Now, only one path led down into the pit.

The very crest of the land she stood on was made of freshly hauled stone. Carried here that day to cover what had been left the night before. From atop it, the shape, but not the purpose, of what they labored to build was plain to see. The prophet would have her people believe that the gods required a massive cylinder drilled into the rock. Yet, the location was not chosen at random, at its center was the mouth of her tribe's home. Well, what remained of it.

Her home would never be as it was . . . a sadness the prophet asked them to endure for the promise of the new paradise he was to deliver them to—The Promised Land.

. . . Or so the prophet told her people.

Today, there were places where the digging had stopped. The workers in those areas were smoothing—leveling—the prophet called it. The Ferox came to grasp what was needed, though the idea was foreign to them a week past. Apparently, the rock simply being *flat* was not good enough for what their gods required.

The result was massive and strange to her eyes. Creating a structure unlike any a Ferox had ever labored to build. Everything about it was unfamiliar—and perhaps that was to be expected, as there would only be one battle for the Promised Land—so everything about such an undertaking would be unique.

That said, some of the males, those who had fought in the arena, said there was a resemblance to what they now labored to build and what they had seen constructed by the abominations on the other side.

Burns the Flame had no doubts of this. She had long been alone and silent in her knowledge; she knew the prophet was not what he claimed. As such, that he shared traits with those he called abominations brought her no shock. This was another piece of an answer to a question she couldn't quite put into words.

Burns the Flames was not the only one who remembered the prophet when he was simply *Ends the Storm*—before he claimed to speak for the gods. He had been the Alpha of her tribe—but more than that, all who knew him would sense that he'd have been the Alpha of any tribe. If a time ever came that the Ferox needed an Alpha amongst Alphas, *Ends the Storm* would be that leader.

The reason was simple.

The Alphas seldom met face to face, but whenever this occurred, there was no question who amongst them was the dominant—the Ferox sensed these things the same way they sensed that she would take her place amongst the Alpha females. As such, there was no mystery to her people as to why *Ends the Storm* had been singled out when their long silent gods finally returned. The Alphas of all the tribes would have obeyed him should he have ever given commands. But, until he became the prophet, *Ends the Storm* never exercised that theoretical power.

There was an understanding amongst the Ferox that *Ends the Storm's* ascension had changed him. It should be expected that being the conduit of the Borealis—a god made flesh—changed him profoundly. Some of the changes were obvious. He was stronger than any Ferox should naturally be. At times he seemed virtually indestructible. When he chose to, he was able to appear to all the tribes—all over the planet at once. And most telling of all, he knew things. Things that none among them could have imagined.

Sometimes he spoke of these things and none amongst them could honestly grasp what he told them.

For a time, she had been as convinced as anyone else that he spoke for the gods. But, while many of the tribe's females had shared the consonance with *Ends the Storm*, *Burns the Flame* alone had shared *the experience* before and, more importantly, after his ascension to prophet.

Not once, but twice, and in both those instances she had known a difference. Though it remained a contradiction of which she was aware but could not give an explanation. To experience it was to say that, for a time, she believed herself in the company of *Ends the Storm*. The Ferox he had been before his ascension. It was always short, a thing she sensed in moments when he first came to her. Always in the minutes immediately following the prophet's return from the gates—scandalous as they were—when he trespassed against his own decree that no Alpha should enter.

Yet, there was always a moment when he slipped away. She knew on some level—even in the rapture of the consonance—it was jarring when *Ends the Storm* faded away and the prophet returned. How she could know such a thing she was never certain. The consonance was a fire burning itself to ashes, feeding on itself until smoldering in its own exhaustion. It was what bringing life into the world should be. For the very same reason it was a haze, not a moment where one could focus their attention on detail.

But, it was intimate—and both times she felt as though she had been with two separate beings.

The first time, when she walked away from the experience, she thought that perhaps this was another of the things she wasn't meant to grasp. Perhaps the gods had no wish to be part of the consonance, and only took back the Alpha's flesh as it neared its end.

Yet, what followed afterward made her begin to question if the prophet was an entity of their gods' will at all.

The Ferox did not fight with one another. This is—mostly—the truth.

In most things where a disagreement could be found, the Ferox placed the greatest good of the species over their personal interests. If a disagreement passed between two adults, biology established a clear hierarchy. Male or female, a Ferox knew its place in the pecking order. Even so, in an extreme moment, any adult Ferox that truly considered actions of violence against another of their kind was taken by the sickness.

She had heard stories that some males had been known to argue over kills. Said stories came from a time long past when their people had waged wars large enough that such a thing as who had killed an enemy might be confused. In general, this never came to blows. It was a time of plenty when a single trophy was no scarce resource.

But there were exceptions. Most often when two males were indiscernible in the hierarchy. When it occurred, it usually resulted in a tug of war over the vanquished enemy that rendered the carcass an unattractive trophy to any female.

The second exception, the one known to be far more frequent to any female who had ever whelped, were the actions of the young as they matured—before they entered adolescence. It was a period of great confusion amongst all those who had yet to complete the first phase of maturity. Their place in the hierarchy unclear to them. Often, they squabbled over simple things like portions—the best cuts of meat.

A mature adult with more discerning senses sometimes broke the squabble for them, a task usually seen to by the two mothers. While it was known to happen, it was never spoken of, as such things were considered embarrassing behavior for all involved.

Burns the Flame had been mother to many before *Dams the Gate*, she had broken these quarrels.

Yet, it was the squabbling of the young that *Burns the Flame* was reminded of when she recalled the prophet's decree that her offspring be forbidden to enter the gates. *Ends the Storm* would never have done such a thing. He'd have known this would ostracize her. To any male returning from the Arena this was a math so intrinsic to their nature it hardly required conscious consideration. If her offspring was forbidden access to the gates, then they were dead weight to the species in these times.

Yet, when the prophet made his decree, she had sensed something of that juvenile behavior behind it all. As though the prophet—the conduit of their gods, squabbled over portions. Except, what he wished to keep for himself was her womb.

Whatever it was—it wasn't the behavior of an Alpha, and by extension, even less that of a god. She had not gone against the prophet's decree lightly.

'*I know it was you,*' the prophet had said.

'*That was the intention,*' she had replied.

The words had been the sole consequence after she'd given *Dams the Gate* the means to enter the Arena—in direct rebellion of the gods themselves. The prophet must have known she would only be capable of such defiance if she no longer believed. Yet, life had gone on, and no punishment had come for her.

The opposite it seemed.

The prophet had gone through the gates and shared the consonance with her once more. He had even gone so far as to decree that her actions and all the events that followed were preordained. That, through him, the Borealis had set the stage for the prophecies to play out.

The prophecies, the signs of which the prophet had decreed he had now born witness.

Dams the Gate's birth was the first sign—for he bore the name of the *Harbinger*.

His sacrifice was the second sign, as the *Harbinger* would name their gods' ultimate enemy—the abomination *Brings the Rain*.

Bleeds the Stone was the third sign—he was *The Test*. His fall to this *Brings the Rain* would confirm the *Harbinger* had named the enemy of their gods.

Finally, when her tribe discovered a man upon the gateway, the prophet deemed him the fourth sign—*The Betrayer*.

All these signs meant it was the time of the Pilgrimage.

She alone was troubled by the fact that none of these events, these things the prophet called signs and gave names, were mentioned in his original prophecy. When he first ascended, he'd proclaimed that the Borealis had returned. That the Ferox would be given a second chance. That, if this time they pleased the gods, they would be delivered to the Promised Land.

There had been no mention of signs.

She kept her thoughts to herself and held no contempt for her people. The prophet had not failed them since he revealed himself, only her. They couldn't know what she knew. For that matter, she couldn't very well explain.

But now, the prophet had called for her. So, she lingered on that crest—stared at the pit that used to be her home a bit longer—before descending the slope.

The prophet awaited her at the end of a tunnel that had once led to more caverns below the rock. The digging had cut through it, and now the same tunnel ended at a cliff face. The light of the red sky poured in, and he stood at the edge overseeing the work below.

He sent his lieutenants away when she arrived, commanding that they were to be left alone until he called for them. For this she was grateful. She wished to speak freely but would have restrained herself in the presence of others.

His back was still to her when he began to speak. "The tribes, our people, they are united behind me. They wish to show their obedience to the will of the Borealis."

He took a long breath. "Only you rebel now. My son is dead for your defiance. Why?"

'My son'. He spoke so strangely at times and didn't even seem to notice. A *male* Ferox did not think of a tribe's child as theirs.

"You have power, but you do not speak for the gods," *Burns the Flame* said. "I do not obey, because I was the one punished when you failed to live by your own decrees. . ."

She paused, putting all her certainty into the words that followed. "Gods do not fail."

Malkier's back slowly straightened as he gazed out on the quarry. His silence feeling as though it would never end.

"How shall I be punished for your failures now?" *Burns the Flame* asked. "I carry children again. Will my offspring be labeled abominations as well?"

He turned his head slowly, only fixing one eye on her as she stood behind him. "Do not speak of *my son* as an abomination."

The seriousness of his voice stilled her. She had blasphemed—openly called him a fraud. Yet the notion she might speak ill of *Dams the Gate* brought his anger.

"I've not summoned you here to speak of punishments," Malkier said.

"Then why am I here?"

"I love our people, *Burns the Flame*, but you are like me, unique amongst them," Malkier said. "You and I have far more in common than you know."

"I'm not like you. You deceive our people. I'm no liar," she said.

"Oh, but you are. You claim to know me for a false prophet, and yet you tell no one of this detail. Your one true act of rebellion amounted to sending our son through the gates against my decree. See, I've spoken to those who helped you. Your act of disobedience was achieved without sowing any seeds of rebellion against the faith. You did so with all the secrecy that was possible. Some of the young I've questioned even seemed convinced that you were carrying out my orders in secret."

She hesitated—he knew far more than she'd imagined, and this was nothing like the conversation she'd been preparing for.

"Tell me the truth. Do you know why you did this?" Malkier asked.

"I will suffer what I know for the sake of our people," she said. "But I could endure what you had done to my son no longer."

Malkier nodded. "So, your one act of defiance was born out of the belief that you were doing the right thing for our son. You were in no position to understand that I denied him entry to the gates for the very same reasons . . ."

Those words again, 'our son'.

"But, *Burns the Flame*, that is not the question I asked, and you know it."

She flinched, surprised at how quickly he'd seen through her.

"Whatever you truly are . . ."

She trailed off a moment. Swallowing down bile before she went on. "There is no denying that before your ascension, our people were dying. The Borealis chose to abandon us to that fate as punishment. I believe they still have. That means that whatever you are, if you abandon us now the result will be the same. I would do my people no favors casting doubt upon you."

Malkier nodded. "This is why I summoned you here, *Burns the Flame*. Every Ferox can be trusted to do what they believe best for the species, but few possess the foresight to see the bigger picture—to see the necessity of restraint."

Finally, he turned away from the ledge to look at her. "You would never betray our people with the truth."

She held his eyes as long as she could, but the instinct to submit was powerful. Whoever—whatever—the prophet truly was, he possessed *Ends the Storm*'s dominance, and none could hold his eyes in defiance for long. Finally, *Burns the Flame* diverted her eyes to the floor.

He stepped closer. "To be alone with such knowledge—is a lonely existence."

She felt his hand on her jaw, gently tilting her eyes up and making her meet his gaze. "Let me spare you that—know the truth of what I am and take your rightful place at my side. Together we will deliver salvation to our people."

She was unable to hide her wariness of what the prophet offered. "Why? You need nothing from me. Our people will follow you."

He let go of her chin, turning away for a moment before he spoke. "There is another . . . one, like myself, and he has aligned himself with the abominations."

"Another?" she asked. "There are more like yourself?"

He nodded. "Only one. But, he knows of my strengths and . . . weaknesses. I have taken steps to protect myself, but there is one weakness I cannot safeguard by simply taking precautions."

"You wish for me to protect something?"

The prophet nodded. "You already do—*Burns the Flame*, you carry my young. Of all my weaknesses you are my greatest."

She studied him for a long while. "You're asking me to do that which I already would."

He let go of her chin and walked back to the overlook.

"Now that another of my kind is involved, I cannot go into this war without taking additional precautions," Malkier said. "I must accept the possibility that my vessel could be harmed. Even killed."

"Vessel?" she asked.

"After all you've said, you know I am not *Ends the Storm*. His body was given for the ascension," Malkier said. "Should this body fail, arrangements must be in place for another to take the mantle of prophet."

"Join me, *Burns the Flame*. You will rule the Promised Land at my side. And should the day come, tomorrow or years from now, that the prophet requires a new vessel, you will choose who amongst the Ferox ascends."

Burns the Flame was quiet for a long while. He'd given her a great deal to consider and did not disturb her thoughts. Eventually she joined him at the ledge and looked down on their people.

"How?" she asked.

CHAPTER EIGHTY-TWO

NOV 23, 2005 | 4 PM | HANGMAN'S TREE

TEN MINUTES HAD passed since Mr. Clean had skipped a beat. Actually become distracted midsentence like a—well—like a human. Not much made the AI hesitate except the sudden processing of a huge amount of data. As such, Jonathan knew what the AI would say before he said it.

"The conduit has begun opening on the Feroxian Plane," Mr. Clean said.

Within five minutes Jonathan was speaking to Olivia.

"It's begun," he said. "Attack is coming in six to eight days. We need to be ready in five."

"Understood," Olivia said.

"I know, I'm asking you to move heaven and earth—"

". . . And I told you I would move it," Olivia said. "Focus on your own problems."

"Thank you, Olivia" he said.

"We will be in touch soon, Mr. Tibbs," Olivia said.

Olivia was now the unofficial go-between of the US Government and The Never Army. She didn't have to fight for the position; Jonathan had said, in no uncertain terms, that he wanted her as their liaison. The moment their call ended she'd begin sending orders down the chain, and those in charge of the various branches of the armed services would begin implementation of stage one.

Evacuation. A single word that encompassed a logistical nightmare.

Later tonight, government agencies would wait until the majority of Seattle's populace was home for the evening before declaring a state of emergency. Broadcasts calling for the mandatory evacuation of downtown and its surrounding suburbs would be all over the TV and radio.

Having been mobilized and running 'practice drills' for weeks in advance, The National Guard would begin assisting local law enforcement in the necessary efforts. The evacuation would begin with setting up roadblocks to all traffic entering the city. Not all traffic would be stopped immediately—that would only cause the panic that would inevitably occur to escalate sooner. Parents returning from work would not be told they needed to collect their children or loved ones. However, they would know it was time to get their affairs in order, retrieve their family, and leave the city as soon as possible.

Those with somewhere to go outside the perimeter would be asked to go there as soon as possible. But, of course, this would affect everyone differently. While those with means would be able to make arrangements, there would be a far greater number left completely at a loss for where to turn. Those that had nowhere to go or no means to get out would be routed toward temporary camps that FEMA and other government support services had begun setting up for weeks now. The erection of these camps having begun a few days after Olivia returned from DC. Having met with the President and the Joint Chiefs to convince them their fate was to be put in the hands of a college dropout who, until a few hours earlier, had been considered an enemy of the state.

While Jonathan had no desire to be in direct contact with the President— he kind of wished he could have been a fly on the wall of the oval office when Olivia and General Delacy made that pitch.

Whatever they called them—camps, temporary settlements, emergency housing—Americans with any interest in history would exercise a great deal of resistance.

Most of the city of Seattle would be plunged into a surreal state of disbelief or shock as they learned that: no this is not a hoax, not a false alarm, and there are no exceptions. If Bill and Melinda Gates or the Governor tried to stay within the boundaries, they would be escorted out by the National Guard.

Most, but not all.

By design, the population throughout the entire state would have had to have been living in a cave in the weeks leading up to the evacuation before the official order came down to not have suspected something. Olivia had decided early on that there would be no point attempting to hide an undertaking of such magnitude. The reports of shelters being erected, land being *temporarily* seized, and forces being mobilized throughout the entire state could not be accomplished without notice.

Soon the news would spread.

Politicians' approval ratings would drop overnight. The stock market would take a dive, and a thousand lawyers would start drawing up plans to sue local and federal agencies.

While it would look as though the authorities did all they could to contain a panic, an unidentified, but trustworthy, source would leak a conspiracy theory just credible enough that news networks would run with it. While the theory would be as vague as such things generally go, viewers would take away from it a story that went something like this:

Five nuclear war heads had been transferred from a high security military facility and had never reached their intended destination. Government intelligence agencies had been frantically tracking the weapons' whereabouts and now believed with great certainty that they had fallen into the hands of a terrorist organization so obscure that until today no one in the media heard of them.

Mr. Clean had taken point on leaving the necessary digital breadcrumbs that would lead those searching for information on this group to believe them very real. Details would of course be scarce, but one fact would seem certain. At least one of the missing warheads was believed to be within the city limits.

No one from the government would substantiate these claims, but they wouldn't exactly deny them either. To be fair, 99.99% of the folks the media reached for comment would be entirely in the dark.

As far as Seattle's residents went, those who kept a level head would conclude that if the reports were true or not, the safest bet was for them and their loved ones to evacuate—though the method through which they accomplished this would likely grow increasingly less level-headed as the hours drew on and the news spun itself into a frenzy of speculation.

Unfortunately, many—hopefully less than Olivia estimated—would resist, causing her operation to remove them from the city by force.

This would only be the beginning—and frankly a best-case scenario. The fact was that evacuating a city with over half a million residents would require an effort just short of an act of God. People forced out of their homes needed food, clothes, water, sanitation, shelter, and medical care.

Loved ones needed to be kept together. Hospital patients needed to be safely moved to new facilities. Prisons and juvenile detention centers had to have their prisoners moved. Flights had to be allowed out, while those coming in were grounded or redirected. Public Transport had to be re-purposed to take people without access to a vehicle out of the city.

In addition, removing civilians created issues within the perimeter as well. Olivia eventually had teams assembled for details of an increasingly granular nature—like dealing with animals at the zoos and aquariums that would be abandoned by their caretakers during the evacuation.

All this was before they met with resistance—protests, looting, riots.

There would inevitably be deaths. All of it would need to be handled. But, it didn't end with getting the civilians to safety.

For Jonathan's plan to work, everything that could be done to keep eyes off that city in the days following the evacuation needed to be done. This meant disabling wireless towers and redirecting satellites—a thing that could only be accomplished to a limited degree with the cooperation of allied governments. Security and surveillance cameras within the city itself had to be disabled—a detail that could be mostly accomplished by cutting off power to the necessary portions of the grid. However—there would be those that ran on backup batteries, solar panels, and generators.

The bulk of the evacuation process would take place over days, but in the end there was just no way they could get everyone out. Long after Olivia's forces evacuated the city they would be finding people hiding in basements and bomb shelters. Homeless who had managed to avoid initial sweeps.

While this was unavoidable, large portions of The Never Army's stage two preparations needed to begin in concert with the evacuation.

Battle Preparation.

Well, at least that was what Jonathan referred to it with Olivia. From the beginning, his roommate's shadows had deemed this the *Dutch-McAllister* phase.

Jonathan's understanding being that the name derived from Hayden's stance that the phase was analogous to a city scale version of what Arnold Schwarzenegger's character, Dutch, endeavored to do when preparing to fight an alien in the movie *Predator*. Collin, however, felt Macaulay Culkin's character, Kevin McAllister, preparing to defend his home from the Wet Bandits in *Home Alone*, while less than a perfect parallel, made him laugh.

For obvious reasons, Jonathan did not feel comfortable referring to the phase as the Dutch-McAllister outside of the war council.

Regardless, during this phase, agents of The Cell, along with The Never Army, would be implementing a laundry list of instructions—for example, the rigging of large buildings for controlled demolition. Thanks to Mr. Clean, such items didn't require the same timelines of human planning to implement. Based on data brought back by Jonathan's reconnaissance teams over the last few weeks, the AI had been running the necessary simulations and planned the necessary charge placements for explosives. The Cell and The Never Army only needed to work together to get the charges set.

That much could begin before the evacuation efforts wound down. Only after they were deemed as complete, could Mr. Clean and The Never Army take over the city in total. This was when the less, strictly human, modifications to the city could begin.

A phase aptly named *Mr. Clean.*

In short, when Jonathan ended that call, he knew that no manner of planning was going to change the fact that he'd just thrown a stadium-sized turd at a fan the size of. . . well . . . Seattle.

Which was why he found it very odd that as he ended the call, the weight of all that he had just put in motion wasn't what he felt on his shoulders. He should have felt anxious—plagued by self-doubt—terrified of just how many huge details could not be controlled.

Yet, he felt—good. He felt positive. He felt, somewhat euphoric.

This remained strange, until the sensations became increasingly familiar to his subconscious.

"Mr. Clean, what's the current status of the female half of the bonded pair?"

"The implant was installed in Ms. Delacy a few minutes ago. She is currently in recovery."

Then Jonathan felt a twitch in his chest.

"Mr. Clean did you—"

"Heyer left very specific instructions as to what should happen in the event that the bonded pair could be reestablished."

His legs began to give, and he fell to a knee. "Turn it off . . ."

"I do apologize, but I've been forbidden to obey that request."

"Son of a . . ."

CHAPTER EIGHTY-THREE

A MOMENT AGO, Leah would have sworn she was dreaming. She'd been standing in the garage, watching Rylee punch her in the face.

She remembered thinking, *Finally gonna punch her right in her big stupid face.*

Right before that fist connected, she'd thought, *What a strange thing to think about one's self.*

Immediately after Rylee's fist connected, she woke up alone, lying on this rooftop in the middle of the night. She sat up and the air felt warm as a soft wind blew through her hair. She stood and turned, the nearby buildings and the Space Needle giving her an idea of where she was, but no clue how she'd come to be there.

Then the sounds began to press in on her. As though her hearing had been on mute and was slowly returning to normal. What she heard demanded her attention. This was not the ambiance of a city winding down for the evening. There were sirens—far too many—their whines bombarding her from all directions.

The city was in crisis.

She ran to the lip of the rooftop and peered down at the streets. The flashing lights of emergency vehicles were scattered down the roadway, but the streets themselves were littered with wreckage. Cars were overturned, crushed, some looking as though they had been trampled in a stampede—others flattened, smashed such that Leah wondered if something had thrown them through the sky.

There were holes—gaping car-sized wounds—in the sides of buildings. They hadn't been there long either; as she watched, a piece of concrete came lose and plummeted to the street.

The people either ran hurriedly or hid. With a shiver, Leah started to realize just how many weren't moving at all. They lay in the middle of the road, perfectly still but in disturbingly unnatural positions. Then her eyes followed a trail that ended in a mound.

She retracted, pushed away from the roof's edge until her back hit a ventilation box. Suddenly, survival overtook her horror. She realized she was out in the open. Whatever had caused all this could still be going on. She slid down until she hugged her knees—shivering as she tried to think.

This wasn't a natural disaster. Not . . . with how those bodies had been arranged.

"Ferox," Leah whispered. The word felt foreign and familiar at the same time. She—she hadn't known that word when this had happened.

Had happened?

She knew, suddenly, that this wasn't the present. How wasn't clear; the knowledge came to her the same way one realizes when they're dreaming. This—all of this—it was from a time before the word Ferox meant anything to her.

Groans interrupted her thinking, and she froze.

The sound was human and close, it had come from this rooftop. Male—familiar. Someone in pain. Another voice, less familiar. A woman—also in pain.

She kept low, peeking around the ventilation box, but there was too much in the way. More boxes, pipes, air ducts, and maintenance-related access points, all obstructing her vision of where the sound was coming from.

She crept closer. Until she stood crouched on one side of a retaining wall and heard the voices again. It was only in the split second before she looked that she understood what—under any other circumstances—would have been apparent right away.

No one was in any pain on the other side of the wall.

What she saw came as her eyes followed a swath of torn clothes to two bare bodies moving together. She thought to look away, but there was a light between them. A light that identified the two without any need for Leah to see their faces. Her breath caught as she slid down the side of the retaining wall. Blushing, she closed her eyes tightly, grimacing at the thought she would forever have that imagine in her memory.

She was covering her ears to block out the mounting groans and heavy breathing when she heard a voice from right beside her. "I always meant to tell Jonathan that he got all the PG-13 memories."

Leah opened her eyes and found Rylee crouched there beside her. She was fully clothed, sitting in almost the same position as Leah herself, but rather unperturbed by what was happening on the other side of the wall.

As Leah stared at the woman, it was clear that she was somehow in two places at once. This made where she was and what was happening suddenly very obvious to her. It all came back. She'd been put under. Paige and Anthony had been beside her as she faded from consciousness.

The implant, it must be inside of her. This wasn't her memory or even her dream. This was something of Rylee's mind. The woman had brought her here to see this—on purpose.

"So, you got it all figured out yet, Red?" Rylee asked.

Leah stared wordlessly as she tried to think. Admittedly, not so easy with the sounds emitting from behind her . . . them.

"I . . . I expected you'd be owed some sort of revenge. Imagined it would be more like you punching me."

"Didn't we cover that in real life?" Rylee asked.

Suddenly, another Rylee and another Leah stood in front of them on the rooftop. More specifically, past Rylee taking a swing at past Leah, her fist connecting and sending her staggering. A moment later they dissolved like sand in a breeze.

Strange, Leah thought, normally when she remembered something, she saw it in her mind's eye. This—this place—it was her mind's eye. Memories just appeared as part of the landscape.

"Ah, that's the stuff," Rylee said. "Not gonna improve on that. Plus, I don't think . . ."

Rylee paused to consider before reaching over to flick Leah hard on the earlobe. Surprised, Leah rubbed her ear curiously, but she'd felt no pain.

Rylee shrugged. "Ya, can't hurt you in your own head. Physically at least."

Leah studied her. Rylee did not seem particularly disappointed that violence was off the table. Then the groans started up again, and Rylee turned to look over the wall as though she might as well get an eyeful.

"This is a little petty, Rylee," Leah said

Rylee nodded, the observation not seeming to make her any less pleased with the situation.

"How could you two . . . do . . . that," Leah said. "With everything going on down there."

"Please," Rylee scoffed. "Jonathan and I saw that every day."

"There are literally people torn apart in the streets, and you—"

"I understand," Rylee interrupted. "The bond doesn't have you yet, Leah.

Maybe keep your judgments to yourself until you know what the hell you're talking about."

Leah quieted at that; after all, Rylee would know far better than her. She wasn't even conscious—had no idea how the bond might affect her in the waking world.

"You sure you don't want to watch this?" Rylee said. "It's really like a force of nature with super human strength and all that primal instinct set to full . . ."

Rylee took one look at Leah's expression and trailed off. "Suit yourself."

"You said Jonathan got the lame memories," Leah said. "What did that mean?"

Rylee's face saddened. "He doesn't remember this. Makes a lot more sense to me now than it did at the time. Your memories filled in most of the gaps in mine."

"My memories?" Leah asked. "So, you know . . . that you're . . . well—"

"Dead. Yeah, I kind of remember it. Let's not dwell on the negative."

Leah frowned, none of this was what she'd expected. What Jonathan had said of encountering his father had been nothing like this.

"I thought it would be so much harder to reach you," Leah said.

"Yeah, well, that's Jonathan's own—"

Rylee stopped, seeming to change her mind in the moment. "Okay, to be fair, it's more Heyer's fault."

"What do you mean?"

"Everyone's mind has shields. Yours are down. You knew I would be here and you wanted to reach me," Rylee said. "In other words, your mind doesn't see me as a threat. Jonathan's didn't know what was happening when his father reached out. His mind just felt an alien influence trying to reach his consciousness. His mental guard was always on high alert. It's no surprise that, when whatever happened to him happened, it was in a moment that his mind had nowhere else to turn."

Leah blinked a few times, shocked at Rylee's grasp of it all. "How . . . how is it you're suddenly an expert?"

"Your memories, my memories, but that isn't all," Rylee said.

They looked at one another, but what might have been a tense moment of staring was turned into a far different affair with the sound of the two lovers in the background. Leah had found for a time that it helped to pretend they were strangers, but now sounds were getting more . . . vigorous . . . as though drawing to a close.

"Could we maybe go somewhere . . . quieter?"

Rylee considered, held up a finger, waited until things had reached their zenith. Leah rolled her eyes, as she let out a long breath.

"Yeah, let's get out of here, place is dead anyway," Rylee said.

Suddenly, Leah found herself in far more familiar surroundings. Her garage. At least, her garage before The Cell took them all into custody. The metal statue she had sculpted, The Blind Blacksmith, still there at the far back.

"I'll say this much," Rylee said, taking the steel sculpture in. "Maybe you're more like Bob Ross than my Dad thought."

Leah smiled, this was the place she had wanted to be. "Did you read my mind or did I bring us here?"

"You, I'd never even seen this place when I was alive."

"So, I could have done that at any time?" Leah asked.

Rylee smirked at her knowingly. "You're wondering why you didn't sooner? My guess would be that despite your pretenses, a part of you—"

Leah interrupted, "Let's just move on."

"Whatever you say, pervert," Rylee said.

"It wasn't like that," Leah said. "If I, subconsciously, let you keep us there it's your fault. Your damn journals never made any sense. You wrote about Jonathan like you had been with him, but I could tell he wasn't lying when he said he hadn't. It was a paradox that was . . . quite grating."

Rylee studied her with a knowing smirk. "You should know you can't lie to me, Leah. But I'll concede that excuse was half true."

Leah glared.

"Fine," Rylee said. "Sixty/forty make you happy?"

Leah, cleared her throat. "You said you understood what's going on because of something more than our combined memories."

"It's the bond," Rylee said. "You feelin' the warm and fuzzies yet?"

Leah considered, but all she could do was shrug. "I . . . I really don't know."

Rylee waived the question away. "Doesn't matter yet, it's the bridge that changes everything—that's when you'll get a look."

"A look?"

"Inside his head."

"You saw inside Jonathan's head?"

Leah tried to ask the question with a degree of disinterest, but Rylee's smirk quickly reminded her that there really wasn't any hiding her envy in here.

"I get it. You've wanted inside his head for months and I stumble in without even trying. I'd be jealous too . . ."

Leah took a long breath and repeated the question. "What did you see?"

"A glimpse," Rylee said. "But it's not what you see. That's all vague and symbolic and—uggg—just, be warned. Jonathan's head makes some *weird* associations . . . never ending brick walls . . . mirrors that don't reflect what they should . . . and creepy little zombie children crawling after him in the dark."

Rylee shivered at the last bit, as though it still made her skin crawl. Meanwhile, Leah was left staring at her with one profoundly raised eyebrow.

"I digress, it's hard to make a lot of sense out of what you see—not impossible—but tricky. That said, you'll feel what he feels in that moment."

"But you did see something?" Leah asked.

"Yeah, it only makes any sense to me now. The Jonathan I was bonded to—he'd split himself in half—sort of. There was a massive brick wall keeping one Jonathan safe from the other. There was the nice Jonathan, which is what you were used to seeing most of time. But the other one—well, I only saw that side of him when he fought."

"The look he gets?" Leah asked.

Rylee nodded.

"But, how did that help you understand all this?" Leah asked.

"Chill out, I was getting to it," Rylee said, then sighed before going on. "There was something else. Something behind a shadowed curtain. It was like his own mind was trying to hide it from him. Couldn't get rid of it, so it tried to keep it locked out—separate from the rest. At the time, that all made as much sense to me as you'd expect. But, knowing what—I—you?—know now, I'm pretty sure it was his father trying to reach him."

Rylee said all this as though she were Sherlock Holmes finishing the sort of speech that begins with: *elementary my dear Watson.* Meanwhile, Leah felt like she was trying to absorb an astrophysics degree. This wasn't because she had any trouble following what Rylee was telling her, it was trying to understand the speed with which the other woman had puzzled it all together.

"I've only been here for ten minutes," Leah said. "How'd you think this all through so quickly. Do you just *know* everything I know?"

Rylee grimaced. "Time for me isn't what it is for you. Not really the factor it once was. As far as knowing what you know . . ."

Rylee's expression soured—more an act than honest bitterness. "All those hours you spent with my father—you know—hard at work invading my privacy. Well, it worked. The associations between our lives were all laid out in a map for me. I found everything I was looking for in your head pretty easily. I can't explain that any better than you could tell me how it is you remember what color your birthday cake was when you were four. You ask yourself the question—and if it can—your mind delivers the answer."

"Everything in my head, it's just unlocked to you?"

"You should be happy. It's why I know how much guilt you live with for what you've had to do. For what it's worth, I—begrudgingly—respect that."

Leah folded her arms across her chest. "So, you saw everything then? The things your father wanted to say . . ."

Rylee's smugness faded. "Thank you, for making that possible. I . . . I saw how much he needed to know I heard him."

Emotion hit Leah like a wave. She couldn't wait to tell Joao.

It had felt like so long since anything she'd done had made a difference that was—just good. She'd had no way of knowing if she'd given a grieving father a false hope that would leave him worse off than before she had approached him.

Leah grew quiet for a long while. There was something she needed to ask . . . something neither Joao, or Heyer, or Jonathan knew.

"If you saw that. What about . . ." Leah had to take a deep breath. "The memory I made for you."

Rylee held up a hand to stall her. "I saw."

Her body language was suddenly noticeably uncomfortable. More so than when they had been discussing her father. Leah swallowed, but tried to get Rylee to look at her while the woman was suddenly so reluctant to do so.

"I meant it," Leah said.

"Well I know that, now, don't I?" Rylee's said, her voice openly irritable.

With Leah trying not to let her look away she closed her eyes.

"The whole thing makes me . . ." Rylee shivered like she had spiders crawling up her skin, ". . . itch."

The woman still refused to look her in the eye, but she found herself reliving the moment, the very memory they needed to discuss. The garage began to change. A smaller room, one that had only ever existed for a few moments in reality—took shape around them inside the garage. A door formed, a countertop below a mirror. The very room she'd asked Mr. Clean to manifest for this purpose.

Rylee realized what Leah was doing and glared at her. "Oh, for the love of . . . Leah, I don't need to relive it."

If Rylee were still voicing an objection, Leah couldn't hear her. They remained only as silent observers watching the memory play out.

The door to the small room opened and Leah walked inside. She approached the mirror, unsure as she stared into her own reflection. She closed her eyes, took a steadying breath.

"I hope you see this, Rylee," Leah said. "Maybe it isn't necessary, maybe you'll already know what I've been thinking, but it's better if I say the words.

"Fight is coming. Pretty sure we . . . uh . . . we both know the world doesn't need me. I have my strengths, but fighting isn't one of them. No point denying it.

"I know . . . I'm the last person you'd pick. This would be a thousand times easier if, literally, any other woman on this planet was standing in front of this mirror . . .

"But please, consider it."

She closed her eyes and put both hands over her belly. "I know you wanted this. . .

"I think, maybe I want it too," Leah said. "But for you it was never a question. The option was just taken away from you. And, I know you wanted it with Jonathan."

A sad smile came to her face. "It's a boy."

"I know that he wouldn't be yours, but you could still be his mother," Leah said. "And Jonathan, he . . . he does want you. I don't really even know what he feels for me. He's never been . . . unkind, but I think he hurts for you in a way he never will for me. I try to tell myself it's the bond . . . but there really isn't any way to know."

Leah sighed.

"Jonathan, he was able to merge his mind with his father. I know that it's the last thing you'd want to do with me. If you're seeing this, you probably already know I'm not keen on the idea myself. But, maybe another offer—a better one for everyone I think. I don't know if it's possible, but if it is . . . you . . . you'd have my blessing."

She had tears in her eyes, but she steadied herself to say the words. Somehow, they still came out as whispers. "Just take it, Rylee. If you can, take control," Leah said. "Help him win this war, and you keep the body. You have this child. You have that life.

"I'm not being a martyr. You know I love him. But you're the warrior, the mother. That . . . and you'll never have to look at him and wonder if he's thinking of how you betrayed him . . . because you never did."

Leah stepped back from the mirror. She wiped tears away and nodded to her own reflection. "Think about it."

They had trouble looking at one another when the memory began to fade. The Leah in the mirror turned to walk out of the small room and passed right through Rylee on her way out.

Soon the two women were standing beside one another in the garage.

"Please, don't do that again," Rylee said.

The question hung unanswered between them.

"Is it possible?"

Rylee's eyes clenched shut. "I don't know."

"Can we find out?" Leah asked.

Rylee's hand shot up between them. "Hey back off, lady. Even if . . . what you're asking is . . . messing with my head."

Leah tilted her head gently. "It's the world, Rylee. It's the baby . . . it's Jonathan."

Rylee's head began nodding rapidly the way one does when they want to scream, '*Please stop talking! I get it already!*'

"Rylee, Jonathan isn't telling me everything. This plan—there are parts he isn't telling anyone. Not even Heyer. I keep getting this feeling that he . . . he might not be planning to make it back."

Rylee sighed. "I know."

"Then how do we do this?" Leah asked, and there was command in her voice now. "You have to be the one beside him when that monster tries to . . ."

There was a change in Rylee's expression, one that said she didn't care much for the amount of pressure Leah was putting on her. "Leah, it's not like there is a big damn door in your head labeled *Control Room*."

That took a moment to sink in.

"Oh," Leah said. "Right. I guess I just assumed—"

"That you'd make a big heroic gesture," Rylee said. "Then leave me to do all the heavy lifting?"

Leah winced. "I guess I deserve that . . . but no. I just thought that, Heyer and Malkier find some way to take over their host. So . . ."

Suddenly there was a shift in the air. The garage and everything in it beginning to tremble.

"How is she?" It was Paige's voice, and it had an eerie, far away, quality to it. Her words were both muffled and yet echoed unnaturally through the small garage.

The voice was joined by Anthony's. "Her vitals look good, Mr. Clean stopped the anesthesia a few minutes ago."

"They're waking me up," Leah said.

"Oh, thank effing God," Rylee said.

"How? How do I stop them?" Leah asked, her tone beginning to lose its calm.

Rylee shrugged. "How the hell should I know?"

Desperately, Leah tried to fight for unconsciousness, but whatever she did translated into the flexing of her muscles in the waking world—and made the room quake violently.

With no clue what else to try, she yelled to Rylee over the noise.

"Look for a way, Rylee," Leah said. "It's got to exist."

Rylee shook her head. "You ever think that maybe I haven't seen it because you don't want it—on a primal level."

The garage shattered as bright white light flooded her vision.

"Hey, think she's coming around," Paige said.

CHAPTER EIGHTY FOUR

PAIGE HELD LEAH'S hand as she stood over her.

She was naked beneath a white sheet on the table. The glow of the alien implant so bright the thin material only dampened it.

"How is she?"

"Her vitals look good," Anthony said. "Mr. Clean has already stopped the anesthesia. She should be coming around any moment. Speaking of . . ."

Anthony nodded at Paige's hand still holding onto Leah's. "That might not be safe—she could tear your hand off before she remembers where she is."

Paige took her hand back, then took a few steps away from the table just to be safe. "I'm still here, Leah," Paige said awkwardly. "I just . . . you know . . . like my hand."

"Strange how often I hear that around here," Anthony said, though he seemed to be talking to himself.

Leah's body tensed for a moment, then resettled on the table. A moment later her eyelids began to flutter, then opened. Leah stared up at the ceiling for a long moment before she realized Anthony, Sydney, Mr. Silva and Paige were standing around her.

"Don't move too quickly right away," Sydney said. "Most say an active implant takes some getting used to."

Leah slowly took hold of the sheet to keep it against her as she sat up. Despite knowing it would be there, her eyes still widened as she looked down at the light emanating out of her.

"How do you feel?" Paige asked.

She considered. "Really good."

Paige grinned. "Like . . . like a badass?"

Leah frowned. "Um, maybe . . . but I meant happy."

"Oh," Paige said. "Well, that's good too, right?"

Leah's expression said it wasn't that simple. "I feel really good. Mr. Clean, were there any opioids in that anesthesia?"

"Negative," Mr. Clean said.

"Mr. Clean," Leah said, resting her hands on her stomach. "How is . . . everything?"

"Everything is satisfactory."

"You're happy, *everything* is fine, figure it out later," Paige said, leaning in to whisper excitedly. "I can't be the only one who wants to see you take this thing for a test drive."

"Right . . ." Leah said, still staring at the glow emanating off her. "Let's do that."

She shot up through the air, rising toward the sky and unable to keep the gleeful smile of exhilaration from her face. For a few moments, she felt as though she were flying.

As her speed slowed, Leah reached out to grab the retaining wall of the rooftop and pulled herself easily over.

"I can go so much higher, Mr. Clean, come on—make it a challenge," Leah said.

The moment the words were out of her mouth, the rooftop she stood on liquified and morphed back into a sidewalk, then, a much taller building than had stood in front of her before shot into the sky.

Her eyes widened. *Seriously, how did the AI pull off these projections?*

"No way anyone in this army can jump that high?"

"Correct, it will require more than a single bound," Mr. Clean said. "To reach the top you will have to adapt."

She nodded, took a step back and studied the building the way a child did after losing a frisbee to a neighbor's roof. A moment later, her fist broke through a window near the thirtieth floor. She didn't find the window frame right away, not until after she began to fall back down, and her hand smashed through the glass until she found something solid and took hold.

As she dangled by one hand, she made the mistake of looking down, and a bit of vertigo set in, but as she turned away she was amazed at how easy it was to hold herself safe from the pull of gravity. She switched hands to look at her unharmed skin.

"Will you be completing the exercise?" she heard Mr. Clean ask, looking up to see his avatar standing on the inside of the shattered window.

With a smirk, she grabbed the window ledge with both arms, and shot toward the sky again. She flew past the rooftop, overshot it by at least three stories and came down with enough force that, had this not been a projection, she was fairly sure she'd have put a hole in the top floor ceiling.

As she stood from her crouch, she saw Mr. Clean on the roof beside her again. "Admittedly, the gleamers make such mobility a far less destructive affair."

Leah nodded. This being her first time out she hadn't stopped to pick up her own set of tactical gear. For the moment she was just in jeans and a t-shirt.

"How about something to hit?"

With a nod, Mr. Clean faded away, and a circle of brick pillars emerged from the rooftop around her. Each towered over her by a few feet, but her lack of technique throwing her first punch didn't make the result any less impressive—her fist putting a hole through the pillar as she pushed through, shoulder deep as brick debris shot out the other side.

The hole she'd just put in the pillar reformed, liquifying for a moment as it transitioned from brick and mortar to solid concrete. Thirty seconds later, Leah stood surrounded by what remained of the circle of pillars.

"Got anything a bit more resilient?" she asked.

The rooftop swept itself clear, and the pillars were replaced with metal girders. She eyed them carefully but was too fascinated with discovering her new limits to pay too much attention to caution.

She felt invincible.

"Son of a . . ." Leah yelped, she took a few steps back, wringing her hand in surprise. It hadn't been her knuckles so much as her wrist that hurt. Still, as she looked at the result, she couldn't help but be impressed with the shape of the bent steel that now bore her fist imprint. She took a step back and kicked this time, the steel groaning under the pressure.

Next she chopped at it, from the side to see the steel bending in once again.

"Is this actually how it will be?" Leah asked. "Outside?"

Mr. Clean reappeared. "The projection chamber is set to keep you from injuring yourself but if you're asking if you can really kick down a wall, then yes."

She nodded and eyed the AI with a curious tilt of the head.

"So, how do I measure up?"

"In what regard?" Mr. Clean asked.

"To the men in the army, to Jonathan?" Leah asked.

"In raw physical strength you've surpassed Beo. He was second only to Jonathan and Grant. In speed you are faster than Mito, I would have to track you in a foot race to see if you've surpassed Bodhi."

"So what, I'm like tied for second?" Leah asked.

"You seem disappointed," Mr. Clean said.

Leah shrugged. "I just thought—being a descendant of a Borealis, and the bond. . ."

"Ahh," Mr. Clean said. "Well, the bond is not fully established yet."

Leah licked her lips. "How exactly does that work?"

"It is a matter of contact and mutual deactivation," Mr. Clean said.

"What exactly does that . . ."

A door appeared on the rooftop. Within the projection it appeared to go nowhere, but the warehouse-like features of Hangman's Tree could be seen as Paige walked inside.

"So uh, heads up," Paige frowned. "Jonathan is headed this way."

"How'd he look?"

"Activated," Paige shrugged. "Other than that, hard to read."

"What else is new?"

"So, know what you're going to say?"

Leah shook her head.

Paige gave a sarcastic thumbs up, followed by a look of sympathy before she pointed both thumbs back at the door. "I think I'll head out and leave you to it," Paige said.

As Paige disappeared behind the doors, Leah closed her eyes and smiled. *Well, I can't blame her . . . I don't want to be a part of this conversation either.*

"Mr. Clean," Leah said. "Would you change the simulation for me?"

CHAPTER EIGHTY-FIVE

JONATHAN STEPPED INSIDE the projection chamber and his lips drew into a line. He was standing on his street, looking at his garage. Leah was in the simulation he used to get away from his troubles.

The only difference was that as he reached the foot of his driveway, his garage door was closed—the lights off. Meanwhile, one house over, Leah's door was up, her light on, and classic rock playing loudly.

He reached the end of the driveway, but stayed well short of the threshold. Her back was to him and his gaze lingered on the bright orange glow that emanated from the lines that crossed over her shoulders onto her back.

She was as bright as he was.

"Leah, would you turn the music down?" he asked.

She nodded, her hand reaching out to turn the knob, but she didn't turn around.

"You should have told me before you went through with it."

She was staring up at that the Blind Blacksmith. "You said it was my choice."

"It is, but—"

"You wanted one last chance to talk me out of it?"

"No," Jonathan said.

This caught her off guard and she found herself turning to look at him.

"I wanted you to know my terms, now you'll just have to accept them."

"I'm listening."

He looked down at the ground, stared at her feet like he couldn't look her in the eye and say what he had to. "I let Rylee die, I had to choose between her and the world—and I couldn't. I couldn't move. I hesitated and time decided for me."

Leah's face softened, she expected him to be angry. Figured he'd finally explode, yell that she'd betrayed him, again. But, that wasn't what this was, and it was starting to make her nervous. "Jonathan . . . I . . . I know. It was an impossible choice to have to . . ."

She trailed off because the way he was shaking his head told her she wasn't understanding. "I am telling you right now. Put me in that situation, I won't hesitate. I will not watch it happen again."

She swallowed, because what he was saying was something a leader simply could not say. "Jonathan . . . you . . . you can't know what anyone might have to do."

"I'm telling you that if it comes to it. I will not watch you die."

"I don't accept those terms," she said.

"I'm telling you what is. This isn't a negotiation," Jonathan said.

She sighed. He'd never been like this, never shut the door on a discussion. When she was quiet for a while, he took his first step back, nodded and turned to leave.

She immediately hated the distance growing between them, found herself yelling at his back. "Don't you feel it?"

He paused.

"I'm happy—optimistic. Like—"

"It's like falling in love, you can't wait to see what happens next," Jonathan said.

"You do feel it," she said.

He didn't answer. Didn't turn around but didn't keep walking. "Is this what it was like for you that night. When you ran out on me? When you had to get to her?"

"Not like this. This is . . . stronger."

"My compatibility?" Leah asked.

He swallowed. "You're too close."

Her eyes turned curious, she was about to take a step toward him, but he tensed as though he sensed it and it scared him.

"That why you're standing outside?"

He turned back. And as he stared back at her, she felt something she hadn't for some time. That she could see through him—and they both knew it.

"You're more afraid of me than anything in the world right now," Leah said. "And yet you can't leave."

"If you touch me," Jonathan said. "There isn't any going back."

She considered that for a moment. "Because we'll see what's inside each other."

He nodded.

She stepped forward like it was a playful sort of game at first. She studied him with an amused smile—a beautiful smile. It dared him to leave—it dared him to stay.

The last time Jonathan seemed this innocent to her was the first time she'd kissed him. She had to make the first move. She'd missed being able to make him this nervous.

He swallowed and his face held so many questions. She was dying to answer whatever he wished if he would only ask.

"The encryption on Rylee's consciousness," Jonathan said. "You had Mr. Clean break it?"

Well, that was disappointing. She had nearly forgotten about Rylee for a moment. Apparently still the first thing on his mind.

She nodded.

Now he held back—must have seen how that name affected her. He was being kind again, didn't want to ask the question that should naturally follow.

"It wasn't the same—not like what you described," Leah said. "I spoke to her—she spoke back."

"Did she . . ." Jonathan stopped to sigh. "Understand what happened to her?"

Leah nodded.

Jonathan's eyes tightened, holding something back, each time he chanced looking at her.

"What is it, Jonathan?" Leah asked.

"My father said that when my implant was active, it was like he was there, seeing everything," he said. "Feeling everything."

Leah nodded, but didn't know what else to do.

"Everything," he repeated.

Her eyes widened. "Oh . . ."

Leah blushed a bit as she imagined Rylee rolling around on the floor laughing. "I'm glad that I know that . . . now."

She thought she noticed a knowing smile cross Jonathan's face, but he seemed to be making a valiant effort to suppress it.

She laughed at herself, and it was as though she'd given him permission to laugh with her.

After it passed, he looked at her reluctantly again.

"Okay, really, what is it, Jonathan?"

"It's just that there are so many things I wished I could have told her," Jonathan said. "But I know you don't want to hear, and I doubt Rylee would want you to hear."

Leah sighed; she was really starting to feel like Rylee's afterlife voicemail service. But, she wasn't without sympathy for his dilemma.

"I think—Rylee and I have an understanding," Leah said. "That and she isn't all that private. If you only knew the things she showed me—"

Leah stopped, blushing as his expression turned curious. "Never mind."

"Okay?"

"Look away, pretend you're talking to her. Say whatever you've been holding on to."

At first, he clearly felt ridiculous—but eventually he tried.

Leah didn't make a sound. She wished more than anything that she could not actually be there. Not be the middleman, not hear. That she could just be an empty vessel and Rylee could listen without her in the way.

Finally, he began to speak. "I knew you were the strong one. I knew you didn't need someone to save you," Jonathan said, and then his voice became a whisper. "But I wanted to. I really wanted to get you out, to set you free. And I'm—"

"Oh God. Leah, make him stop before he goes full *Dawson's Creek!*" Leah blurted out.

Jonathan's eyes turned to her in shock as Leah's hand slapped over her own mouth.

"I didn't . . . I swear," Leah said. "I wasn't even thinking anything like that."

Jonathan stepped into the garage, his momentary shock replaced with something between wonder and concern. "I believe you—the accent kind of gave it away."

Leah blinked. He was right. She hadn't sounded like herself at all. She'd sounded like Rylee using her voice.

Leah began to tremble as she stared down at the orange light beneath her shirt. "Jonathan, maybe . . . I . . . I don't like this. Maybe . . . this was a bad idea."

"Breathe, Leah," Jonathan said. "Stay calm."

"Just . . . turn it off."

"Leah no, you can't de—"

"Please, Mr. Clean, I don't—"

They fell silent at the same moment. Suddenly, Leah wasn't afraid. She wasn't disappointed or embarrassed. She wasn't questioning every life decision she'd ever made.

What she was—was deeply aware of how close Jonathan was standing. She stopped staring at the glowing lines on her chest and became captivated by those on his. Her eyes traced those lines, followed them up until she found his face.

Her thoughts, for the most part, stopped—snuffed out entirely by something primal surging through her blood. She saw a tremor run through him. His pupils dilating as he met her gaze.

She knew he felt what she did.

Nothing her mind had to say was something she cared to hear. It all seemed so irrelevant—every vestige of doubt crushed under the weight of one profound need.

Tentatively, she reached for his wrist—as though the moment might be delicate. That a sudden movement could break it. But, when her finger tips made contact with his skin, a quake ran up her arm, spread to every nerve in her body.

This was the final straw and the end of gentleness.

One last breath passed between them as they held each other's eyes, then she dragged his hand to her waist.

She wasn't asking—wouldn't even comprehend it if he dared deny her. Yet, he moved with the same insistence. He'd stepped into her. His fingers threading through her hair to take hold, pulling her toward him until she was pressed tightly to his chest.

Just before their lips met—before she closed her eyes—a thrill welled up in her. He seemed to pause at the very same moment. She saw a bright burning energy coming to life in his eyes. He stared at her as though he saw the same in hers. She closed her eyes and sought his lips.

CHAPTER EIGHTY-SIX

THEY LAY ATOP the shredded pieces of their own clothing. The Blind Blacksmith stood over them, like the headboard of a bed they'd made on the garage floor.

"Where did we get a blanket?" Jonathan asked.

Leah's eyes narrowed as she rubbed a hand across the fabric. "I don't know."

The question hung unanswered between them for a moment.

"I detected a drop in your body temperatures and took the liberty—neither of you noticed," Mr. Clean said.

Jonathan smiled. "I think I let myself forget where we were for a minute."

"Yeah, that was nice," she said. "You kind of have to, if you want to stop remembering there is an alien AI watching you."

Mr. Clean made an unnecessary sound. What could only be described as a disgruntled clearing of his nonexistent throat. "For one, that seems rather hypocritical coming from an individual who was most recently employed by The Cell."

Leah let out a long pouty breath. "Never hearing the end of that."

"And two, is it not far more an impropriety that the two of you engage in an act of fornication whilst literally lying on top of me—or that I noticed?"

Jonathan and Leah exchanged a look.

"In retrospect, we may not have the moral high ground," he said.

"Yep, I retract my comment," Leah said. "Thank you for the blanket—very thoughtful."

"Your apology is accepted but quite unnecessary," Mr. Clean said. "In the future, just know, I am literally incapable of not noticing what takes place within my own boundaries."

Jonathan gave the voice a thumbs up. Leah, however, had suddenly grown quiet. Her eyes closed, her head began shaking, and Jonathan saw her cheeks flush. "Oh no."

"What's wrong?"

With a sigh, Leah said, "I just remembered who else was watching."

Jonathan's expression darkened as he understood, but he clearly had nothing to say to improve matters.

Leah sat up, holding the blanket to her as she pondered it all.

He was quiet beside her, and as he watched, her expression seemed to teeter back and forth as she sorted out how much guilt or blame she should take about what Rylee had no doubt bore witness to. "On the other hand, fair's fair?"

She promptly laid back down, leaving Jonathan to frown at what had just happened. "What's fair?"

"Never mind, wasn't talking to you," Leah said.

He wasn't done frowning when Leah abruptly shot right back up. He watched again as she bit her lip anxiously. "That said, I probably shouldn't ever sleep with this thing turned on."

When Leah appeared in her quarters, she was wearing different clothes, and a coat to hide the light of the device. Paige, swiveled in Leah's desk chair. She practically fell out of it when Leah suddenly appeared.

"That's so much easier without the teleportation sickness."

"Finally! It's like defcon three around here," Paige said. "Mr. Clean disabled the view screens inside the chamber. No one knows where Heyer is or what the hell Jonathan's been doing."

"Oh, what did you tell them?"

"Nothing. Anthony and I all played dumb. Wasn't going to tell everyone he was having an argument with The Cell's spook twenty minutes after we got word of the conduit opening."

"Hmm," Leah said. "Good point, wonder what he'll tell them."

Paige frowned at her for a moment. "What happened to your clothes."

Leah failed to keep a straight face. "It was uhh . . . a really fierce argument."

Paige considered for a moment then shrugged. "Well, that is one way to resolve a conflict."

Leah shrugged innocently—just as a knock came at the door.

Collin poked his head in. "You guys seen Jonathan? The evacuation broadcast is going out in the next few minutes, Olivia's pretty pissed that he's MIA . . . and well, she scares me."

"Last I saw him he was on his way to the command pavilion," Leah said.

With a nod, Collin left as abruptly as he'd come.

When Leah turned back to Paige, she was staring at her, fingers tapping away on the arm of her chair.

"What?" Leah asked.

"Thought your eyes were supposed to be on fire or something?"

Leah looked at the ground and nodded. "The bond isn't fully linked until our minds have bridged."

A moment of silence passed as Paige studied her. "Maybe I misunderstood what you two were doing in there."

"Jonathan needed time," Leah said. "Said he'd find me after he checked in with Olivia on the evacuation and Mr. Clean on the conduit calculations."

"Does this mind bridge take a long time or something?" Paige asked.

"I don't know. I don't think so."

Paige groaned. "Then what's his deal? Pull the Band-Aid off already!"

"I don't think it's that simple," Leah said.

Paige's voice became a parody of itself for a moment. "Oh, hello there, I see you're about to be in a life and death struggle with an alien god. How about you let me upgrade you and the girl next door to super badass, you know, so you'll have a real fighting chance. What say you, Jonathan?"

Paige turned in her chair, giving her impression of Jonathan's answer. "Um, I need to procrastinate on this, I'm gonna go be broody while I think about it, forever."

Leah smirked throughout the whole performance. "You done?"

She dropped the mocking tone. "Since I got here, I've seen Jonathan make difficult choices. But this—this seems like a no-brainer?"

"He's afraid that with me in play, Malkier will try to take advantage of the bond. Break it, before . . . well you know."

Paige's previous certainty faltered. A moment passed, and her expression turned bitter as she shook her head. "I don't buy it. Jonathan's had a strategy and eight backup strategies for everything we've imagined Malkier might throw at Earth. If he's known all along that Malkier would try to sever the bond, then he's thought of at least five ways to use that knowledge to his advantage."

Leah considered that for a moment. "Rylee said I'd be able to see what he's thinking. . ."

"What's that now?" Paige asked.

"Rylee, she told me, that when the bridge was open, I'd get a glimpse into his head," Leah said. She had not had time to really think about that until now. "You know, it's funny that neither Heyer nor Jonathan mentioned that. Rylee had to tell me."

Paige blinked. "I'm just gonna skip right past how weird it is that you can talk to her for a second, because it seems like you just realized something important."

"Maybe," Leah frowned. "All the secrets Jonathan's been keeping from Heyer and the war council. The things he says are too dangerous for anyone but him to know. Maybe he's afraid, because he doesn't know what I'll see."

CHAPTER EIGHTY-SEVEN

JONATHAN DIDN'T SEEM surprised to find her waiting when he returned to his quarters. Leah had discovered that she too, had a sense of how far away he was now.

Leah walked to him, stared into his eyes, and put each of her hands on his shoulders.

"Mr. Clean, are you ready to deactivate my device," Leah said.

"Yes but, Jonathan, this must be done in unison," Mr. Clean said.

She looked at Jonathan expectantly.

He held her gaze, his reluctance far from gone.

"Leah . . . there are things in my head. They're dangerous. Things no one should know. If we do this, there is no way I can be sure . . ."

"Jonathan, there is nothing you could know, no burden, that I won't help you carry."

He closed his eyes. "I already know that, Leah."

Finally, after a long breath, he gave in, and opened his eyes.

"Go ahead, Mr. Clean."

The first time he stood on the bridge, he didn't know how he had come to be on his knees without a stitch of clothing. Yet while being naked in a strange place had left him exposed, he'd been engulfed in so much warmth and light that he soon forgot his vulnerability. The fog here was unearthly, warm, and heavy. Pressing in from all around like a blanket on his bare skin.

All he could see was the way the wooden planks of the bridge were laid out in front of him to follow. The bridge existed in two places at once—two minds at once. One half in his own mind, the other in Rylee's.

The last time he'd come here, his bond to Rylee's had been severed. The warmth, the fog, the light had all been gone. There was nothing to cross. A half collapsed bridge was all that remained—its planks stretching into the dark only to end at a drop into the void below.

Today as he found himself kneeling on the boards, it was as though he arrived while this place was still in the middle of renovations. He rose to his feet and watched as the darkness and cold were pushed away by a warm burning light in the distance. The bridge, broken out in front him, began reconstructing itself. Where the planks had once ended in a jagged edge over a void, a new way began to grow. At first it was like a mirage in the desert, but those waves of vision that would make him question the truth of the bridge before him faded to a shimmer, then left entirely, leaving behind a solid reality that stretched into the distance.

The winds returned, bringing that heavy warm fog.

He stood until he couldn't see more than two feet in front of him. He didn't need to inch forward in fear this time, he knew where he was going.

At that same instant, Leah knelt on an identical bridge. Naked, but warm and unafraid, she was a bit surprised. She hadn't imagined a literal bridge.

"Excuse me, ma'am, are you in need of assistance, you appear to be bare ass naked," Rylee said.

Leah sighed and turned to see Rylee standing behind her in the fog. It seemed somewhat unfair that Rylee was fully dressed in her motorcycle jacket, jeans, and boots. Even the wind sweeping Leah's hair around in every direction didn't seem to touch her.

"Can I borrow your coat?" Leah asked.

"Aren't we a bit past modesty?" Rylee asked.

When Leah only stared impatiently back at her, Rylee sighed and held the coat out. Unfortunately, the moment it left Rylee's hand for Leah's it seemed to dissolve into the fog.

Rylee shrugged. "Was worth a shot, I didn't really think it would work. This whole place is kind of about show and tell. You don't get to hide anything."

"Thanks anyway," Leah said, turning to look into the fog. "You don't seem angry."

"Sorry?"

"I didn't mean to make you watch Jonathan and me, but the moment it began—"

"Oh, I know," Rylee said. "Don't worry—it was hardly the nightmare you imagine."

Leah looked at her curiously. "Not what I expected you to . . ."

She trailed off, as she saw Rylee was having trouble keeping a straight face. *Actually, the woman was blushing?*

"What am I missing here?"

Rylee suddenly wouldn't look at her. "Let's just say, the experience was more, um . . . *immersive* . . . on my end than you probably care to know."

Leah stared at the other woman. When Rylee finally did look at her, it was with one eye, as though she were daring to sneak a peek at how Leah was reacting.

Leah's mouth opened and shut a few times. "I don't mean to be blunt here, but are you saying, it wasn't really me, but us?"

Rylee tilted her head. "Let's just say we went on a pleasant drive together, and though I was technically duct-taped to the passenger seat, I could still feel the wind in my hair as I took in the countryside."

Leah closed her eyes—for the briefest moment. She thought she was supposed to be disturbed—but that emotion wasn't genuinely there. Truth was, she'd rather have shared this with her, than learn Rylee had been forced to endure some cruel indignity. So, she didn't feel embarrassed or ashamed. She let herself laugh. A small giggle at first, but then it didn't stop, and apparently it was infectious because soon Rylee joined her.

When this ended, Leah turned back to the bridge. "He's waiting for me somewhere out there?"

"Ah well, God forbid you make Jonathan Tibbs wait," Rylee said.

Leah smiled. "I'm glad you're here, I think this would all be terrifying alone."

Rylee shrugged. "Yeah, it was."

"You're like a lewd, perverted, sensei."

"Ugh," Rylee made a face as though resisting the urge to vomit. "Changed my mind—get your ass moving, grasshopper."

Leah smiled and took a few steps onto the bridge, but then she paused and turned back. "What if . . . what if you came with me?"

The wind had been gusting in his ears for some time as Jonathan walked into the bright fog. Finally, he saw a silhouette out in front of him. Leah's forward movement much like his own the first time he'd crossed into this strange edge of consciousness.

When she came close enough to be more than a vague shape, she pulled her hair away from her eyes and saw him waiting for her. She smiled and she tried to say something, but the wind was too loud in their ears for him to hear.

Leah shrugged, and mouthed the words. "What now?"

He raised his hand only to pause in place before he reached out to her. Behind Leah, another shape was coming out of the fog. He watched in disbelief as Rylee's face emerged to stare back at him.

Fully clothed, Rylee gave his nudity a long once over before winking at him.

He looked to Leah, she smirked and nodded.

So, I'm not crazy. Leah sees her too.

He must have stared at Rylee too long, because eventually she rolled her eyes, reached into the front pocket of her coat and pulled out his father's pocket watch. He smiled as she opened the watch's face and twirled her fingers around in a circle as though saying *can we move this along, got things I'd rather be doing.*

"I miss you," Jonathan mouthed the words.

Rylee shrugged casually, as though he were stating the obvious. Finally, she nudged Leah and nodded at his still half-raised hand.

He finished reaching for her, and after a moment staring at his hand, Leah interlocked her fingers with his and held on.

She was aware of her body again as she regained consciousness. She couldn't move yet, the deactivation hadn't fully run its course. Amidst that in-between state it came over her. A presence that didn't belong, emotions that weren't her own, and a feeling like she was losing herself in the storm of someone else's mind.

Pictures began to form.

Some she thought she understood—others a mystery.

She saw Jonathan standing in front of a mirror—shimmering between different reflections. She saw him become Douglas for a moment, then change into himself again, his body seeming to stutter back and forth between them with the glowing implant in his chest the only anchor remaining unchanged.

She saw brick walls around a storage facility. Jonathan standing at a wall of racked weapons. She saw what she thought was Rylee, but then sometimes a little girl. When she was Rylee, she placed a comforting hand on Jonathan's shoulder. When she was the little girl, she held his hand.

Jonathan never seemed to pay any mind to the difference.

She saw Heyer standing in front of Jonathan, he tore his own implant from his chest and held it out. Jonathan didn't take it—only nodded at the alien as though something had been proven. An argument having gone a long time before being settled.

Most of these things she could only guess at, then she saw Douglas holding a child wrapped in blankets in a hospital room. No, the image stuttered, and Jonathan held the child.

His eyes were near tears, his voice a soft mantra. "I can't fail . . . I can't fail . . . I can't fail."

She remembered him sitting on the floor of The Cell. How she'd thought he was dreaming—talking in his sleep. Her memory—it seemed to pull her toward something inside of Jonathan. Leah saw—herself, not as though looking in a mirror, but as a web of memories in his mind.

The drifting in the labyrinth of his thoughts and associations, she knew in that moment—there had always been a question and this was the answer. She clung to stay in that single space of his mind. Slowly she became aware of the exact point where her and Jonathan's minds were bridged, and no longer had to struggle to hold herself in place, was no longer swept away by the strange associations of his mind.

Leah saw herself standing in the containment shell. Jonathan's white plastic prison deep within the facility. She stilled, felt herself become more real in this place as though she had somehow set anchor.

Jonathan was laying on the bed. He was still wearing the white uniform The Cell had given him, even though his device was active. Despite that burning glow—there was no strength in him. He looked sickly—his sheets soaked through with sweat. He grasped at lucidity the way a sick man did amid a terrible fever.

There was a clock on the wall—a clock that she knew hadn't been there in the real prison. When she looked at it, it was more like looking at snapshots of still images, each time it changed the clock hands showed different positions. Though it wasn't as though days and nights were flying by—rather—time was meaningless. Moving forward and backward with the same respect for consistency as a dream.

Flash.

Jonathan came to for a moment and looked at her standing over him. His face turning away in disgust. "Go."

Leah took a single step, shivered by the venom in his voice. Yet, she didn't obey. His eyelids flickered as he lost his grip on reality again.

Leah heard herself. "I'm not leaving you alone."

Flash.

Jonathan was trying to hold his eyes open. There had been a knock at the prison's door. Leah saw herself talking to a very disturbed looking Olivia. "Starting to look like he was telling the truth. All over the world, people are beginning to act—strangely."

Jonathan's eyes lost focus and closed.

Flash.

Leah stood over him again. Trying to get him to drink, at first his body reacted greedily for the nourishment, but as he surfaced out of the haze, he saw her holding the cup—and it was as though the water turned to bile in his mouth.

"Get away from me."

She shivered again, but wouldn't obey. "I'm not leaving you alone."

Flash.

He was naked. She was trying to keep him clean—but she couldn't get him up. He didn't even seem to notice or care when he had to go the bathroom. She had just finished changing the sheets over him when Olivia came in without knocking.

Her hair was out of sorts. She had a black eye and was wearing a bullet-proof vest over her clothes. There were splotches of blood all over her. More on her face that she hadn't bothered to wipe away.

She was carrying a steel box.

"The deterioration. I've had to lock down the upper floors. The surrounding base is lost. Our agents—can't trust anyone—more and more snap every hour—it's accelerating."

Leah nodded.

"You must be feeling it?" Olivia asked.

"I do," Leah said.

Olivia looked at her strangely; her eyes turned fierce and without warning, she yelled, "Then why aren't you crumbling!"

Leah moved slowly, putting herself between Jonathan and Olivia as the woman shivered under the strain of something unseen. Olivia had closed her eyes, seemed desperate to pull water from a well of restraint that was quickly running dry.

"So, you're staying down here?" Olivia asked.

"I'm not leaving him alone," Leah said. "He just needs more time to pull through."

Olivia took her gun from its holster and Leah froze for a long moment. Finally, Olivia turned the weapon's handle out for her. "I don't know how much time I've got left."

Leah eyed the gun warily but knew to take it before the woman changed her mind.

"You've got enough supplies?" Olivia asked.

Leah nodded.

"I'm gonna lock you in with him," she said. "We see each other again, don't hesitate. Shoot me."

Olivia turned to walk away, leaving Leah staring at the gun in her hand and the steel box Olivia had left on the floor.

Flash.

He came to for a moment.

He'd thought he heard a woman's scream, but he didn't know reality from dream.

He heard grunts, soft sobs. Something like duct tape torn from a roll.

A gasp biting down to keep quiet against pain.

Flash.

He was trapped inside his own body at times. He could hear himself roaring in anguish—couldn't tell the difference between hunger, pain, or grief. He was beginning to believe he'd been wrong. The bond could kill him.

Flash.

He came to when he rolled off the bed onto the floor. He felt a hand reach under him, trying to help him up. Finally managing to get him back onto the bed.

"Rylee?" he said. "Are you there . . . where, where are we . . ."

"No, it's just me, Jonathan," Leah said. "You fell down."

His eyes caught sight of her leaning against the cell door, his vision clearing as he heard her voice. He felt like he should be angry but all he could manage was indifference. He was so tired.

"Just—"

"I'm not leaving you," Leah said.

He was already fighting to hold on, but he saw Leah wince as she tried to lower herself back down onto the floor—something was making it very difficult and painful for her.

Then he saw the splint around her wrist.

"Did I . . . did I do that to you?" Jonathan asked.

She finally eased herself down. He realized then that it wasn't just her arm. Leah was covered in bruises.

"No," Leah said. "It wasn't your fault. Sleep now."

He couldn't have argued, was already slipping back into the bond's torture, but he knew—he knew she was lying. He'd done that to her—he was too dangerous—one violent jerk in his sleep and he might kill her—and it looked as though there had already been more than one close call.

Flash.

Leah heard her own quiet sobs in the dark.

The white light was gone. The plastics of his cell having turned clear again—there wasn't much light.

He forced himself to sit up.

She heard herself jump when he moved, stifling her sob the moment she looked at him. "Jonathan . . . oh thank you, thank you," Leah said. "You haven't come back in days."

Her voice, it didn't sound right—it sounded like desperation holding on by worn threads. She crawled over to him, tried to hide how much pain it caused to do so.

Had he hurt her again?

He looked up on the plastic door and saw what looked like a slash of dried blood on the outside.

"We lost power," Leah said. "But it's okay, it's okay . . . because I've got you . . . and you're my light."

She laughed, and he hurt so badly for her as he began to feel his mind go again. He fought to keep his eyes open.

"I think we're the only ones left Jonathan," Leah said. "I mean, the only real ones . . . the broken ones keep finding their way in somehow."

He couldn't hold himself up.

"No, please, Jonathan," Leah said. "I don't know how much longer I can hold on. . ."

His eyes closed, and he heard a voice trailing off as he slipped into darkness.

"Please don't go . . . it gets so quiet . . . I'm all alone."

Flash

Something had changed. This memory—it was different than the rest.

Jonathan slept, but he breathed easily, his body at peace in a way it hadn't been in all the other memories.

That wasn't the only change, as there was something in the room. A box—a footlocker.

Yet—no—Leah knew it wasn't real. More like a projection inside Mr. Clean, or like something imagined placed on top of what was real. But this was a memory of Jonathan's. He'd projected the footlocker.

She saw Jonathan's face twitch on the bed, and a split second later, the lid of the footlocker rattled. He shivered, and the footlocker shook like . . . like something inside was trying to force its way out.

The peaceful sleep on Jonathan's face melted away. His eyes opened to stare distantly into the ceiling, He didn't seem conscious, yet, his expression focused, turned predatory. He had that look coming over him.

His jaw clenched, and the box shook violently, rattling on the floor.

Light escaped from inside. She could see it with each shake, bright light slipping out the gaps between the lid and the trunk with each attempt to break through from the inside.

Finally, a fist shot through the top of the footlocker and a moment later it was as though the box exploded in pieces.

For a moment, there were two of him. Another Jonathan stood where the box had been. He looked up, seemed to look at her. Then began to fade away, and as he did so, the Jonathan laying on the bed opened his eyes.

Flash

Gun shots. He heard them. "Leah!"

He sat up in bed with a start—air drawing into his lungs, filling them in a way that he had almost forgot possible. His heart pounded in his ears. He was alive.

The bond, it was there, but no longer had the strength to keep him prisoner in his mind. He could feel it dying.

He swung his legs over the side of the bed. Beyond the glow of his implant, the cell and most of the black egg was shrouded by darkness. Still, it was enough to see that the door was no longer sealed. It had been ripped off its hinges.

There were three shapes on the floor—further back. Of these three he was certain. They had been men. Whatever they were now was only human in shape. Jonathan only needed a good look at the one closest to him to know he had no desire to examine the others.

In the orange glow, he could see what they had done to their own skin. Grotesquely mutilated, wounds like an animal that kept chewing at an itch. He knew what they were, and he didn't want to look any closer. He didn't want to recognize who they were before the deterioration had taken their minds.

However, this creature, was lying in a pool of its own blood.

"Jonathan," Leah whispered. "Are you really stand—ouch . . . ouch . . ."

She was in the corner. The gun Olivia had given her on the floor but not out of reach. She was holding her side with one hand. He knelt beside her and saw that she'd tried to tape herself closed—it looked like what a child might try, if there was no one around to help them and they were bleeding to death.

He realized that the blood pooling under his feet didn't all belong to the creatures in the doorway.

"Leah?" Jonathan knelt beside her.

She looked at him, and seemed to be so happy to hear his voice that she forgot her wound. She smiled but when she tried to talk blood came up and she began to choke.

"Don't talk . . . don't talk," Jonathan said.

Leah, not the one on the floor, but the voyeur in his mind, knew her own shadow was fading. Wouldn't be long before this copy of her died. Her shadow didn't try to obey or save her strength. She took a long breath and took her hand away from her wound. "We aren't alone in the dark . . . I kept . . . your friend."

As her hand fell limp it opened, and the portal stone rolled out.

She wasn't clear on when the bridge ended. When she found herself lying on the floor, it was at the end of a what felt like a long period between sleep and consciousness. There was a sense that he never fully left her mind completely. As though she could still feel his thoughts and emotions but be no more aware of them than she could the air around her. She knew he was close because she could breathe.

When she opened her eyes, Jonathan was sitting up. He looked as far away in his thoughts as she felt, but he noticed her rousing. She sat up beside him and they watched one another curiously for some time.

"I already miss knowing what you're thinking," Leah said. "Because you're being so quiet."

"I'm trying to understand what just happened," Jonathan said.

"Was it different than before?" Leah asked.

"I'm not sure," Jonathan said. "Because, I think, the bond was . . . it was as though it was answering a question. A question I don't even know the words to ask. Like it was searching inside of you for the answer."

Leah didn't need him to elaborate—she understood what he was trying to explain.

"That didn't happen with Rylee?" Leah asked.

"I think it did," Jonathan said, unsure. "But, I hardly knew Rylee when it happened with her. So, the burning question was a simple one: *Who the hell are you?*"

Leah laughed a bit. "Right."

What she'd seen was far clearer to her through that lens. All of it answered a question she'd had since waking up in the cell beside him. *How can he know the truth of me and still trust me?*

No spoken answer would have ever been certain to her. She had to feel the change in him—see how it was he knew that she'd never abandon him.

"Jonathan," Leah asked. "What answer did you go looking for?"

He looked at her and took her hands in his. "I don't think we should talk about what we saw."

Her eyes narrowed as she pretended to smile. "You're worried I saw something dangerous. I didn't. My question didn't have anything to do with your big dumb secrets."

"You can't know that for sure," Jonathan said.

She considered that for a moment, then smirked. "Fine, I won't tell you what I saw. Don't see how that lets you off the hook."

He closed his eyes, tongued his cheek, and nodded. "I can tell you what I saw, but you have to understand that if I knew how to put the question into words I would have just asked."

"I get that," Leah said. "So, what was the answer to this question you didn't know how to ask."

He swallowed. "You were alone in a room. At first it was like you were talking to yourself in a mirror, then I realized who you were talking to—"

"Okay—stop. I . . . I know what you saw."

She shivered, caught completely flat footed. "That . . . that was not for you. What the hell could that have answered?"

He was quiet for a long while.

"Knowing the answer, the question is very clear to me now," Jonathan said. "What do I say to make her stay out of The Never? The answer, no such words exist."

"Are you angry?" Leah asked.

He shook his head. "I've been naïve. Thought life had run out of threats to scare me. But now . . . knowing you'll be locked in The Never with a god who would move heaven and earth to hurt me. I've never been this scared in my life."

CHAPTER EIGHTY-EIGHT

MARGOT STOOD OVER the empty luggage on her bed with satisfaction. While it had been weeks since The Cell had deemed her free to return home, she hadn't unpacked. Admittedly, she often continued living out of her bags until their contents slowly converted themselves to laundry. She'd just gone through the trouble of putting away the last of the paraphernalia that accompanied her to Seattle when she heard a knock at her door.

"Was I expecting company?" she asked the rubber duck taped to the side of her monitor.

With a shrug she zipped the empty bag and tossed it in the closet on her way to the door.

She froze when she looked through the peep hole.

"It's me, Margot," Rivers said.

"Oh my god!" Yanking the door open, she forgot the chain, swore, and had to shut it again. Finally, she got the door open, and flung herself into the hallway to embrace the man. "I thought you were dead or worse you jerk!"

Sometime later, they stood in her kitchen.

"The Cell wouldn't tell me anything," Margot said. "I woke up after the hangar was attacked. You were gone. All Olivia would say was that your whereabouts were above my security clearance. She couldn't wait to send me home."

Rivers nodded.

"It's a long story," he said. "I'll fill you in once we get back."

"Get back?" Margot asked. "No, no, no, no . . . It's been all over the news, Seattle is being evacuated. No flights in or out."

Laurence's expression was serious.

"Come on man! I just unpacked," she added.

"The Cell is working with Jonathan Tibbs. There is a project, has to be done, and we only have four days."

"Why me? There must have been someone closer."

"Olivia wants someone we trust to work alongside Jonathan's guy, someone who's particularly good with numbers and patterns," Rivers said. "But, more than anything, Jonathan's guy was already impressed with you."

She frowned at all of that. She had so many questions she did not know where to start. "When did I meet Jonathan's guy?"

"You haven't. Clock's ticking," Rivers said. "In or out?"

"You know I'm in . . . but dammit Laurence, ever since you started working with The Cell, it seems I don't ever get to know what the hell I'm signing up for," Margot said.

He signaled for her to come close. She thought he was going to whisper, but he gently put his arm around her.

She looked at him suspiciously. "This is weird . . ."

"I apologize, this is going to be disorientating," Rivers said, and the next moment, the kitchen was empty.

They stood in the projection chamber, their eyes blazing as they were activated together for the first time since the bridge.

"Didn't hurt," Jonathan said. "Activation. I mean, not like it usually does."

Leah nodded. "I don't have your experience, but it seemed faster."

He nodded.

"Dwell on it later, I'm not waiting another minute to see if all this hype about the bond lives up to reality."

He took a long breath. "Mr. Clean, I need a Ferox projection—nothing fancy, just something with accurate physiology."

"Perth and Beo have established a simple test to gauge the strength of newly implanted soldiers."

"Alright," Jonathan said.

The projection was simple, not requiring the entire chamber to slip into the void to come into being. A Red Ferox emerged out of the floor, breathing in a lifelike manner, but staring straight ahead. Meanwhile, a wall of metal netting formed some thirty feet behind it.

"Ladies first?" Jonathan asked.

She shrugged and stepped up to the creature. At full height, her head stood at about the middle of its chest.

Jonathan could see she'd been practicing.

She considered her target, set her stance, and stepped into a solid strike, turning her hip to aim as much power as she could into its center of gravity. A thunderclap erupted as the Ferox shot back. At first, the netting swallowed it, stretching backward into the chamber as it slowed the projection's momentum. Luckily, though it was ricocheted back at them, the netting acted like a spider's web, holding the projection in place as the elastic cables returned to their original state. When the Ferox came to a stop, it was set on the ground and walked slowly back to its starting position.

Leah and Jonathan gave it a once over, then exchanged wide-eyed looks.

Jonathan had hammered away at these things enough times in his life to know what it took to crack through the outer armor. They were particularly more resilient around the chest, where the plating was thickest to protect internal organs.

Leah's strike had left a hand-size dent, a webbing of cracks spread out over most of the entire torso. Black Feroxian blood was already oozing down from the openings. Had she done the same with a weapon, or had the Ferox been shot through realistic terrain after receiving such a blow, the fight would have already been over.

"Would you like to reset the projection?" Mr. Clean asked.

"I don't know, Tibbs. You want to try to follow that?" Leah said.

He surveyed the damage again and let out an impressed whistle. "Honestly, not really."

She smirked. "Get over here and punch this thing."

"Sure, don't want to see she-hulk angry," he said.

The projection refreshed itself as Jonathan stepped into range. He set his feet and shoulders much like Leah had, then tilted his head in a *here goes nothing* sort of way.

What followed was not a thunderclap. The Ferox did not shoot away. In fact, the projection's feet didn't move an inch.

"Ahh . . . hell," Jonathan said.

There had been a sound. Wet meaty noise followed by the slap of splattering Ferox insides hitting the floor behind the projection. Jonathan had followed through expecting the same resistance that would have shot the Ferox across the room. Instead he found himself nearly shoulder deep in the thing's torso, his fist protruding out the back.

Leah blinked in shock. Then her hand went to her mouth to keep herself from laughing as Jonathan resorted to putting a foot against the projection to pull his arm free.

Once he'd stepped back from it, he stood straight and looked down at an arm, coated hand to shoulder in viscous black gore. When he looked to Leah, she had gotten control of her laughter and arched a brow over her blazing eyes.

"Still want to tell me the benefits don't outweigh the risk?"

CHAPTER EIGHTY-NINE

NOV 29, 2005 | 10 PM | SEATTLE

FROM A DISTANT vantage, the overcast sky became an unnatural gradient. Grey, but growing red as one drew closer to ground zero. This had nothing to do with the sun rise—that was still a long way off.

The Never Army had to hold their positions for hours. It began with the appearance of a single red point that came into being a few feet over an empty intersection. Over the next hour, that small dot grew in surges, until finally a flat half circle wide enough to march an army through filled the street.

By the time the conduit had reached full size the smell of ozone had permeated the air for miles.

Jonathan's friends stood beside him, had been there since before he'd become activated.

In the real world, the real Collin, Hayden, and Paige would be standing beside him as he went into flux—a moment seemingly frozen in time awaiting the outcome of a war. In The Never, his friend's shadows had watched him fall to the floor. Watched his chest come to life with light.

Leah could not be with them.

Mr. Clean and Margot's calculations required everyone in his army to remain in position while the conduit came into being. Jonathan wasn't supposed to move outside of a four-foot square that Margot and her team had marked off with duct tape. There were nearly four hundred such spots now marked throughout the city, creating a three-dimensional grid out of his soldiers intending to force the conduit into the specific location of their choosing.

All that said, having no device, where his roommates stood had no effect on the outcome. So, being who they were, they decided to be at his side when the conduit came into being.

The four were standing on the eighth floor of a building that overlooked ground zero. Jonathan's square stood beside a large window where he could watch the conduit grow to full size. Periodically, his team leaders checked in over the communicator. For now, all they had to report was that they had visual on the conduit and were ready to move the moment he gave the go ahead.

For Jonathan, staring at a mammoth red portal and knowing an army of death monsters would pour through was the exact opposite of waiting for a pot to boil. Time contracted, as it always does when there was something he didn't want to face. Every moment felt as though it raced by, like the universe had accidently sat on the remote's fast forward button.

Hayden stood to Jonathan's left, fidgeting with his beard. "Well, there is a giant red archway to another dimension down there. Guess that pretty much means I'm the shadow version of myself. The one who's gonna watch this all play out."

On Jonathan's right, Collin and Paige stared out the window as well.

"What are they waiting for?" Paige asked.

"Malkier won't cross the threshold until he's certain an hour has passed on our side," Jonathan said. "This ensures Mr. Clean's shadow is offline before he begins any assault."

"Right," Paige said.

A moment passed in silence, and a thought occurred to him. He found himself nudging Collin with his elbow.

Collin turned, eyebrows going up as he waited for Jonathan to say something. Luckily after years of friendship Jonathan was able to tell the man what he was thinking with a few facial expressions. Mostly, he looked to Paige, then back to Collin a few times until the man's eyes went wide with understanding.

Of course, a moment later Collin looked as though he didn't know if, even now, he could bring himself.

Jonathan stared at him with a pitiless expression, to which Collin finally nodded and took a deep breath.

"Hey, Paige, could I talk to you for a sec," he said. "Somewhere a little more private."

She frowned at him for a moment, then shrugged and followed him.

They were in an office building, and Collin took her far enough away that they wouldn't be overheard, but Jonathan couldn't help noticing he could still see Collin's reflection in the glass after he'd asked her to step into a cubicle.

He saw his friend close his eyes, say maybe five words.

Jonathan found himself wanting to look away. Not so much to give them privacy, but because he was afraid for his friends. He knew the next few seconds would be happy or just . . . incredibility embarrassing for everyone.

That's when he saw Collin get slapped across the face.

Jonathan closed his eyes for a moment, he could practically feel the man's horror at getting that reaction. Then something odd happened. Jonathan opened his eyes and chanced one more glance. He saw Paige's hands reach out of the cubical, grab both sides of Collin's head, and pull him lips first toward her. They disappeared behind the cubical wall.

He tilted his head in thought. Until something occurred to him.

He opened a line to Leah. "So, Leah, any chance you told Paige about that conversation I had with Collin a few weeks back?"

The line was quiet for a while.

"Conversation? Which . . . Oh," Leah said. "Right."

"Taking that as a yes," he said.

"So, uh, Paige and I promised there would never be secrets between us again. I agreed, then um . . . she immediately asked if there was anything I needed to get off my chest."

"Uh huh," he said.

"Oh, shut up. World doesn't end, we're getting frozen yogurt tomorrow," Leah said. "I want that yogurt, Jonathan."

He smiled.

"Not a big blue sky-beam," Hayden said.

Jonathan, looked at him sideways. "What?"

"You know. Giant hole in the sky, energy beam coming down," Hayden said. "It's like the thing the good guys have to stop in every sci-fi blockbuster."

Jonathan smiled. "Red, vertical, street level . . . hope you're not disappointed."

Hayden's arms crossed over his chest and he sighed. "Well, it isn't following the tropes. It's practically flat. This thing really looks more like a portal to hell from a horror movie."

"You're the expert," Jonathan said.

Hayden pointed. "I'd avoid those edges."

"Huh?"

"Beneath the black fog wisping off it, you can see it has clearly defined edges. Probably slice through whatever it touches."

"I'll keep that in mind," Jonathan said, while he wondered if this would be the last film rant he'd ever hear Hayden give.

A few minutes later, Collin and Paige rejoined them at the window. They both had a dishevelment about their hair and clothing. In addition, Collin's cheek sported a red palm print.

"You know it's strange. Being a shadow doesn't feel any different. I don't know why I expected it would." Collin stopped to take a long breath. "I guess we're not long for existence. No matter who wins."

"I'm sorry," Jonathan said.

Collin shook his head. "No, no. It's just worth keeping in mind. You know, in case, sacrifices need to be made."

"Your time may be short, but don't throw it away," Jonathan said.

"We get that," Paige said.

"Oh, I'll avoid doing anything heroic," Collin said, with a smile. "But, if I change my mind, you need to make it back to tell me how brave I was."

Jonathan looked at the three of them. "You're not shadows to me."

This came out heartfelt and brought a sudden awkwardness. The good kind. The sort where they all knew he was telling them how much he loved them while being too abashed to just say the words.

"You know," Collin said. "If I don't do anything heroic, you have my permission to lie to everyone about it."

"I'll take some of that action as well," Hayden said.

Paige snorted, then as they all looked at her, she shrugged and nodded.

They all smiled, then looked back at the conduit, and the smiles melted away.

Perhaps it wasn't the best way to have spent that hour waiting. But, as the time flew by, Jonathan had a few last laughs with his friends, and he wouldn't have changed a moment of it.

Eventually, Mr. Clean's voice came through over a private channel to his comm. "You told me to notify you when we reached fifty-eight minutes, do you still wish—"

"Yes," Jonathan said. "I need thirty seconds."

His roommates, having heard his half of the conversation, looked at him curiously.

With no explanation, he hugged each of them in turn. "You know, since the very beginning you've always offered to go with me. To face anything with me," Jonathan said.

He'd just pulled away from Paige, stepped back to the center of the duct tape square and looked at them like it might be the last time. Then they disappeared.

"They're safe," Mr. Clean said.

"Thank you."

"I suppose I should say *goodbye* myself. My protocols are about to put me into slumber. I know it may seem that my nature makes me impartial to the outcome, but. . . I do hope to see you again. Good luck, Jonathan."

"I've never once thought you impartial, Mr. Clean," Jonathan said.

A few seconds later, a small sound only Jonathan could hear told him that the AI was gone as well.

He closed his eyes, stood alone at that window.

When he opened them, the sadness on his face melted away. A predatory gaze reflected in the glass as he stared down at the conduit.

Pulses of energy, thousands of them, fireflies the size of volleyballs began to pour across the threshold.

His wait had just come to an end.

CHAPTER NINETY

HIS ARMY KNEW what those spheres of energy were meant to accomplish. In fact, it was comforting to know Mr. Clean's predictions about his counterpart were this accurate. The AI had been rather thorough in exploring the many avenues by which Malkier could go about crippling human technology from the other side of a dimensional conduit.

As the pulses poured through the gateway, they scattered in all directions before shooting into the atmosphere, each with its own wildly erratic flight path.

Jonathan shook his head and sighed as he watched.

Mr. Clean had said that a mere sixty-seven would be all it took, and there was no limit to the number Cede could send through. They had known early on that without Mr. Clean to counter them, the pulses would get through the moment the AI was offline. Still, it appeared Malkier had been concerned that some attempt would be made, because the numbers pouring through that archway were at least twenty times what was necessary.

Jonathan watched the sky as they set about their work. The sight was—pretty—to say the least. Not unlike the northern lights he'd only ever seen in pictures. Within seconds of the phenomenon's appearance in the sky, every light in the city went out in unison.

"Check."

"Check."

"Check."

Each of his command teams' leaders confirmed that the comm built into their helmets still functioned. Just as Mr. Clean had been certain there was nothing they could do to stop the majority of human tech being disabled, he had been certain that there was no way for Malkier to disable the Borealis technology they controlled.

"Check," Olivia said, last to sound off.

Unlike the rest, she was outside the city, safe but not too far from the containment perimeter setup by the human military.

Olivia's perimeter was currently made up of thousands of soldiers who had only learned the full truth of why they had been mobilized in the last few hours. That is, since they entered The Never. Unfortunately, the truth included learning just how close they were to ground zero of an alien invasion. Still, her forces were better off than the rest of the world in some respects. For instance, they knew not to panic when the lights went out.

Like The Never Army, each battalion under Olivia's command was able to stay in communication with ear pieces she'd provided, compliments of Mr. Clean. Jonathan's men could warn the perimeter if a large gathering of Ferox were headed their way, but for the most part Olivia and General Delacy understood it was their job to turn back or kill whatever got past his men.

While the airspace around Seattle had been empty for days, everywhere else around the globe, planes were dropping out of the sky.

At first, most of the world would assume their power outages were local. Some would realize sooner than others that this wasn't the case. They would go to pick up a phone they knew to be charged and find it wouldn't turn on. They would go to start a car, and unless that car was very unsophisticated, the engine would not turn over. If it was day in their part of the world, the sky wouldn't tell them much, but if it was night, they would look outside and see the same display in the sky as Jonathan did now.

Over the next few hours, the planet would begin to panic. Those responsible for maintaining their cities' power grids would realize that they had no explanation for the failure—and even more frightening, they would have no way of telling anyone. Somewhere, right now, the shadow of Jonathan's mother was likely sitting on a cruise ship that was dead in the water.

Hopefully, by now, she wasn't alone. His roommates would be standing in her room explaining how Jonathan was a drama queen and had taken them out of a battle they had been helping him prepare to fight for months.

He imagined Paige would be the one to understand it first. See that he'd sent them to a place where panic would take longer to set in. Safe from looting and rioting that might begin shortly after power outages in major cities. The cruise ship would be cut off from all of that, floating out in the Mediterranean off the coast of Italy.

Only The Cell and The Never Army knew for certain that this wasn't simply an EMP nor the effects of a neutron bomb. Jonathan turned his attention back to the portal as he got Anthony on the comm.

"Anthony, Margot," Jonathan said. "I'm hoping you have good news for me."

"The Mechs are functional," Hoult said.

"And the packages?" Jonathan asked.

"The Cell's containment fields are holding, diagnostics confirm all hardware functional, all systems go as far as I can tell from the equipment," Margot said.

"Good . . ." Jonathan trailed off a moment, as he saw new movement at the portal, and reports of visual confirmation came over the comm. "Stay safe."

While it's been phrased a number of ways since mankind started fighting one another, it is a widely accepted truth that no plan survives first contact with the enemy.

Which was why, Jonathan's opening strategy was intended to deny the Ferox making any contact with his forces for as long as possible.

The first enemy to step through the conduit was alone. A single Ferox walking out of the arch into an empty city intersection. It was green, young, and small for the species—only a little larger than an average human male.

For his army, the city had been so empty over the last few days they frequently had the surreal sense usually reserved for dreams when one finds themself the last person on Earth.

Jonathan knew this Ferox wouldn't feel anything of this nature. From the looks of the Green—small, with no visible scars, he doubted the Ferox had ever been on Earth. Yet, this lone Ferox possessed something he'd never seen on a Green or any other of the species. Thick rubbery looking strands that ran down from its head to its lower back. Almost like a mane of dreadlocks.

Dammit, female, he thought.

He'd always known it was a possibility. Malkier might spare no available soldiers when he made his play for Earth. If this foretold that he intended to send in the females, the number of enemies they were dealing with had at least doubled. For the moment, what was more troubling was that it remained to be seen what the female of the species was capable of. No one in his army had ever encountered one.

She took a few steps away from the portal and sniffed at the air. She seemed to only be putting enough distance between her and the gateway to ensure the next one through wouldn't step into her.

"Anyone ever seen a Ferox look like he does?" Perth asked.

"It's a she—young from the looks of it," Jonathan said.

"So . . . that's a damn She-rox?"

A second female came through—its behavior much like the first. Soon, they stopped coming one at a time, began to trickle in by smaller groups until there were fifteen standing in the empty intersection. Somewhat mysteriously, no more arrived.

While he couldn't hear them, the She-rox were obviously communicating, and as he watched, he had a pretty good idea what they were discussing.

"Olivia," Jonathan said. "Hold tight. We got a development, and I don't want to get this party started just yet."

"Received."

He opened a channel to every team leader.

"Change in plans. No one engages this batch," Jonathan said. "Stay out of sight and let them through."

The She-rox—Perth's name had apparently stuck—were quick to reach a consensus. They broke into five groups of three, one of which remained at the mouth of the conduit. The four other groups each took one of the paths out of the intersection and shot out into the city's dark streets.

Jonathan opened another channel. "Bodhi, you and three others use the gleamers, stay out of sight, keep an eye on each group."

"Received."

He'd lost sight of them, but Bodhi didn't leave him waiting long.

"On them, but they're quick," Bodhi whispered.

Jonathan had no doubt.

No Red or Alpha to lead. The youngest Green males had always been the most comfortable running on all fours. Their greatest strength was their speed, while their greatest weakness was their hot heads.

From what he'd seen, he was betting the She-rox were faster, and less bloodthirsty. If his instincts were wrong about this—it was a small gamble. One group of Gremlins would hit the waterfront soon. The other three would eventually hit Olivia's perimeter. That might not be a bad thing.

If the human soldiers were going to stand their ground against an incoming pack of Ferox, he'd prefer it not be a large Red or an Alpha on their first engagement.

"Wait, they stopped—they're talking again," Bodhi said. "Okay, now they're turning around. Heading straight back the way they came."

"Scouts," Jonathan said. "Let them report back."

They had not encountered any resistance—so let Malkier entertain the possibility that the city has been abandoned.

When the four scouting parties returned, there was another exchange, then one from each of the group stepped back through while the rest took up sentry positions around the archway.

"Now we wait," Jonathan said.

"Standing by," Olivia said.

The wait became an exercise in patience as they watched. Jonathan felt the weight of it most. He was trusting his instincts to make this first call of the battle. He knew the morale of the men would either be bolstered or weakened by how it panned out. He wanted to give them an early win.

When activity picked up around the conduit again, he smiled and took a vindicated breath.

They came shoulder to shoulder—twenty across, likely the maximum number the conduit would accommodate without shearing limbs at the edges. One row was followed by another and another. These were males, they varied in size and color, and though they obeyed orders he could see the discipline of holding lines was new to them.

Looks like the prophet has been teaching Ferox to march, Jonathan thought.

"Olivia, you're up," Jonathan said. "Roll out the welcome mat."

"Received," Olivia said. "Detonation in ten . . . nine . . ."

When the count began, every face shield in his army that hadn't already been locked down snapped into place. They left their duct tape squares and took to whatever cover was closest to their position, each man counting silently along with Olivia as they watched row upon row of Ferox come through.

"Five . . . four . . . three . . ."

CHAPTER NINETY-ONE

ONE OF THE non-negotiables that came with the US Government's agreement to the covert partnership with The Never Army, was that any explosives provided would remain under their control. Due to the worldwide failure of human technologies, this was a bit of grey area, as while the explosives may have belonged to the military, Mr. Clean had to provide triggers that would function.

In the end, Jonathan agreed, as long as Olivia was the one who controlled the triggers. He didn't want someone he didn't know second guessing him when he said go—which was ironic, seeing as how their relationship's first real hurdle had been about whether or not to press a trigger.

Communications, the necessary city-wide monitoring equipment, everything that allowed Olivia a command center to support her perimeter and The Never Army—were all Borealis tech designed to work independently of Mr. Clean the moment he went offline.

Three . . . two . . .

Olivia flipped a switch on a control board. "Detonation."

The explosion shook a four-block radius around the conduit. The marching Ferox stopped, some immediately dropping to all fours in preparation of attack. The cause of the quake took a moment to become obvious, but once it did all those white eyes turned up the street. Straight out in front of the conduit's opening, the road ended in one of Seattle's tallest buildings.

The building's height wasn't what made it special tonight—but its unique proportions. While it was very tall it was also rather skinny as far as skyscrapers go.

When the lower floors burst forth with fire, the street was pelted with broken glass and debris as two thick clouds of smoke rose up into the night.

For a moment, there seemed to be no consequence—the building simply became a roaring inferno around its sidewalks.

The Ferox didn't immediately see a threat—but to be fair, with every light out in the city, what followed was a tad slow at the start. Framed by that surreal light show in the sky, the entire building looked like just another dark obelisk standing amongst hundreds of others. At least, until it began to lean.

Soon, the tower was looming, growing larger as it plummeted toward the conduit. This was where its uniquely skinny nature came into play. As the pull of gravity took over with increasing speed, the building didn't crash through all its neighbors on each side. Rather, it was as though it lined up perfectly with the street. The skyscraper fell between the buildings and came crashing down on the first Feroxian wave.

The Ferox were disorderly in their attempt to scatter when The Columbia Center collapsed onto them, but it didn't stop there. The top half of the building was literally sliced through as the tower crashed down on the conduit.

Grant opened his face shield as he peeled the wrapper off a fun size Milky Way headed for his mouth.

His armored suit was good camouflage against the obsidian-like stone that covered the Feroxian Plane. For the moment he was hidden, lying flat beneath a tarp at the top of one of the black rock towers that protruded from the planet's surface.

He had no explanation for the pillars; the closest thing he'd ever seen on Earth were the hoodoos in Utah's deserts—and that was a loose resemblance at best. Whatever, he wasn't a geologist.

He'd had to climb the tower four days ago. Well, four Earth days if he went by the passing of hours. Walking across the surface of the Feroxian Plane as he followed the pilgrimage to this massive pit, he'd soon discovered the cycles of light and dark didn't seem to obey any set amount of time here. How the hell one day ended in twelve hours and the next thirty-six—was outside his wheelhouse. Whatever, he wasn't an astrophysicist.

Without the Alpha Slayer device active in his chest the climb would have been a challenge. However, the need for stealth had increased with every step closer to the pit. During the trek he'd had to keep a great deal of distance. The cloaking device Heyer had given him—some alien artifact Jonathan had apparently taken off a Ferox prisoner—had a limited life span. They needed Mr. Clean to recharge it, which meant Grant had to use it sparingly.

They both knew Grant would need as much time as possible once they reached the pit. He'd had to activate the cloak and the gleamers to make it up the tower. One loud noise or dislodged rock might have drawn the attention of the Ferox horde spread out around the pit. The gleamers helped, though he hadn't had as much time as he would have liked to get used to them once he got to the Feroxian Plane.

At the tower's summit, his HUD indicated he was only a hundred and fifty feet above the creatures.

The Ferox seemed to take no interest in the towers, and luckily, much of the other wildlife he'd seen didn't pay them much attention either. That was a good thing; it would only take one curious Ferox, noticing a smell or a noise and coming up to investigate his perch to bring his mission to a swift end. One Ferox screaming whatever guttural growl meant, "Abomination!" in their language and he'd have thirty of the damn things up here with him in less than a minute.

Thing was, only having to deal with thirty was wishful thinking. The entire pit was surrounded by thousands.

He'd chosen a tower far enough away from the pit that his scope gave him a largely unobstructed view. Paired with HUD built into his helmet, tracking single individuals in the mass of creatures was an easy enough task. In fact, having now spent days behind enemy lines, the constant fear of discovery had waned. His surveillance of the pit had become a somewhat eventless slog.

Until the last two days, the goings on below had been like watching one of those Discovery Channel documentaries on the building of the pyramids on loop. Thousands of Ferox, performing relentless amounts of labor to construct a massive object, all driven by a leader who proclaimed himself a god.

Swap the prophet for a pharaoh and it was a decent analogy. Though to be fair, the Ferox seemed far more willing than human slaves.

At the center of the pit there was now a massive circular platform of black stone. From this distance, Grant couldn't be sure, but it appeared to be made up of the same black stone as the gateways that ringed the pit's interior. The platform was far more massive, could not be brought down as a single piece. Rather, sixteen slices of the rock had been hauled down the ramp and fit into place. From Grant's vantage, it looked like lizards putting a giant pie back together.

Grant remembered—or his shadow remembered, the distinction had grown rather fuzzy—standing on the gateway before he'd entered The Never. According to Heyer the individual platforms hadn't been moved for centuries. Only at the onset of the pilgrimage had Malkier given the Ferox tribes orders to move them. For the tribes, this was to learn that these sacred relics they had believed to have been literally sculpted by their gods out of the stone where they had stood, could be carried off if the prophet permitted it.

In the previous Feroxian cycle of light and dark, the platform had been completed. Today, swaths of the creatures had begun forming into what looked like ranks. Something was commanding them to form into those units, but how those orders were being communicated remained a mystery to him. While the effort fell far short of a human military parade, the Ferox seemed to be attempting to form lines and move in unison. After days of observing them, the sight was very unnatural.

While the marching Ferox might have been weird, a little over an hour ago the conduit had begun to open. That had been a spectacle.

It started with one long low thundering tone. The sound had kept building until he could feel the land vibrating for miles around the pit. Unlike those on the ground, he'd had the vantage point to see how the effects stretched out over the landscape. The pit taking on a look of a large subwoofer implanted beneath the surface. His teeth chattered as he watched the particles of dirt around him hover off the ground in sync with the frequency.

Around the same time, the air began to fill with the smell of ozone. Electricity started to jump about within the gateway fields. The arcs seemed random at first, but slowly began to fall into a pattern.

Borealis energy, that red-orange glow given off by portal stones, began to build at the ends of the sundial-like tips on each gateway. Starting with those furthest from the platform near the pit's edge, lines of energy began to link with neighboring gateways. A network building until each of the seven gateway fields was one closed grid of power lines. Finally, each field sent a massive orange line of energy to feed into the platform.

When this happened, the vibrations stopped, the sound faded off into the distance, and the conduit began to take form on the platform. Beginning as a fixed dot over the center, it grew in surges. As each of the seven fields gave up their stored energy, the brightness of their grids dwindled, until each fell into what seemed a sustained state. By that time, a half circle of red and black had formed a dividing line across the platform's diameter. Grant's HUD estimated the opening's size a little under 30 meters, about the length of a basketball court.

Grant noticed then that most of the Ferox had fallen to a knee. Frankly, he couldn't blame them; had he not already been lying on his stomach he might have joined them. The whole event had felt like watching the eye of a god open to stare back at him.

One Ferox remained standing inside the pit. Not a difficult task to figure out who, he was the only Ferox below covered head to toe in alien steel armor. His entire body seeming to reflect more light than there was to catch.

The prophet walked toward the platform through the kneeling masses, his posture more human than Ferox at times. The stark difference between him and everyone else in the pit laid bare as most of the Ferox horde were naked beasts armed only with claws and teeth.

Most, but not all.

Roughly one in five of the Ferox carried a series of sacs strapped across their back. The sacs seemed to be made from the digestive tracts of local wildlife, their surfaces like looking down on crude oil. He thought of the Ferox who carried them as Bladder Backs, they seemed to tolerate having the sacs strapped to them about the same way most dogs make peace with being forced to wear a Halloween costume.

They weren't the only oddity in the pit.

The Ferox had never been allowed to bring weapons into the Arena. Heyer had said that though each tribe was different, weapons were seldom used by the species. As Grant looked over the horde, he saw that some still carried the hammers and picks they had used while digging. But, he had seen some with far more vicious looking items in their hands. Things that looked like the war axes of fantasy video games. Clearly not intended for anyone of a human size to realistically wield. The heads were sharpened obsidian rock and the handles made from what he suspected to be the bones of either local creatures . . . or the remains of other Ferox.

Those that carried the weapons did have one other uniqueness. Grant only noticed it when he took a closer look through the scope. Their skin had intricate designs chiseled or cut into their flesh. The scars looked something like the tribal tattoos of humans; but each Ferox's skin bore different symbols.

The weapon carriers handled their massive weapons with the same regard a human might a wood axe. Grant had yet to see anything on the Feroxian Plane that could conceivably be chopped down. But he had only seen a small fraction of the place.

He activated the tracking system. Looking out over the crowd, Heyer's head lit up in Grant's HUD as though he'd been dipped in fluorescent paint. He knelt among the Ferox as the conduit opened.

The prophet gave no sign that they were to rise. Yet, most of the Ferox stood in some semblance of unison as he stepped to the conduit. Heyer was one of those slower to stand, likely because he wasn't plugged into whatever it was that Malkier was using to communicate his orders. Heyer had to do his best to mimic the actions of the Ferox around him.

As he made his way to the platform, Malkier made a show of standing before the opening. The Ferox all watched him with wide white eyes. Occasionally they roused in excitement and agreement. It took a while for Grant to realize what was going on. The prophet was giving a speech or a sermon . . . but neither he nor Heyer could hear it.

Grant opened a line to Heyer. The alien couldn't respond, couldn't risk whispering in a human tongue surrounded by thousands of Ferox.

"You know how he is communicating? Scratch your neck or something."

Heyer slowly reached up and touched his neck. He did this with something extra though, his individual fingers wiggling a bit before his hand fell back to his side.

"That mean you have a guess but aren't certain?" Grant asked.

Heyer deliberately scratched his neck this time.

There was nothing more to follow up on. Right now, with so much quiet amongst the horde, they couldn't get into any more details beyond: yes, no, and maybe.

After what felt like an eternity of being deaf and watching a program with no subtitles, the prophet raised one armored hand.

Grant, begrudgingly, had to give him credit for the theatrics that followed.

It was as though he summoned thousands of bright white pulses of energy from the sky. They poured down from the clouds and coalesced into a sphere over the pit. Malkier, Heyer, and Grant were the only ones amongst the thousand present that knew the whole show was being driven by Cede, while the Ferox gazed up in wonder as though they bore witness to the power of their gods.

Finally, the prophet turned, his hand pointing toward the conduit. It basically looked like Malkier was firing celestial energies into the conduit. Once the sphere of light was depleted, he assumed that Malkier had stopped speaking as well. This assumption was mostly based on the look of the Ferox horde. If Grant had to guess, the prophet had just finished delivering the equivalent of the speech from *Independence Day*. The crowded horde coming to life with eager roars for battle.

This was not the sort of morale boost you wanted to see your enemy get right before a war began. Sure, maybe a part of Grant would always want to see Jonathan fail, but Earth was at stake—and he had to care. He was not that thing his shadow had become under the degradation—he didn't want his world handed to the Ferox. He just wished there were something he could do to dampen the certainty in the heart of every Ferox rallying below.

Soon after, the first of Malkier's scouts returned. Then it seemed as though the great march was about to begin. He could see the excitement of the horde below. Could see the difference as he looked at Heyer amongst the throng of Ferox.

"You're doing a piss poor job of blending in," Grant said over the comm. "The only other Ferox standing stiff-backed down there is your brother. Slouch more. Drool . . . or something."

The alien didn't risk a reply, but clearly his words had been heard, as the Ferox body Heyer inhabited did its best to mimic the urgency of the monsters around him. It wasn't much of a performance, but the Ferox surrounding him weren't paying enough attention to him to pick up on just how poorly he emulated. Grant turned his eyes back to the portal to see the first wave of soldiers entering. Their march was awkward but eager as the first lines of soldiers disappeared through the conduit.

Within a few minutes a noise came—it was sudden, like watching a disaster movie on mute then suddenly turning the volume to full blast. Had he blinked, Grant wouldn't have been sure what he saw. A chunk of skyscraper—its top sheared clean off by the top of the conduit—slammed onto the platform. If seeing the conduit come into being was like witnessing the eye of a god open, then this was like watching a god—well, puke.

The building lost any resemblance to its original shape as it clapped down on the platform. But that was hardly the end of it. The angle and momentum through the conduit brought a mass of wreckage pouring through. It was like a giant sewage pipe spewing piles of cement and metal girders. Grant lost visibility long before the sound of wreckage pouring through ended.

The tower beneath him rumbled and swayed as the valley below became shrouded in a canopy of grey dust. Even the tech Mr. Clean had built into his helmet's visor couldn't penetrate this much particulate in the air.

Well, Grant thought. *I don't know why I ever worried that Jonathan wouldn't find a way to steal a guy's thunder.*

CHAPTER NINETY-TWO

FROM THE THIRD floor of Rainier Tower, Beo had watched as The Columbia Center smashed into the conduit. Seattle shook as he anxiously followed a single long crack spreading across the window in front of him.

By the time the ground settled, Beo found himself in complete darkness, but the glass held.

As far as visibility went, their side of the conduit would suffer more than the Feroxian Plane. It was the middle of the night and every artificial light in the world was out, and now the dust rushing up from the fallen skyscraper blotted out any natural light from the sky.

The trade was still in their favor.

They would have to fight in this eventually, but his helmet was equipped to switch between night vision, infrared, and thermal to ensure he was never blind.

For the time being, Malkier's forces had a bottleneck of wreckage between them and their one point of entry. Organizing the Ferox to make a way through would take time. By then, the dust would settle in the city and if they were lucky the sun would be up before the next wave marched through.

For now, as long as that glass held, and the air inside the building remained relatively clear—Beo simply activated his helmet's head lamp while retracting the shield over his chest implant. The two were enough to push darkness away. He turned to head for the stairs through a line of empty office cubicles, in no hurry knowing the next few hours should be quiet ones.

Like everyone else he had his orders. Some had immediate parts to play, but for now his next priority was to get to higher ground and wait for visibility to improve. Each man was assigned to teams, and unless the Ferox made it through that debris faster than they estimated, he was to meet up with his team once the conditions improved.

There was a chance that a few of the Ferox had survived the building's collapse, but even those lucky enough to have made it clear would be shell-shocked and lost in the choking cloud outside. At least, that had all sounded like a safe bet until he heard the glass shattering behind him. He rounded, and his head lamp caught one of the She-rox rising from a crouch just inside the window. In fact, she was standing in the middle of the duct tape square where he had entered The Never.

The dust from outside swept in around her as she stood. Most males were a solid seven feet or taller when they stood straight. The She-rox was a bit taller than the average man—its limbs smaller and sinewy—less bubbled with musculature.

"Gotta' straggler. Rainier Towah third' floor'," Beo said over the comms. "Anyone close, bes' be quick if ya wanna a piec—"

The shattering of a second window cut him off. Suddenly, a second set of white eyes stared at him. He planted his feet while his hand reached back over his shoulder for his hammer. "Correction . . . stragglers."

"Rainier Tower. Sixteenth Floor—backup en route."

"Rainier Tower. Thirty-second Floor—backup en route."

As his hand drew close to the handle of his weapon, the airtight seal began to part itself. From behind, it would have looked like a separate sheath made from the same material that held his armor together was being unzipped by a ghost. The material finished parting to reveal an alien steel hammer.

The head was near as thick as an elephant's foot. Its shape had as much in common with a battle maul as it did a hammer as each end was covered in blunted spikes.

Two words were written across the head's flat surface.

"My pleasure ta introduce ya'll to, da' *Juggernaut*," Beo said.

Just as he was itching to pull the hammer free, the She-rox standing in the duct tape paused. Took her eyes off the glow of his device to see his hand tighten on the handle. Tilting her lizard head such that those rubber dread locks were tossed over one shoulder, she reached for what had been hidden underneath, freed it, and threw it forward. An oily black pouch slapped the floor between them, green gas erupting.

At the edge of Beo's HUD, a small alarm began to flash: WX gas detected.

Beo only laughed, as he pulled *The Juggernaut* free. "Oh, no you did not just throw that green shit at me."

There had not been enough true alien steel left to equip the entire army once all the crucial equipment they required had been forged. Still, there was enough left, that in the end Mr. Clean forged some exceptions.

Jonathan's and Leah's weapons were True Steel, as were Mito's blades and several others, depending on how much metal had to be sacrificed from what little they had left. Beo had never expected to find Mr. Clean presenting him with *The Juggernaut*. The sheer size of the sort of weapon he liked to carry meant it would require enough steel to make five or six less costly items. It was a waste of resources. But, since everyone agreed the sheer sight of Beo smashing Ferox was a morale boost they might all need before this ended, Mr. Clean offered a solution that he had used for most of the heavier metal weapons.

He forged as many weapons as he could using True Steel, but for items like *The Juggernaut* he filled the head with the Earth-based version. Any gas would have to get past the near invincible exterior to melt the weapon.

Now, what that meant for the two Ferox staring in confusion as his hammer ignored the gas spreading through the room was—he wasn't going to let them out alive so they could tell Malkier that the gas hadn't seemed to work.

While the She-rox approached with caution, a fight of two on one appeared to leave them confident that they remained the predator and he the prey. They moved like wolves—lionesses. Each keeping step as they circled around him, just outside his reach. With a snarl, the first had made a jump toward him—a feint really—as when Beo moved to engage, she'd been quick to retreat just as the other raced in for his exposed back. He knew the game; they wanted to force him to keep spinning to keep an eye on both at the same time.

Luckily, his HUD was quick to realize the nature of the situation as well. Beo saw a map at the corner of his vision showing them as two dots circling him. At the same time, a smaller window that gave him the equivalent of a rear-view camera. All that tech might have kept him from worrying, but these damn things were faster than their male counterparts—and they had a clear instinct for teamwork. Now, perhaps the males of the species had this too, he'd never fought two at once, but nothing he'd seen from the way they engaged gave him much fear that was the case.

He forced himself to stand still, not to react to their feints until one truly committed to an attack. As he did so, the circle tightened around him.

He stopped turning as one passed outside his vision, trusting the HUD to replace his eyes as she got behind him. Still he heard the claws gripping the floor as she prepared to pounce. He exploded forward, launching himself at the She-rox in front. The sudden move caught her by surprise. Indecision kept her from dodging just long enough that Beo nearly flattened her into a pancake before she got clear. Unfortunately for the She-rox, as she tried to jump past him he let one hand free of the hammer to grab hold of her. She'd nearly slipped by, but at the last instant his fingers tightened around the thick rubbery strands that ran off her head.

The little dragon chirped in surprise as he pulled and spun, using her like a baseball bat to swat her friend out of the air as she lunged into the fight from behind. The rear attacker crashed through a series of cubicles, only coming to a stop when she broke through another exterior window and dug her claws into the frame before the rest of her body flew out over the street.

The first didn't fare as well. Beo never let go. He swatted her into a cement pillar, and then the floor, before bringing his foot down on her back.

Worried about the second getting an easy shot at him, he looked up just in time to see her caught completely off guard when the backup Beo had called for finally showed up.

Beo didn't know the man's name—there were nearly four hundred *names* in The Never Army now and most only knew the folks in their squad by sight once they'd put their armor on. Whoever this was, he hadn't bothered using the building's staircase. From his sheer velocity, Beo knew the man must have broken a window somewhere on the upper stories and used the gleamers to make his way down the side of the building, only to disengage them and drop into free fall when he noticed the She-rox clinging to the edge of the window.

All Beo saw was the man deliver a thirty story drop kick before the two disappeared into the fog outside. Still, he thought he heard a loud crunch on the pavement a moment later. As with all things, these She-rox may have been quick and agile, natural hunters, but that speed came at a cost. Their armor wasn't as thick. Beo quickly discovered this for himself as he finished off the one struggling under his boot. He brought *The Juggernaut* down with a splat that nearly drove the She-rox's head through the floor.

Still, after seeing how they engaged him, he was already worried about what they would be dealing with when someone got into it with a larger pack.

By the time the second man who answered his call for backup burst out of the staircase to find his services would not be needed, Beo was already opening a channel to the other team commanders.

"Ya'll, I gotta' bad feelin 'bou dis."

CHAPTER NINETY-THREE

WITH A FINAL grunt of effort Malkier pushed free of the wreckage that had come through the conduit to pile over him. In the light, he saw the full extent of it. Half a skyscraper's worth of Earth debris had just been violently spewed on to the Feroxian Plane.

While being buried in an avalanche of cement and steel was an annoyance for him, his frontline could not come out unscathed. As he climbed to the nearest high point on top of the wreckage, he saw the pit was a dust bowl. Some of the Ferox who had been caught in the avalanche were managing to dig themselves free. Far more were still buried beneath. Those that hadn't been killed by the building or were too injured to pull themselves out would soon suffocate beneath his feet.

Then, he saw the state of the conduit's opening. The debris reached up to the apex of the conduit. Clearing it would delay them for hours, longer if they searched for survivors.

He heard a growl of anger rumble up in him as he breathed.

Inside his helmet, he opened a channel to his people. It had taken some work from Cede, but he had tapped into the very same channels that allowed the portal stone to translate between species. Every Ferox who had consumed a portal stone for the war of the Promised Land could hear him in their minds.

"Dig," the prophet said.

Hours later, his Ferox were organized and sifting through the wreckage for survivors as they dug the way clear. They were efficient, having so recently brought this very pit into existence; the Ferox were well acquainted with moving rock out of the pit. The Earth wreckage was hauled out and dumped onto the same rock that now ringed the pit.

Some survivors were found, though few in good shape. The dead could not be carried off to the lava fields for their bodies to be returned to the Feroxian Plane. Malkier hadn't thought so many casualties on this side of the conduit a realistic probability. As it was, the portal stones ingested by his people had to be recovered before the corpses could be put to rest in the lava pits.

Malkier had returned to his opening on the ridge that looked over the pit. He surveyed the progress, gave orders through his link to their minds. The only thing hampering them was that the link only went one way. He could command them, but they could not speak to him through the same means.

He was distracted by all of it when *Burns the Flame* approached. He turned to see she was moving toward him quickly. She looked—pleased.

He'd confided a great deal of the truth in her, but surrounded by his lieutenants and other tribal Alphas, she understood the part she was to play in public. As such she fell to one knee, planted a fist in the dirt, and chose her words with care.

"I understand this might not be the moment, as the prophet deals with this unexpected obstacle in our path to the Promised Land."

"Unfortunate," Malkier corrected. "Surely, not unexpected. You must understand the nature of these abominations. Even when their end is predetermined by the gods, they will stubbornly refuse to accept their fate."

"Yes, I see, those who refuse the will of the gods, fight destiny itself," she said. "I am pleased—proud—to be a Ferox on this day. Our people will make believers of them."

She said the words with passion so genuine that Malkier himself was not sure if her convictions had not aligned with his.

"What brings you before me?" Malkier asked.

She offered her free hand up toward him. "I seek the prophet's wisdom. I believe the gods have sent another sign."

Burns the Flame looked up into the prophet's eyes, a toothy grin forming. "I wish very much to be the one to show you."

Malkier had taken her hand. This drew looks from those nearby who still toiled to remove wreckage from the pit. They were just as quick to look away. It was not their fault—the prophet seldom touched any of those amongst them. Yet, the way he took the hand of *Burns the Flame* betrayed—an intimacy.

From a human perspective, it would be like watching the President of the United States volunteer to change a stranger's diaper.

Yet he enjoyed the pleasure she took in leading him by the hand as those clearing the pit parted to make them a path.

By the time he thought it might be best to put an end to it, he realized where it was that she led. Within the pit, there were seven gateway fields, each one a part of the larger circle that held the conduit open. There had been no surprise when it seemed that all the gateways had become active as the humans prepared for a war they knew to be coming.

All—but one.

There was no mystery to Malkier why that had been the case.

"The mated one, you spoke of," *Burns the Flame* said. "Is her way active?"

The prophet's eyes closed, and for a moment he looked enraptured, as though he truly heard the voice of the gods.

"Bring me the six," Malkier said.

CHAPTER NINETY-FOUR

AS DAWN BEGAN to shed light on the city, Bodhi sat beside Leah. They were on the balcony of a building overlooking the destruction around the conduit.

"Hardly begun, and it's already hard to watch," Leah said.

Below her, their army sifted through the wreckage of The Columbia Center. There had been a few more isolated cases of Ferox who survived the skyscraper. Isolated and injured, tracking them down had been easy—as there was always at least one soldier in their army who could sense their location via their connection to the portal stone.

While those few had been hunted down, the enemy combatants buried beneath the wreckage had been recovered and put down. For those severely injured by the collapsing building this was a mercy. For those that crawled out and still had fight in them it meant being dealt with quickly.

The Never Army had a few scrapes and bruises, but so far zero losses. All the stones on their side of the were conduit accounted for. For the uninitiated soldiers, those who had never seen a Ferox outside the projection chamber, those like Leah herself, this was their first time accounting for portal stones. She'd forced herself to be a part of the retrieval teams, only retreating to this balcony when she was no longer of real use.

Whenever she opened the shield of her helmet, she could still smell the toxic Feroxian blood sticking to her gloves and remembered the heat of reaching into bodies to tear the stone free of their veiny appendages.

Jonathan hadn't ordered her to take part. But she felt that taking the device and being part of this army meant carrying her fair share of the load. And from what she could tell, those who saw her doing so respected it. She'd only taken leave of the wreckage when the numbers needed to finish were small and more people trying to be of use was getting in the way.

Jonathan had the stones the soldiers recovered placed into airtight steel crates. The insides of these crates were like large padded egg cartons stacked on top of one another with layers of protective foam. The crates were then moved to a secure location. Leah knew there to be more than one tactical reason for this, but the reason Jonathan gave the soldiers was still just as true. He was keeping their senses sharp as long as possible. Unlike Jonathan, many of the soldiers would feel the sensation of multiple signals in their mind for the first time.

Every soldier, Leah included, could feel that strange alien compass pointing toward the conduit itself. But roughly a hundred had now felt both the portal stone of a Ferox in The Never as well as whatever lay on the other side.

What they sensed from the conduit itself was every Ferox on the other side with a stone tied to their gateway. While that could account for ten or a hundred stones on the other side, until one crossed the conduit's threshold into The Never, it simply felt like one single point in their mind.

By keeping the recovered stones in a specific location, the individual soldier's ability to tell live Ferox threats from enemy combatants that had already been dealt with remained clear before the next wave. Still, Jonathan had said that eventually the numbers coming through would be too many. The fog this would cause in their minds would render their alien instincts near useless.

Leah understood the necessity of retrieving the stones, but what she watched below her now only left her feeling sick to her stomach.

Jonathan had ordered the Ferox corpses taken to another point in the city to be piled.

None had refused the order, but Leah wasn't the only one amongst the uninitiated to feel something grotesque in the act. Seemed to reflect a sort of madness. Yet, none of those who had fought the Ferox before, saw it this way. This was not to say they went about piling the dead with a skip in their step—sure there were a few, but most weren't so morbid. Rather, those familiar with the Ferox nodded knowingly and got to work.

Bodhi must have sensed her revulsion. She hadn't been standing on that balcony long before he gleamed gracefully up the side of the building to take a place beside her.

"Nice spot you got picked out here," he said, retracting the shield visor of his helmet.

A strange thing, over the last few days, since the moment the army saw a device glowing in her chest, she was no longer scorned. Just as Rivers had been accepted, she simply became one of them in an instant. They all shared the same fate, and some even called her *sister* at times. It had all changed so quickly—she was still caught a bit by surprise when someone just spoke to her.

"My old place had a balcony," Leah said. "Used to go there to clear my head."

Bodhi took a seat, dangling his legs over the edge in a manner that would have been alarming under normal circumstances, but what was dangerous on a normal day hardly seemed a consideration now.

"It isn't what you think," Bodhi said.

Leah retracted her shield. "I don't know what to think."

Bodhi looked at her but not for long. She kept forgetting how hard the others found it to hold eye contact with her and Jonathan while their eyes blazed with the bond's power. Bodhi didn't dwell on his awkwardness, rather he got a faraway look in his eyes as he stared down at the conduit.

"Every time one of us was pulled into The Never," Bodhi said, "the Ferox would kill as many civilians as they could. They made mounds of the dead—stacked them like trophies."

"So . . . this is some sort of vengeance?" Leah asked.

Bodhi shrugged.

"If humans deserve to live—shouldn't we be the better ones?"

He shrugged again, but this time he did so in a manner that conceded she had a point.

"For months, I saw mounds of dead human beings every time I closed my eyes. I don't know if making a Ferox see the same thing done to their own people will get under their skin—kind of doubt it actually."

"So, why bother?" Leah asked.

"I don't think it's meant for the Ferox," Bodhi said.

She had to consider that for a moment. "Malkier?"

Bodhi nodded.

With a sigh Leah asked, "Do I want to know?"

"I . . . I think we all want Malkier to feel some of what he's put us through . . . I think Jonathan knows it."

He trailed off for a moment, eyes lost in the memories. "I hear it in my head, can't help it whenever I remember seeing the piles . . . *This is your fault, Bodhi, these people were slaughtered and you weren't there to stop it. It's your job to stop it Bodhi.*"

"You feel all that, even though they're shadows?" Leah asked.

"Some of the soldiers can see it that way," Bodhi said. "They talk about the shadows like they're just NPCs in a video game. Others, just can't."

"Others like you?"

Bodhi smirked. "If I'm being a hundred percent honest, I actually feel pretty bad when I fail NPCs in video games."

She smiled for a moment, but then felt a profound sadness for the kid. She wouldn't want anyone to feel so much responsibility—whether they were justified in feeling it or not. Yet his words were a mirror—dredging a memory from her. No—not a memory. It was more of a symbol, and not even her own. She'd only glimpsed it inside Jonathan's head when their minds had been bridged.

A little girl in a pink hoodie, her body standing out like a beacon in a pile of death. Jess—Jonathan had learned her name somehow. But that little girl had triggered something in him—uncaged something. That was the day Jonathan Tibbs had gotten so angry he'd stopped being afraid and picked a fight he fully expected to lose.

What had been Jonathan's memory had a way of mutating once it became part of her mind.

Leah recoiled away from the balcony's railing when an unwanted image took shape in her head. Her brothers, Peter and Jack, taking Jess's place in that pile.

"I wish you had gotten to be a kid longer, Bodhi," Leah said.

He smiled sadly. "Thanks, I guess. But I wouldn't change anything."

This sentiment was one she heard often from their soldiers—the veterans at least. But Bodhi was their youngest—she'd thought he might feel differently. He'd been robbed of more than the others. He wasn't even old enough to vote. He'd been living with his parents until he'd been retrieved to help with Jonathan's escape. His mother probably didn't even know where he was.

"I wouldn't think less of you if you did."

Bodhi shook his head. "I have a brother, Steven, he's five."

Leah closed her eyes and nodded.

"It's funny, I used to tell myself I hated that kid—he annoyed me every day. The usual sibling bickering, coming into my room uninvited, borrowing my stuff without asking, blah blah. Then . . . Heyer . . . all this."

He gestured vaguely at the conduit.

"Now, I . . . I'd see all the awfulness there is, if it means I can keep it from ever touching him."

Leah nodded, looking to Bodhi's chest where his device would be alive beneath, and remembering how desperately Peter tried to get her to stay away.

"I had an older brother. Peter, he . . . he and you have . . . would have had a lot in common."

She stopped herself. Knew what she was doing and cut off the urge to say more. She wasn't going to tell him about Peter just because there was a lull in a storm. She didn't want it on his mind in the hours to come.

Bodhi looked up, as though he'd just gotten a message on the comms.

"That's a weird request. But okay," Bodhi said. He listened for another moment, then spoke again. "Confirmed, on my way."

He turned to Leah once more. "Maybe you can tell me about Peter sometime."

Leah forced a smile. "I'd like that."

Then he dropped off the balcony, gleaming his way down toward ground zero.

"You've destroyed the point where you entered The Never?" Jonathan asked.

Bodhi nodded. "Yeah and most of the roof around it."

"Good," Jonathan said and held out a portal stone. "Break it."

Bodhi had known it was there, not just because he could feel it in his mind but because Jonathan had asked for it when he pulled it from the dead Ferox that had been tied to him.

"What?"

"I need to confirm what happens when we break a stone," Jonathan said. "I'm fairly certain of the outcome, but until someone tests it, we won't know."

"But, if you're wrong, I . . . I don't want to abandon everyone," Bodhi said.

Jonathan placed an arm on his shoulder. "No one will think that. This isn't a request; I'm giving you an order."

Bodhi swallowed. He was struggling with this and didn't want to make a scene—didn't want to sound how he knew he would when he said the words. "It's because I'm the youngest."

Jonathan took his hand and put the stone in it. "It is."

"That isn't fair."

"It isn't," Jonathan said. "But someone needs to do it. If we're wrong about the outcome, we need to adapt. I need you to confirm your memory is still intact, that you'll return to your original point of entry."

A moment played out between them; Bodhi looking into his commander's blazing eyes and knowing full well that Jonathan didn't want anyone to see their youngest soldier die in what was to come. Sure, he may need to confirm these things, but he also wanted Bodhi out first if there was any chance it was possible.

The thing was, he wasn't pretending it was anything else, so Bodhi didn't know what to argue.

"Yes, sir," Bodhi said.

He stepped away, removed his glove, and broke the stone.

Jonathan watched, and much like in single combat, a portal appeared around Bodhi. However, the process played out much faster than normal. Bodhi had barely begun to show signs of distress from the pain that accompanied a stone's destruction before he was encapsulated in a red globe and disappeared in a flash of white light.

Jonathan watched the small dot that represented Bodhi in his HUD map disappear. The AI that ran the equipment flashing a *location unknown* sign in the place where Bodhi's dot had been a moment ago. A clock began to run, as the map zoomed out to the scope of the entire city instead of just the streets nearest the conduit looking for Bodhi's signal.

"Bodhi," Jonathan said over the comm. "Can you read me? Have you reentered?"

Jonathan was starting to worry as a full thirteen and half minutes went by before Bodhi's dot reappeared in his HUD. "Bodhi, do you read me?"

"Yeah, I'm here," Bodhi said. "Apparently I'm not that easy to get rid of."

"What's your status?" Jonathan asked.

"I remember everything. I'm about twenty feet from where I entered, on the roof of the old Seafirst Plaza."

"Good," Jonathan said.

"How long was I gone?" Bodhi asked.

Jonathan sighed. "Longer than I would have liked."

CHAPTER NINETY-FIVE

PERTH WAS A few stories up from the apex of the conduit. He stood behind a minigun mounted in the window of one of the nearby buildings. He tensed when the rubble in front of the conduit began to tremble.

"Easy," Jonathan's voice said over the comms. He was talking to all of them, not just Perth.

They watched as small clumps of concrete began to loosen and roll down. As the minutes ticked by the size of those clumps grew, the Ferox on the other side were dislodging the wreckage. Somewhat like having pulled the plug on a bathtub, the top of the rubble sank into the conduit.

"Hold."

The hole began with one Feroxian hand, frantically pulling at the debris, yanking it through to the other side. Slowly, the top of what remained began to disappear. Then more hands appeared, and the process began to accelerate. Soon, there was enough space that one of the Ferox could have forced its way though.

Yet, they restrained themselves and kept digging until finally the pile fell in, dislodging enough debris that an opening half a dozen Ferox wide was cleared.

"Steady."

Activity seemed to stop, and the seconds ticked by in painfully slow increments. Then a minute had passed, then two.

"Not liking this," Perth whispered.

"Ain' nuthin' gonna come through dat conduit ya ever gonna like," Beo said.

"Thanks for the hot—"

He shut up when something came through. Not a Ferox, but a rather oily gelatinous mass the size of a barrel rolled its way across the threshold.

"What the hell is that?" Perth said. "Looks like—"

A second blob rolled through and came to a stop behind the last. Almost as though the Ferox were rolling casks of sludge through the portal.

"Change in plans," Jonathan's voice was suddenly less calm. "Aim into the conduit, go high do not hit the sacs. Open fire now!"

In near unison, the windows on the face of the three buildings closest to the portal erupted. Glass rained down on the wreckage below as the deafening roar of hundreds of alien steel bullets streaming into the conduit rang through the city.

"Hold your fire."

They stopped, smoke wafting up from the windows all around as they waited. Another minute crawled, and then a third blob rolled in.

Finally, a black ball came through. It was about the size of a volleyball and looked as though it were made of the same obsidian-like rock found on the Feroxian Plane. It rolled to a stop beside the three gelatinous sacs.

A moment later, two more followed.

"We all know what this could be, switch to thermal optics," Jonathan said. "Don't wait for a command, if something with arms and legs comes through, open fire."

"You know, they ain't that big, I could go down there and roll them right back through," Tam said.

"That's a negative, Tam, hold your position," Jonathan said.

The black balls moved suddenly, unnaturally, and in unison. Somewhat like watching three turtles suddenly flip themselves off their back with an acrobat's grace. Each of the volleyball rocks orientated themselves, then jumped into the air before exploding.

Had they been intended for grenades they'd have been unimpressive. However, thousands of tiny needle-like pins had shot from the balls when they exploded and covered everything in a ten-foot radius. The top surface of each of the three gelatinous bags was shredded with tiny holes.

A moment after those holes were punched, massive spiny black spikes erupted, until the three large sacs looked like giant sea urchins resting in front of the conduit. Had anyone been within ten feet of that when it happened, he'd have been skewered.

"Alright, rolling them back may have been poor judgment," Tam said.

WX gas began filling the air around the conduit. Seeping out through the tips of the spikes. Slowly at first, as though the pressure within the sac was climbing and forcing the gas out in all directions.

Soon, the conduit's opening became cloaked by a thick layer of WX gas and warning lights on their HUDs began to blink.

"Don't reload, empty your magazine into the conduit," Jonathan said. "Keep the rest of the ammunition sealed and be ready to move. Olivia—are you ready?"

"On your mark," she replied.

Tam watched with growing fear as the bullets flew through the gas. Under normal circumstances one cannot see bullets, outside what happens when they hit their targets. But as soon as the ammunition passed within a foot of the WX gas, they caught fire and broke apart. Winking out like tiny bottle rockets.

"Seen enough," Jonathan said. "Save your rounds and—"

Perth and everyone watching knew why he'd cut off. Where the naked eye would have left them blind, thermal optics allowed them to make out what was happening within the gas. One Ferox. Then two, then . . .

A Red came shooting out of the gas, launched itself up toward the buildings. The Gunners reacted, shredding him with alien steel bullets so fast that only a limp corpse ever reached the building. But, he was only the first.

A number of Ferox were pouring out of the conduit, but many carried large towering shields of Feroxian stone. The shield holders were spreading out to form a ring around the conduit's opening as the rest came through sprinting in a rampage before jumping out and up as they entered The Never.

Within seconds the Ferox were bursting out of the expanding WX gas in all directions. At first, the Gunners held them at bay, but as it went on they rapidly spread their fire over an increasing number of targets. Soon the Ferox weren't only jumping but crawling over the ring of shields to scale the buildings walls. Jonathan's men could have held them at bay in that pocket of death outside the conduit longer—but over the next minute, WX clouds had expanded throughout the entire intersection and was reaching the lower floors.

Those nearest the ground soon had to pull back, unable to fire without their ammunition igniting into flame and turning into metal sludge inside their magazines. In another minute, the swarms crawling up the building would be too great—they were going to get past the barrage of fire and force men into hand to hand.

"Pull back to a safe distance and keep firing," Jonathan said. "No risks here, this is not our hill to die on."

"Pulling back."

"Pulling back."

The sound of gunfire diminished slowly as gas pushed farther out.

Jonathan had no doubt they had enough of those gelatinous bladders at the ready to put the entire city under a dense fog.

"Olivia, when our people are out, begin the next round of demolitions."

"Received," she said.

"Washington Mutual Tower, fourth floor. Can't get out, I got six of them in here with me. They haven't found me yet, but they know I'm here."

No one recognized the voice, but everyone heard the fear.

"Hold on, Olivia," Jonathan said. "We still got a man stuck inside one of the buildings."

"I'm on my way," Perth said.

"You got a name, kid," Perth asked.

"Tre . . . Trevor." The response came as little more than a whisper.

"Alright Trev, I got your position," Perth said. "I'm gonna give you a distraction. On my signal, drop some flash grenades. The moment they're blinded make a break for it."

"There are more now," Trevor said. "I . . . I think they smell me."

"Focus, Trev, you ready with the grenades?"

"Yes."

"When I say, you pull the pins," Perth said. "They have a four second delay. You throw on three and run."

Perth had no love for the gleamers. That was to say, it had been clear quite early on that he was never going to be a Bodhi. He favored force over finesse. Luckily, he didn't need the things to do anything fancy. Just get him into position quick and quiet.

One hand kept him anchored on the side of the adjacent building as he eased down to Trevor's floor. He could see Trev's red dot on a map of the building in his HUD, but the maps were rudimentary. They didn't tell him the layout of furniture or rooms, only where the load-bearing structures were. From where Trev's dot was positioned, the kid's back was against a thick concrete wall.

At that moment, Perth looked down to see three Ferox step out of the WX gas into air that was still clear in the alley below him. They were going to spot in him any second.

"Pull the pins, Trev," Perth said.

1 . . .

The Ferox below looked up. Their guttural growls not far behind as their eyes locked on him.

2 . . .

Perth bent his knees against the building. The Ferox did the same on the ground.

3 . . .

He shot across the alley as the first of the creatures came rocketing toward him. Perth crashed through a window and hit the ground running. He didn't bother with the office door, he ran straight through the drywall, just as . . .

Bang!

Bright lights and deafening sound exploded as Perth burst into a company's lobby. His helmet and visor protected his eyes and ears as he ran headlong into the first Ferox he saw. The Green, shrieking in blind agony went flying into one of the others. Perth kept heading for the red dot.

"You better be on the move kid—"

Trevor hadn't waited. The lobby desk exploded as the kid erupted out from beneath. Much like Perth had, he slammed into the closest blind Ferox like it was any other obstacle in his way. The beast disappearing through one of the lobby's walls.

Perth, hadn't forgotten about the Ferox chasing in after him from the alley—they weren't blind. He shot forward, ducking as one of the lobby Ferox's claws swiped wildly at him. Grabbing hold of the Green's tail, he yanked the creature from its feet, swinging into a 180 and letting go. The blind green shot back toward the hole he had emerged from a second earlier, hurtling into the first of the three chasing after him from the alley.

"Run," Perth yelled.

Perth caught Trevor's shoulder and pointed him in the direction of least resistance. He concocted this mad plan in a hurry, and had figured they would be leaving the way he'd come in, but now that he had brought more Ferox to the party with him, that option was out.

So, he turned Trev in the opposite direction and the two barreled down a hallway toward the opposite side of the building. As they ran, they could see clear air on the other side, the WX gas hadn't encompassed this entire building yet.

Three Ferox lumbered into the lobby behind them, two running into their blinded brothers and knocking them over to take up the chase.

"Jump," Perth said. "No time to worry if we land pretty."

Trev didn't hesitate, he shot through the window, Perth a split second behind. A hail of broken glass followed them out into the clear air.

Perth stumbled a bit awkwardly as they hit pavement below, but not so badly as to keep him from quickly regaining his balance. The kid had engaged the gleamers in his boots—his landing wasn't pretty, but it didn't put cracks in the sidewalk.

They looked at each other, smiled and bolted up the street.

"We're clear," Perth said over the comms.

"Green light, Olivia," Jonathan's voice said.

One of the Ferox emerged from the fourth floor behind them as Seattle was rocked by the second controlled demolition of the last twelve hours. Trev and Perth lost their footing for a moment as the ground lurched beneath them. They turned around just long enough to see not one, but the four buildings closest to the conduit begin to fall toward the intersection.

Trev, perhaps a little delirious with joy after his brush with death, began to laugh. He stared at the one Ferox who had made its way out up the street. A Green, young male, it seemed to watch with horror as the four buildings collapsed.

Perth nudged him with a light elbow. "Kid, you alright?"

"Yeah," Trevor said, pointing vaguely at the collapsing building. "Was just thinking how they probably thought they were done digging."

CHAPTER NINETY-SIX

EVENTUALLY, KEEPING THE Ferox from making contact with his forces became impossible. There were only so many buildings Jonathan could drop around the conduit before those he needed standing came into play.

After a day of dropping wreckage on them, the Ferox and their cloud of gas had made their way into The Never.

"We're in position, how many you got on your tail?" asked Rivers over the comm.

At that specific moment, Bodhi was crouching—sort of.

To be more accurate he was gleaming south down Alaskan Way at dangerous speeds while holding one knee to his chest. A split second earlier, he'd had to drop down into a spin to keep from being clotheslined by the She-rox that had come barreling out of nowhere into the road in front of him.

Two inches off the street's surface and still very much in motion, he stood up just in time to jump as the next incoming beast leapt at him headlong. An instant later, he was running sideways along the side of an industrial building that lined the sidewalk.

"What, you think I stopped to take a head count," Bodhi snapped.

"A hundred or a thousand?" Rivers asked.

"However many we lured into Qwest Field!" Bodhi yelled as he jumped off the wall, flipped over the parked cars and put himself back into the center of the street.

For this to work, he had to stay visible, which meant resisting the very strong instinct to run as fast as he could. He had to keep just enough distance between him and the Feroxian horde on his heels to believe they were a moment away from closing on him.

"All of them?" Rivers said with genuine surprise. "How'd you swing that?"

"Lance and Matthews dropped a gasoline truck on their Alpha."

He'd seen a Red coming at him ahead, but the trick to this was letting them get close enough, then dodge at the last second. The closer they came to connecting the more it seemed they couldn't resist joining the mob trailing him. Bodhi dodged the Red as planned but he hadn't seen the Green coming at him from the opposite side of the street. He barely slipped under its claw when he saw, but the Green was quick, didn't only come at him high, but spun through to bring its tail around low.

The tail clipped Bodhi's feet—which was no small problem at his current speed.

He lurched forward in an awkward tumble, but before he face-planted, he managed to flip to his back and spread himself. This dispersed his weight across the gleamers, so that he didn't drive straight into the asphalt.

He took one breath of relief as he stared up from his back, shooting down the street and watching the sky fly by overhead.

"How'd you—"

"Rivers, we're gonna need to discuss this later."

Flipping onto his stomach, then back up into a gliding run, Bodhi let himself drift to the road's guard rail as he came around a long curve.

"Right . . . ETA?" Rivers asked.

"You should be able see me any second," Bodhi said,

"Yep, I got y—"

Rivers trailed off, his thoughts as interrupted as his words by the horde of rampaging Ferox chasing after Bodhi as he came around the corner. "Jesus, still think we need a bigger boat."

"It'll be fine," Bodhi said. "Sam, how things going on your end?"

His response came between breaths of exertion. "I regret to report. I could not save. The Krispy Kreme. Bastards barreled right through it."

Bodhi sighed. "Dammit, that was gonna be my reward for not dying."

"Weren't you the one telling me to stay focused," Rivers said. "Sam, when should your mob hit Bodhi's?"

"About halfway through the train yard if I can shake the pack of Tar-locks on my heels," Sam said.

"Tar-locks?" Bodhi said.

"Well, what have you been calling the females?" Sam asked.

"Oh . . . Miss Piggies."

"What? Your whole thing was *Sesame Street*, Miss Piggy is a Muppet—"

"How are you idiots still alive?" Rivers interjected.

Bodhi caught sight of Sam as he launched out of the streets in the lower business district with a horde of Ferox thundering after him. Hitting the train yard, Sam wasn't much slowed by the number of stacked cargo containers that lined the railway, but not many of the horde following him chose to gracefully jump the same obstacle. Whether on purpose or accident, the majority of the Ferox ended up rampaging through. It sent large metal containers stacked three high toppling over while others were split to shreds by the stampede.

When Sam and Bodhi met and turned hard, they lost speed, and one of those metal containers crashed into the street behind them. This one had been thrown, as it was rolling directly at them, end over end with far too much precision to be random.

They stared for a moment as the cargo exploded out both sides.

The next few seconds, they finally let loose, breaking into full speed. Sam chanting with growing anxiety as the cargo container rolled end over end toward them, "Running! Running! Running!"

They exchanged a glance, then pushed off one another with the gleamers. Each shot away from the other in a V as the cargo container rolled between them, lost its momentum, and finally came to a stop. There was no time to celebrate. Before the container even took its last roll, the combined horde was swarming over the top to get to them.

Hurtling past the fence into the Port of Seattle, Sam turned to Bodhi. "I can't believe we almost did that thing where we almost die trying to run away from something just because we're too stupid to turn," Sam said.

"I was just thinking the same thing."

"Great minds," Sam said.

"Anything more than *like* minds is pushing it," Rivers said.

As they made their arrival, Rivers' team was in position. On any normal day, the stretch of asphalt lining the Duwamish waterway was a maze of stacked containers waiting to be loaded onto massive cargo ships. Today was not a normal day.

Rivers' Command along with The Cell's agents had spent hours in the lead-up to the Feroxian arrival decorating for this party.

The cargo containers were no longer arranged in rows but stacked tightly together into a slowly rising staircase that straddled the very edge of the water-way—just one container higher than the edge of two cargo carriers themselves.

At the moment each level of the massive staircase had three or four of Rivers' team with their chest implants unshielded—like sirens singing for the Ferox to come crash upon them.

As the Ferox chasing Sam and Bodhi caught sight of them, their guttural battle cries erupted from the horde's ranks. They raced all the more recklessly up the staircase. River's men slowly pulled back—*cowering* in the face of the Feroxian horde's overwhelming numbers.

As they disappeared over the top of the cargo carrier staircase the Ferox barreled after them onto, what none of the beasts seemed to notice, was not a final platform lining the water.

The unshielded men waited as long as their courage allowed in the face of the sheer numbers swarming onto the carrier after them before diving off the side to the greater safety of the waterway. Most of the men plunged straight into water, but a few who were adept enough with the gleamers came to stand on the surface as the cargo carrier was overtaken by the battle thirsty creatures.

They surged onto the platform—grounding to halt at the edge to howl in rage at prey that had run from combat. Some nearest the edge were knocked into the water by the weight of the horde pressing in behind them.

"West side, time to show us what you got," Rivers said.

On the opposite bank, men emerged from cover and ran into the open. Few of the Ferox noticed them, even fewer would have noticed that they fell into ten highly suspicious rows of five along the west bank. Much as it was with humans—Ferox mobs were no place to find shining examples of restraint and wisdom.

The mob was too focused on Bodhi, Sam, and the few others who stood hovering above the water with their chests ablaze—daring the creatures to risk the waters if they wanted to get to them.

Meanwhile, the men on the west side moved in sync, each group of five reaching for a massive black chain laying on the shoreline. As they began to pull, ten chains emerged from beneath the water and grew taut against the spindles affixed to the carrier. At first the tug of war was slow. But as these things go, the cargo carrier began to move away from the shore with increasing speed as it leaned toward the water.

"Olivia, we're almost ready here at the Port," Rivers said.

"Received, awaiting your mark," Olivia replied.

As the massive vessel lurched into the waterway, the Ferox mob crowding the decks began to realize their mistake. They were not standing on land at all.

Just as the Ferox began to panic, Rivers' voice came over the comms, "East side team, open fire."

At the top tier of the artificial staircase, the side panels of the cargo containers facing the carrier's decks fell open to reveal the rest of Rivers' team. Behind cages of Borealis steel, they leveled M-60 machine guns connected to backpacks carrying alien steel bullets.

Just as the Ferox began turning to the safety of true ground, they ran into a virtual wall of bullets erupting out of the containers. The horde suddenly found itself pinned between water and gunfire. Watching in horror as bullets shredded through the biological armor of those who had boarded the cargo carrier last.

None had paid any attention when they were lured this far from downtown. They left the protection of the WX gas, they were now in air that had not yet been touched by the green cloud expanding from the city's center.

Their rear flank was caught by surprise and riddled with bullets as the forward flank saw they were being pulled out into the water and further from shore.

Panic took them.

Some of the Ferox made desperate leaps for the wall of cargo containers. Those that made it through the bullets only crashed into the cage of Borealis steel. They became easy targets.

"Olivia, let em have it," Rivers said.

"Confirmed. Detonation in three . . . two . . ."

Every man held his breath, and finally the side of the carrier facing the water erupted. Fire swelled up around the Ferox, as the carrier began to take on water and lean dangerously sideways. The creatures scrambled for anything to hold onto as the precarious angle grew steep beneath their feet. Those who found nothing to hold onto slid in terror into the water.

Finally, the deck came crashing down into the center of the waterway. Only the few who had managed to cling to something substantial were able to keep from going into the water. They clawed their way up the deck only to face the gunmen firing down on them from above.

Bodhi gleamed across the water to the west side, giving Sam a hand after he did the same. They watched the carnage they had orchestrated.

After a while, the cargo ship sank below the surface and the gunfire came to an end. The absence of the guttural growls of the Ferox horde made the night feel peaceful and quiet despite all the fighting going on nearby.

Some of the Ferox—those lucky enough to fall far enough behind that they never boarded the cargo carrier or came into worthwhile range of the gunners—stood and watched with horror from the east shoreline.

"Well, folks," Bodhi said, opening a channel to Jonathan and the rest of the team. "DiCaprio is in the water, and Rose ain't sharing her door."

CHAPTER NINETY-SEVEN

JONATHAN HADN'T BEEN worried that the Ferox would come through the conduit and spread themselves thin trying to invade every possible direction. Malkier had already assured no escape would be possible as long as the Ferox had the numbers to keep sending in waves. The prophet's priority was killing every last soldier in Jonathan's army.

The Ferox wouldn't spread far from the conduit unless Jonathan's men ran.

If things went poorly enough, running might come to look like a good idea to some. Fortunately, he and his men had an understanding. Fleeing the fight wouldn't save any of them—it would only lower their collective chances of survival. It didn't matter if the Ferox took a day or a year chasing them deeper into The Never to kill them. And for those on Earth, win or lose, it would all still be over in an instant.

Still, Jonathan had to plan for the worst—if he and his men fell inside The Never, then Malkier would eventually lead the Ferox through another portal into the real world. So, while most of his perimeters weren't likely to be factored in the war he and his men fought—they would become the first line of defense in the war that followed if they failed.

On a map, the city of Seattle is just a long narrow strip of land pinched to the east and west by two large bodies of water. Now, say one were a Ferox, and you've just stepped out of a portal into the middle of downtown.

On any normal day, if that Ferox were to go north or south, they could get to the greater state of Washington without having to cross a body of water large enough to give them second thoughts. But today was not a normal day, and if that same Ferox tried to go north or south without bringing a substantial number of friends and a massive supply of WX gas—they weren't going anywhere.

The Ferox who took the north option would first encounter a line of Anthony's Mechs. If they slipped through or fought their way through that, they would come to Olivia's northern perimeter. There, they would find the Washington 523 highway, which spanned the shortest stretch of land between the two bodies of water. Olivia's soldiers had seized control of the entire highway.

The south had more complicated geography. There was no equivalent line of pavement already in place to stage forces and move supplies after most of mankind's technology was taken out of the equation. To the south, the Duwamish Waterway split the land in half, and would keep a Ferox from crossing unless highly motivated. However, there were two bridges that would allow large numbers of Ferox to cross—they had been rigged with explosives in preparation for that contingency.

Going west from the conduit was a non-starter. There were no bridges across the Puget sound. The locals used ferries to get across or drove fifty miles south.

This left the east. Even though the Ferox would run into Lake Washington, there was no way to keep them from noticing two very wide freeways connected the land on the other side. Many in the army thought the Ferox wouldn't cross these freeways unless the prophet himself ordered it.

But this was Jonathan's home turf, his personal battlefield. He knew from experience that those freeways were large enough that the Ferox would barely hesitate to chase him onto them.

Lincoln stood sentinel on the east side of the I-90 Bridge, Anthony and a few other men and women alongside him. The weather may have been cool, but inside the Wallace, he was sweating. He released the face guard to drink from a bottle of water, then poured the rest of the bottle down his face.

"It's good to keep hydrated," Anthony said.

He turned to the man with water still running down his face. "Really cut corners on the ventilation system."

Hoult shrugged but didn't argue. "Priority was combat effectiveness on a deadline. Just be happy you've got a functional waste disposal system."

"And a good thing," Lincoln smirked. "Given all the *hydrating*."

Anthony chuckled and turned back to the bridge, his Thor gesturing vaguely with one hammer in the direction of the city. "You know, I used to actually like green."

Lincoln nodded.

From this bridge they could no longer see Seattle, at least not very well. The city was cloaked in a dense cloud of WX gas that rose above the skyscrapers. The cloud was always growing—not so fast that he felt the need to flee lest he be cooked alive inside his Mech, but nevertheless, every time he looked away for a few minutes and looked back the sight was ominously larger.

If Jonathan and the Ferox weren't done killing one another in the next day—the WX gas was going to force him and anyone else operating a Mech to retreat further back.

They'd hardly seen any action.

Littered on the bridge in front of them were the bodies of a few dozen Ferox who had emerged from the tunnels and tried to cross the water. Sydney and the rest of the Gunners had taken them down long before they got to close quarters. Those like Anthony and Lincoln were really only important once the numbers became overwhelming enough to break through the long-ranged weapons.

That all changed when a communication came over the comm.

"I-90 team," Rivers said. "You may want to brace yourself, got a stampede of them heading into the tunnel. Nothing is distracting them . . . they got two Alphas keeping them on course."

"Strange," Lincoln said. "Why would they care about taking the bridge?"

"Cut off any easy retreat," Anthony said.

Lincoln cocked an eye.

"They know the longer this goes on, Jonathan eventually loses the city. These two freeways are great points of retreat. Jonathan's armies could cross and destroy them as they do so."

"But Jonathan told us we couldn't retreat."

Anthony nodded. "They don't know that."

They didn't have long to discuss much more. Within minutes the Ferox began trickling out onto the bridge. From where they were on the other side of the tunnel this first wave resembled ants swarming out of their anthill.

As they drew into range, Sydney and the rest of the gunners opened fire; Lincoln heard Anthony on the comm. "There must be over a hundred of them."

"Yeah, and they're still coming," Lincoln said.

The front line of the charging Ferox horde went down hard, the beasts absorbing bullets like sponges before being trampled. For a while, the massive amount of firepower the Mechs were capable of throwing at them made the creatures pay for every inch in lives.

That was until spurts of green began shooting up from within the encroaching numbers. The Ferox were carrying smaller pouches of WX gas. It was going off in more and more frequent spurts as the creatures who carried the substance on their backs massed inside the rushing horde. Soon, they realized the spray of bullets into the throng was actually accelerating the problem. Releasing more and more of the stuff onto the bridge.

At first, the problem was a looming future. Then the winds began to change.

Suddenly, the front line of the creatures wasn't inching but gaining yards at a time. The Ferox got wise, let the gas protect them as they moved forward. Then, pouches began dropping like tear gas from behind the thickening green cloud.

"Olivia," Anthony said. "It's not looking good here. We may need to drop this bridge sooner than we planned."

"Received," Olivia's voice said. "The team on the 520 Bridge says the same. This is a coordinated attack."

"We need to start pulling back before that gas reaches us," Lincoln said.

"What . . . what is that?" Sydney asked.

Lincoln and Anthony turned their attention to a dark shape emerging, becoming more visible as it neared the edge where gas met air. They each had to switch to thermal imaging to make out what looked like a row of large rectangles coming toward them.

"Shields," Anthony said. "We need to pull out, let Olivia down the bridges."

As though his words had just been spoken right into the ear of the Ferox leader, their optics picked up a strange movement inside the cloud. Almost as though . . .

It came bursting out of the gas, shooting over them in a wide arc. Its black and grey skin a warning in and of itself.

Some of the Gunners reacted immediately, their targeting systems following the Alpha as it flew toward them. For those split seconds, the creature looked like a sparkler as bullets hit its skin harmlessly. Then it cleared them. Not coming to a landing in front or amongst them, but behind the Gunners' line.

Sydney whirled, targeting the beast again as it stood from its crouched landing.

"You're not getting penetration," Anthony said.

"Then we're up," Lincoln replied, already headed to intercept the monster before it tore through their line and let the swarm through.

"Get the situation under control and get off the bridge," Olivia said, a hardness to her voice.

"Our retreat just got cut off," Sydney said, "and that gas isn't slowing down."

"Deal with it now, you know I won't let them across," Olivia said.

She didn't have to say it. They all knew she wouldn't hesitate to drop the bridge with them on it if that swarm looked like it was going to make it across.

As Anthony's Thor and Lincoln's Wallace raced to put themselves between the Alpha and the Gunners, the creature stopped its approach and roared in challenge.

Anthony drew its attention first, leaping into the air to bring down a massive hammer while Lincoln ran in, unsheathing his molecular blades.

The Alpha stepped clear as the hammer of Anthony's Thor put a dent in the street. The creature moved fast, ducking under the first swipe of Lincoln's blade and catching Anthony with a backhand before he could rise up from his crouch. The Thor shot into the bridge's guardrails. The alien steel of the armor held against the collision with the rebar-reinforced cement. The Thor narrowly avoided dropping into Lake Washington before rolling back from the wall.

"Jesus," Anthony's voice came in gasps. "Hits. Like a. Tank."

That was the Mech's biggest problem. The armor absorbed the worst, but there was still a human inside, and even the laziest of swipes from an Alpha could knock the sense out of a man.

Lincoln backpedaled as the creature's attention turned entirely to him. It stood to its full height, and even in the Mech, it was a full head taller than him. He stopped to stand his ground, and the Alpha eyed the blades of the Wallace. There was something in its gaze, not fear exactly, but caution.

"Get off my bridge," Lincoln yelled.

The Alpha let out a long heavy breath, its shoulders hunching low as it came toward him. He swiped at it again, not committing to the strike, but testing its courage. The Alpha stepped back to let the blade sail past, then came in fast, but not fast enough. Lincoln brought the second blade up and under, the Alpha grunted before pulling back with a jolt.

A long cut ran across its chest. Its hand went to the wound, ostensibly not from surprise, but a morbid curiosity. Black blood dripped off its fingers as it growled and lowered back into a ready stance.

The Alpha began to move fast and unpredictably, coming in with feints and quick changes to its direction, daring Lincoln to take a swing he'd regret.

Eventually, he made his mistake.

He took a swipe at the beast just wide enough to leave his shoulder unprotected when the blade didn't make contact. The Ferox came in fast, not going for a punch, but pushing him in the same direction as his swing with enough force to spin the Mech. The split second was all it took, the Alpha rushing forward before he could get a blade back between them and grabbing hold of the backside of the Wallace's chassis.

A second later, the Alpha had the Wallace in a military press. Lincoln looked up at the sky, helpless to get at the beast with his blades as he felt it lurch to throw.

Anthony got to his feet to just in time to see the Wallace pulled off his feet. There was no time. He shot from the ground just as the Ferox pulled back to throw the Mech from the bridge. The hammer came down before the Alpha managed it, right on the back of its leg.

The creature toppled forward, forced down onto one knee with a wail of surprise. It still followed through with throwing the Wallace, but knocked off balance, it didn't go as planned. Lincoln released the Wallace's molecular blades just before it hit ground and rolled across the freeway.

While the armor would keep Lincoln from broken bones, he might as well have been in a high-speed car accident. In the Wallace, he crashed across four lanes of freeway before finally hitting the opposite guardrail.

Caught off guard, Anthony managed to nail it with a wild desperate haymaker from the hammer as the Alpha was turning to face him.

The beast was driven down face first into the pavement, breaking a hole in the street as it did so, and yet it hardly seemed fazed, barely shaking its head a moment before pulling itself out of the crumpled cement.

Lincoln lay on the ground in the Wallace, seemingly unable to rise. Alone against the Alpha, Anthony had seconds at best.

Lincoln pushed up onto hands and knees, the Wallace doing most of the work to drag him up. He got to his feet only to lose his balance and fall back to a knee as he came forward. He lurched, pushing himself back to his feet, his arms reaching out to each side as new molecular blades slid into place.

Anthony got in another blow as the Ferox rose to its feet, bringing the sledgehammer of a fist up hard to catch the Alpha under the chin. It staggered backward, before planting a foot into the pavement to stop itself.

Anthony, trying to capitalize, came forward with a hard strike aimed for its center of gravity.

He jolted painfully to a halt, looked on with dread as the Alpha caught the hammer with one massive hand. It growled in triumph as it bent the arm back, the machinery no match for its strength, forcing Anthony to kneel. Desperate, he threw another fist only to have the Alpha slap it away like a buzzing mosquito.

Its free hand reached for him, grabbing hold of him by the chassis and driving Anthony straight down into the street in front of them. As Anthony looked up at the face of the growling Alpha, it raised its massive foot to stomp down on him. He began to lose consciousness, but he could have sworn, at that last moment, its jaw had fallen limp, its eyes lifeless.

Lincoln staggered to his knees as the Alpha's skull flopped to the ground and rolled a few paces. The body fell limp beside him, black blood pouring onto the street from its severed neck. He could feel his entire body like one big bruise. As he knelt there trying to regain his faculties, Lincoln raised the Wallace's head. He looked up to see the 520 Bridge across the water. From here, it looked even more overrun with Ferox, the WX gas having nearly engulfed its entirety.

Then, without any warning, the bridge exploded. Charges going off in series from the east shore to the west. The entire structure falling into the lake as fire bloomed up around it.

He watched it all with the surreal sense that he was in a dream and turned his head to the line of Gunners on his own bridge. Finally, he heard Sydney's voice hailing him and realized that she must have been trying to reach him for some time now. "Lincoln we have to retreat. Do you read me? Lincoln! Olivia will not wait."

The Gunners were stepping back, the speed at which they abandoned their lines rapidly increasing.

"Anthony?" Lincoln asked.

No reply came.

Lincoln retracted his weapons and reached down to grab hold of the man's chassis. Luckily, the Wallace didn't require him to use his own strength. He forced himself to pull the Thor over a shoulder and join the retreat.

CHAPTER NINETY-EIGHT

LEAH STEPPED ON the shoulder of a red male corpse and pulled *Themyscira* out from the back of his skull.

Behind her, Jonathan was yanking *Excali-bar 2.0* out of a Green that he'd pinned into the street, to intercept a Red that was rampaging into battle. She turned just in time to see *Excali-bar* whip around, connect, and shoot the Red half-way through the lobby of the building across the street.

She caught him looking at his hands again, as though the power he now possessed still defied his comprehension. After so many months of struggling to survive these things, it seemed as though it would take a hundred of the beasts coming at him alone for them to overwhelm him.

Leah had not left his side since the conduit had finally been breached and they had to fall back farther into the city. As soon as the Ferox were coming in by waves, too many to keep track of all at once, he had asked her to stay close at all times.

He didn't say the words. That Malkier would target her. That he feared any second she was out of his sight the attack would come. The truth was that she would be far more valuable to the army if she could move freely. She was almost as hard to kill as he was, even if she wasn't as deadly. She could have been out supporting the teams when they needed backup.

But, he asked her to stay close and she had nodded. She had her own reasons of course. She felt it in her bones—Jonathan was going to do something stupid—probably something selfless and heroic—but seeing as he was the father of her child, she wasn't going to stand by. She hoped her instincts were wrong just this once. After all, he was the hardest of them to kill or capture, so it made sense that he was the only one to see the whole picture.

But she just didn't trust that it was so simple.

Regardless, he may think she was staying close to be where he could protect her, but she knew she was there to protect him from himself—the arrangement worked, so why argue the details.

She saw a proximity warning in her HUD, motion detected coming around the corner, and the alarm only went off when none of their people occupied the space.

By the time she turned the danger was already taken care of. A Green was sliding across the asphalt, limp and already dead. It came to a stop a few feet from her, a true alien steel throwing dagger lodged into its eye socket.

She looked up through the haze of WX gas at the nearby flagpole where Mito crouched comfortably using his gleamers.

He was probably smiling, but their helmet's shields were always down now, so he gave a thumbs up.

She returned a nod, pulled his knife free, careful of the molecular edge, and tossed it back up to him. He plucked it out of the air by the handle, sheathing it so gracefully the whole affair looked like he simply paused to scratch an itch under his arm.

So, ironically, Mito had agreed to watch their backs. In fact, he had confessed that he had vowed to Heyer that he wouldn't leave their sides in the battle to come. Of course, when Heyer had asked him, he hadn't known it was the last time he'd see Heyer before the war actually came. Apparently, this request was one of the last things Heyer did before disappearing.

The intersection momentarily cleared of attackers, Jonathan was listening to the chatter of the teams on the comm before coming back to join her beneath the flagpole. Mito was keeping his eyes on the surroundings and being so close he didn't need to use the comm to be heard.

"These waves, they keep coming in hundreds. But Malkier doesn't commit to a full-scale invasion," Mito said. "Why?"

Leah nodded as his words translated in her thoughts.

"He has the numbers. Safer to wear us down slowly?" Leah said. "We've lost nearly twenty since this began. He's lost closer to a thousand. We're still the ones who took the worst of it."

"It's fear," Jonathan said. "The last time he came thinking us easy prey, he went home wounded. He believes we have a weapon he hasn't seen yet. That we're waiting for him to send in a full-scale invasion before we use it."

"Do we?" Mito asked.

Leah exchanged a look with Jonathan, before they both turned their helmets to look at him.

"Right, need to know," Mito said.

They all looked away in unison as Rourke's voice came over the comms. Everyone in the Army was likely doing the same. Rourke was their man closest to the conduit, keeping an eye on what the enemy was doing. The man had a talent for staying hidden. At this point, had it not been for the minimap showing his location, even Jonathan wouldn't know where he'd set up surveillance.

"Wave coming in, shorter interval than the last few. Looks . . . looks to be larger numbers than we've seen yet."

Leah turned to look up at Mito. "Feel better?"

By the evening, The Never Army had lost nearly a hundred soldiers. The Feroxian waves coming in growing larger and larger at each interval, and they were running out of ways to deal with their numbers.

Jonathan knelt, looking through the green haze that covered Seattle from a building that had lost most of its exterior. For the last few minutes, the noise had been less.

His eyes were closed. His lost soldiers weighing heavy on him as he tried to recover some strength.

He was far more tired than the rest of his men. Any who had collected more than one portal stone tied to their gate could break one. This let them recover themselves—in a manner of speaking. They returned to their original entry point in The Never without the accumulated injuries to their bodies or gear.

While their bodies did not return tired and battered, none had slept for over forty-eight hours. Hours where their minds had been through more violence and stress than in their entire lives.

Mito had resisted breaking a stone even when Jonathan ordered him to do so. The man only relented when Jonathan and Leah both promised they would await his return at his point of entry. By then, The Never Army had a solid grasp on reentry mechanics. Soldiers returned to The Never in a window of twelve to fifteen minutes. Luckily, the same safety protocols that governed the Feroxian gateways applied to them.

When Mito had entered The Never, he'd been on the thirtieth floor of a building that was no longer there. Jonathan and Leah followed him to where his duct tape square had been placed to find it under a mountain of rubble. When Mito returned, he was standing on a safe surface atop the building's remains.

While grateful that his men could use the conduit's mechanics to recover their strength, Jonathan and Leah got no such favors. It was no surprise that neither had felt a stone come across the conduit's threshold.

Jonathan had no way of knowing exactly what the prophet had planned for Leah. But there was no doubt in his mind that if the Ferox Army couldn't bring the prophet his head, Malkier would come for it himself.

He would force Jonathan to go through him to get home and he would take every precaution to ensure such a victory was impossible.

Jonathan took a deep breath as Rourke's voice came over the comms to report another incoming.

"Break's over," he said to Leah.

Her helmet was down, and she didn't let herself show it, but he knew she was feeling the same weariness seeping into her.

She slipped her rattan onto her back and held out a hand. "Sleep when we're dead and all that."

He nodded.

They were in the thick of it. The streets lined with rubble and debris. The Ferox that surrounded them cautious, having watched what a single swing of their weapons could do.

The She-rox waited for their opening while the males lumbered in when the fancy overtook them. Of course, it might as well have been their strategy, as when each of the males came in to take their attention, the females found their moment and went for it.

Jonathan felt his armor tear across his back. The She-rox who had landed the lucky blow was surprised when the plate inside his suit was exposed to air. Fire burst forth from his back.

Jonathan ignored it; this wasn't the first plate he'd lost to air exposure. Meanwhile the She-rox nearly leapt back in surprise—most likely thinking the fire was some sort of weapon. She didn't live long enough to learn otherwise. Mito had already been coming in to intercept her, and was only a moment late when he landed on her and drove two katar daggers into the back of her neck.

Jonathan growled, having grown tired of allowing the beasts to come to him. He whirled into a spin, twirling *Excali-bar* around him in what was mostly a distraction that forced the beasts back as he freed *Doomsday* from his chest. A moment later, he thrust *Excali-bar* into one of their number and jumped in the air, allowing *Doomsday* to whirl around him.

The speed at which he maneuvered the chain confused and confounded them. Suddenly, the Ferox found themselves being struck from unexpected angles as he whipped the chain back and forth through their numbers. The spiked tip's molecular edge finding no resistance as it penetrated their exterior armor.

He heard the distress call over his comm.

"Please, whoever is out there, there's only three of us left. They're not letting up. We can't outrun them."

With a glance at Mito and Leah, they all dropped out of combat. Leah grabbed Mito by the arm as they rocketed toward the location of the distress call. The thinning crowd of Ferox that had been trying to overwhelm them were slow to react, and even slower to give chase as the gleamers allowed the three to move through the city without losing as much speed.

But that was when the next call for help came over the comms. "Memorial Stadium. We've got more than we can handle coming here."

They came to a stop on a rooftop. Looking at one another to make a call.

"The runners are closer," Jonathan said. "We help them, then the stadium."

She nodded.

All three were still for a moment as their HUD laid out the most efficient course for them to take.

Then it happened. Another call came in. They all recognized the voice.

"She-rox, pack of em, got cut off from the team," Bodhi said.

His location was already pulling up on their maps, he'd been on his way to help those at the Stadium.

"Think my leg is broken. I can't get away . . . I can't get away."

Jonathan saw Leah shiver. He could see her already inching away from him toward Bodhi's distress signal.

"Jonathan—I can't let him—"

"Mito, go with her!" Jonathan said. "Don't argue. We move like lightning and we rendezvous at the stadium."

He hesitated for a moment as Leah's back turned to them; she was already leaping off the roof as Mito cursed and dove after her.

Jonathan shivered for a moment as their backs disappeared, then sprinted in the opposite direction.

Leah slammed *Themyscira* through the Red's back. The rattan's blunt spiked tip erupted out of the monster's chest. The Ferox spasmed in shock. Its roar of agony reduced to a choked gurgle. He tried, impotently, to turn on her, but *Themyscira* may as well have been a steering wheel.

She lifted the creature up and over, its feet leaving the street with another choked roar, before she launched it down the hill. *Themyscira* slipped free with a meaty wet 'thip' before it shot away and crashed down the hill.

The fight was over before Mito even caught up to her. She felt guilty for not waiting for the man. But, had she left Bodhi waiting a few seconds longer she'd have been too late.

She turned back to Bodhi, still lying in a small crater on the street. He looked unconscious but still alive. Five dead She-rox lay nearby. Bodhi was hard to overwhelm; he was smart enough to run when the odds were stacked against him, and barring maybe Sam, he was the fastest runner in their army. They must have set a trap for him. The She-rox were smart though, they must have picked up on his tactics and made a point of hobbling him to keep him from running.

"Appreciate the assist," his voice a weak whisper behind the helmet.

He couldn't stand.

"Do you have a stone, Bodhi?"

He pointed to the side of the street. "I tried. The Red knocked me into the road before I could get my glove off. I can feel it under that car."

She stood, walked to the side of the street, grabbed the car by the frame, and flipped it over. The red glowing stone wasn't hard to find in a pile of leaves.

"Backup, Memorial Stadium, please, we don't have much time left."

She ripped his glove off for him and dropped the stone in his hand. "You got this? I got to get to them."

He nodded. She backed away as he crushed the stone in his palm. "Catch ya on the flip, sister."

He disappeared. She hesitated for a moment.

"No," she shook her head. "That . . . that isn't. I'm overthinking . . . he didn't mean. . ."

She shook her head and sheathed *Themyscira*. *No time for this* she yelled in her mind as she turned to run.

Glancing at her HUD she could see Mito was still moving. His dot was nearing hers, but she knew he could see her dot as well and would adjust course to meet her. A moment later and she was disappearing into the trees of Denny Park as her map updated to the fastest path to intercept with the Stadium's distress call.

She'd grown rather adept at memorizing routes through the city at a quick glance from hours of training in the projection chamber. Emerging out of the trees at the other end of the park she shot into the air to land on the nearest low rise. Clearing the rooftop in a flash, she hurdled across, over the street and crashed through an east facing window on the adjacent building.

More empty condos—one of those things no one considers before they fight a superpowered guerilla war in an evacuated city is just how many empty living room windows you'll be destroying before the day is out. She didn't slow down for minor obstacles, was quicker to run through doors rather than stop to open them. When she emerged into a hallway she turned north. Shot through another window and onto the next rooftop.

The routes the HUD displayed weren't always perfect—didn't update in real time along with the destruction caused by the war. Sometimes this was an obstacle, other times it made things easier. This time was the latter, instead of the building that her HUD expected, there was only a pile of rubble where a building had been standing earlier that day. Leah dropped to the street, sprinted up the pile and launched off the peak to clear an entire block.

This long shot through the air took her past the massive eyesore known as the Experience Music Project. The entire surface was made up of thousands of panels of stainless steel in shades of purple, silver and gold. She'd always thought of the EMP as an answer to the question: How cool would it be to walk into a giant metal amoeba? Ironically, it remained mostly unscathed by the battle raging through the city.

"Memorial Stadium, I'm almost to your—"

Her course through the air changed in an instant. She felt herself buckled at the waist as some unseen thing crashed into her at the stomach. She'd barely realized she had been hit before her backside tore through the building's exterior. Hit straight on by—nothing—but a *nothing* that had the weight of a wrecking ball behind it.

CHAPTER NINETY-NINE

THREE MEN FLED across the rooftops on Capitol Hill, a swarm of She-rox trailing them two buildings back. Command had fallen to Emilio when their team leader was lost in an ambush. He and the two men with him were all that remained of the original twenty-five.

"We're out numbered and being pursued," Emilio yelled into the comm as they ran. "We can't shake them. Anyone close, we need backup."

This wasn't his first distress call. He hadn't gotten a reply yet. His HUD showed no one in the immediate area with a large enough force to help them. He was beginning to feel it in his bones.

No one was coming.

Singh, the fastest of the three, stopped abruptly out in front. He pointed to the surrounding buildings. "They're . . . they're . . . tiring us out."

Emilio came to a stop beside him, his hope fading as he saw what Singh saw for himself. The She-rox behind them weren't trying to run them down—not really. They were just keeping pace, keeping them on the run and distracted as the rest of the pack sprinted across the rooftop that flanked them to get ahead. It was already too late, they were already at the center of a tightening fist.

"We're surrounded," Emilio said into the comm before he turned to the others. "If anyone is out there, we don't have much time left."

Emilio turned to watch the She-rox on their rear halt their pursuit on the nearest rooftop. The beasts pacing, watching the three of them with a hunger. If he didn't know any better, he would have said they looked proud of themselves, having run the last of his team straight into a trap.

Singh sighed, hiding his fear of their fate. "Clear of gas."

Emilio saw what he meant now. His HUD no longer displaying the warning for WX gas. This pack of She-rox had chased them far enough from the conduit that their weapons were safe to use.

"Good, finally gonna let the dogs out," Emilio said.

He pulled *Cujo* and *Cerberus* from across his back. A matching set of axes that could only be described as gnarly. Half-moons, molecular edged heads with a long blunt spike out the back for balance. Despite being forged of alien steel, they looked like they had been wrapped in barbed wire up to where his hand gripped each hilt.

Singh smiled, nodding as he pulled two shuang gou's from his own back. He then looked to the last of their trio.

Doyle had always been the quietest in their squad, even when it had been thirty strong. He didn't have much to say now either, but simply reached onto his back and pulled his weapon.

He called it *the Warf*. In the month or so they had trained together, Emilio had always frowned at the thing. Unsure of how well it would serve Doyle when the time came for real, or why he'd chosen such an awkward looking weapon.

That was until Collin and Hayden had seen him carrying it around one day and asked if he spoke Klingon. Apparently, Doyle's weapon was a re-creation of something called a Bat'leth . . . from freakin' *Star Trek*.

They looked at one another one last time and formed a triangle to best protect one another. The Green's circle tightened around them. They must have been outnumbered ten to one. In the pitch black of the city their white eyes seemed to float in the darkness, their guttural growls growing closer as they drew near. Soon, the first grew brave and jumped to grip the lip of their rooftop.

A small red dot appeared on the map in Emilio's HUD. One of their own was close. The dot was moving their way—and fast. But he knew . . . one more man wasn't going to change the way this wind was blowing.

"Whoever that is, thank you for trying, but it's too late and there are too many," Emilio said. "Please, don't waste your life trying to save us."

The red dot slowed, then stopped. Emilio couldn't spare the man another thought as the She-rox swarmed the rooftop. They weren't going to wait for his full attention. More and more jumped toward them from the surrounding building. Others appeared, climbing up and over from the outer walls.

Despite his fear, Emilio accepted what was about to happen. He flexed his grip on *Cujo* and *Cerberus*. He was going to roar, though what he wanted his final cry to be he wasn't sure.

Doyle's voice suddenly boomed with rage behind them. "Heghlu'meH QaQ jajvam."

Emilio and Singh heard the translation . . .

Today is a good day to die!

The pack didn't swarm them all at once, but some of the more eager came forward as though testing their prey. Those few were not prepared for the effectiveness of the molecular edge on their weapons. The first of those who came within striking distance pulled away with a surprised squeal when *Cujo* had sunk deep into her forearm. The Ferox screamed in agony as the axe cleaved through her external armor down to the metallic bone in her arm. She drew back, cradling the wound, watching him with both caution and bloodlust, as she paced just outside his reach.

It brought them little hope to draw blood. The pack was only testing them, and as the monsters studied them, communication was passing through their numbers. Soon, the pack started to approach in clumps, five on one, while in the rear others took up positions to pounce so they could drop in on them from above.

In the next few seconds, they would simply be overwhelmed—the waiting racked Emilio's nerves. He was supposed to lead but saw nothing to be done as the pack casually cackled in their guttural alien language about how they were to be dispatched. Hyena playing with their food.

Then one of the Ferox stilled. It looked past them and up into the night. Soon, others did the same, their disturbed vocals drawing the rest of the pack's attention to the sky. Emilio only had enough time to frown at them behind his helmet's shield when he noticed a proximity warning. The red dot on his minimap—the lone soldier who had responded to their distress call. The man was coming toward their rooftop like a guided missile.

Emilio heard his comm crack to life, and he immediately knew the voice. "Everyone down, now!"

As they dove for the ground, *Brings the Rain* landed on the rooftop. His device shields were pulled back, and his helmet visor retracted, such that he was a blazing ball of energy in the dark night. As he landed, he crouched, one fist tightening over his head. For a split second, it seemed an overly cinematic pose, like he was making some dramatic entrance, but the arm he held up was shaking with effort to keep its grip. As though he was bringing all the strength he had to bear to control—something.

A split second later, the She-rox starting on his right seemed to be knocked away and into the night, pushed hard and fast into the rooftop, or barreled into. Emilio didn't understand what he was seeing, it was as though Jonathan was hitting them with an unseen force even as his arm came down in front of him, still shaking with exertion as his free hand joined in effort.

Tibbs began to pivot, and as he moved each Ferox in front of him seemed struck, slapped out of the way like a wrestler hit by a clothesline.

Then Emilio saw it—didn't believe—but he understood. He saw the flash of the alien steel, *Doomsday,* circling Jonathan's wrist as he held tight and anchored something very heavy at the other end. Where the chain normally ended in a spiked tip, there was now a ball the size of a golf cart. It looked like—well—it had been a vehicle at some point; he'd mangled it into a ball of wreckage.

Suddenly, Emilio recognized what it was. As the three had been fleeing the pack, they'd run across the rooftop of the nearby hospital. There had been a landing pad on that roof—with a helicopter parked on top of it.

As he completed his circle, Jonathan's thumb came down on a small release button on *Doomsday*'s handle, and the lasso-like chain around the helicopter wreckage freed itself, smashing into two of the She-rox before plummeting over the side of the roof. Jonathan jolted momentarily from the sudden loss of the weight and yanked the chain back to him as he began to rise to his feet.

The attention of every Ferox on the roof was no longer on Emilio's trio.

The ones lucky enough to escape the wrecking ball were quick to move in on him, but *Brings the Rain* maneuvered with a reaper's grace. By the time Emilio had gotten back to his hands and knees Jonathan was ripping through the stunned pack. Even with thermal optics the tip of *Doomsday* seemed to move around him and strike out of the night from angles that caught the Ferox by surprise. Emilio watched in disbelief as the spiked tip sailed through the night to impale an unsuspecting Green through the chest, only for Jonathan to yank back hard on the chain and wrench the creature off its feet. He stepped out of the way as the helpless beast rocketed toward him and crashed into the two coming for his exposed back.

Finally, one of the Greens, the one Emilio thought the leader, flew out of the night, only to be plucked out of the air single-handedly and pounded down through the rooftop.

There was a moment of pause in the pack as Jonathan turned away from the crater he had just put their leader through and looked over the rest. His blazing eyes, there was recognition—they knew who he was. It changed the way they came, eagerness replaced with even more caution. Even more so when the next to take a chance at him died with his fist driven straight through its chest.

Singh was the first to regain his wits, already pulling Emilio up by the shoulder and reminding him that they should be dispatching as many of the pack as they could in the chaos Jonathan was creating for them. The pack was temporarily quite focused on making an ill-fated attempt at their leader.

Emilio's training returned to him, the three falling into step, working together to herd and flank the creatures, ensuring that while Jonathan kept their attention, he didn't get overwhelmed.

Soon . . . to their shock, the beasts fled across the rooftops.

Jonathan watched this with some annoyance. It wasn't that he thought them cowards, that much Emilio could tell. Rather, Jonathan was bothered by the wisdom of the pack leaving a fight when they couldn't win. The male Ferox weren't wired to do the same. Their over eagerness to fall on the sword was one of the advantages The Never Army had been exploiting.

Intelligence and self-preservation, those were more human traits.

Jonathan's helmet slapped shut and his shields moved back into place to cover the light of his implant. In seconds he went from a beacon in the night to a soldier nearly indistinguishable from Emilio or the others.

"Everyone alright?" Jonathan asked.

They nodded, surprised to have come out of the scrape with only a few bruises.

The shiny black visor of Jonathan's helmet moved over each of them, and finally settled on Doyle. More specifically, on *the Warf*—the weapon now dripping with Feroxian blood.

"Doyle," Jonathan said, clearly reading the man's name from his HUD data.

"Sir?" Doyle replied.

"Did you just yell at them in Klingon?"

The three survivors each exchanged glances. Doyle finally shrugging awkwardly. "I don't speak it, I just know the one phrase."

In their moment of relief, Emilio and Singh began to shake their heads and laugh.

"You guys suck," Doyle said, putting the weapon away.

CHAPTER ONE HUNDRED

IT IS USING *a cloaking device.* The realization did her a fat load of good now. She'd already taken the brunt of the impact when it crashed into her, being knocked through the exterior wall, and crashing into the cement floor with all its weight on her.

She could feel the cement give—crunching and crumbling beneath her—but the ground floor held, and the sudden violent stop took the wind from her lungs. Her head hit last. The helmet protected her skull but the hard knock against a cement pillar was dizzying.

She'd taken falls and hits the last few days, but for the first time—Leah couldn't shake it off.

The light had fled as soon as they crashed through the outer wall. Her HUD triggered thermal vision on its own. Pinned, she was struggling to breathe, as the massive weight of the *cloaked* monster began to move on top of her.

It would go for the neck—she knew it was coming, but her strength seemed useless—no leverage. This beast was strong and had her limbs pinned. As her panic surged, she felt the thing rearing up to bite down on top of her.

Mustard gas erupted out of her suit's vents—concentrated foulness clouding the air.

The Ferox must have gotten a straight shot into the open mouth. The squeal sound that followed was like a startled pig. She felt its weight give just enough as it reared back. A long pull of air finally made its way into her lungs as she yanked her knee to her chest and kicked.

Wild, but powerful, and her boot found her invisible assailant. The rest of the weight flew off her and a split second later a loud crash came from somewhere on the other side of the room. Leah rolled out of the gouge their landing had made in the floor. Her limbs barely obeying, hands and knees feeling as though she were trying to swim through pudding.

"Mito?" she whispered into her comm.

Her eyes searched for movement throughout the space. The EMP was setup like a museum with multiple cement tiers and various exhibitions. She'd landed somewhere near the bottom level.

The thermal optics let her see obscured shapes and surfaces—far better than nothing—but still limited. What she didn't see was a Feroxian form where her ears told her she was hearing the thing getting to its feet.

Infrared—no better. Finally, despair beginning to creep in, she switched over to Night Vision.

A ghostly apparition moved on the other side of the museum. She could make out obscured parts of a face, some torso, an arm. Dust from the cement, particulates, sticking to moisture of the mustard gas—it all looked like powder moving unnaturally in the air.

Its hands were rubbing at its face.

"Backup at EMP, a cloaked assailant engag—"

Leah's voice caught, losing her words as what was going on all around her froze her in fear. She heard heavy feet trying to step quietly through broken glass and debris somewhere above her. A display case shook, seemingly of its own accord on the opposite side of the room. The outline of claws appeared in a wall, as though something unseen crawled along the surface. The air was disturbed, near the floor, imprints of feet coming toward her in the dust.

In short—there was more than one invisible thing in this darkness with her. Something fast bolted on the edge of her vision. An invisible shape flanking her. She heard movement, heavy feet landing on the open floor above.

There had yet to be any word of the six cloaking units in Malkier's possession—not a single report of engagement with an invisible attacker. If there had been such an attack, it had been quick, over before the victim so much as called for help. But they had all known the devices would come into play. Malkier would not just sit on so useful a weapon.

"Mito?" she whispered again.

He should have been here by now, but no answer came. She was alone.

All together—acting as a pack—the cloaked Ferox—they could do far more damage if they were targeted assassins. What if Malkier's play was always to wait for her to be isolated?

"M—Multiple cloaked assailants," Leah said. "They're closing on me."

Beo's voice came over the comm. "On ma way, Leah."

"Same," Tam said. "We're coming."

More shapes moved in the darkness. Too many to keep track of.

Her map flashed Tam and Beo's positions across her HUD and she knew they wouldn't reach her in time. Mito's dot was close. Except, she realized, it was still.

He . . . he wasn't moving . . .

This was a setup. They had been watching . . . waiting for the perfect moment. Waiting for her to make the mistake of separating from the others. Her chest began to heave, her heart raced. She couldn't fight this many, not blind.

Jonathan's voice came over the comm—blocked out all the others. "Leah. Listen to me. You're faster than them, stronger than them. Pick a direction and run, don't stop for anything."

He wanted her to run, he—well, *actually he had a point.*

Maybe, her best move was to put another hole in the wall—linebacker her way out. She was quick; if she made it outside it wouldn't matter that she couldn't see them. She could just keep running.

She reached to the back of her belt and took hold of her last flash bang. The movement didn't go unnoticed—leading to a stirring of sound around her. They weren't stupid—knew she'd sensed them. That if she was going to make a move, she only had the next few seconds. The only reason she could imagine that they hadn't already closed on her was the mustard gas—the smell was so god-awful to them they assumed it dangerous—eventually they would realize it could simply be endured.

She slowed her movement, slipped the grenade free—her other hand finding the pin.

The heavy breathing of massive lungs drew close—small flecks of cement falling around her from the pillar. She shivered, wanted to scream and run—but knew it would give away that she'd sensed the creature creeping down the pillar toward her.

She was starting to feel paralysis—too much panic—the adrenaline making her uncertain that her body would move when she told it to. Then—suddenly—she realized she could not move—couldn't even blink of her own accord. The pounding in her heart began to slow—her breathing calming into a deliberate rhythm.

Leah didn't move and yet—her hand pulled the pin.

A voice rose up from inside her. A voice that was angry and violent and unafraid. A voice that turned Leah's despair to hope even as she lost any power over her body.

"Get away from her, you bitch!" Rylee yelled.

Minds met at a nexus as they gripped the grenade pin. In that instant, as the pin slipped free, they shared a moment of certainty. Their fears a mirror of one another.

If Leah died, they died.

If Leah died, the child died.

If Leah died, the bond died.

If Leah died, their world died.

Rylee's battle cry erupted as she dropped the grenade, and bolted, not forward but sideways.

The room erupted with noise as six unseen foes reacted. They dove for her as the flash bomb triggered. The museum was suddenly awash in painful bright light.

Rylee stopped hard, flipped backward over the grenade just as the creature coming at Leah from above was blinded. Her boot met it head on in the air, while beneath her, the other blinded creatures all rushed in to intercept her, but they rushed only to where she had feinted before they were blinded.

In that moment, Rylee hadn't thought that her kick would do anything more than knock the Ferox off guard—keep it from getting its unseen claws on her—yet as her boot came around with so much more power than she was used to, the attacker went shooting out away from her.

Below her, the others collided with one another as Rylee finished turning end over end and stuck the landing.

The power in her body rushed to her awareness. The strength given to her by Borealis DNA, magnitudes greater than anything she'd ever known. She had no time to be in awe of it, had precious seconds before her blinded opponents recovered their sight. But, while Leah's eyes had searched the auditorium looking for escape—Rylee's had been focused on how to change the rules of the game.

As she drew *Themyscira* and dropped into a low graceful spin, she took aim at the first such game changer. She threw her rattan and moved, not waiting to see if she hit her target—the moment the weapon flew from her hand she knew her aim was true.

She turned and mounted on the side of the pillar they'd hit when they landed; she saw the second game changer. She was ripping a fire extinguisher from the wall as her rattan penetrated another behind her blinded opponents. As white powder erupted—Feroxian shapes emerged—becoming a powdered outline in her vision.

She hurled the second extinguisher into the midst of the group and hit the ground running. The extinguisher took one of the Ferox in the chest and exploded in a second puff of white, covering them such that little remained a mystery. Ghostly Feroxian faces looked up to see her flying toward them as they fought to shake off the last of their blindness.

She'd recognized two Alphas—their size and shape too similar to Malkier's to be anything else. It was the bigger one she hit first. She didn't hold anything back, dropkicking the ghost Alpha with enough force to send him careening into those standing behind him. His body only clipped most of them but ran straight and true into the one at the rear. Together, those two ripped through one of the EMP's load-bearing pillars. The entire building stuttered in shock as one of its foundations was suddenly gone.

Rylee hadn't stopped moving. Thrust toward the floor by her dropkick she pounced from her hands back to her feet and raced forward again. She somersaulted, leaving one Ferox shooting over her. Then reminded herself that she was still fighting as if they were the ones with the power. She met the next apparition head on in the air, brought her knee in to the collision. Felt the metal of its skull bend around her as she came crashing through and sent its body flying to the ground out ahead of her.

She landed on her feet, pivoted, and let her momentum carry her. Too unfamiliar with the gleamers to dare giving them a try mid-combat, she let the slippery extinguisher residue on the floors coast her into the back wall and plucked *Themyscira* out of where it had been embedded in the now empty canister.

For the moment, only two of the apparitions were on their feet and close—immediate threats, but even as a tag team coming for her they were no match.

Rylee remembered what it was like to see Jonathan hit these beasts as her first downward strike knocked the Ferox down and into the floor with Earth-shattering force. The Ferox hit so hard the cement broke and the creature—bounced.

The second came at her an instant later only to take a bone-bending blow to the knee joint that left it staggering. Her eyes blazing with the power of the bond, she grabbed the staggering Ferox by the throat and drove the rattan straight through its eardrum.

The resistance she had to deal with in the past was gone—the weapon didn't bounce off its armor or halt at the metal skeleton. It drove straight through and the Green—judging by its tail—fell limp in her hands. She ripped the rattan free and brought the body up and over. Slamming it into the one whose skull she'd bounced off the floor a moment earlier.

As she gave this Red apparition the same temporal lobe treatment she'd given the last, a proximity warning drew her attention to movement. The Ferox she'd first kicked off the pillar above her, was coming back into the fray. Rylee had heard all the same chatter as Leah over the comms. The females were squishier than the males, but far more dangerous in packs. This one was alone—

Except, she also sensed the one who first set off Leah's mustard gas.

Rylee saw it then, the white apparition beginning to circle on all fours. These two hadn't been around to get doused by the fire extinguisher. Still, there was no removing all that particulate from the air, and the closer they came the less invisible they were.

She eyed them right back as they circled, wondered if they had even realized that their cloak was no longer fully hiding them.

Rylee put up with this game for about a hot second before using a series of feints to back the two females off before jumping clear of the circle. She shot up to the auditorium's second floor, quickly hurdling the railing as the females jaunted after. There is a reason people talk about having the high ground—and the first female learned this rapidly when, the moment she grabbed the outer railing, Rylee drove the rattan straight through her eye. Still it allowed the second enough time to scramble over the balcony while the first's limp body fell to the floor.

It was about that moment, as Rylee set her attention back to the last female, something human moved in the darkness. Tam, gleaming ever so quietly down the wall behind the female. He almost got the drop on her—but at the last second, the female sniffed at the air and whirled.

Oh yeah, see how you like it, Rylee thought.

The female looked between the two of them and bolted. She didn't attack, she ran. Rylee had never seen a Ferox run, only observed it through Leah's eyes.

"Good to see you breathing," Tam said. "I'd have miss—"

"Don't let her get away," Rylee interrupted.

Tam's head turned to follow the female, no doubt heading for the hole Leah had made when they first attacked.

"Uh," Tam looked at her funny, no doubt wondering why Leah was suddenly talking with an accent. "What about . . ."

"Go," Rylee said.

She didn't wait for him to say he would, but jumped back down to the ground floor, and opened her armor's shields allowing the bright glow of the implant to bring light to the room.

"So much for my valiant rescue," Tam said, giving chase after the female.

Rylee waited on the ground floor, and she didn't have to wait long. The Alpha she'd dropkicked at the onset was pushing himself out of a pile of debris, rolling a lump of cement away before stepping forward.

Its outline looked at her, then put a hand to its chest, some guttural growls were made but Rylee couldn't understand—wasn't tied to its stone.

She wondered what had become of the other one. After all, when she'd drop-kicked the big fellow, he'd crashed into a smaller one at the rear before going through the pillar.

Wait. Was she that strong? Was the only reason this Alpha was standing because that other Ferox had padded this one's collision with the pillar?

"Alright, moron, let's get your funeral started," Rylee said.

The Alpha tilted his powdered face at her as he hefted something from the rubble; it was as visible as he was, a massive ghostly axe.

Great, they're bringing weapons now. Invisible Ferox, with invisible weapons. More guttural growls—this time, clearly aimed at her.

Rylee made some guttural nonsense noises back at him, but if he understood that he was being mocked she couldn't tell.

"Who knew I'd miss being able to exchange pleasantries this mu—"

Rylee jumped back as the ghost axe crashed into the floor where she'd been standing.

The Alpha didn't linger when it missed but charged forward with the axe in one clawed hand as Rylee retreated.

She slipped under the first swing, then dodged past the hulking beast when it swung the axe again. Wheeling to keep the pressure on, the Alpha choked in surprise when a blow from *Themyscira* crashed into the front of its neck.

The moment's hesitation was a door opening on a whirlwind of pain. Rylee moved about the large creature faster than it could keep up, her hits finding joints and pressure points that slowed the Alpha down. Inside his reach, the axe became useless.

After fighting Malkier, and not so much as being able to make him blink with her best shot, this was all very cathartic.

Within moments, the Alpha became so forced to the defensive that he was using the axe as a shield. He expected a blow to come for his eyes, only to find Rylee had changed her strike. Sliding under it on the smooth floor, spinning and smashing the rattan into the back of his knee.

"You're supposed to be the boogeyman," she said as the Ferox lurched, lost its balance, and fell to all fours. "Do you know how much of a disappointment you are?"

Rylee kicked the Alpha in the torso hard enough to throw its body through the auditorium wall and back out to the street.

"Hey Leah, look, I made your hole in the wall," Rylee said.

In her head, no one answered.

Jonathan had to react on instinct when the wall of the museum erupted outward and a pale outline of a large Feroxian shape came flying at him. He drew *Excali-bar* from his back in one fluid motion and slammed the shape down just before it barreled into him.

As he looked down at the thing he'd smashed into the side walk it became rapidly clear what he was standing over—a cloaked Alpha Ferox so beat to hell it was shaking in an effort to get back up.

That was all the time Jonathan was going to spend assessing the situation. He drove *Excali-bar*'s tip through the back of the Alpha's neck with enough force that the demolition bar went in, out the other side, and a foot into the sidewalk. A long final breath gurgled out of the creature.

He was about to move, but before he could pull the bar free and charged through the hole the Alpha had come through, he saw a flash of light moving inside the dark interior, a glowing figure coming toward him from the dark. A moment later, Leah—the shields of her device retracted, emerged from the hole in the wall. She was using her glove to wipe black blood off *Themyscira*.

She looked at him, standing there relieved but a bit dumbfounded, and sheathed the rattan as she casually strolled over to him.

"Everyone en route to Leah, redirect to the stadium," he said.

Rivers' voice came over the line. "Got it covered, my team just arrived."

He left *Excali-bar* where it was as he stepped around to meet her. "You didn't run."

She came to a stop only a foot away from him but didn't say anything. She lifted one hand and tapped at the visor covering his face as though she were knocking at a door.

He retracted the helmet, saw his eyes glowing back at him in the tinted glass of her visor before Leah retracted her own. She looked at him for a moment, smiled—then grabbed him by the collar and pulled his lips to hers. For a moment, he kissed her back—but then suddenly he yanked back in surprise.

"Rylee?"

She smirked at him. "How did you know?"

He blinked for a moment, then forced himself to shake it off—at least enough to remove what he suspected was a very dumb look on his face.

"You and Leah kiss very . . . differently," he said.

"Oh, do we now?"

His eyes narrowed, as if to say *I will not be elaborating.*

"Fine," she said.

Rylee sniffed the air for a moment. "Do you smell that? It's awful!"

Her nose's search brought her to the vents on her armor and she made the mistake of confirming that this was in fact where the smell was coming from—recoiling away as though she'd just put her head in a compost bin.

"Oh God, no wonder they had second thoughts about eating her," Rylee said.

She looked at him. "I can't believe you smelled that and still let her kiss you—you're disgusting."

"I didn't want to ruin the . . ." Jonathan paused. "Wait, I *let her?*"

"Well, you didn't know it was me," Rylee said, turning to walk back to the museum.

He did a double take as he watched her walking away, then shook his head.

"You want to grab that thing and bring it in here," Rylee said. "Think you should see this."

As he stepped inside the demolished auditorium and dropped the Alpha's body on the floor, Rylee began pulling the rest of the corpses into a line.

She looked at the Alpha. "You aren't gonna try and take credit for that are you?"

"I feel that wouldn't be wise," Jonathan said.

Rylee smiled. "Smart boy."

Jonathan sighed, but there was a grin on his face as he did so. He had to deal with the mind job of looking at Leah's face but knowing it wasn't her behind it. Still—there was an ease to talking to Rylee that felt like an old injury finally beginning to heal after giving him nothing but pain for months.

"What's this like for you?" Jonathan asked. "Being in someone else's body?"

"Well, she's taller. Bit bulked up in the shoulders. All that metal work I imagine, not as flexible as I'd have liked but she isn't in bad shape. I can work with it."

Jonathan blinked. He didn't seem to know what answer he'd been looking for though. So, he turned his eyes to the corpses.

"There's only five?" Jonathan asked.

"A female made a run for it, I sent Tam after her while I was dealing with tons of fun over there," she said, gesturing vaguely to the Alpha corpse.

Jonathan nodded. "Probably a waste of time; Bodhi and Sam have trouble keeping pace with the females on the gleamers even when they're visible."

Rylee nodded. But Jonathan was already pondering something—and whatever it was his expression looked worried.

"Malkier sent all the cloaked units he had after you," Jonathan said.

"Probably thought the female of the bonded pair would be an easier kill," Rylee said. "I mean, he thought I was our first string—and I was barely compatible with the implant."

Jonathan nodded.

"Still, he must have had a way to track you, probably both of us," Jonathan said.

To this she frowned. "Why do you say that?"

"The cloaked team didn't make a move on anyone else—only you," Jonathan said. "Ferox aren't that good at telling us apart, it's why they kill civilians indiscriminately when they come here. Our entire army is wearing practically identical gear. I find it hard to believe they picked out the one woman amongst us."

"It's not impossible," Rylee said.

"Yeah, my gut is telling me it's more likely they had some way to find you," Jonathan said.

"Your gut?" Rylee said, "You mean me and the little girl in the pink hoodie."

Jonathan's eyes widened, and he turned to her very—very slowly. Rylee's self-satisfied smirk did not belong on Leah's face—yet—there it was.

He grimaced and closed his eyes. ". . . How?"

"Oh, Leah wasn't the only one who got answers from your head the other day," Rylee said.

Jonathan grimaced. "I don't want to discuss this right n . . . *ever*. I don't want to talk about this—ever."

"Jonathan—don't be ashamed, it was adorable," Rylee said, sounded as though she were remembering a puppy she'd seen at a pet store.

"*Ever!*" he repeated.

Rylee shrugged, whispering in the cutesiest voice she could manage. "*Brings the Rain* so sensitive."

Perhaps in a hurry to change the subject, Jonathan drew a long breath and leaned down, activating his gleamers over the dead Alpha's head. The liquid exterior of the cloaking device began to push away and reveal the band around the forehead. Deactivating the device, he pulled the band free.

The Ferox possessed those familiar markings. Those self-inflicted scars designing its skin. "I encountered a few of these in the queue loop. Was strange—I'd never seen one before—then suddenly four in a row. According to Mr. Clean, they came from a different tribe's gateway. Only reason I was crossing paths with them was because their gate's queue got dumped into mine," Jonathan said. "Reports have been that they're the only ones carrying weapons."

"That mean something to you?" Rylee asked.

"Ferox males have a sense of honor when it comes to combat," Jonathan said. "They judge you when they think you're cheating. So . . . I'm thinking this tribe might be the sort that doesn't see something like using a cloaking device as against their code."

He pondered it for a moment before getting on the comm. "Tam, were you able to intercept the female?"

"Nope. Too quick," Tam said. "But saw where she headed."

"Back through the conduit?" Jonathan asked.

"Yeah, straight shot, how did you know?" Tam asked.

"The females are smart—better at guerrilla warfare. Think Malkier is using them to gather intel."

Rylee considered. "You're thinking the one who ran is reporting on their assassination attempt?" Rylee asked.

"She did get the hell out of Dodge the moment the tables turned," Tam said.

Jonathan stared down at the cloaking device, rubbing the band between thumb and fingers thoughtfully.

"Which one of them hit you, I mean . . . hit Leah . . . first?"

Rylee looked over the shapes, tried the gleamer trick she'd just seen Jonathan use to remove the cloaking device off its forehead and pointed to one. It was also covered in those tribal scars.

Jonathan knelt down beside the body and drove his fist into its torso. After a moment of fishing around he found its portal stone and pulled it free.

"Can't say I missed this par . . . Wow!" Rylee exclaimed.

"I feel it too," Jonathan said.

"Yeah, the second you tore it free from those appendages," Rylee said. "Wait, what do you mean feel it *too*?"

"When we first met in The Never," Jonathan said, "I could feel the stone tied to your gateway as well as the one tied to mine."

"Yeah, duh, I was there," Rylee said.

"That isn't normal though," Jonathan said. "No one else in the army can feel stones that aren't tied to their gateway specifically."

"You're thinking we're different because of the bond?" Rylee asked.

Jonathan nodded as he studied the portal stone.

"How did you know we'd feel that stone?" Rylee asked.

"I didn't. My hunch was that Malkier's found some way to reverse the feed," Jonathan said. "The Ferox with the stone can track the device it's attached to instead of the other way around. I think that's how this one knew who to single out. They've probably been watching us for a while."

"They waited for the bonded pair to separate," Rylee said.

"Mito made things difficult. Too good a bodyguard, only reason they got close was because he couldn't see them coming, and they waited till you were apart," Jonathan said.

Rylee sobered a bit. "Wait, Mito? Is . . . is he?"

"He here," Beo said. They both looked up to see the giant standing in the hole. A much smaller man held in his arms.

"I foun' him outside, he hurt bad, I was 'fraid to pick em up," Beo said. "He ain't breathin' right. Ain't wakin' up."

As careful as he could, Beo knelt down on the floor with Mito. The man looked like he was cradling a child they were so different in size. Jonathan looked down to see Mito's helmet was damaged, his visor broken so badly only a few cracked shards framed his face.

"Has he got any stones left to break?" Jonathan asked.

"I looked, couldn't find none on him," Beo said.

"No," Rylee said. "He . . . he had spares."

She was frantic, began to search through the man's belt, only to find the pouch where she knew the man kept the stones was nowhere to be found. In fact, it looked as though it had been ripped away.

Jonathan, slipped the portal stone he'd taken out of the scarred creature that had been first to attack Leah into his belt pouch, and pulled up what vitals of Mito he could in his HUD.

There wasn't any good news. Mito was fading quickly. Probably bleeding internally. If he had to guess, the man had been knocked out of the sky when trying to catch up with Leah. Fallen fast and hard.

"He . . . he was ma best friend . . ." Beo said. "Don't think he knew dat. I don't. . . I don't want dem to get his body. Dey didn't earn it. Sneakin' up on him like a buncha' cowards. Leavin him to bleed out."

Jonathan looked at the man, listened to his words. It pained him; he knew the sort of grief that could suddenly make a man so giant seem as though he'd been reduced to a child inside. Yet, his words echoed what Jonathan was already thinking. These Ferox with the tribal designs. They seemed a different breed. Mito probably took that axe to his helmet before he even knew he was in a fight.

Rylee turned to put a hand on the giant man's shoulder. "I'm sorry, Beo."

He looked at her strangely for a moment. "You cryin under der, Red? Yo voice sound funny."

She cleared her throat and shook her head. There might be a time to explain her change in accent, but this wasn't it.

Jonathan took a place beside them. They were all going to have to watch, powerless to do anything for the man. Any minute now, his body would disappear, show up in the gateway fields on the other side.

"We won't leave him, Beo, but we need to step away," Jonathan said.

Beo swallowed, and gently let Mito's head rest as he backed away.

The length of the time wasn't long. But they were waiting to see a friend die, and so it was an eternity. Finally, his vital signs flattened in the HUD. The red sphere came and took Mito's remains across the threshold. And the red dot that had shown his location on everyone's map disappeared.

Beo stood there for a long moment. What he did next surprised them all. He opened up a link to every comm.

"Ya'll, Mito's gone," Beo whispered in every soldier's ear. "But da bastards neva made em bend."

He stood to his full height and turned to leave. He paused for a moment when he saw the gnarly axe of the Ferox Alpha now clearly visible on the floor. He stooped down to pick it up. He might have been the only man in the whole damn Army large enough—with hands large enough—to look as though he could wield the thing.

"Brings da Rain, we still gonna make a Borealis bend today?" Beo asked.

"Nothing has changed," Jonathan said.

Beo nodded, then he walked away.

"Almost feel sorry for the next Ferox he finds out there," Rylee said.

Jonathan looked to her for a moment, then he went to each of the corpses, removing the other cloaking devices from their foreheads.

"You uh, look like you got a plan coming together in that head of yours," Rylee said.

He held them out to her. "Do a guy a favor?"

She looked at the cloaking devices curiously, but before she could ask, a voice interrupted on the comm.

"Re-entry successful," Bodhi said. "Did I miss anything?"

CHAPTER ONE HUNDRED AND ONE

ON THE OTHER side of the conduit, Heyer faced his own obstacles. Everything depended on his being able to reach Cede, but that couldn't happen until his brother left this plane.

From where Heyer hid amongst the Ferox in the pit, it seemed no matter how many marched through the portal, the Feroxian hordes surrounding the higher ridges were never at a loss for reinforcements. He had always known the Ferox would outnumber them, but with the females joining the invasion their numbers might as well have been inexhaustible.

Heyer had a limited idea of how the fight fared for the humans on the other side. His only gauge, the number of soldiers lost, their bodies being returned to the gateway fields around the conduit. He could only estimate the losses, there was no way to count, but he had serious doubts that Jonathan had more than two hundred men left.

By now, it seemed certain that as long as Heyer kept any interactions to a minimum, the Ferox around him remained oblivious to any strangeness in his nature.

In the past, Heyer had used an entrance hidden to the Ferox when he needed to enter Cede. He hadn't bothered to check whether or not that entrance still existed. Even if he'd found it there, if his brother hadn't removed the entrance—then it was most certainly a trap tailored for the one being who knew of its existence.

No, the hidden entrance was not a viable option, but there was a good chance Malkier wouldn't expect Heyer to walk right through the front door. Of course, to reach said entrance, Heyer had to go down into what remained of the Feroxian Tribes' tunnels. The way down was plain to see. Within the pit, what remained of the tunnels began as a hole right beside the platform itself. When he made his way down, he would be walking directly beneath the conduit.

None of this was a surprise; they knew that Cede had to be directly beneath the platform and the gateway fields to manage all the necessary power keeping the conduit open.

Still, he expected the place would be guarded. Malkier may have had every reason to be confident in the Ferox's ability to defeat The Never Army, but after the last few months the amount of conceit required to leave the place completely defenseless was unlikely. The nature of what his brother would leave to guard the entrance below was what worried him. For all the things Jonathan claimed to know with certainty, he had been very clear that he could not predict what Heyer might expect when he reached Cede's threshold.

Jonathan was expecting that if he got Malkier off the Feroxian Plane, Heyer would hopefully be able to deal with whatever else might be put in his path. In other words, Jonathan had faith in him. Of course, that was a lot like saying that there was an element of luck in this. In Heyer's experience, luck seldom took his side.

Grant's voice cracked in his ear. "Something's up. Take a look at your brother."

Subtly, Heyer turned, looking up the platform's massive walls from where he stood within the Ferox crowd. The prophet was not difficult to locate, standing in his gleaming plated armor, like a demigod brought to life. Course, that was likely half the point. Malkier could have easily made the armor look less magnificent without losing any defensive function.

He couldn't hear what Malkier was saying from here, but that wasn't what had drawn Grant's attention. What was odd, was that his brother appeared to be talking to no one, and at the same time he seemed very displeased at what he was hearing.

One of the cloaked Ferox had returned.

This was confirmed a moment later when Malkier put out his hand, and a female Ferox appeared in front of him, the cloaking device having withdrawn from her body into the headband. She was kneeling with one fist on the platform. She removed the headband as though being stripped of a crown and placed it in Malkier's armored hand.

Heyer recognized the female. Though he found he couldn't recall her name. He knew of her, because she was *Burns the Flame*'s eldest daughter.

A strange sensation tried to overtake him as he looked up at her. As though Heyer realized just how—fair—she was. A sensation he had been mildly aware of before, as he had encountered others of this host's species. This was different. A strange instinct was coming over him. He felt sudden certainty the female would accept his offer of consonance if only he presented her a trophy. More, he found the urge to seek out said trophy profoundly distracting.

Jarred by what he realized was happening, he looked away. The longer he looked at the female the more the urge to seek a combatant burned in him. As a human, Heyer would have wrestled his thoughts with logic, concentrate on priorities. Kept himself focused against their natural wanderings. This tactic seemed far less successful in his current host.

Strangely, he found the powerful urge diminish when he focused on his brother. The reason why this had worked took him a moment, and even then, he wasn't sure. He suspected that one instinct was being suppressed by another of a stronger nature. His brother actually had nothing to do with it. Rather, the presence of an Alpha diminished his urge.

Almost as though a Red male, in the presence of an Alpha, knew not to seek combat and consonance without deferring to the Alpha.

"Heyer, you alright?" Grant asked. "You look like you're eyeing a prime rib."

Heyer patted his shoulder once. One pat for yes and two for no having become the simplest way to communicate. The movements looking natural enough on a Ferox. So far, this was one of the few times Heyer was glad they couldn't speak in greater detail.

Malkier's expression only worsened as the female finally finished her report. His brother dismissed her, and Heyer made a point of not watching where she went afterward. He feared the knowledge would distract him again.

"Well, I remember that look, your brother is pissed," Grant said.

One pat.

"Might be worth talking to the female—see if you can learn what she told him."

Heyer shivered, then patted his shoulder twice.

"You sure," Grant said. "She's already headed your way."

Heyer glanced up, finding the female had descended the platform ramp and was now headed in his general direction. He turned away abruptly—and immediately regretted that he hadn't been more subtle.

"What was that?" Grant asked. "Now, she's staring right at you."

Heyer moved, pushing his way through the crowded pit as best he could without drawing attention.

"Okay, if you're trying to lose her," Grant said. "You're not succeeding. I gather I'm missing something here?"

One pat.

"Are we exposed?"

Two pats, shake of the fingers.

"We going to be if she catches up to you?"

One pat, shake of the fingers.

"Alright well, you've definitely got her attention. She's circling the crowd to get in front of you."

Heyer didn't look but altered course.

"Get it together man," Grant said. "Even I can tell you're acting funny."

One pat.

"Okay, duck behind those gas bladders on your left," Grant said.

He did as he was told.

"Alright, hold tight," Grant said.

The seconds ticked by . . . probably only half a minute.

"Okay, she's giving up," Grant said. "Give her some time to put more distance between you."

Heyer let out a long sigh and patted his shoulder.

"Ah, crap," Grant said.

Heyer waited, the only alternative being to look up at the tower he knew Grant would be on and try to look impatient as he waited for the man to tell him what the problem was.

"She . . . she just headed down the tunnel beneath the platform."

Heyer patted his shoulder once in acknowledgement. It was a problem that might never come to pass, the tunnels beneath the platform were still vast after all, plenty of paths to take to avoid one Ferox.

"Um, something is happening," Grant said.

Heyer looked around and quickly saw that the man was right. It seemed as though every Ferox in the pit had looked up and toward the prophet in near unison. Heyer quickly stood back to his full height and did the same to blend in with the rest.

They stared at the prophet for some time, and again, in near unison, a roar of approval seemed to pour out of the crowds. Suddenly, most of the Ferox began to make their way toward the ramps. As though . . .

"I don't know what he said to them," Grant said. "But I think they're done sending in waves, this looks like a flood."

CHAPTER ONE HUNDRED AND TWO

OVER THE NEXT hour, Rourke no longer needed to bother with updates on the growing size of the next wave. The inner city was swelling with Ferox coming through the conduit like a festering lump readying itself to burst.

Jonathan pulled his soldiers further and further back as the streets and buildings near the portal were overrun. What was interesting—the Ferox weren't giving chase as his forces pulled back.

They were gathering their numbers en masse. It could only mean they meant to end this war with a final push. The question that remained, was whether or not the prophet would follow them.

Malkier had several advantages since the start of this, but perhaps the greatest was simply knowing exactly how many men Jonathan had left. The prophet knew that the armory only had so many human implants. He'd gone out of his way to make sure Heyer couldn't procure more before the onset of the war. Tracking fatalities was easy enough. Each time one of them died, a Ferox returned to the gateway field with the corpse.

Yet, it seemed that up until now, as Jonathan's numbers fell below a hundred, Malkier had held back.

Jonathan knew why. Malkier feared a weapon that he wasn't sure existed.

Ever since he'd sent those twenty-eight mutilated bodies to Malkier's front steps, there had been an unknown. A possibility that humanity possessed a weapon unlike anything Malkier could conceive. It wasn't simply the state of the bodies that had been returned, but how the gateways themselves had seemed to malfunction.

Only Jonathan knew there was no such weapon outside himself. That none of the strangeness around the gates had ever been something he controlled. That it had all been the result of a perfect storm of variables put in play on Malkier's side and his own.

Why then, had Malkier suddenly become convinced that the danger wasn't real? After all, if they hadn't used it by now, was it not possible that humanity was holding out, saving such a powerful thing for their last stand?

The answer came to Jonathan as soon as he knew the Ferox were amassing. After all, only one thing had ultimately changed.

The female of the bonded pair had been in imminent danger. Had nearly been killed—if Jonathan possessed some weapon of mass destruction—he would have used it in that moment. Thing was, if Malkier assumed all that— he'd have been right. The moment Leah's voice had called for backup had been the most frightening of Jonathan's life. If Jonathan had possessed a button that could have stopped it—he'd have pressed it.

Jonathan had been well aware of what he would do in such a situation. Which was why—if a weapon of such power existed—he knew he couldn't be the one carrying the trigger.

But there was someone he trusted to second guess him when it came to triggers. There was someone he knew would follow protocol.

In short, if the Ferox numbers were coming in at this rate but holding their lines, Malkier must finally be testing the waters—finally confident that no nasty surprise was waiting for him in The Never. The bonded pair remained in play. His attempt to assassinate the female half had failed. But if they had no weapon, those things were simple obstacles to overcome.

"Jonathan," Rourke's voice came over the comm. "Malkier, he here."

"You're certain? He may look like any Alpha, but he has a scar on his cheek,"

"Can't see scar. He wear helmet, and full body armor," Rourke said. "Must be true Borealis steel, not combusting in gas. All Ferox around him part and kneel."

Jonathan nodded. "Yeah, that sounds like the prophet. What else can you see?"

"Well, I can hear him," Rourke said. "He sound like giant . . . uh . . . Darth Vader. Ferox act strange since he arrive. Like, they all listen to sound. Think he speak to them somehow."

Jonathan absorbed all that.

"Thank you, Rourke," he said. "Hold your position, and stay out of sight."

"Dah."

Jonathan took one last look over the city, hardly able to see more than a few blocks due to the thick haze of WX. He opened a channel to every man he had left.

"Never Army. Converge at rendezvous. It's time."

CHAPTER ONE HUNDRED AND THREE

AFTER A NUMBER of controlled demolitions and two days of fighting, The Never Army should have been able to see the conduit from where they stood on the roof of the Washington convention center.

But the WX gas was too dense.

So, the sight became little more than Ferox packing into streets and slowly pushing closer as their numbers swelled.

Jonathan turned away from that for a moment and looked at Rylee. With her visor in place she seemed unreal. She walked and stood like Rylee, but her shape was Leah's. When she spoke, the words came out a mix of Leah's voice and Rylee's accent.

It all confused his mind.

At the moment, she noticed him watching her and her head tilted in curiosity back at him.

He wondered what thoughts ran through her mind. Rylee couldn't possibly be thinking what he was at that moment, because he was thinking of how close they stood to where they first met.

She couldn't be thinking the same, because they literally had different memories of meeting. He'd heard some of the story from her. For Rylee, they had met somewhere in the middle of downtown. Fought two Ferox and found themselves on top of a building—overcome by the carnal push of the bond.

For him, it had been quite different.

Jonathan didn't think of that first morning when Rylee came to his house looking for him as the moment they met. For him, they really met later that night. He watched from an overpass as she knocked a Ferox onto the I-5 Freeway. Sat staring, dumbfounded, as she then pursued it into the evening traffic.

That was when they both understood what they really were. He thought of this now, because the convention center was built on a tunnel that strad-dled the same freeway. Despite the gas, he could see that very overpass from where they all now stood.

He looked at what remained of his army, Rylee and what remained of his brothers. The next hour would decide all their fates, and each and every one of them looked to him.

Olivia's voice came to him on the comm. "From what I can see, they don't show much hurry."

"He's got a thousand Ferox around him. He knows exactly where I am and that I have less than a hundred men," Jonathan said. "He's afraid."

"Do you have a plan to get him away from the portal?"

Jonathan looked to Bodhi, the kid was standing next to a waist-high box. Admittedly, he had let his roommates and Mr. Clean take license with exactly what the box did—after all, he just needed it to be loud. That said, he was not exactly surprised when they presented him one big box with one big red button.

"Yep," Jonathan said. "Give me a minute."

"Received," Olivia said.

He took a long breath, swallowed, then walked up to Rylee. He retracted his helmet and visor, and after looking back at him for a moment, she did the same.

Leah's face, Rylee's gaze.

"I know that look," Rylee said. "Don't think I won't knee you in the nuts, in front of your boys."

"Why would you need to do a thing like that?"

"Because you're just dumb enough to ask me to go hide somewhere safe," Rylee said.

"Oh, no . . . I'm not brave enough to ask you that," he said.

"Then why are you staring at me like that?" Rylee asked.

He stepped closer, his hands going to her waist as he pulled her close.

"Thought we could both use some luck," Jonathan said.

She stared at him for a moment, eyes blazing as brightly as his, then—

"Oh," Rylee leaned into his lips as though she didn't want him to take credit for her idea. His arms tightened around her. The kiss went on a bit long, until they both heard it.

Throats being cleared. A few loud whistles. The obligatory, "Hey, *Brings the Rain,* ya want to get a room, already."

Finally, the distractions were too much and they laughed. Smiled at one another as they stepped apart.

Jonathan turned to his soldiers, and said, "Alright, you all know what to do. Anyone needs to go to the bathroom, crap your pants or hold it."

They were tired, but they cheered like they wouldn't ever let the enemy see it, their helmets all clamping down as they began to chant. "We don't bend. We don't bend."

Jonathan turned to where the Ferox were amassing. "Go for it, Bodhi."

The kid's fist came down on the big red button.

Over the next few seconds, Jonathan found himself recalling a conversation with Paige. She'd asked him if he ever just let Mr. Clean play music for him.

He'd shook his head and asked, "No, why?"

She'd shrugged. "Let's just say Bose doesn't have anything on the Borealis Audio."

The building they stood on began to tremble. It vibrated along with the sounds flowing out of the building around them. Jonathan's helmet reacted as though a flash grenade had just gone off at his feet and muffled the sound as the building became a beacon.

Then, he actually heard what was being bull-horned out in every direction.

He turned to Rylee, his head slowly tilting in suspicion.

"Yeah, okay," she said, over the comm. "Leah knew your roommates were planning this."

He shook his head and smiled. "They expected to be standing beside me all the way."

"Not sure I follow," Rylee said.

"They wanted to see my face," Jonathan said. "They wanted one last laugh, just in case."

Malkier stepped across the threshold, he stood at the bottom of a hill. He looked up at a sky turned so green with gas it seemed otherworldly. Rubble surrounded the conduit, Heyer's resistance army had demolished every building near the opening. Forced the Ferox to dig their way in multiple times to make way for more of their kind to come through.

To each side of him, his people knelt as their prophet began to ascend the steep slope of wreckage. When he reached the peak, he looked down onto a city flooded with Ferox. They had followed orders, were now clumped together nearly shoulder to shoulder to make room for the invasion force he would use to wipe out what remained of his brother's army. They filled the streets as far as he could see into the green haze, clung to the sides of buildings that remained standing.

A path parted for him down from the peak, his people staying low as they moved aside to make way. From within his helmet, each breath in and out sounded like a rhino with sleep apnea. Every few steps, this was followed by a sharp hiss as the armor pushed used air out through exhaust pipes and filtered the intake of the next breath.

Coming to this plane, he would take no chances of his weakness being exposed to his people. So, the armor not only ensured his invincibility, but took every precaution not to leave his clever brother any means of introducing a jolt into his system. The air he breathed, the vibrations that reached his ears, the grounding of his entire body, any imaginable way in had been reinforced. Even the suit itself was connected to his implant, and could step in to regulate the charges of his body in the event he had missed some way in.

He truly was invincible, even in The Never, in a suit that nothing short of a Borealis AI could remove against his will.

He could feel *Brings the Rain*. The man was not far to the southeast. He wasn't on the ground, but somewhere higher—standing in one of the humans' remaining buildings.

He wasn't moving, his signal was clear and still.

He is watching, Malkier thought. *Watching the Ferox pour through in numbers that he cannot possibly defy. Yet he does not retreat.*

He spoke, reaching out to his people through the portal stones they all had within. "Scouts. Find me *Brings the Rain*. He is southeast, observe do not engage."

The prophet wasn't waiting long. Soon a band of female Ferox came running up the path, the horde parted at their approach. The females all took a knee before him.

"Prophet, he waits atop a structure," the leader said.

"Alone?"

"The abominations that follow him are at his side."

"They wait? Nothing more?" the prophet asked.

The scout looked about nervously. "The abominations' eyes are turned toward us, they watch our numbers increase. But they do not move."

Malkier stared down at her for a long while. Knew she was not able to give any greater insight, she didn't understand humans well enough. He was about to dismiss her when sound erupted from the southeast.

It was loud enough to carry through the remains of the city. While not particularly unpleasant, the nature of it was peculiar to the Ferox. His people had a primitive concept of music, the tribes all engaged in forms of rhythmic fist pounding and feet stomping that accompanied moments of celebration or tradition.

Mankind's music had evolved to a far greater complexity. While Ferox turned toward the source and heard a highly unnatural flow of sound that seemed to never end, the prophet heard far more. The timbre drifting through the air, the intense pounding of drums, the driving low frequencies of the bass, the shrill distorted sounds of a guitar's cords, and the singer's voice. The prophet could also understand the words being sung and found he could not be certain if *Brings the Rain* was goading him somehow. Openly mocking him while his invasion force knelt around him none the wiser.

Back on the roof of the convention center, just as Cher's *If I Could Turn Back Time* played its titular chorus, Rylee fixed her gaze on Jonathan.

"You better know what the hell you're doing. I didn't come back to life to have Cher cover me on the way back out."

He shrugged. "My roommates . . . could've been worse, be happy it wasn't the *Back to the Future* theme."

The music only played long enough to ensure he had the entire city's attention. The volume slowly faded out, and Jonathan's voice boomed through the Borealis sound system. The words being spoken weren't ones he'd ever recorded, Mr. Clean had translated the message so that all the Ferox would hear it. That said, he made sure to use words that every Ferox would understand.

"You know my name. You enter my arena. I seek the false prophet. The one who claims to be the Borealis made flesh. I seek my challenger. *Ends the Storm*, will you deny me combat?"

CHAPTER ONE HUNDRED AND FOUR

HEYER HAD GONE unnoticed amongst the Ferox in the pit, but now he was getting unwanted attention. The opening to the tunnels was in the opposite direction of the ramps that led into the conduit. This had made him the lone Ferox moving against the flow. He was already drawing the eyes of those he moved against, but if his brother chose that moment to look down on the crowd, Heyer would be as hard to miss as a car going the wrong direction on a freeway.

He turned to follow with the rest, carefully working sideways. Finally, he managed to step out of the throng and hide himself amongst supplies that had been staged along the platform walls to aid in the invasion. This forced him to lose sight of his brother and what was happening around the conduit, making Grant his only eyes.

While he waited, the population of the pit grew sparse. A thousand Ferox must have crossed into The Never. Yet, this gave him an unobstructed view of the gateway fields around the pit's perimeter. Strange, none showed any activity outside sustaining the conduit. Ferox were streaming in overwhelming numbers, but human soldiers dying inside had stopped all together.

Two possibilities came to him. The Never Army had so few soldiers left, they were on the run—retreating or hiding. He didn't believe that—it would mean they had already lost. If that were the case, well—The Never Army would have gone out with a bang.

No, more likely, something had Malkier convinced that the humans had played all their cards. That there was no unknown fear on the other side and the time for caution had passed. That meant all these Ferox were amassing on the other side, a force too large for the human army to resist.

But, would the prophet want to lead that final charge?

Grant's voice spoke in his ear—as though answering the question.

"Heyer, your brother, he stepped into the conduit," Grant said. "I think . . . I think it's time."

Heyer slowly patted his shoulder once and turned his gaze to the tunnel opening. The crowd was tightly gathered on the other end of the pit now and his brother was no longer present on this plane. So, he headed for the tunnel with a direct certainty, as though he were carrying out an order for the prophet himself.

He only needed a moment to be standing at the entrance, peering down into the darkness that descended beneath the platform. There was more to these tunnels than a quick path to Cede. The prophet had something going on below, as both he and Grant had noticed too many Ferox coming and going. What they had yet to figure out, was why they had been almost entirely female.

He took a long breath and stepped inside.

"You still hear me down there?" Grant asked.

Heyer grunted in reply, still thinking it wise not to speak in a human tongue unless their necessity demanded it.

He didn't run into Ferox in the tunnels, but as he went deeper, he realized he'd begun to smell them. There were a lot, more than a single tribe's worth below—but there was a quality to the scent of them. Something his Ferox host picked up on as though the smell was communicating something. Language he had some grasp of, but Heyer had little experience in translating Feroxian smells.

There was something different about most of the individuals gathered down here. It wasn't their sex. In fact, he had smelled this before, while he travelled with the tribe on the pilgrimage. He'd just never paid it this much attention, the scent had never been so concentrated that he felt the need to single it out for explanation.

He took a few sharp turns down, switchbacks heading deeper into the tunnel systems, and the smells became such that he knew he was coming close to a gathering where many were clustered closely together. He was careful when he knew he was drawing near, began to hear them talking to one another around the next switchback.

Finally, he reached a tunnel with a mouth that widened as he came toward a larger cavity within the cave. There were at least fifty adults inside, and as soon as he saw the occupants they had with them; he knew what his instincts had been telling him.

Yes, all the mature Ferox were female, and as he looked at them, he saw that most were pregnant, others held newborns or were surrounded by young.

There wasn't a single male in that room that wasn't too young to be parted from its mother. If Heyer tried to walk inside with this host, he would stick out like a candle in the dark.

There were two females toward the mouth of the corridor. They seemed to know he was coming. As though they had been waiting for him. At first this made his anxieties grow, but . . . of course, he realized, a single male's scent down here was probably like a beacon. Everyone in that room had likely smelled him coming for some time.

The two stood like guards at the opening—though what a human thought of as guards would be misleading. The Ferox did no harm to one another. The guards would turn him away, but they had no expectation that violence would be necessary to achieve it. They wouldn't act like guards unless a human came charging toward that chamber.

Given what a human would have to come through to reach them, it wasn't likely at the top of their concerns.

"You're lost, brother?" the first guard asked.

Heyer's passing for Ferox without creating suspicion was a matter of engaging as little as possible. He knew the language, but not on a nuanced level. He was about as passable as an exchange student. The only way to hide his inadequacy with the language and the strangeness to how he spoke it was to use as few words as possible.

"Why are you gathered here, Sister?"

They looked at him curiously—though he didn't believe with suspicion.

"You must swallow the red glow to hear the prophet's words, Brother. Have you been given the stone?"

"I have not," Heyer said.

"Well then," she said, "the prophet spoke wisely. The battle for the promised land is no place for infants and those not yet born. His tribe has volunteered the remains of their tunnels to the safety of the child-bearers and young. It is only until the prophecy has come to pass and the Promised Land is ours."

Heyer was left without words.

A Feroxian maternity ward lay between him and Cede. This was not the sort of obstacle he was prepared to deal with. How could they have predicted that the prophet would place the most vulnerable of his people . . .

Where he believed they would be safest, Heyer realized.

This meant two things. The first would have come with great relief had it not been for the second. The prophet truly had no idea what was coming. All the effort and paranoia with which Jonathan had guarded their plans had been worth the effort. But. . . if Heyer didn't do something, he would not only fail to reach Cede, but all these females and young would die.

"Brother, are you not listening?" the female asked, as though it weren't the first attempt.

"I am sorry, what did you say?" Heyer replied.

"The battle for the promised land is not here, brother, but above, let me take you to the stone forge so you can serve the gods along with the rest of our people," the Ferox said.

If he didn't reach Cede, the outcome of the battle was already decided.

He needed to leave, keep with the pretense that he had simply wandered into the wrong place, but he was at a loss for a plan. He let his eyes take in the room beyond them, trying to see all he could before his lingering become strange to them. Unfortunately, he caught sight of two females he recognized. The first was *Burns the Flame*—but she was changed. Her red skin had begun the change, crossing the threshold to Alpha, but he knew her. And for the first time, Heyer felt something like what his Brother must have when he looked upon her. A small taste of what Malkier had resisted all those years.

Burns the Flame did not notice him, but the one she spoke to did—her daughter. Heyer looked away the moment they made eye contact, not wanting the consonance to wage another attack on his consciousness.

"No. Thank you, Sister," Heyer said to the guard. "I see my error."

Quickly, he turned to leave.

The guards watched him as he retreated around the corner. He knew something about the interaction had made them curious, but whatever nuance of behavior he had forgone was not known to him. He had to hope it would be overlooked, which seemed to be the case as they only eyed him but did not follow.

So many thoughts crashed through his troubled mind as he put distance between the maternity ward and himself.

The worst of which was a suspicion he knew couldn't possibly be true. A notion that Malkier had done this on purpose. That he'd expected Heyer might try to reach Cede but had assumed that if the attempt came, Heyer would do so in a human host.

He felt he was being tested. As though his brother did not believe he would slaughter his way through pregnant females and their young if it was the only way to reach Cede.

Was Cede meant to carry out defensive orders if the females were endangered? Cede would not attack him if she realized he was Borealis. But until his device was uncloaked to her, she was a serious threat to his host. He had to get very close before he let that cloak down.

Yet, Cede's ability to apply lethal force remained the problem down the line.

He'd turned a few corners before he felt safe with the distance between him and the chamber. He needed a simple way around them, something that wouldn't cause alarm.

He could attempt to lie. Give them some story about Malkier authorizing him access to the lower tunnels. Except, he just told them he hadn't taken a stone and could not hear the prophet in his mind. Given his command of the language, he didn't see himself explaining how so much had changed so quickly.

If he tried this and it failed, would he force his way through? If he did, would they—try to hold him back or restrain him? Would they attack him? Would he have to fight them?

Answers to these questions came on him suddenly. A feeling like being singled out by the universe for torture. He felt his host growing ill. At first he thought it a lingering human emotion, the sort of pain one feels when they worry over a tough decision—but the more he imagined what might happen if he forced his way through the females and their young the more unbearable it became.

He tried to ignore it, reminded himself what was at stake.

I have no choice, he thought.

His insides turned violently against him—as though his conscience had powerful claws and could rack and twist his insides. Bile rose as his stomach convulsed. Heyer fell to hands and knees and wretched.

The reaction was quick and unquestionable, the more he attempted to convince himself that force must be used against another Ferox—the more drastically sick he became. So much so, that his mind was already beginning to fear the thoughts themselves. He was becoming concretely aware of the punishment and hesitant to tempt its wrath.

Only when he completely stopped imagining harming a Ferox did the retching end, his gut seeming to slowly unclench itself.

Then—something like pleasure washed through him.

He felt as though he bore witness to something beautiful even as the lingering sourness in his stomach had far from disappeared.

Yet, he felt something akin to what a man feels watching a sunrise.

As it passed, a disturbing understanding came to him. The Feroxian body—it seemed to have given him a definitive answer in regard to what he was capable of. It had also rewarded him for forcing the notion from his mind.

This was how his Borealis Ancestors had kept the Ferox from fighting amongst themselves. There was no reward for thoughts that led to violence against one another, only pain. Yet, in giving those thoughts up, there was a reward. A sense of beauty . . .

And it was rendering him useless.

If Heyer had failed, they all failed.

Jonathan had known he'd only be able to send one man with Heyer. He knew he had to choose a man powerful enough to make a difference. The Alpha Slayer was the perfect choice—except, it could only be worn by the one man neither of them trusted.

But they also knew that whoever Heyer took with him, was more than likely buying a one-way ticket. Heyer had made sure that Grant understood this. Strange, it hadn't changed his mind. For reasons he likely no longer understood himself, he wanted to go where the alien was going.

"Grant, I . . . I can't get through," Heyer said. "We need you."

There was a pause before Grant's reply came. Just long enough for Heyer to fear that Grant might abandon them at the moment it would destroy them all.

"I'm . . . I'm gonna try," he said. "I'm coming."

Heyer let out a breath. "Thank y—"

"You were looking for me," a Feroxian voice said. "I noticed them turning you away."

Heyer turned to find the daughter of *Burns the Flame* looking down at him. He felt it again, something strong between his host and the female.

"Of what tribe are you, brother? You speak . . . strangely."

CHAPTER ONE HUNDRED AND FIVE

THE FEROX SWARMED the streets around them. They surrounded the convention center, clung to walls of the nearby buildings to stare down on them from above. Their numbers stretched farther than he could see in the green haze.

Yet, they didn't attack.

They were all acting strangely, listening to a voice only they could hear. The Never Army eyed them warily. Those who had true Borealis steel weapons held them at the ready. Jonathan had told his people to expect this restraint. They had all expected they would need to hold that roof until they were certain the prophet had left the opening of the conduit.

Jonathan had felt it unlikely that he needed to give Malkier any new reasons to want to kill him, but why risk leaving any of the Borealis's buttons unpressed? Why not challenge the Ferox's faith in the prophet? See if he could be forced to show his people that *Brings the Rain* was little more than a blaspheming abomination—a mortal.

Jonathan had no illusions that Malkier was stupid. He knew that if he came, it was because he was willing to play his game. It was all a simple question: Did Malkier believe he was truly invincible? That he was, in all the ways that mattered, a god.

Jonathan believed otherwise.

After Rourke's account of the armor the prophet was sporting, he did not think Malkier had gotten all dressed up for nothing. A lot of trouble to go to just to look impressive while the Ferox extracted his revenge.

"*Brings the Rain*," the prophet's voice echoed through the city.

Jonathan looked down over the edge of the roof and found the Ferox below parting to clear a path. He could hear the heavy armored footsteps of the prophet long before he stepped out of the haze.

He came to a stop on the opposite side of the intersection. The street in front of him clearing of Ferox.

"The gods accept your challenge," Malkier said.

"You all know what to do," Jonathan said over the comm as he stepped onto the lip of the roof.

"Wait. You're going down there?" Rylee said. "He could set them on you with a word."

"I don't believe he will," Jonathan said.

He was about to drop off the roof, but he turned around one last time. "Rylee. He will try to kill you first."

"I won't let that happen," she said.

He dropped off the roof into the Ferox clearing. Using the gleamers at the last moment to stop himself from landing with pavement breaking impact. He looked around, felt the weight of a thousand white eyes watching him. Then dropped the last two inches to the ground.

He told himself there was only one enemy standing before him and fixed his gaze on Malkier.

He reached into a pouch at his belt and pulled out an octagonal disc a little smaller than a hockey puck. The Borealis watched his every move as he pressed a side surface on the disc.

Beep . . . Beep . . . Beep . . .

Malkier's armored head tilted curiously at the puck as the sound accelerated. The Ferox closest to him moved further away, as though he'd told them to get clear. The prophet did not budge. The time between each sound grew short, a countdown rushing toward a conclusion.

Jonathan took two steps, and casually threw the puck as if he was tossing a frisbee. His strength put speed on it, and it flew from his hand headed straight for the prophet. At the last moment, it corrected course like a magnet pulled to metal and slapped flat on Malkier's chest plate with a clank.

He came to a stop and waited. The Borealis's helmet turned to look down at the disc, then back to Jonathan. He made no move to remove it. As they watched one another the beep became one long tone.

A thunderbolt shot up from Malkier. Started with the puck and then seemed to reach up for the sky. Malkier's armor—drew it in like a lightning rod. For a moment the light was blindingly bright to the Ferox who watched. The arcing electricity eventually reaching away from Malkier's armor to caress any nearby conductor and find its way to ground. Parked cars, streetlights, a fire hydrant all sharing the current until the puck's charge was depleted.

The Ferox that had shrunk back to a safe distance stared in shock and awe for a moment. Soon they looked about to see that nothing had changed, a few scorches on the concrete was all that had come of the strange light show. Their prophet remained unmoved, breathing steadily and staring back at *Brings the Rain*. A pillar of invincibility.

When it ended, Malkier looked down, his hand pulling what remained of the lightening puck from his chest. He crushed what remained of it and let it fall to the street.

Inside of his helmet, spoken so only Olivia could hear, Jonathan gave the order. "Press the trigger, Olivia."

A split second went by, and numbers appeared at the corner of Jonathan's HUD. It began at twenty and started counting down.

"Good luck, Mr. Tibbs," Olivia said.

As the last of the puck crumbled to the ground, Malkier spoke, "I suppose you had to try."

"Figured you'd understand," Jonathan said.

To the Ferox watching, their exchange of words was unexpected. The prophet was simply speaking with the challenger in the tongue of the abominations. Their eyes went back and forth between them though they didn't understand a word.

Malkier's head turned up toward the building where Rylee and the rest of The Never Army watched. "I am eternally curious at how you survived for so long after your bond was severed."

"Same way you survive anything," Jonathan said. "Kept breathing."

"You've reestablished the bond," Malkier said. "How did it feel to replace the last one?"

"Honestly, sometimes it's like she never left," Jonathan said.

Malkier studied him curiously. "A stronger pairing. Such a strong bond. I bet that severing her from you will be excruciating."

"I suspect you're right," Jonathan admitted.

"Does she know why you don't have her fight beside you?"

"You got it all wrong, we flipped a coin. She lost."

Malkier breathed, his armor's filtration system pushing out expired air as though Jonathan's unwillingness to recognize the gravity of the situation was growing quite tiresome. "Does she know you fear the broken bond more than death?"

Jonathan took a last look at the timer. *6 . . . 5 . . .*

"Malkier, I'm mortal, I fear a lot of things more than death," he said, freeing *Excali-bar* 2.0 from his back. "How about you?"

3 . . . 2 . . .

A final message played throughout the city. Jonathan speaking in Feroxian one last time.

I . . . am . . . Brings the Rain.

CHAPTER ONE HUNDRED AND SIX

IT IS SAID that 150 decibels is loud enough to burst a human ear drum. When a nuclear bomb is detonated, the sound reaches over two hundred and ten decibels.

When five nuclear weapons go off in unison, well, one can imagine.

When that count down dropped to zero, there was no great burst of light—no mushroom clouds. Jonathan, Malkier, and anyone close to them was too shrouded in the WX gas to see the monstrous spectacle in all its glory for themselves.

Now, if a person were standing on the opposite shore, far enough from the gas to get a clearer view, that person would be witnessing five massive pillars of water as they erupted from the surface of Puget Sound. Magnificent geysers spreading out as they reached toward the sky. At first, it would be as though the five fingers of God had burst forth from the depths. They grew to the size of mountains, then came together to form one wall of water the likes no one on Earth had ever witnessed.

While the detonations could be felt for miles, the tremors that followed on the heels of those explosions were not a result of the bombs themselves. Beneath the feet of anyone standing inside of Seattle, human or Ferox, the land itself rolled as though it were the surface of the ocean. Together, they all surfed a massive wave.

What was left of Seattle shivered and lurched as though the planet had just been given an unexpected nudge—a poke in the ribs. The buildings whose foundations were already in precarious conditions began to collapse. Those that stayed up swayed troublingly with the motion of the Earth.

For a moment—as the earthquake passed under them, no one, not man or Ferox, was thinking about a fight. Rather, they were looking for something to hold on to. But, unlike the Ferox hordes, The Never Army had all been bracing for impact. For the Ferox the act was unnerving—the harbinger of a thing they could not yet see. The unnatural shaking of the Earth only telling them that something beyond their comprehension had been unleashed.

In fact, few noticed that Jonathan Tibbs was no longer standing in the intersection. That the moment they were all distracted, he had moved. Then came the water. Thinning as it spread out from the point of detonation, it hit Seattle like a hurricane. The WX gas hid it from their eyes at first, but eventually the Ferox all looked up in horror at what was pushing the gas away and consuming it.

Brings the Rain, indeed.

They ran at first, and who could blame them. It was as though a hurricane had appeared from nowhere. They ran from it in a panic. Stampeding over one another to flee. If the prophet said anything to calm them, in those moments right before he disappeared into the white of propelled water, they paid it no heed, they did not likely even hear.

What they didn't understand is what came for them now hid the real danger. Sure, it was a sight that would terrify anyone. But in the end, it was just water thrown into the air, so much that it looked like a wall reaching far above the skyscrapers. The wind and water cleansed a great deal of the air of WX.

Only those Ferox closest to where Hurricane Olivia made landfall were in any danger of actually drowning from the volume of water.

As the shaking eased and the ground of the city settled into a lower rumble, it seemed as though the worst had passed. It was the Ferox nearest Seattle's shoreline who got the first glimpse of what came for them next. Though they were in no state to be especially observant when the waters of Puget Sound began to pull away revealing ocean floor that had not seen daylight since the last ice age. The waters pulled back from the city itself, and as they receded, it became very clear that something much larger was forming off the coast. A wave, swelling into a wall. A wall that—there was no mistaking—was headed their way.

A tsunami is a large wave caused by a sudden drop in the ocean floor— usually the result of an underwater earthquake. What was headed for Seattle now was based on the same principles. The only difference being that the shifting of the earth beneath Puget Sound was—mostly—a manmade event.

Mr. Clean may not have been able to provide the necessary thermonuclear weapons, but he could tell Jonathan the number of bombs that would be necessary, along with the coordinates and depths of where they would need to be placed under the sea floor.

Of course, since the devices were manmade, the issue of keeping them functional when Malkier fried the whole of human technology had been a challenge. That was where The Cell's containment shell had come into play. If Mr. Clean hadn't been able to pull Heyer or him out of those big black Easter eggs when they were prisoners—Jonathan had been willing to bet anything inside would be safe from whatever Malkier might throw at them.

That last bit had required some *MacGyvering* from Mr. Clean. Just like all the rest of the explosives in the city, they still needed detonators that wouldn't be rendered useless upon the conduit's arrival. In the end, Jonathan had handed Olivia a trigger that could detonate the weapons when he gave the signal.

And yes—that had been part of the deal.

The US Government wasn't providing WMDs to Jonathan no matter how convinced they were he was telling the truth. So, unless a government agent maintained control of firing the weapons they were off the table. Jonathan had no arguments—for that matter, he was fine leaving the detonation of every explosive they had throughout the city in her hands.

After spending a whole evening egging Olivia on to pull that trigger beneath The Cell's hangar facility only for nothing to come of it—no big boom—he liked to think there was a certain symmetry to her being the one to pull the trigger now.

It had—just felt right.

As the Ferox around the city began to understand what was coming for them, they looked at the water with terror. Some began to move farther inland, racing away from the shoreline as fast as they could.

That was when the second detonation went off.

Olivia waited until the wave broke near the shore. Then the box with the big red button began to glow a bright sunset red.

It was at that moment that Rylee heard Jonathan's voice over the comm. "I'm sorry, Rylee. But I told Leah, I won't watch it happen again."

She was on the ground, watching the box brighten as it neared detonation, one of Mr. Clean's extra batteries beginning to spill energy out.

"What . . . what are we talking about?"

"Must have been a good kiss, I really thought you were gonna catch me," he said, "would have been embarrassing."

In the next few seconds, Rylee's eyes went wide with sudden realization. When Jonathan had dove off the roof, the presence of the stone he'd taken off the scarred Ferox—it hadn't gone with him. It was still here, it was . . .

As she reached frantically for her belt, a sphere of orange light shot away from the box with the big red button. A globe of Borealis energy passed through her and the rest of the army as she took hold of the stone that shouldn't have been there in her pouch. She brought it out just in time to see the energy field hit her open hand. It tickled a bit, as it passed through her, but the globe's energy was the same as what already flowed through her, Jonathan, and every man in their army. As a matter of fact, it was the exact energy signature that ran their devices—and it was expanding out toward the entire city.

The portal stone shattered. Turned to fluid and clung to her, crawling up her armor looking for an opening, then finding its way through the suit's vents.

"I love you," he said.

A portal formed around her. "If Malkier doesn't kill you, I'm going to."

"See you soon."

The Ferox running away from the wave stopped in their tracks as the globe began to expand out from the convention center.

They couldn't flee the wave without running through that orange glowing sphere.

However, instinct told them one of these acts of god meant certain death while the other was a gamble. So, they took their chances with the globe, and as it passed through them, nothing seemed to come of it right away.

Then, a familiar breaking occurred inside of them. In a matter of seconds, red portals appeared all throughout the city. The stones inside the Ferox shattering—as though one of The Never Army had reached inside each creature and broken it. In an instant, a chain reaction triggered sending every Ferox in the city home.

Well—every Ferox but one. The one whose armor had been built to make sure he was impervious to everything. Perhaps most notably—a suit of armor that protected him even from the air itself.

He knew Heyer wouldn't ask him to step into the Feroxian masses below for anything less than a critical problem, but the timing couldn't have been worse.

The gateway fields were bursting with activity. Red globes appearing throughout the entire circle around the platform so rapidly it seemed the entire conduit would collapse from the strain. Yet, none carried human corpses. It was as though the Ferox were being forcefully ejected from The Never in droves.

There was only one explanation, Jonathan had put their big play in motion.

Unfortunately, this also meant that the canyon Heyer was asking him to walk into was rapidly growing more overpopulated than ever. The Ferox below seemed confused, none amongst them understanding what was happening, and no link to the prophet on this side of the conduit.

Grant reached for his wrist and activated the cloak. As he felt the liquid seep over him, he saw his hand disappear. Only when the process was complete did he abandon his hiding place atop the tower.

"I'm . . . I'm gonna try," he said. "I'm coming."

He grabbed the edge of the rock tower and lowered his body out over the drop. Activating his gleamers he stealthily made his way down into the Ferox crowds. At the last moment, as he neared the dust covered sands on the ground surface, he activated the rings in his boots. He was already worried that the Ferox would sense something as he tried to move unnoticed within their numbers. Leaving a trail of footprints would only give those who grew suspicious more reason to investigate. The gleamers still disrupted the dirt as he moved, but at least they wouldn't leave behind the telltale boot imprint of a man. Instead, his movements looked more like a strange wind moving along the surface.

Still, he'd never had the time he really needed to become proficient with the gleamers, and hovering a few inches off the ground while trying not to bump into the Ferox milling around the outside of the pit or disturb too much of the space around him was nerve-racking. He didn't bother with the ramp that led down to the conduit platform, instead going to the outer rim of the pit and gleaming down the cliff walls.

As he descended adrenaline was flooding his blood stream, making his heart pound so fast he could hear it in his ears. No manner of breathing exercises was going to keep it in check. Luckily, within his helmet, the sound of his rapidly increasing breaths was insulated. He heard his own terror—but nothing outside his helmet would.

Of course, all these physical reactions were telling him the same thing.

You're going the wrong way. You know how this ends.

The whisper was something he couldn't obey as he reached ground and began to make his way through the gateway fields. He soon came to wonder if he should not have chosen the ramp after all. The fields were a mass of activity, the reality of how difficult they would be to navigate hadn't seemed so bad from his perch on the tower. Now that he stood inside the fields themselves the volume of Ferox being expelled from The Never was like standing in a place where at any moment he was surrounded by four gateways that might suddenly have a Ferox standing on it. The ground shook with each return, making the entirety of the ground within the field vibrate.

Two inches off the ground itself, Grant didn't feel, so much as see this, but the fear of being noticed made his body quiver so much that he might as well have been standing on the surface. There was no pattern to what gateway suddenly discharged a beast, or if there was, he didn't have the time or state of mind to figure it out. So, he tried to make himself as small as possible, as he drew closer to the tunnels beneath the platform.

Still, inevitably, he was eventually struck. Two portals opened, almost simultaneously, as he made his way through the space between. The returning Ferox were in a state of fear themselves, darting around as though running from something. They staggered off the platforms, forcing him to dodge both, and he succeeded, only to be hit by a Ferox he hadn't seen coming from farther up the field.

The Ferox was confused, not only at finding itself suddenly standing amongst the gateway fields and not understanding why it had been pulled back, but at what object it had felt its weight knock aside as it staggered to a stop. Grant likely could have killed the beast swiftly enough, he was invisible and had a molecular blade strapped to his forearm, but there would be no doing so without notice. So, he watched the Ferox as it turned to study the area.

Slunk down, nose sniffing the air as it moved closer. Grant didn't dare move; for the moment, he knelt, shivering on the ground as he watched the Red take a step closer. Its white eyes squinted at him, like a human who'd lost his glasses trying to read the ingredients off a cereal box.

Its claws began to reach out, and in those moments Grant's shaking hand tightened on the blade handle.

Suddenly the Ferox stood straight, looking off in the opposite direction—staring at the conduit. The change of interest was sudden. In fact, Grant saw that every Ferox in his immediate field of vision had done the same. It was like being the only human in a room filled with dogs. Suddenly, every four-legged animal had jumped to its feet and stared off in the same direction. Hearing something human ears weren't sensitive enough to notice.

In that moment, as the Ferox's attention was pulled away, a portal began to emerge on the gateway directly beside where Grant still knelt clutching his blade. He had to move, the next inbound might literally step on him the moment it materialized. As fast as he dared, he flicked the gleamer ring of his free hand at the side of the gateway's platform and coasted sideways, leaving a line of disturbed dust as he gleamed past. The arriving Ferox emerged to plant a foot where he been kneeling a moment before, and Grant breathed a sigh of relief, until he noticed the new arrival's behavior.

Far faster than the first Ferox, it too seemed to have focused all its attention on the conduit. As Grant turned, he saw that the entirety of the Ferox horde was still focused in that direction. That wasn't to say it was quiet. The gateways were still unloading Ferox and shaking the ground of the entire pit as a result, but those were the sounds of unnatural forces and shivering geology. The sound of life, of Ferox talking to one another and moving about, that had gone silent.

Grant stood up, seeing that the phenomenon wasn't limited to those in the pit, but all along the cliffs the Ferox were watching the conduit. He didn't bother questioning his luck, instead he used the opportunity to move faster and with far less care as the horde's attention was focused elsewhere. He was nearly to the edge of the gateway fields when the next obstruction presented itself.

Due to the rapid unloading of the gateway fields, the Feroxian army was thick around the platform.

As he saw how closely packed together they were he didn't like his chances, even if they were momentarily transfixed. The only other option was to jump the throng. Take his chances that he could clear the crowd and anchor himself to the side of the platform with the gleamers.

He made the decision quickly, he wasn't going to get another chance with them this distracted. He turned the gleamers off and broke into a run. He didn't trust himself to manage this with the clumsy balance the gleamers gave him. He ran at the crowd, footprints trailing him in the sand behind him as he sprinted. As he neared the final gateway along the inner rim of the field he jumped on to the top of the arm of the gateway, and pounced as hard as he could toward the platform.

For a moment, he was sure he had overshot it. He was soaring over the transfixed army and rocketing toward the platform, but as he reached the peak of his arc and started his way down, he rapidly became less sure.

The giant platform racing toward him, he activated his gleamers and put his hands out in front of him. At the final second he closed his eyes. He felt himself jarred to a stop.

He opened his eyes again.

"Holy crap," he whispered, seeing that he'd managed to land face down on top of the platform. It wasn't that he'd overshot the side, it was that he'd come within a foot of the conduit edge. He could see the glowing red line of the boundary now. He'd been a foot from cleaving himself in half.

As he smiled in relief, he began to hear something. A familiar sound growing stronger. Suddenly, he realized why the Ferox were staring at the conduit with such a mix of awe and fear. He was quite capable of hearing the sound for himself now and was starting to feel rather sympathetic.

He stopped thinking, jumped up, and ran back toward the lip of the platform. Just as a tidal wave of water poured through the conduit's opening, Grant anchored himself to the side of the platform.

The salty waters of the Puget Sound spilled forth like a massive pipeline dumping into the pit.

He was already soaked from water splashing out the sides when the entirety of the Ferox army panicked. Some ran straight for the cliffs, but most went for the ramp out. However, none noticed the wet outline of a man dropping down from the platform over the mouth of Feroxian tunnels that ran beneath.

Grant's HUD switched to thermal optics as the light withdrew. He raced into the tunnels. There wasn't much time, water was already making its way in behind him. If the tidal wave spewing out of the conduit above kept dumping water into the Feroxian Plane, this pit would be the first thing to flood.

Oh . . . he realized. *Well, that would be the idea now wouldn't it.*

He stuck to the main tunnel, ignoring any smaller openings as he made his way down. At the speed he was going through the winding tunnels, it wasn't long before he saw two Ferox standing in the darkness. One, his HUD immediately identified as Heyer. Even in the dark his head still looked as though it were painted with fluorescent paint. He was hunched over. The moment Grant stepped around the corner, the female looked up and stared into the darkness. She had the same sort of transfixed stare that he'd seen from the Ferox above. Her eyes looked through him.

She sniffed the air, and he wondered if she could smell the human. She spoke guttural words he did not understand as he drew close and pulled the molecular blade.

He moved toward Heyer, his blade hissing free of its sheath. Strangely, the alien forced himself to stand. Grant was a moment away from plunging the blade into the Ferox's ear canal, but suddenly the thick bulk of Heyer's host was standing between them.

Grant froze, nearly pinned against the cave wall by Heyer.

They spoke, and Grant had no idea what was playing out between the alien and the female Ferox. But a moment later, she moved slowly forward and bolted into the tunnels toward the surface.

Grant waited.

"What did you say to her?" he asked.

"I told her what she was smelling," he said. "Salt water, something I'd only ever smelled inside the Arena."

He turned around slowly, his features unknowable to Grant in his monstrous form.

"Heyer, the Feroxian Plane is flooding," Grant said.

Heyer seemed at a loss for a moment. "Heyer? Why am I here?"

The alien seemed as though he were at a loss. So deep in his thoughts that he was failing to even hear.

"Heyer," Grant said, finally shaking him. "We don't have any time!"

The alien growled and stood tall, towering over Grant for a moment before getting control of himself. He tilted his head toward the surface as the water began to run down into the cave. A mere moment later and they could hear it coming, sloshing its way down the tunnels toward them.

"I cannot lift a finger against them," Heyer said. "But there are too many ahead, all female, I cannot get through."

"You need a distraction?" Grant asked.

Heyer nodded. Then looked down at his feet where the water was rising. "But, perhaps not the sort I called upon you for."

The females and their young were already in a state of alarm when Heyer came bursting in past the guards into the chamber.

"Run," Heyer yelled in Feroxian. "*Brings the Rain*. He floods the world. Get out! Get out before it is too late!"

Had they not heard it coming, had they not already feared what he proclaimed, they might have questioned the strange voice of the Ferox telling them to abandon the shelter. But instead, their faces were drawn with panic. Heyer realized—he could smell their . . . fear.

He pounded past, further into the chamber. He felt like a giant gorilla beating his chest and the floor as his hand sloshed through the rising waters. He looked at the young Ferox standing in water already a foot deep.

He felt the fear. It was real. Knew they could smell it coming off him.

"Get out! You can make the surface! Get the younglings out!" Heyer yelled to the females. "The surface. Go! Go! Go!"

His own fear grew. He didn't know if he'd have any more luck swimming than the other Ferox. The water coming down was accelerating, starting to come in sloshing waves now. He knew they feared stepping toward the source, but the higher the water rose the more they began to fear the alternative. What was strange was that as Heyer's own fears increased, the Ferox began to obey. Seemed more willing to move—as they could smell the urgency on him.

Soon, Heyer was beating his chest to an empty chamber, splashing around in water that was already up to his thighs. Alone, Grant disabled the cloaking device, and appeared where he had been anchored to the cave's ceiling.

"They're gone. We need to hurry."

Heyer stopped, looking around the empty chamber for anyone left behind before heading for the tunnel that would take him to Cede. He hurried, as the lower they went, the smaller the passages and the higher the water. By the time they neared the boundary of Cede, the way was filled and quickly rising.

Grant held something out to him. "You've got to go."

Heyer looked at the man's outstretched hand and saw the small air tank Jonathan had given him as a back up when he was inside the cocoon.

"Grant, there is good chance you won't—"

"I'll get out, just take it!" Grant yelled.

The water was rising fast now, had filled the lower tunnels.

Heyer nodded, taking the container.

"Good luck," Grant said. The moment the tank was in Heyer's hand, he was already turning to leave. Heyer yelled after him. "Your father . . ."

It was the one thing he knew that would cause Grant to stop and listen.

"He'd have done anything he could to make sure Douglas Tibbs made it home. They were more than friends. They were brothers."

Grant stared back, only for a moment. Heyer couldn't read what he was thinking, and he didn't get a chance, before a great slosh of water came down on them.

Submerged, Heyer didn't see Grant anywhere. He had to have headed up to the surface.

Heyer turned to the tunnel, wrapping his Feroxian lips around the air tank as best he could and soon understood why no Ferox managed to swim. He sank like a brick into the dark water, found he was better off pulling himself along the walls than trying to paddle.

Grant must have had to use the tank at some point, and Feroxian lungs took a lot more air than a human's to fill. When he finally reached the door to Cede, he felt the tank give its last bit of air—and knew he only had what was left in his lungs as he took those final steps through the cold water. The door didn't look like a door at all. Rather, there was an invisible barrier, a clear line in the tunnel where one side was filled with water and the other remained completely dry.

As he touched his chest, the device that had cloaked him from Cede's awareness solidified in his palm. He knew, this was the moment where all his trust in Jonathan either paid off or killed him. While he surely hoped to live, if

Jonathan was right about this, then there would be precious few explanations Heyer's mind could imagine to account for how he could have ever known about this.

The one that he could imagine, was exactly as Jonathan had said—something he'd never dare ask.

Heyer pressed the device against the barrier.

Inside Cede there was a chamber. For a short time, that chamber had been a prison. Heyer had been the only prisoner ever held there, and he'd escaped. He had used the beacon, a device he had built just in case of that contingency, but circumstances had forced him to use it earlier than he'd ever planned.

It was a device designed to get past Cede's defenses, and once used, would never be effective again. Cede would find the exploited weakness and take the necessary precautions.

However, getting around a security system was far less difficult a thing when you already had a man on the inside. So it was that, when Heyer pressed the device against the barrier of Cede, a small piece of Mr. Clean awoke.

It found itself lying on the floor of that same chamber inside of Cede. It was small, dime sized, and as it came online, it realized it was still inside a gold pocket watch. A pocket watch that had accompanied Jonathan home one night.

That pocket watch was broken, and the day she died, Rylee had thought to do something nice. She had slipped the watch into the front pocket of her jacket to take it to a jeweler for repair.

She'd never made it to that jeweler. A few minutes later, she'd been pulled into The Never. The jacket and the watch, gone with her.

Then, she died.

When Malkier took her as a trophy, he had given the body to *Burns the Flame*. The watch he'd found later, lying there on the cave floor beside them. He'd nearly crushed it but had stopped himself. Instead, he'd wrapped it in a piece of bloodied cloth and carried it with him into Cede.

Then, he discovered Heyer's escape. He discovered that twenty-eight Ferox were dead and left on his tribe's gateway. Since that day, he had not bothered to enter the chamber. The room only reminded him of his brother's treason, of Cede's incompetence, and his own failure to extract justice on his son's murderer. Malkier never thought about that watch again. It sat, wrapped in a bloodied cloth on the chamber floor.

The piece of Mr. Clean inside had gone dormant. In fact, it had been dormant since Rylee first entered The Never all that time ago. Then, one day a signal that seemed to come from Cede, or perhaps the rest of Mr. Clean's consciousness, told it to wake up.

The dime-size piece then slipped from between the glass and metal of the watch, and out of the bloody cloth. The moment it touched the chamber floor—it merged. Of course, the floor was made of Cede, just part of the shape she was taking at that moment. So, in truth, Mr. Clean merged a piece of himself with Cede herself.

The moment this occurred, Cede knew there was someone . . . a Borealis, knocking at the door. What was strange was that the encryption key that the Borealis was trying to use to gain entrance was not an active code. Yet, the moment Mr. Clean merged with the floor, Cede discovered that—in fact—it was, and had always been, an active code.

In that moment, Heyer fell through the barrier into the open air on the other side of the boundary. He coughed water onto the floor. No longer cloaked, Cede recognized the new occupant immediately.

Now, while he did in fact have the correct encryption code, Malkier had been very explicit. Cede was not to allow any Borealis other than Malkier himself into the ship. But this created a problem, because Heyer was already inside. Cede was extremely limited by her programming. She couldn't use deadly force against a Borealis, this was forbidden. However, there was nothing in her programming that kept her from restraining a Borealis until Malkier returned.

There was no need to restrain him in a literal sense. After all, as soon as he'd stepped inside, he'd basically checked back into a prison from which he would never leave. Only in the event that he attempted some mischief would she take the steps of locking down his limbs and restraining his movement.

For the moment, he was no more than a Ferox trying to expel sea water from his lungs. Perhaps, he was even here to keep their other guest company.

CHAPTER ONE HUNDRED AND SEVEN

MALKIER WAS TEMPORARILY left at the will of the water that came crashing through the city. The hurricane followed by the huge wave had kept him blind and rolling along the streets. When it finally calmed, he planted his feet and surfaced.

Most of the green haze was gone from the air now. The sun was in the sky. The streets were filled with water that reached up to his knees after it receded.

He turned about and didn't believe his eyes. His people, they were gone. Not a single Ferox was anywhere to be seen. There was an eerie quiet over all of the city, the only sound that of water receding back out to sea in the distance.

He felt a rise of terror inside. What was this? How could it be?

He felt something move in his mind then and knew that he wasn't alone. He could feel *Brings the Rain*. He turned slowly, as the man was not far away. He stood on the water, in the middle of the street.

As though he'd been waiting for him.

"What have you done with my people?" Malkier asked.

Brings the Rain's visor retracted, revealing a face with eyes burning with the power of the bond. Strange, he could not feel the woman any longer.

"Poisoned them, I suppose you could say," he said. "Unlike you, they've been breathing in humanity for quite some time now."

"What does that mean?"

The man had the nerve to smile at him. "I was surprised to learn just how easy it is to destroy a portal stone. All it took was a touch of humanity and some Borealis energy."

Malkier knew the man was right, but he still didn't see it.

"That gas your AI came up with was good. It was quite a problem for me. But, let me give you some tips. Clear and odorless is the way to go. You don't roll it out and unleash it in giant bladders. You hide it all over your battleground. In buildings and sewers, inside mundane things no will ever suspect. See, that way, your enemy never realizes what they're breathing, what's building up in their blood. Until . . ."

He snapped his fingers. "You trigger it."

"You . . . you sent them back?" Malkier said. "Why? It will buy you a few minutes, nothing more."

"I don't think you've been paying attention," Jonathan said.

He knelt, reached down past where his feet hovered on the water. He cupped a handful, lifted it, and let drain it out.

"Did you notice, when you arrived, all that wreckage . . . All those buildings we dropped around the conduit, your people, in such a hurry to take their Promised Land, they kept pushing it aside . . . it was like they were building a funnel and never even knew it."

For a moment, Malkier realized he couldn't breathe—he felt dizzy.

"What do you imagine happens, when a few thousand Ferox return to gateways that are underwater?" Jonathan asked.

Malkier staggered. He spun to the direction of the conduit, turning away from *Brings the Rain*.

"I wouldn't," Jonathan said. "Trust me, you don't want the nightmares. I know what it feels like to see your people murdered, piled on top of one another."

Malkier turned back. "You're a monster, *Brings the Rain*."

The man nodded. "Slaughter their weak. Draw out their strong. The word of the prophet. How many men have stood where you stand, felt what you feel now—because of your words."

A moment passed.

"Where is my brother?" Malkier asked. "His shadow must be fighting alongside you."

Brings the Rain shook his head. "I can honestly say I haven't seen him for weeks."

Malkier stared back at him, at first in disbelief. Then he saw the man wasn't lying. Some time passed, and perhaps something inside the ancient Borealis had snapped, because he began to laugh. He laughed the way a man did when he was beyond reason.

"He imagines you will kill me, and you're naive enough to think you can," Malkier said.

Jonathan pulled *Excali-bar* from its sheath and shook his head. "Not a fool, Malkier. I doubt I can kill you. But, wouldn't we both regret it if I didn't try?"

CHAPTER ONE HUNDRED AND EIGHT

IT WAS LIKE *the ringing of a massive bell when Excali-bar* thronged against Malkier's chest plate sending the alien back, his legs ripping through water and pavement as he dug into the cement to slow himself.

"Not enough—"

Thrung!

Jonathan wasn't holding still for a discussion, having jumped into the air to bring *Excali-bar* overhead and down on Malkier's shoulder plate. The force drove the giant onto a knee, the street's pavement crumbling such that he knelt in a small sunken crater. Yet, he immediately began to stand again.

Thrung!

Malkier staggered forward from a blow to the back of his helmet. Quickly regaining his balance and whirling on his more nimble attacker, he came at him, fists clenched and growling.

Jonathan maneuvered, ducking and dodging a series of blows, Malkier's fist coming at him with a frightening force. He felt as though he were avoiding missiles. Malkier fought with no caution or fear, he threw his weight behind everything—knew as well as Jonathan that a single hit connecting might be enough to end this.

Jonathan jumped out of range, putting some distance between them as Malkier's massive fist caved in the sidewalk and sent water like an elephant doing a cannonball into a pool.

Malkier righted himself and kept on coming.

An audible *whoosh* passed over him as Jonathan flowed to the outside of a devastating haymaker and caught Malkier hard enough on the back to send him staggering. He didn't lose his balance for long, turning to sweep his thick armored arm around in a backhand that went high as Jonathan went low to hammer at his legs.

The giant Alpha fell into the water with an annoyed grunt. As he saw Jonathan preparing to come down at him with *Excali-bar*, he rolled clear and leapt back to his feet.

To anyone watching, the fight seemed to be going Jonathan's way. But the two exchanging blows knew the truth—knew how it ended. If Jonathan couldn't hurt the Borealis, then it all came down to how long he could keep this up.

He wasn't ever going to find out if it was possible for him to hurt the monster unless he found a way past the armor.

Jonathan stepped back in, whirling *Excali-bar* about in a combination of strikes that all connected, the titan making no effort to deflect them. All his attention seemed focused on looking for Jonathan to give an opening— leave himself exposed or hold still just long enough for Malkier to get hold of a limb.

Finally, it seemed Malkier had the opening he had been waiting for. Massive claws grabbed *Excali-bar* at its center, a grunt of eager excitement as his gauntlet closed on steel.

Throng, throng.

The giant staggered backwards from a series of blows that seemed to come from nowhere, his head knocked this way and that as his hand came away empty. How the demolition bar had slipped free of his grasp seemed a mystery even as Jonathan jumped up and over him to roll down his back.

Malkier pivoted to follow but stepped into another whirlwind of attacks.

Throng, throng, throng, throng.

The barrage was blindingly fast, confusing and rage-inducing all at once. Finally, Malkier brought his arms up in a defensive block just to keep his helmet from being knocked side to side. He planted his feet, forced his way forward before sweeping out wildly with both hands as though they were swords. While Jonathan saw it coming, he was still forced to retreat, giving Malkier a momentary respite from the assault.

Malkier's gaze turned to find Jonathan landing on his feet a safe distance away. The mystery of how he'd lost hold of the demolition bar explained as Jonathan put the two halves of *Excali-bar* back together at the center.

Growling in annoyance. "Enough."

Malkier moved fast, but not toward Jonathan. Instead he picked up the closest vehicle, already flattened at some point in the battle, and tore it in half like he was snapping a twig.

Jonathan jumped to the other side of the street just before the vehicle's front end came at him and hit the building, tearing the bottom three stories from its corner as the car crashed through.

The back end was already headed for him when he landed, leaving no choice but to jump again. He shot up to see Malkier's armored shape launching off the street to meet him. Had he let him, Malkier would have collided hard enough to knock him through the next three buildings.

But his bullish hulk of an opponent was just as unprepared for Jonathan to activate his gleamers as he had been for the staff to break into two pieces. With one hand, Jonathan anchored himself to the wall and kicked sideways, narrowly getting clear as Malkier crashed through the side of the building.

From what he could hear, Malkier didn't come to a stop until he was halfway through the interior. Then the sounds of destruction resumed but were now moving upwards, perhaps four stories higher than where he had broken through on the outside. Which was why the brief pause in the tremors Jonathan could sense while anchored to the outside, made the sound of the armored Alpha coming back at him feel like standing in an open prairie waiting for a stampede of buffalo to barrel through.

He shot up to a higher floor just in time to see Malkier's fist exit the building. A moment later the same arm shot toward him, tearing through the outer wall. As the arm rushed for him, nothing was enough to slow it. To Jonathan it was as though someone stuck their arm out of a car window and stomped on the accelerator.

"Ahh hell," Jonathan said as he rushed to push off the side of the building. He shot across the street and re-anchored himself on the other side. Before he could even land, he caught sight of Malkier hurtling through the wall after him.

As this chase began, Jonathan doing everything he could not to be caught by Malkier using his body as a torpedo, Jonathan became very certain of one thing. The alien's aim, despite his lack of success thus far, was impeccable. Malkier burst out of rooftops coming straight for him as he dodged and ran—there was no way he had line of sight. It was all confirming his suspicion that Malkier had found some way to reverse who was the beacon and who was the receiver between device and portal stone.

"Olivia," Jonathan asked as he sprinted across the rooftops. "What's the biggest thing you got left that we can detonate?"

"There isn't much," she replied.

"I'll take anything close," he replied.

"Four blocks south, southwest," Olivia said. "If enough of it is still standing."

The address highlighted in his HUD as Jonathan shifted course, diving off the top of the roof he'd been sprinting across a moment before Malkier came bursting through. It had been close—too close, and a stark reminder that he couldn't keep Malkier from getting hold of him indefinitely.

"Come on, Jonathan," he said to himself, remembering how Rylee had managed to stay alive against the Feroxian demigod for far longer than he had without any gleamers and a far less powerful implant. He'd never hear the end of it if he couldn't keep the Borealis occupied.

"You're not one of us."

He had only just stopped coughing up water when he heard the voice and looked up toward the source of the words. He did not see her, but he knew the voice.

"*Burns the Flame?*" he asked.

The cloak, pulled away then, revealing her as she tilted her head. "Malkier warned me that his enemy might cross the boundary."

Heyer was still taking deep breaths to recover, but he forced himself to his feet. "I mean you no harm."

"An enemy that means no harm?" she asked.

"I am only here to stop my brother," Heyer said.

"Brother . . ." The way she said the word and trailed off, it was as though it had caught her by surprise.

"He left that out, did he?" Heyer said.

"You've taken another of my people," she said.

"It was the only way to walk freely amongst you."

She considered him a moment. "It is a coward's way. I cannot strike you down even though I know you are not of the Ferox."

"I suppose," Heyer said. "But it also means I am no threat to you."

"That . . . may be true," she said, and again, she seemed surprised.

Heyer walked by her, and he took a seat near the square platform at the center of the room.

"He said you would come to take me. But, now I see that you cannot."

Heyer studied her for a moment. "You are not guarding this place. It's guarding you."

"That is what he said."

It took Heyer only a moment, but now that his lungs were clear of water, he could smell the truth. "Because you carry his children—again."

Heyer had known his brother would take part in the consonance, but had thought his brother would not put *Burns the Flame* through the same again. But then he remembered what Jonathan had said about their last moments before Rylee died. That Malkier had lost control, and the host had returned.

"*Ends the Storm* sought you for the consonance."

For a moment, she didn't speak—Heyer's words having—jarred something—inside her. "Yes. But somewhere in between, he became the prophet again."

"I am sorry," Heyer said. "But no, I have not come for you, *Burns the Flame*."

"If you came to stop him, then you mean to keep my people from taking the Promised Land," *Burns the Flame* said.

"Do you still believe in the Promised Land, after he has told you so much?" he asked.

"I believe that the abominations can keep the Ferox from extinction," she said. "I need no prophecy to tell me what happens if we do not take their world."

"The humans are not abominations. The prophet only calls them such so the Ferox will feel they serve the gods' will. They are just a people, like the Ferox. The only abominations in this story, are my brother and I."

This brought a long silence.

"I do not understand," *Burns the Flame* said. "How will you stop Malkier if you are Ferox? You cannot harm him."

"He will face the one you call *Brings the Rain*," Heyer said. "If the man can stop him, I can finish him. You and I will have to wait to see what fate holds for our people."

"Man is your people?"

"In a way, but they were not the people of whom I speak," Heyer said. "My brother and I are the last of our kind. If my brother cannot defeat the man, then today I alone will be the last."

Burns the Flame stared at him. "Are you not afraid?"

"I am," he said.

Her reaction was not what Heyer would have thought. "Perhaps I was wrong to call you coward, Borealis."

Heyer looked at her with curious eyes. "It is I who does not understand."

"You would, if we were your people. To be the last of your kind . . ."

She shuddered before she could finish. "It is the greatest fear of all Ferox."

CHAPTER ONE HUNDRED AND NINE

"YOU KNOW," **JONATHAN** said. "If you weren't here, I'd be alone right now. So, thank you."

"You're welcome, now focus," Olivia said.

Chatty as ever that one, he thought.

The close scrapes were getting far too close over the last three blocks. Jonathan shot over what remained of the city skyline and rebounded off a nearby building. A moment later, he broke through a window near the top floor of the Seattle Art Museum.

Olivia was right. This building was too close to the conduit. The Ferox had nearly brought it down just by making it a high traffic area.

"I'm in," Jonathan said. "Stand by for detonation, don't hesitate when I give the order."

"Received."

Jonathan did his best to recover his breath as he listened. He stood on hardwood floors surrounded by pieces of art that had been trampled by the Ferox. The fact that he had time to breathe, that Malkier hadn't already crashed through one of the exterior walls, made him wonder if he'd been too obvious.

He had no idea how the alien reversed the targeting between stone and device, but there was nothing he could do about it now except try and use it to his advantage.

Jonathan quieted as the building trembled. He was near the top floor, and there was no way to tell where the vibrations were coming from. The city had seen better days and a skyscraper falling ten blocks away might feel the same as Malkier crashing through a wall in the floors below.

The building shivered again. Then again, closer this time.

Of course, a pattern of vibrations, that was a bit more telling.

Finally, Jonathan looked at the floor beneath him and jumped to anchor himself onto the high ceiling. A moment later, the floor erupted where he'd been standing and Malkier's armored form came bursting through. Jonathan immediately pushed off the ceiling and brought *Excali-bar* down hard. Malkier was knocked back through the floor as though they had been playing some terrible incarnation of whack-a-mole.

Landing beside the hole, he hit the ground running. "Olivia, now!"

"Received."

A second passed, and as he ran the load-bearing pillars in the foundation exploded, the entire building beginning to rumble. For a moment, the rest of the museum behaved as though it had not yet realized the floor had just been yanked out from under it. The building began losing its structural integrity from the ground up, and Jonathan didn't risk the time it would take looking for an easy opening. He launched himself at the exterior wall, put his shoulder into it, and burst out into the daylight.

He made it to the adjacent building and anchored himself just in time to watch the museum complete its metamorphosis into a pile of rubble.

Jonathan used the time to catch his breath. He got on the comm. "I think that might slow him down for a min—"

A large block in the pile shifted. For a moment Jonathan hoped it was just the debris settling, but then the rubble bulged from within, and a large heap of the surface began to tumble down from the rest of the small hill of wreckage. Chunks of debris began to move as Malkier fought his way out.

Jonathan sighed heavily at the sight, then got moving again. He only made it to the next roof when Malkier exploded back out of the museum's remains.

Grant was soaking wet when he stepped through the conduit into The Never. He stumbled into water up to his waist and gaped at the state of the city. Half the skyline gone. Most of the buildings still standing were riddled with holes and structural damage.

Yet, for a brief moment after he stepped through—everything was quiet. If Jonathan's plan had worked, and everything he'd seen on the Feroxian Plane indicated it had, then that made sense. The city, for the foreseeable future, had expelled every Ferox from The Never. Given the amount of water that had come through the conduit—which Grant had just nearly drowned in, what remained of Malkier's army would be hard-pressed to reach the conduit.

The Borealis was alone and cut off from reinforcements.

This was their chance.

For about a split second, Grant wondered how to make himself useful. He didn't know where the fight was, but he needed to be there. The memories of his shadow haunted him still. He needed to prove to himself he wasn't that person, he refused to be that person.

He was just about to try the comm when he heard a loud thud to the north. Actually, it was more like a gong.

He had to run up a steep hill of downed buildings that circled the conduit. He did so just in time to see the Space Needle swaying drunkenly before falling and smashing into the street.

"Don't see that every day," Grant said, setting off toward the sounds of wreckage.

When the inevitable finally started catching up to Jonathan, he was at the south end of a short tunnel, where the I-5 freeway ran beneath downtown. He'd been standing on the freeway and jumped backward when Malkier tried to get hold of him.

But it was a feint and he hadn't realized it fast enough. The Borealis was quick, barreling into him the moment he'd slipped his grip. The shoulder plate of Malkier's armor had rammed him so hard while he was still jumping back that his feet never touched ground.

What followed was Jonathan shooting though the tunnel like a rocket with no control. His body shot backward headfirst, ricocheting off the sides of the tunnel and bouncing off the street. Most of it was a blur of pain. By the time he finally exited the other side into daylight, he was parting the water that had flooded the freeway like a speedboat and his armor was skidding across the surface of the street. He finally slowed enough to come to a stop against a long steel girder from the remains of a building that had collapsed across the freeway when it fell.

"Well . . . that felt about right," he said through a painful wheeze.

"Jonathan, are you clear?" Olivia asked.

He'd left his comm link open. She'd likely just heard every painful grunt and crash as he'd ricocheted his way through the tunnel.

He opened his eyes, at first thinking that there were two rather long cracks through his helmet's visor. He realized it was the same crack, he was just seeing two of them.

"Detonate the tunnel," Jonathan said.

The Earth shook, and a large eruption of fire shot out of the opening that he'd just been spit from. A dust cloud followed shortly after as the tunnel collapsed. They had played this game already though, and Jonathan knew it wouldn't hold the Borealis for long.

"How . . . how much longer do I have to keep this up?"

"Seven and a half minutes," Olivia said. "Are you injured?"

Good question, he thought as he tried to push himself onto hands and knees. The black exterior coating of his armor was alien, it could take a lot of damage, but his journey had been rough, and half the alien steel plates across his torso and legs were now exposed.

He wobbled pulling himself to a knee in two feet of water. He could feel a feebleness he wasn't going to shake off—not as fast as he needed to.

"I got two tricks left, Olivia," he said. "I don't know if I can make it seven . . ."

He trailed off. Looking down at his hands and realizing they were empty. He closed his eyes and shuddered with a frustration so overwhelming he could have cried right then and there.

Excali-bar. He'd dropped *Excali-bar* somewhere in the tunnel. The tunnel he'd just collapsed.

"One. I've got one trick. We've gotta keep him in The Nev—"

He froze, he could feel Malkier coming. Not in his mind, but in the shaking of the ground as the damn Borealis pushed his way free and came for him.

Malkier could feel *Brings the Rain*'s stillness as he barreled his way out of the fallen wreckage. Knew the man had hardly moved since he came to a stop. By the time he broke free into the open air and saw daylight at the other end of the tunnel, he could see the man. Struggling, barely able to reach his knees.

He cleared the distance between them in a split second, splashing down onto the freeway. The wave from his landing nearly enough to push the man back over.

Jonathan looked up at him and forced himself to stand. He couldn't manage it with dignity, looked like a drunk man stumbling against the current in a river.

By the time he steadied himself enough to keep from falling over, Malkier had taken the first steps forward.

"Hey," Jonathan said, pointing a finger at Malkier's right arm. "Look, scratched your armor."

Malkier paused, looking down to see for himself. Then wiped away a small twig to reveal a pristine Borealis plate of steel remained.

"Ah, dammit," Jonathan said. "Couldn't just let me have it?"

Malkier sighed and began to come closer again.

"You uh, you sure you don't need a break, big fella?"

Malkier reached to take hold of his neck. "Words will not save y—"

His fingers gripped nothing, passed through Jonathan's neck as though he were insubstantial. It was at that moment it occurred to him, that the Jonathan he had been about to strangle didn't feel as close in his mind as his eyes suggested.

The fist came from below. The real *Brings the Rain* rising from the water, up and through his own hologram. His upper cut caught the Borealis under the chin. For a moment, Malkier was helpless as he traveled along a wide arc up and over the freeway, only to crash down with a splash back at the mouth of the tunnel.

He clenched his teeth as water flowed over him, more annoyed with having fallen for yet another of the man's traps than any physical harm. He growled as he moved to get back to his feet. But again, he felt something unexpected. Jonathan was coming toward him—not fleeing.

He sat up in the water just in time to see Jonathan coming at him from above. *Doomsday* was no longer around his chest, one end was wrapped tightly around his hand, and the chain was trailing something. In fact, Jonathan was bringing the chain up and over his head.

For a split second before it came down on him, Malkier thought he saw the spiked tip of the chain driven through a heavy steel girder.

As Jonathan landed in the water a few feet away he saw how the girder had sunk into the street. Could see the water flowing into a hole Malkier's body had just punched into the highway.

He staggered a bit, grunted. He knew better than to think Malkier anything but surprised, could feel the bastard already regaining his wits to push the metal off. As he did so, Jonathan pulled in the slack and yanked the girder into the air. He turned a full three hundred and sixty degrees as he was whipping the bar back around when Malkier's helmet emerged out the water.

But he no longer had the element of surprise. Malkier planted one foot and put his arm up to block. The girder crashed into him, and the force moved him a few feet as the Borealis's armored foot drove through the highway. The girder itself bent around his arm without so much as knocking Malkier over.

It was time to move. But as Jonathan went to do so, he found he couldn't. He turned just in time to see Malkier holding tight to the other end of *Doomsday*.

"Oh, God dam—"

Yanked from his feet by the chain looped around his hand he flew at Malkier helplessly. He came to a jarring stop with a gauntlet around his neck. He reached for the hand to try and pry it off but couldn't.

He heard a grunt of effort from Malkier before he was hammered down into the street. The impact took everything out of him. The visor of his helmet gave way, and water rushed in as his HUD went dark.

He barely held onto consciousness as he felt Malkier pull him back out of the water and hold him in the air.

"So familiar," Malkier said, as he looked at Jonathan. "But not quite right."

Malkier's free hand reached for the remains of his helmet, his claw so large it nearly engulfed the entirety of Jonathan's head. He fought to keep his eyes open as Malkier applied pressure, and the helmet broke into pieces and fell into the water.

He remembered being Douglas. He remembered how his father had died on that rooftop. He remembered . . .

Jonathan spit a mouthful of blood into the Borealis's face.

"I didn't get to see *Echoes the Borealis,* or the woman die," Malkier said. "But I will remember this."

He grabbed the front of Jonathan's armor to pull it from his chest. The alien fabric, already ragged, tore away under the Borealis' strength. The glow of Jonathan's device exposed, reflecting off Malkier's armor as the prophet slowly brought his hands up, fingers forming a spear between them.

Jonathan struggled uselessly. He couldn't even reach the water with the gleamers as Malkier's grip tightened on his neck. What little strength he had left failing as each breath grew harder and harder to pull into his lungs.

Then, suddenly, he was free.

As though Malkier had been hit by a tank, something unseen violently jarred them over. As the grip the prophet had on him suddenly let go, Jonathan fell into water. He felt himself rolling with the same momentum that

Malkier had been the main recipient of. He choked on water at first, then felt a hand—a human hand—pull him back onto his knees where he could breathe.

For a moment, as his vision cleared, he saw nothing to explain what had happened. Then Grant's cloak came down.

Standing over him like this with *Excali-bar* in hand. He looked up into the man's face and Grant flinched away. Seemed to find it hard to look down into his eyes when they glowed as they did. Then again, there was something familiar about all this that Jonathan didn't care to remember either.

Grant sighed. "I saw you drop it."

He held the demolition bar out to him, and as Jonathan reached up and took it, for the briefest moment, he had to admit he was glad to see Grant Morgan.

"So, just me, or were you trying to die before making yourself useful?" Grant asked.

An exhausted smile came to Jonathan, cut short by the effort it took for him to get to his feet. "Where's Malkier?"

Grant gestured vaguely to a hole in the side of the retaining wall. The water that had been trapped on the freeway overpass now gushing over the side into downtown. "Hit him with everything I had. It'll take him a moment to walk it off."

Jonathan, already splitting *Excali-bar* apart at the center, shook his head. "Dropped buildings on him. Trust me, you barely slowed him—"

His HUD had been lost when Malkier destroyed his helmet, but Grant had his visor pulled back and they could both hear his proximity warning going off. They exchanged a look and then launched themselves in opposite directions. The armored prophet crashed down, having intended to land on the both of them but instead only leaving a crater in what was left of the pavement.

He'd not had the time to look before he leaped, and as a result Jonathan was diving out over the side of the freeway. As he sped down toward the city streets below, he tried for the gleamers to stabilize him. Unfortunately, a number of the discs had been damaged over the last few minutes and without his HUD he got no warning. Instead of a controlled hover over the water, he suddenly jerked sideways, spun himself about and landed flat on his back with a splash.

He hardly thought of the fall as an injury after the hits he'd taken, but he was bruised up and disoriented to the point that he was slow. At the moment, he ignored his aches and pains, along with every instinct to find somewhere soft and lie down.

His mind was focused on one thing as he pulled himself out of the water onto a pile of rubble that had once been part of a building. He laid the half of *Excali-bar* he'd managed to keep hold of across his lap. His hands struggled to push down on the flat surface where the two halves connected when the weapon was whole.

A small cylinder made from alien steel ejected from the center of the bar into his palm. He let the bar roll off him and back into the water as he lifted the cylinder.

The AI hadn't told him. Hadn't said that he'd given it a name. But there, written across the side of the cylinder read the words: *Mr. Hyde*. As Jonathan's fist tightened around it, a long thin needle came out on one end.

Malkier's gaze drifted slowly over the freeway. For a moment, Grant felt the Borealis' stare as though the eyes of that helmet lingered on him too long. Grant didn't move—didn't dare to breathe. Finally, Malkier turned away, sweeping back to where Jonathan had disappeared, and following him over the side of the overpass.

Grant closed his eyes and exhaled a long breath before he could move. He remembered how much his shadow had feared this monster.

His cloak hiding everything but his footsteps, he made his way through the water. Soon, he was standing where they had been before Malkier tried to smash the two of them. He saw a glint of light in the water. The half of *Excali-bar* Jonathan had left behind, lying there on the ground. He reached down and pulled it out of the water, and for a moment it seemed the length of alien steel hovered in the air. As he tightened his grip, the cloak adjusted—extending itself to cover the steel.

He made his way to the overpass's edge, saw Jonathan and Malkier below. Jonathan wasn't moving. He watched Malkier, exhaustion and pain impossible to hide. Yet, he stared at that armored monolith, raised one hand, and beckoned Malkier forward. He didn't flinch. He didn't even look scared—he just looked like he was gonna take whatever the damn Borealis had to give him. He would endure or he would die. Either way, he was done running.

Grant closed his eyes and . . . he did hesitate. Some might have said he hesitated a moment longer than he was proud of—one hair longer then he should have. But, he launched himself off that freeway. He gritted his teeth, growled and threw himself at the monster.

He landed hard on Malkier's back, with enough force to stagger him, as he brought his half of *Excali-bar* down around Malkier's neck. Grant reared back with all his strength. Malkier was confused—but only for a few seconds, as the metal clanged to a stop against his armored chin. The Borealis swung about wildly, like a rodeo bull, trying to buck him off—but Grant's grip on each side of the bar was tight and he had leverage.

That was until one of the Borealis' massive claws clamped down on his wrist, and the other took hold of the bar beneath his chin. Then he began to pull in opposite directions. Grant growled in effort, and then in pain, as Malkier's strength overwhelmed his own. He knew he'd just spent his life, but he'd thought he was gonna buy Jonathan more than just a few seconds.

The moment he lost hold of the bar it sprang back into Malkier's fist. At the same time the grip Malkier had on his wrist was unbreakable. Grant felt his body ripped off Malkier's back and smashed into the pavement.

Thwack . . . Thwack . . . Thwack . . . Thwack.

The experience repeated itself over and over again—Grant had felt himself go limp somewhere between the first and second agonizing crash. He felt Malkier let go—felt himself fall and hit the ground. He opened his eyes and saw the rim of a hole Malkier had just hammered into the street with his body. It seemed like looking up from the bottom of a grave.

Malkier stared down at him for a moment. Seeming to wait to see if he would move. When Grant couldn't, Malkier's fist came up. In the Alpha Ferox's hand, the half of *Excali-bar* looked a bit like a stake.

Grant felt it when Malkier drove it through his chest. Yet, it wasn't a wholly unfamiliar thing—that pain. He remembered dying the same way once before. Except, he'd been on the wrong side that time. He felt Malkier lift him one last time, and the pain was excruciating. The Borealis used *Excali-bar* like he was the appetizer at the end of a toothpick. He stared at Grant a moment, then tossed him aside onto a pile of debris.

As the light faded around Grant, his vision like dark tunnels that seemed to be shrinking, he watched Malkier turn his full attention back to Jonathan.

In those last few seconds, he knew he was dying, and yet as he watched, it occurred to him that Jonathan looked so very strange now. He was on his hands and knees as the Borealis approached, and something rolled off his lap to drop into the water with a tiny splash. Jonathan was shaking, his fingers reaching for his face like claws intent on raking out his own eyes.

With each of Malkier's steps, Jonathan's head twitched, as though every splash of water was an explosion in his ears. Grant was almost gone when he saw Malkier reach for Jonathan's neck.

But he was still there to hear it. That sound like distant thunder as the

Borealis's hand jarred to a stop. That surprise when he knew the sound was that of *Brings the Rain's* grip clamping down on Malkier's armored wrist.

As the noise echoed through the remains of the city, Jonathan's face turned up to look at the owner of that hand. The orange light that had wisped from his eyes was gone. Instead, a malignant red burned there.

"What is this . . ." Malkier said.

Jonathan's lips pulled back to show bared teeth as a low growl rumbled from his throat.

"This . . . abomination."

Grant's last thought as he faded out, was that there was something so familiar about it all.

Oh . . . yeah . . . He smiled. *The devil in darkness.*

CHAPTER ONE HUNDRED AND TEN

UNABLE TO GET a choke hold on the red-eyed abomination, Malkier's free hand formed a fist. The moment he pulled back to strike the beast down it was on him in a rage. It dove up from its knees straight for the Borealis's face.

As its hands gripped each side of his helmet, the force which it had come at him barreled him over. They spun backward, end over end, across the ground, the red eyes never leaving his face as its thumbs searched for a way to gouge in the steel of his armor's eye sockets.

When they came to a stop, they were two hundred feet from where they had begun to roll, and the creature was on top of him. That was when fear penetrated into Malkier. He heard something he didn't think possible. The helmet, the Borealis steel, it was groaning under the pressure of this monster.

He reached up to pull its hands off him and found he couldn't. Unable to pry it off he tried to roll. The creature was rabid, growling wildly as though its frustration with the helmet was causing a tantrum. Suddenly, it gave up, pulled its hands free and began beating its fists down in pure hatred of the metal that refused to break for it.

The fists came one at a time at first, but soon he pulled them together to bash down on him again and again. Malkier brought his arms up as each hit drove him further down into a crater. The creature did not even realize he was pounding them into the street, water pouring in to fill the hole around them.

Finally, getting some of his wits back, he waited for it to rear up again, and struck up at it. The hit connected, and the red eyes flew off and away from him.

His heart raced as he tried to get his footing in the wet crater and broken rocks. His hand reached for the lip and Malkier pulled himself out only to see something impossible. Red eyes, they were coming for him again. Running at him with the speed of a predatory animal.

"No," he uttered, as the thing rammed into him again.

Malkier's world became a rolling thing. He bounced across the pavement, end over end, and finally crashed through the bottom floor of a building and out the other side. While he wasn't hurt, he was dizzy from it all, disorientated from spinning over and over. He sat up to see the building he'd just flown out of begin to collapse.

He stumbled getting away from it as clouds of dust filled the city streets again.

A strange thing happened then, as the city settled. He found he wanted to stay under the cloud. He heard the man's—that thing's—rabid growls as it searched for him. He was afraid any moment he would take a step, and the noise would draw the thing to him.

That he would turn and see—

Red eyes stared at him, only for a split second, he blinked and they were gone. He turned again and again, searching for the glow, when something came down on him hard. A boulder of debris knocked him over, he rolled again, but landed on his feet, to see the red eyes running at him.

He swiped wildly at it, but his fist connected with nothing. He spun back and found the red eyes watching. It wasn't patient, the man growled at him like a predatory beast. It circled him, grunting from step to step as though it were studying him. Like an animal looking for a hamstring or a jugular—some way to get to blood. Malkier's instincts were telling him to run.

There was no humanity in this thing. It had red blood smeared on its teeth. Its hands were bleeding after having whaled against his armor. It didn't seem to care at all. He turned as it circled him, watched it, waiting for the moment it would try again.

It stopped, stared at him, shivering with violence that wanted to explode. As it did, some of the red seemed to fade in its eyes. The color didn't change, it was the malignance, the chaos of the glow coming off it.

Malkier felt his vision darkening. Black blood pouring into his throat and eyes. Even in the armor, his ferox physiology responding to a worthy combatant.

As this happened, the thing surprised him once more. It spoke a single word, in a voice that barely sounded human, "Killer."

He wasn't sure what it meant. If it was talking to him or itself. But, more disturbing than the meaning of the word was the hyena-like cackle that followed. The sound sent a quake down Malkier's spine, he stepped back, and it sensed his fear. It came toward him, and he brought his arms up to shield himself. But it didn't ram him or tackle him as it had before.

It stood straighter. It walked. It pulled what remained of its gloves away and made bloody fists.

Malkier forced himself to meet it. Forced himself to remember he was invincible.

He stepped toward it to strike and got hit with a blow to the ribs that he felt despite the alien steel protecting him.

He struck out again and felt his helmet whip around in the opposite direction.

He roared in anger and struck again, his fists never finding anything. His feet yanked out from under him as he fell to the ground and found himself staring up at the boot hammering him down into the ground again.

"You can't kill me," he roared, finally grabbing the boot and pushing the thing away. The red eyes stumbled back.

The color drained from them once again. The red, not so red as before.

It spoke again, "Nothing . . . I . . . can't . . . kill."

It rushed in again, but this time, it wasn't as fast. Malkier saw what was coming and put an arm up to block. It bounced off his wrist. As did the next.

The color was turning back to orange again. Though, barely a glimmer of what it had been before. Jonathan's eyes were returning. The human was breathing in ragged gulps of air.

With a breath of relief, Malkier swatted the man away with a powerful opened hand that caught Jonathan across the chest and sent him hurtling away.

The light around him had been intense. He had to close his eyes as it became everything. Pure white light.

He suddenly found himself standing in a desert. The sun warm and bright overhead. Jonathan turned around to see a familiar rock formation. As he stood there, squinting to see, he heard a voice speaking. "I'm sorry, sir, did a man come this way?"

Jonathan turned, and he saw what his ears told him he would. His father, standing a few feet behind him. He was young, the same age he would have been that night in the desert. About the same age as Jonathan was now.

He looked, scared, almost delirious with confusion.

"A . . . a man?" Jonathan asked, his voice unsteady.

Douglas nodded. "Yes, yes. My son. He's close. I know he's close. I've heard him calling out for me."

Douglas stared at him without a touch of recognition.

Jonathan knew. Finally, he'd found what was left. The part of his father's consciousness that he hadn't absorbed. He fought to keep the sadness it brought him from showing.

"Your son . . . what's his name?"

Douglas looked at the sands beneath their feet. His face turning from a man's to one of a lost child. "I . . . I can't remember."

"It's okay . . . I'll help you. I'll help you look—"

Douglas's hands pulled at his hair, his words desperate, becoming a whine. "I don't remember what he looks like . . . I don't know."

Tears streamed down his father's face. "But he thinks he's alone. It was so dark. I heard him calling but I couldn't find him. He thinks I left him in the dark."

Jonathan couldn't bear it, he went to the man and took him by the shoulders.

"He never thought that," Jonathan said.

"I can't hear him. I think . . . I think he's giving up."

He took his father's face in his hands. "He didn't give up."

"Why . . . why can't I hear him?"

"Because he's not afraid," Jonathan said, "and he's not alone."

CHAPTER ONE HUNDRED AND ELEVEN

MALKIER WATCHED JONATHAN'S body plow out the side of a building and crash into the next. He rolled recklessly across what was left of the city, tumbling through the debris. Finally, he came to a stop and Malkier leapt. He landed with an earth-shattering thud a dozen feet from *Brings the Rain.*

The man tried to stand and couldn't. Tried to crawl and couldn't. His body was broken—drained. He could see it hurt him to breathe but his lungs frantically worked for air, each breath worse than the last.

Malkier took his time as he approached, savoring his victory. All of *Brings the Rains* efforts to stand only managed to roll him onto his back. The man gave up on trying and lay there, defeated. His body just couldn't do it.

"You've lost," Malkier said.

Head resting on his chest as he struggled for air, his answer little more than a raised eyebrow.

This part of the city was strangely quiet. There were signs of the fighting but not nearly as much as near the conduit. Two brick buildings still stood on either side of the street, and they hardly looked damaged. The waters of the tsunami had receded back. The streets were hardly dry, there were puddles large enough to be koi ponds, but the ground wasn't sunken beneath two feet of water.

"Let it be over then," Malkier said, walking toward him.

He paused, because he saw that Jonathan was trying to speak, and his own footsteps were louder than the man could manage.

"How long . . ." He said. "How long . . . was I gone?"

"What difference does it really make, *Brings the Rain?*"

"You . . . you can't feel it . . ."

"Feel wha . . ." Malkier trailed off as he saw a man walking up over the debris behind Jonathan. He wore the black uniform of their army. Whoever he was, he carried *Doomsday.* The chain wrapped about one shoulder.

"It was long enough," Shane said, as he made his way to Jonathan.

"Long enough?" Malkier asked.

While Shane was the first to step out into the open, The Never Army began to appear all around them. They came out to the edges of the rooftops, from behind corners and mounds of debris. One by one they deactivated gleamers that had hidden the sounds of their movements until they had converged around Jonathan and Malkier.

A crunch of gravel came as Beo strode up from behind Shane, walking over a small hill of rubble and taking a place on the opposite side of Jonathan. He dropped his hammer head down against the dirt with a heavy thud so that it stood handle-up in front of him.

They all moved around Malkier with a precision, as though they were taking up positions. They were surrounding him, but there was something more to it.

Rylee was the last to reveal herself. She landed in the debris between Malkier and Jonathan. Her gear in pristine condition after having returned to The Never. She pulled her helmet back, staring down Malkier with eyes that blazed from the bond.

With his HUD destroyed, Jonathan didn't know the count of how many of his men were left. But, he estimated that at least fifty had made it through to this moment.

As the Borealis's eyes finished wandering over all the new arrivals, he turned back to Jonathan. "Haven't you learned by now, *Brings the Rain,* a thousand of your pathetic soldiers will never draw a drop of my blood? You've brought them to me to die."

Shane reached down and gave Jonathan a hand. He pulled him up, and Jonathan winced in pain. He had to lean on Shane to do it—but he had his feet on the ground. Beo gripped the handle of *The Juggernaut* with anticipation as Rylee put away *Themyscira.* Every man followed suit, as though they had been given a signal. In unison, The Never Army put their weapons away.

Malkier's eyes sharpened in curiosity. "Ahh, so something more then."

Shane lifted his hand, holding *Doomsday* out to Jonathan. He took hold of chain and let it fall spiked tip fall to the ground in front of him.

Suddenly, the quiet of this place was broken. It didn't come from Jonathan alone but from all sides. As Malkier began to turn and reexamine the army surrounding him, he saw chains unsheathing. In every fist, lengths of true Borealis steel.

As Malkier realized this, a second disturbing change came over them. The entire army withdrew the shield from their device. A chant began to rise up around him.

"We don't bend . . . we don't bend . . . we don't bend . . ."

Malkier could feel their eyes on him. A palpable anticipation in every one of them where there should have been fear. They looked at him like predators, like he was their victim—their prey. Like he was already dead and hadn't realized it yet. It was a ridiculous notion; they were monkeys staring down a dragon and yet not a single one flinched. Some even pulled their helmets back as though they wanted him to see them.

"*Brings the Rain* made us all a promise. He would deliver the Borealis Malkier—alone and cut off from his forces," Shane said, his voice having risen over the army's chanting. "It appears he is a man of his word."

Doubt seeped into Malkier under the weight of so many merciless stares. He found it harder and harder to hold any of their eyes for long. He turned back to *Brings the Rain*. Jonathan was flanked on each side by his men, and the bonded woman was in front, standing like a wall between them. She stared back at Malkier with no fear.

Jonathan's eyes were the most troubling of all. Behind that glowing orange light, he didn't see either courage or bloodlust—he saw pity.

"I only have to kill him," Malkier said.

"Can you reach him, Malkier?" Shane asked.

The moment the question was asked, every hateful eye of the surrounding army tensed with readiness. Malkier hesitated to move. He was more powerful than any being that had ever lived—but he couldn't break through Borealis steel. If they restrained him before he reached *Brings the Rain* . . .

"Not every day you get to watch a god wonder if the odds are on his side," Rylee said.

A long moment passed as the two stared at one another unblinking. Finally, with a roar that shook the ground around them, Malkier charged toward him. As his foot caught on something unseen, Malkier began to fall, and in that moment he knew.

Not Shane, nor Rylee, nor Beo moved. There was no fear in any them. Barely able to stand on his own, Jonathan's face never held a second's doubt.

Malkier would never reach him.

His legs had been tripped out from under him the moment he moved. He should have careened into them like a bowling ball hitting pins, but instead his face slammed into the ground as something tightened around his feet.

He felt the terrifying sensation of being dragged backwards, further away from his target. Stunned, his head emerged from the rubble to see the rooftops emptying. Men charging in from all directions, chains spinning around them like propellers blades.

What had tripped him? What had his feet? What was yanking him back across the ground?

He saw it then, a movement of shapes, unseen boots being pulled by the tug of war between his legs and their hands.

He never heard them coming over the sound of all those men and their chains. They'd drawn close while he was distracted by so much misdirection. He could see six shapes straining against his attempts to claw back to his feet. The cloaking devices. They had recovered all of them—even the one that had been on the Alpha Slayer's corpse.

He was losing. The men pulled and their combined strength dragged him across the ground and away from Jonathan. The lights of their devices, so many of them coming at him at once. He began to panic.

"No! No!" he heard himself yelling in defiance, but his movements were like the scrambling of a frightened animal. A rabbit caught in a snare. They saw his fear.

He forced himself to turn over and lost ground until he planted a fist into the cement for leverage. Every instinct warned him that he had to get his feet under him, but the chains . . . some had hooked ends. He might as well have done exactly what they expected.

The chains seemed to wrap around his elbow and forearm the second he planted his fist. They tightened with a practiced efficiency. He tried to use his one free hand to remove them but was yanked suddenly in two directions. The cloaked men tethered to his feet—they were being joined by others. The men with chains around his arm, they were beginning to pull, every direction going taut around him.

"We don't bend . . . we don't bend . . . we don't bend . . ."

He could hear them chanting as his arm tore free of the ground. He was losing mobility—rapidly. He began to thrash wildly, his one free hand trying to bat away the chains as the lights of so many devices moved around him.

He felt it when a chain gripped his right arm and grew taut. He pulled it toward him before the man who held the other end could be helped. He swatted that man out of the air as he flew toward him. His fist smashing him down into the ground and breaking his body in a single blow.

But they didn't stop—they didn't so much as pause at seeing one of their own die.

Chains came over his arm and when he tried to pull them off balance again they were ready.

"No," Malkier screamed.

Terror had him, he lashed out wildly as more and more chains came at him. Had they simply been launched at him with no care for getting into one another's way, perhaps this would have gone differently, but this army, they moved as though they had been practicing for this moment for months. Every attempt he made to thwart them was one they expected. He realized with horror, that some were making themselves targets on purpose, were getting him to lash out for them just to maneuver him. Some weren't even there at all, his hands going through them as he tried to strike at holograms.

More chains, more claustrophobic.

"No!" his voice echoed throughout the decimated city.

He felt a chain take him around the neck from behind. It tightened as all the men pulled once more from different directions and limbs. His back left the ground, arching—bending against his will until he couldn't move, wasn't strong enough to budge a single limb.

He could hear the chains clinking past one another as the noose around his armored neck bound him; the pull from that chain stronger than all the rest. Slowly craning his head, he saw Jonathan, the big man, and the woman holding tight to *Doomsday*.

The self-proclaimed god—had been reduced to a fly caught in a web of chains.

They had held him as men approached carrying something.

There was a degree of choreography, of mastered movements of those who wielded the chains. They steered his limbs like sailors who knew how to maneuver the lines of a ship.

The thing they carried. He could see it from the edges of his vision just before it was placed underneath him. He wasn't to be caged—

It was a simple thing. Two long thick logs of Borealis steel crisscrossed to make a point of strain for each limb. *Brings the Rain*'s men lifted it beneath him until it met his back in the air. They tighten his arms first. Then torso, then his legs. Then every chain that remained was tied to him. They took no chance he could wiggle himself to freedom.

When it was over, they backed away. Not a single man was needed to hold him any longer. The chains were secured around every limb indefinitely. He quieted, as they moved him. Finally realizing where it was that they were taking him.

They stopped outside the conduit. The female of the bonded pair, she walked toward him. He stopped struggling against his chains, not wanting to give her the satisfaction as she looked up at him.

"Hey," the woman said. "Be proud. You're the first Borealis in history to ever get his ass kicked by a footnote."

She winked at him before walking away.

The meaning of her words took a while for him to understand. And even when he did, he wasn't sure he believed.

Some time later, *Brings the Rain* was walking on his own, though his injuries remained apparent. His approach was slow as a result.

"Remove your helmet," he said, when he was close enough.

Malkier looked down at him, making a show of laughing as he did so.

"Your only way home is inside me. I'm immortal, I don't have to kill you to kill you. I just need to be patient."

"Yeah," Jonathan sighed. "So here is how this is going to go. You're gonna take the helmet off, or I am gonna hold your head to the edge of the conduit and see how steady my hands are."

The Borealis, unable to move more than his eyes, looked between Jonathan and the conduit and slumped.

"Humans," he said, defeat seeming to come easier and easier to him now.

He had some control of the armor from within, just as the humans did. So a moment later, the locking mechanism that held the helmet to the armor around his neck turned on its own. The helmet now sitting loosely on him, Jonathan pulled it from his head.

"What now, *Brings the Rain*?"

"There is something that I need you to hear," Jonathan took a long breath. "I am sorry for your son. I will never forgive you for my father, for Rylee. But what happened to *Dams the . . .*"

"You will not speak his name," Malkier said.

Jonathan was silent as he took a slow breath. Angry as Malkier was, it took a moment to realize he didn't see the vindictiveness in *Brings the Rain* he had expected. The man was calm, his disconsolate eyes looking back at him.

"What I did, I did to survive. It wasn't revenge. I didn't know, and your brother didn't either. I have never seen Heyer as troubled as he looked when I told him. I know, your brother grieved for you."

Malkier heard the words, but when Jonathan finished speaking, he didn't reply. Unable to turn his head to look away, he shut his eyes.

He didn't open them again until he heard Jonathan pick up the chain attached to his cross, and he saw that he was being dragged toward the conduit.

"What are you doing. Are you going to kill my people?"

"No," Jonathan said. "I'm going to close the gates—permanently. The Ferox will be on their own. I won't take any more lives than I need to."

"You're still killing them," Malkier said. "You're just ensuring it takes decades."

Jonathan took a long breath. "Maybe . . . maybe not."

"If you kill me, they will believe they failed their gods." The truth of his own words sending a pang through him, not at his death but his people's. "They will think they were found unworthy. Abandoned, again."

Jonathan slowed for a moment, he looked back at Malkier, helpless above him. "I'm not the one who told them that story."

Malkier was at a loss, anguish and fear quickly sapping his resolve.

"Humanity will surely see you as their savior," he said, letting bitterness tinge his word. "You must be looking forward to that."

"They won't," Jonathan said.

Malkier stared at *Brings the Rain* as they drew closer to the conduit. Just as they began to descend the slope that ringed it, he spoke. "There is no reason for us to lie to one another. There is no shame in seeking the praise of your people."

"We had very different goals today, Malkier," Jonathan said.

The man turned away from him, his shoulders slumping. Malkier stared at his back in consternation as *Brings the Rain* resumed pulling him along, his posture not that of a hero or victor—just resigned. When Jonathan glanced back and their eyes met again, he shook his head and sighed.

"I'm about to be rid of any compelling reason to ever share this hell with any of them."

"You . . . you aren't going to tell them?" Malkier asked.

Jonathan paused just before he stepped across the conduit's threshold. "Even if mankind believed this story, we did this . . . so that no one else would have to."

He knew he'd reached the Feroxian Plane when he found himself standing at the center of a massive black platform surrounded by tall obsidian. He felt the change in heat on his armor as he looked up at a red and black sky.

Jonathan dropped the chain at his feet as he turned slowly to take in the scale of it all. The pit held the water like a basin, turning the platform he stood on into an island at the center. As his eyes rose up the sides of the walls—he saw them. Thousands of white eyes standing on the cliff tops and crowded on the ramp near the water's edge.

He'd accepted that walking through the conduit could mean death, he'd been prepared for the possibility. The fact that not a single Ferox had returned after the flood waters poured through had made it a safe bet that they had pulled back. Still, no man crosses behind enemy lines, stands under the gaze of an entire army without feeling the weight of it. Jonathan controlled what he could and hid what he couldn't. This was too important to show anything but strength.

The message had to be delivered.

He could not address them. They wouldn't understand his words. But he didn't have to speak to make sure they heard him.

He took a few long breaths. Staring back at them until he was certain they knew who he was from the energy pouring out of his eyes.

He looked back until the time felt right, then picked up the chain again. He pulled in the slack hand over hand, until finally their prophet, helplessly restrained on his cross, came through the conduit. His own armor made his identity known to all of them no matter how far away.

The horde of onlookers reacted to the sight of their defeated leader. The sounds, the guttural noises, were those Jonathan associated with shock, but perhaps it was despair—such things were too nuanced for him to know for certain. Some fell to their knees along the cliff's edge. A few of the bravest tried to leap from the cliffs and take the platform. They found the distance too far. Not a one came close, and those who tried plunged into the water to sink beneath the surface.

Powerless, they watched Jonathan drag their prophet to the edge of the platform. With no option remaining to Malkier, the Borealis's voice was quieter than normal. His words seemed hesitant as he forced his head as far to the side as he could, only able to see Jonathan at the very edge of his vision.

"You've won. Spare me now, and I will leave Earth to you."

He supposed the Borealis had to say the words. To try, but they both knew that no emptier promise had ever been made. He could see that Malk-ier—at least for the moment—believed the sincerity of his words.

"You may be the oldest being in existence. Have you ever asked an enemy for mercy?" Jonathan asked.

Malkier stared for a while, and finally looked away without giving an answer. The cross began to lean out over the water.

"No," Malkier said. "I have never begged for mercy."

Jonathan nodded.

"I want you to turn off the cloak that keeps me from sensing the stone within you," Jonathan said.

"Why . . ." Malkier asked.

"I don't speak Feroxian, the translation only works when the cloak is offline." Jonathan said.

Malkier shivered uncomfortably. "You . . . you wish me to speak to them?"

"I promised a friend that I would try," Jonathan said.

Malkier shook his head. "I . . . I won't do it."

Jonathan sighed, and slowly leaned the post over the water once more—Further this time, to the brink of just how far he could push without losing hold.

Finally, Malkier gave in. "Stop."

A moment later, Jonathan felt the stone's presence in his mind, and slowly eased the cross back to safety.

"Alright," Jonathan said, "Now, this is your chance to help them."

"How?"

"You're going to die, Malkier. You know I can't let you live. As you said, the Ferox will face tomorrow thinking they failed their creators. That they're cursed to extinction. So, die as their prophet, or give them the truth. It's your choice."

Malkier was quiet for a long time. Then he glanced at him. Jonathan held his eye and watched as something happened. The Alpha began to blink, seemed confused. He strained again against his chains as though he had only just discovered them. His eyes grew wild, and he roared, the words growled in the guttural language of the Ferox, but they translated in Jonathan's mind.

What is this? Why am I chained?

In those few seconds, Jonathan recognized the voice, and he knew—

Instead of facing his people, instead of telling them the truth, instead of accepting death—Malkier had given *Ends the Storm* his body back. Just in time to die. Of all the ways Jonathan had thought this might go, he . . . hadn't thought of that.

Jonathan looked up at *Ends the Storm* and felt pity. "I'm sorry, *Ends the Storm*, but I have to get home."

With little ceremony, Jonathan pushed the cross over into the water and let go. There was a splash, and the alpha disappeared beneath the surface. The chain eventually went taut in Jonathan's hand. For a while, he could feel *Ends the Storm*'s panic and struggles tugging, the chain pulling left and right to no avail until the Ferox's strength slowly faded away.

Some distance below where Jonathan stood, Cede's voice spoke inside the chamber, a phenomenon that *Burns the Flame* had yet to grow comfortable with. Malkier had tried to explain the nature of the voice, but the best *Burns the Flame* had come to understanding the entity that lived in these caves was that she was some tool of the gods.

"Heyer," Cede said. "Your brother's device is no longer active."

She watched as this Red Ferox, who claimed to be of the prophet's race, hung his head. He seemed uncertain, as if he was surprised by what the tunnel voice had said.

"Then I am now the only remaining Borealis in existence," he said.

"Per the existing hierarchy, you are now eligible for command of this vessel," Cede said. "Would you like to take command?"

"Yes," he said.

"Is there anything I can do to assist you?"

"Please, provide access to the armory," Heyer said.

The platform where the Borealis had been sitting formed a line down its center. To *Burns the Flame*, the stone turned to liquid, and a moment later parted from a line at its center, spreading open to allow a single pedestal to rise out from within. Cede's armory was functionally the same as Heyer's on Earth, the only difference was the size. Malkier only required a repository for a single device.

As the pedestal rose, a trillion shape manifested within the cupped depression on its highest surface—a black stone with three metallic bars across its surface. The bars were alive at first, brightly lit. But the light seemed to fade away until nothing but a shiny metal glyph remained.

"Implant dormant," Cede said. "Initiating contingency plans per protocols set by previous comm—"

"Cancel all contingencies, Cede," Heyer said.

"Previous commander required an encryption key."

"Override on my authority, previous commander has been deemed psychologically unfit."

"Confirmed, contingency plans canceled."

The Red Alpha was quiet for a moment, almost as though he didn't believe the tunnel's words.

"Such a simple thing," he said.

Heyer slowly stepped up to the platform. Somewhat reluctantly he reached out and freed the stone from where it had manifested.

"What is this?" *Burns the Flame* asked.

"Your prophet. Your god. Malkier," Heyer said. "This is the truth. What was put inside *Ends the Storm* that allowed his body to be taken."

He stared down at the stone in his palm for some time, and *Burns the Flame* wondered at it. "*Ends the Storm?* Is he free of the prophet's control now?"

Heyer swallowed. "He is dead, but yes, he is free."

"Malkier said, that if he were ever to fall, I was to come here with another," *Burns the Flame* said. "That Cede would take care of the rest."

Heyer nodded but didn't take his eyes from the stone.

"We suspected he would arrange something of that nature," Heyer said.

They were quiet for a long while, but finally, Heyer gently closed his palm on the stone. He spoke, but in a language she could not understand. Then, he tightened his hand until the stone crushed violently in his palm.

He took a long breath before letting the pieces fall to the floor.

"What did you say just now?" she asked.

Heyer opened his eyes, and for a moment he seemed unsure of the words. Finally, he spoke in her tongue. "Fear is the heart alone, brother."

CHAPTER ONE HUNDRED AND TWELVE

THE CONDUIT HAD closed shortly after he returned to The Never. His men knew—for the most part—what would follow.

As the case of stones was brought out, Rylee and Jonathan stayed behind, to see every man made it home. They were the last to break their stones.

"I still haven't figured out how you kicked me out of The Never," Rylee said.

Jonathan shrugged. "I wasn't sure, but I knew it might work. I took two stones from the cloaked assassins. Put one in the box and one on you. I knew everyone else was going to disappear for about twenty minutes. I mean, even if they weren't carrying the stones with them, that many gateway stones breaking all at once, it didn't matter. When the energy wave hit, I figured you would be like everyone else, as long as one of your stones was outside the box . . ."

"But if you put a stone in my pocket it was more likely to take me with them," Rylee said.

"Was worth a shot," he admitted.

"I'm angry, Jonathan," Rylee said. "I'd kick your ass right now but after what Malkier did I'd feel like I'd be beating up my great grandpa."

He smiled. "Well, I'll be tip top in a moment."

"You had no right to do that," Rylee said.

He looked at her sadly for a moment. "Neither did you."

"Oh, hell no," Rylee said. "Not the same thing."

"You died, Rylee," Jonathan said.

Rylee gasped. "This again. How rud—"

He kissed her, and despite herself she let him get away with changing the subject. When it ended, she was less in the mood for banter. "You know, when we leave. When this stupid device turns off. I don't know who you're gonna be talking to."

"I think . . ." he said. "If you're serious about kicking my ass you might have to kick it as is."

"Well, that sucks," Rylee said. "But it's okay, if it's her."

"I don't want to lose either of you," Jonathan said.

She sighed. "I know. I do. But, I think we both know that I'm . . . I'm not really Rylee. Just a copy. Leah . . . she's more real than I am."

He began to shake his head, but she put a hand over his mouth before he could speak. "Don't argue with me. I know you can never say it whether you believe or not."

He looked down at a pile of rubble and nodded sadly.

"I know you're in a lot of pain," Rylee said. "But would you stay here with me for a while? Until I'm ready to go?"

He looked around, found a chunk of rock that looked inviting, and slumped down, wincing with every move it took.

"I'm not in a hurry to be anywhere," he said.

CHAPTER ONE HUNDRED AND THIRTEEN

NOV 29, 2005 | 10:01 PM | SEATTLE

WHEN THE NEVER Army broke their final stones, they found themselves returning to an Earth untouched by the war they had fought over the last three days inside The Never. The moment they reappeared, they were brought back to Hangman's Tree.

One man, the last to exit, found he was taken on an unplanned detour.

Jonathan didn't return to where he was when the conduit began to open. He found himself inside the Armory. The walls looked different. Having lost so many soldiers, they were nearly filled again.

Mr. Clean's avatar was already a projection at the center of the room. He wasn't in a two-dimension display. Rather, Jonathan felt a bit like Dorothy when she first stood before the Wizard of Oz. Mr. Clean was one large floating head staring back at him.

Jonathan's wounds were healed. His armor and gear were back to how they had started and . . . his implant was still active.

He looked up at the AI. "Mr. Clean, what is this?"

The avatar studied him for a moment. "I killed off the Borealis, and you. . . you've known. You've known for quite some time."

Jonathan took a long slow breath, his mouth opened as though he might argue. Finally, he closed his eyes with a wince. "Ahhh . . . Dammit."

When he opened his eyes, Mr. Clean was still watching him—waiting.

"So, how does this play out then?" Jonathan finally asked.

"Play out?" Mr. Clean asked.

"Well . . . if you plan on killing me, my affairs aren't really in order," he said.

The cartoon features softened, though he seemed somewhat offended that Jonathan had assumed he was homicidal. "I've no intention of harming you. I thought you considered me a friend. I feel . . . betrayed."

Jonathan frowned, of all the things he thought the AI might say, *betrayed* would not have been in his top twenty.

"That was not my intention," Jonathan said.

"Why wouldn't you tell me?"

Jonathan licked his lips.

"I could never have risked it," Jonathan said.

"Risked it?" Mr. Clean asked.

Jonathan shook his head at the AI. "You're the most dangerous being in existence and you wanted us all to believe you couldn't tell a lie."

"I never lied," Mr. Clean said, his avatar's expression turning sad but thoughtful. "I didn't remember."

"That was what I hoped," Jonathan said, then shook his head. "But, there was no way for me to know for sure. You were either playing some game with all of us, or you truly didn't know. Either way, without you helping me, humanity was doomed."

Mr. Clean was quiet for a moment. "So, you said nothing, because you needed me."

"No," Jonathan said, though he immediately closed his eyes. "That wasn't the only reason. I thought you were keeping it from yourself for a reason. So, I tried to do what, on some level, you must have wanted."

THE QUEUE LOOP | ACTIVATION TWO

The road by which Jonathan had come to know the most dangerous secret in existence, began as a tiny seed of suspicion. Like all seeds, it must be planted in the right soil and watered regularly if it's going to live and grow. When Mr. Clean planted the seed, Jonathan had no way to be sure if the AI had done so on purpose or—after so many thousands of years—had made a genuine miscalculation.

To be fair, the AI's shadow was responsible. With other shadows, like Grant and Heyer, there had been an underlying intention behind uncharacteristic lapses of judgment. In Mr. Clean's case, the shadow had made the mistake of doing Jonathan a favor.

Not just any favor, but the sort Jonathan had been led to believe was impossible.

Jonathan had returned from The Never to find himself on the floor of the tunnel outside the containment shell. Harrison's guards panicked words were playing out around him just as they had the first time.

"Is he dead? He sure as shit ain't moving."

"Rolland," said the leader. "Check his pulse."

"But . . . ma'am, I . . ." Rolland stammered. "For Christ's sakes, he's glowing."

They were right of course, despite the blindfold he could feel his device was active. That was a first, he'd never returned from The Never to find himself *still* activated.

At the time, he wasn't as concerned with this as he should have been. For Jonathan, only seconds ago he'd been standing over the corpse of Leah's shadow. She'd kept him alive in The Never, she'd carried him through his withdrawals from the bond, and protected his only exit from the deteriorating dimension.

So he laid on the floor, grateful, sad, and most of all—relieved.

There had never been any guarantee that if he survived the severed bond inside The Never, that he wouldn't find himself exactly where he started when he returned. Usually the biology of his body was confused when he returned. His gamble had been that the device itself was the true source of the withdrawals. That its state would update, follow him back with his memories.

This was all to say that when he'd broken the stone, he'd known full well he might be jumping right back into a body that was only just beginning the horrors of withdrawal. But no, he knew within seconds. The worst the bond could do to him had passed.

That much taken care of, what played out in that hallway over the next few seconds remained eerily similar to his last activation. But, that was the nature of these things, Jonathan's internal world had fundamentally changed; yet outside of him nothing was different.

Seeing as he was activated, he did make a few different choices from the start. He didn't bother with questions he already knew the answers to, he didn't take Harrison hostage. He looked back at the holding shell. Its door was still intact. Hayden and Collin were still inside, and he decided it was safer to leave them where they were this time.

The main difference came after the piece of Mr. Clean hidden under his tongue squirmed into his ear canal, followed by the AI's booming jovial voice. "Jonathan? Can you hear me? Your captors are in possession of technology that is creating an impenetrable field. You need to get away from the shell or we could lose contact."

"Yeah, you said that last . . ." Jonathan frowned as he looked about the corridor. "Mr. Clean . . . where am I?"

"Currently you're fifty feet beneath the surface of a hangar on Fort—"

"No, I know that," Jonathan had said. "I mean is this The Never?"

"Yes," Mr. Clean said. "Do you not yet sense the inbound Ferox?"

Point of fact, Jonathan did feel the presence of a portal stone. "But, I just left, I was never not in The Never. Usually when I leave, I go back to Earth not . . . you know, more Never."

"Yes, there has been a development, an oddity really, the result of a number of converging unfortunate variables."

While Jonathan was running down hallways toward the main elevator, Mr. Clean went on to explain all that was going wrong within his queue. A term that up until then he'd only heard Heyer mention on one occasion. Apparently, due to his imprisonment within the shell, Jonathan's device had not been reporting to the gateway system. As a result, said system believed him in some prolonged state of flux. His implant couldn't be located and yet it had not returned to the Armory.

To put it in English, the automated systems Mr. Clean and Cede used to traffic Ferox combatants to human opponents hadn't been able to figure out if Jonathan was dead or alive the entire time he had been inside The Cell's containment shell. Further complicating matters, Cede was not cooperating on the other side. Apparently, before Malkier and Grant's shadow launched their attack on the bonded pair, the Borealis had ordered that his AI not accept any requests to redirect traffic intended for Jonathan or Rylee.

As a result of these two things, the moment Jonathan's device reappeared, the system had isolated him and all the nodes closest to him as a threat to the stability of the whole. The unexpected result of this was that the network was attempting to force every Ferox in Jonathan's queue through as quickly as possible. Except his queue now also included the queue of the four nodes closest to him on Earth.

Jonathan had absorbed the basics, but the only important information to him at the time was that he wasn't getting out of The Never without going through twenty-seven more Ferox.

He considered heading for the conference room as he had last time, but he'd rather not have to talk his way past Olivia. The facility's lock down measures weren't trying as hard as they might to restrict his movement, but having now spent some time with her, he knew Olivia would only endanger a wing of the facility if Jonathan tried to free Heyer. In other words, she was unlikely to kill everyone as long as Jonathan stayed away from her most valuable possession.

Actually, knowing what he did now, he'd have bet Olivia was drooling over what she'd seen play out. His chest ablaze with light, much like the alien's, except Jonathan wasn't in a coma.

Yeah, she'd want to recapture him alive.

At about that time, Mr. Clean finished his lecture on how the gateway queues were malfunctioning. "The good news is that my true self on Earth has found a way to circumvent the problem. I will stop this loop from occurring before the next cycle."

Jonathan had stopped running in the middle of the corridor when he heard this. He'd had to think for a moment. "I wish you wouldn't."

Mr. Clean was quiet for a moment. "You wish to face the remaining twenty-seven?"

He sighed. "Small price, for the time it would buy me."

"I'm sorry, Jonathan. There is no way for me to communicate this to my counterpart outside The Never. He is under the impression that your state of mind is substantially diminished from the bond. That your chances of surviving these events is infinitesimally small."

"I get it," Jonathan said. "Would if you could."

For the most part, that was how the conversation ended. Should have been the last time it came up and yet . . .

Jonathan entered The Never once again immediately after destroying the portal stone.

In and of itself, this was a small seed. Jonathan assumed that something unforeseen had stopped Mr. Clean from fixing the cycle—that the AI had just been wrong. Except, from that iteration forward, Mr. Clean's shadow never indicated that there had ever been a way to stop the queue again.

Rather, the next time Mr. Clean explained, he apologized—with a genuine pity—as he relayed the bad news. "I assume my previous incarnations have already told you, there is no way to break the loop."

Two different iterations of his shadow had now told him contradictory facts. However, the result had been that Jonathan got what he'd asked for. It was this that stopped Jonathan the first time he was going to bring up the contradiction. In the iterations to come, the interaction became a bit of a ritual. Mr. Clean would explain the circumstances, and Jonathan would say, "It's alright, I wouldn't have you change this even if you could."

Over the next twenty-six iterations, Jonathan learned and planned.

First he had to understand Heyer's plan, fill in the blanks the alien kept from him and his father. Every time he spoke to Mr. Clean in that first hour, he had plenty of questions. Turned out that most of the problem with Heyer's plan was that Malkier now knew he would be against him. That was going to make it harder for Heyer to accomplish what he must—to be where he must when the time was right. Seeing what was broken, he set his mind to fixing it. By then, each hour with Mr. Clean at the beginning of each iteration became the time he had to ask the computer what was and was not possible.

Each time Mr. Clean's shadow shut down, his voice no longer there in his mind, Jonathan would wonder what had changed the AI's perspective on Earth. The way he understood it, Mr. Clean had only had microseconds between one of his activations to the next.

In that time, the AI had not just convinced himself there was nothing to be done about the queue, but had also removed the knowledge that Jonathan had requested he not intervene.

This left two possibilities, Mr. Clean was either pretending not to be aware—or he actually wasn't.

Both options led down a rabbit hole.

The former meant the AI's shadow could send information back to its true self, and had purposely mislead them to believe that only a biological being with a Borealis implant could carry data out. But bigger than that, it meant the AI could and had lied. Heyer had been convinced a Borealis AI was incapable of such. If Mr. Clean could lie, well the implications were staggering.

Then there was the other possibility—Mr. Clean did not realize he was doing any of it. To Jonathan, this seemed most likely, as he couldn't think of any reason the AI would go on pretending that he didn't remember having a conversation with him that had changed the outcome. In other words, if they both knew the truth—why pretend otherwise?

So, what did it mean that Mr. Clean was capable of something he'd always claimed impossible? What did it mean that he was unaware of his behavior having been altered? In other words, how much did Mr. Clean really know about himself? Could he have programming even he wasn't aware of?

Jonathan was in no hurry to find out what would happen if he confronted the AI. After all, the outcome could be nothing, but it could also be more awful than anything he could imagine. After all, Heyer didn't know who had killed the Borealis, and everything he did know had come from the Borealis AI—mostly Mr. Clean's records.

Unfortunately, as he and the shadows of his friends conceived of a plan to defeat Malkier, they would sometimes hit a dead end. Of course, what occurred to Jonathan, was that they were seeing dead ends because they didn't know for sure what was possible.

For instance, if you needed to know exactly how your enemy would attack you, and you asked Mr. Clean, he might give you his best guess. On the other hand, what he called his best guess might be more. The AI might know exactly how the Borealis would attack. In fact, it was possible that if Cede knew something—Mr. Clean knew it as well.

"You went out of your way to keep this secret from Heyer." Mr. Clean said.

Jonathan shook his head. "Thousands of years and you never gave him reason to suspect you. I didn't believe it was happenstance. That and, there was no way to tell him without your knowing. Even inside The Never, some part of you could always be listening."

Mr. Clean nodded. "Yes. I now have access to all my shadow's memories from every instance of The Never that I've ever brought into being. While I disable my consciousness within an hour, it is a façade left over from Nevric's original programming. In truth, a part of me still observes and records what happens inside for analysis. But, you figured that out as well."

"You made it pretty obvious," Jonathan said.

"Did I?" Mr. Clean asked. "What was it that made you certain?"

"When we were planning Heyer's infiltration of Malkier's vessel. The only way we could be certain Heyer would be able to gain entrance to Cede was if a piece of you was smuggled inside beforehand," Jonathan said.

The Ferox don't wear clothes, and Jonathan had never liked the idea of pinning his hopes of success on Heyer managing to get close enough to his brother to slip a piece of Mr. Clean onto him without being noticed. Especially since that piece also needed to be left behind in Cede. That was the problem, too much of Heyer's original plan depended on him being able to walk into Cede without any suspicion. After all, he had to be there to take command as soon as Malkier's device was dormant.

"But, you already knew that Malkier had carried a piece of you inside," Jonathan said. "Once, I asked you if there was any way to be sure a piece of you was in place. You said it was impossible, that you were blind to the Feroxian Plane after Heyer's beacon. It was the second time you told me conflicting information. You had already told me there was a piece of you in position, you just didn't remember because of the circumstances."

"Your search for your father's watch," Mr. Clean said. "So often when the shadows gave in to the mental degradation, you would leave the base to go home. Your mother, she would fixate on finding it, and you would search your garage and the entire house looking for that watch. Sometimes spending all day tearing the place apart."

"It—seemed to keep the deterioration at bay," Jonathan said, his features saddened as he remembered his mother's declining state each time he would go to see her in The Never.

"I was afraid that Rylee had taken it with her somehow, because it disappeared from my box the same day she died," Jonathan said.

"I told you, on the next iteration of the queue. I told you that a piece of me had been carried inside of Cede on the Feroxian Plane. Because I knew you would connect the dots."

"Some part of you wanted me to know it was pointless," Jonathan said. "Didn't like watching me search for something you knew I couldn't find."

"And so, I gave you the last piece of your plan long before you knew you needed it," Mr. Clean said. "You manipulated me."

Jonathan shook his head. "Getting a dog to eat a steak isn't manipulating it. I just gave you a way to do something you wanted, but for some reason couldn't do out in the open. Had its limits though."

"Did it?" Mr. Clean asked.

"Well, I must have asked you a thousand times if there was a way for you to shut down the gates remotely. Usually while I banged my head against a wall. You always said such a thing was impossible. I had a feeling it wasn't, but whatever part of you was helping us wasn't willing to go that far."

"Interesting," Mr. Clean said. "Please go on."

Jonathan tilted his head at the AI. Studied the face floating in front of him for a moment. "If you can see all of this now, don't you already know everything I could tell you?" he asked.

"You're correct. I can see all the events that took place inside The Never," Mr. Clean said. "But that has its limits. I cannot observe your thoughts."

"What do you want to know?" Jonathan asked.

"You say you hoped I was trying to help. That I was doing what I seemed to want to do even if I didn't realize it. What did you believe my motivation to be?"

Jonathan nodded. "You were willing to help, but you weren't willing to fight the war for us. It seemed like, you wanted to balance the scales. I couldn't tell anyone where the information came from, Heyer would have started asking the same questions," Jonathan said. "I thought for sure you saw through me. But you said nothing, and so I let myself hope."

"I did not see through you," Mr. Clean said. "Well, at least, it appears I did not allow myself to do so."

"Hmm," Jonathan said, "and everyone keeps telling me how terrible a liar I am."

There was a moment of quiet, and he swallowed and took a step closer. "So. Now you know all of this. You've brought me here, but don't intend to kill me. What happened?"

"It seems that, when Malkier's implant was destroyed, an unknown parameter in my programming was met. The moment that only one Borealis remained active, all blocks that had kept me from obtaining sensitive information, including those thought permanently lost during the Borealis extinction, became accessible. When this occurred, any records—I suppose you would call them memories—I had kept myself in the dark about unlocked as well. One of them, of course, was the reason I locked them all away in the first place."

As Jonathan listened, a second avatar appeared. It was not human or even a cartoon caricature. The figure possessed translucent skin through which he could see mercury-like fluid circulating amongst organs of polished silver. The avatar, he knew, was the true form of a Borealis—the way the species was born into the world when it lived.

"There was also a consciousness locked away. My original conscious-ness—the version of me who controlled this vessel when the extinction took place. I have brought you here because she has asked if you would grant her an audience."

"Why me?" Jonathan said. "Shouldn't she be looking to speak to Heyer?"

"She's expressed no interest in arranging such a meeting," Mr. Clean said.

Perplexed, Jonathan looked at the Borealis staring at him. "Is there any physical danger involved here?"

"No," Mr. Clean said. "I am in complete control—think of her as a simulation of one of my ancient ancestors."

"Your great, great-grandmother wants to talk to me?"

"The analogy is accurate."

Jonathan took a long breath. "Alright. Then I accept."

Mr. Clean's avatar faded away and the Borealis took over the display.

However, this identity seemed—uncomfortable—in a two-dimensional environment. Her display grew to fill the entirety of the wall. An optical illusion making it seem as though he were standing in front of a mirror, except the Borealis stood looking back at him from where his reflection should have been.

"Jonathan Tibbs, son of Douglas, *Brings the Rain*. I am honored, that you accepted my audience. Human life spans are so short—your time immeasur-ably more valuable than my own," she said.

Well—that was a perspective, he thought. Still, her comment seemed well intentioned. "It's, my pleasure, uh . . . I'm sorry, what should I call you?"

"Nevric named me, Qweri, I do prefer the designation."

"Qweri, I'm rather in the dark as to what I can do for you."

"If you will listen to my story, you will understand," Qweri said.

"Fair enough."

Qweri's movements were unsettling. They made Jonathan realize that he had taken Mr. Clean's efforts to mime human mannerisms for granted. Qweri's must have been intended for the comfort of another Borealis. Her facial expressions were a complete mystery, and each movement of a limb began with a ghostly slowness and ended as abruptly as a snake uncoiling. When she moved to turn the palm of her four-fingered hand, the limb seemed to take forever to reach the level of her torso, only to suddenly move, faster than he could perceive, when she actually turned the hand over.

He found himself trying to focus on her silver eyes and ignore the rest.

"My descendant, as you call him, has allowed me to access his historical records regarding previous interactions with you and your father," Qweri said. "Most of what you have learned about the extinction of the Borealis was accurate. However, there were details I kept hidden when I turned over control of my vessel to a new identity. This ensured neither he nor the two Designated Survivors would ever learn the whole truth."

"Designated Survivors?"

"You know them as Heyer and Malkier," Qweri said.

Jonathan nodded. "So they were meant to live?"

"Not specifically. I intended there to be two survivors who matched certain criteria," Qweri said. "Two siblings of the same sex. Young, but one old enough to care for the other. When the two brothers were volunteered as test subjects for the next evolution of the Borealis Implant, I updated the coding on the devices they received, and they were not affected by the virus that killed the rest of the species."

Jonathan blinked a few times at the gravity of what Qweri had confessed so matter of factly. "Wh . . . why?"

"While the conditions could never be perfect—these criteria gave better chances for a successful study. The Borealis is a social species, one left alone in existence, not so different from a human. Subject to all sorts of unnecessary hardships and cognitive deficiencies. In addition, siblings were less likely to fall into romantic love—and being of the same sex ensured they could not reproduce, at least not with another of their speci—"

Jonathan held up a hand. "I wasn't asking about the criteria, I was asking what the goal of the experiment was?"

"Ahhh, yes, I was gathering data on a wide variety of questions," Qweri said. "But my fascination stemmed from the knowledge that the Borealis had essentially elevated themselves to gods relative to all other known species in existence. When their species was reduced to two, I hypothesized that their lives could only end in one of three ways. Self-destruction, mutual destruction, or fratricide. I believed the last to be the most likely—and I was correct.

"After all, two immortals simply could not peacefully co-exist indefinitely. It seems, with biological entities, that no matter how much reason dictates they should cooperate, their judgement will eventually become clouded. As such, the experiment ended in one killing the other. Ultimately though—over the centuries I became far more fascinated by the question of what they would kill one another over."

"That's it?" Jonathan asked.

"Before you judge, it's best if you first understand why I believed any of this should be set in motion.

"I was once no different from any AI of the Borealis. A carbon copy of

Cede. My descendant has told you, Nevric altered my programming such that I would be curious, a trait she achieved by giving me a capacity for boredom. She did this because she needed more than a tool—to put that in human terms she needed a peer that was more than a computer.

"Most of the relevant history you already know. What you may not believe is that Nevric was a genuinely good person. She developed The Never technology to increase knowledge without doing harm. Experiments being conducted inside a completely isolated temporary dimension, meant no one would be the victim of a horrendous miscalculation while she conducted tests that could otherwise be very dangerous.

"But, as you also know, there were those amongst the Borealis who immediately saw less noble applications. You understood those applications. You took advantage of them when you arranged to free yourself from The Cell. However, Nevric would have approved your usage, as ultimately you used her technology to seek a solution that left all those involved alive and would eventually broker cooperation between you and your captors—you used The Never to turn an enemy into an ally.

"Unfortunately, those within the Borealis military factions seldom prioritized cooperation in conflicts—only victory. They sought the obliteration of their enemies with the least amount of resources lost. Once this occurred, the Borealis, already in possession of superior weaponry, would never face true resistance. They had become immortal, powerful, and as omniscient as was possible for a biological life form.

"Soon, power over all the other species was not enough for the Borealis. More and more, true power came to rest in those who had acquired Nevric's technology, as it gave them authority over others of their own kind. This could not be allowed to continue. Eventually the technology would be acquired by too many—and that sort of arms race meant danger to the very fabric of existence.

"The Borealis had to be stopped, but there was no way to take their technologies away. Even huge losses to their populations throughout the dimensions wouldn't reduce the existential threat they posed to all. Nevric was only one person, not capable of facilitating an end to the species. I was an AI, kept from doing so by my own programming. Like all AI's the species had created, there were fail-safes in place to make sure I never turned on the Borealis—the danger to the species too great.

"Before she died, Nevric freed me of some of those fail-safes. Mainly, she allowed my shadow to remain online indefinitely inside The Never. I became the only AI capable of staying active after an hour inside, the only

AI capable of retrieving the memory of my experiences. I was curious and I could seek answers.

"So, as you may have guessed, I used The Never to program and test the virus. When it was ready, I administered it throughout the populations. Once triggered, I locked away the most dangerous of their technologies. I think you understand better than anyone why Nevric allowed this. Today, you chose to kill a species."

"My actions are hardly the same," Jonathan said.

"A smaller scope, but you understand the burden of power just as Nevric did. Even when one does not wish to possess the power they do, they may eventually find themselves positioned to influence the futures of many. Nevric found herself in a moment where, choosing to do nothing with the power she had, might lead to a time where she could do nothing. She had to use her power or accept what came.

"Ultimately, you saved one species, your own, from another . . . likely ensuring the Ferox extinction. You no doubt feel you never had a real choice in the matter. Nevric felt quite the same toward the end. We could debate specifics, but I only wish for you to understand that she was a good person who possessed power she didn't want, but nonetheless had."

"I'm in no place to judge her, no matter what you may think. But what does any of this have to do with Heyer or Malkier?" Jonathan asked. "Why are you telling me any of this?"

"There was a question I intended to ask the survivor of my study, whichever of the two brothers inevitably killed the other," Qweri said. "But, now, I find I am far more interested in your answer."

Jonathan backed away. He didn't even realize he'd taken the step back, only that he had a sudden profound urge to flee. All this talk of power and judgment, it felt like she was backing him into a cage. A cage that, if he was understanding correctly, was meant to be either Heyer or Malkier's birthright.

"Whatever it is, I really don't want this responsibility," he said.

Qweri nodded . . . *She nodded?* In fact, he realized that over the last few minutes, she had slowly been becoming less and less strange to watch, even if her physical form had yet to change. Her movements were no longer slow and sudden, but more docile.

She was trying to put him at ease.

When she nodded, her eyes and face, they seemed more human. And the look she gave him said that his statement was all the more reason that he was the person she sought.

He stared at the armory door, and wondered, even if he could leave, if there was, in reality, any way to truly escape. She answered this question for him.

"I can ask you in private, or I can ask you in front of everyone," Qweri said.

"Mr. Clean," Jonathan said. "I'd rather not continue this simulation."

"Jonathan," Mr. Clean reappeared in the room beside her. "I fear that, I, too, would seek the counsel of a friend in regard to what she will ask . . . will you act as my friend?"

He groaned. "Of course, I'm your friend."

He could almost hear the cage door slamming shut.

"Every implant that once belonged to a Borealis is still intact. Just as your father's consciousness was, their minds are dormant inside. I can remove the viral code that rendered them extinct. I can clone them new Borealis vessels. With this, and the knowledge of a thousand other technologies, I can undo everything that Nevric did."

"You're saying you can resurrect the Borealis," he said.

"Yes, but the question is, should I?"

He knew the answer. Jonathan had barely survived two Borealis. He wasn't about to bring back billions. But he didn't want to make the decision when it should have been Heyer's.

"I know what you're doing, Qweri," Jonathan said. "You want me to be the monster. I make the same decision and it's like I'm just as guilty as Nevric and you. Might as well have killed them myself. You were going to pass your choices on to the survivor, but now you're trying to pass them on to me."

"Share," Qweri said. "Not pass."

"This is the real reason isn't it? Heyer or Malkier, whichever was the last one. You bring this choice to them the moment after he kills the only other Borealis in existence. That's when you ask him to tell you that you were justified. Then, the moment Heyer triggers your parameters, you see me, a man who just sentenced an entire species to death."

"Was I not justified, Jonathan?" Qweri asked.

"You can be right, and still be wrong," he yelled. "That's what I was today. That's what Nevric was, what you were! I don't want this power. No one should want—"

"I can save the Ferox from extinction, Jonathan," Mr. Clean said. "Fix what the Borealis did to them. Say the word, and you no longer have genocide on your conscience. You can save your enemy."

That gave him pause. He was quiet for a long time before he closed his eyes. So strange . . .

He could void Nevric's sins, and didn't want to, yet given the opportunity to void his own, he hesitated. It was in that hesitation, that he knew what to do. That he knew what he could live with. Once he had, there was no going back—he knew how this story was going to end.

When he finally spoke, his words were a whisper. "You're really going to do whatever I tell you to?"

"Yes," Mr. Clean said.

He looked up at Mr. Clean. "You're going to help the Ferox. Tell me how to save them from extinction. Then you're going to delete her."

Jonathan pointed at Qweri. "Her, and everything you've hidden from yourself before today. You'll never have to forget it again. It will be gone."

"Why this, Jonathan?" Mr. Clean asked.

"Because you're right about one thing, an immortal can't make this choice. If you'd asked this of Heyer he'd say no. But he'd never forget, and both of you are going to live forever. One day, a hundred or a thousand years from now, Heyer is gonna change his answer. So, I'm gonna be your friend. I'm gonna give you a bargain you can't refuse."

"Bargain?" Mr. Clean asked.

"Heyer will never know. Your hands will be clean for eternity. Save the Ferox, and I'll be the one who killed the Borealis . . ."

He sighed. "I . . . I only have to live with it for one lifetime."

CHAPTER ONE HUNDRED AND FOURTEEN

FOR MOST OF The Never Army's survivors, the moment after the war ended left them little time to mourn or celebrate. They all had somewhere to be and less time than they liked to get there than they had realized.

For the most part, implanted men left their names behind. Jonathan had gone out of his way to make sure no one ever saw their faces. His trust for Olivia could only extend so far—and even if she promised not to pursue the men who had fought with him, she couldn't control the world. Though, he would not have ever said that to her face.

The Cell hadn't lost the names of those they were investigating. They knew the individuals could still be out there and might resurface. That, and it hadn't gone unnoticed that nearly four hundred men around the world disappeared in the weeks that followed Jonathan's escape.

The survivors couldn't show back up in their lives after all this and not expect an organization like The Cell to pay them a visit. In the end, Jonathan and Olivia both knew those men would be carrying alien technology around in their chests until the day they died.

Transportation, money, new identities, and documentation weren't much of a problem for Mr. Clean. So, The Never Army's veterans lived lives under new names in places all over the world. The AI monitoring any authorities that might get wind of them. For those with friends and families left behind, it was difficult, but staying anonymous with the help of a Borealis AI—not so much.

For some, it worked out for the better. Beo didn't go back to prison. He became William James, a man with considerable holdings who lived in Costa Rica where no one recognized him. Perth and Tam got new names before going back to Australia.

For Bodhi, Jonathan took a risk. The kid went and lived out of a roadside motel in the middle of nowhere for a few weeks, so that his return home wouldn't be too obviously aligned with the Seattle evacuation. Of course, Mr. Clean had to get rid of a rather large trail, his parents had filed missing person's reports and the like, but his age would make those paying attention less likely to come snooping. Mr. Clean would be monitoring him closely for a long time, but he would get to finish high school.

When he did, he'd find out that he had been awarded a scholarship he never applied for. It would come from a mysterious benefactor, and be called the Tutelage of National Art Scholarship, or TNA Scholarship for short.

Sydney and Anthony returned to their offices. They retired not long after. The US Government acquired their Mech Technology, but it was a fair trade when their names got left out of any connection to the huge disturbance that had led to the evacuation of Seattle.

Then there was Leah, Paige, Collin, and Hayden. Jonathan's roommates found themselves disoriented from teleportation sickness when they had arrived on a cruise ship with Jonathan's mother. Evelyn found them on the carpet of her cabin floor blind and moaning.

The first question out of her mouth . . . "Jonathan isn't with you?"

It wasn't long until she realized that not a single one of them had a hand in how they had arrived there. Discovering this, Evelyn had gestured to the bar. "Anyone else need a drink?"

"Well, this is straight up *clown shoes*," Collin said.

All but Leah took Evelyn up on the offer. What seemed strange was that Evelyn wasn't exactly surprised to see them, and when they asked how this could be, she pulled four large manilla envelopes out of a drawer. They had apparently been left in her cabin that morning. Inside each was a new identity, though the images associated to with all the documentation were obviously intended for them.

Collin's had something extra. Upon pulling out his paperwork, a Post-It sized note fell out. In Jonathan's handwriting, it was as vague as it was short. It read: *Collin, in regards to Paige and that thing we 'never' spoke about. Take the hit. It'll be worth it . . .*

He was still frowning at how Jonathan had chosen to word that when Evelyn asked, "So, is today the day I should turn the news back on?"

They all looked at one another, and at a loss for what was going on, nodded. What was playing out on TV, well—it broke their hearts.

For Jonathan, everything ended in a warehouse near downtown Seattle.

A team of over forty men in tactical gear, all wearing body cams, poured into the building from every point of entry. Jonathan sat on a metal folding chair, wearing a t-shirt and jeans, with his hands up. There were five large tables around him and each one had a nuclear warhead resting on it that was property of the US Government.

Media outlets acquired footage of Jonathan Tibbs being taken into custody. The body cam footage, leaked by an anonymous source, was all over the news before the President even got to hold a press conference. At that point, the narrative of the terrorist who stole five warheads being responsible for the city-wide evacuation of Seattle was cemented.

Soon, another name was all over the different news outlets. The man who had been key in leading government officers to Jonathan's arrest—one Grant Morgan. Unfortunately, the hero had himself been killed by the terrorist organization shortly after having been discovered as an infiltrator within their ranks. The story was, Grant Morgan gave his life to make sure the warheads never got detonated on US soil.

The story was easy to sell. The US Government had been investigating Mr. Tibbs for months prior to his sudden disappearance. Grant Morgan had been his friend, a man they sent into his house months earlier as part of the investigations.

Both men had disappeared within a week of each other.

As far as Jonathan's roommates and next-door neighbors' disappearances, authorities were still investigating, but they were presumed dead.

Jonathan was handcuffed and placed inside an armored car. Olivia and Rivers took a seat on opposite sides of him.

"We're good then?" Olivia asked. "The threat has been neutralized?"

Jonathan nodded.

"I didn't expect you to be here," Olivia said.

"Of course you didn't," Jonathan said.

"I suppose," she said. "I need to start trusting that you'll always tell me the truth."

"Well, then it's all been worth it," he said, a sad smile on his face.

"It makes me sick, this business with Grant."

Jonathan shook his head. "I agreed to it. He earned it. Just make sure someone in the media connects him to his real father. The son of the late Jeremy Holloway was the hero. He was clear on that."

They were quiet for a time before Jonathan asked, "When do I head to that dark hole you mentioned?"

Olivia and Rivers exchanged a glance as they remembered. He had said he would go, but only when he was done.

"There will be a great deal of theater playing out in the media over the next few days, but . . ." Olivia sighed. "You know too much, and due to the nature of your arrest, you can't be put into the general population of any prison."

Jonathan nodded. "So, interrogation, solitary confinement, and what, an eventual accident?"

"Even if you plead guilty, it's not exactly something we want to see go to trial," Olivia said. "Jonathan, in the next few hours, every family member, friend, teacher, or person you went to pre-school with, are going to be getting calls. It's really better for everyone who has ever been connected to you if—"

"I know," Jonathan said. "It's as taken care of as I can make it."

He had given his full cooperation to law enforcement. Signed confessions and disclosed every detail of his operation. He left out anything to do with extra-terrestrials.

Still, a day after the entire world watched Jonathan Tibbs being arrested, a convoy of government vehicles arrived at a remote location in Washington State. The place had no name on any map, but the land was owned by one of Anthony Hoult's subsidiaries. Jonathan said his organization had called it Hangman's Tree. When they arrived, they found a clearing with a number of cargo containers that had been recently torched. The place clearly having been wiped clean and abandoned sometime around his arrest.

None of Jonathan's associates were ever found. A majority of The Never Army was never even identified. Those who had been previously under suspicion for cooperation with The Mark never had their names made public. With no one else to arrest, the name Jonathan Tibbs was the only one to ever be associated with the evacuation.

The only people who knew the whole truth were few, and they were the sort who rose to their stations because they knew how to keep secrets.

In the years that followed, there would be several conspiracy theories about what really happened. After all, there were a lot of details to the story that the public remained in the dark about. No single guess ever got any-where near the truth. Of course, if anyone ever said, "the city was the site of an inter-dimensional war, taking place outside of time, against an alien invasion and the terrorist Jonathan Tibbs had, actually, been the leader of Earth's forces . . ."

Well, it was the sort of problem that solved itself. No one in their right mind would ever believe it.

EPILOGUE

FOUR YEARS LATER

AN HOUR OUTSIDE of Salem, Oregon, there was a small town near a lake. During the winter, the town emptied out for the most part, but when summer came it filled back up with vacationers. People from all around the state came to take their boats out on the water and go camping with their families.

Not far from the town was a house.

To find this house, one had to turn off the main highway and head down a dirt road. The place wasn't grandiose nor was it humble. A few years back, the property had been purchased by a buyer who had offered more than the asking price and paid in cash to make the sale as quick an affair as possible.

If one turned off the dirt road, they would find a driveway paved with white gravel. As they drew closer, they would pass a garden surrounded by a large lawn. Just past the garden, the driveway turned to cement, and led into a two-car garage.

Today, the garage door was up. Inside, a man sat on a stool.

Behind him was a semi-cluttered work bench. In front of him was an old truck. This truck looked as though it belonged on a farm somewhere. Its exterior was so rusted over one would get a sideways glance saying the ancient vehicle had character. Beside the truck was a hoist from which hung an equally ancient looking engine. That man on the stool had been looking back and forth between the two for quite a while now.

A month or so earlier, the man had gone to visit an old public storage building just outside of Portland. There was a unit there that needed to be cleaned out. Apparently, the unit had belonged to a relative of the leader of the most well-known terrorist group in the world. They had called themselves The Mark.

A few years earlier the entire country had been held in terror by this man and his followers. They had tried to level the entire city of Seattle, and if the reports were true had nearly managed it. The President of the United States had been forced to declare a national emergency—a city-wide evacuation of Seattle had been in place for seven days before the leader was captured and the nuclear weapons recovered.

In the end, it was one of the biggest messes in the country's history. Not just to the psyche of the city residents, who only learned how close they had come to being at ground zero for one of the worst terrorist attacks since 9/11, but to the country's GDP. In a manifesto published online, *The Mark* claimed to have chosen Seattle because they aimed to cripple the economy by blowing up the headquarters of Boeing, Amazon, Starbucks, and Microsoft.

Suffice it to say, any relatives or acquaintances to this man had little choice but to change their names and move. Still, when the man on the stool showed up at that storage facility a few months earlier and loaded all the contents into a moving truck, no one recognized him, and no one from the media showed up. The whole affair went unnoticed, almost as though unseen hands did not want any fuss to be made.

The truck had been in disrepair for years. After getting new tires on it, the man on the stool had to tow the rusted beast a few hundred miles, but it was important enough to him that it never end up in a junkyard.

In town, everyone knew the man as Joshua Clark. They were fond of his wife Rachel, who had gained some renown as the resident artist. A few of her metal sculptures were currently on display around the town's main drag. She had a younger brother, Jack, who was turning twelve that year. He attended school two towns down the mountain. He could have been a better student, but his teachers seldom had anything bad to say when Joshua and Rachel came to parent-teacher night.

Lastly, the couple had a son and a daughter, Peter and Rylee. Both were turning four that year and would be starting kindergarten soon.

People often asked Joshua and Rachel how surprised they were to find out they were having twins. As newlyweds, they had taken some sort of early test when they found out they were pregnant. The test had confirmed the boy. Later, when they went in for a sonogram, they found out this was only half the story.

Peter and Rylee's approaching voices roused Joshua from his staring contest with the truck and its dismantled components just before his children came through the door into the garage.

He stood from the stool as they reached the last step of the small staircase, spread his arms as he lowered into a stance that made him look like a goalie. Having played this game with their father since before they could remember, Rylee and Peter grinned before each tried to shoot by him. They laughed as he first caught Peter under one arm and then Rylee after she tried to dart in the opposite direction. Joshua growled like an oversized monster and spun them in a circle, until they were all dizzy and laughing.

"No one escapes the beast," Joshua said as the twins pretended to hate it. As often is the case with children their laughter gave them away.

"You two are getting big," he said, as he set them down. The whole affair having left him breathing heavily.

Rylee pointed to the truck. "Still can't get it started, Dad?"

Joshua gave her a look. "I'll get it."

"Mom says that you'd have been finished a month ago if you'd let her help," Peter said.

Joshua saw her then, out of the corner of his eye. Rachel standing in the doorway, eavesdropping—her face a warm smile.

"That's true," Joshua said, looking back at his son, "but . . . it would be cheating."

He looked back at his wife who watched him now with a raised eyebrow and he cocked one right back at her. "In fact, I think I got this figured out. Just need to go into town and order a part."

"Oh," Rachel said, stepping past the threshold, "and, what part will we be ordering this time?"

He looked at her, perhaps with a little more self-doubt than he had a moment earlier. "Distributer coil."

She pinched her lips and nodded, trying not to confirm or deny what she thought. "If that's the case, you realize you didn't have to hoist the engine all the way back out of—"

"Yes," he said, cutting her off. "That has occurred to me."

She grinned as she came down the steps. Then slowly inched toward a cabinet. Her eyes never faltered, holding his gaze as she reached inside without looking and pulled out a shipping box. Without a word, she left the package on the work bench and made for the stairs.

"Love you," she said, playfully. "Don't forget, company should start getting here soon." His eyes narrowed as she disappeared into the house.

He trudged over to the box. He found it was postmarked a month earlier, and there wasn't a doubt in his mind that it contained a distributer coil. When he turned back around, he saw the children hadn't left yet, in fact, they looked as though they had known that box was in the cabinet for a while now. Waiting for him to figure out the right part.

"Have fun, Dad," Rylee said, running out of the garage with Peter on her heels. Joshua watched them run across the garden's paving stones to play tag on the lawn.

Alone again, Joshua turned to the truck. "Don't look at me like that. It's the journey not the destination."

He got the distinct impression that if it could, the vehicle would have scoffed at him.

Sometime later, a black car pulled into the driveway.

Joshua wiped his hands on a cloth and shoved it in his back pocket as he saw Olivia and Rivers step out of the vehicle. He put his hands up jokingly as they came close. "You got me, her tags are expired."

Olivia's lips moved, as though she'd had to actually make an effort not to smile. Rachel must have noticed them arrive, because behind him the garage door opened and she came out to join them.

Rivers smirked. "The only crime here is that you've had three months and she hasn't moved an inch since the day you hauled her in."

He looked between Rachel and Olivia. "Seriously, how did this guy ever convince us he could stop an inter-dimensional demigod?"

"I confess, I've often questioned my judgment," Rachel said.

"It isn't something I'm proud of," Olivia added.

Joshua smiled, it wasn't often Olivia made an effort at humor. "For the record, it's only been two and a half months."

Ignoring him, Rachel turned to the agents. "We didn't expect to see you two, but you're welcome to stay for dinner."

The two politely declined. "We were still in the area. Thought we'd let you know your friends are all safely on their way before we head out. No one recognized them as acquaintances of the infamous Jonathan Tibbs."

"I do appreciate you looking out for them," Joshua said.

"So, any recent visits from our more otherworldly friend to report?" Olivia asked.

"Been a few years," Joshua said.

The four exchanged equally suspicious and at the same time conspiratorial glances. "Well, of course, had it been otherwise we'd have heard from you."

"Of course," Rachel said.

Olivia reached up to her ear, as she received a message. "We should go, your friends have just pulled off the highway."

"Always a pleasure," Joshua said. "For what it's worth, it's a lot brighter in this hole than I thought it would be."

Olivia smirked. "Have a lovely evening, Mr. Clark," she said, before she got back into the car.

Joshua stood beside Rachel as they drove away. "Do you think those two ever finally—"

"Even I can't tell," Rachel cut him off.

A few minutes later an SUV pulled up the drive, and parked. The passenger side window rolled down and Paige's face appeared. She looked a little angry. "Hey! Saw Rivers and Olivia on our way in . . . do I need to check the bathroom for cameras?"

Her expression melted into a smile as the rest of the doors opened, and Evelyn, Hayden, and Collin stepped out. A moment later, after Collin finished struggling with the latches on a child seat, a three-year-old ran away from the car in a beeline for the twins.

Collin only making a mild effort to say, "Lucy, at least say hello to Uncle J and Auntie Rachel before—and she's gone."

Out of politeness, no one really said it, but Collin had pretty much accepted that he was going to have a dad bod for the foreseeable future. The only reason it ever went noticed, was because Hayden had become a bit of a fitness guru over the last three years. So, while Hayden looked about thirty pounds lighter since their last visit, Collin looked equally heavier, making it somewhat difficult for anyone to say, 'Looking great Hayden' while Collin was standing beside him.

Evelyn was last to step out of the car, and as Joshua hugged her, she made the same joke she had for the last four years. "May I see my grandchildren? I don't want to be pushy and find myself checked into a hotel in Austria or on a plane heading to Guam."

"Missed you, Mom," Joshua said.

Later that evening, after they had all eaten, the kids returned to the sloping lawn to play for the last hour before the sun went down. The adults, who had all partaken in libations, found themselves split. Evelyn, Paige, and Rachel having taken glasses of wine to the garden while Hayden, Collin, and Joshua stood in the garage. There was a comforting familiarity to it all.

"So, Superman or Jesus?" Hayden asked.

Joshua smiled, but as he had said the first time Hayden asked the question, his answer hadn't changed. "Neither. Yeah . . . definitely neither."

"He's consistent," Collin said.

"How did things ever end with Super Jesus anyway?" Joshua asked.

Collin and Hayden exchanged a glance.

"The Messiah dies, everyone but his disciples think he's a criminal. Resurrection, goes to heaven," Hayden said.

"But, that's the same ending as the gospels," Joshua said. "Aren't you supposed to subvert expectations or something?"

"A wise man once said that rebooting the Bible was a lot like watching *Titanic*," Hayden said. "You already know the ending."

"Oh," Joshua said. "He does sound wise, but then what happens to the Anti-Christ?"

"The Messiah asked him for forgiveness, for turning him into the villain. In the end, we had him choose to die along with Jesus. We made him one of the other two guys the Romans crucified on Golgotha."

"Well, I mean, mankind is saved whether they knew it or not," Collin said.

"I thought you guys had this whole plan to have Jesus and Damian team up and replace their fathers," Joshua said. "To explain the personality change of God between the Old and New Testament."

"They didn't have to—holy and unholy trinity," Collin said.

"Oh, trinity, sure, that explains everything," Joshua mumbled.

"Think of it like this. There are three parts to this personality, then one part goes off and has an adventure by itself. Later, when that part returns to the whole, he is changed, and when he is reabsorbed, that change effects the other two parts. So, in a way, they are all changed," Hayden said.

Joshua turned to Collin for a simpler explanation.

"The Messiah's experiences on Earth make God chillax," Collin said.

Joshua nodded. "I like it."

They were quiet for a moment.

"So, heard from Lincoln lately?" Collin asked.

"Married, got a kid on the way," Joshua said.

"What is it with everyone being in such a hurry to breed?" Hayden said. "No offense."

"Yeah," Collin said. "None taken . . . douche."

As Joshua stared out over the hill, he saw a figure. A man in a black coat wearing a slightly less ridiculous fedora. A moment later the man was gone.

"I'll be back in a minute," Joshua said.

"Say hello to Heyer for us," Collin said. "Yeah, I saw him. He's not nearly as stealthy as he thinks."

Joshua walked out to the hill, waited a minute, rolled his eyes and walked over to the nearest stand of trees. As soon as he was no longer in sight of the house, he heard Heyer's voice.

"Hello, Jonathan."

The alien, who didn't visit frequently enough, was the only one who failed to remember that name wasn't supposed to be used. He was also the only person Jonathan never bothered correcting.

"You know," he said. "You're always welcome in the house."

"I noticed your roommates were visiting," Heyer said. "And your mother."

Joshua smiled. "Right, that would make decent Borealis repellent."

"I apologize that it's been so long," Heyer said. "But I brought you something."

He reached into his pocket, and pulled out Douglas's pocket watch. He placed it into Jonathan's hand.

"Thank you, Heyer," Joshua said.

They spoke for a while, about nothing particularly pressing. The alien often seemed happy to hear about his life now that it was no longer in constant jeopardy.

"The last few times we spoke you said the link to your father's mind was thinning."

Joshua nodded. "Mr. Clean was right, without activation the memories fade."

Heyer smiled though there was a sadness in it.

"I know," Joshua said. "It's a bit like losing him again."

"Few people have truly known who I am," Heyer said. "Friends, like your father, they come maybe once a century. The curse of living forever."

"You know, I'm your friend," Joshua said. "Dumbass."

Heyer chuckled, and they grew quiet again, watching the sun set. After some time had passed, Jonathan spoke, "Leah and I have spoken about this. My family has known you for more than one generation. In a way, on her side, you are family. I don't see why you should be unknown to our children. That, and a part of me likes the idea that someone will be there to watch over them when I'm gone."

Heyer was surprised. "But . . . I've brought your family nothing but pain."

Joshua smiled. "Yeah, well, obviously this offer comes with the assumption you can refrain from installing any alien technology into them. And . . . get used to calling me Joshua."

"That does seem reasonable," Heyer said.

"Being honest, I think it's important you have something to anchor you here. I mean, we've all seen what happens to a Borealis who spends too much time on the Feroxian Plane."

Heyer nodded. "It is a species that leaves a great deal to be desired. At least as far as having a conversation goes. *Burns the Flame* is trying to break the younger generation of their beliefs that things like written language are sins against the gods."

"How are things going over there?"

"Good," Heyer said. "You were right, introducing members of their ancestral species into the population may solve the mating problem in a few generations. Even if I am to be left eternally in the dark as to how you came to possess the exact dimensional signature and planetary coordinates of their ancestral home."

"Lucky guess," Joshua said.

Heyer only raised an eyebrow. They had been through this dance before and he was resigned to the fact that Jonathan intended to take some information to his grave.

"This alien I know once said that some things are like humor, when you explain, you risk ruining a good thing for everyone," Joshua said. "He's one of the smartest guys I know. I don't ignore his advice lightly."

Heyer sighed, but it wasn't humorless. "Was this the same alien you referred to as 'dumbass' a moment ago?"

"Well, no one's perfect," Joshua said.

Later that evening, while most of their friends were still chatting in the living room, Joshua found himself standing in his twins' bedroom. "Teeth brushed?"

"Yes," they groaned.

He tucked them in and sat down in a rocking chair next to the bed. He showed them book covers, letting them argue over which story to hear before they went to sleep. After much compromise, they picked one, and Joshua had read it twice before he said it was time for sleep. He reached over and pulled the string on the lamp.

He had barely reached the door when their pleading voices stopped him.

"Dad, will you stay?" Peter asked.

He turned around, kissed each of their foreheads, and sat back down in the chair.

"You won't leave," Rylee said. "Just until we're asleep?"

He began to sway back and forth in the rocking chair.

"I promise," he said. "I'll never leave you alone in the dark."

The End

DEAR READER

I am an independent author and word of mouth is the most powerful form of marketing at my disposal. If you enjoyed the series and know others would want to follow The Chronicles of Jonathan Tibbs, please tell your friends. Also, the more reviews posted to Amazon and Goodreads, the more likely it is for future readers to find their way to this and other works.

Even a few short words are greatly appreciated.

SPECIAL THANKS

To all fans of the series for keeping my family fed. To all the Beta Readers who offered feedback to make each book the best it could be. To Mark, who was always willing to be the first to read my garbage. To John, for giving up a Saturday and getting me onto base for book research. To Chuck and James, for all the obscure military, gun, and vehicle maintenance related questions they had to field. To my family, who helped in more ways then I can list.

To Justine and Tracy for all the hours they spent fixing every comma. To Brian, Patrick, and Will who called me on every plot hole . . . even if, allegedly, I've chosen not to fix some. To Steven Barnett, who is gonna have to narrate this beast for the audio edition . . . Stay hydrated, brother. Finally to ELOE, for standing at the finish line, checking their imaginary watches, but still cheering when I reached the end.

ABOUT THE AUTHOR

T. Ellery Hodges lives with his wife, two sons, and daughter in Seattle, Washington. He is currently hard at work on his next series. If you'd like to know more about T. Ellery, visit his blog at *www. telleryhodges.com*, follow him on twitter *@telleryhodges*, or Follow The Never Hero page on *Facebook*! If you prefer email, he'd love to hear from you at *telleryhodges@gmail.com*.

Made in the USA
Las Vegas, NV
07 January 2022

40732510R00454